The memories came in a tumble, of her mother laughing and running across the sands holding her hand, of the words of the psalm that she sang to lull her children to sleep. Catriona remembered secrets shared and promises made and the happiness that had always filled her home . . . In the whisper of the wind Catriona could hear her mother's voice and she vowed then that she would not forget the memories nor the promise that she had made.

Kirsty White was born in London of Scottish parents. She has worked as a newspaper reporter and in broadcasting and programme-making before turning to full-time writing. Kirsty White lives in Dumfriesshire and is currently working on her next novel.

MY LITTLE OYSTER GIRL

Kirsty White

ORION

An Orion paperback
First published in Great Britain by Orion in 1993
This paperback edition published in 1993 by Orion Books Ltd,
Orion Hous, 5 Upper St Martin's Lane, London WC2H 9EA

A CIP catalogue record for this book is available from the British Library

ISBN 1 85797 097 7

Typeset by Datix International Limited, Bungay, Suffolk
Printed in England by Clays Ltd, St Ives plc

Prologue

The beach was a magical place. It existed only on the whim of the tide; sometimes, in winter, the sea was so high that waves crashed against the rocks and the shore disappeared completely and when you looked out from the path all you could see was the expanse of the Sound, sombre and grey as the northern sky.

In spring, the beach came alive with the calls of newborn seals and gannets and terns and oyster catchers; at low tide, oyster beds stretched out as far as the eye could see.

Once the beach had been famous for oysters, because there was a river nearby that fed the shellfish until they were fat and lush, but in the hard years when the people had risen against the landlords a man had been prosecuted for stealing the oysters and over the years that followed people stopped going to the beach not through fear but pragmatism because there were other beaches nearby where the oysters were nearly as good that were further from the landlords' prying eyes.

The new century brought hope to the island.

A man had security now, the Crofters Act countered the threat of eviction so long as the rent was paid and although many of the crofts were so small that they would not support a healthy chicken there were other ways that a man could earn his living.

The people lost the habit of going to the beach to gather shellfish; there was no longer the need and revenge against the landlord was more easily achieved by poaching the occasional stag. Only the tinkers still scoured the shore for sustenance and although they were pitied they were also ashamed because of all those who lived in the island only the tinkers were without hope because they were also without land.

On the island, land was everything. A man's croft put food on the table and eased his existence from dire penury to poverty that was relentless but not as overwhelming as it once had been when the threat of eviction hung over the land. In Skye, a man considered himself rich if he earned a few pounds at the summer fishing and had a few shillings left over when the rent was paid and the necessities of life purchased from the merchant in Portree.

Of all the people who lived in the villages of The Braes, only Mor Nicolson loved the beach. When she was just married, she found it one day in spring when the sun breached the clouds in columns of light that danced over the waves like wills-o'-the-wisp brought to life by the promise of summer. When Mor closed her eyes above the music of the sea she heard the caw of gulls and the soft cry of newborn seals; the sun on her face was so warm that she threw her shawl down and ran over the sands, as playful and joyous as a puppy seal.

When Catriona, Mor's first born, was but a babe-in-arms Mor would take her to the beach and let her play as she gathered carrageen. Later, when Catriona learned to walk, they would stroll over the sands together for hours, deep in talk.

Mor shared her secrets with Catriona, and also her dreams.

Chapter One

*D*eath came with the storm.

Catriona's eyes opened as her father ran out into the night to fetch the man who had the gift of healing, who knew the prayer that would stop the flow of blood from her mother.

The new baby followed him, a tiny scrap of life in the arms of the midwife's daughter, whose howls rang out above the sound of the wind.

The door of the bedroom was open. Catriona crept in and saw the spreading stain of crimson on the bedclothes, the colour discordant in the dull glow of the oil lamp.

The midwife tried to hustle her out, but by then she was at the bedside and Mor reached out for her.

'Catriona?'

'Hush, Mama.'

Mor's face was pallid, waxy pale and suddenly old, as if she had lived her whole life out just in these last few hours. Her hand in Catriona's was limp and cold.

'Care for them,' she whispered, 'the newborn too, and your pa.' Her voice was urgent, taut with pain.

'I promise you, Mama, I will.'

'Away, Mor, and don't be daft,' the midwife said in that way of hers that was both sharp and kind. 'It's only a little bleed, that's all, and Tom's away to see Coinneach Mor and you know Coinneach's stopped worse bleeds than that.'

On the bedclothes the stain was spreading. Mor looked at the midwife and then at Catriona. 'I'm sorry,' she murmured.

And then she died.

In the evening of that day Mor Nicolson was buried in the yard of the church where, a few moments before, her baby son had been baptized.

The minister spoke of life as a journey whilst her children watched their father throwing earth into the grave. Tom Nicolson was a big man and his shadow blotted out the setting of the sun. Methodically he filled the grave until all that remained was a patch of freshly dug earth making a scar on the winter grass. The knot of mourners dissolved into the dusk.

Eileen MacInnes, who lived nearby, came into the cottage and bustled round until Tom Nicolson's icy silence forced her to leave.

'It's a great shock for your pa,' she said to Catriona, 'but don't worry, now, I'll come back tomorrow.'

'Catriona,' her father said in a voice thick with grief, 'close the door and don't let that interfering bitch back in.'

Catriona did as he said and then fed her brothers and sisters and put the younger ones to bed. 'Where's Mama?' Sine asked, too young to comprehend the meaning of death. 'Mama's gone,' Ailish said, and Catriona felt the void in her soul then as, in the darkness, her sisters sobbed.

Her father sat up that night, in front of the fire in the main room of the cottage where his children slept. His brother came to the door but Tom sent him away, and Angus must have told the others because nobody else came after him and Tom and his children were left alone with their grief.

When morning came Catriona rose early, stoked the fire and put water on to heat.

'You were with her,' he said, moving his chair to let her pass.

'Yes, Papa.'

'What did she say?'

'That she was sorry, Papa.'

She never thought that a man could cry the way her father did then.

'You understand,' he said, after a long time, 'I don't want anyone coming in, not just yet.'

'Don't worry, Papa. I can manage.'

At school that day the teacher took Catriona aside to tell

her that she was sorry her mother had died. Though Catriona felt she must rush away because she had left her young sisters at home, Miss Anderson firmly led her through to the little room in the school house and made her sit down by the fire as she fetched milk for Catriona and a cup of tea for herself.

Miss Anderson was not from Skye, but she was born of island parents and understood something of the way that islanders lived. Their lives were hard but the harshness was tempered by the companionship that comes of troubles shared. Or so it seemed to her, an outsider, a young woman dedicated with evangelical zeal to the task of educating the young. Catriona's pain was sharp but it would fade in time and the survival instinct had always been strong in these parts. The islanders were used to taking care of themselves.

'Don't be afraid to cry,' she said.

Catriona flinched, appalled by the thought that she might break down and sob in front of a stranger. She had not cried yet; her pain was still too acute for tears.

'You must tell me if I can help at all.'

Abruptly, Catriona stood up, suddenly nauseous in the heat of the room and wanting to distance herself from this woman who smiled hesitantly as if by that gesture she could ease her pain.

'I must go,' she said. 'I'm very sorry.'

'You must tell me,' the teacher said again, 'if there's anything I can do ...' Her voice tailed off then, helplessly, as she realized that Catriona had already fled.

Catriona ran until her chest threatened to burst; stopping then, she sagged for a while, panting until she caught her breath. The wind was cold, ripping at her skin with icy tendrils; her eyes stung with the salt of her tears. For a time she waited, then she walked on.

She was nearly home when she heard footsteps behind her; she turned and saw Lachlan Maclean. He was a few years older than her and had left school now, but he still followed her as faithfully as he had always done. In early childhood they had been firm friends, but she was almost ten years old, and in growing up she had also grown away from him.

Her father used to tease her that she would never want for anything when Lachlan was around.

Lachlan blushed, winded, the flush of his face clashing with his sandy-red hair. He smiled and frowned all at once. 'I'm right sorry,' he said, 'for your mother.'

His eyes were fixed to the ground.

'Thank you,' she said.

'I'll walk with you.'

Catriona shrugged.

'How's your da taking it?'

She did not answer.

'My ma said, she said he'd be taking it hard.'

The wind howled suddenly, turned to a keening note that tore at her soul. Lachlan shivered, then reached for her arm.

'Catriona ...' he began, but she didn't stop, she just walked on with him clinging to her like a dog to a bone. He had reached adolescence and his voice dived an octave, but the sound he made was not the sound of a man. 'I'll help,' he said, 'I'll help all I can.'

She ignored him.

'I mean, it was your Ma who kept things going. Your da'll not know what to do with her gone.'

She spun around. 'Go to hell, Lachlan.'

His mouth opened.

'Don't you dare say another word.'

'But Catriona ...'

She began to run again, not stopping until there was enough distance between them to preclude the chance of him catching up.

When she got back to the cottage her father was standing outside, glaring in the direction of the MacInnes house.

'The bitch,' he said, 'came with a pot of barley soup. Wanted to say a prayer, she did.'

'Papa,' she said carefully, 'she was only trying to help.'

'I'd rather go begging than sup Eileen MacInnes's barley soup.'

There were only potatoes and oatmeal in the cottage. She realized with a start that the cow had not been milked since the day before. Maire was crying and Sine was damp and her brothers and Ailish were nowhere to be seen.

Quickly she changed Sine and then went to the byre, but her uncle Angus had milked the cow and left the milk in the churn.

Leaving the byre, she saw Eileen MacInnes waddling up, her breath trailing in wispy little clouds. Eileen was plump and clumsy and too friendly and eager to help, in the way that fat people sometimes are.

'Catriona, I've been looking for you. Your da's a bit touchy yet, it takes them like that sometimes. But if you pop in to me for your dinner, I've plenty soup and bread.'

'I'll send Ewan and Alec and Ailish.'

'You'll come yourself, won't you?'

'I've things to see to, Eileen.'

The beach, she thought, there's always plenty food on the beach. Sometimes, not often, she had gone there with her mother, who wasn't ashamed to gather shellfish like the tinkers did. Her father brought food – venison or salmon or herring, a lamb in springtime and maybe a bit of beef for salting. He didn't like to hear of her mother gathering shellfish, it offended his pride to think that people might say big Tom Nicolson could not feed his wife and children; yet Mor had to, at times, as everyone did, because there wasn't always enough to go around.

So Catriona fetched the pail for shellfish. On her way to the beach she found Ailish playing with her friends, and told her to take her brothers to Eileen MacInnes for the barley soup their father had spurned.

At low tide, below the cliffs, the sands stretched out in a golden crescent where, far away at the water's edge, gulls wheeled and dived. This place was precious to her, had been ever since her mother had said that the sands appeared by magic only when the fairies had the strength to drive the sea away.

Long before she knew the secret of the tides, her mother had made her listen to the music of the sea.

She could hear it now, faint as a whisper, and she listened carefully to see if it had something to tell her. But the message eluded her, made indistinct by distance and the cries of the gulls.

The wind was sharp and spiked with rain, so she went to the oyster beds and filled her bucket.

As she turned for home the clouds suddenly lifted and the sun shone; in a moment the wind withered and died. A flock of birds flew overhead, their fleeting shadow streaking the sand.

She knew then that her mother was there, her spirit so close that Catriona felt she could reach out and touch her across the void of the afterlife. For a moment she paused and listened and then she said, 'Yes, Mama, I'll take care of them. Believe me, I will.'

The memories came in a tumble, of her mother laughing and running across the sands holding her hand, of the words of the psalm that she sang to lull her children to sleep. Catriona remembered secrets shared and promises made and the happiness that had always filled her home. Her mother had been gentle and docile in a way but strong too, so strong that she could calm the rage of her husband; with her his anger never lasted for more than a moment. Mor Nicolson was, had been, laughter and light; in a way it was fitting that she had died during the darkest night of the year, in a storm so violent that dogs howled and cows bellowed and roofs had been clean whipped away. On the morrow of Mor's death the resurrection of the sun gave her daughter hope that the promise of heaven was more than just a reason to pray to a God whom she had never seen.

In the whisper of the wind Catriona could hear her mother's voice and she vowed then that she would not forget the memories nor the promise that she had made.

In a pool left by the tide she saw her shadow, sharply

defined and strange now that it was alone because always before her mother had been beside her and there had been two sets of footprints in the sands.

In the winter, evening came quickly. When she saw darkening clouds gathering over the hills she wrapped her shawl around her and walked quickly home. The pain then was so raw that she felt as if she, too, was bleeding to death.

That evening, after the oysters had been cooked and eaten, she walked over the grazings to Annie Macdonald's house. Annie had a brood of children and a husband who worked all summer at the herring fishing to make the money to feed them. Annie had milk and the midwife had given her the baby to care for.

Annie was sitting by the fire with the child; she did not look surprised as Catriona walked in.

Catriona felt a stab of pain when she remembered how her mother had laughed with Annie here in this cottage only a few days before.

'Have you eaten?' Annie asked as her husband rose to give Catriona his chair.

'No, Iain,' she said quickly, remembering her manners.

'Don't be daft, pet,' he said, 'sit yourself down for a moment. I was off for a walk anyway.'

'Do you want a cup of tea?' Annie asked.

Catriona nodded, grateful that Annie had put baby Allan down in a crib, that she had not asked her to hold him. She could not bear to touch him yet.

Annie's hands were shaking as she handed across the mug.

'How are you, pet?' she asked in a voice as soft as the mist.

'I'm ...' Catriona began, and then, 'Ohh, Annie.' The tears came in a flood as Annie put down the teapot and rushed to her side.

'I mustn't cry,' Catriona sobbed, 'I'll wake the children.'

'Ach, pet, cry all you want,' Annie whispered.

For a long time Annie held her tight and Catriona cried her heart out in an embrace that was tender and caring but strange to her because the arms that held her were not her mother's.

Afterwards she sat huddled by the fire, drinking a mug of warm milk and honey.

'Why, Annie? Why did she die? Was it God?' she asked.

'No. Not God. Leastwise, I don't think so. I'd say it was fate, pet.'

Allan began to cry and Annie picked him up and began to feed him again. Catriona felt drawn towards her new brother and slowly moved over to stand at Annie's side. The baby stopped feeding and she saw the innocent blue of his eyes and the faltering smile that crept across his face. She took him from Annie and felt the warmth of his body, the fragile flutter of his tiny heart. The hair on his head was downy soft and she brushed a tendril from his forehead. In her arms he settled and slept.

'You don't know, do you?' she whispered, as she realized with surprise that she felt love for the tiny child.

'I'll take care of him,' Annie said quickly.

Catriona knew what she was saying, that despite all of her brood she could take in another, that Iain wouldn't mind and nor would she.

'No, Annie.'

'I'll have to keep him here the first month or two. To feed him. And look after him while you're at school.'

'Yes, but he's my brother. He'll have to come home.'

'It won't be easy, Catriona.'

'It's what Mama would've wanted.'

Annie looked at Catriona and saw the determination ingrained on her young face. Mor Nicolson came from Arisaig, she had met Tom when he had spoken at a Land League meeting there; her family was miles away on the mainland and in any case her sisters had emigrated years before. Mor had been determined, too, Annie thought, remembering the way that she had run the croft and smoothed the edges of Tom's anger when the Land League had faltered and then given up. He had loved her so deeply that her death for him would be a burden almost too great to bear.

8

'I can manage, Annie, I will,' Catriona said, and a wave of pity overwhelmed Annie for the girl's plight.

'Aye, pet,' she said, 'and I'll help you all I can.'

The first months were hard, almost too hard for Catriona, as she struggled to keep her home together whilst her father sat listlessly in his chair, subdued by the inertia of his grief.

The village women watched her carefully and helped when they could, but Tom Nicolson was too proud to let them do much and eventually they realized that, anyway, his daughter could manage.

Catriona already knew how to cook because she had helped her mother, and other things she learned by trial and error. She became a familiar figure as she hurried around the village on some errand or another, caring for her sisters and brothers and working on the croft. At low tide she always set off for the beach and walked far across the sands in search of shellfish; at these times she found respite in the stoic beauty of the island, and also peace.

In time her pain subsided and was replaced by a sense of loss which echoed in her soul as she tried to fill the gap in her life that her mother had left.

When, one day, her father rose early from his bed and went to dig his potato patch she felt relieved, happy even, because it seemed that at last he was emerging from the chasm of his grief.

Four years had passed and she had become used to the obligations of motherhood; she had taken her baby brother home and reared him as best as she could; her other sisters and brothers were now all at school and life was easier for that.

Tom had not paid the rent and Catriona had been worried that they might be evicted until she discovered that her uncle Angus had been paying it along with his own.

'Don't tell your da,' he'd said, 'but I thought it was for the best and it wasn't so much after all.'

'Oh, Angus,' she said, 'I've a little put by, I could pay you back.'

'Don't be daft, pet. That was money your ma left for you. You keep it, pet, and use it if you need it, but not to pay me because I made plenty at the fishing this year.'

Sometimes she felt a desolate loneliness at the burden of care and consolation and then, just as things threatened to overwhelm her, something always pulled her back from the edge. As she gathered shellfish she would talk aloud to her mother in heaven and although she never heard a reply it was as if Mor was listening nevertheless.

As the island slowly emerged from the gloom of winter her father became like his old self again. He worked hard in the fields and with the lambing ewes; he whistled and sang and joked with the other men and it was only at night in the cottage that the aura of despair settled over him.

And his daughter felt hope again.

One day she began to dream, a silly dream, an idle dream of the kind she and her mother had once shared to ease the burden of their work. It was nothing, it meant nothing until she realized that she had taken pleasure from it, that at last she had gained the courage to dream again.

That day on the beach she saw that the frosting of snow was melting from the Cuillin Hills and a sea thrift bloomed shyly amongst the tumbled rocks.

It's true, she thought then, though she had never believed it so before. It's true what the old men say, that spring is a promise and time eases all pain.

She wished then that her mother could have been with her to share the wonder of that day.

For a moment she stopped to watch the first of the eider ducks nesting in the scrawny dunes, plucking at grass that wavered softly in the breeze.

The duck noticed her and paused too and then continued, unconcerned.

Catriona cast a last glance over the sands and continued homewards. Far away, where the cliffs rose high above the sea, she saw the figure of a man and waved, realizing it was her father, but he did not see her or pretended that he did not, because he made no move to acknowledge her.

Early that spring, when Tom's interest in life awoke again, he often came out to meet her and they would walk home in silent companionship. He even carried her bucket for her once, saying that he never thought the day would come when Tom Nicolson was seen in The Braes with a pail of mussels.

Catriona laughed then, glad that her father could make a joke of his pride.

'To hell with it,' Tom had said. 'I'll be up there in Portree in September, with oysters for the tourists. Sixpence a dozen, Hector said they get for them in Glasgow.'

'Sixpence a dozen?' Catriona's interest quickened. As the winter months had passed she had realized what Tom did not. The money that her mother had left her, the precious hoard saved by knitting and selling socks, had dwindled over the years and now there was nothing left of it. The need for money was acute – to buy cloth to make new clothes and for meal to ease them through the empty months that augured the harvest. Catriona did not want to burden him with that when his optimism was still so fragile.

'That and more,' Tom said knowingly. 'The daft buggers who kill stags for pleasure don't know that if you go for a walk on the beach you can get oysters for free.'

'I'll go to Portree in September,' she said, 'you don't have to bother, Da. I'll do it myself.'

'You bloody won't, Triona. No girl of mine'll go around with a bucket like a tinker.'

Catriona fell silent as Tom strode on, the bucket swinging in an arc with the motion of his arm. When they got indoors he put the bucket down, took off his cap and wiped his forehead. 'I never thought the day would come,' he said again as he sat down on his chair. 'Put on the kettle, will you, pet?'

Catriona waited until the tea was made.

'You'll go, will you, then?'

'What, pet?'

'You'll go to Portree to sell oysters?'

'Don't be daft, lass. I was only joking. And I doubt there'd be any business in it, because that fellow in the Royal Hotel gets them from the shore like we do and he'll sell all there is to be sold.'

'We could sell ours cheaper.'

'No, Triona, and don't be arguing about it either. You'll not do it, over my dead body, and I'll not do it either. Yon man in the Royal is a selfish bugger and he'd find some nonsense to stop us if we tried that.'

'But Da . . .'

He silenced her with one of his looks, when his brow furrowed into craggy folds and his eyebrows joined together in a dark line to shade eyes hinting of anger. If she went on he would erupt, standing up and ranting on like a madman until the object of his annoyance had been silenced. For just a minute she wondered whether she should persist, because she hadn't seen Tom like that in years, not since her mother died, and she wondered if it might do him good to get his temper back again, or to lose it as he had done in the old days. Then, as she saw his face relax again, she thought better of it, sensing that his good humour was a pose; it would not do to risk him lapsing once again into the melancholia that had shadowed him for years.

'Remember, Triona,' he said, smiling slightly, 'I'm still a wanted man in Portree. It wouldn't do for me to get arrested and I might well do if I got into a ruck with that man at the Royal.'

She smiled and began to peel the potatoes for the evening meal.

Her father had been a hero in the days when the people of Skye had risen to fight for the land. Tom Nicolson was just a boy then, but he was old enough to throw the first stone on the day when the crofters had chased the landlords' bailiffs and the constables from The Braes.

He had never forgotten those days, though nearly thirty years had passed. In his mind he still fought the same battles; the cause, eroded for others by time and despair, was still vibrant to him. Other men settled down to work the tiny crofts that had been the fruits of the Land League's struggle, and their sons grew up to a meagre birthright. The leakage of people continued – as each year passed, more men left the island to search for work; but men like Tom stayed, to believe in the cause and rise again when the time would come.

Tom believed that, Catriona knew. He believed that the justice that was theirs by right would be recognized by law. He did not recognize the boundaries of the landlords' lands; he ignored dykes and fences and ranged far and wide, taking the stags that roamed the hills and the fish that swam in the rivers. And although the gamekeepers knew him well they dared not stop him because there was no man on the island brave enough to challenge him.

The early years of Catriona's childhood had been easy ones; the harvests were good and Tom's poaching provided the food that the croft did not and earned the money to pay the rent as well.

The poaching had stopped when Mor died. A year passed during which Tom hardly shifted out of his chair and after that Catriona did not dare ask him, but used the money from her mother to buy meal, and made up the food by scouring for shellfish herself.

And now that he had said he would not go to Portree and would not let her go either, another chance had gone.

She felt a sudden rush of frustration as he sat there smiling to himself.

Years before, when she had been very little, her father had flattened the estate factor during an argument over a croft. He punched him square on the jaw and the factor fell to the floor in a daze; and Tom paid the rent to the groundsman and then walked home as if nothing had happened. And nothing did happen to him – because the factor was new in the islands and did not know who Tom was, and nobody else would tell him. Even the police in Portree were not helpful, aware that arresting Tom Nicolson would be more trouble than it was worth.

Every now and then, though, when Tom wanted an excuse to avoid going to Portree, he would say it was because he was a wanted man.

Catriona thought about the price of oysters as she made the supper that night, mulled it over as she fed her family and helped Allan and then Sine and Maire to get ready for bed.

Sixpence a dozen, and she could get five dozen or more easily in one bucket, ten dozen in two; and although Portree was ten miles away it would not take her more than a couple of hours to walk there. Sixpence a dozen, for shellfish that were there for the taking by anyone who went to the beach.

After Tom went out for his evening stroll she asked Ewan about it. Ewan was the more thoughtful of her twin brothers, he was not as impulsive as Alec or her father and sometimes he even had good ideas.

'I've not heard that,' he said, as he whittled away at a bit of driftwood that he was trying to turn into a shinty stick. He turned to his brother and asked him.

'I've heard something,' Alec said. 'Iain MacInnes said the man in the Royal'd give you a farthing for a bucket of whelks.'

'Oysters,' Catriona said, 'not whelks.'

'Aye, oysters too. A farthing a bucket, but a creel, like, and not the wee bucket like you use. Anyway, Iain and his brothers were getting them but they said the man's a thief, like. A farthing a bucket, they thought, but when they took half a dozen it was only a farthing in all that they got, and not a penny ha'penny.'

Catriona turned away and began to darn a pile of socks. What her father said was true; the hotelkeeper in Portree was a rogue. She felt a sudden rush of anger at the men who owned shops and hotels on the island, who bought the islanders' wares for a pittance and sold them on to the summer tourists for many times what they had paid.

Mor had built up her nestegg by knitting dozens and dozens of pairs of socks and selling them to the merchant. Each evening, after dinner, she plied her needles whilst

Catriona sat on a stool at her feet. Once Catriona had asked Mor to teach her too, but Mor would not – Catriona had a brain and she would do better to use it for studying than knitting socks.

Over the years Mor had saved four pounds by selling her socks. The money was in an old tobacco tin, together with a guinea coin that had been a wedding present to Mor, hidden under the big wooden dresser.

It pained Catriona to spend the money that had been so hard earned, because although four pounds was a lot of money it represented the fruits of her mother's toil for every evening of her married life. Catriona had never seen Mor at night time without knitting needles in her hands, working so fast that the motion of her fingers was almost a blur. It took her a couple of evenings to knit a pair of socks, and after setting aside spare sets for Tom and the twins, every pair that she made she washed carefully in lye and then packed in her basket until the day came to sell them in Portree.

Catriona would go with her and watch the merchant carefully counting the socks and then taking a pair or two at random and holding them up to the light to check them for holes or joins in the wool. The merchant wouldn't buy socks where the wool had been knotted together because his customer's comfort might be disrupted by the bump. When the merchant's inspection was finished he would count the socks again and then the money, carefully, counting each coin twice before he gave it to her. Catriona felt her mother's satisfaction then, as she gave the merchant the list of things she needed and paid for them out of money that she had earned herself. Afterwards, Mor always bought her a something, a ribbon once though more usually a piece of candy that she could chew on the way home.

'I don't know why you bother, *annsachd*,' her father said once when they arrived home. 'I'd get you what you needed, whatever it was.'

'Yes,' Mor had said, 'but I like when I do it myself.'

Tom Nicolson was capable of leaving the house of a morning to go poaching and returning at nightfall with two or three pounds, and Catriona knew that he also made money by selling whisky that an old man brewed illicitly in a still hidden deep in the hills. Thing was, Tom was an easygoing man and nothing worried him, least of all the lack of money. Each rent day Mor would go through an ordeal of worry until at the last minute Tom would go out to get the money he needed and return a few hours later with coins ringing in his pocket.

A few months after Mor died, Catriona took out the basket of socks and found more than sixty pairs, which she decided to take to the merchant to sell herself.

Mor had told her once that she got fivepence a pair, and Catriona thought she would get more than a pound. She bundled up the socks and discarded a few pairs which she found to be flawed, realizing with a pain that cut like a knife that when Mor had winced with the pain of her last pregnancy she had also dropped a stitch.

The merchant looked at her with disdain until he remembered that she was Mor Nicolson's daughter, and then said grudgingly that he would give her five shillings for the lot.

'What?' Catriona gaped. 'You gave Ma fivepence the pair.'

'I wouldn't take them at all, lass,' he said, ''cept they were Mor's, because I've got more than I know what to do with.' He opened a cupboard to demonstrate that it was full.

'You see,' he went on as he counted out the money, 'I'm doing you a favour. I've more than enough to last the season and I can't afford to have all my money tied up in stock.'

'No,' Catriona said.

'What?' The merchant stopped counting and looked at her.

'You are not doing me a favour,' Catriona said as she began to gather up the socks.

'I am that,' the merchant insisted, 'and you've no need to do that, lass. I'll put them away myself.'

'You will not,' Catriona said, 'because I'm not selling them to you. You can keep your money and I'll keep my socks and that'll be an end to your nonsense.'

'What?' The man was astonished; he had never known a woman to talk back to him.

'My father'll use them, or my brothers. It's not worth it, selling them at a penny the pair. My mother'd be turning in her grave if she knew.'

'Your mother would be turning in her grave if she heard you talking to me like that!'

Catriona paused, framed by the doorway. 'She'd be laughing, because she'd know you deserved it. A penny for a pair of socks? That's highway robbery, even by your standards. Goodbye, Mister MacLeod.'

The merchant stood at the front of his store, watching Catriona as she cut a swathe through the fishermen passing the time of day and the tinkers selling trinkets.

An old man joined him, and nodded his head knowingly.

'A bonny lass, Catriona is. She's got her mother's looks for sure.'

The merchant stared at him. 'Maybe, Coinneach.'

'Aye,' the old man said. 'Her da came to me on the night, you know. When Mor died. He wanted me to say the prayer.'

'And didn't you?' The merchant was surprised, because everyone, even men like him who thought of themselves as educated and modern, knew the power of Coinneach's prayers.

'I did that, and many times, too. But it was too late, Callum Og. The woman was already dead when Tomas reached me. I sensed that. And Tomas, he knew too, but he wouldn't recognize it. There was the look of a wild man in his eyes and I prayed all I could, but I was praying for him and the children. Mor had already passed on. But Tomas is lucky to have Catriona, no? A bonny girl, and she works as hard as her mother, they say.'

The merchant turned to go back to his stock and his ledgers. 'She's bonny, yes, she's got Mor's looks, I grant you. But she's got her father's temper and all.'

'That's some woman she will be. Some wife.'

'Don't be daft,' the merchant said. 'A spirit like that'll soon get beaten out of her, by her husband if not her father.'

Coinneach Mor, the healer with the gift of stopping blood, walked away because otherwise he would have argued and everyone knew it was a waste of time to argue with the merchant MacLeod.

Catriona put the socks back in the dresser and used the rest of the money that Mor had saved.

The money had run out the previous year, when only the guinea was left, and for a year now Catriona had been making do with what she had and a couple of shillings that Angus gave her. Annie always helped; if there was anything that she needed then Annie gave it to her before she asked, but it offended her pride to rely so much on Annie when her father spent his days in idleness.

This year, she thought, as she walked home on that gentle spring day ripe with promise, she would have to make money somehow. The boys' shirts were done again, more thread than cloth, and her own blouse was a tapestry of darns; Ailish needed a new dress, as did Maire and Sine, Allan was clad in cast-offs from Annie's sons. But even if she managed to make Maire a dress from the remnants of Ailish's old one, she needed cloth to make dresses for Ailish and Sine. The potatoes were just about done and so was the meal; she had told her father but he had just shrugged disinterestedly.

What Alec said was true; there was no money to be made by selling oysters in Portree and it would be an insult to her mother's memory to let the merchant have her socks for a penny the pair. In any case, the twins and her father were getting through them, although she repaired each pair carefully and then when the holes defeated her carefully unravelled the wool and knitted a new pair from the old.

As she passed Annie's, Allan ran out joyfully to join her and she took his hand and walked the rest of the way home with him, as she let the sun calm the worst of her worries and listened to his chatter.

Old Hamish was standing by the dyke as usual, smoking the air through his empty pipe and watching the world through eyes as blue as the sky.

'It's a fine day, Catriona.'

'It is that.'

It was Hamish's job to keep the dyke in good order so that sheep would not stray onto the growing grounds, and every spring he would spend days gazing at the dyke before he got around to making the repairs. That day, Lachie the carter had brought some stones from the quarry and Hamish was staring at them as if by thought alone he could fix the gaps in the wall.

'You wouldn't have a spot of tobacco, Catriona?'

'I would not, Hamish. Da's not had any for months.'

'Ach, a pipe helps a man think, I always say. These cursed stones, I don't know what Lachie's thinking about. They are all the wrong size, every last one of them.'

Catriona smiled suddenly, remembering what her father said about old Hamish, that nothing was ever good enough for him but the excuse that it wasn't.

Allan tugged at her hand and she began to walk on, but Hamish stopped her.

'Who was that lass I saw Tom with?'

'Must've been me,' she said airily, wondering if he would ever get around to fixing the dyke before somebody else had to do it for him.

The potatoes were old and soft now, with skin wrinkled like an old man's cheeks. Ailish complained that they tasted bitter but Catriona knew there was nothing wrong with them beyond the effects of time; they had been in the pit for nearly a year. Allan fetched the potatoes for dinner; it amused him to climb into the pit and choose them one by one, discarding the ones that were too small or had sprouted. In September, just after the harvest, the pit had been full to overflowing and Catriona had been quietly content that there was enough to last the winter.

There never was quite enough; the spring months were the worst, with the old harvest done and the new harvest not in yet, the fields would be thick and green with sprouting tubers but the store would be bare. Tom had grown some turnips last year, but in March during the lambing they had begun to go bad so he cut them up and fed them to the sheep. In the old days Mor always had a boll of meal in the cottage to see them through the lean months but there hadn't been a whole boll of meal in the cottage since she died. Now when she needed one Catriona knew that her father did not have the twenty-four shillings he needed to buy it from Portree.

Even the precious guinea that she had saved as a keepsake and for good luck wasn't enough to buy the food she needed.

Allan came back to the cottage holding the potatoes in his smock, grinning duskily underneath the earth and straw that smudged his face.

Catriona took them and thanked him, and wiped the worst of the muck away from his hands and face; she always bathed him before bedtime but until then it was futile to try to keep a small boy neat and clean.

'You're sad,' he said pensively, 'you've got that look on your face.'

'I have not,' she said. 'I'm serious, that's all.'

'Why're you serious?'

She paused as she cleaned the potatoes. 'I'm not even serious, Allan, just thinking.'

His face creased into a puzzled look that lightened into a smile as Maire and Sine came in from school. Maire sighed deeply as she put down her school book. It was in English – she hadn't spoken a word of the language until she went to school, and the unfamiliar words bewildered her. Some of the island children never learned English, despite the teacher's efforts; they grew into adults who spent their lives in a kind of fuddled estrangement because they understood nothing of the tongue of the world beyond.

The twins came in next, breathless and smelling of sweat because they had been playing shinty; they had grown fast in the past year and they filled the cottage with the clumsy arrogance of adolescent boys. Alec sat down on his father's chair, his legs splayed wide; Ewan threw his jacket off and then put it away on his hook as Catriona shot him a look.

The cottage was suddenly full of noise, familiar, comforting noise and banter; only Ailish was missing and she always came in last of all. There was something flighty about Ailish, a restlessness that curtailed her attention. Although she was just two years younger than Catriona, she did not help with the work indoors. She had hair the colour of the dawning sun and big eyes as green as the sea, and a way of asking questions helplessly that made whoever she asked determined to help her. In The Braes she was thought of as pretty and treated with friendly reserve because looks like hers often went with vanity, and vanity was not a trait that was respected.

As Catriona watched Ailish grow, she realized that her sister knew she could get by with her smile and her pleading, misty eyes; in years to come, Catriona imagined, Ailish would marry one of the men who had a job fishing all year round who could make the money that a woman like Ailish needed to give her a life of comparative ease.

Catriona smiled to herself, because Ailish had told her a few weeks ago that since she was twelve now she had decided to think about getting a husband and she was wondering which one of the men would do, because, after all, in three or fours years it would be time for her to be wed.

Marriage seemed distant to Catriona; her mother had been dead for going on five years now and the tail end of her childhood had vanished into the obligation that had fallen upon her. She had grown up in these years, she knew; she had heard the old women say she would make some man a fine wife, but she had never thought of herself as that although some girls of her own age were already promised. She was content with her life, such as it was, and beyond that there was the distant prize to be gained if she fulfilled her mother's dreams and went to the city on the scholarship that Miss Anderson said she would win if she worked very hard.

Mor had plotted and schemed for that right from the day when Catriona won first prize in the infants' class.

Her father said it was stuff and nonsense. What did a

woman need to know – or a man for that – of life outside the island? The island, after all, was their home.

Mor had said she wouldn't listen to that nonsense, it was the daft talk of drunks and old men; there was a whole world outside the island where there was knowledge to gain, and also profit. The rigid barriers of the past were crumbling like the dykes around the potato patch because all men had the vote now, or most of them; and if they chose the government, then the government would have to listen and not just ignore them as it had done before.

'Men,' Tom said, clutching the word as if it was a lifeline against the force of his wife's will, 'men, that's right, *annsachd*. Men and not women. It's men who work in the world out there and not women. Women don't have the vote and they don't work, either.'

Mor stopped what she was doing and stood facing him, her hands braced against her waist. 'Oh, no, Tomas? What is it that I'm doing now? If the Land League had had its way, women would've had the vote as well as men, and it's nonsense to say that women don't work. They cook and clean and skivvy and earn good money for doing what I do for you for free, and besides that there's education for women now. There's women who are teachers and doctors and women lawyers, too.'

'No child of mine will become one of these scoundrels.'

'I'm not saying she will but God gave her a mind and she should have a chance. If she wants to learn, let her learn, and if she became a teacher you'd be proud of her, and don't you lie about it, Tomas, because I know you.'

Tom turned to Catriona, who had been listening intently. 'Is that right, precious? D'you want to go away and study all that lowland nonsense and come back knowing more than I do and thinking that you're better than us all?'

Catriona cleared her throat and looked at her father and then her mother, her father's face indulgent and her mother's radiant with hope.

She was only seven years old and she did not know what she wanted to do; she had never thought about it until she heard the teacher tell her mother that she had a good head on her shoulders and could get an education if she studied hard.

Mor winked almost imperceptibly in that secret gesture that sometimes passed between them when she wanted to get the better of Tom.

'I do, Da. Why not?'

'Ach, bloody hell, I don't know. Women.' He sat down, took his pipe out of his pocket and began to puff away at it, although he was only smoking fresh air because he'd not had tobacco all year. 'Away you go, Catriona. Become a lawyer, become a bloody judge for all I care.'

'Not a lawyer,' Mor said quickly. 'A teacher, maybe.'

'Whatever,' Tom said. 'Whatever you want, my precious, you just go and do it. I have to say that else your ma would be going on at me and coming away with all that lowland nonsense.'

'D'you mean it, Da?' Catriona said, suddenly glimpsing the possibilities that shone so brightly in her mother's eye.

'I do, precious, 'cept if you come back thinking you're better'n us I'll bring you down so fast you won't know what's happened, till you're not even a herring girl but a wee skivvy carting salt for a ha'penny a week.'

That was the way it was all decided, not by Catriona but by her mother. And once the decision was made she felt happy with it, because although she was very young she was also keenly interested in the world beyond the island where so much was happening that she did not understand.

Ailish and her father came in together, Ailish feigning tiredness and Tom strangely subdued as Catriona took the pots from the fire and served the potatoes and oysters with oatcakes and the butter she had churned that morning.

The calf, she thought suddenly. Tom's two milk cows had calved the previous year. One of the calves was a stirk that had been killed and salted for the winter; the other was now a healthy yearling that would fetch at least fifteen shillings at market.

'Da,' she said suddenly, 'Beathag's calf. Can you not sell it next month?'

He looked bemused for a moment until he realized what she was talking about. Both of his cows had names and he used to treat them like people until he lost all interest in the croft and its stock.

He smiled. 'I thought you were talking about old Aggie's lass for a minute.'

'The calf, Da, the yearling. There's a market in May, isn't there? Can you sell it?'

'Aye, pet, 'cept you'd get a better price if you waited till September.'

'I don't want to wait till then, Da.'

'Why d'you want to sell her, Triona?'

Catriona looked down at the food that was going cold on her plate. She'd never asked her father for money, not in all these years, but sometimes she had told him that she needed things and watched in dismay his reaction of impatience as he replied sharply that she was not to bother him with things like that.

Then she looked at Ewan's shirt, which had sprouted a rip right down the back since this morning, along the line of a patch she had sewn into it to make way for his growth.

'I could do with some calico, Da, and the potatoes ...'

He cut in quickly. 'I saw that, pet. They're just about done and I doubt they're good for seed. I've been planting the same for ten years now, must be. It's about time I got fresh seed. How much d'you need for calico, pet?'

'I'm not sure. About half a crown is enough, but it's cheaper if you buy a bolt and that's about ten shillings. It'd do for a couple of years, though.'

Tom put his hand into his pocket as he looked at her sorrowfully. 'If you needed money, pet, you only had to ask. I'm blind to all these things, your Ma used to say. Here's fifteen shillings, if that's enough. I'll get some meal when I buy the seed, and if you need any more, mind and tell me now.'

Catriona was so surprised that she forgot about her food

and had to eat it all in a rush when she realized that the others were finished.

She had worried so much for the last few months that she was dizzy with relief when she saw her father counting the money out. She was light-headed now, exultant even as she realized that she no longer had to worry, that there'd be meal to see them through to the harvest and cloth to make new shirts.

Her father had changed again, not to the old Tom who she had seen in glimpses these past few months but to another man who was no longer indifferent to his family's needs. In the first few months after Mor had died, his grief had frozen him until he was almost like stone as he sat on his chair by the fire, rarely moving unless the need to relieve himself made him get up slowly and go outside only to return shortly and resume the same huddled pose hard up against the flames, as if the warmth would melt the ice in his soul.

He had hardly eaten then. Catriona became used to leaving his food for him on a plate on the warmer, knowing that he wouldn't eat as she watched but much later in the depth of the night because he no longer slept properly, only sometimes his eyes closed in the afternoon and he would doze for an hour or two.

He seemed so fragile that she became reluctant to touch him for fear that he would falter and then collapse completely into his loss.

In the autumn of the year that Mor died, one evening he suddenly sat up and talked to her. He did not stop for many hours and she sat listening, sensing that otherwise he would lapse into silence again and maybe remain silent for ever.

'It was me,' he said, 'you know, it was me as much as the boy.' He couldn't yet bring himself to call Allan by name. 'Mor had a bad time with Maire, but she thought I wanted another son. I didn't. I didn't need another son or the making of one either. Some men do and there's them that say I'm one of them, but I loved your mother, pet. I wouldn't've touched a hair of her head if I'd known I would harm her.'

Not sure what he meant, Catriona went to him then and he folded her into his arms and sobbed like a baby until long after a fresh dawn leaked through the cottage's only window. He told her then that he would never take another wife.

After he'd finished digging the potato patch that spring, Tom moved Mor's chair back to its place opposite his by the fireside and told Catriona to sit there because she was growing too big for her stool. In the evening when the others had gone to bed they would talk for an hour or two in pleasant companionship about the little things that had happened during the day.

Once or twice Catriona caught him looking at her in a strange way and then as soon as he saw her watching him he would shake his head and change suddenly, almost as if he was ashamed of himself. He became distanced again, oddly detached as he pecked at her cheek before she went to bed and he no longer hugged her as he used to, in the way that had reassured her so much of his love. Sometimes, if she touched him to attract his attention or even accidentally as she passed him in the overcrowded cottage, he jerked away as if he wanted to avoid all contact with her. That hurt Catriona, although she did not let him know it.

After the evening meal was over, Ailish stood up abruptly as usual and said that she was going out to see her friends.

'Sit down,' Tom growled, so sharply that the twins stopped talking and Ailish gaped in amazement. 'You're aye gallivanting all around the place, Ailish. Is it not time you gave your sister a hand?'

'Catriona doesn't ...' Ailish began, before she hushed because of the way her father was staring at her.

'Maybe Catriona doesn't and maybe she does, but you don't know because you've never asked her. In any case, I've something to say to you, Ailish. Something to say to all of you.'

Catriona finished wiping the dishes and took Allan on her lap as she settled herself in her chair. Tom waited until the whole family was seated in a circle by the fireside, the twins with their grubby knees and shirts that dangled outside their trousers, Ailish in her dress that was bleached by many washings but adorned nevertheless with some lace that she had scrounged from a friend, and Maire and Sine looking bemused at the family gathering, a new ritual for them because it had fallen into disuse in the years since Mor died.

Catriona remembered, though, the way she and the twins had sat at their father's feet as Mor put the younger children to bed and had listened for an hour or more as he told them stories; Tom's children had grown up enchanted by the world they perceived through his eyes. Tom had not travelled far in the world, it was true, the furthest he had been was to Inverness and to Edinburgh, and both times he had ended up in gaol; there were those who said that every time he set foot off the island he went to gaol, but Tom had been to Kyleakin many times, and to Arisaig often when he was courting Mor, and he hadn't even been arrested then.

Of course he had mellowed since those days. Catriona could remember the time years before when the Land League was in its death throes and men came to persuade Tom to stand for Parliament. Even though the power of the League had waned, the name Tom Nicolson was known throughout the Highlands and if he stood for election he would win for sure. Tom had been interested, even flattered by the idea until he had learned that if he won he and Mor would have to go to live in London, or he would have to leave her in the island for most of the year. As soon as he realized that, he told the men to stop joking, because wild horses would not drag him away from his wife or the island and they were bloody daft even to suggest as much.

Mor had begged him to think again, carefully, before he refused, but Tom's mind was made up. He gave the men a drink, several drinks, and it was dawn when they left the cottage. The night hours had been rich with history and anecdotes but as a virgin day spread over the island he walked to the door with them, threw his arms towards the horizon and told them they were madmen to believe he would leave any of that.

As she watched him now, Catriona wondered what would have happened if her father had listened to her mother and become an MP.

Her father's expression changed again, as he took out his pipe and put in a tiny plug of tobacco which he lit with a spill from the fire. There was no laughter in his eyes any more, but then there had not been for years; the moment was portentous because there was a purpose in the measured calm of his face that was belied by the tremor in his hands.

'Right, well,' he said quickly, 'now you're all here, I'd best get on with it. I wanted to tell you all 'fore anyone else did, 'cos there'll be gossip, I 'spect. Not that there's aucht to talk about. I'm getting married again in ten days' time and the new wife, she'll be moving in with us and cooking our meals and the like. It'll be a weight off you, Catriona lass.'

Hamish's knowing face flashed before her: *'Who was that lass I saw Tom with?'*

'Must've been me.'

For a moment Catriona's world stopped.

Then she heard her father's voice going on, saying that he was going to marry Marsaili MacKay, from the next village, a pretty girl just a shade older than she should be for marriage because, the old women said, she had inherited her mother's nagging tongue.

The twins' heads hung in embarrassment or shame, she did not know which because the meaning was the same; it would be a terrible thing to see their father marrying a girl hardly older that his eldest daughter.

Maire and Sine were shocked into silence, only Ailish seemed unconcerned. Allan tugged at Catriona's sleeve, and she got up and made him ready for bed, settling him as quickly as she could because her mind was churning.

As her father talked on she took her shawl from the hook, wrapped it around her shoulders and slipped out before he could stop her.

In the dunes at the edge of the beach, the ducks and geese settling for the evening noticed her and their chatter ceased momentarily and then continued as she walked amongst them, careful not to disturb their nests.

Further out a heron stood one-legged, poised to catch a fish as the setting sun cast its shadow upon the water, the image and reflection merging briefly as the bird delved for its prey and then parting again in the way that lovers might if a stranger disturbed their bliss.

The air was alive with birdsong and the melody of the sea. There were oystercatchers and kittiwakes, terns and gulls, puffins and auks; even starlings, as audacious as gnats, as they guarded the shore that they thought of as their own.

Catriona walked on across the edge of the tide as soft waves lapped at her feet. The sands stretched for a mile or more; there was a sense of timelessness about this place that was lulled by the endless motion of the sea and the passage of clouds in the sky.

As the sun set far to the west, the last light of the day cast a glow over the ocean that scorched her eyes. The beach had absorbed most of her sorrow over these years; it had given her food and also joy. Just briefly, for a moment an hour or two before, she had believed that at last her life had changed – not completely, but just enough so that she would have time to dream again.

She sensed someone behind her and turned and saw her father, striding towards her with his trousers rolled above his knees. The sunset coppered his auburn hair and lit the hard set of his jaw; she saw then what it was that women wanted in him.

He stopped and stood there, staring at her so hard that she would have flinched if she had not been so angry.

The sunset coloured her brown hair in the same way; her eyes were the colour of her hair and when she was startled she had the nervous grace of a young fawn. Tom Nicolson loved her in that moment for being who she was, what her mother had been, would have been still if she had not died. His daughter had beauty, but none of the arrogance that usually tarnished it.

For a long time they stood there in silence looking at each

other, Catriona wondering what he had come to say and Tom trying to find a way of saying it.

'Catriona,' he said in a hushed voice. 'Don't judge me harshly. I'm doing it for you, you know.'

She stared at him for a long time and then she turned away. 'Don't ever say that to me again, Father. Don't ever say that to me again.'

Chapter Two

Catriona knew nothing of Marsaili MacKay, beyond what people said.

She was spoilt, they said. They said that she'd turn like her mother, and her mother was a notorious nag who made her husband's life hell. Archie MacKay had to be working every hour that God sent to keep Mary MacKay and Marsaili in the style to which they'd become accustomed.

Mary MacKay was known for her airs and graces in a place where nobody else ever had either. She wore ornate hats that cost five shillings each and she'd had a new stove fitted in her cottage that went on fire and burned the roof off. She hired Lachie to drive her to Portree in his cart when she wanted to go shopping; she was too proud and too lazy to walk like everyone else. And Marsaili was just as bad, or so they said. Catriona did not know.

It was said that Marsaili MacKay was so vain that she had turned down three or four Braesmen because they were not good enough for her and that she had actually tried to entrap a monied tourist and made a terrible fool of herself by turning up at the Royal Hotel in Portree dressed in a ballgown when the tourist had asked her and her mother for tea. It was said that she painted her lips to make them red and spread powder on her skin to whiten it and that she preened for hours before a mirror before she deigned to set a foot out of the house. And her language was polished and deft, her English affected like a landlord's, but when she was crossed Gaelic curses tripped from her lips like raindrops in March and she could swear like a tinker when the mood took her.

Annie told Catriona that Tommie Matheson once fancied Marsaili and had taken her to a dance, but he told Annie that when he touched her she felt like a barrel because she had a corset on and that dancing with Marsaili was like dancing with a corpse. When she laughed the corset burst and her dress ripped and her stomach swelled like a cow's udder.

Catriona smiled as Annie went on: 'Tommie says she's really fat underneath it all and she had so much lavender water on that he sneezed when he got close to her. When her corset burst she got really upset and slugged him one when he laughed at her and teetered off home in those daft shoes that she wears, but he says that Niall MacArthur actually kissed her one day and she tasted really strange and afterwards when Niall went home everyone was laughing at him because that stuff she wears on her lips was all over his mouth.'

Catriona laughed then, despite herself.

She had to attend the wedding for her father's sake. It was so strange, the way that her life had been turned in on itself in the space of just a few days.

She hardly knew Marsaili at all; she had only exchanged a few words with her before the day that she watched her walk down the aisle and become Tom's bride.

Tom's voice as he made his vows was hesitant and uncharacteristically quiet; there was something furtive and hurried in his manner as if he wished the ceremony to be over in a trice.

As Tom and Marsaili turned to face the congregation, Catriona caught a glimpse of his face.

She knew then that he had been lying when he promised to love Marsaili and cherish and honour her.

There was no expression there beyond regret and she felt an impulse to run to him and urge him to recant before the register was signed.

But she was wedged tightly in the pew with Allan on one side and her uncle Angus on the other. Her eyes met her father's briefly; he turned away and then, afterwards, it was too late.

Marsaili was triumphant, victorious as Tom's bride; as she stood outside the church with Tom, Catriona realized that she hated her, not for being the woman she was, but for trapping Tom into a marriage that he did not want.

What was it that Iain Macdonald had said to her, late at night after she had spent long hours talking to Annie? 'Tom Nicolson always did have his sense in his trousers before her married your mother, pet. Maybe that's what's happened; his sense has gone back to the place it always was.'

Catriona looked at Marsaili again and felt a flush of disgust.

Annie's cottage was quiet after the forced gaiety of the wedding dance.

'Sit down,' she said, 'you'd best get a rest while you can. There'll be mayhem later.'

The Nicolson children were staying at Annie's to give Tom and his bride privacy on their wedding night.

'I don't know, Annie. They all looked pretty subdued.'

Carefully, Annie measured tea into the spoon and tipped it into the kettle. It would be September before Iain earned anything and she had only half a caddy left. For weeks she had been ekeing it out leaf by leaf so that it would last until then and drinking tea so weak that it tasted more of water than anything else. Abruptly, she cursed and put a whole extra spoonful in.

'To hell with poverty,' she said. 'That's what Mor used to say, d'you remember, Catriona? Things would get so bad, like the year the fishing was terrible and there was hardly a potato left. Your da went off and did a bit of poaching and Mor sold a gross of her socks and she came round here with a half boll of meal and a side of venison and tea, even. "To hell with poverty," Mor said. "To hell with all that."'

Annie laughed at the memory, shaking her head. 'That was your da in the old days, pet. Your Ma as well.'

Catriona fell silent for a moment as Annie added honey and fresh milk to the tea. Allan had settled in her lap and his body turned heavy as he slept. Gently, Annie carried him over to the cot.

'Maybe I shouldn't be talking like that, pet. Maybe you don't want to remember.'

'No, Annie.' Catriona smiled. 'I want to remember. Sometimes I think memory's the only thing that keeps me alive.'

The image of Tom's face stayed in Catriona's mind as the day passed, the rest of her family arrived and they all ate and then went to bed. In the twilight of the evening her sisters chattered and she could hear the noises of boisterous games coming from the barn where Ewan and Alec were supposed to be sleeping with Annie's sons. She lay with her arms behind her head, oblivious to the sounds of glee and Annie's occasional whispered hushes.

Her father was a big man in The Braes, in the whole of Skye. He'd been famous since he was a lad and men and women too still looked to him for leadership, looked to him to make sense of the world outside that sometimes they did not understand.

Only Mor and later she herself had seen the shadows of doubt that haunted him still, the endless consideration of the past.

Tom's bitterness had come out rarely when Mor was alive, more often when he was alone with his thoughts and his dreams of what might have been.

The frustration and the injustice of it all plagued him still; in the depths of the night she often watched him sitting at the fire staring at the flames as the old dilemmas nagged at his mind.

One night she watched as he took the copy of the Napier Report that contained the testimony of the men of The Braes and put it on the fire and then, as it turned to ashes, put his copy of the Crofters Act on top and raked the peats until the flames roared and danced.

'Why, Da?' she asked.

'Because it's a lie, pet. It's a fucking lie.'

He gazed at the fire until the books had been reduced to blackened leaves that splintered and drifted upwards on the draught.

'Once you read the words and get the meaning from them, you realize that their bloody justice is the biggest lie of the lot. See, pet, what they gave us, these bloody crofts and security of tenure and fair rents and all that blah, see, pet, that was what we had already.'

'No, you didn't Da,' she said sleepily, remembering the stories of the clearances, of people by the thousand being driven off the lands as their cottages were burned to the ground. The memory of those years haunted the island; here and there, on land long given over to sheep, there were the skeletons of houses, charred rectangles burnt onto the ground where the sound of sheep chomping grass rang hollow against the echoes of the past.

'Ah, but we did, pet. That was it. This Crofters Act, this bloody nonsense about tenancy and tenure and fair rents and improvements and all that; we always had that. *Duthchas* it was called; a man's right to the land. We didn't know we'd lost it till it was far too late; they'd been clearing the glens for fifty years before they started on the islands, and people said, the landlords are different here, they're not strangers, they're clan chiefs. But all the bloody landlords, bloody so-called clan chiefs, did the same; they cleared the people. And cleared them and cleared them; it went on for half a century before it stopped. And why did it stop? Because they realized that we'd become wise to their lie and men would stand and die before they let themselves be driven out of their homes, women as well. And so they didn't dare try it because they didn't want another war with the people like they have in Ireland; we had the crofts then. The Crofters Act made no difference, and nor did anything that's happened since. The whole bloody nonsense was just an excuse to put a few uppity rascals like your father in gaol.

'Bloody babble,' Tom said, raking the ashes. 'Pure bloody babble. We threw a few stones and they said it was a crofters' rising, pure revolution in The Braes. They sent gunboats to arrest Big John from Glendale. Bloody gunboats in Loch Poolteil!'

*

As soon as Catriona heard Annie rise from the bed behind the curtain, she got up herself and went outside to fetch the pail of water, looking dismally towards her own house, vaguely defined against the mist. Quietly, in words as sharp as the morning air, she cursed Marsaili and then prayed to a God that she did not usually trust to keep her father safe from the wiles of his wife.

After breakfast she thanked Annie for her hospitality and then walked to school slowly, her eyes scalded with fatigue. In school, she listened uninterestedly to the lesson as knowing looks passed between her brothers and their friends. Disjointed thoughts drifted around her mind; she found herself thinking of her father and Marsaili and of the way her father had been with her mother, and what Mor would have felt had she known what would happen to him.

The reality of it hurt her, as if her deepest dread had suddenly become true; the knowledge alone was hard to bear.

Two years ago a woman had come to visit once or twice, a kindly widow from Balmeanach who would bring scones with her and once a honey bannock. Tom treated her hospitably but with distance; after she left he cursed and threw the honey bannock on the fire and Catriona's mouth watered as the sugar fizzled and burst.

'Why, Da?' she had asked him.

'The bitch, the bloody woman, she wants me to wed her. Doesn't she know I'd never wed anyone else after I married your mother?'

He had said that twice to her, he'd made a promise that had been broken. What was it he had said when she reminded him of it? 'Things change, Catriona.'

Only that.

At the end of school she would return to a home that had been invaded by a stranger; she hardly knew Marsaili yet suddenly she had entered her life and swept all of the past aside in one easy gesture.

'Your Da was bound to take another wife,' Annie had said, yesterday, after the others were settled in bed.

'Why?' Catriona asked. 'He doesn't love Marsaili.'

Annie turned away so that Catriona would not see the look on her face, but Catriona caught it anyway.

'There's other things in a marriage apart from love, pet.'

'What things?'

'Ach, it's just men.' Annie's manner changed then, became almost flippant. 'They need us more than we need them. A widow'll get by and work the croft herself, but a man, well, he'll wander around the place like a foundling until he's found another wife. And your da's a young man yet. There's many good years left in him. You'll grow up and make your way in the world and Tom'd be left alone with his memories.'

'He doesn't love her, Annie. He doesn't.'

Annie brushed her hair from her brow. 'For a man like Tom, Triona, love only comes once.'

'Why did he marry Marsaili, then?'

Annie shook her head. 'I don't know, pet. As God's my judge, I do not know.'

'Catriona?' Miss Anderson's sharp voice cut into her thoughts. She had not realized that the teacher was talking to her and now the whole class was looking at her and she felt colour rise in her cheeks.

'Yes, Miss Anderson?'

'Could you show us where Montenegro is on the map?'

'Yes, Miss Anderson.' Catriona rose obediently and walked to the front of the schoolroom.

At the core of Europe, the Balkans blurred and melted into one. She could remember Montenegro somewhere at the edge of the Adriatic but all of a sudden she could not remember exactly where and pointed instead to Albania, recognizing her mistake almost as soon as she had made it.

'I'm sorry,' she said, as Miss Anderson corrected her.

'Don't worry about it, Catriona.'

Catriona returned to her desk and gave her attention to the lesson.

'Now' Miss Anderson was saying, 'the members of the Balkan League are Bulgaria, Serbia, Greece and Montenegro. The Balkan League is at war with Turkey, the former colonial power. What is the name of the old Turkish empire?' Her eyes swept the room, falling on the twins. 'How about you, Alec?'

Alec looked down as Catriona mouthed the word 'Ottoman' to him.

'Alec, I asked you a question.'

'Miss Anderson, I'm sorry, but I don't know the answer, Miss Anderson.'

The teacher's lips formed a taut line along the edge of her mouth. 'If you ever listened you might, Alec. And what about you, Ewan? Do you know, by any small chance?'

'I'm very sorry, Miss Anderson, but I'm afraid that I don't.'

'It's as well Catriona's your sister, isn't it? Otherwise I'd think that the angels were looking the other way when the Nicolson family brains were handed out.'

The twins reddened but said nothing.

'Does anyone else know, apart from Catriona?'

'Yes, Miss Anderson, I know,' Michael, the minister's son, said. 'The old empire based in Turkey was the Ottoman empire but there was a revolution four years ago and some army officers took over and deposed Sultan Abdul Hamid.'

Ewan tittered and a frisson of mirth spread around the room.

'I wouldn't laugh, if I were you,' Miss Anderson said, 'because the great powers are very concerned about the situation in the Balkans. Germany is seeking influence there and the King's advisors are concerned about the Kaiser's intentions. That could mean war, you know.'

Catriona looked at Ewan and Alec, then remembered that the remnants of the Land League had driven the army recruiters out of The Braes. No, she thought then, that can't be right. There'll not be another war again, how could there be if men refuse to fight one?

The teacher stopped her on her way out, putting a proprietorial arm on her shoulder in a gesture that Catriona resented for its intimacy.

'I'm sorry,' Miss Anderson said, 'I should have known that you'd be tired today.'

Catriona smiled weakly. She did not like the way the teacher took such a close interest in her.

'Congratulations,' Miss Anderson said, smiling broadly.

'What?' she said, rather rudely, but she was too surprised to be polite.

'Your father getting wed again. It must be a weight off your mind.'

Catriona must have flinched then, though she did not mean to, because suddenly the teacher's expression changed and became wistful.

'I know,' she said, 'it won't be easy, but it's for the best in the end, Catriona. It's no life for a man on his own. It'll work in time, if you give it a chance, and you will, won't you? You're not a stupid girl, Catriona. Everything in this world takes time, and people most of all.'

'Yes,' Catriona said, thanking the teacher and hurrying away before she gave vent to the anger she felt gathering inside her, as insistent and ominous as the sky that darkened before a storm.

That evening, as she sat eating the stew Marsaili had cooked, nausea rose inside her.

After a mouthful or two she pushed the plate aside.

Tom shot her a warning glance.

'It's not the food, Da. It's just I'm not hungry.'

'There's some bannocks my mother baked in the tin,' Marsaili said.

'Really, I'm not hungry.'

Mechanically she began to gather together the plates after the meal was finished until she realized that Marsaili would clear up now; it was her role, as the woman of the house. She put the plates down with a clatter as Marsaili looked at her askance and then walked abruptly out of the house.

'I'll go to her,' she heard Marsaili saying.

'No,' her father said, 'leave her be.'

Much later he came outside, filling his pipe with the plug of tobacco that Iain had given him.

'Give Marsaili a chance, pet, she's not that bad.'

She gazed at him and saw the doubt in his own eyes, and something else that was too fleeting to catch.

Don't say anything, she thought, don't say a word because you'll make it worse. But Tom was looking at her intently, waiting for her to speak.

'Really, Da, I wasn't hungry.' She shrugged and hugged herself as she felt the evening wind begin to bite.

'I didn't like it either. She'd boiled all the taste out of it. I said, "Why didn't you roast it?" I mean, it was a good bit of lamb from Angus, and d'you know what she said, "What do I roast it in?" I said, "Over the fire, of course." But she said you need a stove for roasting and when I said you and Mor always managed she said we were living in the dark ages without a stove and everyone had a stove these days and I'd have to get one for her if I wanted roast meat. I said, "Over my dead body, only a madman would pay five guineas for an iron box to hold a fire ..."'

As Tom gabbled on she watched the flickering changes of mood on his face, the way he tried to mask his feelings with mirth as he usually did, but the anger flowing just below the surface shaded his grin with a scowl that made his voice melt into a blur of words whose tone held more meaning than the words themselves.

'Da ...' she tried to interrupt but the flood just continued the way a river continues to run once its banks are burst, and so she just stayed silent and let him talk.

Marsaili came to the door of the cottage, smiling brightly and wiping her hands on her apron. 'Tom,' she said, and then 'Tom!' louder, in a voice sharp with frustration.

Tom ignored her and rattled on.

'Goodness' sakes, Tom. Catriona, has your father gone deaf?'

Catriona made a helpless gesture.

Marsaili walked over and grabbed Tom's arm, tugging at it twice before he paused and looked down at her.

'What is it?'

'Your tea's ready and poured. It'll get cold if you don't come and drink it.'

'What ...' He hesitated for a moment and then turned and followed her in with a resigned shrug.

You're not his wife, Catriona thought as she watched Marsaili usher him indoors.

You don't even know him, she realized as Marsaili's high-pitched voice rang out from the cottage, impatiently telling Catriona to come in for her tea.

Meekly she entered the cottage and took the cup, content that Marsaili could never take her mother's place.

The beach became her refuge. Each afternoon after school she walked there, sometimes alone and sometimes with Allan.

The sound of the sea lulled her; she would sit for hours gazing at the waves and then return home calm to face Marsaili's chatter and do her schoolwork as best she could.

The atmosphere had changed; her father's humour was forced and everyone knew it except for Ailish, who lived in the clouds as she always did.

Sometimes, as she watched Marsaili at work, Catriona felt like a stranger.

One day as they searched for lobsters stranded by the tide, Allan clutched her hand too tightly and she sensed that he was worried, but when she asked him he wouldn't say why.

She picked up a razorfish shell and began to draw patterns in the sand, at first random shapes to catch his interest and then a map of the Balkans.

'What's that?' Allan asked and she explained the shapes of the countries and told him about the Balkans and the King and the Kaiser.

The game amused Allan for a time until the tide turned and waves came in, and the boundaries of the Balkans melted and disappeared into the sand.

'Da says it's a lot of bloody nonsense,' she said.

'What is?'

'Miss Anderson says there'll be war but he says there won't be because half the country'd rather fight for the Kaiser.'

'What's war?'

She looked down as his innocent face. 'I don't know, Allan. The King declares war and then all the men join the army and go to fight, but Da says they won't.'

'Would you go?'

'No, Allan. Women don't go to war.'

'Will you go anyway?'

His expression became intense suddenly, as if that was what had been troubling him all along.

'What d'you mean?'

The words came out so fast that they tumbled together and she had to ask him to repeat them.

'Ewan said you were going away once you'd finished school because you'd get a scholarship. Alec said that Ma used to say you were the only one in the family with a brain.'

Catriona smiled. 'That was Ma and me, Allan. Ma had a dream that I'd win a scholarship and go away and come back a rich woman.'

'Will you?'

'I doubt it, Allan.'

'D'you want to go?'

'Not till you're grown yourself and then we could go away together.'

As she took his hand and they raced the tide along the shore, she had a sudden sense that Mor was talking to her, telling her not to forget the dream, but when she stopped to listen there was nothing there.

Spring ripened into summer; the island transformed like a chameleon from the monochromes of winter to bright sunlit colours as sharp as the sunrise.

The parched, wintry bracken faded on the hills and the grass grew until the grazings were ripe for cattle once more; as clouds drifted overhead their patterns fell in glancing shadows that textured the earth. Of all of Skye, only the Cuillins resisted the changing seasons; in spring, snow clung to the peaks and even in August the heights remained stoically unchanged despite the growth that flourished all around. The mountains were the only constant in a landscape that changed like a kaleidoscope; the passage of the sun formed sculptured shapes that moved like windswept driftwood over the backdrop of the peaks.

In July the school year ended and Catriona won first prize as usual; she had hoped that her father would come to see her receive it but when she looked around he was not there and instead Marsaili sat in his place, clapping energetically for everyone but particularly when Catriona shyly walked up to the podium and accepted the leather-bound copy of *Pilgrim's Progress* from the minister.

Catriona swallowed her disappointment and walked home with Marsaili and her brothers and sisters; when they passed the potato patch she realized what had gone wrong.

Tom was standing by the dyke, his sleeves rolled up, as Angus ushered the last of the sheep from the plants. His good jacket was slung over the wall and she saw that his tie hung loosely about his neck.

'I'm gey sorry, pet,' he said as soon as he saw her. 'I was all dressed and ready to come when I saw that the sheep had got in.'

Old Hamish was standing there as usual, smoking the air and nodding his head sagely. Tom turned to him and loosed off a string of Gaelic curses that left Hamish looking not contrite but indignant.

'Tom, Tom,' wailed Hamish when Tom paused at last to take a breath, 'but Tom, you're not listening.'

'Bloody right I'm not,' Tom growled. 'You make as much sense as a barking dog.'

'Ach, Tom, listen, will you? I'm trying to tell you, it isn't that I didn't fix the wall, it's that I fixed it and it fell down again.'

'And whose fault was that?'

'Not mine, for certain, because I left it standing. It was either Lachie's fault or God's fault. Not mine.'

'And you just left the sheep to wander about the potatoes?'

'I was just walking along to the brow of the hill to see where Lachie was with the stones, and bugger me if they didn't get in when I wasn't looking.'

'They wouldn't've got in at all if you'd fixed it right in the first place.'

'You can't say that, Tomas, because you don't know if they would or they wouldn't. You weren't here, were you? You were playing around with that new wife of yours.'

Tom finished wedging the stones together and turned to Catriona. 'I'm sorry, pet. I really am, but when we came up here, me and Angus, the sheep were all over the place and we had to fetch them out before they'd eaten the whole crop.'

'It's all right, Da,' she said. 'It wasn't your fault.'

'And not mine either,' Hamish cut in.

She ignored him.

At home she put the book carefully on the dresser with the others. Almost immediately Alec took it down and began to peer at it.

'Bloody hell,' he said, 'that's useless. You've got *Pilgrim's Progress* already, Triona.'

She did not care. She had read only the first of her prizes, a vapid and earnest book of religious tracts. The stories held no interest for her; their chaste morality had little relevance to her life.

Marsaili's plump hand shot out, snatching the book from Alec. She looked entranced as she fingered the burnished leather of the binding.

'A good book,' she said, 'I've heard about it. If you don't mind, Catriona, then I'll have a read at it in the evening.'

Alec looked at Catriona and sniggered. Marsaili could not read at all, they had realized that one day when she was watching Maire trying to write on her slate.

'Clever girl,' Marsaili had said, when she thought Catriona was out of earshot. 'What does it say?'

Alec and Ewan had nudged each other and giggled and spent the rest of the afternoon writing rude words on their slates and trying to get Marsaili to copy them.

Ever since Marsaili married Tom she had been nagging him to buy a stove as she served food that was either burned through or barely cooked at all.

Nobody could be that stupid, Catriona thought as Marsaili continued to dish up hard potatoes and bannocks that were soft inside but scorched at the edges. They did not really need a stove, for they had plenty of good cooking pots and a heavy griddle that never burned anything if it was fixed properly to the rack. Mor had cooked with these utensils all her life and Catriona had learned to use them easily within days of her mother dying.

But Marsaili groaned and bitched and Tom viewed it all with bored resignation, as if he knew what was going on but would do nothing to change it.

'I've been thinking,' Marsaili said to him one day, when they had all crunched their way through a fish that was charred to the colour of soot, 'you can get a wee stove for only three guineas and I got one guinea from Ma for my wedding. Pa'll give me another and then you can give me a third and we'll have our stove, Tom, and no more nonsense about making me cook like a Druid.'

'If it was good enough for Mor and Catriona it's good enough for you,' Tom grunted as he thumbed his way through a month-old copy of the *Glasgow Herald* which someone had brought back from the city.

'But times are changing, Tom,' Marsaili went on. 'Even Eileen MacInnes is getting one.'

'Over my dead body,' Tom said, turning a page.

Marsaili seemed to think for a moment and then sat down in front of him. 'Tom?'

He ignored her.

'Tom?' Her eyes were wide and moist with tears. Marsaili put her face in her hands and began to sob. 'I've done all that I can, Tom. I've never cooked on a fire and Ma, she says it's a lot of nonsense, making us live like heathens. Everyone's getting a stove now and you can afford it.'

Tom shifted his chair to catch the evening light to read his paper.

'Tom, it's nothing, really nothing. Only a guinea.'

A shaft of sunlight flooded the cottage then, as far to the west the sun slid towards the horizon. The light caught Marsaili, glinting off the tears that slipped down her rosy cheeks and making her contorted face ugly in the harshness of its scrutiny.

Tom fixed her with his stare. 'Stop it, Marsaili,' he said, in the same detached way that he might tell Maire to stop playing with the cooking pots if she was making too much noise. His attention rested with her for only a moment before he returned to the paper.

Marsaili stood up. 'That's enough. I've had it. If you're too mean to get a stove, then I'm not slaving over the fire like a tinker.'

She flounced out, banging the door, and from the dim recess at the back of the room Catriona watched Tom reading the paper as if nothing had happened at all.

Much later Catriona walked out into the evening as the sky turned to violet in the north and the hills cast long shadows over the sea. Over the sound, the isle of Raasay floated gently; the landscape faded with distance, the rise of the mainland beyond was just a faint outline against the clouds.

Seagulls wheeled above and the last rays of the sun caught them and sharpened their image as they soared and dived; the wind paled into a whisper as the day finally died.

She had expected to see Marsaili weeping somewhere but the path was empty; Eileen's door was closed and so was Annie's.

She turned and saw Ewan and Alec ambling towards her, kicking stones.

'What happened?' Alec asked.

'Da and Marsaili had a row. I thought she'd be bleating somewhere but she's not.'

'She's gone,' Alec said. 'We saw her on the way to Balmeanach. She went home.'

Catriona wanted to stay out for longer, but she saw Lachlan Maclean in the distance; when he waved at her she got up and walked home with the twins.

In the cottage Tom was still sitting reading the paper. He made no move to go to bed as Ailish and then the twins settled down.

When the cottage was quiet Catriona saw that he was not reading any more, just staring listlessly at the print. The paper had been open at the same page for ages. After a time he put it down and looked away briefly before his gaze fell on her.

'Ach, away, Catriona,' he said. 'It's long after the time you should be in your bed.'

'Can I get you anything, Da? A bite to eat?'

'No, precious. I'm not hungry.'

She waited for him to say something because she could see the pain in his face.

'You could fetch me a drop of whisky, if there is any.'

Mor had always kept a flask or two of the special whisky that her father distilled in the dresser, in the drawer to which only she had the key, which Catriona now kept hidden in the old holed kettle that had never been fixed.

Quickly she fetched one of the flasks and poured some into his mug.

Tom drank deeply and then sighed again. 'You're your mother's daughter, pet. It's well seen who you are.'

He drained his cup and she poured him a little more.

'You'd best leave it with me, precious. It's past time for you to get to bed.'

'I'm not tired, Da. I don't mind.' She so much wanted him to tell her what he was thinking that she hardly dared to move.

'Ahh, but I do, pet. A growing lass needs her sleep and it's not for you to sit up all night with an old man like your da.'

'I said I don't mind, Da.'

'Triona, pet, I do. It's best if you get to bed.'

Very slowly, her limbs stiff through inertia, she rose.

'I never thought I'd taste the like of this again,' he said as he picked up the flask.

'There's a bit more put by, Da, if ever you want it.'

He chuckled and for the briefest time the sound of his laughter lifted her heart. Then he became sombre again, and spoke words that, Catriona recognized, came from her mother: 'Never let the river run dry, Triona. Keep a drop or two for the morn and then the sunrise will give you some more of her own.'

There was a pause, and then: 'Catriona?'

'Yes, Da?'

'You've a drop more put by, pet?'

'I have, Da.'

'Well, precious, keep it well hidden from me because this is not the water of life but the tears of angels. I'd not want to drink it again until I'm ready, pet. You understand that.'

'I do, Da.'

'Now get to bed, pet, because you need your sleep.'

She hesitated. 'Da?'

'What, Catriona?'

'Don't let Marsaili hurt you, Da.'

He shook his head. 'Yon'd never hurt me, Triona. Yon might nag but I hear it no more than I hear the noise of cackling hens. Don't even think about it. And Triona?'

'Yes, Da?'

'These years of your childhood, they're precious years, pet. Don't wish them away for years you've not lived yet.'

He opened his arms to her then and hugged her for a long time until her eyelids were heavy and she was ready for sleep.

Marsaili came back the next day and Tom took her in as if nothing had happened, and Catriona felt despair in the pit of her stomach when she saw the look of patient resignation on his face.

Marsaili got her stove two weeks later. Catriona took Allan home early one day – he had a summer cold, as the island children often got because even on the hottest day the wind could suddenly turn chill.

As soon as she walked into the cottage she realized that something had changed. The table and chairs were pushed up against the wall and Marsaili was on her knees spreading a ragged old rug that her mother had given her. The dresser had been eased out of its place and wedged in between the back door and the wall.

'You're home soon,' Marsaili said, ignoring Allan's pale face.

'Allan's not well,' Catriona said. 'And the wind's turned fresh. He'll be better indoors.'

Marsaili looked at him. 'Ach, nonsense, Catriona. He's right as rain, aren't you, pet?'

Allan hid behind Catriona's skirt and did not reply.

'He's got a chill, so I thought I'd put him to bed to sleep it off.'

'Whatever,' Marsaili said, vague as always when it came to anyone's interests apart from her own.

'You won't believe it,' she said, after Allan had been tucked up. 'We're getting a stove.'

'How's that?'

'Well, when I pulled the dresser out this morning to lay the rug, I found an old tin.'

'No,' Catriona murmured.

'I did so,' Marsaili said, ignoring the pained look on Catriona's face. 'And there was a guinea in it, so I said to Tom, was that his savings like and he said he knew nothing about it.'

'It was Mother's money,' Catriona said. 'A guinea my gran gave her on her wedding day.'

'Ach, well, I spent it. I gave it to Lachie and he took it to Portree and he's just back this minute. He says the stove'll be here tomorrow.'

'Marsaili, that was my mother's money. She left it to me.'

'Nonsense, Catriona. When she died, it was your Da's, and since he didn't know about it, he'll not know anything about the loss.'

Catriona went to the door. 'It was my money, Marsaili. You had no right to spend it.'

'Where're you going?'

'To Portree. To the merchant. To get it back.'

'Ach, away and don't be daft.'

'I am, Marsaili.'

'You are not, Catriona. I've spent it on my stove.'

'You had no right to do that, Marsaili. I know the merchant. If I speak to him, he'll give me it back.'

'Away and don't be stupid. The merchant might not have it any more. Lachie was away at the back of seven o'clock this morning and it's the afternoon now. The merchant'll have dozens of guineas in his shop. How'll you know which one is yours?'

Catriona closed her eyes. That's true enough, she thought, it wasn't a guinea, it was *the* guinea, and how would the merchant know which one, when there would be so many in his coffers?

Marsaili was looking at her indignantly.

How come, Catriona thought, how come you can be so stupid and then when it comes to money, you've more sense than any of us?

The anger made her weak. All of a sudden she felt faint, her knees buckled and she swayed briefly before she regained her equilibrium. In the cot in the corner Allan slept, and so, very quietly, she tiptoed out and then ran and ran up to the top of Ben Lee where she was miles away from the village and Marsaili and her wiles.

From afar the cottages looked tiny; there was her own, all alone in its patch beyond the others, and Annie's, surrounded by children, and Eileen MacInnes's with the potatoes sprouting all around because Eileen planted extra to feed her greed.

She sat down on a patch of grass, folded her head in her arms and cried until she felt the weather change. The wind dropped and the clouds drew back so that the sun burned like a beacon, blinding her at first, and she had to blink several times before she got used to it.

When her eyes closed she saw the vista of her home and Annie's and Eileen's and then all the others, outlined in a ruddy monochrome that faded fast into blackness as the image dissolved.

Way out to sea, an ocean steamer smeared the horizon; in the distance she imagined that Uist blended with the ends of the earth.

She remembered what her mother had said about the island: 'To us it's the universe, pet, but in the whole wide world it's just a tiny part.'

She felt very small then amongst the power of the mountains and expanse of the sea.

She tried to hear her mother's voice but there was silence, bar the faintest hint of a laugh that was the last of the wind as it disappeared into the funnel of the Cuillins.

In a strange way she accepted the hurt; she did not argue with Marsaili again and when the stove came she acquiesced to it and did not protest when Marsaili rearranged the contents of the cottage around it. She said nothing to Tom at all.

'I know,' Allan said the next day.

'You know what?'

'Marsaili took the guinea. I heard her tell you.'

'Don't worry about it,' she said.

When Tom was at home Marsaili bustled around the cottage cooking and cleaning, but once he was gone she would turn to Catriona and ask her if she didn't mind doing this or that because she felt a headache coming on. Catriona always did the jobs that Marsaili disliked, like milking the cows and mucking out the byre. She did not mind, but she felt Marsaili's disdain and she resented that.

Marsaili nagged Tom; Catriona could hear the sound of her voice at night from the other room, whining constantly that she needed money for this and that. The strange thing was that Tom always gave her what she wanted. The sound of them together sickened Catriona. Is it worth it, Da? she would ask herself as she heard the rhythmic movement of the bed against the wall. In the mornings her father would avoid her eyes as he ate his breakfast and then quickly leave the house. She never knew where he went, only that he wasn't poaching because he never brought anything back.

There had been a change in him ever since the stove arrived, as if he had given up the struggle and had left his life up to fate and his wife.

One day Tom stayed at home in the morning because he had sold a cow and was waiting for a man to come from Balmeanach to collect it. For days since, Marsaili had been nagging him for the money to buy a new dress.

Marsaili made a great play of taking the churn and going out to milk the cows, returning like a scalded hen a few moments later and complaining because one of them had kicked her. Catriona sighed and went instead, seeing the knowing look that passed over her father's face as she passed.

The cow gave up her milk meekly. Catriona noted the yield with satisfaction and left the fresh milk to separate because she wanted to make cheese.

Tom had gone when she returned to the cottage and Marsaili was sitting by the fire rubbing comfrey into her bruised ankle.

'How dare you do that?' she spat.

'Do what?' Catriona asked.

'You knew the cow would kick me. Tom says it kicks everyone except you.'

'A cow kicks anyone it doesn't know, Marsaili. And you went too quick for me to tell you.'

Marsaili stood up. 'I'm tired of you, you little bitch. You treat this place like it's a castle and your da's a king, but it's only an old black house and your da's my husband before he's your da.'

'He was my da before he even knew your name.'

'To hell with you, Catriona. I don't know why he puts up with you.'

'I don't know why he puts up with you, either. Or perhaps I do. I'm surprised that a man as clever as my da fell for it.'

The slap hit hard, drawing the breath from her as she felt her balance falter.

'Don't you ever say that again,' Marsaili said.

Catriona sensed the door opening as Tom came in.

He stood and stared at them both. 'What are you arguing about?'

Marsaili shot Catriona a look of venomous hatred.

'She called me a whore, Tom.'

He turned to Catriona.

'Did you?'

'I said I didn't know why you married her.'

Marsaili's face was a mask of disdain. 'I don't know,' she said to Catriona, 'why the hell you stay around here. If you're as bright as they say you'd've realized that you'd be better off being a maid and earning some money like the other girls do.'

Catriona felt panicked, all of a sudden. She turned to her father. 'Da wants me to stay at school. That's what he wants. Don't you, Da? Don't you?'

Tom looked at her for a long time and then at Marsaili. 'You're both as daft as each other,' he said, 'if you think that I'm going to say as much as a word to either of you.'

Catriona followed Tom deep into the hills, where she found him thigh deep in a lochan. There were half a dozen fish on the bank and she could see that he had another two in the trap. When he noticed her he told her to wait for just a minute until he had pulled the nets in.

She sat down on the grass and breathed in the warm air of summer. The calm waters of the lochan were a mirror of the hills beyond. An eagle floated high above, seeing first the salmon and then the people and then wheeling away in search of other prey.

Her father had taken off his shirt and rolled his trousers up around his thighs and he worked with such precision that his movements in the water hardly caused a ripple.

Catriona felt tiny beads of sweat forming on her brow; she brushed them away just as her father lifted two fine fish in his nets and strode to the water's edge, where he killed them swiftly with a single blow.

As he sat down behind her he took his pipe from the pocket of his jacket, added a little tobacco and then looked around for something that he could use as a flint.

'Here,' Catriona said, handing him the flint that she always carried in her skirt pocket. She had misplaced one too often ever to leave it to chance.

Tom lit his pipe with the flint and a swatch of dried grass. The smoke from the burning tobacco was the only blemish on an otherwise cloudless sky.

You've changed, Catriona thought. Tom never used to smoke during the day, nor in the evenings except on the rare occasion when someone else had tobacco to spare. Now he smoked at all times, from when he left the house in the mornings to the time he went to bed.

'What Marsaili said,' he began, 'yon's got a sharp tongue in her mouth. I wouldn't give it too much thought.'

Catriona did not say anything for a while and so they sat in silence, each alone with their thoughts.

Tom wondered if his mistake could ever be undone.

On his wedding night he had lain awake as Marsaili slept beside him. The room seemed different then and he felt alone; the ghost of Mor that had lingered so long was gone since the moment he had taken Marsaili, as if the act of sex was also a ritual of exorcism. There was something dead about the place, a feeling of cold that he thought was because the fire had gone out until he realized it meant that love had gone.

He had loved Mor beyond understanding and it was not to slight her memory that he had married again, but because if he did not he thought he would lose his mind.

Every time he looked at Catriona, he saw only Mor. He knew that Catriona would never understand this and he would never tell her, so he took another woman quickly, before the longing drove him mad.

To have another body beside him in his bed would help to take the edge off his pain, he had thought.

In the cold of that morning he rose and looked at the island outside his window, seeing a landscape blurred by mist and rain. In the distance Catriona was outside Annie's fetching water, and he watched her until she was back indoors again.

Then he found the flint and some kindling and worked until he got the fire going. It was a terrible thing for a fire to go out in the islands. An omen, he thought fleetingly, before he cursed himself for being silly.

It would not do to let Catriona discover that the fire had gone out on the night when he took his new wife home.

But he had to get on with his life and so when one morning Marsaili told him that there was work on one of the estates to prepare for the hunting parties, he went off meekly, knowing he was no longer the man he once had been, that he might never be again.

But he couldn't tell Catriona any of that.

On that day, shaded with a calm that rarely came to the windswept islands, when the breeze was so still that the landscape looked like a photograph, Catriona did not know of the doubts clouding her father's mind. She wanted reassurance only that she still had a place in it.

'You want me to stay at school,' she said. 'You want me to learn all I can, don't you? Don't you?'

For a while Tom looked into the distance, to the blue peaks of the Cuillins shimmering in the heat of the sun.

'I don't know, do I? It's what you want, lass.'

'But you want it too, don't you, Da?'

'I'm not sure what I want these days. There's girls of your age work as maids and bring home good money.'

'You don't want me to do that?'

'There's always a use for money, Catriona. All you ever learn in school is a bunch of irrelevancies. All that bloody nonsense about the Balkan League and Kaiser Bill. When did that woman Anderson ever teach you anything about yourself?'

Catriona got up and ran away so fast that she was over the crest of the hill before he realized she was gone.

*

55

That night, on the beach, Catriona ate raw oysters freshly picked from the beds, careless of the risk of dysentery or worse.

Through the window of the cottage she had watched Marsaili serving the evening meal, and had walked away in disgust at the image of contented domesticity. Only Allan gnawed at her soul; she knew that the others were old enough and strong enough to survive without her. Ailish was even friendly with Marsaili; on Sundays before church the pair of them paraded in Marsaili's dresses, looking for all the world like visitors because their lace and frills were foreign against the wilderness of the hills.

She sat on a rock above the sands, still warm from the heat of the sun, and closed her eyes.

Mor came to her, smiling gently.

'Catriona, precious, why so sad?'

'You don't know what's happened, mama.'

'Oh, but I do, and I always knew it would.'

'Couldn't you stop it?'

'No, precious, I could not, because fate is not written by the hand of man – or woman, come to that.'

'Who does write it, then?'

'Oh, Catriona, I don't know. God and the Devil, they both try, but life has a force all of its own.'

'I don't understand, Mama.'

'Don't worry, my dearest. In time you will. Why don't you think back, Triona? Think back to the time you won your first prize at school. You were only six ... d'you remember what I said then?

'You've got brains, Catriona, more sense than your father and me put together. And you can use them. You won't have to spend your life knitting socks for a pittance or stealing the landlords' deer. If you use your sense, Catriona, you'll find a much better way of making your living than that.'

'But, Mama. I haven't won the scholarship. Not yet.'

'You don't have to, pet. You could manage without it.'

*

Catriona opened her eyes to the new day defined by the jubilant sunrise over the mountains on the horizon. Although she had slept only briefly, she felt refreshed.

'But you're not here any more, Mama,' she whispered. 'You're not even here.'

'Oh, but I am, precious,' Mor said in a voice as clear as the new day. 'I'm with you on this earth with every step you take, as I'm with Ewan and Alec and Ailish and Maire and Sine and Allan. I'm even with your da. Love never dies, Triona. If you really love you can never die, my pet, because love will keep your soul alive.'

For just a moment she saw her mother standing there on the beach in the glow of the sunrise and then she blinked and Mor was gone, and she turned to see Allan running towards her; she knew then that she'd never be certain if it had been a dream or not.

'I knew you'd be here,' he said. 'You always come here when ...'

She tried to make light of it; she tickled his chin as she asked him when what.

He brushed her hand away. 'When Marsaili hurts you. Triona, you go if you want to. Annie always said she'd look out for us.'

'I wouldn't leave you, Allan.'

A tear formed in his eye and sparkled as it caught the light. 'I don't want you to be unhappy, Triona.'

She hugged him tightly and held him close for a very long time as she thought.

'Are you sure, Allan?'

'What the bloody hell will we do when Marsaili starts having children?'

Catriona knew then that it wasn't just Allan talking, but Ewan and Alec, Maire and Sine, Ailish even. Over the years she'd cared for them and now they were asking for her care again, in a way as kind as they could manage.

'You're the only one of us who's any good at making money,' Allan said.

'That's not true, Allan. I've never earned a penny in my life.'

57

'But you could if you tried.'

She looked at him intently and wondered how much of her worry he had absorbed over the years. Though she knew her father would never forsake them, Tom had weakened since he married Marsaili; in a way she was stronger than him and when his children grew up she would turn on each of them as she had turned on Catriona.

'That's true, Allan. And don't you worry because I will. I promise you that.'

Catriona reached Portree as the church bells chimed six times.

The Church of Scotland minister lived just outside town in a large manse that was far too big for the ageing bachelor who had taken on the parish twenty years ago. During the years of the clearances and then the Land League, the islanders had joined the Free Church in their thousands, sickened by the way the established Church had vacillated in the struggles against the landlords.

The Church of Scotland minister of Portree now, the Reverend Angus MacPherson, was different to his predecessors. Those who knew him spoke of a humble man ready to do the deeds of the Lord before he did for himself.

He drank, it was true, but then again, so did most people, even some Free Kirk ministers who foreswore the Devil's brew. The Reverend MacPherson had bad rheumatics and gout, and the water of life eased a little of his pain; nobody begrudged him that.

He had arranged scholarships for many young people and found many more a good job in the city, and gave not a thought to whether they worshipped in the Kirk or the Free Kirk or even the Conventicle that a maverick young preacher had begun to conduct recently when he had fallen out with his Free Kirk colleagues.

Catriona knocked boldly at the manse door and waited as she heard the slow movement of elderly legs along the passage.

'Reverend MacPherson,' she said, 'I'm sorry to trouble you but I'm looking for a job.'

'What? What time is it?' He looked hard at the sky until from indoors he heard the chime of a grandfather clock. 'Heavens, lass, come away indoors. It's only a quarter after six.'

In a kitchen that was warmed by a huge log fire he put a kettle on the hot-place himself. 'You'll take a cup of tea, lass? You'll have to do with what I give you, because the housekeeper doesn't come on until half past.'

Catriona waited nervously, trying to sum up the courage that she needed to tell a lie.

'Just give me a minute, lass, till the kettle's boiled.'

The sound of water pouring on to leaves calmed her.

'Will you take a bite to eat? No, lass, I must be daft because if you've come a way you must be hungry.'

The minister waited until she had eaten two scones before he spoke again.

'First of all, lass, tell me who you are.'

'Catriona Nicolson.'

'Now, wait, let me think.' He studied her intently for a moment. 'Aren't you that clever wee lass from The Braes? You aye win the prizes, and your da's Big Tom Nicolson of the Land League? Your ma died a few years past, isn't that right?'

She told him that it was.

He shook his head. 'But what do you want a job for, lass? A girl like you'd win a scholarship easy, for the teaching college maybe. And you can't be more than fourteen.'

'I'm sixteen,' Catriona said defiantly, praying inwardly that he would not bother to count.

The housekeeper came in and the minister shooed her out as he got up and shuffled some papers in a drawer.

'Are you quite sure about this?' he asked.

'I am, Reverend.'

'As it happens, there is a job, a junior clerk's job in a law office in Glasgow run by an old curmudgeon called MacKenzie. The lassie MacLeod from Breakish was going to take it, but her family's just fallen with the typhoid and MacKenzie'll not take anyone if he thinks they've got germs. But you'd have to leave tomorrow, lass, because the job's to start on Monday. I can send him word that you're coming on the telegraph, because he's been hounding me for the last month, but you'll have to get your references yourself.'

'References?'

'From your parish minister. Since that's a Free Kirk and MacKenzie's ours, I could maybe give you that, but you need a note from school as well. The exams you've passed and the like. Your teacher'll give you it.'

'I'll ask her,' Catriona said tactfully.

'Aye, well, if you wait a moment, I'll write you out one from the church. Mind and don't lose it, now. MacKenzie'll have you out on your ear. And here's the address of a woman to stay with. She's expecting Mary anyway; it's best you stay in a decent house.'

And so it was arranged, in the space of a day, that Catriona would go to work in Glasgow. She had to beg and plead for a reference from Miss Anderson, and finally threaten that if she did not get it she would not go back to school anyway.

The news spread along The Braes like wildfire; before she reached home with her references Eileen MacInnes met her on the path and pushed a pair of shoes into her hands, and then one of the women from Balmeanach gave her a new shawl and Annie gave her a cotton dress that her sister who worked as a maid in Perth had been given by the lady of the house. It was always the same when someone left; the whole village would turn out bearing gifts and good wishes. Lachlan Maclean gave her a blouse from his sister, looking so sad that she could not turn him down.

Tom took the news stoically, Marsaili with feigned indifference, although when Tom put his hand into his pocket for money for Catriona's fare she grudgingly gave her a ten-shilling note and then another one when Tom looked at her sharply.

'I don't need this money,' Catriona said. 'Reverend MacPherson said he'd advance the money for the fare.'

'You can't be leaving with empty pockets,' her father said.

In the evening, Miss Anderson came to the cottage to say she was sorry if she had been brusque but she had been upset because she had had high hopes for Catriona if she had stayed at school. Strangely shy for once, the teacher gave her a parcel that she hoped would help, and when Catriona opened it she found a dark skirt and jacket with a new white blouse that would be perfect for her work.

'Stuff and nonsense,' Tom said, 'aren't your own clothes good enough?'

'Are you blind as well as daft?' Annie said.

Tom walked out of the house.

'Don't worry about a thing,' Annie said. 'I'll watch everyone. And write to me.'

'I will,' Catriona said.

'You'll not be gone for ever.'

'No,' Catriona said. 'I'll come back. I promise you that.'

Chapter Three

*C*atriona rose before dawn, when the island was still shrouded with the pale twilight of the Hebridean summer night. By candlelight she checked her bag; she had the references and the flask of whisky, the suit Miss Anderson had given her and her nightgown and underclothes.

She turned and saw that Allan's eyes were open. She went to him.

'I'll miss you, Triona.'

'I'll miss you, little one.'

She held him until his eyes were closed in sleep again and then she drew the blanket over him and kissed his forehead gently. She had said her goodbyes to her sisters last night and as they slept she did not want to disturb them.

Ewan was awake, curled against Alec's sleeping body. 'Good luck,' he whispered, '*beannaich leibh.*'

'*Beannaich leibh,*' she replied.

The island was still as she walked outside and drew her shawl tightly around her shoulders against the chill. A breath of wind blew shivers through the rye and in the distance the Cuillins stood tall against the night. She paused for a moment and whispered a prayer, then walked briskly down the path.

From the rocks above the beach she stood and watched the surge of the tide. It was too early for birdsong yet and the only sound was the rhythm of the sea. As she turned away dawn was breaking over the land and as she walked she knew that behind her the beach was coming alive.

Her father was standing at the crest of the hill.

'I knew where you'd be,' he said. 'You didn't think I'd let you go alone.'

'I can manage,' she said firmly.

'You're still my daughter,' he said, taking her bag.

They walked in silence to Portree.

As she was boarding the steamer he reached into his pocket and gave her a handful of coins.

'This isn't what I wanted,' he said. 'If aught goes wrong, pet, come home. There's always a place for you in your father's house.'

She looked at him. 'You said you wanted me to work as a maid.'

'What I said was that there was always a use for money.'

'Don't worry, Father.' He flinched when she called him that. 'I'll bring in money, you can be sure of that.'

The foghorn coughed and the boat drew away from the pier. Tom Nicolson watched until the ferry was only a streak of smoke in the distance.

Catriona stood on the deck, proud and defiant, and he cursed himself again for the foolery of his marriage.

'Goodbye, my little oyster girl,' he whispered as he watched her grow small with distance. 'God be with you.'

Catriona stayed on deck until the ferry had rounded the headland and all the other passengers had found seats for themselves or at least shelter from the sharp wind that began to blow as soon as they were out in the open waters of the Minch. Turning then, she saw that the benches were taken and so was the space at the stern where steam from the funnel heated the air. Tired already, she brushed the hair from her eyes and looked again, and when she still found nowhere turned back to the railing, shrugging as if she did not care.

Already her hands were cold and turning blue. She ignored them for a while and when she could stand it no longer, turned around and cupped her hands to her mouth, blowing sensation back into her fingers. A shadow fell across her and she looked up and saw a man, his face covered with what looked like a mask. Startled, she gasped and pulled away, before she realized that it wasn't a mask, just coal dust.

'I'm sorry,' the man said in Gaelic, 'I didn't mean to

disturb you but there's a place by the funnel where it's warm.'

'I'm fuh-fuh-fuh-fine,' she stammered, her lips numb with cold.

'The Devil you are,' he said, picking up her bag and leading her along the deck to a place where tarpaulins were piled up against a lifeboat. He put her bag down and lifted the tarpaulins easily, leaving just one in place and plumping it into a seat. 'There you are,' he said, grinning broadly, his teeth brilliant against the soot on his face.

'It's suh-suh-supposed to be summer,' she chattered, as she sat down and felt the shock of heat melt the chill in her back.

'It's a northerly,' he said, looking into the direction of the wind. 'Straight from the Arctic and cold as sin.'

He left her and she heard the fall of his footsteps as he went below and came back again with a mug.

'Tea,' he said, 'lousy tea, but it's warm.'

She drank half of it before she thought to thank him. 'Ach,' he said, dismissively, wiping his face and bringing a circle of skin back to its normal colour. 'Nice day, despite the wind.'

There was something vaguely familiar about him. He spoke Skye Gaelic, but it was more than that. His shoulders were broad and very powerful, he was tall and lean and moved with grace; though his features were blurred by dirt his face was strong and honest; his eyes were grey flecked with green, the shade of the sea on a dull day. When he smiled he made her want to smile back, the first time she had felt like smiling all day.

'Rory MacDonald,' she said, remembering.

'I am,' he admitted. He came from the next village along The Braes.

He had been a heroic shinty player when he was young. One year he had scored so many goals that his team won the Camanachd. The whole of The Braes had cheered him – the whole island, in fact; the village men had carried him home triumphant from Portree with the cup.

'Do you still play shinty?' she asked him.

Almost angrily he shook his head. 'I've been working on the boat for six years now. I don't get time for any of that.'

She had watched him play herself; she would've thought great things would come to a boy who could play like that.

'I'm the stoker,' he said, 'I keep the boiler going.'

'Oh.'

'But the engineer left a while back. I do his job as well, though not on paper because I never sat the exams for it.'

He still has his pride, she thought.

'I'd best get going,' he said, 'don't want the boat to stop.' He grinned again as she handed back his mug. 'I'll bring you another later. If you want anything else, just stamp on the deck.'

She tried to smile, but knew she probably looked as if she was frowning, so she hugged herself instead, because the wind still felt fresh. As he turned away she watched him thoughtfully, wondering if the lowlands did that to everyone, if the city would devour her promise like it seemed to have taken his.

By the funnel, her body thawed as she listened to the cries of the seagulls gliding in the wake of the boat. She watched the coastline of Skye pass as the ferry sliced the waves, the tip of an arrow heading relentlessly south. For a while she thought of the stories of witches who crossed the sea in eggshells, wishing that she could be one of them, that she could be anyone but herself. Just as tears formed and threatened to break again, her strength surged and held them back. For a long time she sat rigid, then, very slowly, she let herself go, lulled by the warmth and the rhythm of the engine. After a while she slept.

An hour later he came again with a mug of cocoa, which he thought was a little better than shipboard tea. When he saw that Catriona was sleeping he dumped the cocoa over the side, then went and fetched blankets, which he draped over her.

Belowdecks, the thrum of the engine told him that all was

well. He listened for a moment to make certain and then, satisfied, picked up a book and began to read. It was a text on maritime engineering, a dry, stolid piece of prose that would have bored anyone else. Within a few months of starting work on the ferry, Rory had known its engine as well as the engineer did; since then, he had studied hard and taught himself a lot. There wasn't an engine on this earth now that he couldn't have running as sweetly as an accordion once he'd stripped it down and checked the moving parts. When the engineer left he was not replaced because Rory could do his job at the same time he did his own. The problem was that because he had left school so early, without exams, he couldn't become an apprentice, never mind qualified, so he did not get paid for that part of his work. He did both jobs stoically, hoping for better days.

The wage he got was good for a stoker, good for a lad just twenty years old. He gave it to his father to make up for the shortfall of the family croft, a few windswept, sandy acres on the edge of the sea. In a way the work he did was a penance, a penance for the land.

After a while he realized that his thoughts were drifting, so he put the book aside and sat there thinking. Tom Nicolson's daughter was young, he knew; he didn't know her precise age but he supposed she was sixteen or so. She had been good at school, had won all the prizes; great things, even a scholarship, had been promised for her future. He wondered what she was doing on the ferry; if she had won the scholarship already he would have heard of it. There was a determined look about her, a strength in the way she had continued to face the wind when everybody else sought shelter, but he sensed a vulnerability too, as if her resolve was as thin as ice on a winter's morning. He did not want the city to hurt her, he didn't want her to end up like him, to have to give up her future for the sake of the money her family needed now.

The waters were choppy, getting rough; as a wave slapped the bows the boat reared for a moment then settled on its course. Quickly, he climbed the ladder and looked at Catriona; if she was frightened by the motion he wanted to reassure her. She was still sleeping gently, the sun catching her hair and turning the brown into fireshot amber. He had noticed that about her first of all, that her hair was auburn and so were her eyes; she was very lovely, he thought, with all the freshness of a budding flower.

Belowdecks again, he checked the burner and then picked up his book, reading a page before the captain's footsteps made him put the book aside and pick up the shovel so it would appear that he was working.

The captain looked around and smiled at him. 'Don't mind me, Rory. It's going easy.'

'Are there any cabins free?' Rory asked.

'Aye, mibbe,' the captain said. 'Why?'

'There's a wee girl from home. She looks like she could use a rest.'

'Aye, mibbe,' the captain said. 'Jist mak' sure she's no' there when we dock, acos yon buggers would hae my job, an' yours an' aw. An' mak' sure the burner's richt afore ye skive aff tae join her.'

Rory's face flashed anger. 'I said a *girl*.'

'Aye,' the captain said. 'We wis all young once.'

Rory was used to the bawdy humour, the easy camaraderie of the men who worked the boats. The sea was in his blood now and he shared that bond with the other men on the ferry, but the captain had annoyed him and he was not sure why. He had the name of being a ladies' man, but it wasn't true, not all of it, he liked women too much to use them as easily as some did, and he never had the money to court them at all. Only fools married early, most island men had to work for years to make the money they needed to survive. Of all the promises the future had once held for him, only one was left; that was, his promise to himself that no son of his would have to leave home as he had and no daughter would have to work as a maid, when the toil would take the shine off her beauty long before she reached marrying age.

Much later he climbed up to the deck, where Catriona was

still sleeping. For a moment he watched her and then, not wanting to disturb her, brought a tarpaulin to lay over her to prevent the mist from soaking her. Despite the care that he took, she woke up.

'There's a cabin below,' he said. She started like a deer as he sat down beside her, and he thought again how lovely she was. Her mother had been like that too, he remembered, the woman who'd tamed the wildest man of The Braes, whose beauty was such an entrancing mixture of fragility and strength.

She reared away and for a moment he was angered until he realized that he'd come straight from the engine room without bothering to put his shirt on or even wipe the dust from his face. It was so hot there that sometimes he worked naked; even then, he only had his trousers on.

'I'm sorry,' he said, looking down at himself. 'The wind's getting fresh and you'd be more comfortable below. There's a bunk and blankets, you could have a sleep.'

'I only have a deck ticket,' she said softly.

'There's plenty cabins empty.'

'I'm fine here,' she insisted.

He shook his head, shedding a whisper of coal dust on the deck. Below the dust his hair was light brown but it was usually so filthy that people thought it was black. As he moved the muscles of his back rippled, sheened as they were with soot and sweat.

He unfolded the tarpaulin and carefully arranged it over the blankets that covered her. 'The mist is wet,' he said, 'this'll keep you dry.'

She smiled very slowly, her face like the sky when the day is dawning. 'It's very kind of you.'

'Ach,' he said, embarrassed, 'you'd be better in a cabin. The devil with a ticket.'

Catriona shook her head; he realized there was nothing he could say to persuade her.

'Would you like a mug of cocoa?'

'No, really.'

'Ach, well, like I said, if you need anything, just stamp on the deck.' He left quickly, not wanting her to know of the thoughts running through his head, that he imagined she might see on his face.

She smiled again and then turned over to sleep.

Below, the captain was waiting for Rory, his face covered with a leer.

'She's staying on deck,' Rory said gruffly.

'Better luck next time.' The captain grinned.

Rory had to grip his fists together to stop himself from hitting the man. 'She's not like that,' he said tersely.

'Awa' tae hell, laddie,' the captain said, 'ye've the look o' a man wha's fallen fir the lass.'

Rory scowled at him. 'Don't be daft.'

The stillness of arrival woke Catriona.

'There you are,' Rory said. 'I was just about to come looking for you. I'm off for an hour or two in a minute. If you wait at the pier I'll take you round to Mrs Gordon's. It is Mrs Gordon's you're staying at?'

'Yes.'

'Well, lass, just you wait and I'll have you round there in a flash. You might get lost if you tried to find it yourself.'

Numbed by his kindness, Catriona waited at the end of the gangway for him, watching as he helped the other passengers off and then went below.

She remembered him on the boat, the way he had spread the tarpaulin around her; she'd been afraid, momentarily, but when she saw it was him she had felt comforted instead. There was something about him that she felt drawn to; she had never felt that for a man, though a couple of island boys had wanted to court her. She had dusted off their efforts as easily as she swatted midges.

She wondered if Rory would try, and if he did, what she would say. But then she thought of her father and that memory drove all pleasant ideas from her mind.

She had not come here to do things like that.

The city was cast in shades of grey which marked the streets from the sky as if the place was swathed in a veil that removed all colour like a photograph. She heard English being spoken in a Scottish way, with an accent so thick and fast that she could not discern one word from the next but listened instead to a constant flow of guttural wrath.

People moved quickly, jerkily, like jiggers in a reel but without the pattern, so that they looked like palsied dancers to the beat of the trams that thundered past.

The roar of man and machine made her shrink inwardly, almost in fear, until she realized her arms were clutched around her body so hard that in a moment she would lose all sensation and faint.

No, she said to herself, and then again, 'No!' aloud, so loud that the last of the ferry passengers turned and stared at her.

This is the city, she said to herself. This is the place where I have to learn how to win.

She relaxed and stood firm against the confusion, determined that amidst the chaos she would find the will to begin.

Rory found her there, after the last drunk had been coaxed from the ferry under the threat of the police if he did not leave there and then.

'Ach, lass,' he said, looking down at the bare feet peeping out from under her skirt, 'had you not better put your shoes on?'

She looked at him, surprised. The shoes were strung to the handle of her father's bag, carried in the way tinkers carted their pots and pans. 'I ...' she began, nervously clearing her throat. 'I don't think ... perhaps I should leave them for the time being. They'll only get filthy in all this muck.'

He laughed and shook his head. 'That's just it, Catriona. This muck's muck, real filth like, not the clean soil of The Braes.' He traced a line on the cobblestones with his own boot and she saw a crescent of mire build up around his toe. 'You can't walk around in bare feet in this, 'cos if you do you'll end up with an abscess or tetanus or Lord knows what.'

One side of Catriona's mouth twisted into a confused grin as she looked again at the shoes and her feet. She had not put them on when Eileen gave them to her, she had just thanked her quickly, embarrassed, and then left before Eileen became maudlin and cried on her shoulder. She was too close to tears herself to be able to cope with that.

The shoes were little leather lace-ups, shiny and stiff – unworn, Eileen assured her, because her husband Tarlach had bought them for her one day in Wick after a good day's fishing and a few glasses, no doubt. Eileen's feet were far too broad to fit into them and so she had stored them away until the time came when they would be of use. Catriona looked at them now and saw the way that the leather caught dully the light filtering down through layers of clouds that obscured all but a pallid glow. When Eileen gave them to her she had meant to ask how to put them on, and then later on board the ferry she had meant to fiddle with them to discover how they worked, but with one thing or another she had not and now when she needed to she simply did not know what to do first.

Rory was looking at her in a kindly way and her eyes fell away from his in confusion and despair.

Suddenly he picked her up and carried her through the crowds as easily as her father would pick up an ailing lamb.

'Don't worry,' he said quickly, 'I'm not kidnapping you and carrying you off to darkest Africa. We're just going around the corner to Maggie Drummond's, where we can sit down and decide what to do next.'

The crowd gave way as he strode through them and from his shoulder she had the briefest sensation of the parting of the seas until he reached a small door in an alleyway. He opened the door with one hand as he put her down.

The room was smoky and dark and filled with men drinking mugs of tea, and the smell of food.

The floor was wooden, she realized with surprise, as the stoker edged his way to a table and pulled out a chair for her.

A woman came up to him and he smiled playfully at her

71

and ordered some tea and scones, and Catriona wondered briefly if she had fallen into one of those dens of iniquity in the city that Eileen MacInnes railed on about (and Annie said were more the product of Eileen's imagination than anything else).

The woman sat down beside her and touched her arm in a friendly gesture that made Catriona shrink like a sea anemone.

'This is Catriona Nicolson,' Rory said, 'Tom Nicolson's lass, just down from Skye to work.'

'Och,' the woman said, 'it's a gey awful shock the first few days; it's the noise, they say, the racket of the place.'

The sounds and words were still a blur to Catriona, so she sat back and listened, praying that soon all the strangeness would begin to make sense.

'Maggie,' Rory was saying, as the woman poured tea as thick as treacle into blemished china mugs, 'Catriona here, well, she's just down from the islands and ...' He leaned over and whispered something into Maggie's ear that caused her to laugh and ask Catriona something that at first she did not catch.

'Have you got any stockings?' Maggie asked again.

'What?' Catriona knew only vaguely what stockings were; she had never worn them, nor had her mother, but she knew that Marsaili had several pairs because the day after the wedding she had washed them and put them out to dry and cursed roundly when the breeze had quickened and carried them away.

'Stockings, lass,' Maggie said, 'you'll need 'em to get into your shoes. It'll be pure murder otherwise.'

'I ...' Catriona deflated in an instant; felt shocked at her own omission. 'I didn't know ... '

Maggie turned on Rory. 'What're ye thinking of? Of course, she disnae ken about things like that.'

'I was thinking,' he said, 'that you might have some?'

'Ach, away to Hell. I'll send Greta out for her own pair for the few pence it'll cost.'

'I was thinking,' he said, handing over a coin, 'that I'd look pretty silly if I went to get them myself.'

'Why d'ye no say so, ye daft limmer?' Maggie stood up and disappeared into the cloud of smoke that shrouded the back of the room.

'Help yourself,' he said as he picked up a scone riddled with currants and smeared butter onto it.

Catriona had never seen currants before except in a case in the merchant's at Portree; one day he had given her one to taste but it was so small that she swallowed it before she got a chance.

'I'm sorry,' she said, 'I didn't know.'

Suddenly her face felt hot with shame and her eyes misted as she tried to find the words to apologize.

'I can pay for the stockings.'

'Ach, don't be daft. I got a sixpence bonus.'

'What?'

'I got a sixpence bonus. I helped load the coal at Oban because the lad was sick twice this week and so I got a sixpence extra in my wages. I can afford a pair of stockings for you. I would've got them myself but I wouldn't've known what to do, going into a woman's shop to buy a pair of stockings.'

He picked up a second scone and cut it open and a whiff of steam escaped as he spread on butter that melted in an instant. He handed it to Catriona and urged her to eat.

She did so slowly; at first the taste was masked by the heat because the scone was fresh from the oven but as it cooled the unfamiliar, rich blend of eggs, butter and currants felt comforting. She finished the scone and ate another, and sensing that she was hungry Rory ordered some stew and sat watching her until she had finished that.

Catriona felt full and tired all of a sudden and her eyes closed briefly as the chatter faded to a murmur.

'I'm sorry,' she said, as she forced them open again.

'Don't worry,' he said easily. 'We'll be off, soon's Maggie's got your stockings.'

She looked around and for the first time realized that most of the people were islanders like herself, seamen and artisans who spoke Skye Gaelic and Lewis Gaelic interspersed with the odd word of English.

There were no women apart from herself and Maggie Drummond and a couple of girls who rushed through doors carrying plates of food and mugs of tea.

'Maggies's not bad,' he said in Gaelic, 'though it gets a bit rough later. She serves ale, though she's not supposed to.'

Catriona looked at him uncomprehendingly.

'A shebeen, you know, like the excise in the islands.'

Maggie returned suddenly and looked at him sharply. 'You're not turning the lass's head, are you, Rory? If you come with me, lass, I'll help you get your shoes on.'

Catriona followed her through a kitchen full of smouldering pots and bubbling kettles to a back room stacked with sacks of flour.

'Rory's aye one for the patter,' Maggie said. 'It's true that the polis came, but not about the ale. They were after some laddie fra' Skye after a ruck in Buchanan Street and they came here looking for him.'

'Rory played shinty at home,' Catriona said wistfully.

'You teuchters,' Maggie said, 'there's only ever one place you call home, no matter how long you've been away.'

'He was really good at it.'

'That's not all Rory's good at,' Maggie said in a tone that made Catriona look at her wide-eyed.

'I didn't mean it like that, lass,' she went on hurriedly, 'Rory's no' bad, he's jist a bit of a lad.'

A bit of a lad, Catriona thought. Though she knew what a lad was in English, she didn't know enough of the language to understand what Maggie meant beyond that.

The stockings were thick and dark and Catriona pulled them over her feet and fixed them on with the garters that Maggie gave her, then watched as Maggie loosened the laces of the shoes and held them for her to step into.

Standing up, she stumbled at first, awkward with the extra half inch of height that she had gained.

'Take your time,' Maggie said, 'walk up and down a bit. You'll soon get used to it.'

When she walked back into the throng, Rory was waiting with her bag at the door.

The sky had darkened and the air tasted of rain.

'Mrs Gordon's in the Gorbals, just over from the Cross,' Rory said, 'it's about a five-minute walk from here.'

They crossed the Clyde on a bridge that was held by wires stretched like a spider's web from pillars on either side of the river; the sensation was so strange that Catriona felt dizzy at first. The only bridges on Skye were ancient ones, crafted from stones wedged tightly into the shape of an arch.

Once over the bridge Rory turned into a street lined with buildings and then from it into another one, so quickly that Catriona lost all sense of where she was.

'Ach,' he said as he noticed her hesitate. 'I was forgetting you've not been here before. It's strange at first but it's just like weaving. The streets work like the warp and the weft crossing each other and you get to know your way around them in no time at all.'

He turned another corner, pausing to show her where the name of the street was written on a plate on a lamp post.

'At night time the lights come on and you know where you're going. It's gas, like, here, but there's electricity as well.'

Catriona had only ever read the word in textbooks and listened to Miss Anderson's patient explanation of the invention that, she said, would change the world. She had no understanding of any power that did not come from nature.

Halfway along the street Rory stopped and pointed to a house like all the others, distinguished only by a burnished brass plate that carried a number.

'Maybe it's best I leave you here,' he said, 'Mrs Gordon's a right one, like.'

She faced him, reluctant to leave his company. 'What d'you mean?'

His face cracked into a scowl. 'Ach, she's a wizened old bat that thinks any man turns into the Devil when darkness falls. The captain took a girl to her once and she chased him away with a broomstick.'

Catriona laughed. 'I don't believe you.'

He winked. 'You will, soon's you meet her. I'd best leave

you here, Catriona. She's not that bad, 'cept if she saw me she'd be lecturing you till dawn. For God's sake, don't tell her I bought you a pair of stockings.'

Catriona shook her head, bewildered.

'In any case, there's a girl from Skye here and a few others. You'll not be lonely, Catriona, and if you come to the arches in a week's time, I'll tell you what's going on at home.' He touched her arm in a gesture of farewell, but she sensed that he, too, was reluctant to go.

'What is it?' she asked him, hoping that they could meet sooner than next week, perhaps tomorrow even.

Rory looked away for a moment, as he jingled the coins in his pocket. It wasn't true about the bonus, he'd spent the money he kept from his wages to pay for his meals, and a bit more from the money he usually gave to his mother.

He would have to explain it when he got back, not because he had to account for every penny that he earned but because his father needed his money – the calf he was planning to sell at the September market had broken its leg and he would be short of the Michaelmas rent. Rory would have asked her to meet him, but he didn't have a spare farthing.

'Ach,' he mumbled, 'I was just going to wish you luck. That's all.'

'Thank you,' she said slowly.

'I'll see you next week, Sunday noon at the wee tearoom under the railway arches.'

She nodded.

Gruffly he put his hands in his pockets and strode off, thinking that the captain had been right after all, that he had fallen for her. He shook his head to get rid of the thought, because he was too young yet to think like that, too poor to think about anything but how to get the money he needed to pay the croft rent. There would be a poker game that night, he could risk a penny or two, perhaps; he would certainly win if the captain was drunk enough. For a moment he thought of turning back and asking her to meet him after all, before he decided against it because if there was anything worse that the thought of disappointing his parents, it was the thought of disappointing Catriona. He could make up the rent money if he did without most of his meals for a couple of weeks.

Catriona stood watching him for a while, sad once more now that he had left her, thinking of the days that would pass before she saw him again.

Mrs Gordon's door opened suddenly, long before she had worked out how to use the heavy brass knocker, and a woman looked out suspiciously, sweeping her eyes over Catriona before she looked up the street and saw Rory turning the corner.

'You'll be Mary MacLeod,' the woman said sharply. 'I've been waiting for you since just after noon and it's past six o'clock. Where've you been?'

Catriona quailed. 'I ...'

'You'd best come in,' the woman said. 'I'm Mrs Gordon, by the way, though I suppose you know, and it's a pity you're late because you've missed your dinner.'

The door swung open on a hall that smelled of camphor and lavender and toast, and Catriona stepped in diffidently, stumbling on a thick carpet, not regaining her balance properly before Mrs Gordon opened another door and ushered her into a room filled with furniture and lit by lamps that gave off a smell that she suddenly realized must be gas.

Mrs Gordon was a woman in late middle age whose leaden hair was twisted into a bun so tight that her face looked as if it was carved from stone. As she spoke her mouth moved but otherwise she was expressionless and the coldness of her gaze made Catriona shiver inwardly despite the fire that blazed in the hearth.

'I'm Catriona Nicolson,' she said quickly. 'Mary MacLeod couldn't come. The Reverend MacPherson said he'd tell Mr MacKenzie. I have his reference, if you want.'

Mrs Gordon fixed a pince-nez to the bridge of her nose. 'It would do no harm, girl.'

Catriona found the papers in her bag and handed over the minister's letter.

77

Mrs Gordon glanced at it. 'Very well. And the other one.'

Catriona gave her Miss Anderson's letter, suddenly resenting her nosiness.

Mrs Gordon made a sound like a dog with a bit of food trapped in its throat.

'You're bright, I see. It's a pity you're not clever enough to find your way here. I was about to send the constables after you but I suppose they'd not have gone far if they were looking for someone called Mary MacLeod.' She stopped and fixed Catriona with a steady glare that dared her to tell anything other than the absolute truth. 'Now, do tell me: what was it that kept you all that time?'

Catriona was still standing there and suddenly she noticed the ache in her feet that tightened into a sharp pain as she moved. She shifted her balance slightly and winced as the pain intensified.

'I ... we arrived about noon, it's true, but I ...' She faltered for a moment and then decided that she might as well tell the truth, or at least a part of it, because she simply had no time to think up a decent lie.

'I didn't know where to go, Mrs Gordon,' she said defiantly. 'I've never been to the city before and I thought I'd just ask someone where you were, like we do at home. And then, well, once we arrived, I didn't know so I was about to ask but luckily there was a man there who's a friend of my father's and he said if I waited for him he'd take me, so I waited and he said I looked hungry so he took me for some food because I didn't eat on the boat and then we came here.'

Mrs Gordon stared at her for an age, as Catriona blushed as ruddy as a winter sunrise and waited for her to speak.

'This man,' Mrs Gordon said finally, 'he's the laddie I saw at the end of the street.'

'He is, Mrs Gordon. He is Rory MacDonald and his father is Niall MacDonald and they have the last croft in Peinchorran before you reach the grazings.'

'Half of Skye is called MacDonald, so I'm none the wiser, girl, and that's maybe just as well, because it doesn't do to break the rules before you even arrive, as you've done. But I'm not one for putting young girls out on the street, so we'll forget about it for the time being and so enough's been said. You've missed dinner, but I'll fetch you some bread and dripping and tea, and if you go and sit yourself in the dining room I'll explain what's what.'

Mrs Gordon swept out and Catriona shuffled after her, finding by instinct a gloomy room facing the street that was filled by a long oval table surrounded by chairs. The air was chill, the grate empty. She put her bag down diffidently and heard the silence, split only by the ticking of a clock.

The windows were veiled by lace curtains and bordered by heavy velvet drapes the colour of parched summer earth. The lace reached only halfway up the windows; above she could see the houses opposite and above that the dismal sky. Slowly she walked towards them and saw between the threads of the lace the figure of a man walking past, and then a woman, bent against the wind. She had noticed the city wind as she had walked to Mrs Gordon's with Rory; it was not like the island wind which blew with a rhythm of its own but rather a squall of fractured puffs that gasped down between the buildings and threw up eddies of dust. The dust lifted like a cloud and she felt particles strike her face and her eyes before she closed them; it made her pause for a moment but Rory shrugged his powerful shoulders and strode on.

A horse cart clattered past, hard against the cobblestones, its driver tightening the reins as the horse struggled against the load; heavy leather patches shaded its eyes and Catriona realized with surprise that the horse was blinded and only the driver could see the road.

Children then, two little girls walking meekly beside their mother and two slightly older boys skipping along as her brothers would have done, but oddly indifferent to the hard city streets.

On the other side of the street a door opened and a man came out, standing for a moment on the threshold as he looked either way along the street, as if uncertain of where he should go. He put a pipe in his mouth and cupped his hands together to light it and then marched off purposefully, trailing a smear of smoke that drifted upwards, curved into a blur and faded into the sky.

She felt the draught as the door opened and heard the sound of Mrs Gordon putting a tray down on the table.

'I'm sorry,' she said, taking her seat as Mrs Gordon poured the tea and handed her a plate with a slice of bread covered with streaks of greyish brown fat.

Mrs Gordon ignored the remark and sat facing her, holding a brown folder filled with papers.

The bread tasted stale and the mix of meat and fat turned her stomach for a moment before she forced herself to chew and swallow the food quickly, before it made her sick.

When she finished Mrs Gordon grudgingly lifted a lid from another plate and served her a slice of cake, pursing her lips grimly in a gesture of forbearance.

'You'll be hungry after your journey,' she said, in a quieter voice than she had used before. 'The girls get cake on a Saturday and you missed yours but there was a bit left over and it's better to go to you than the birds.'

Catriona felt bile rise as she looked at the cake, crumbling on the plate, the texture of the sponge riddled with vivid red globes.

'Oh, Mrs Gordon, thank you, but I couldn't. Really, I've had enough.'

Mrs Gordon's eyes widened. 'You don't want my cherry cake? The other girls adore it. It's a special treat that makes the week for them.'

Catriona tried again. 'It isn't that I don't want it, Mrs Gordon. I do, but I've eaten so much, it would be greedy to eat any more. Can't I keep it for later?'

Deftly Mrs Gordon slid the cake back onto the serving plate and banged the lid down over it.

'No food in your room, that's a rule of this establishment because it encourages rats. But you can have it later, I suppose, at supper time, which is an extra; I charge a farthing for tea and sixpence a week for cocoa, which is a very fair price.'

She opened the folder and ran her finger down a column of names, stopping at one that read Mary MacLeod which she obliterated by sticking a bit of paper over it and writing 'Catriona Nicolson' on top of that.

'Tsk,' she muttered, as she angled the piece of paper into place. 'It never does with you girls to plan ahead. I only take a few boarders, you know, I've given most of my places to the Vigilance Society but they can't pay a commercial rate and I have to earn my keep like everyone else.'

She blotted Catriona's name carefully and then continued: 'The rate's two shillings a week which covers your bed and your board, which is breakfast and dinner at night. I don't do lunches, 'cept I will make up a flask of tea for you and a sandwich, but that's an extra. On Sundays dinner is after church and there's a supper as well at tea time. Tea at nine o'clock is a penny ha'penny a week; cocoa's sixpence but I give you a biscuit as well. I launder your sheets once a week; you leave them out on Mondays and I leave fresh. You change your own beds. Personal washing you do yourself, either on Tuesday evening or Friday evening. You have use of the facilities at both these times, but at no others.' She paused then. 'Do I make myself clear?'

Catriona flinched. 'You do, Mrs Gordon.'

'You put your smalls through the wringer and dry them on the pulley in the pantry. No smalls on the outdoor line. Is that clear?

'Now for the rules . . .'

Catriona drifted away somehow, back to the island, where the boys would be coming in from the shinty game and dinner would be ready, and Allan would be rubbing his eyes sleepily.

The cottage would be full of people; Ewan and Alec would be jostling each other and Ailish preening as best she could in the crush, Maire and Sine would be sitting at the table chattering and her father would be taking off his jacket and washing his hands.

The image was an old one and she realized with a start that it had changed; the cottage would be subdued now as

Marsaili served the meal but even so her brothers would be there and her sisters, there would be the easy familiarity of life with her family which was gone now, never to return.

This house was cold and comfortless; one in which a person's life became a business which had to be paid for, penny by penny.

She had never heard of anyone charging for tea in the islands; even in Maggie Drummond's although Rory had handed over some coins she had supposed that the money was to pay for the food and not that.

Island etiquette was such that it was a terrible insult to offer to pay for food or drink; even more to ask for money for it.

And this woman – who sat before her with glasses poised on her nose, like birds perched alert to watch the harvest, ready to swoop when a grain of seed escaped, as if to catch the slightest of Catriona's needs and turn it into a farthing here, a ha'penny there – bewildered her beyond belief.

'I can pay you now,' she said suddenly, lifting her bag from the floor and searching for the pouch that held her money.

The pride of the Gael rose in her then, the same emotion that had led her people to conquest and also to defeat; with them she shared the brittle sense of dignity that would not allow her to owe a woman like Mrs Gordon so much as a penny piece.

Marsaili's money, she thought, as the landlady snatched the proffered ten-shilling note, marked it in the book and then counted out a shilling and some pennies in change. Marsaili's or her mother's, it made no difference because although the motive was different the result was the same.

'Put it in your purse, then,' Mrs Gordon said as she watched Catriona fingering the coins.

Catriona put the pouch back into her bag and let the coins drop into it. Her father's coins were all she had left of him; she decided then that she would never spend them because his gift was worth more than the money it was.

'And now,' Mrs Gordon said, closing the ledger firmly, 'I'll show you to your room.'

Catriona would have turned and run then, fled in despair if her feet had not been so sore that every step was torture and if she had not realized that if she returned to the island by the next boat she would be the laughing stock of The Braes for years to come.

Over the years many young women had gone to be maids and young men had gone to dig the roads and the railways; some came back cowed after months or even weeks and then the old women would nod their heads knowingly and say that it didn't take much to bring young so-and-so back to earth.

Catriona did not even have that choice because it had been her destiny since childhood to leave the past behind along with the island and learn the ways of the world.

The landlady led her out into the passageway and up the stairs.

Each step was agony for Catriona, like the pain of being cut by a razorfish shell not just once but again and again, each time she lifted her foot to climb a stair and then put it down on the next one.

At the landing Mrs Gordon paused. 'You're not ill, are you? You look awfully pale.'

Catriona shook her head and bit her lip, and carried on until they had reached the top of the house.

Mrs Gordon opened the door and then fretted and reached into her skirt for a match to light the lamp.

The room was very cold and rain spattered against the window.

It was small and shaped by the fall of the roof; at one end a bed rested in an alcove hardly higher than Catriona's waist. Facing that there were two other beds, leaving only just space to walk past and reach the twin chests of drawers braced again the wall.

'Now, let me see, you're under the roof, I think, but it's not so bad because you've got this little chest all for yourself.'

Catriona was gazing at the sky that leaked through the skylight.

'That's it,' Mrs Gordon said briskly. 'I'll leave you to settle in. Beth and Tia will be in shortly. The convenience is downstairs, by the way. You do know how to use it, don't you?'

'Of course,' Catriona said.

'You fetch your own water. Bowls and jugs are under the wash stand.'

The door clicked shut behind the landlady and Catriona sat on the bed and then leaned back and took the weight off her feet.

Much later, Beth and Tia came, making a sound like a drum as they climbed the stairs.

The door opened and they found her there, lying half on and half off the bed so that her shoes did not sully the bedclothes, shivering with the chill and the pain in her feet.

'You must be Mary?' Beth asked before Catriona had a chance to speak. Beth was young, with wispy fair hair curled into a twist; some of it had escaped and it hung about her face in damp tendrils.

Tia was older and careworn somehow, although Catriona thought that she could not have been more than twenty. She hung back for a moment as Beth chattered, and then knelt down beside Catriona's bed.

'Your feet hurt,' she said. 'I can tell.'

'I've never worn shoes before.'

Beth sniggered.

Tia gently eased the shoes off and then swore softly in Gaelic. Catriona looked down and saw that her right heel was a bloody mess that had stuck hard to her stocking; her left foot was not so bad but the toes had cramped and her ankle was swollen.

'Away and get some water,' Tia said to Beth. 'See if you can get some warm, and fetch some salt from the kitchen. Tell her I've got a sore throat if she asks.'

The door closed behind Beth as Tia tried unsuccessfully to ease off the stockings.

'I'm from North Uist,' she said softly, 'at least, I was. I've been here a while now.'

'How long?'

Tia smiled weakly and pushed the hair from her face with a tired gesture.

'Only a few months here. I ... before that, I was a maid, but I'm a seamstress now. I make a good wage, least they tell me it's good.'

'I'm from Skye, The Braes.'

'Seonag's from Skye. She's in another room, with a girl from Inverness. They're at the college training to be teachers. She ...'

Tia shrugged and stopped talking, but Catriona waited for her to carry on.

'I shouldn't say, but she's a bit of a toff. The girls that are training to be teachers, they look down on us workers. You work too, don't you?'

'I'm going to. A lawyer's office. I don't know what I'm supposed to do there, but it's supposed to be a good job.'

'It might be. I don't know.'

Tia looked at her hands, which were pitted and scarred; the tips of her fingers were callused where she held the cloth.

'I think this's bad. It'd be worse if I was a herring girl.'

'You wouldn't make as much money.'

'The herring girls can make as much in a season and they don't have to pay for this.' She made a sweeping gesture around the room and its shabby furniture. 'I manage, though.'

'Do you ... how d'you manage Mrs Gordon?'

Tia looked away for a moment. 'Beth gets on with her, but she's from Perth. Down here, it's different, Catriona. It isn't like the islands.'

When the water came she bathed Catriona's feet and gently eased off her stockings. Then she added salt to the water to kill the germs and bathed them again, dried them and put ointment on the blisters, and bandaged them with a strip of calico that came from her drawer.

'You should've worn them for an hour or two indoors first,' she said knowingly. 'It hurts like hell if you're not used to them.'

They were chatting naturally in Gaelic and Catriona did not realize that Beth was sitting on her bed with an expression of slighted interest on her face. Tia saw her and switched rapidly back into English, as Catriona asked her in Gaelic how in hell's name was she supposed to go to the 'convenience' without her shoes and why was it that Mrs Gordon did not leave a po under the bed like everyone else?

Tia laughed and found her an old pair of canvas slippers of her own which were big enough to fit around the bandages. Catriona managed to limp down to the WC and back upstairs.

A bell chimed in the bowels of the house and Beth rose dutifully to go downstairs.

'Supper,' Tia said. 'I'll try to bring you a cup of tea when she isn't looking.'

Catriona lay back and folded her hands behind her neck. Through the skylight she could see the darker tones of evening; the dull of the afternoon had lifted and the sky was an odd shade of grey-blue now, streaked like a bruise with the advent of night.

So much had changed in the space of a day that she was dizzy with the pace of it all; too stunned yet to understand how different her life was.

She looked around at the drab wainscoting that was faded and blistered in places where the veneer had dropped off, and the shabby furniture that gave the whole room an uncared for look, like a widow in the first throes of grief who is too distracted to tend to her hair or dress herself in more than rags. I must get out of here, she thought, but only briefly as she heard Tia climbing the stairs.

'I've got you cocoa,' Tia whispered as she handed her a mug and reached into her skirt, 'and a biscuit.'

'I . . . doesn't it cost sixpence?'

'*Galach* sixpence,' Tia spat.

In the morning Catriona's feet ached and when she put her weight onto them the ache turned into a sharp pain as the scab that had formed overnight on her heel splintered and fell off.

Tia, hearing Catriona's sharp intake of breath, turned over sleepily, reached for the tub of ointment that was on the chest of drawers and handed it to her.

'Take the bandage off and put this on. It'll help.'

Catriona did so and found that the pain eased.

The sound that the WC plumbing made embarrassed her in the still of the morning as it echoed through the house. She had heard four o'clock chime somewhere and waited for five, then six to pass before she got up and went to the bathroom. In the island she would have had privacy at a time like that, there was no roaring torrent of water to mark the passage of her waste.

Beth shuffled past her on the stairs, wearing a robe over her nightgown. In the morning light Catriona could see that the other girl's nightgown was made of fine cotton, embroidered and edged with ribbon. Her own shabby cambric, grey with many washings, made her feel ill at ease. She sensed disdain in Beth's glance as she passed, in the way that she smiled fleetingly and hurried on without a word.

Tia had filled her water jug the night before and she washed quickly and not properly, suddenly ashamed that she had to do so in front of strangers.

Breakfast was a strange meal of slices of bread and butter and a single egg perched in a cup. She had to eat it with a spoon and not as she would have done at home, by removing the shell and eating it from her fingers.

Mrs Gordon said a prayer first, for ever it seemed as Catriona opened her eyes briefly and saw steam rising from the eggs.

The girls ate in silence as the landlady glowered over them like an angry crow.

'We leave for the kirk at ten,' she said as Catriona rose from the table.

'I . . . I don't think I could manage it today,' she said, 'my feet are so sore.'

Mrs Gordon looked down at her feet. 'You don't have to make excuses to me, girl. It's Our Lord you have to answer to, and I'll imagine you'll have quite a bit of explaining to do.'

Catriona slowly climbed the stairs; when she reached her room she threw herself down on her bed and sobbed.

Years back, when her mother had talked about the college scholarship that Catriona would win in time, Tom had once tried to punch a hole in her dreams by saying that it was a lot of nonsense because no island girl could face the city alone.

Mor had looked at him in that way of hers, with her arms a defiant triangle braced by her hands against her waist: 'Don't be daft, Tomas. Even you're not so stupid, less you're putting it on. Half of The Braes lives in the Gallowgate and there's people from Breakish and Portree all over the place. Not strangers, friends, mind you, unless your memory's gone along with your brain. Your cousin Hugh and his wife Jenny, he's a carter in Govan, isn't he? Have you forgotten him?' Without giving him time to reply, she went on, 'There's my uncle Iain in Motherwell, wherever that is, and my cousin Kirsty who's a housekeeper in Hillhead and my cousin Ceit who's married to Jocky *beag* who's a coalman, and Silis' husband's brother who's a foreman on the railway, they live in Partick. Any one of them would take Catriona in and care for her just like their own; so there's no nonsense about the girl going down to the city and being alone.'

The list of names echoed in her head, all relatives she had never met who would be glad, she knew, to see her and take her in. That was the way that island girls went to the city, to stay with kin, not like this in the house of a landlady whose usury matched the worst excesses of Lord MacDonald, who had the cheek to charge a farthing for a cup of tea.

She smiled wistfully as she dried her tears. I could go to see them, she thought; she could ask Rory to find out where they lived. The impulse vanished with the realization that they would know the lie; that they, having heard of Mor's hopes for her eldest daughter, would expect her to be going to college on a scholarship and not just to work as a lowly office clerk. Worse even, they would know without being told that she was fourteen and not sixteen; they would

88

wonder why she had left suddenly without the prizes and the scholarship and she would have to tell them about her father and Marsaili. So she would tarnish the glow of her mother's memory; she did not want to feel their shame, to have to bear it along with her own.

'Catriona?'

Tia was back from church and Catriona felt colour rise in her cheeks because her thoughts were so powerful that she was sure they could be seen in the cast of her face.

'I'm sorry,' she tried to say, but her throat was dry and the words came out in a croak. She cleared her throat and tried again.

'Don't worry,' Tia said gently. 'It takes time to get used to it at first. I've got a pair of old boots that you can wear to work tomorrow. I'll take you there as well; it's on the way to the store where I work.'

'Thank you,' Catriona said. 'I can pay you for the boots.'

'Don't be daft. They're old, like I said, but they'll do for a week. There's a market called Paddy's, if you go there you could probably sell these shoes for the price of a decent pair.'

At seven o'clock in the morning Catriona stood shivering outside an office opposite a building that looked like the drawings of Roman temples she had seen in a schoolbook.

The brass nameplate read: 'MacKenzie MacLure SSC'.

The wooden door was shut tight; she had already tried the door knob and it did not move.

The Reverend MacPherson had warned her to be there on Monday at first thing, but Tia told her that the offices did not open until eight o'clock, if that. She went to the shop early to iron the clothes.

Tia had become distanced that morning; the friendliness of the day before had vanished into a polite but reserved attitude as she showed Catriona the way to Royal Exchange Square. Catriona sensed that something in Tia's past made her so; she wondered if the city affected everyone like that, making them either arrogant, like Mrs Gordon, or otherwise vaguely sad.

The quarter hour chimed and then half past. A man selling newspapers marched by, shouting, 'Balkan War: latest'.

Catriona remembered Miss Anderson's prediction and shrugged; the Balkans were two thousand miles away on the other side of Europe.

At a quarter to eight a woman hurried up, carrying a bunch of keys.

'You must be Catriona Nicolson, she said. 'I'm Mrs MacIver, Mr MacKenzie's manageress. You've been waiting since the crack of dawn?'

'Just seven o'clock.'

'Och, you Skye girls are all the same. You'll have to learn to keep city time now, lass.'

The door swung open on a marble-floored hall of sepulchral gloom. Mrs MacIver bustled in and lit the lamps.

'Well, come in, lass,' she said, opening another door leading to an office packed with ledgers in piles that stretched from floor to ceiling.

'You've worked in an office before?'

Catriona wondered what she meant.

Mrs MacIver caught the confusion on her face. 'Och, that Reverend MacPherson, Mr MacKenzie tells him to send a lass with experience and he aye sends a wee girl from school. You've no' worked afore, have you, lass?'

'No.'

'Och, well, no bother, though that'll cut your wages back. You'll pick it up, soon 'nough.'

Catriona reached into her pocket and handed over her references.

'Ach, lass, yon's not for me. Mr MacKenzie'll look them over later. He wants an honest lass, more'n anything. The city girls are flighty, like.'

'My wages, what'll that be?' Catriona blurted before she wished she had not asked.

'Och, a couple of bob a week, I suppose. Two and six, I think, though he'd've paid a bit more if you'd a year or two's work behind you.'

Catriona's face fell and she turned away so that the woman would not see her expression. She had imagined that she'd make more than that, enough at least to send a shilling home each week.

'That's more 'n a fair wage for a wee lass like you,' Mrs MacIver said. 'It'll pay your keep, won't it?'

Catriona said that it would.

'That's just it, lass. You can't expect more 'n that, not till you know your way around.'

Catriona listened in silence as Mrs MacIver explained the work that she would have to do.

Outside, a church bell chimed the quarter hour.

It was too late to go home.

Time passed very slowly that day.

Once Mrs MacIver had explained the filing system, Catriona was left alone in the file room with a pile of papers, and a clock that ticked pedantically in the corner. When she finished she watched the clock sweeping the minutes away. She did not know what else to do, except to watch and wait.

Mrs MacIver came back an hour later, twenty minutes into Catriona's reverie. 'Oh, you're finished,' she said, 'That's quick. But I hope it's right. I'll just check that it is because if it isn't it'll all have to be done again. There's no point in doing something quickly unless it's done right.'

Catriona watched her flicking through the files, checking at random that the papers were in the right place. She seemed surprised to discover that they were.

She was astonished that Catriona managed to count out the money for the bequests from a Mr Matheson's will to 'children of the indigenous poor of the Cowcaddens' in a few moments, and took twice as long to check the sums herself.

Pursing her lips, she set Catriona to copy out an accounts ledger, and left her at it all day, taking another from a pile on her desk when Catriona finished just before the office closed at six o'clock.

She went back to the cold, quiet room in the Gorbals, ate a tasteless meal and spent the evening watching Tia Macleod concentrating on her sewing, and trying not to think of home. The next day was a repetition of the first, and the next one the same again.

The only break in the monotony came on Friday, when after checking the petty cash twice Catriona became certain that there was more money in the box than there should be.

'Excuse me,' she said to Mrs MacIver, who was bent over an account file, 'I'm sorry, but I think there's a mistake. There's five shillings too much here.'

Mrs MacIver tightened her lips as she checked the addition. 'Well, Catriona. You're quite right. I got five shillings change from the coalman, but I didn't make a note of it.'

Catriona knew then that she had been tested, and she bit her lip and swallowed a retort.

On Saturday, when the office closed for the week, Mrs MacIver told her that she had done very well, especially for an island girl who had only just left school.

'I was first in my class at home,' Catriona said reflexively, remembering for a moment what Mor had hoped she would achieve.

'Aye, so it said in your reference,' Mrs MacIver said, 'but ye ken, lass, being clever up there is no' quite the same as being clever down here.'

Catriona walked away hurriedly before her anger showed.

She counted the hours before she was due to meet Rory MacDonald under the railway arches on Sunday at noon. During the week she had thought about him often; when Mrs MacIver spoke sharply to her she thought of the way he had wrapped the tarpaulin over her on the boat, almost as if he had been hugging her. She would've liked that, she realized.

Back home people spoke of Rory as a good man, the sort that any woman would be glad to marry, but he was young himself and his father's croft was one of the tiniest on the island; Rory supported his family with what he earned on the boat. She felt a splinter of guilt when she thought of what her stockings and the food he'd bought her must have cost, then she told herself again that she was in the city to work and she shouldn't be thinking these things, especially of a man she hardly knew. Then she decided that if she liked thinking like that, why not? It was a way to pass the hours after all; it caused no harm to anyone. There were girls prettier than her who would die for a man like that; Catriona had never thought much of her own looks, especially now that in the city she had to dress every day in funereal colours. Mrs MacIver had been quite clear about that, only black was permitted and her navy suit would do at a pinch, but only until she got something better.

Catriona was mourning, in a way – mourning the loss of her home and happiness, the colours and textures of a land she loved.

If the days seemed long, the week passed in a flash; when Sunday came round she walked briskly along Argyle Street until she reached the railway arches, where she paused and checked her reflection in a shop window. Her dowdy clothes merged with the reflected brickwork, but her hair hung loose and thick, newly washed with flower-scented soap that Tia had given her. She smiled and watched her face lighten; thought that she didn't look so bad after all. The prospect of seeing Rory again in just a few moments made her feel happy, though the summer sky was the colour of lead.

A few yards before she reached the tearoom, the door opened and she heard the burr of Skye Gaelic, the tail end of a story followed by raucous glee. It wasn't a tearoom really, just a booth with a few chairs and tables behind a window misted with condensation. Peering through, she saw a table of girls, Rory in the middle of them, his head rising way above theirs. She recognized a couple of girls from The Braes who worked as maids, another from Portree who was a seamstress and three sisters from Breakish who helped in their uncle's shop. She stood back, watched for a moment longer as Rory said something and they laughed, flinched as he threw his arm around Mary MacKinnon and tickled her side. Sinking down on her heels, she felt her heart fall as a bell chimed noon. She had imagined meeting Rory alone for a moment, to have a chat just between the two of them; she hadn't thought there'd be so many people with him, and all of them girls.

The door opened again; a man whose face she faintly recognized held it for her to go in.

'No,' she said, turning quickly. 'Really, I don't have the time.' She could post her letter to Annie instead of giving it to him.

Just as she reached the light beyond the railway arches, Rory caught up with her.

'Catriona' he called, 'didn't you see us inside?'

She half turned towards him. 'Oh ... yes, Rory, but I didn't ...'

'Ach, come away in,' he said, grasping her arm as he turned back to the tearoom. 'I wasn't sure if you'd find us or not. I'd just persuaded Mary to go to Mrs Gordon's for you when I saw you outside. It was hell's own job, I tell you.'

He likes me, she thought, he does like me.

The other girls made room for her; one poured her tea as another offered her a plate of cakes.

They were talking about someone she didn't know; she smiled obediently at the funny bits.

Rory reached into his pocket and handed her a letter. 'From Annie Macdonald' he said.

It was too soon to expect anything from her father.

'Did you see Allan?' she asked anxiously.

He smiled. 'I did that. He was at Annie's when I went for your letter. I saw the twins and your sisters. They all send their love.'

Catriona smiled, relieved.

'What are you doing down here?' Mary MacKinnon asked her. 'You haven't won the scholarship already, have you?'

'I ... no, I didn't win the scholarship, Mary. I'm sorry, I have to go now.'

'Don't be daft,' Rory said.

'No, really' she said, rising. 'I'll see you next week.'

He walked to the door and held it open for her. 'Catriona, are you sure you're all right?'

'Of course I am, Rory.'

'I'd walk you over the river,' he said, 'but I have to wait for Jean MacPherson. Her granny's not very well, and her mother asked me to be sure to tell her. Jean'll be worried. I don't want to leave news like that with anyone else.'

'I understand,' she said, very slowly, feeling slightly ashamed of herself for not being sorry for Jean and her granny, for not being strong enough to withstand the inquisition of the other island girls.

Rory touched her cheek gently. 'Till next week, then.'

She walked away quickly, so that he wouldn't see the disappointment on her face.

One of the other girls fell in with her, calling out for her to wait as she caught up. 'I've to be back early,' she said, 'I promised the missus I'd make afternoon tea.'

Catriona shrugged, wondering why it was that her own job was considered better than domestic work. She did not want to talk to the girl, but she had to do so for politeness' sake.

'Takes time to settle in,' the girl said, 'but you'll manage it, I don't doubt.'

'It was nice to see Rory,' Catriona said softly.

'Ha!' The other girl grinned. 'I wouldn't get any ideas about Rory MacDonald. He's fun, but he's a tease and a flirt.'

Catriona stopped dead. 'What do you mean by that?'

The girl's eyes rolled upwards, as if Catriona was daft. 'Haven't you heard about him? Everybody else has.'

The girl went on, oblivious to the crestfallen look that came over Catriona's face. 'He's like all sailors,' she said. 'He's got a girl in every port.'

'He only goes between here and Skye,' Catriona said.

'Well, he's got plenty of girls here.'

'I don't believe you.'

'He has,' she said, nodding to emphasize the point. 'Not island girls, but girls he meets in the city.'

'How do you know?'

'My cousin Willie, his friend Malcolm works the other ferry. He knows Rory and he told my da not to let me near him. My da'd kill me if he knew I met him.'

'That's just gossip,' Catriona said.

The girl smiled easily. 'Have it your own way.'

They crossed the bridge in silence. The air felt chill, even cold.

'I'll see you next week,' the girl said, when they reached the tram stop for Pollokshields.

'If I can,' Catriona said mechanically, trying to make her voice sound light.

'You should be glad I warned you about Rory,' the other said, 'it wouldn't do to get yourself hurt.'

Catriona's lips curved slightly. 'Don't worry about me,' she said.

'So long then.' The girl waved cheerfully as she held her skirt down to stop it blowing up in the tide of the tram.

Along the street a bit, Catriona turned a corner and then another, bunching her hands into fists, punching them into her pockets as she walked along. The day had turned sour for her; suddenly she felt as sullen as the weather. She walked around a square of streets, then started again when she returned to her starting point.

She didn't believe what the girl had told her, not for a minute. Rory was not, could not be like that.

Then she remembered the way he had put his arm around Mary MacKinnon, the disappointment that had felt as sharp as a slap. She hardly knew him, after all. Perhaps the girl was right, that might've been what Maggie meant when she said he was a bit of a lad. Catriona completed half a dozen circuits of the block, telling herself she was glad she knew, just in case. They would be friends, no more than that. She was too young, she told herself, for the last time, to be thinking of any man.

She walked back to Mrs Gordon's, flexing her shoulders to throw off the hurt that cut as keenly as the cold city wind.

Chapter Four

*W*inter came quickly to the city.

By October, Catriona walked to work in the morning in darkness, and when she left it was dark again; all she saw of the day was the pale, thin light that filtered through the office windows and occasionally a smudge of the sun veiled by cloud if she was sent out on some errand.

Her work bored her. Along with the filing and the endless copying of ledgers, she had to clean the hearths in the lawyers' offices and then set the fires and light them, polish the desks and put out fresh paper and sharpened pencils, refill the inkpots and change the blotters, have a pot of tea ready when Mrs MacIver and Cameron, the shorthand writer, came in with the messenger Maloney at eight o'clock. Although Mrs MacIver was pleasant enough there was a condescension in her manner that irked, particularly the way she had of seeming so surprised that Catriona could cope with her work. Cameron ignored her, MacKenzie and the associate lawyers hardly knew she existed; only Maloney spoke to her when he was having his tea by the boiler in the basement and she was replacing files in the archives. He had been with the firm for forty years, from the time that MacKenzie was an apprentice and Arthur MacLure had been the top lawyer in the city; his name was still the firm's though he'd been dead for twenty years. Catriona thought there was something odd about that; she felt vaguely squeamish when she handled the notepaper with the dead lawyer's name engraved along the top.

At the end of the month, when the bills were sent out, Catriona was astonished at the sums involved, did not understand how even MacKenzie's professional services could possibly cost £100 or more.

'Alchemy, it is,' Maloney would say, 'he casts a spell upon his clients.'

Catriona thought her work could have been done just as well by a trained monkey. There was an organ grinder who stood at the corner of Buchanan Street with a monkey who danced for farthings; she had been terrified of the animal at first until a passer-by had told her that was just what it was, an animal and not the Devil come to life and doing a jig on the streets of Glasgow.

In the evening, when she left work, she went home to Mrs Gordon's and sat in her room listening to the hours pass. At first she thought the church bells rang so often because the city people were particularly devout, she did not realize they sounded only to tell the time.

After that Sunday when she met Rory with the other island girls, she invented a mythical cousin with whom she had Sunday lunch, and so avoided the questions the other girls would be bound to ask.

She felt a dull dread when she thought how easy it would be for MacKenzie to find out she was only fourteen, to give her the sack because she had lied.

After that she met Rory early on a Sunday morning; he did not complain when she threw stones against the cabin of the ferry to wake him up after he had been out most of the night with his friends. She felt ashamed when she gave him a letter to take home to her father that contained only coins, not a note.

After a month of recriminations in the Free church that Mrs Gordon took her girls too, Catriona told her that she would go to the Gaelic church in Renfield Street instead, held firm when Mrs Gordon threatened damnation upon her soul and prayed that her landlady would not discover that she just wandered the streets.

The city began to fascinate Catriona then; she would walk up Buchanan Street and gaze into MacDonald's, entranced by the costumes on display that cost her annual salary or even more. She used to stare for ages, wondering how anything could cost so much, pulling back when she saw the mark that her breath had made on the window, ashamed of the smudge and rubbing it with her sleeve to remove all traces of her presence. Then she would walk to Sauchiehall Street, past the cinemas, Trerons, and Copland and Lye to the mirrored glass windows of the Willow Tearooms where she would stand, imagining the lives of the people who could afford to spend her weekly wage on lunch. The tearooms intrigued her; all of Glasgow talked of Miss Cranston and her splendiferous Room de Luxe. Catriona never saw beyond the mirror work of the windows, the stylized notice that told her lunches started at 10d for poached flounder, to a whole high tea for 2/6d. Once, when Maloney was elsewhere, Mrs MacIver had sent her to deliver an urgent letter to Miss Cranston at Buchanan Street, and Catriona had been so astonished by the murals of white-robed women, lithe as reeds against a golden sun, the tables set with green-handled cutlery and china and flowers in little silver bowls, the sensation of stepping into a painting, that she had gaped in wonder and not noticed at first the manageress who impatiently asked her what she was doing there.

The people fascinated her too; the ladies who owned and managed tearooms all on their own, Charles Rennie Macintosh, architect and artist, responsible for the strange, stylized effigies of nature that set Miss Cranston apart from her competitors and who MacKenzie, WS, was suing for breach of contract. 'Has the man no soul?' Maloney exclaimed when she handed him the writ to serve and then, when he returned, 'The laddie's scarpered, Catriona. Jist file the writ, lass, it can't be served if we don't know where he is.'

Macintosh's work was all over Glasgow that year, adding grace and style to the Victorian buildings of the city centre.

At the fringes the town's grandeur was frayed, faded, as the buildings became tenements that turned into slums along the Gallowgate and to the south of Argyle Street. The tempo of the streets changed; sophistication became exuberance.

Catriona found Paddy's Market one Sunday, where she sold Eileen MacInnes's shoes for sixpence to a woman who there and then held them up in her hand, bawling, 'Fine calf lady's shoes, jist a shilling', and then bought a pair of black leather boots, worn but re-soled, for ninepence, the cost justified, the man told her, because the soles were as good as new – new in fact – and would last for years if she took care of them.

The market was an anarchic sprawl of stalls, hawkers and dank little shops that filled the lanes between Jail Square and the Briggait; years before the Corporation had opened a building for the old clothes traders but they had resented the imposition of order and taken to the streets instead. At the market you could buy anything from an evening gown in pristine condition to a set of underwear washed but yellowed with age. It was the haunt of the opportunistic and the impoverished; rag merchants toured the stalls to buy bundles of cloth that could be recycled and women in shawls picked through the jumble to find something for their children to wear. Long ago, in the hunger years, the market was started by an Irishman so poor that he had to sell the shirt off his back; now the Irish had made the place their own together with anyone who shared their need. A man called Donoghue ran the place, a big bluff Glasgow Irishman with a shock of ruddy hair and a voice that soared above the trains that trundled towards St Enoch's. Catriona watched him at his stall all day one Sunday, and realized that he must have taken twenty or thirty pounds although every time he sold anything he acted as if he had lost out. There was money to be made from old clothes and rags, things that islanders would be ashamed to give away. Remembering Mor, she got Annie to send her a hank of wool and knitted a pair of socks which she sold to Donoghue for ninepence, then Annie sent her half a dozen pairs which she sold for four and sixpence, sending Annie the money with a letter telling her of the strange ways of the city. Donoghue offered her a job then, which was what she had wanted all along, the chance to make a little more money in the only free day she had in the week.

'I've got a job,' she told Rory, when she woke him up at the crack of dawn.

He scratched his head sleepily. 'What, another one?'

She flinched, because her father had sent her an angry letter in which he said he didn't know what she was doing with an office job, because she would earn much more as a maid.

'At Paddy's Market.'

His face cracked into a smile. 'Come on, Catriona, we'll have a cup of coffee to celebrate.'

They stood at the stall by the dockside, blowing on the steaming mugs.

'And I'm going to get another one,' Catriona said, explaining that she was teaching herself shorthand so that she could become a senior clerk. Cameron had derided her efforts and Mrs MacIver was sceptical, but Catriona was grimly determined to take a chance.

'I'm going to find another place to live as well.'

'You've been busy, Catriona.'

She nodded.

'You know, I thought you didn't come to the arches because you were angry with me.'

She looked at him. 'Why would I be angry with you, Rory MacDonald?'

He remembered the thoughts about her that sometimes ran through his head. 'I wouldn't know. Women.'

For a moment she considered, then told him the truth about her age, also how she resented the questions about her father.

He seemed shocked; like everyone else he had assumed she was sixteen. 'In all the time I've known you,' he said, 'you were always so grown up.'

'Rory?'

He looked away. 'I used to see you on the beach gathering oysters. When I was coming home from Portree.'

'Oh. I'd best go, Rory. The market starts early.'

'Come next week, then. Come early and we'll have a blether.'

'You need your sleep, Rory.'

'Sleep? I'd rather see you, Triona.'

She went off to the market, feeling very light all of a sudden, despite the morose city weather.

When Donoghue discovered that Catriona stayed at Mrs Gordon's he told her she was mad because there were better boarding houses that charged half as much; he gave her two addresses and the first woman she went to offered her an attic room which could be shared by two for a total rent of a shilling a week without meals but with an oven where she could cook for herself.

She asked Tia to share with her, thinking she would be delighted to leave Mrs Gordon's.

Tia put down the blouse she was working on. 'I don't think so,' she said, 'it'd cost as much once you buy food.'

'It wouldn't, Tia. It wouldn't cost more than a shilling a week for food for us both. We'd be a shilling better off.'

Tia picked up the blouse. 'I'm sorry, but I can't, Catriona.'

'Why not?'

'I'd rather not, that's all.'

Catriona persisted.

'You don't understand,' Tia said.

'This isn't a prison.'

'I can't leave, Catriona. Please don't ask me again.'

Catriona went round to Mrs Campbell's and explained that she could not take the room because she did not have anybody to share it with.

'Och, that's no bother, lass. You can take it all for yourself, if you like.'

'I would like to,' she said, softly. She could manage the rent, and still save sixpence.

The landlady looked at her in a kindly way. 'Tell ye what, lass, if ye'll get up early and help wi' the breakfasts, and the dinners at night, I'll let you have the room for sixpence, an' yer meals an' a'.'

'That would be wonderful,' Catriona said, almost unable to believe her luck.

'Good riddance,' Mrs Gordon spat, when Catriona told

her that she was leaving. 'I want you out of this house on Friday night.'

Catriona remembered the monthly rent paid in advance; she was due three weeks back. 'Six shillings,' she said, 'you owe me six shillings.'

'I owe you nothing at all, girl.'

'You do, Mrs Gordon. If you check your books you will see.'

'I'll check nothing, girl; how dare you tell me to? If I hear any more of your cheek I'll be in touch with your employer.'

Very slowly Catriona walked up the stairs, holding her anger until she was back in her room, when she cursed like a fishwife.

Tia looked up. 'You see what I mean. I daren't risk it.'

Catriona sat down and began to pack the few things she owned into the bag she had brought from home. 'She can't do anything worse to you than keep you here.'

Tia went back to her sewing.

At Mrs Campbell's her life became easier. With the landlady she made the breakfasts and dinners, cleared up afterwards and still had plenty of time to herself. The landlady prided herself on her baking, taught Catriona how to make pies, cakes, sponges and scones with the fine flour people used in the city, passed on the tricks she had learned when she had been a cook in a big house.

'Ach, lass, it's such a pleasure tae work wi' ye, I feel almost guilty tae ask you for rent.'

'No,' Catriona said quickly, 'I'd rather pay.'

In the evenings she stayed in, knitting socks or studying shorthand and practising dictation with the landlady. When she remembered her mother, the irony of it all struck her; here she was in the city where all of their dreams were supposed to come true and what was she doing but knitting socks to make a few extra pence?

With the money she saved, and the extra she earned at the market, she was able to give Rory two ten-shilling notes to take home to her father two weeks before Christmas. The obligation had weighed heavily upon her, the thought that she had not even managed to repay what Marsaili had given her; she felt the burden lift as she handed over the money, smiling brightly as if it had cost her nothing at all.

Rory put the envelope in his pocket. 'I was thinking, Catriona, next week, I usually have to work on the engine on Saturdays, get it right for going home, but she's just had a new compressor fitted, running as sweet as a bird since then. I've Saturday free mostly, and there's a dance at the St Andrew's hall; a good band's playing, I thought you might like to come.'

For a moment, she didn't realize what he had asked her; he had spoken so fast that the words took time to sink in.

'I've got tickets' he said quickly, praying that the five shillings they cost would be worth it, that she would agree to come with him.

'Oh, Rory,' she began.

'It starts at eight, Catriona, and doesn't finish till midnight, but if you've to be in early, I'll see you right to your door.'

'Oh, Rory,' she said, 'it isn't that. Mrs Campbell's doing a church social on Saturday, and she asked me to help her especially, because there's hundreds coming and she can't manage herself. I said I would and I have to, my rent's cheap because I help her out.'

'It doesn't matter,' he said quickly.

'Rory, I'm so sorry. I'd love to come. I really would.'

'Doesn't matter,' he said, 'I got the tickets for nothing. The mate bought them and gave them to me because he can't use them.'

'Oh. Maybe, maybe if the church social finishes early, but it starts at eight, too.'

Rory's old pride surged; he had never asked a girl out before, never needed to because they always asked themselves.

'I could maybe get away by ten?'

'No, don't worry. I can take someone else. Only asked you

because you look like you need, a night out. It doesn't matter, Triona. Really, it doesn't.'

The start of the war took her by surprise. She read the *Glasgow Herald* every day, after it had been discarded by Mr MacKenzie and pored over by Mrs MacIver and Maloney. For months the paper had predicted conflict, but on the day the war began, the front page was full of sales notices for the city stores, the news about the King's ultimatum buried on an inner page. The weather that day was dull, cold for August, the streets spattered with rain, but something about the moment trapped Catriona in the streets; when she left work she joined the crowds in George Square waiting in stoic anticipation for war to begin.

Walking home, she wondered what it meant, listened to a man saying that the Expeditionary Force would pop over to France and send the Kaiser packing.

Two days later, when Cameron resigned in order to answer the call to arms, MacKenzie offered her the job as his shorthand clerk, if she learned to type in her own time and at her own expense. Catriona did that, knowing she would recover the cost from the salary she would get, of seven and sixpence a week.

A few months into the war when people were still saying that it would all be over soon, Catriona hugged herself and relished her luck.

The war to end war, they called it in the beginning, a brief foray into France to dent the Kaiser's optimism. At first it meant opportunity for Catriona and other women who took jobs normally done by men.

Men joined up in their thousands, buoyant with the promise of victory. They left from Central Station, telling anyone who would listen that they would be back within a few weeks.

At Christmas the newspaper told of troop fraternization on the Western Front, news that augured defeat for the Germans, people thought; the paper had said nothing about the calamitous defeat of the Expeditionary Force.

The truth seeped through, in snippets; Catriona overhead a soldier on leave saying that the war in the trenches could last for ever because attack was certain suicide. That was when the newspapers and MacKenzie were still predicting swift success; Catriona was so shocked that she asked the man to explain, and when he did she was filled with horror at the thought of men forced to live like rats.

Every week Rory brought letters from Annie and her family; her brothers always wrote even if Tom did not, and Allan managed a line or two since he had started school in the autumn. Annie usually sent some socks as well, for her to sell at the market; because Rory told her the news as well she did not feel as if they were far away. She had wanted to go home for a week, but her father told her he'd rather she sent the money because things were tight on the croft.

It was in the April of 1915 that Rory told her he was leaving the ferry to join the merchant fleet, to run the gauntlet of the German navy to keep the country supplied.

The weather was crisp and clear, still cold, but the sun had risen and the gulls drifting on the breeze told her that it would be warm later. She stood staring at him for a long time, willing him to change his mind; she had known from the start that something had happened because he was waiting for her at the coffee stall and she did not have to wake him up as usual.

'Kenneth MacDonald's taking over as stoker,' he said, 'Kenny from Portree. You know him. He'll carry the mail as well.'

'But . . .' she began.

'But what?'

Kenneth isn't you, she thought, biting the words back.

'Why?' she asked.

'I have to, Catriona.'

'You don't. It's volunteers only, no conscription. The government's given its word.'

He grinned cynically. 'The government can change its mind, Catriona. It'll have to. They're not going to win the war tomorrow. They'll have to conscript sooner or later, so I'm going now, while I still have a choice.'

'When?' she asked, blinking.

'Tomorrow.'

'I wish you'd told me, Rory.'

'I only knew myself last week.'

She was still staring at him; suddenly she leant a little closer, peering at his chin. 'What happened, Rory?'

Two days ago, he had happened on Tom Nicolson as he walked back from Portree, said 'hello' in a friendly way as Tom glowered at him from the dyke he was working on. 'You meet that girl of mine down there, don't you?' Tom grunted.

'From time to time, I do,' Rory replied.

Tom stood up and brushed the grit from his hands. 'Just keep your hands off her, that's all I want to say.'

Rory's expression sharpened. 'And what do you mean by that?'

'You know what I mean. I know too. Just not my daughter, y'hear?'

'You've no right to say that to me,' Rory said, angry at Tom for what he had done to her himself.

'Have I not, Rory MacDonald?'

'You have not, Mr Nicolson, because I wouldn't dream of harming a hair of her head.'

In a flash Tom's right fist drew back and lashed forward, the blow so hard that Rory was thrown to the ground and winded.

'That's what I mean,' Tom said.

'But I haven't,' he spluttered, 'I didn't ...'

'That's exactly what I mean,' Tom told him, 'don't you even think it. That's just a taste of what you'll get if you do.'

His jaw still throbbed. 'Ach, nothing, Catriona. I had a dram or two last night. I fell up the gangway going back onto the ferry.' He had not shaved since Tom hit him, so that the stubble of his beard would hide the bruise. Rory's anger surged; he should have hit Tom back, he would've done if they hadn't been out in the open, if people hadn't been able to see and relay the story back to his own father.

Catriona's eyes dropped to the ground. She had been hoping that he would ask her to another dance; when he hadn't she had talked to Mrs Campbell and asked if she could have him to tea.

'Of course, lass,' the landlady said, 'any day but Saturday, because I do the socials at the kirk.'

'Saturday's the only day he's here,' Catriona had said.

The landlady frowned slightly. 'I don't like to miss the kirk socials lass, ye ken, but if it means that much I'll see whit I can do.'

She had not asked again.

'I don't want you to go, Rory,' she said, softly, and then, on impulse, she threw herself into his arms, hugged him so tight that for a moment he couldn't breathe.

'Whoa, lass,' he wheezed, unhitching her as she blushed deeply.

She smiled shyly. 'I'm sorry,' she whispered.

His heart fluttered, then settled; he was reeling from the feel of her body. 'You don't have to be sorry for doing that.'

'I'll write to you, Rory. I promise I will.'

He touched her cheek gently. 'Don't be daft, Triona. You can't write to everyone who's gone to the war.'

'You're special,' she said.

Tom's snarling face swam before him, but it wasn't the thought of her father that troubled him, it was the fear that if he was killed it would break her heart.

'Will you write to me, Rory?'

'Ach,' he said, fumbling with his hands, 'I'll be that busy I'll not have time to write to anyone. You take care of yourself, girl. I'll come back, don't you fear.' He grinned to hide his embarrassment. The truth was he was wary of the war; though the merchant navy wasn't the military, the risk was just as great – greater even, because if the Germans could stop the merchant navy bringing in food and other supplies, they could throttle the country into surrender.

He looked away, remembering what the officer said when he had signed up: *'It's best you're a bachelor, lad. War's not the time to make any promises.'*

'We should keep in touch,' she said, hating the words for their distance, the hollow sound they made.

'If,' he said, 'you'll hear if . . .'

Their eyes met. 'I'd rather we wrote,' she said.

'I'd rather we didn't,' he replied, more gruffly than he felt.

Catriona listened to the silence then, the city sounds in the distance reminding her only of how alone she would be when Rory went. Her eyes drifted towards the clouds, then returned to him.

His face creased into a smile. 'Come on,' he said, 'the war's a lot of nonsense. They say it'll be over in a month or two.'

'They're wrong. You know that. You even said it yourself.'

'Ach, they've been wrong so often, maybe next time they'll be right.'

'For God's sake, the war's not a joke!'

He reached out his hand to take hers. 'It's still early. I've time to walk you along to the market.'

'No,' she said, 'I'd rather not.'

'Catriona . . .'

'Goodbye, Rory. *Beannaich leibh.*'

'Catriona, I'll come back, I promise,' he started to say, but already she had turned away. For a moment he thought of going after her, but the distance between them was already too great. When she wanted to, Catriona could run like a deer.

The rushing wind dried the tears that sprang to Catriona's eyes as she careered blindly along Clyde Street, not slowing down until she reached the Saltmarket.

She paused for breath, and then, as she walked on, the rhythmic click of the iron tips on her boots brought her back to reason, reminded her why she was in the city, why she had to work so hard.

At first her instinct had been to escape, to flee the humiliation that Marsaili heaped upon her. It was only later, when she heard that Marsaili had given birth to her first child, that her purpose became defined. With Marsaili adding to her father's family, even the pittance he might once have set aside for her brothers and sisters was gone. Ewan and Alec had already left school and they would need money to stock a croft of their own, because her uncle Angus had promised them a share of his land. Angus was a bachelor and he had made the twins his heirs but they would still need sheep and a cow of their own, material to build a cottage beside his, and though building a cottage had once cost nothing more than a man's time, now the islanders had to buy wood and cement, even pay for the stones that came from the quarry. In peacetime the twins might have earned the money they needed at the summer fishing, but she didn't want them going off into the North Sea now that German U-boats lurked in the deep. Apart from that there were her sisters, who needed clothes for school and help later, maybe, when they left school to find a job; after them there was Allan, who already at the age of six could write a creditable letter and who she had vowed would have the education she'd given up.

One day, not long after the start of the war, she had written down all of their needs, estimating each item carefully before she added it all up, realizing with horror that she needed to save nearly a hundred pounds by the time the twins came of age. With her salary and the money she earned at Paddy's she could save one pound a month at most; to get the money she needed would take more time than she had. For a moment, the prospect daunted her, until she decided to get on with it and do the best she could.

That morning, when she turned off Clyde Street into Shipbank Lane, she paused for a moment to fix a smile to her face, and then walked determinedly to Donoghue's main stall, where he was unwrapping a bundle of shirts left unclaimed at the laundry.

'Thaur ye go,' he said, handing Catriona a bag of collars. 'See, if we match the twa up, we'll get a florin a shirt at least.'

Catriona thought for a moment. Looking at the collars, she saw they were either very large or very small. The shirts were virtually new, stiff with starch and snowy white. 'Maybe it'll be better,' she said, 'if we leave them separate. Working men don't bother with collars, and the shirts are worth a florin as they are. If we try the collars for threepence, people'll think they are getting a bargain, and they won't worry that they're not the right size.'

Donoghue paused, scratching his brow as he did when he was thinking. 'Ye've got something there, lass. Aye, ye're right. Sell them separate at threepence a collar. I got them fir naithin' onyway. Woman gied me a bundle acos they're aye losing them at the laundry.'

At the end of the day, when he had counted the money, he handed Catriona a whole florin for her good idea. 'Ye should gie up that daft job in the office, lass. Ye'd mak a fortune if ye came in wi' me.'

Catriona smiled as she thanked him, thinking that she didn't dare risk the vagaries of market life. She liked the status of her office job, humble but higher on the hierarchy than a maid or, God forbid, a ragwoman at Paddy's Market. The law was no longer a mystery to her, but a language with rules that, once learnt, could ensure her livelihood for life. Although most of the legal fraternity howled with derision, one firm in Glasgow had taken on a woman as an apprentice. If she worked hard, Catriona might be taken on as an apprentice too.

The loneliness set in once Rory was gone, the sense of emptiness that made her mood as dull as the city weather, as heavy as the smoke that flowed like lava from the foundry chimneys and settled over the city like a lid. She missed her family and friends, most of all the light of the island, the sun that always shone somehow, even on the coldest winter day.

Sometimes, in the evening as she walked home, she felt the wake of a tram as it passed, closed her eyes and thought of the breeze at home, saw the colours deepening into the evening and felt briefly the sense of peace that came over the island when the day was done. Then she would open her eyes to the angular shadows of buildings, air tainted with the exhaust of motors, seeing the sky only when she crossed the bridge over the river, the water too filthy to hold the reflection of the colours above.

Mrs Campbell was a kind woman, they often spent the evening together, baking mutton pies and pastries which the Women's Guild took up to Bellahouston for the wounded men sent home from the war. Catriona appreciated the landlady's friendliness, but felt the distance between them that came from her being a paying guest in a stranger's home.

The seasons passed; the winter of 1915 was grim and she did not notice spring, feeling the difference only when the rising sun pierced the clouds for the first time in months. She was pleased with herself, though, quietly satisfied that she had managed to save twenty-five pounds towards the twins' croft. Catriona told nobody about her pledge, not even Annie; it would be too cruel to tell Ewan and Alec if something happened and her plans went awry.

It was on a Friday in March when, leaving the office, she noticed a vaguely familiar figure in the khaki kilt of the soldier.

She smiled distantly until she recognized Lachlan Maclean. Amazed then, her face fell as his took on all of the pathos of a beaten dog. 'Annie told me where you worked,' he said shyly. 'I hope you don't mind.'

For a moment her thoughts churned until she realized that she was glad to see him; as she looked at him now she felt a rush of homesickness so acute that tears came to her eyes.

'Of course not,' she said, remembering his simple ambition to have a croft besides his father's; the day he had asked her to share it with him when she was five and he was eight. Later, in the hard years, his humdrum dreams had stifled her, his cloying adoration had driven her away.

The years had not changed him much apart from making him a few inches taller, as if the child had been put through a mangle, wrenched and pulled to make him a man. His sandy hair had been savagely cut to within a quarter inch of his head where he wore a military cap scarecrow fashion, held by a strap under his chin; every now and then he would touch the strap, to make sure that the cap had not been swept away by the wind. He coughed nervously; she noticed the soft down on his chin where his beard would grow, felt sorry for him because he was young to be a soldier, a child still, despite his age. The soldier's uniform looked like a costume on him.

'I'm off to France tomorrow,' he said in a shaky voice, 'I thought I'd come to see you first. We could go for a walk, have tea, go to the cinema if you'd like.'

It was a gentle spring evening and starlings sang in their thousands, so loud that at first they drowned his words. Catriona looked up and saw the sky above the buildings, the silhouette of the roofs hard against the clouds. Even the thought of Lachlan was peculiar in the city; his uncertainty marked him out as a stranger, though he was dressed the same as hundreds of other men.

'What made you join the army?' she asked, shouting so that he could hear her above the birdsong.

He shrugged. 'They say there'll be conscription any day now.'

'Did you talk to my da?'

'I never talked to anybody, Catriona. I just signed up. They're sending out the pink forms you have to fill in, to show if you're military age; conscription'll be in before the year's out.'

'What regiment have you joined?'

'The Sutherlands or the Royal Scots, I'm not really sure. It doesn't matter, Catriona. They're all on the same side. We've done a week's training and now we're off to France.'

'Why, Lachlan?' she asked again, sensing a reason behind his evasion.

He leaned close to her, as if to impart a secret.

'Lord MacDonald said, the factor said, that special consideration would be given to men who join the army, for a croft when they get back. So I decided to take my chance. I might as well.' He paused. 'I'm nineteen now, Triona. I've not had any work this year, not since the game beating in September, and I only got a few pennies for that. It's either the army or the lowlands. Either way I've to leave home, but this way I might have something to come back to.'

You bloody fool, she thought, before she remembered the land hunger that gnawed at the soul of her people; suddenly her heart went out to him.

'Who else's joined up?' she asked, her fear for her brothers making her voice too sharp.

Lachlan flinched. 'Not many. MacIain and MacCallum, a few boys from Breakish. Andy and Angus MacPherson, the MacKinnon boys. Men aren't minded to go and fight, not with the trouble with the land. There's ten boys from Skye in the regiment with me. We get called teuchters or some bloody thing.'

She noticed that his uniform kilt was too short, that his knees looked cold.

'Have you time to come for tea with me?' he asked again, so eager that it would hurt to refuse him.

'I'll have to go back to my boarding house first, to tell my landlady I won't be in for supper. But I'll be back in twenty minutes, if you wait here.' She did not want to take him with her – she was afraid that kindly Mrs Campbell would ask him in.

When she met him again he was holding one of the roses that flower sellers sold outside the station for departing soldiers to give to their girlfriends. She took it from him, so embarrassed that she did not know what to say.

'I've been thinking about you,' he said as they headed along Sauchiehall Street, in the vague direction of Kelvingrove Park.

Catriona tried to smile.

'D'you remember, when we were little? We were going to get wed, you and me.'

'Times've changed,' she said quickly.

'Folks are angry. Folks are angry, back home, about what your da did to you ...'

'Da did nothing,' she cut in angrily. 'It's none of anyone's business what he did.'

'That Marsaili, it's a terrible thing.'

She looked away. 'Lachlan, you've no right,' she started

to say, before at last he realized how she felt and began to talk about the trams instead.

To distract him she said they could take one to the Kelvin Hall and then walk back through the gardens.

'I was going to write to you,' he said, when they got off at the other end, 'in fact, I did write to you but when I gave the letter to that Rory MacDonald he said I was wasting my time because you'd be too busy to read it.'

Vaguely, she wondered why Rory had done that; when he left, it had hurt so much that she tried not to think about him but, even so, he still crept into her thoughts every time she read about the German U-boats lurking in the deep.

'Have you heard anything about Rory?' she asked him.

Lachlan thought for a moment before he said that he hadn't, but he would have done if anything bad had happened. 'Is that true, Catriona? Would you have been too busy to read a letter, if I had sent you it?'

There was a man sitting on a bench throwing bread to the pigeons, each waiting patiently for its scrap.

'I do keep busy,' Catriona said, 'I have a job in the market as well.'

Lachlan tried to take her arm then, but she shrugged him off, then immediately felt sorry because of the hurt expression that came over his face.

She looked towards the darkening sky, glad that night was coming to bring all this to an end. She knew now how the years had changed her from the little girl who had once played happily with Lachie and the other island children. Lachlan, though, did not notice the reticence in her and prattled on about how much fun their lives had been back then. Once they reached Charing Cross, she heard the clock chime and reminded him of the time – she had to get back to the Gorbals to prepare for the next day.

His face fell again. The uniform, like that of a toy soldier, made him look even younger than he was. She thought of the casualty lists, the lengthening toll of the dead in France.

'We've still time for a cup of tea,' he said as they passed a tearoom, a drab, tired place quite unlike the exotic Willow Rooms, Miss Cranston's flagship just along the road.

They went in and sat down; Lachlan grandly ordered tea for two with a choice of cakes.

'I have to be in at ten,' Catriona said, 'and it takes twenty minutes at least to walk back.'

'I'll walk with you,' he said.

She drank the tea so quickly that it scalded her throat. The bill came, for 1/6d; shocked, Lachlie asked the waitress if it was right.

'Aye,' the waitress insisted.

'I thought the Food Order said that teas couldn't cost more than sixpence,' Catriona said.

'Plain teas,' the waitress said, 'that's wi' a teacake or a scone. Youse've had cakes. Cakes's no' on the Order.'

Lachlan counted the money twice, to be sure that it was right. Catriona felt angry on his behalf, but when she offered to pay her share he shook his head. 'I earn a shilling a day as a soldier,' he told her.

They walked to the river in silence. Once they reached the pedestrian bridge she suggested that he leave her there, so that he could find his way back to the barracks.

'I'd rather walk you all the way.'

She shook her head. 'I've only a wee bit further to go.'

He grabbed her hand suddenly. 'Will you marry me, Catriona?'

She smiled uneasily; she had been scared that he might ask her. 'It's nice of you to ask, Lachlan,' she said carefully, 'but I can't make any plans just yet.'

'I'd make you happy,' he insisted.

'Lachlan, I can't. I've too many things to do.'

'What things? I'd help you, I would. I could get my pay sent to you, not my ma.'

'No, Lachie.' She prised his hand away gently.

'Are you seeing that Rory MacDonald?'

She began to become angry. 'It's none of your business, even if I was.'

'Why won't you marry me?' he insisted.

She shook her head tiredly. 'Because I won't, and that's that.'

'Will you write to me, then?

She thought for a moment. 'Of course. I'll do that.'

He began to say something else, but she ran then, swift as the wind, had crossed the bridge by the time he started after her and then she lost him when she turned the first bend.

Later, she felt the sadness of unrequited love; was sorry for the pain she'd inflicted upon him.

She told Mrs Campbell about it all over a pot of tea.

'A girl like you, that's not the last heart you'll break,' the landlady said.

'But I didn't want to hurt him. I'll be so embarrassed when I see him again, and he'll be embarrassed to see me.'

'I wouldn't worry, lass.'

'Why not?'

'I wouldn't bet on anyone coming back from that mess,' the landlady said tersely.

Annie wrote a few days later, to say that Tom refused to fill in the pink form and so he was fined; he escaped gaol because he was above military age.

Catriona heard that boys below military age were joining up because there was no work; she wrote an anguished letter home about the twins and Tom promised her that they would not go to war, even over his dead body, since his ghost would surely keep them at home.

The news from the front was not good. The newspaper was silent for a while, the notion of victory so remote as to be incredible, but after a time the tenor of the reports changed, became hopeful again. Maloney drew the line on that, with the cynicism of the Irish. He read out loud the report from the Western Front one day:

'"Our artillery was active last night in the neighbourhood of La Bassée. Otherwise there is nothing to report." That isn't news,' he spat, his Irish brogue breaking with anger, 'that's lies, so it is. This' – he turned to the casualty lists on another page – 'this is the news: "286 officers, 2,657 men killed." That is the war news: 2,657 men killed and there is nothing to report? So many men dead and all they did about it was fire a few shells at La Bassée? Mother of God, men join the army to be soldiers and they're used as sitting ducks. It's a crime, so it is. A crime, and that bloody Haig should be prosecuted. I wouldn't sup his whisky if they paid me.'

Catriona silenced him with a glance, handing him a pile of messages. Mrs MacIver, at work on an overdue ledger, stared after him.

'He didn't mean it,' Catriona said quickly.

'I hope not,' she said, 'it's against the law to say things like that. But what can you expect from the Irish? Yon was probably a Fenian in his youth.' She turned back to her ledger, the conversation at an end.

Catriona picked up the paper to fold it and put it away. As she did so, she noticed the name of one of the regiments that Lachlan had mentioned. The regiment had lost 1,243 men; Lachlan Maclean was third on the list.

She dropped the paper and ran, gagging, to the WC in the basement. For a long time she vomited, until her stomach felt raw, dimly perceiving a knocking at the door.

'Are ye a' richt, lass?' asked Maloney. 'For God's sakes, answer, else I'll have the door off.'

'I'm all right,' she said, 'I won't be a minute.' She sluiced her vomit away, wiped the bowl and then ran water over her hands and face.

'He's dead, Maloney.'

'I know, lass. I didn't mean anything bad, what I said.'

'I wish to God he'd never gone, Maloney.'

'There's more'n you wishing that today.'

Forty thousand Allied soldiers were killed on the first day of the Battle of the Somme, so many that the paper had taken weeks to print the full casualty list.

Maloney took Catriona's arm and helped her slowly back up to the office.

'Are you all right, Catriona?' Mrs MacIver asked, handing her a cup of hot, sweet tea.

'I'm fine.'

'If he was a relative, you're allowed compassionate leave, you know that.'

Catriona shook her head. 'He was only a friend.'

As she left work that evening she saw at every corner women collecting money to care for injured soldiers, as the setting sun cast geometric shadows over the city streets.

The twins arrived on her doorstep in the spring of 1917, just as she was praying that the Americans would turn the tide of war as the papers promised, before they reached the age of nineteen when they would be forced to go to war – or to gaol instead.

Annie had written to her a few weeks before: 'I don't know what'll happen next, Catriona. There's been tribunals and men gaoled, and there's been boys as young as fourteen joining up because the landlord's promised land. Your da's against it, but the boys think it's all a big adventure . . . '

'We came to see you,' Ewan said, after Mrs Campbell had shown them into the front room, making an exception, because they were Catriona's brothers on their way to the front, to the rule that prohibited male visitors.

'Can we go to the pictures?' Alec asked.

She sat down, stunned for a moment.

'Does da know you're here?'

Neither of them said anything.

'Ewan, I asked you a question.'

'He knows we've gone,' Ewan said.

'Triona, can we go to the pictures?' Alec asked again.

Distractedly, she fetched ten shillings from her savings and took them to La Scala.

Ewan hesitated so she gave Alec the money to go himself, telling him that they would wait in the tearoom. Ewan's face was pale as they sat down.

'You're just sixteen,' she said. 'You don't have to go.'

'A lot of lads our age are gone.'

'Why, Ewan?'

For a long time, he didn't answer.

'Ewan, was it Da?'

He was looking at a boy only a year or two younger than himself eating an ice-cream sundae and she ordered one thoughtlessly and handed over the ninepence it cost. Wages had risen sharply during the war and although MacKenzie grumbled about it hers had now doubled to fifteen shillings a week.

'Ewan?' she asked again when he finished the ice cream.

'It wasn't Da, Triona.'

'Who was it?'

'We've not been working since we left school, we've been helping Da, and this summer we were going to go dyking with him but the man said we couldn't because we were army age. And Marsaili, she nags a bit.'

'Couldn't you have tholed it, Ewan?'

He avoided her eyes. 'You did the same yourself, Triona. You should understand.'

'You could've waited,' she said, 'you've another three years till you're draft age.'

'For what?' Ewan reasoned. 'This way we get a soldier's pay now ...'

'Ewan, soldiers die. Lachlan Maclean was killed. A soldier's pay's no use if you're dead.'

'Lachie always was a bit daft, Triona.'

She looked at him. 'So are you.'

He avoided her eyes. 'We'll be stretcher bearers for a long time, we'll not be fighting till we're nineteen and then the draft'd get us anyway.'

Alec came out of the film then, laughing, and they walked together down Buchanan Street, the twins jousting, Catriona earnest.

At the tram stop she grabbed them, one with each hand. 'Don't go,' she begged. 'I've money. I'll give you enough to see you through.'

Very gently Ewan prised her hand away. 'We have to, Catriona. We've signed up. We're the King's men now.'

She shook her head. 'I'll not forgive you if you get killed.'

The tram came and they jumped onto it, waving brightly as it pulled away.

*

She went to Central Station early in the morning of the day they were due to leave. After she had waited for hours she asked the woman at the WRVS stall and was told that their regiment had gone in the early hours whilst she slept. The knowledge made her cry with despair and she stood in the crowds murmuring a prayer of helpless regret.

'For God's sake, woman,' an officer said, snapping a swagger stick impatiently against his shin, 'stop bleating, will you? Don't you know that crying's bad for morale?'

Catriona looked at him wordlessly and he glared at her as if she was threatening the whole of the war effort on the Western Front.

'Awa tae hell,' a woman roared, a simple old soul in a ragged dress with a shawl clutched around her shoulders. 'How many of your sons are at the front?'

The officer turned, his contempt the squeak of his polished boots on the station concourse, and strode away.

'Och, lass,' the woman said, taking Catriona's arm and guiding her back to the tea stall, taking a cup of hot sweet tea and holding it to her lips, 'see an' try tae dry yer eyes, hen.'

Catriona heard the hour chime, and realized that she would be late for work.

'See, hen, yin day this'll aw' be a memory. Dinna shed yer tears till ye have tae, an' pray ye never do.'

Mumbling her thanks, she hugged the woman briefly and stumbled out into the sunshine.

That autumn the battle of Passchendaele was fought. Catriona's days passed in a blur after she got the little white printed card that was all that men were allowed to send from the front. It carried only a tick beside the line that said 'I am well'; the other lines were all crossed out. A letter came later from Ewan, telling her that he and Alec were stretcher bearers, that they spent most of the time in Ypres, miles from the fighting.

She nearly fainted in the street one day, when she heard a man saying that the whole of Passchendaele was a sea of mud, that as many men drowned as were killed in the fighting.

In late November, a week after the little village had fallen to the Allies, Catriona heard a wail as she fell asleep, the sound of gunfire mixed with screams. She came awake and listened, but heard only the crackle of the last tram rolling towards the depot.

A dream, she hoped for a moment, before she felt Alec's death, heard Ewan crying out at the end of his life. She stayed awake that night wondering at the games her mind played with her, because the papers said that the Western Front was quiet, the great battle of the year over at last.

In dull dread she went to work, trying to smile because she did not want to spread her fear.

The twins' names were in the lists of the casualties at Cambrai, a battle so insignificant that she hadn't even known it had been fought.

For the first time in four years Catriona went home, on a week's compassionate leave.

As she crested the hill before her village, a small figure ran towards her out of the gloaming; she put her bag down and cradled Allan in her arms.

'I knew you'd come,' he said. 'Da got the telegram from the army yesterday.'

She took his hand and they walked home. As she passed the path that led to the beach Catriona saw that the tide was in, pounding the rocks with angry spray that obliterated the sands. Allan had grown taller, but he was so thin that she could feel the bones of his fingers.

'I'm glad you're back,' he said in a small voice, 'I miss you.' She saw the tracks of tears on his face.

'I do it for you,' she said, 'you know that.'

He squeezed her hand.

The cottage was silent. Sine and Maire hugged her speechlessly; Ailish wasn't there.

Her father got up and took her bag. 'I'm glad you're home, pet.' His eyes were raw.

'Did you get my telegram?' he asked.

'I read it in the newspaper.'

'I sent a telegram last night.'

Marsaili began to make another place at the table. 'I wish you'd told me you were coming, Catriona. I don't know if there's enough.'

Her father's face turned to ice.

'I'm not hungry, Marsaili,' she said quickly, remembering the chocolate bars in her bag for Allan and her sisters.

'So long as I live in this house,' her father said, 'there'll be food for Catriona at the table.'

They ate without talking. Catriona felt Allan close to her and she squeezed his hand under the table. Ailish came in when the meal was over; Marsaili told her angrily that if she did not come in time, food would not be kept warm for her. Ailish kissed Catriona perfunctorily, looked away when Catriona asked how she was.

'I'm all right,' she said defiantly when Catriona asked again.

Marsaili left the clearing up to Maire and Sine, went into the bedroom and firmly closed the door.

Catriona felt the old hatred rising inside her, and struggled to keep calm.

'Sit down, lass,' her father told her.

She looked around, noticing the changes. Tom's hair was white now and Sine's and Maire's hands were red, the way hers had been when she cooked and washed and cleaned for them all. Allan had grown but was still a child; she felt his innocence in the way he looked at her. Ailish sat in the corner, twisting her hair into knots.

'Sit down,' her father said again, 'you're making me nervous.'

Ailish fled, banging the door. Tom half rose as if to stop her, then turned back to the fire, shaking his head.

Catriona's eyes met his for a moment; sickened then, she turned to walk out.

'Wait, pet,' he said, 'I've things to say to you.'

The wind was bitter, sharp as a knife. That didn't change, nor the island landscape, but she had never seen the hills as bleak, felt the pall of night like a shroud. Allan's footsteps cracked the grass; she looked down and saw his feet bare, remembering the pain of walking on frost.

'Listen,' she said, because she'd seen it all already, felt the loveless, bitter place in what had once been a home. 'I'll find a place for us all. I'll find us a home in the city, and you can come with Maire and Sine. And Ailish.'

She was walking aimlessly, the sounds of the wind and the sea so strange after the noise of the city.

'When?' he asked, and she remembered how long time took to pass for a child, the way a day felt like a month, a year even. She had never been unhappy, had never felt despair, but she recalled the sense of endlessness of it all, and how far away dinner could seem when she was hungry after play.

'As soon as I can. A year, maybe two.'

'Promise?' he asked.

'Yes.'

Annie was waiting at the door of her cottage as Catriona and Allan arrived. 'It's been too long, pet. Far too long,' she said as she folded Catriona into her arms. Inside, she saw Iain, wondering for a moment what he was doing at home from the navy before she saw the blankness in his eyes.

'He's safe from the war, Catriona,' Annie said, smiling bitterly.

Taking small, uncertain steps, Iain rose and walked towards her, reached out and felt for her shoulders, touched the contours of her face. 'You've grown, pet.'

Annie went to the fire and put the kettle on.

'When?' Catriona asked, feeling like crying for the twins, for Iain, for the years since anyone had called her pet.

'A few months past, pet. A gun exploded at Rosyth. In the bloody dock.'

Annie put the mugs down. 'It could've been a U-boat, Catriona. He's not been demobbed yet.' Her voice was brittle, tight with strain. 'Do you want to stay tonight, pet?'

'I …' The tea was too hot, too strong, too sweet as always. 'I'd best not, Annie.'

Annie walked out into the night with them. Allan stood silently while for a long time the two women hugged each other. Rain as gentle as tears began to fall from the sky, and Catriona realized it was past the time Allan should go to bed.

Far from the cottage she heard raised voices, Ailish's and her da's, felt Allan's hand tremble in her own. Ailish was swearing, cursing in Gaelic; her father was calling her a bitch, telling her he'd take his belt to her if she said any more.

Allan sighed, a resigned sound like an old man would make, one who was tired with the world and its sorrows.

Catriona opened the door and silence fell, the anger so strong that the air had turned sour. Her father was standing, swaying slightly, his breath thick with the smell of whisky. Ailish slipped away to bed, followed by Allan.

Catriona faced Tom.

'The bloody little bitch,' he started to say, 'hasn't shifted herself for years. Not like you, eh?'

From behind the curtain she heard Ailish sob. Tom reached for the flask of whisky on the top shelf of the dresser. 'You'll take a glass with me, Triona? What age are you now? Eighteen, nineteen? You look like a woman with your hair up like that.'

She was so used to the pins that she had forgotten them. With an impatient gesture she pulled them out and shook her hair free. 'Don't bother, Da,' she said, as he took another cup from the dresser.

'Tea, then?'

She shook her head.

'For pity's sake, pet.' He sat down and stared at the fire.

'You don't know what it's like, Triona. There's no work, not for a man like me. I should be in the war, they say, and I've them to feed and Marsaili and the babes. We wouldn't have managed without you, you know. The Nicolsons would've been on the parish.'

Not you, she thought. You'd never be on the parish.

'They'd've gone anyway, the lads. With the draft. They-

'd've been gone by now and nothing would've been different. D'you hear what I said, pet? When the army recruiters came?' He laughed hard, forcefully: 'I said, how much does the Kaiser's army pay? 'Cos I'd just as soon fight for him as the King ...'

Tom couldn't stop talking, once he started. Words spilled from his lips like vomit as the whisky loosened his tongue. For a long time she listened, then she saw beyond his talk, saw that tears were rolling down his cheeks and he sniffled in between the words, snorting like a pig as he swallowed his phlegm. He stopped talking, cried instead. She went to him, feeling compassion rise despite her anger, but he shoved her away.

'God's sake,' he spat, 'can you not leave a man to grieve in peace? Your trouble, girl, is you're too much of your mother.'

She picked up her bag then, from the place where she had left it, and quietly walked out into the night.

In the light of the moon she followed the path to the bothy in the lee of the hill, to the place where rocks overlooked the track and a small boy, hidden, could distract a whole flock of sheep, to the stretch of sandy ground where the twins had played shinty and plotted to win the Camanach. As the wind rose and fell she felt her skirt whip around her knees, stopped and took off her shoes and felt the shock of the earth beneath her feet. In the distance the Cuillins rose, shadow faint against the night. The wind dropped to nothing and all was still. In that moment she said farewell to her brothers, wished them Godspeed in their journey to Tir nan Og.

The arctic terns hardly stirred in their nests on the rocks as she walked towards the sands. Far away, waves broke over the mussel beds; a gull cried harshly then wheeled away, flashing white against the grey of the sky. The wind changed and all was hidden by cloud.

Very quickly she scribbled a letter to Allan, repeating the promise to find him a home, to find a new home for them all in the city, promising that it would not be four years before they saw each other again.

*

Catriona drifted through the weeks that followed, not caring that at last the tide of the war had truly turned, that talk of victory was no longer a hollow joke.

Mrs MacIver retired at the end of the year; shortly afterwards MacKenzie called her into his office and told her that the position of senior clerk was now hers, along with a salary of one guinea a week.

Once she might have been pleased, but she felt only a dull annoyance at the arrogance of the man who assumed that she cared. Even Mrs MacIver had admitted that she was the best shorthand clerk who had ever worked for the firm, that if she had been a man she would certainly have been taken on as an apprentice. She would have left years ago but for MacKenzie's refusal to give a reference unless an employee left with his consent. If not for that, she'd've taken munitions work, earned thirty shillings a week or more and perhaps saved the twins from going to war.

It was only on the day the Armistice was declared that Catriona realized nearly a year had passed since the twins had been killed.

She had been so numb with grief that she had not even begun to look for a house.

The sounds of the Marseillaise rose from the square below, a great roar came from around the corner; she watched people surge towards it, arms flailing in their eagerness to get through.

The streets were so busy that Maloney could not deliver his messages; Nina, the clerk typist she had hired, had not even arrived at work.

MacKenzie called her into his office to dictate a telegram congratulating Field Marshal Haig; told her to take the rest of the day as a holiday because the city corporation had ordained as much.

Catriona cleared the papers on her desk, then damped the fires and closed the office.

Outside, she stepped nimbly into a gap in the throng that vanished instantly as she was jostled and tossed like a cork on the waves. For a moment she fought the flow, trying to turn in the direction of the footbridge over the Clyde, but the force was too strong and she was pulled headlong towards George Square, catapulted into the celebration there.

A young man – an injured soldier, she knew, from the ragged scar that twisted half of his face into a scowl and a wooden arm that stuck out at an angle from his chest – grabbed her with his good arm and spun her around, his face so close that she could smell the whisky on his breath: 'Wees've won, hen,' he yelled, 'wees've bluidy jacked the Jerries!'

She tried to smile but managed only a grimace.

'Aw, hen, whit's the matter? Gie's a smile, fir God's sake!'

She tried again, but his friend, less drunk than he, pulled him back: 'Kin ye no' see, Tam? Lass's lost someyin. She's no' smilin' acos she's still greetin'.'

'Och, see, abdy's lost someyin. It's o'er the now, but. It's a' o'er.'

His friend pulled him back and the ex-soldier disappeared into the crowd as Catriona murmured her thanks. The crowd was tight now, almost motionless, a mass of bodies stranded on the tide. From the distance there was a call for silence, then the reedy tones of the National Anthem rose from George Square. Catriona looked down, saw her mud-splattered feet, a rip in the thick woollen stockings she had bought only the previous week. As the anthem played, the crowd fell still, finding its voice again when the last notes of the anthem sounded and the band swung into 'Scotland the Brave.' A cheer rose then, drowning the music; Catriona turned and saw, a bit away, a face that brought tears to her eyes.

The old woman edged through the crowd and gripped her shoulders with fingers gnarled with age: 'It's ye, isn't it? The wee lass fra the station?'

Catriona nodded, swallowing a sob.

'Thaur deid, lass, aren't they? I can tell by yer face.'

'They are.'

'Och, hen, it mak's nae sense, the men whau've gone. Forty thousan' fra Glesca, they say, they dinna ken fir sure.'

Catriona looked into her eyes, saw that her soul was awash with grief.

'It's guid tae see ye, hen,' the woman said, pinning a sprig of white heather to her shoulder. 'Fir luck, ye ken?'

The crowd surged and they were pulled apart.

It took Catriona two hours to work her way to Argyle Street, another hour to get through St Enoch's before she reached the bridge over the river.

Walking across, she noticed that the heather was slipping from the pin and so she took it off and put it in her pocket for safekeeping.

By the time she reached Mrs Campbell's, it was early afternoon.

'Is that you, Catriona?' the landlady called from the kitchen, where she was baking a batch of apple pies for the celebration in the Gorbals Hall.

'Yes,' Catriona said, as she started up the stairs.

'There's a visitor for you, lass,' Mrs Campbell said, 'waiting in the front room.'

Catriona opened the door slowly, wondering who it could be. The fire was lit and Ailish hunched over it, fast asleep.

Very gently, seeing the blisters on her swollen feet, Catriona eased her awake.

'Catriona,' Ailish murmured, her voice thick with fatigue.

Catriona hugged her.

'I had to leave,' Ailish said.

'Don't worry,' Catriona told her, 'you can stay here with me.'

'I'm sorry.'

'Don't be. Really. You've nothing to be sorry about.'

Ailish began to cry.

Catriona held her sister and felt the shroud of loneliness begin to lift at last.

Chapter Five

Catriona eased Ailish's feet into a bucket of steaming water, biting her own lip in sympathy. Her sister's feet were ragged, with a red line right around the instep, garish blisters on her heels and every toe.

Ailish shivered then relaxed. When the water had cooled, she lifted her feet out and Catriona dried them gently, then smeared zinc ointment over the ruddy flesh.

'I doubt I'll be able to walk again,' Ailish smiled thinly.

'It happened to me too. You'll heal quickly.'

Mrs Campbell bustled in with a tray of soup and bread, a mutton pasty and a slice of apple pie, still steaming from the oven. 'Here, lass,' she said, 'get this inside you. There's some for you too, Catriona. I'll just bring it through. There's a social at the kirk tonight.'

Ailish began to eat hungrily as Catriona thanked the landlady.

After they had eaten, Catriona took Ailish's bundle and helped her upstairs, seating her at the table while she fetched the bath and began to fill it with hot water.

'Don't,' Ailish said quickly. 'I'm so tired I'd rather just sleep.' She was still tightly wound in her shawl, two or three jumpers under that.

'I'll help you,' Catriona said.

'No,' Ailish said sharply, then: 'Please, Catriona, just let me get to bed.'

Catriona had only one nightgown, which she gave to her sister, wondering fleetingly why she turned her back as she undressed.

Ailish fell asleep quickly, her hair like tousled wheat strewn over the pillow. Catriona crept downstairs and borrowed Mrs Campbell's *Evening News*, turning to the To Let pages to begin her hunt for a place to live.

'Ach, lass,' the landlady said, 'the wee lass can stay here, long's you want. It'll not be easy to get a place, not wi' the men coming hame fra' the war.'

'It's not only Ailish,' she explained, 'I've another two sisters and a brother as well.' The landlady had been kind to her, and she did not want to risk an insult. 'I promised them last year I'd find something.'

'Aye, well, tak' yer time, lass. As I says, it'll no be easy.' She smiled. 'But the war's o'er, lass. Ye'll be glad o' that.'

Catriona shook her head. 'The dead'll not come back from the trenches.'

'No, lass, but there'll be no more of them, thank God. Get yer coat, an' come wi' me.'

'I'd rather not.' She stared at the fire, seeing the faces swim before her, Ewan and Alec, then Lachlan, then Rory, still smiling. 'Rory,' she said suddenly.

'What's that, Catriona?'

She shook her head again. 'Nothing, Mrs Campbell. Just a friend, the only one I had who wasn't killed.'

'See, lass,' she said, 'that's something ye can be grateful for.'

'I suppose,' Catriona said, wondering where he was, if she would ever see him again.

She tried to begin her search for a flat that night, but when she reached Clyde Street and saw a tram stranded in the crowd, heard the mêlée as a brass band and a pipe band playing different tunes marched into each other, she turned and went home again, thinking that the flats would still be vacant tomorrow, because nobody could get through the madness on the streets.

Next evening she went to a dozen flats from that day's *Evening News* and six from the day before's. Most were taken before she arrived; she found out that people waited outside the newspaper offices for the first edition and the best places were gone by mid-afternoon. She only reached the top of the queue at one place, two rooms and a kitchen off Byres Road for a usurious 15/- a week. 'I'll take it,' Catriona said tiredly, reasoning that the rooms were big, that Allan could sleep in the alcove bed in the kitchen and she and Ailish and Sine and Maire could share the other rooms.

'Not so fast,' the factor said, 'I need references, your husband's name and rank.'

Catriona handed him a letter from Mrs Campbell and the pass signed by MacKenzie that let her into court.

The factor grunted. 'Your husband's name and rank?'

Catriona hesitated, fingered the brooch she wore that the army gave out to all relatives of the dead. She had thrown hers away in disgust at first, but retrieved it from the rubbish when she realized that it was all she had left of her brothers. After they'd been killed she had gone to the regimental offices to collect their things but the clerk just consulted a list and told her that there were no effects, their bodies were so badly maimed that they'd been buried as they were found.

'Are you a widow?' the factor asked sharply.

Catriona looked away; he asked her again and she had to admit that she was a spinster.

'I'm not allowed to rent this property to a woman,' he said.

'I have a good job.'

'You could lose it.'

She did not argue further, just turned tiredly and walked out into the rain, consoling herself that there were other flats, would be better chances. As she crossed the bridge over the river she looked down and saw water the colour of lead.

On Saturday she rushed home at midday and helped Ailish into the pair of boots she had bought from the shoe shop in Candleriggs. Although they were second hand, they had been re-soled and heeled and were made from soft calf that would not hurt Ailish's healing blisters. Ailish looked at her quizzically; she was still wrapped in sweaters, though she had washed the hem of her skirt.

'Come on,' Catriona said, taking her by the hand, 'we're going out to buy you some new clothes.'

Ailish hesitated for the briefest moment, then smiled. 'You don't have to, Triona, honestly. I'm fine as I am.'

'You are not. You can't go out looking for a job in a shawl. You need a coat and a dress too, or a blouse and a skirt.' She had planned this for days, to be a surprise. Ailish wasn't Ailish any more, not the arrogantly beautiful child she'd known of old, or even the strong-willed young woman who had fought her father; she had changed, been deflated by the loss of her brothers, perhaps by the shock of the city.

The stores on Argyle Street were different from those of Buchanan Street and Sauchiehall Street, the windows were not crystal clear and sometimes the paint on the name sign was chipped. In the Royal Pavilion she had seen skirts on sale at 9/11d; in Currie and Thompson three-quarter-length cashmere capes were 12/6d. There, she could outfit Ailish with change from £2; she could afford that easily and still have enough to rent a place. She thought of the bulk of the money she'd saved as belonging to the twins; they'd want her to spend some on Ailish, because they had loved her so.

Walking across the footbridge, she noticed Ailish's arms folded defensively over her chest, her brow furrowed in thought.

'Come on,' Catriona said, putting a hand out to take her sister by the arm, 'we'll have you looking like a mannequin in no time.'

Ailish's face flinched and she shrugged off Catriona before smiling dismally. 'It's the wind, Catriona. It's awfully chill.'

Catriona looked at her, wondering how she'd forgotten the wind on the island, which made the worst Glasgow gale feel like a breeze.

In the Royal Polytechnic department store Ailish became her old self for a moment, looking in wonder at the painted ceiling of the shopping hall, the display of waxworks around the store. 'Let's look at their skirts,' Catriona said as Ailish's eyes fell upon a stand of paste jewellery, glass baubles in peacock's-tail colours.

'Isn't this wonderful?' she murmured.

Catriona looked closer, caught the shallowness of the sparkle. 'It isn't real,' she said.

'But it's so pretty.' Ailish reached out and touched a garlanded necklace, the design heavy and years out of date. As the rhinestones moved, they sparkled like crystal; Ailish sighed aloud and then picked up a little brooch in the shape of a flamingo with pink-tinged feathers and gold-dipped legs.

Catriona saw her face, and decided quickly. 'Which one d'you want?' she asked, not caring about the price.

'Oh, Catriona, I couldn't.'

'You can too.' Catriona pulled her aside and told her that she had saved the money for Ewan and Alec, who'd want her to have it.

Ailish thought for a long time before she decided on the brooch; Catriona handed over 4/11d, thinking that if the brooch cheered up her sister it was worth twice that.

'We'll look at the skirts now,' she said.

'No,' Ailish said, flushed slightly. 'I've been thinking, Catriona. I was working as a kitchen maid back home and I ate far too much. I've put on some weight and it'd be a waste to buy anything new till I lose it.'

'A dress then. The style's loose this year, hardly any waist at all.'

'I thought just a coat and a hat, if that's all right. I can wear that to get a job, then buy what I need when I know what I'll be doing.'

They walked along to Currie and Thompson, where Ailish chose a calf-length cape with a velvet trim and a matching cloche.

'It feels so nice,' Ailish said as she studied her reflection in a shop window. In the new cape she looked elegant beside Catriona, whose skirt was too short. She looked away quickly because she imagined she could see the sheen of too many launderings on the cloth of her jacket.

They linked arms and wandered up Buchanan Street, Ailish inspired by MacDonald's and then entranced by Sauchiehall Street, where just on one block there was Pettigrew and Stephens next to Copland and Lye, opposite the grandiose Les Magasins des Tuileries. The cinemas blared newsreels of the Armistice and Charlie Chaplin's *Shoulder Arms*.

'Would you like to see it?' Catriona asked, but Ailish shook her head, looking at her feet as if the old blisters had begun to hurt.

When they reached the Willow Tearooms Catriona told the waitress that they wanted to have tea in the Room de Luxe. The waitress led them to a table by the window and then offered to take Ailish's bag. She hesitated for a moment until Catriona reassured her that was all right.

'Have you been here before?' Ailish whispered after the waitress left.

Catriona shook her head as she gazed at the the mirror work of the windows, the pale lavender silk-covered walls, the silvered doors that carried an enlargement of the leaded glass panels lining the walls. She had to look at it for a time before she saw the trace of a tree in the pattern, the branches that frayed from a point halfway up the trunk, the single leaf on a thin lead twig. The chairs were painted silver, upholstered in purple velvet; the overall effect was almost too much. From every angle, the room echoed itself in the mirrors; Catriona saw a fragment of herself, caught the reflection of Ailish's smile. Even the light was tinted pink by the rose chandelier.

'What d'you think?' she whispered.

Ailish looked around. 'I don't know ... it's too perfect to eat in, somehow; perhaps they should just charge you to come and have a look.'

Catriona remembered a drawing in the *Evening News*, which had caricatured the fantasy as 'the Room de Looks'.

The menu came, Ailish ordered chicken and ham rissole with sauce, Catriona a mutton pie and tea and cakes for two. The bill came to two shillings, more than Catriona spent on food in a month.

'Thank you,' Ailish said, as they walked home in the strange city gloaming fractured by headlamps, the air resonant with the crackle of trams.

'It's nothing,' Catriona said, satisfied that she'd had tea at Miss Cranston's at last, wondering distantly how she had started, dreaming for a moment of what she would do if she could manage to start a tearoom herself.

At Argyle Street a tram drew to a halt as a car flashed past in the inner lane, throwing up a wave of muddy water that made Ailish flinch first, then swear roundly at its wake.

'It's frightening,' she said, in a moment of candour. 'This place, I mean.'

'Don't worry,' Catriona said, 'you'll get used to it soon.'

As they passed by St Enoch's, Ailish trembled at the noise of the trains.

On Monday MacKenzie, WS, called her into his office and asked her to sit down. 'I want you to sit in court with counsel,' he said, 'the MacAlpine case. You know.'

Catriona looked at him. A washerwoman from the Cowcaddens was suing the corporation because she had slipped and broken her leg on a cracked paving stone which she did not see, she claimed, because the streetlights were out. Mackenzie, acting for the corporation, had written the case off as a no-hoper; so, too, had Arthur Farquharson, the King's Counsel he had instructed. Catriona had researched the precedents; the corporation had no defence, no real defence, the matter was being fought only because the corporation feared a flood of similiar claims if they settled out of court.

'Well?' MacKenzie glared at her.

'Of course,' she said, hopeful all of a sudden because to sit in court and take notes during trial was the job of an apprentice, not a clerk.

'You'd best get down there,' he said, 'and mind and come back at lunchtime, to make sure that wee girl's doing her work.'

Catriona ran along Ingram Street, arriving in the courtroom with the judge. In a whisper she introduced herself to the KC as she got her pencil and paper out.

'Just don't fall asleep,' he said. 'I already told Jimmy we haven't a chance in Hades.'

She looked around, watched the plaintiff's lawyer rise to outline the claim as a bored expression came over the judge's face.

At lunchtime Farquharson sent her to Lang's for sandwiches; she had to wait outside the lunch bar until one of the waiters noticed her and came out, because women were not allowed to enter. Once she had delivered the sandwiches, she had time only to check Nina's work before she went back to court.

The plaintiff's advocate announced that his client would be taking the stand.

'She's a decrepit old hag,' Farquharson hissed. 'If we could've postponed a bit longer she'd've croaked.'

Mrs MacAlpine was a small, warped woman with tightly curled grey hair. She walked with a stick, making very slow progress to the witness box as her advocate smiled and Farquharson glowered. Her eyes were rheumy – sad, Catriona thought at first, until something about the vacant way she looked around the courtroom made her think again.

Her advocate took all afternoon to tell her story, playing out the drama for all it was worth. It was a tragedy, even if a very minor one, the skilled and honest washerwoman who could no longer work because the corporation did not repair the streetlights. Catriona felt her sympathy rise, until she remembered she was on the other side.

She worked late into the evening finishing the typing and other office work, and went to court early the next day, waiting on the steps until Mrs MacAlpine arrived with her soldier son, back from the war but still wearing the uniform of the machine-gun corps.

Farquharson was testy as he fiddled with the papers on the table before him, cursing the luck that had allocated the case to him, ruing that he had not handed it over to a junior.

'Excuse me,' Catriona began.

He ignored her, muttering a curse.

'Excuse me,' she said again.

He looked up. 'What is it? Can't you see I'm trying to organize myself?'

'Mrs MacAlpine's eyesight's bad,' Catriona said.

'What?'

'She can't see properly,' Catriona said. 'She has cataracts.'

'How do you know that?'

'I saw her yesterday. I watched the way she walked into court today.'

The KC's eyes narrowed. 'Cataracts, you say?'

Catriona nodded. The condition was common in Skye, throughout the highlands and islands. 'I was thinking, if she has cataracts, that might've been why she tripped.'

The KC looked at his notes, the law texts piled on the table. 'If I ask her and she isn't, we'll lose, d'you know that?'

'Is there any chance that we'll win?'

He thought for a moment, as the court was called to order. 'I just hope you're right,' he whispered as he rose to begin his questions.

Slowly, the KC began, his manner disarming, almost that of a friend. The washerwoman, caught off guard, agreed that she was aging, that with the women discharged from munitions work, there was more competition for domestic work anyway. The KC continued, throughout the morning, striking viper-like only at the end, when the judge looked at his fob watch and then looked as if he might call a break for lunch.

Mrs MacAlpine faltered, and when pressed said rather lamely that she had managed just fine with her cataracts before the accident.

The KC bore down on her relentlessly. 'How many people walked along the street that evening? Can you tell us why you were the only one who slipped and fell?'

The washerwoman turned away, brushed a tear from her eye and admitted that she could not when he asked her again.

'Could it not have been that it was your bad eyesight that prevented you from seeing the paving stone?' he asked, not giving her a chance to reply before he nodded to the judge and sat down.

He shook Catriona's hand as the washerwoman's advocate withdrew her claim and the judge awarded costs to the defendant.

They walked out into the brisk winter wind. On the steps of the court the son turned away from his mother: 'Bastart,' he spat, 'ye bluidy bastart. Her eyes ar'ny that bad. Bastarts, the lot o'ye.'

Farquharson hurried Catriona away. She turned briefly, watched the old washerwoman cross the road slowly, her cane echoing above the sound of the Argyle Street trams.

As they parted, the KC pushed something into her hand.

'But what about Mrs MacAlpine?' she asked. 'How's she ever going to pay your costs?'

'Oh, I wouldn't worry about that, Miss Nicolson. She'll get a couple of angry letters from the City Treasurer's department. That's all. There's some debts that you don't collect till you get to heaven.'

She watched him striding off towards his chambers, his umbrella tapping against the pavement in time with his step. Opening her hand, she found a pound note, crumpled and damp with her sweat. Her instinct was to give it to Mrs MacAlpine, but when she turned back, the washerwoman had disappeared.

MacKenzie was at his desk, thrawn with rage at an adverse ruling at the Court of Session, burping dyspeptically after a hurried lunch. 'Send the girl out for stomach salts,' he barked, 'and make sure your notes are on my desk by the close of business. I'm seeing Baillie Cuthbert tonight and I need a coherent reason why we've wasted the corporation's money.'

'We haven't,' she said quickly.

'What d'you mean?' he growled.

'We won,' she told him, relishing his amazement for a moment before she explained.

'So Farquharson came through in the end,' he said, 'I suppose I'd best write to thank him.'

Catriona said nothing.

'And by the way,' he went on, 'the overheads are way too high. I don't see why I should provide tea for the staff, although I'll continue to do so for myself and the clients. If you buy your own, I'll contribute the hot water. That's quite enough. This is a legal firm and not an outpost of Miss Cranston's. There's a recession on the way, there always is after a war; we'll have to pay the price, you can be sure, and the war has already cost this firm a fortune . . .'

As he barged on, Catriona thought of the young men from her village, the boys even, who had gone to France and who would never return. Almost every family had lost someone, many, like hers, had lost more than one.

MacKenzie continued, oblivious to the look on her face. Pausing finally, he glared at her for a moment before asking if she had anything to say.

'Have you any idea what your war cost my people?' she said, not giving him time to reply before she turned and walked out.

She reached Mrs Campbell's just as the bells of the Gorbals Church chimed nine times; she had spent the evening queuing for flats, being turned away time and again because she was not married, because the place had been taken by someone else. As she walked in, Mrs Campbell put her head around the living room door:

'Hae ye found ony place yet, lass?' and then, seeing the look on her face, 'I dinna want tae hurry ye, Catriona, but seeing the way yer sister is, it'd no' be richt, no' wi' the ither lodgers.'

Tiredly, she climbed the stairs, wondering what Ailish had done. Like all the Nicolsons, Ailish had a quick temper; unlike Catriona, she had never managed to fetter it, had never been obliged to. Catriona flinched when she thought of what she'd said to MacKenzie, wondering if she'd have a job the following day.

Ailish was hunched over the stove. The room was cold because she did not know to open the latch to let the heat circulate.

'You didn't find anything,' Ailish said, as she gave her sister a mug of tea. The drink was hot and Catriona blew the surface, sending ripples lapping at the rim of the mug. After a moment she drank, scalding her tongue.

'I will soon,' she said, 'it's just ...'

'Just what?'

'They don't like renting to an unmarried woman.'

'That's stupid.'

'It's true. They'd rather have a man to pay the rent, though God knows my job's as secure as a man's.'

Ailish smiled as she rubbed the small of her back. Catriona saw the bulge then, the curve of pregnancy that had until now been concealed by heavy jumpers. Ailish opened the oven; the smell of scorched dough filled the room. 'I made bannocks, but I cooked them too much.'

She handed Catriona one, once she'd picked off the black bits.

'They're not bad, honestly,' Ailish said. 'They taste just fine.'

Mechanically Catriona began to eat. 'Why didn't you tell me you were pregnant?' she blurted, once she'd finished and Ailish was rinsing the dishes.

Ailish froze.

'You are, aren't you?'

Ailish shook the bowl and put it back on the rack, then sat down heavily. 'I didn't ... hoped ...'

'Hoped what?'

Ailish's eyes misted with tears. 'I hoped you wouldn't notice. I hoped ... I just wished I wasn't, that's all.'

'But you are.'

'Yes.' Ailish began to sob then, and Catriona went to comfort her, holding her sister as she cried her heart out. The anger Catriona had felt mellowed into concern.

Much later she helped Ailish into bed, first filling the bath with hot water and bathing her as tenderly as when she was a child.

'Ailish,' she whispered, when they were ready for sleep, 'the father, the man who ...'

'Dead,' Ailish murmured, 'dead since the summer. Hector MacKie, maybe you knew him. Killed in France. I'd've been married, if not for that.'

*

Maloney handed her a scrap of paper with an address in his spidery writing. 'I ken ye're looking, lass,' he said. 'There's a place jist aff the Briggait, it's no' a palace, mind, but them that lived there did a moonlicht this very morning, I saw them myself walking down the Gallowgate wi' their beds on their backs.'

Catriona knew the place; one of the old tenements not far from Paddy's Market that had escaped the slum clearance of the turn of the century and survived in the shadow of the railway lines.

She had tried to talk to Ailish, suggesting cautiously that she could go home where Annie would care for her even if Hector McKie's mother would not, but Ailish turned hysterical at the idea, she could not bear to face the shame. Catriona understood that.

She went to the address at lunchtime, so forlorn that she hardly had any hope left.

The landlady, her breath thick with gin, looked her up and down. 'D'ye ken thae wha's gone?' she demanded. 'Yon scunners owe me fir a month.'

Catriona smelt for the first time the strange, tangy odour of cats and stale bodies. 'I don't,' she said, in her soft island voice. 'I heard they had, that's all.'

'Ach, ye're a teuchter,' the landlady said, taking a key from a nail, 'youse arny as bad as the Paddies.'

The room was small, about ten feet square with a recess for a bed; there was an old-fashioned range and a coal box, a cupboard and shelves beneath the space for the bed.

'Tak' it or leave it,' the landlady said, 'soon's I put a line in the windae, it'll be gone jist like that.' She snapped her fingers, but the sound she made was masked by the rattle of the trains.

'How much?' Catriona asked.

'Five shillin' a week, a pound fir the key.'

She counted out the money. 'It's me and my sister,' she said quickly, 'she's a widow.'

'I dinna care if it's the Kaiser himsel', so long's the rent's paid, hen.'

On Saturday afternoon Catriona went to the Barras and bought a bucket and a scrubbing brush, Lysol and Monkey Brand scouring powder, and black lead for the range. As she scrubbed the walls, the colour changed from brown to ivory; the floor looked decent, once she had polished it. From Donoghue she got two mattresses, chairs, a table, and a bundle of laundered bedding that he swore was almost new – all delivered by the lad who fetched and carried at the market – for sixpence, since Donoghue said he was glad to be rid of the stuff because it was taking up space.

On Sunday morning, before she went to the market, she took Ailish there, saw the way her face flinched when they turned into the dark alleyway, and was grateful that she tried to smile once they were indoors.

'It's not as bad as you said, Catriona. It's very cosy'.

Catriona left her to settle in.

The tenement stank although the women who lived there took turns to scrub the stairs every morning. The smell never went completely, though sometimes it faded for a time under the assault of bleach. It was the aroma of despair and hopelessness, so pervasive that it had worked its way into the fabric of the building, the chipped plaster and the fractured skylight. At the Barras Ailish had bought a bunch of dried lavender along with the brass curtain ring that she wore on her wedding finger and which left a mark like a bruise. She hung the flowers over the door, the scent mingling with that of the WC on the landing below.

In the morning Catriona would breathe deeply before she opened the door and then hurry downstairs, not inhaling again until she was out of the close. The smell followed her though, as she walked the streets of the city; she was afraid that she would carry it on her, that it would mark her out as a resident of the slums.

MacKenzie called Catriona into his office during the week before Christmas to tell her to clear out a desk for the shorthand writer Cameron, who was coming back to the firm as an apprentice.

Catriona took a deep breath. 'I'd like to apply, Mr Mac-Kenzie.'

He stared at her. 'What?'

'If there's an apprentice's job, I'd like to apply. I could do the work. You know that.'

'Don't be ridiculous, woman. The law's a job for a man.'

'Two or three firms have taken on women apprentices, Mr MacKenzie. I want a chance, that's all.'

He gazed at her and then, when she did not falter, at the signet ring he wore, the design a strange *mélange* of a divider and scales. 'The very idea is out of the question. You're a good shorthand typist, Miss Nicolson. Best stick to that.'

'Is it because of what I said about the war, Mr Mac-Kenzie?' she blurted.

'It's because, as I've said, the law is not the place for women. Even you can't question that.'

Catriona walked home slowly, as the wind dried the tears that leaked down her cheeks.

Ailish gave birth to a boy on Christmas morning in the Maternity Hospital on Rottenrow. When Catriona arrived, she was already sleeping, the baby swaddled in a crib with a tag marked 'Jamie Nicolson'.

'It's so sad,' the midwife said.

Catriona said nothing.

'I mean, to lose her husband when she's so young, so close to the end of the war.'

'The war was a tragedy for everyone,' Catriona said.

'It was that, Miss Nicolson, it was that. Still, I hope this young man's the last to lose his father before he was born. There's something especially sad about that, Miss Nicolson, whatever the reason. But he'll have the medal, I suppose. His father was a very brave man.'

Catriona didn't know what to say.

'I mean, the VC,' the nurse said. 'Ailish told me she's keeping that for him. It's all such a tragedy.'

Catriona left the hospital, thinking she must persuade Ailish to stop spinning her stories, to keep her dream-world in her mind, where it belonged. She'd always been a dreamer, Ailish, always dreamt of being anyone but who she was. Tom used to say that she lived in *tir nan sgeulachd*, the land of fairy tales.

Ailish tried hard with the baby. She fed him every two hours, kept him clean and dry, sang lullabies that were really popular songs sung to different tunes because she didn't know the right words.

Catriona felt her heart ache when she saw the trapped expression on her sister's face, the panic when Jamie cried and wouldn't stop. She remembered Allan at the same age and folded him into her arms with the skill born of experience.

'He cries so much,' Ailish murmured, 'perhaps he doesn't love me.'

'He loves you,' Catriona told her, 'all babies cry like that.'

In March, when Jamie was three months old, Ailish said that she wanted to get a job.

'You could, I suppose,' Catriona said, 'but you don't need to. I make enough.'

Her sister's face flashed bitter before she hid her anger with a smile. 'There's a dance on Friday,' she said. 'Can I go?'

Catriona looked at her, wondering why she no longer mourned Jamie's father. Ailish had made friends with a girl from the next close, often spent the day talking to her.

'I'd rather you didn't.'

Ailish got up and took a brush to her hair. 'I never get out, Catriona.'

'Nor do I.'

'You go to work every day, to the market on Sundays.'

'That's different.'

'Is it? At least you get out.'

'All right,' Catriona said tiredly. 'You go to the dance. I'll take care of Jamie.'

On Friday night, once she had finished her tea, Catriona

filled a bowl with hot water and bleach and began to scrub the stairs, putting Jamie's cot on each landing as she worked. It had been Ailish's turn that day, but she had forgotten all about it and when Catriona had reminded her, she was already dressed for the dance.

When she finished the last landing, she stood up and rubbed her back, and tickled Jamie's chin as he slept. The door of the flat there opened; a woman peered out.

'Jings, lass, I thocht ye wis a rat.'

Catriona laughed as she lifted the pail to carry it to the drain.

'Och, lass, gie that to me, an' come in for a cup o' tea. Bring the wee lad wi' ye.'

Catriona hesitated.

'Don't be daft,' the woman said, drawing her into a room filled with the clean smell of drying washing.

She sat down, smiling shyly at another visitor, the Irishwoman who lived on the ground floor and ran a shebeen that opened in the early hours after the pubs had closed.

'I'm Jess, an' this is Kate,' the woman said, as she handed her a mug. 'This is Catriona, Kate, Ailish's sister. Works in a law office, don't ye, lass? She wis doin' the stairs, Kate, acos Ailish forgot. Ye should'a left them, lass. I'd'a done then mysel', 'cept I'd tae bring the washing in.'

Kate stood up, flexed her back. 'I'd best get back, Jess. I'll be busy, the night. Cheerie-bye, Catriona.'

'I'm sorry,' Catriona said, after Kate had left.

'About what, lass?'

'Ailish,' she said.

Jess shook her head as she rearranged the washing in front of the fire. 'She's gey young tae tak' whit's been thrown at her.'

'She should've remembered.'

'I wis the same mysel', lass. Mind ye, I'd twa bairn by the time I wis that age, but it's no' easy wi'out a man.'

Catriona said nothing, thrown for a moment by the easy tolerance of the other woman's manner.

'It's no' easy fir ye, either,' Jess said, sitting down and picking up her own mug.

'I manage,' Catriona said.

'Don't we all? I hae Jack, ye ken, he wirks on the railways, wirked there a' through the war, an' the bairns. But ye hardly look auld enough tae wirk yersel', lass.'

Catriona smiled. 'My twentieth birthday just passed.'

'Where did ye live afore?'

'Over the river. In a boarding house. But with Ailish ...'

'I ken,' Jess said wisely. 'This isna much, but at least it's shelter.'

The rumble of customers rose from Kate's shebeen. 'I've bided here a' my days,' Jess said. 'Used tae be a great place, afore they knocked maist o' it doon. Used tae be shebeens a' nicht, singing in the back courts, coffee stalls at every corner. It's changed, but.'

Catriona was thinking.

'Abdy wants one of thae new places, like the City Trust places on the Trongate. The slums're bad fir health. I managed, but. See an' ye could eat yer dinner aff the stairs, they're that clean.'

'How d'ye run a coffee stall?' Catriona asked.

'Och, lass, did ye no' see them afore the war? Jist a wee trolley thing, like, wi a burner, an' an urn fir yer coffee and anither fir the water.'

She remembered the old trolley behind Donoghue's stall, where he kept rags, dusters, things that he could not sell.

Annie had written last month, to tell her that Allan was wheezing a bit, not badly but he was chesty so she had taken him to the doctor. 'Don't worry,' she wrote, 'I just wanted you to know.' Catriona sent a ten-shilling note to pay for his medicines and a pair of warm woollen vests that she bought from the Royal Polytechnic; Annie would never ask, but she would need it, with Iain blind and unable to work. Her savings were dwindling; Ailish bought the food but she didn't hunt the markets and nor would she wait until five o'clock on Saturdays before going to the butcher and the fishmonger's. Catriona gave her five shillings to last the week; by Wednesday it was usually gone. At the end of the week she had only pennies left from her wages, but she still sent money to her father every month. As she lay awake at night listening to the sounds of the city in darkness, she often wondered where she'd find the money to keep the rest of her family once she'd found somewhere to live.

'I'm going to start a coffee stall,' she said suddenly.

Jess looked at her thoughtfully. 'Why not, lass? Best pitch's going begging, efter a'. Best place in the whole o' Glesca is jist by the Britannia Theatre, twa minutes up the road. I'll get ma boys tae help ye wi' the water.'

In April, as the biting winter wind softened to a breeze and on Glasgow Green the grass was growing in unruly tufts, Catriona opened her coffee stall at the corner on the Trongate, outside the Britannia Theatre. Donoghue had given her the stall in the end, for nothing more than a smile, when she explained what she wanted it for. It had taken nights of scouring to clean the fittings, but now the trolley gleamed in the glow of the street lights, piled with mugs she'd bought for a ha'penny each. Jack Calvert, Jess's husband, had repaired the canopy and painted Catriona's name on it, in big white letters that made her blush.

The smell of freshly brewed coffee drifted down the Trongate; the urn held two gallons and on the brazier she had two gallons of water keeping hot. Dougy Calvert, son of Jess, waited with her.

Until seven o'clock she waited, in dull dread that no one would come, until the queue started for the music hall and she began to sell, slowly at first. Then a line formed and she was so busy that she had no time to think until the rush died when the show started at eight o'clock.

'Ye're doin' no' bad,' Dougy said when she counted the coins and gave him fifteen shillings to take home when he went to get more water.

Standing beneath the canopy in the light drizzle, Catriona felt hope rise again, the feeling so strange that she hardly recognized it at first. In less than half an hour she had taken half of what she made in a week at the office. She had enjoyed it too; enjoyed meeting people and talking to them, their thanks when they said they were glad someone had started the coffee stall again.

When the show finished, she was busy again, not pausing until she heard a familiar voice in the queue.

Tia Macleod stood there, dressed elegantly in a black velvet dress with an ocelot jacket. 'I recognized your voice,' she said.

'How are you?' Catriona stumbled; they had not seen each other since she had left Mrs Gordon's, and she felt vaguely ashamed that she had come to this.

'I work at MacDonald's now,' Tia said, 'I left Mrs Gordon's. And you?'

'Still at MacKenzie's. And this. I want ...' She paused then, because her ambition sounded so fragile when she voiced it out aloud. 'I'm going to start a tearoom,' she said, 'a tearoom all of my own.'

Tia smiled, and handed her a card with her new address. 'I wish I had your guts, Catriona.'

She walked away with a group of friends.

Donoghue arrived when she closed the stall, with a tall Irishman she recognized from Paddy's Market. 'I jis' wanted tae mak' sure ye'd get home safe,' he said.

Dougy and his wee brother Jock were with her, blowing their cupped hands to counter the chill of the night.

'This's Liam Devlin,' Donoghue said. 'Ye ken, he's got the builder's yard behind the Saltmarket.'

Catriona felt herself blush, and wondered why.

'I've bought three coffees from you tonight,' Liam Devlin said, in a brogue that sounded like the waves of the ocean, 'and the best scones I've ever eaten, though my mother'd not forgive me for saying that.'

'I'm glad you enjoyed them,' she said.

'Come on,' Donoghue said, lifting up the folding legs of the trolley and turning it around, 'I'll see ye home, lass.'

'No need,' Liam said. 'I'm going that way. If you don't mind, Catriona?'

She shook her head, suddenly exhausted, watching the way he pushed the trolley as easily as if it was a pram. Liam

Devlin was a big man with broad shoulders and muscled arms that strained the seams of his old tweed jacket. Though it was early in the year his skin was tanned mahogany; it carried the mark of the open air.

'You can sit on top if you like,' he said, as Dougy and Jock ran home, whooping over the sixpences she'd given them.

She smiled as she gazed down at the cobblestone pavement. She was too shy to smile at him. 'I couldn't,' she said.

'You could too,' he told her. 'A girl like you could do anything she wants.'

She turned away as her cheeks flamed, suddenly wondering what she was doing walking down the Briggait with Liam Devlin. He was older than her, a decade at least though she knew that the city could age a man quickly. In the market on Sundays she'd heard the girls talking about him. He had been in America during the war and had done well there, so well that he had his own yard and employed dozens of men who worked in gangs at the docks. There was always money in his pockets, and an easy smile for the girls, but he had never been seen in the dance halls or tearooms, and he did not have a lady friend although a man like him could have several. He flirted madly with the market girls. Glancing at him, Catriona saw his rugged features, the shock of black hair just beginning to whiten at the edges, his forehead furrowed with experience and wisdom. A man like that, she thought, could have any woman he wanted. What on earth does he want with me?

Just then, he turned and smiled at her. His expression was naked somehow, almost shy.

As they passed under a street light, she saw that his eyes were the colour of the morning sky, as innocent and as kind.

Catriona opened her coffee stall on three evenings a week, and all day on Sunday at Paddy's Market. On an average evening she made ten shillings, on a good one a pound. Her savings began to grow, more so when she made meat pies and bridies, and currant scones that she sold for sixpence a bag. During the day she worked at the office, ignoring the slights that Cameron delivered by habit, so conscious was he of his position as an apprentice while she was only a clerk. In the early evening the anger faded as she baked a fresh batch of scones and pies; she found catharsis as ever in lots of hard work.

Ailish had been out to hunt for a job, but given up in despair when she found that the best she could get was five shillings a week as a junior in a shop. 'It wouldn't be worth it,' she said, 'not once I'd got someone to care for Jamie.'

Catriona was ironing her blouse for work the next day. 'I've been thinking,' she said, 'I might give up my job soon. 'I'd make more money if I ran my stall down at the docks during the day.'

'I thought you wanted to be a lawyer.'

'I won't get the chance. Not with MacKenzie, anyway.' She had not told Ailish of the hurt she felt when she had been turned down.

Ailish swore.

'With my stall I could make enough to buy a lease of a shop somewhere, with a flat above. And if I wasn't going to the office, you could get a job.'

'At five shillings a week? I won't work for their slave wages.'

Catriona turned the blouse over and held the iron on the collar. 'I only got half a crown when I started, Ailish.'

'*Galach* half a crown. You'd've made more as a beggar.' She did not notice the pain on her sister's face.

Jamie woke up, crying. Ailish looked the other way as Catriona went to comfort him. After he was settled, she went back to her blouse.

'You don't understand,' Ailish said in a low voice.

'You have to start somewhere, Ailish.'

'That's easy to say.'

'It wasn't easy when I did it.'

'Triona, I got almost as much at home.'

Catriona held the blouse up to the light. Satisfied that it was perfect, she put it on a hanger.

'I can't stand it,' Ailish murmured.

'Can't stand what?'

'Here. This place. Everything.'

Catriona looked at the walls she had scrubbed, the rag rug beside the fire, the little cotton cushions she had sewn to soften the hard wood chairs. In candlelight, the range shone dully, the wooden floor gleamed. 'It's not so bad, Ailish.'

'Catriona, it's a slum.'

'It's all I could find, Ailish. It wasn't easy.'

'I'd rather be in prison.'

Very calmly Catriona walked to the sink and poured water into the kettle.

'I hate it. I just hate it.'

She swung round. 'That's enough, Ailish.'

'It's driving me mad.'

'You should've thought of that before you got pregnant. It's too late now.'

'Catriona, don't blame me for that ...'

She spun around, her eyes aflame. 'Why shouldn't I? You blame me for this, and it's all your fault. You got pregnant, not me. I took you in, gave you a home. It's not much, I know, but it's all I can manage. If you don't like it, you can always go.'

Ailish grabbed her cloak, opened the door.

'Go on,' Catriona said, 'run away if you want to. You always do.'

Once she was gone, Catriona made tea, then sat drinking it, humming to Jamie. She changed and went to bed, but did not fall asleep until she heard Ailish come in again.

'I'm sorry,' Ailish whispered. 'I didn't mean what I said.'

Catriona turned over and pretended she had not heard.

The following morning Catriona got up early and counted the money she had saved in the tin she kept in the bottom of the cupboard. There was almost £70 in coins and ten-shilling notes, which she piled neatly on the table before she checked her addition and then put it away again.

Ailish yawned sleepily; you could still see the tracks of tears on her face.

'I'm sorry,' she said again.

Catriona shrugged.

'Triona ...'

'It doesn't matter, Ailish. I've just counted up. I'm making good money. In the autumn we'll be able to find somewhere else.'

Ailish turned over in bed, balanced her chin in her hand. 'When will you give up your job?'

'I'm not sure. I'll have to save a hundred pounds at least, for a lease and all the things we'll need.'

'We?'

'Sine and Maire and Allan want to come down as well.'

'Catriona, they don't know about me. They don't know about Jamie.'

Catriona stood up. 'They'll understand, Ailish.'

'Why don't you give up your job now?'

'Because I make a guinea a week there, Ailish.'

'You said you'd make more on your stall.'

'I have to be sure. Glasgow's in the doldrums. They're talking about striking at the docks. If there's strikes, there'll be no money to be made on coffee stalls.'

Ailish got up and went to Jamie. 'Catriona, last night, I didn't mean what I said. I know you've helped me ...'

'You're my sister,' Catriona said. 'We can talk later. Now I have to go to work.'

That day the paper said that the threatened strike had been called off; the yard-owners were adamant that they had called the union's bluff. Turning to the classified columns, Catriona found a shop with a room and kitchen in Springburn for a rent of 30/-, paid quarterly in advance. Maybe, she thought, as she walked home, maybe it won't be so long after all.

It was a balmy spring evening. Starlings sang in their thousands; the city fog glowed golden in the light of the setting sun.

She did not know where Springburn was, but it couldn't be as bad as the tenement off the Briggait.

'Catriona?' Kate called out as she heard her footsteps on the stairs.

Catriona turned back, seeing Kate still in her dressing gown, her unruly hair tied back with string. 'I've got the wee fella,' she said, coughing. 'You'd best come in, lass.'

Catriona followed her into a room that was dark and too hot, that smelled of yesterday's whisky and faintly of sweat.

'Mother of God,' Kate said, looking at herself in the mirror, 'I didn't realize I looked that bad. It's Jess's day at the washhouse, lass, so Ailish left the wain wi' me.'

Jamie was on a rug laid out in front of the fire, rolling around old biscuit tins.

'I'm never sure what to do wi' wains,' Kate said as Jamie began to bang a tin, 'I just let them play.'

Jamie gurgled when he saw Catriona, then went back to his game. The noise he made was deafening. Catriona gestured her thanks and then scooped him into her arms to carry him home. As he lost his toy, Jamie's face screwed into a frown.

As she climbed the stairs she wondered where Ailish had gone. It was a Tuesday, and Ailish rarely went out at the beginning of the week. When she did, she usually took Jamie with her; once or twice she had left him with Jess while she went shopping, but never with Kate.

The strange feeling settled upon her when she reached her own front door, and opened it to a room that was oddly tidy and very quiet. She looked around, saw that her bag was gone; looked again and saw that Ailish's cape was not on its peg.

There was a note on the table. She picked it up, but had read only the first few words before she heard Kate's footsteps on the stair.

The door was still open; she turned and saw Kate holding one of Jamie's nappies.

'I changed him, Catriona. I didn't have any nappies, so I used one of my towels. I washed it and put it to dry on the boiler. It's dry now.'

Catriona thanked her and then, as Kate turned to leave, asked her, in a very small voice, to come in.

Kate looked at her as she held the letter in a trembling hand.

'Ailish's gone,' Catriona said.

'I was afraid of that, lass.'

Kate waited until Jamie was settled and Catriona joined her in a chair beside the cooling range. Distractedly, she opened the hatch and added a few lumps of coal, fanned the fire until the flame held.

'Where?' Kate asked.

'America,' Catriona said.

Kate shook her head. 'I thought she was just away looking for a job or something. I only thought later, when she didn't come back. I should've stopped her.'

'Nobody could stop Ailish once she's set her mind on something.' Opening the bottom drawer of the chest, Catriona found the tin, rattled it, heard coins but not the soft rustle of notes, and only a few of them.

She began to sob then, as Kate folded her into her soft, forgiving arms.

'Hush, lass. Don't try to talk just yet.'

'It was my fault.'

'How could it've been?'

Catriona looked at her. 'We argued. Last night. Said things we shouldn't've. She tried to say sorry . . .'

'She shouldn't've done it, lass.'

'But I should've forgiven her, Kate.'

'She shouldn't've done it, lass. Shouldn't've gone and left you wi' the wee lad. Doesn't matter what you said, or didn't say.'

Catriona stood back and began to dry her eyes. 'But, you see, that's what Ailish always did. She always ran away.' She sat down by the fire, read the letter again and then tossed it into the flames, feeling a wave of anger that made her almost faint.

'You've learnt a lesson, lass,' Kate said as she put the kettle on. 'The hard way, but there aren't any others.'

Catriona shivered as she cupped the mug in her hands. In his cot, Jamie stirred, then settled again.

'Money's safest in the bank,' Kate said. 'I should've told you. That's where mine goes.'

Catriona was thinking of the trapped look on Ailish's face, of how young she was, despite her years, of the letter that said, at the end: 'You see, I'm not as good as you.'

'I didn't think,' she said, in a daze.

'Jess'll mind the wee one,' Kate said, 'or I will. I was like you, lass, just like you, once upon a time. You don't do your stall tonight, do you?'

'No.'

'Well then, us two'll just sit down and work out a way through this. Liam Devlin lived in America; his friends there could send her back.'

Ailish's face swam before Catriona's eyes; beautiful Ailish, vain Ailish, selfish and silly. She didn't know the cost of the money she had taken, didn't know the value of love.

'No,' Catriona said, shaking her head. 'Let her go, Kate. If that's what she wants, let her do it.'

The next day, at work, she found the old city directory of 1911 and called the Children's Home at lunchtime, when the office was empty.

The voice that answered was arrogant at first, condescending as Catriona explained her situation and made an appointment for that evening after work. Early that morning she had been to the docks; the shipping office confirmed that Ailish had been a steerage passenger to New York, with another girl and a young man. Catriona had been half hoping that her sister would have changed her mind, that she would find her at the pier, full of remorse but too ashamed to come home. Ailish was impulsive, not usually bad. She had lain awake all night and come to the decision in the small hours, only if Ailish was really gone.

After work she raced home and took Jamie from Jess, bundled him up in his shawl and filled a bag with the rest of his things, a pathetically small heap of nappies and a couple of clean baby gowns.

On the tram to Giffnock she held him at a distance on her

knee, not looking into his eyes as she comforted him mechanically, watching the city fade as the tram crackled on towards the suburbs.

The home was a bleak place, built of grey stone a shade lighter than the sky. She rang the bell, waited, and then was ushered into a corridor that smelled of beeswax and dust. As she sat outside a door marked 'General Office' she heard in the distance the sounds of children, and watched through the window as a line of grey-clad little people filed past, subdued and tidy as soldiers. Reflexively she clutched Jamie to her chest and held him there, patting the back of his head.

'It's for the best,' she whispered, 'you'll see,' as he whimpered and settled into the heat of her body.

'Miss Nicolson,' a woman said sternly; she was dressed like a governess and carried a folder of papers. 'If you come with me, we'll take care of the formalities.'

Catriona followed her meekly, and answered by rote the questions she asked. For a moment or two the woman wrote in an angular script, then handed her a form to sign.

Catriona took the pen, then hesitated as she felt the flutter of Jamie's heart.

'You'll find him a good home, won't you?'

The woman pursed her lips. 'We always act in the best interests of the child.'

'But he'll be adopted, won't he? He'll have a mother and father to care for him?'

The woman looked annoyed. 'He's a bit old, you must understand. Newborns settle so much easier. The older ones, sometimes they've picked up bad habits.'

'He's only five months. Your advert said you arranged adoptions.'

The woman smiled patiently. 'Miss Nicolson, we do try. There's more children these days than there are families who want them, and some of them stay with us here. The home is excellent, you know.'

Catriona put down the pen.

'I would think carefully,' the woman said sharply.

'I need to be sure he finds a good family.'

The woman snorted. 'Any family at all would be better than the one he was born into.'

Catriona's eyes narrowed as she rose to leave.

'Miss Nicolson, sit down! If you walk out these doors, don't come back. We won't take him, you know. We haven't got time to deal with mothers who change their minds.'

'I wouldn't dream of letting you,' she said quietly, clasping Jamie to her, 'not in a thousand years.'

Chapter Six

Catriona walked out in the evening towards the river, and then across the bridge until she reached the middle. The Clyde, far below, flowed gently in dark wavelets that made comet tails of the gaslights. In the west sunset was a vivid gash, streaked by the smoke from factory chimneys. For a moment, at dusk, the city looked like a painting, pale grey and softened by mist.

During the day the water was the colour of mud, slicked with oil and sometimes the garish remains of colours pumped in by the dyeworks not far upstream. At night it became soft onyx, crested gently by the light of the moon. Catriona looked down and saw her reflection, distorted and swept away by the flow.

In her arms, Jamie slept contentedly. She looked down at him, wondering if she had a right to his trust. At the children's home she had walked out rather than lose her poise. Waiting for the tram, she'd given rein to her temper, cursing roundly; a woman looked at her strangely and then stepped away as if she was mad. She closed her eyes and saw again the official's face, her outrage and disdain. She swore softly in Gaelic; Jamie stirred and smiled at her as if he was glad she had.

'Don't worry, little one,' she said, 'we'll get through. We'll get through all this, and better times will come.'

She thought of the promise she had made to Allan, to the others, how much harder it would be to make it good now.

Downriver, a tug edged into the current, the horn raucous in the still of the night, its wake a wide vee in the water that sent eddies slapping against the quayside.

It hurt to have to break a promise, but she would make it good in time. They would understand, when she could find a way to tell them.

Tears came to her eyes when she thought of the careless way that Ailish had tampered with her dreams.

In the drawer where Ailish had kept her clothes, she'd found Jamie's birth certificate that read 'Catriona Nicolson, widow' under the place for the mother, 'Ewan Nicolson, decd.' as the father.

She saw Ewan then, smiling, saying that he did not care; she remembered him and Alec in their uniforms. So many people had died since she had lost her mother. Sometimes she felt Mor's presence, willing her on. Not now.

The clock chimed the quarter hour; she had time yet to think a while before she had to go back.

The moon was risen, a crescent in the sky that cast a thin light on the water, fractured by the rippled surface.

Feeling movement beside her, she turned and saw Liam Devlin. He rested his arms on the bridge and she saw his workman's hands, the callus between his thumb and finger made by the spades and hods he had wielded over the years. His eyes were unguarded; they seemed to reach out towards her soul.

He looked at her and then at Jamie; Catriona, sensing that he knew where she had been that evening, raised her face bravely to meet his gaze. 'I'll care for him,' she said defiantly.

'I never doubted that,' he said.

She turned away so that he would not see how she doubted it herself.

'I could get her back,' he said simply. 'I could send a telegram to my brother in New York.'

So Kate had told him. Catriona felt anger for a moment, but it died when she realized that everybody would know soon. There were no secrets in the tenement slums.

She shook her head.

'Don't tell me you don't care.'

'Oh, I care, Liam Devlin. But I know that she'd run again. I'm her sister, not her gaoler.'

'I suppose that's sense of a sort.'

'It's the others,' she said softly, her voice tailing off into reticence to talk about the hurt.

'What about them?' he asked, in a way that demanded an answer.

'I've two sisters and a little brother; they were coming down in the autumn. I was going to buy the lease of a shop, you see.'

'What difference does it make?'

'The difference is,' she said, 'I had the money then and I don't have it now.'

He looked down and watched the water for a while.

'What's wrong with the place you have at the moment?'

'It's a single end, not enough for the four of us.'

'You live in a castle back home?'

'No, a cottage like everyone else, but I'd not bring them down here to live in that.'

'Maybe you should give then the chance to decide for themselves.'

Catriona's eyes flashed fire for a moment. 'I'd not let my family live like that.'

Liam changed the subject. 'That stall of yours. How much do you make in a week?'

'Three pounds. Maybe a little more.'

He turned to face her. 'How much more would you make if you gave up your job and took your bridies down to the docks to sell?'

'I thought of that,' she said, slowly, 'but my oven isn't very big.'

'Catriona, I have a big enough oven. You know my place? It used to be a boarding house when I got it; there's a kitchen big enough to cook for an army. I don't use it. You could. And there's great big baking trays and pans and urns. Just needs cleaning, that's all.'

'I'd pay you rent.'

'The Devil'd pay me rent. I start charging rent when I turn a landlord. That'll be the day.'

'I'll think about it,' she said as they turned to walk back to the Briggait, then: 'I'll do it, Liam. I'll just need a week or two to work my notice.'

When they reached her close, he stopped.

'Catriona,' Liam said, 'if you need money?'

'How d'you know she took my money?' she flashed, still angry with the world.

'You told me,' he replied. 'I know how hard you save.'

'How d'you know that?'

'Because I see the work you do. You earn, but you never spend a penny on yourself.'

'It's not your business,' she said angrily.

He shrugged helplessly. 'It doesn't have to be so hard, you know. The money she took, I'd give it to you, lend it if you insist.'

'No.'

Kate was waiting at her door when Catriona went into the close. 'Come away in, lass,' she said, 'I've a pot of tea just made.'

Catriona hesitated. 'I'd best get Jamie to bed.'

'Ach, he's sleeping well enough where he is. Come in, lass, and we'll get you sorted out.'

'I'm not opening tonight,' Kate said as she poured the tea. 'These buggers'll have to find somewhere else. 'S not worth it, in any case, the beginning of the week. All they want is bloody credit, and you've to haunt them like a phantom to get the money back. There you go.'

Catriona took the mug, her hand trembling slightly. She moved Jamie to one side of her lap, anxious not to disturb him.

'Oh, Kate . . .'

Kate knelt on the rug beside her. 'Don't you go worrying, lass.'

'But Kate, I've to work.'

There was a knock at the door, then Jess came in. 'Catriona' she said, echoing Kate. 'Don't worry yersel'. I'll take the wee one when ye're out.'

Catriona nodded numbly. 'But, Jess . . .'

Jess stood with a basket of washing wedged against her hip. 'What, Catriona?'

'I don't want to impose, Jess.'

'Only way to get by is to help each other, lass.'

'I'm giving up my job. I'm going to run a pie stall at the docks, and my coffee stall at night. It wouldn't be all of the day.'

'Ach, lass, I've that many wains running aroun' my feet a' day as it is. Anither'll no mak' ony difference.'

Jess left, and Kate pulled her chair in to the fire. 'I mind when I came over, lass. Couldn't breathe the air for months without coughing, on a Sunday I just used to start walking along the road till I reached the country. Daft thing that I was; got sacked as a maid for doing that. I walked so far I couldn't mind where I'd turned a corner. I never used to turn corners, used to go straight ahead lest I got lost, but I turned a corner one day because I saw some wildflowers in the distance. I turned off the road to go to see them and then when I turned back I was lost. I was late back and I got tossed out on my ear; I slept rough that night, on the green, but in the morning I got another job in the bakehouse from a man who let me sleep up in the attic above the bakery. A good job, that was, and warm too.'

She smiled. 'Daft things you did when you were young. And here I am now, I could go back any time I want to, and now I've grown old I don't want that.'

Catriona didn't think of Kate as old; she was of indeterminate age, beyond youth but not aged, her face mature but not faded.

'Colmaquillan,' Kate said, 'there were ten McGlones in Colmaquillan, when my da died. Six brothers and four sisters. Five of them died with the typhoid the year I left. Then three went to the phthisis. My brother Sean went to America and Joe went into the seminary. There wasn't a home to go to after that. There's no more McGlones in Colmaquillan, 'cept in the graveyard. But I shouldn't be telling you that. You've got enough yourself without listening to me.'

'No,' Catriona said quickly.

'Yes,' Kate said, drawing her shawl tightly around her shoulders.

'Wait,' Catriona said, as she stood at the doorway. 'Does it ever get any easier, Kate?'

'Yes, it does, lass. It does in time, if you don't let yourself go bitter. If you do that, it never does.'

She wrote out her resignation early the following morning and gave it to MacKenzie, WS, as he was drinking his morning coffee.

He opened it, then threw it aside.

'What nonsense is this, Miss Nicolson?'

'I am resigning, Mr MacKenzie. I'll work out my notice till the end of the month.'

'You'll do no such thing.'

'Mr MacKenzie, I am afraid that I will.'

He picked up the letter and tore it into tiny pieces. 'I won't accept it and that's final. You're paid very well for the work you do here.'

Catriona said nothing.

'Now get your pad. I have work to do.'

'Shall I advertise for another clerk?'

'You'll do no such thing, Miss Nicolson. I refuse to accept your resignation, and that's the end of the matter.'

She did not move.

'Well, get on with it, girl.'

'Mr MacKenzie, I am resigning, whether you like it or not.'

His expression hardened and a vessel began to throb at his temple. 'Miss Nicolson, you will not resign. I will not permit you to resign. You will start work now, or else ... or else ...'

'Or what, Mr MacKenzie?'

'I'll sack you, for God's sake. I'll sack you, my girl.'

She smiled. 'Go ahead.'

A flush spread over his face, turning it the colour of fine port wine. He began to drum his fingers on the desk. 'I'm warning you, Miss Nicolson. I will not be held to ransom by a slip of a clerk.'

'*Tigh na galach*,' she said.

'What's that?'

'*Tigh na galach*, Mr MacKenzie. It's swearing, in my language. In yours, I suppose it means go to hell.'

'Go to what? Now . . .'

She spun on her heel and stalked out of his office, closing the door behind her. Walking into the main office, she picked up her purse, then straightened the papers on her desk. 'You'll have to take over,' she said to Nina.

'Whit?'

'I'm leaving. I just told MacKenzie to go to hell.'

Nina remained motionless as she walked out.

Maloney caught up with her as she was striding down Ingram Street.

'All the best to ye, Catriona. Yon well deserved that.'

She grinned. 'Drawing up a writ, is he?'

'On the phone to that KC accusing him of poaching his staff. He's not got round to suing you yet.'

She laughed out loud. 'When he does, you'll not be able to find me, Maloney, will you?'

'Well, blow me, I doubt if I will. In fact – ' he paused and looked around, moved a step closer – 'don't you worry, girl. It'll not leave the office. Or maybe it will, maybe it'll get as far as the Clyde. Certainly, it'll never reach the courthouse.'

'Thank you, Maloney.'

'I'll miss you, Catriona. I'll see you on that stall of yours.'

The morning was tender; as she walked, the breeze cooled the fire in her cheeks and stoked the embers of her pride.

Liam Devlin left her a note and the key to his building on the Saltmarket. When she first opened the door of the kitchen all she saw was dust; she started work with a brush first and then a cloth, scouring every surface until at last the old range shone and the floor was clean and polished.

Liam was away that week, working, he said, on a contract way down the river at the deep docks, and it was easier just to camp at the site. Catriona had come to an arrangement with Jess about Jamie; during the mornings and the afternoons when she worked in the kitchen he stayed with her and Jess took him at dinner time and in the evenings when she was running her stall.

She met Jack Calvert's cousin Davy, who would drive the

cart and horse she rented to the docks in time for the workers' dinner break. Davy wanted to work at the docks as he had done before the war; he agreed to work for her until then, though she sensed he was embarrassed to be paid by a woman.

Liam came round to the coffee stall on Friday evening, as he always did. 'How's it going?' he asked.

Every last penny had gone on flour, meat, vegetables. 'Fine, I think, if people don't stop eating.'

He smiled.

A week later she was tired and sore but after everything was paid she had made more than ten pounds, which she counted carefully and then put in the account she had opened at the Linen Bank on Ingram Street. She had sold over a thousand pies that week, too many sandwiches to count; when one of the dockers told her that her beef bridie tasted better than anything from Lang's she'd hugged him for joy and been dreadfully embarrassed when he reminded her that he was a married man.

'Do you ever take any time off?' Liam asked her that evening as she served the last cup of coffee outside the Britannia Theatre and then began to close the stall.

Catriona shook her head.

'Don't you ever want to see the show?' he asked, inclining his head towards the theatre that had been packed full all week with a new singer and a pair of child dancers.

'I can hear it from outside. People tell me about it afterwards. I'd rather go to a ceilidh, if you want to know.'

He stood there shaking his head, taking the stall from her as she began to wheel it across the street.

'Catriona,' he began slowly, 'what do I have to do to persuade you to go out with me? I don't care where, anywhere you like, just some place where I could spend some time with you when you're not selling mugs of coffee or making bridies or taking the whole world's cares on your shoulders.'

'All you have to do,' she said, surprised at herself, feeling shy but also happy, 'all you have to do, Liam Devlin, is to ask.'

'And if I ask you, Catriona, would you say yes?'

'Yes,' she said. 'Yes, Liam Devlin, I would.'

On Sunday afternoon, as the market closed, Catriona rushed home and washed her hair in the tin metal bath that she kept below her bed. Jamie watched her from his cot, chuckling as she towelled her hair and then shook it loose in the breeze from the open skylight.

'Daft, amn't I?' The Tron Church clock chimed five; her hair would be dry by seven, half an hour before she was due to meet Liam.

Jamie laughed when she picked him up and held him so that he could see the pigeons on the roof. Since Ailish had left he cried sometimes in the dead of night, the sound making her heart churn as she thought of his future. When that happened she would get up and hold him until he settled, wondering always if he ever felt her doubts. She remembered Allan's innocent trust, knew that Jamie would trust her too in time and wondered how, if ever, she could tell him the truth.

After the doubt she always felt a surge of compassion that made her whisper promises that meant more to her than to him.

In her wardrobe were one cotton dress, two dark skirts and a couple of blouses, carefully starched but plain. She held up one to her chest and moved so that she saw her reflection in the mirror, the island girl again now that her hair hung loose.

'I don't know,' she said to herself. The choice was the dress, too cool for a spring evening, or the blouse, so severe that she looked like a governess. Or an office girl. She was twenty years old, but she had never been courted before, she didn't even know the rules. On the island, love began as friendship, long walks along the beach or over the hills and then dancing at the ceilidhs. In the city, the ritual was different; couples strolled along the streets together, went to dances and the music hall. Young girls went out together, giggling and blushing; if they met a young man who showed interest, they 'clicked'.

Catriona brushed her hair dry and pinned it carefully into a loose chignon.

Jess put her head around the door, a frothy bundle in her hand. 'Here,' she said, unfolding an ivory blouse with a pin-tucked bodice and a wide collar made of lace, 'you can have this if you like. My sister in Canada doesn't know what babies do to a woman's figure.'

'I couldn't, Jess.'

'You could so.' Jess held the blouse up to her. 'It suits you, Catriona.'

Dressed, she looked into the mirror and saw a softer reflection.

'You look fine,' Jess said.

Catriona leant over the sleeping baby and kissed him softly. 'I won't be late.'

'Jis' go and have a richt guid time. The wee one'll not even wake up.'

Liam was waiting outside, leaning against his car, wearing a suit and tie that made him look like an actor cast in an unfamiliar part. He feigned nonchalance, but his fists had been bunched, his hand was pale as he opened the door for her.

'I thought you were joking,' she said, as she climbed in.

He looked at her quizzically.

'About the car, I mean.'

He smiled. 'I needed it, *acushla*. For business. These men that own the yards, they'd not take me seriously if I turned up with a horse and cart.'

She laughed as she felt the edges of her shyness melt. She had never been in a car before, never felt the sensation of moving along so close to the surface of the road and the other traffic. Just in front of them a car stopped, and she held her breath as they seemed about to crash into it, only coming to a halt at the last moment, when she felt safe to breathe again.

Liam tugged at a lever on the floor of the car and the engine note changed.

Catriona looked out at the pedestrians, remembering the

times she had gazed at passing cars and wondered about their passengers.

'It beats a horse, just about,' Liam said. 'It doesn't tire so easily. But if it breaks down it takes the mother of God to get the engine started again.'

'D'you understand engines?' she asked, thinking fleetingly of Rory.

'Not as well as I should. I doubt the man who invented them understands this beast. But I manage.'

They drove west out of the city. The evening sun glinted off the windscreen and shot fiery streaks through Liam's hair. In the city his hair looked black, but now she could see there was an amber tone to it that was brought out by the light of the sun. Catriona felt nervous, wondered what to say to him. Liam concentrated on the road, turning every now and then and smiling when the traffic gave him a chance.

'When the sun catches your hair,' he said, 'it looks like you're on fire.'

'I was thinking the same about you.'

A tram juddered to a stop in front of him and he swore softly in Gaelic. Going through Paisley, he showed her the old abbey, once the home of Benedictine monks.

'Where are we going?' she asked.

'There's a place I think you'll like,' he replied.

Beyond the town the road climbed a hill, the car engine protesting as Liam changed gears. 'Close your eyes,' he said, as the car swung off the road and she heard the engine die. The air was still; she heard faint birdsong and the wind ruffling through grass. He opened the car door and helped her out, still with her eyes closed. Uncertainly, she stood in the open.

'Look now,' he said, and she saw far below the whole of the Clyde Valley, the soft mist of evening mingling with the smoke from factory chimneys, the buildings like toys in the distance. Out here in the country, the city looked so very small, so fragile against the might of the land.

'When I was a lad,' he said, 'just leaving home, I got the coal boat to Ardrossan 'cos our Da couldn't afford the fare to Glasgow and we knew a man on the coal boat who'd take me for free. So I got to Ardrossan and then I'd to walk to Glasgow. I got lost, God knows, spent the night on the hills praying for Mother Mary to show me the way and then when I woke up in the morning, I was here.' He smiled. 'I was twelve years old, Catriona. I would've turned back 'cept there was nothing at home to go back to.'

His eyes narrowed against the harshness of the light, also the memory. 'Ach, what am I saying? Let's go and find ourselves a place to eat.'

'No,' she said quietly, 'not yet.'

They stood in silence as the setting sun cast their shadows before them. Catriona gazed at Liam's image, thought of Ozymandias for a moment, a line or two out of a poem she'd read at school and then, remembering the rest of the poem, of Ossian instead. The sun slipped behind the hill and the shadows faded; the sky turned primrose in the west. The air was very clear and still, so still that far away the sounds of the city were faint as birdsong. A car came along the road, disturbing her reverie as she turned to Liam and wondered again why a man like him was interested in her.

'You're beautiful,' he said, as if he could read her thoughts.

She blushed and turned away. For a while she studied the valley, watching the trail of a railway engine, the evening mist settling like gauze over the Campsie Hills. The air tasted of spring; the doubts that had haunted her seemed to fade as the smoke of the train blurred and melted into the clouds.

'I miss Ireland,' Liam said suddenly. 'I miss the way the mountains go soft with the evening, the taste of the wind. I miss the silence of the hills.'

The other car had parked and a couple got out.

Catriona smiled. 'I miss home too.'

'Why did you come here, Catriona?'

Suddenly she found herself telling Liam about her life; she told him so many things so quickly that when at last she stopped to take a breath she blushed, saying she shouldn't be telling him all that, she must be boring him.

'You could never bore me.'

He took her hand; the gesture surprised her as suddenly she felt a sense of peace. His hands were strong and confident, but he was a thoughtful man too, she could tell that from the gentleness of his touch.

'I've known you for years,' he said.

She looked at him.

'I saw you first at Paddy's Market way back, the year before the war. Donoghue warned me off. Said you were too young and you had a man back home in any case.'

'I don't,' she said, 'I don't have a man at home.'

'I went to America,' he said. 'I wasn't going to fight the Sassenachs' war. I suppose you think I'm a coward.'

'I know you aren't,' she said quickly.

'If I had to fight, I'd fight for Ireland,' he said.

After the day had faded they drove back to the city and stopped at a little Italian cafe where Liam ordered coffee and a strawberry ice for Catriona.

'You know,' he said, as she ate the ice cream, 'you must send for your family, if that's what you want. Ailish took your money, but you mustn't let her take your dreams.'

'I'll start looking for a place,' she said, as he reached over and wiped a dribble of syrup from her chin. His touch made her tremble slightly.

'I'm sorry,' he said, 'but I didn't want it to stain your blouse.'

They talked easily for hours, leaving only when the cafe owner began to extinguish the gas lamps.

She sighed when they turned into Stockwell Street and the dark, tall buildings closed in around them.

The car slowed and Liam honked the horn to alert some boys kicking a can around the street. They were barefoot, filthy, painfully thin. They smiled broadly when Liam waved at them.

Catriona watched them for a moment, and turned away when they noticed her scrutiny.

'They're happy enough,' Liam said.

'At home,' she said bitterly, 'we'd not let an animal live like this.' She had heard so many stories of people who came to live in the tenements who promised themselves that it would only be a year or two before they moved on to something better and then ended up, like Kate, spending a lifetime there.

'Don't fret,' Liam said. 'You'll survive. I promise you.'

'I wonder, sometimes.'

'You will. Trust yourself. Trust me, if you will.' He took her hand again, kissed it so softly that she hardly felt his touch. He shook his head and then smiled gently. 'I'll see you tomorrow, *acushla*, or the next day. Next Sunday, if we leave sooner, we could take the wee lad down to the sea?'

'That would be nice, Liam. Thank you.'

After he left she wanted to be alone, but she found herself in Jess's front room, telling her about the place they had gone and the Italian cafe and the strawberry ice cream.

Liam Devlin, she said to herself as she settled down to sleep. There was something about the sound of his name that brought a sense of security to her troubled mind.

In the morning Catriona sang as she worked. Davy had planned the route last week; they started at the Kingston Dock at eleven where the foreman left his order for the men's dinners with the man at the gate. Then they went down the river to Princes Dock and Harland and Wolff, the Linthouse Yard and Fairfields. Before the dinner whistle went at noon they crossed the river by the ferry and delivered to the yards north of the river, the Meadowside and Point-house, the slip dock and JG Thompson's boiler works.

Catriona sold a bridie and a cup of soup for sixpence – good value for what it was and a decent meal for the men who didn't have a woman to pack a dinner for them.

'You're awful quiet,' Davy said as he pulled the horse to a stop outside the slip dock, where there was a queue waiting.

'I am not,' Catriona replied.

'You've not said a word all morning.'

Catriona eased the lid off a churn of soup and served the

first of the men. They only had twenty minutes for their dinner break, so she worked quickly, finishing just as the whistle blew to call them back to work.

The soup was finished and there were only a couple of pies left.

'You've clicked, haven't you? You've got a dreamy look on your face.'

'I have not, Davy.'

As they were about to leave, a man walked up wearing the badge of the dockers' union. 'There might be another strike call,' he said, as Catriona gave him one of the leftover bridies. 'You'd not sell to the scabs, would you?'

Catriona felt a tinge of apprehension. Davy gave the man a penny for a copy of *The Worker*.

'You see the sense of it, hen, don't you? The forty-hour week would make jobs for the boys back from the war. There's many on the streets without work, you ken.'

'I've not worked since I came back,' Davy said. 'I'm right with you.'

'And you?' The man was gazing at Catriona, fixing her with a stare that forced her to answer.

'I'm with you too,' she said at last. 'I'll not be here if you go on strike.'

'Right, hen. We've all got to stick together.' He turned and walked over to a knot of men standing on the street corner.

As Davy turned the cart back to the ferry, heading for Harland and Wolff to collect the empty soup churns, he looked at her. 'What's the matter, Catriona?'

The movement of the cart made the churns clatter and she had to shout to make herself heard.

'I need the money from this round, Davy. I've two sisters and a brother at home, and my sister's baby here.'

'An' how much does that take? Ye'll manage fine with what ye mak' on yer coffee stall. If they strike and ye don't, that'll be ye finished in Glasgow.' They had boarded the ferry and as it slowly pushed out into the river he looked around at the docks, the shells of ships and the height of the cranes. There was a bitterness on his face that Catriona had not seen before.

'I spent four years in Flanders,' he said, 'four bluidy years in yon hell. They promised us it'd be better, ye ken? They promised us aw' sorts, they promised us heaven on earth, they did. We didna expect heaven, but we thocht we'd get a job after it was o'er, like we had when it began. Jis' a job, ye ken? That's no' too much tae ask, is it? But we didna e'en get that, Catriona. An' that's why we're angry. Ye ken?'

'I understand,' she said slowly. The men had a right to that, but there had already been one strike at the docks that year and another would make no difference.

Back at the Briggait she ran upstairs to Jess's to collect Jamie for his afternoon walk. He was still sleeping when she arrived, so she sat down for a cup of tea.

'You never stop, do you?' Jess said.

'D'you think there'll be more strikes?' she blurted, her anxiety making her voice high.

Jess sat down and picked up some mending from the basket beside her chair. 'There's trouble on its way. There's thousands out of work, and there's not a decent place to be had to live in for love or money. There's been too many broken promises, ye see.'

'I know that,' Catriona said softly.

'They were promised the world, ye see. When they were fighting. An' they came back tae the same thing, but worse. No jobs, no homes, no nothin'. No' even an explanation. It's more 'n any man can take, Catriona.'

'I know, Jess.' She picked up Jamie and wrapped him in his shawl.

'I wouldna worry,' Jess said. 'We'll get by.'

'Maybe.'

Out on the green she held Jamie close to her chest and crooned a Gaelic song that he did not understand but which made him smile and tug at the strands of her hair that had escaped from the pins.

Walking amongst the trees she saw the tramps, not all old and washed out, some young and with campaign medals pinned to their rags. The tramps only rested on the green, when the streets were busy they trawled Argyle Street and George Square with their caps meekly held out for farthings.

Jamie laughed as a crow fluttered its wing, beating the air for a second before it climbed toward the sky. She held him up so that he could watch the bird soar. 'It isn't right,' she whispered into his uncomprehending ear. None of it was right, not the tramps nor the unemployment, nor all of the false promises made to the men who had fought the war. But if a dock strike began again and lasted for as long as it might, her business would not survive.

Later, as Jamie slept in his cot by the fire in Liam's kitchen in Shipbank Lane, she put on stock for soup and began to mix a batch of pastry that she would leave overnight in the pantry because her bridies and pies tasted better if they were fresh.

When she finished it was long after eight o'clock but Liam had not returned yet. There was nothing else to do; everything was ready for the next morning so she checked that the gas was off before she wrote a note to Liam to tell him there was soup in the little pan on top of the oven and a plate of mince and potatoes warming inside. As she left it on the table she noticed a copy of *The Worker*. Picking it up, she read a complicated story on the front page about a company's share dealings that the paper described as a fraud on the working man. There was nothing about any planned strikes.

Sine's letter came the next day. The postman brought it over to her in Shipbank Lane because he knew that she worked there now. Catriona tore it open anxiously and read it twice before she sat down and blinked back tears of relief:

> I didn't say anything before, Catriona, but I've been seeing a bit of Archie MacLellan. He's working as a groundsman just now, so he's got a wage and he'll get a cottage when he's wed. It's too soon for that, but we've been talking about it so I'm not sure that I want to come to Glasgow, least not yet until I'm sure about Archie and me.

Things are a bit better here. Da's working hard on the croft; the sheep he bought with the twins' money have lambed, so there'll be some money coming in apart from what you send us. Maire and Allan send their love, and so does Annie. Don't worry about us.

Sine wasn't yet fifteen. Catriona's heart ached when she thought of her little sister getting wed, but a lot of island girls courted at her age and married when they reached their sixteenth birthday.

The week passed; at the docks there was no more talk of strikes, not that she had time to listen because she was so busy serving soup and bridies.

On Friday, just after the hooter had called the men back to work, the union man drew her aside.

'Name's McGinlay,' he said, taking her hand and shaking it in a grip that crackled her fingers.

'I've been thinking, lass,' he went on, as she noticed the look on his face; there was something about him that she disliked, that made her wonder how a man like him could be voted into a union job.

'Ye make guid money here, don't ye?' He folded his arms and took a step towards her.

'I'm not doing badly,' she replied, wondering what it had to do with him.

'Well, I'm thinking, hen, since you're makin' money fra' the brothers, ye should gie a little sumthin' tae our funds. The welfare fund like, fir the brothers wha havnae work, like. Ye ken?'

'Would a shilling be enough?' Catriona asked, thinking of the men who begged on the streets for farthings.

'A shilling, a shilling?' McGinlay roared with laughter – not mirth, more like derision. 'My, hen, that's guid, that is. A shilling?' He shook his head. 'I've no heard as guid as that fir a long time, hen. A shilling?' His face hardened and his voice dropped to a growl. 'What are ye making aff the brothers? Five, ten pound a week? An' ye offer me a shilling? Nae, hen, there's nae chance o' getting awa' wi' that. A pound, I'd say, at the very least. Mak' it twa pound, an' I'll be happy wi' that.'

He was leering now, the sneer on his face the look of triumph of a man over a woman just because she was that.

Catriona flinched slightly and struggled to hold herself straight because she was nearly as tall as he was and could look him in the eye. Men like that did not, could not frighten her; she would not, must not let him.

'Do I have any choice, Mr McGinlay?'

'Choice?' The question seemed to surprise him for a minute and then his brash arrogance returned. 'Nae, hen, I doubt ye do. The brothers'd not buy a glass o' water fra' ye, not if I gied them the word.'

She thought, but could not think quickly enough. Davy had finished packing away the trays; he was sitting on the cart, ready to leave.

'I'll think about it,' she said, wanting to get away from this man and his demands.

McGinlay shook his head. 'Nae, lass. If ye dae that, ye'll find yersel' wi' out any trade on Monday.'

Catriona reached into the canvas bag she tied around her waist to carry money and counted out the coins. McGinlay checked the money quickly and put it into his pocket. 'Ye're a' richt, hen. Jist think o' it as rent.' He smiled then, seemingly unconcerned, and said goodbye just as if they'd had a pleasant chat.

Wordlessly she got into the cart as Davy flicked the reins and the horse began to lumber towards the Broomielaw.

'Is it McGinlay ye've clicked wi'?' Davy asked when they were halfway down Clyde Street. The teasing look on his face appalled her; he saw her reaction and fell quiet.

When they reached Shipbank Lane he helped her carry the trays and urns back into the kitchen.

'He wasn't troublin' ye?' he asked as she gave him the money to pay for the horse and cart.

'Who?' she asked distractedly.

'McGinlay. He's got the name of a troublemaker.'

'No,' she said quietly, 'he wasn't troubling me. It wasn't anything, Davy. It was nothing, really.'

Davy looked at her for a few moments as if he doubted what she said, but when Catriona managed to throw him a bright smile he smiled back and left.

The pattern started then, two pounds every week to McGinlay who waited for her every Friday at the slip dock until she had finished serving the men. Sometimes he helped himself to a cooling bridie if there were any left over, but he never offered to pay for it and Catriona never asked.

There was something sordid about it all that kept her awake at nights, something in the furtive way he took the money that made her wonder where it went.

It dulled her hope, took the edge off the sense of achievement she had gained briefly when she had realized that with a horse and cart and plenty of hard work, she could make money, real money, enough even for her to start dreaming again.

The money still came in, slightly less of it, but there was enough to save, enough to hope that in a year or two she would be able to buy the lease of a shop in Bridgeton or Springburn or the Gorbals with room above for her family to live in. Rents were cheaper in these places, and though it wouldn't be what she had dreamed of, it would at least be a living.

She thought of that, and prayed for the day to come when she could tell McGinlay to go to hell.

As time passed her trade got better; within a few weeks she was able to rationalize that she could afford the money she paid to McGinlay. There was some sort of sense in what he said about rent; justice of a kind that if she made money from union members she should give something to their funds.

The dockworkers were good men, their wages were low and their hours long, but even so they were prepared to take a wage cut to give work to the unemployed. In the early morning when she went to the market she saw them walking in from the suburbs because they couldn't afford the tram fare.

They waved cheerfully and she waved back; she knew them well now, some of them, especially those away from home who lived in the lodging houses so that they could earn the money they needed to keep their children fed.

They were gruff, humble, humorous men; she often wondered how a man like McGinlay came to be their leader.

She handed over the money to him in the same way that she paid the coalman, the butcher, the merchant.

He never thanked her but took the money as if it was his by right.

Only Liam noticed the change in her, the worry on her face when she thought no one was looking, the way he sensed her hope had somehow been quashed, as a budding flower dies in a late frost.

'There's something wrong,' he said, one Sunday when they were walking along the front at Ardrossan, with Jamie in her arms.

'It's nothing.'

'You're not smiling.'

She grinned determinedly. 'I am so.'

Liam studied her. 'There is something wrong,' he repeated.

'Liam, there's nothing wrong. Nothing at all.'

He looked away, found a niche from the wind behind a boarded-up kiosk and stopped to light his pipe.

'Have it your way,' he said, after a long time. 'But if you change your mind, I'm here to listen.'

At the end of one week, McGinlay did not pocket the money quickly and leave, as usual; he waited, stamping his feet, until Davy was out of earshot and then said he wanted double the money she'd been paying.

Catriona was caught short; she had not expected that.

'I've watched ye,' he said, 'ye're makin' a wee fortune wi' a' this, so ye are.'

'I'm not giving you any more money, McGinlay.'

'Ah, well, hen, we'll hae tae see abou' that.'

He waited as if she'd change her mind, just like that, but she brushed past him, got into the cart and told Davy to hurry because a rain cloud threatened and she wanted to take Jamie for a walk on the green. Once Liam had asked her why she was moody on Fridays; she'd told him she wasn't, only that it was the end of the week and she was tired.

After that, he had not asked her again, and she had made a special effort to be bright when he came in from the docks. But the secret had weighed heavily upon her, created a distance between them that she did not want to be there.

Once Davy had unloaded the wagon and she had paid him, she ran up to Jess's, feeling her mood lighten when Jamie held his chubby arms out towards her.

Thanking Jess, she picked him up and walked to the green, skipping every so often and watching the smile that spread over his face.

'I'm going to talk to Liam,' she told Jamie. 'I'm going to tell him all about McGinlay this evening when he gets home from work. That's right, isn't it? That's the right thing to do?'

Jamie gurgled and smiled, and stretched his tiny hand to the sky, where it looked as if he was trying to catch a cloud surfing the wind.

Chapter Seven

'*W*hy didn't you tell me this before?'

Catriona's attention fixed on the halibut she was cooking for Liam's supper, slowly in a pan with a little vinegar and sliced onion.

'I didn't think,' she began, 'I thought it was, well ...'

Her voice tailed off as the fish sizzled and she deftly lifted it onto a plate.

'Pity's sake, Catriona, the union doesn't go around extorting money. This is Glasgow, not New York.'

Liam ate, and she watched him with satisfaction. Once he had finished the fish, he mopped up the juices with a bit of fresh bread.

'I thought the money was for the union,' she said lamely.

'Catriona, the union doesn't collect money like that. If you'd been giving to the union it would be voluntary, and you'd get a receipt for it. The money you've paid this man McGinlay goes into his pocket and stays there.' He stood up and took his cap from the hook on the door. 'I'll get it back for you, *acushla*. Every last penny. MacLean's speaking in the Gorbals tonight, and every union man in Glasgow'll be there. I'll find out about your man McGinlay, and what he's up to ...'

'No!' she said, suddenly angry. 'Please, Liam. Let me deal with McGinlay. I won't pay him any more.'

'Catriona, a man like that, he's not the union, for sure, but he could trouble you. You're vulnerable down there, on your own.'

'I'm not on my own. Davy's with me. And the men, they're my friends.'

Liam looked at her. With her hands braced on her waist, she was proud and defiant, lithe and tall. There was a quality about her that reminded him of the way a rowan tree bends with the wind, fragile but so much stronger than the tree that defies the wind and so loses a branch or more. But even a rowan tree could break in a storm.

'I'm your friend too,' he said, watching the way she blushed. 'I'll just make sure McGinlay knows it. That's all.'

She started to speak, but he stopped her. 'I'll have to go, else I'll be late for the meeting, but I'll see you later, *acushla*. That is, unless you get someone to watch the stall and come with me instead?'

'I can't, Liam. Not on a Friday, with a new show starting.'

He touched her cheek. 'I'm glad you told me, Catriona. I've known for weeks there was something wrong. Every Friday, you went so quiet. I thought it was me, you know.'

'It wasn't you, Liam. Of course not.'

The big kitchen felt empty after he left. Catriona put her scones into the oven, and sat down to wait for them to bake.

Later, Davy Calvert came up to the coffee stall just after the show at the Britannia had started. Catriona gave him a coffee and offered him a scone, which he would not take. 'Jist passing time, ye ken; he said, 'naithin' on the nicht.'

He often came to talk to her when the stall was quiet. She knew he did not drink or go to the music halls; he saved every penny he earned but for no particular reason since the girl he had been courting during the war had gone off with someone else. Davy was too proud for his own good.

'John MacLean's speaking in the Gorbals.'

'Aye, an' he'll be saying the same's he said last week, an' the week afore that. I've had it up to here wi' the Bolshevists and thaur revolutionary Soviets, Catriona. Aw' I want is a job.'

She smiled. The government had been outraged when MacLean was appointed Honorary Consul for Russia by Lenin himself. He had spent most of the war years in jail for offences under the Defence of the Realm Act; the experience would have broken a lesser man, but he still spoke up for the workers, for the things he believed in.

'I dinna mean that like it sounded,' Davy said. 'MacLean's a guid man.'

'I've never heard him.'

'He's no' bought ony o' yer scones, ye mean.'

She laughed. 'I'd like to hear what he's got to say.'

Davy peered at the Tron clock. 'Awa' ye go, then, lass. I'll watch the stall for ye. Ye'll be back afore the show closes.'

Catriona raced along Argyle Street and then over the river to the Gorbals, arriving at the hall, winded, just after John MacLean had started to speak. The man looked like a schoolmaster, his back was slightly stooped and he wore rounded pebble glasses. He spoke in a nervous monotone, quickly so that his audience had to listen carefully or otherwise lose track.

The words drifted over Catriona, left her feeling numb despite the roars of applause that punctuated the speech.

MacLean spoke of the tyranny of capitalism and workers' solidarity; the phrase meant nothing to her until he said that only if the workers stood together could change begin, that if the workers united change would come because there was no power in the land that could challenge the working man.

The audience cheered; she looked around and saw faces hardened by experience that were radiant with hope.

Catriona thought about the Land League, about the land raids she had heard about on Raasay, Tiree and Vatersay; about the tiny crofts of The Braes on the edge of the vast emptiness of the landlords' lands.

She had heard her father speak like that, just once when she was very little, when her mother carried her out in her arms to hear him speak at a crofters' meeting. Tom hadn't spoken like that in years, he never would again unless he was drunk and talking to himself.

Yet this was the Land League moved to the lowlands; the union repeated the promises that had faded in the islands through time and despair.

She closed her eyes and saw the island men going to war, to fight not for their country but for the land, the few acres the factor had promised if they joined the army. The promise had been broken; that didn't surprise her, she had expected it. In a way, she was glad so many had died before the promise had lost its meaning; the landlords' betrayal would have broken their simple hearts.

Suddenly, she was listening to MacLean, feeling the power of his words, the power of the men in the hall. For a moment she was with the union, she believed that a time would come when the shipyards and docks would pay fair wages and give work to the men who had come home from fighting the war.

MacLean stopped talking, his voice tailing off to a hoarse whisper as men roared and cheered and clapped. He waved them to silence for a moment, thanked them for listening to him, and sat down.

The spell was broken.

Catriona remembered her own promises, first to her mother and then to her sisters and Allan. She could not forego the needs of the day for the union's vision of utopia tomorrow. Bitter for a moment, she wondered if MacLean's pledge was different to any of the others, if workers' solidarity would bring the rewards he said would come; if communism would make any difference to the average man.

She looked around the hall until she saw Liam deep in conversation with another man, and waited until he noticed her, feeling a surge of joy at his smile.

They walked out together into the cool of the evening.

'Your McGinlay wasn't there,' Liam said, not asking a question but stating a fact.

'No.'

'He was on the union committee during the war, but he was voted off last year. He's a foreman now, he's still a member but he doesn't collect for the hardship fund or anything else.'

'Liam, please don't talk about him.'

Liam gazed at her for a moment. 'Whatever you want, *acushla*. But we have a name for men like that in Ireland. A way of dealing with them as well, if it comes to that.'

'Liam . . .'

He stuffed his hands into his pockets as they walked towards the river.

'Did what MacLean said mean anything to you, Catriona?' Liam asked as they crossed the suspension bridge. Halfway over he stopped and took out his pipe and a plug of tobacco.

She smiled. 'That's the first time I've seen you smoke tobacco on a Friday, Liam Devlin.'

The river breeze blew the match out; he huddled over the box, shielding the fragile flame with the whole of his body, and tried again. This time the flame burned for long enough.

'Like I said, did it mean anything to you?'

Catriona looked down to the river, where the evening sky of rose and violet reflected in fragments on the water, the colour tender against the sludge.

'It's like there's two worlds, Liam Devlin, the world of dreams and the world that's real. In the world of dreams, I wish to God it could be the way MacLean wants it, but in the real world, I'll take the only chance I can get.'

The vivid blush of the sunset had vanished; only the faintest trace of pink grazed the horizon. A flock of starlings dusted the sky, cheeping and chattering as their wings beat the air.

'What d'you mean by that?'

Catriona inhaled deeply and then sighed. 'I mean that I won't give up today for the promise of tomorrow. My father did that. He dreamed and schemed whilst my mother fed us all by knitting socks. That's what I do, Liam. I work. I don't have the time to dream.'

She felt Mor's soul for a moment, a shift in her consciousness that told her not to forget the dream, not to stop believing, so briefly that the thought faded before it was fully formed.

'I mean,' she said again, 'sometimes it isn't so easy to dream.'

He put his arms around her and hugged her tight for a moment before he remembered himself. 'I can understand that.

'D'you know,' he said, a moment later, 'there's a man

trying to clear St Enoch's of starlings? Every night at nine he goes out with a shotgun and fires into the air and the starlings leave and then they fly back soon's he's gone.'

Catriona smiled as the tiny birds settled on a warehouse on the other side of the river. A bit away, a shot rang out and then another.

'That's him,' Liam said. 'Another minute or two and they'll fly back. Wait and see.'

For a while Liam smoked in silence. 'This dream world of yours. What would it be if you could make it real?'

'I don't know,' she replied, rubbing her arms against the chill breeze blowing up from the river.

'D'you ever think that if more men had stood like Mac-Lean, and there's thousands like him, d'you think that stupid war would've happened?'

She shivered. 'It doesn't help to think like that.'

Liam watched the first of the starlings flying back to their patch. 'There's the future, Catriona. In Ireland, we believe the future's worth fighting for. A better world's worth fighting for.'

The starlings lifted in a cloud; drifting in the breeze for a moment they hovered mid river and then swirled down again towards St Enoch's. No more shots rang out and the birdsong faded to a whisper.

Liam took her hand and she felt his strength. 'Come on,' he said. 'The show'll be over in fifteen minutes.'

Catriona watched McGinlay all week, as he watched her from a distance, always surrounded by a knot of men.

'D'you know,' she said to Davy Calvert one day, 'Mc-Ginlay's not the union man, he's just a foreman, that's all.' She was thinking about the subtle way he had tricked her into believing that he was.

'The man's a blaw, Catriona. A'bdy kens he's a nyaff.'

On Friday McGinlay came up to her as usual when the rest of the men went back to work. She sensed something different in his manner, in the way he took particular care that nobody else could overhear what was said. He drew her close, so close that she could smell the remnants of whisky on his breath. 'I've been thinking, hen, mibbe I wis a mite hasty tae ask ye fir mair money. Times is hard, efter all.'

She drew away. 'They are that, McGinlay.'

'Ah, well, a coupla quid'll dae. Nae point in fallin' oot about it.'

'We'll not be doing that, McGinlay.'

'Well then.' He held out his hand expectantly. She stared at it, then at him.

'Go to hell, McGinlay.'

He was genuinely surprised. 'Whit?'

'I said, go to hell. I'll not be giving you a farthing from this day on, and count yourself lucky that I'm not telling the union that the money I gave you never got further than McAusland's Bar.'

'Union, whit d'ye mean the union? Whit's it got tae dae wi' the union?'

She smiled. 'You've just given yourself away, McGinlay.'

His eyes narrowed for a moment before he stepped back. 'Jist watch yersel', hen.'

'I don't listen to threats,' she hissed as he turned and stomped away.

It was a warm day and the breeze cooled her face as Davy drove the cart back to Shipbank Lane. Once she had asked him if he would like to do the dock run himself, so that she would have time to bake pies to sell at the market, but he shifted on his feet, embarrassed for a moment, before he found the words to refuse her offer. 'It's kind o' ye, Catriona, and I'm richt grateful fir the chance o' wirk, but it's no' a man's job, is it?'

He had applied for a job on the railways, she knew, and had been promised work by the LNER when something came up.

Quickly, she counted out some coins and gave him a pound. He protested about his wages too, saying that she paid his too much because the rate for a full-time carter was only thirty shillings a week; a pound was too much for only a few hours.

They argued briefly before she convinced him that he was worth that at least to her.

She walked out into the bright afternoon to collect Jamie from Jess Calvert. He was wide awake and waiting for her; when she walked into the room his face broke into a smile and she felt her troubles fade away.

The green was peaceful in the afternoon; down by the river the traffic sounds faded and she could hear the rush of the wind amongst the trees. Cradling Jamie in her arms, Catriona walked to the far end of the grass where on the other side of the river Richmond Park gave an illusion of the countryside; the images of the tenements faded to be replaced by a sense of calm.

She found a seat and settled Jamie in her lap so that he could watch the crows. A passing tramp wearing a military overcoat stood mutely, cap in hand; he sensed that she could afford a farthing or two and she hated to see the gaunt traces of hunger on his face.

A year ago he had been a soldier; she reached for a penny then gave him a shilling instead, extravagant perhaps but she felt good about herself since she had tackled McGinlay.

The tramp looked at the unfamiliar coin and smiled as she waved away his thanks. 'You see,' she said to Jamie, 'things are better already.'

As she walked home she heard the happy sounds of children at play, marvelling at the way they enjoyed themselves with just a tin can and some sticks.

Maybe Liam's right, she thought, as she turned off the Briggait towards her close. Maybe if her family came they would find a sort of contentment here, as she had.

As she turned into the dark close and caught the smell again – that mixture of cats and carbolic, of urine and cooking, the wafts of stale whisky and cheap wine that seeped from Kate's on the ground floor – she gagged reflexively and cast the thought from her mind.

The close off the Briggait had been a refuge when there was nowhere else to go. In a city of slums this was the worst, a place where she could cope, just, but she could only cope alone.

She wanted better for them all, for Jamie as well.

'Catriona,' Liam said, a few days later, 'will you come home with me, *acushla*? Just for a few days, at the Fair. The docks'll be closed then, anyway.'

She thought for a moment about the propriety of going away with a man, then about the friendship Liam had given her, the ease she felt in his presence as if he was a safe harbour to rest from the storms of her life. In the months she had known him, her feelings had changed towards him, deepening from friendship to something beyond. Love, she thought sometimes, maybe this is love; she did not know much of that emotion among adults beyond the magic she had sensed between her parents.

He felt her unease and smiled softly. 'We'll take the overnight ferry, *acushla*, and drive from Belfast. Home is only a day's drive away from there.'

She was thinking of her own home, that she would much rather go there, but then the questions would come – and what on earth to do with Jamie?

'Yes,' she said, deciding. 'I'd like to do that.'

They reached Belfast on a cold grey morning; the city streets were slicked with rain. Catriona held Jamie tightly to her chest as Liam drove like a man possessed, muttering to himself, hunched over the wheel.

After the city the road travelled through towns in the fertile farmland of the north: Lisburn, Lurgan, Portadown. Union Jacks fluttered from every window, like in Glasgow when the war had been won, almost as if the war was not over yet. She said that in passing, wondering why.

Crossing into Tyrone, Liam changed when he saw the hills.

'The war isn't over yet, *acushla*. I sometimes think it never will be.'

Catriona knew little of that, little of the politics behind what the papers called the 'vexed Irish question'. The Irish had voted for Home Rule for so long, why not give it to them?

'Carson's Volunteers,' Liam said, 'they fly the flag to remind us of that. Four fifths of the country wants Home Rule and who do they listen to? The fifth that doesn't, that's who. It doesn't matter about us, it never has done. A million and a half dead in the Hunger and all the time Irish grain was being shipped to Liverpool. You don't forget that, *acushla*, not in fifty years, not in a hundred years. And you don't forget an injured man who couldn't stand, being shot as he sat in a chair because the death sentence had been passed. Stupid fools, they never knew anything about us.'

Needing petrol, he passed a garage flying the Union Jack, and drove miles down a country track until he found one that didn't fly the flag.

'The anger frightens me,' she said, as they drove deep into the hills. The anger she felt on the streets of Belfast, Liam's silent rage in response.

'It wouldn't have mattered,' Liam said quietly, 'none of it. If they hadn't shot the leaders of the Easter Rising in cold blood, if they hadn't killed so many others. But it's true what they say, that the fools left us with our Fenian dead and whilst Ireland holds these graves, Ireland unfree will never be at peace.'

Catriona heard the echo of her father then; she saw his face briefly as she reached into her bag for Jamie's bottle and held it gently to his lips.

Crossing into Donegal, she looked around, felt the thrill of land that she knew, the mountains and the glens, the rolling shadows cast by the clouds on the hills.

'Like home,' she said in a small voice, watching the pattern of the sky reflected in a lochan. She understood more of Liam now, more of the magnetism between them because he too was the product of this place of emptiness where man was secondary to the land and the sky.

Liam laughed. 'See that?' He pointed to a field of young wheat, still green but beginning to bleach in the sun. 'That's not our land, it's owned by an English Duke. When they came they took the best of the land and drove us away from it. We had all of Ireland, once upon a time. Now, we only have the edges.'

Going through a village, Catriona saw the little houses squashed together, potato patches in dry soil, cows grazing on the bald land beside the road.

'On Skye, it's the same. My father . . .' She paused then as she remembered him in her childhood when his rapturous monologues painted a picture of another world, just within reach, in which the land in all its magnificence was theirs again. 'My father,' she continued, 'was a Land Leaguer in the old days, before the Crofters Act.'

'What happened?'

She looked out of the car window and thought for a long time before she answered. 'He says the crofts are a prison without walls, that they settled too soon for something they already had, they didn't realize until later they had been tricked.'

In the late evening, when after sunset the hills softened to the texture of velvet, they reached Liam's village on the coast of Donegal.

Liam turned onto a rough track beside a sparse field in which a solitary cow grazed. 'This is Patsy Devlin's farm, *acushla*, the heritage I bought from William Ellis for the sum of five pounds an acre and the good grace of His Majesty's Irish Land Act.'

At the end of the track the cottage door opened and a tiny woman began to shoo away the hens. 'Liam,' she said, as he bent to hug her. 'And you must be Catriona,' as Catriona stood shyly at his side.

'You'll have to forgive my English,' she said as she stood aside to let Catriona into the cottage, 'heathen bloody tongue that it is, I only spoke it to pay the rent and I haven't done that for fifteen years, thanks to Liam.'

The cottage was warm and smelled of cooking; as soon as Liam and Catriona sat down his mother served them big plates of stew, potatoes and cabbage, with thick slices of soda bread.

'Catriona has the Gaelic,' Liam said, 'it's hers too, except they speak it different up there.'

Catriona saw the pictures lining the mantelpiece, strong

men who looked like Liam waving gaily at a quayside somewhere.

'That's Sean and Francis,' Liam said, 'in New York.'

'I've five sons in America,' his mother said, 'an' two
daughters; more of the family's there than here.'

'Where are the others?' Liam asked.

She looked away. 'Cal and young Patsy's on the run,
Liam. Only Deirdre and Eithne's here but they're away to
the church because the Father's having a prayer week. But
tell me about you, lass,' she said, turning to Catriona. 'I've
waited half his lifetime for this one to bring a woman home.
I'd just about given up hope when he wrote me about you.'

Catriona blushed, tried to say something, then found
herself talking easily to Liam's mother because of the kindness
that shone from her eyes.

'My name's Theresa, lass,' she said, 'but you must call me
Terry because everybody does.'

Deirdre and Eithne came in later. Old maids they were,
though just in their thirties; they wore long skirts, starched
blouses and little hats balanced uncertainly on top of tightly
pinned hair.

'Protestant, are you?' Deirdre asked Catriona immediately.

'She could almost be one of us with these eyes,' Eithne
said, as if she wasn't there.

'You've a child,' Deirdre went on. 'Are you a widow?'

Liam stood up, anger on his face.

'It's my sister's son,' Catriona said calmly.

'You two,' Terry said, 'there's tea on the hob if you want
to sit down and talk like civilized people. If not, take the
pair of you off to bed and leave us be.'

Deirdre yawned, an exaggerated gesture that seemed to
echo in the small room, then took off her coat and climbed
the ladder to the loft. Eithne followed her. 'Liam,' she
called, from the top of the ladder, 'you've to meet the Grady
tomorrow at noon. He said you'd know where.'

Terry shook her head. 'I'm sorry, lass, don't mind them.
It's a lot of nonsense they talk; because they've not wed

themselves, they don't want anyone else to. Don't worry about them.'

Liam took her out into the morning as the rising sun silvered the crests of the ocean waves that crashed against the shore. 'I wanted you to see this place,' he said, gesturing over the land and the sea. 'I wanted you to know who I am.'

'I already did,' Catriona said softly.

'When the war's over, will you marry me? Will you come home with me and make this land our own?'

The question took her by surprise.

She thought of Allan, Sine and Maire, her family far away and knowing nothing of this, of the promise she had made to them that could fade in the wind. And then there was Liam's war, Liam's secret war; she knew little of it but she heard far more in the silence than from anything he ever said.

Yet she was drawn to him, so strongly; in that moment as he stood on the beach with the breeze ruffling his hair she began to love him, began to want to fold him into her arms and never let him go.

'I know,' he said. 'Your sisters and brother can come. There's a school for them, and once we've won the war there'll be plenty of land. I'll provide for them. You know I will.'

'Yes,' she said, not thinking for once beyond the moment, not thinking at all but rather feeling the call of the land again, the call of the land and this man who wanted to give her a home. She loved him then, felt the purity of an emotion that was as warm as the sun and strong as the sea.

Liam took something from his pocket and she saw a ring of old gold that was twisted and coiled into the images of her race.

'You will wear this for me,' he said, 'it's Irish gold, as old as time; all there is of the Devlins as they once were.'

As he slipped it onto her finger, she felt a slight looseness and realized that it did not quite fit.

'God willing,' she whispered, feeling strange that she

thought of God in this place, then remembering the God of the islands, the power that you could feel in the sea and the hills.

Later, when Liam went to meet the Grady, she helped Terry to lift the early potatoes.

'You'll watch out for Liam,' Terry said, when they reached the end of the row and stood for a moment to ease the ricks from their backs.

'I will, if I can.'

Terry looked over the hills, shading her eyes against the harsh sun. 'Liam did well in America, he'd've been a rich man if he'd stayed, but I asked him to come back, see? To take care of his brothers. Now, God knows, he's mixed up in it too, but you'll watch him, won't you, Catriona?'

'I'll try,' she said, 'but I don't know ... I don't know anything about that.'

'None of us do.' Terry smiled. 'All we can do is wait and hope and pray. They say the time is coming, and maybe they're right, but it's something for Ireland, isn't it? Dail Eirean sitting in Dublin, and half the members sitting in gaol.'

Catriona turned suddenly and saw Deirdre and Eithne watching from the shade of the barn, silent but rapt in their scrutiny.

Just once, when they were back in Glasgow, Catriona asked Liam why his mother worried so.

'There's nothing to worry about,' he told her. 'As God's my judge, I've never handled a gun. I never shall because it will be all over soon.'

The newspapers told another story, but Catriona rarely read them these days. Her business was doing well and her savings were growing; in another year or so she would have enough to buy the lease of a shop. Liam smiled when she told him that, and said that by then they would be already wed and living in a little cottage in Donegal; Catriona tried to suppress the foreboding that it would not happen.

In the time that they had known each other they had

never danced together, never been to the theatre or the music hall or courted as other couples did. Catriona had her work and her family, Liam his gangs of labourers at the docks, and when he disappeared for a day or two her instincts told her not to ask him why or where.

The months passed and they grew closer; they never touched beyond holding hands, but sometimes that alone set off a longing in Catriona which made her shudder with its intensity. Sometimes, in the evenings when they sat by his kitchen fire, she hoped the future would bring its own solutions, that the time would soon come when they would be wed.

In December, a few days before Christmas, she came back from the docks and found Liam packing a bag.

'It's Patsy,' he said, as she saw that he had been weeping. 'He's been killed by the Tans.'

She went to him and put her arms around him.

'I'm getting the night boat. I have to go.'

'I'll come with you?'

'No,' he said. 'You can't.'

She felt the longing surge. 'Liam?'

He kissed her then, a long, slow embrace that took her breath away. 'Catriona ... '

'Liam, I love you.'

She had never said that before.

In that moment she needed him, suddenly, as she had never needed him before.

She felt her hands, unbidden, taking off her coat, damp with rain, then unbuttoning her blouse. Her hair sprang out of the pins and tumbled down her back.

Their eyes met; he bent and softly kissed her forehead, then he picked her up and carried her upstairs to the room where he slept, where she had never been before. There was a bed, unmade, an old traveller's chest with shipping labels stuck to it, a gas lamp and nothing else.

She didn't know what she was doing; she had no knowledge, only the instinct that she wanted him.

Dimly, she perceived Liam shrugging off his clothes and

then helping her out of her underclothes, his touch so gentle that it felt like a breeze. His skin against hers was warm, his chest covered with soft downy hairs like a baby's scalp. He kissed her forehead, her eyelids, the tip of her nose, and then looked at her.

'I need you,' she murmured.

His breathing changed, she felt his heart beat under his chest; his hand on her breast made shivers rise that quivered to the roots of her soul. She felt herself moisten and open to him; as the fleeting agony surged then faded, she moaned and then cried softly as he moved inside her.

In that moment, she felt that she was his now, always; the decision was made and the doubts were gone.

The aftermath brought her a sense of destiny fulfilled; she had wanted so much to love him, whatever the world threw in her way, now she had loved him as she promised she would.

'*Acushla*,' he said, 'we'll wed now, soon's I get back. We'll not wait any longer.'

'Yes,' she said, 'of course.'

After he left she took Jamie's crib to Liam's room and then slept herself, comforted by the scent of his sweat on the sheets.

Two days later she felt the crack of his death. She was standing at the slip dock taking money for a bridie; the coins fell to the ground and clattered.

'Ye a' richt, lass?' The man bent over to pick them up and handed them to her. He came from Lenzie and stayed in a lodging house during the week; she knew him well because he often took an extra pie for his tea and sometimes she gave him a bag of scones if there were any left over from the coffee stall.

Catriona swayed briefly and then got her balance back. 'I'm fine,' she said, smiling, hoping that he would not ask any more questions, that he and the rest of them would go away.

Far above, the winter sky was angry; she looked up and saw dark grey, felt the first touch of rain.

In the evening a man came to her, a man she vaguely recognized as one of Liam's labourers.

'I know,' she said, taking her coat. 'But can I come to his funeral, please? Would you mind?'

'Course not,' he said, 'Mother of God, the man loved you. We all knew that. Terry said to tell you to come, she sent the telegram to me so's you wouldn't hurt too much.'

She drifted through the journey on a cloud of pain, not feeling the gale on the sea, nor the hailstones that fell on the streets of Belfast. Jamie was with Jess because he was too young for death; she felt the emptiness in her arms where he should have been.

The mountains of Donegal were brushed with snow. Liam's body was laid out in the front room of the cottage; she looked at him, reached out to brush a stray hair from his brow and felt the coldness of death.

'Come home, Catriona,' Terry Devlin said, 'come home to us.'

Catriona sat down by the fire, and soon fell asleep without even realizing that she was tired.

In the morning Liam's brother Cal led the coffin bearers; the whole village followed the funeral into the tiny church where the Requiem Mass was said in a language that Catriona did not understand.

As Liam was buried she took the gold ring from her finger and threw it into his grave.

'Why?' she asked later, when the cottage was full of people.

'Only God knows,' Terry said. Nobody knew why, only how. It was the Tans, they said, the same soldiers who had killed Patsy a week before killed Liam. The Grady had been there too but he had escaped into the hills.

Cal came back and dared the patrols to arrest him, but they were gone now because they had inflicted enough grief on the village for a while.

'We'll take care of you,' Terry said, 'bring the wee one back and we'll take care of you.'

'No,' Catriona said gently. That was what Liam had

given her, after all. In his love, she had found the strength to care for herself.

The grief numbed her at first; she was too hurt to cry. The tears came when she got back to Glasgow and found that Jess and Kate had made her bridies and Davy had kept the business going.

There was nothing else to do but work.

The men at the docks sensed that she had lost someone, and were kind in the way they did not ask questions.

Only McGinlay stood out, a sneer on his face as he slouched at the back of the line of men, eating a sandwich. Catriona ignored him for as long as she could, but could not avoid passing him as she carried the trays back to the cart.

'Ye'll not be so cocky now that yer Fenian friend's where he belongs,' he said, so quietly that only she could hear.

Catriona froze.

'Lonely, ye'll be, am I no' right?'

She faced him. 'I don't know what you want, McGinlay, but whatever it is, don't bother me.'

'I'm not botherin' ye, jes' expressin' my condolences, that's aw'.' He laughed then, proud of his humour.

Catriona lifted her foot and brought the tip of her heel down very hard on his instep. In a flash, she had noticed that he did not wear tough workman's boots, but soft leather ones.

'Jeezus God,' he swore, hoping up and down on the other foot. 'Christ, ye've crippled me.'

The other men turned and stared.

'If I have, it's not before time.'

She turned on her heel and left him there, thanking fate for the bitter wind that dried her tears before they stained her skin.

The policemen came to Shipbank Lane that evening, when she was in Liam's kitchen preparing food for the next day. One wore uniform and one did not; tiredly, she asked them what they wanted.

'Miss Nicolson, your friend, Mr Devlin. We'd like to ask you some questions about him.'

Through habit, she offered them tea.

'What do you want to know?'

They looked at each other, their faces blank. She put a plate of scones onto the table, then sat down with them. They said nothing as they drank their tea.

'You were close to Devlin, weren't you, Miss Nicolson?'

'I was . . . I would have married him. That's all.'

'You must have known him well.'

'Liam Devlin was a good man,' she said slowly.

'He was an IRA man, Miss Nicolson. Do you know how many of our soldiers have been killed in Ireland this year?'

'Would you like some more tea?' she asked, lifting the pot to pour.

'Devlin supplied explosives,' the older policeman said.

Catriona's hand on the handle of the teapot faltered, spilling tea into his saucer.

'They use dynamite at the docks, you know,' he continued. 'Devlin had enough of it to blast the whole of the Clyde basin and all he moved was a few feet of rock.'

'If you knew that, why didn't you arrest him?'

Their eyes met for a moment; his were the first to turn away.

'Did you know, Miss Nicolson?' the other one asked.

She thought for a long time before she responded with just the merest shake of her head. From the counter she got a clean cup which she filled with tea, watching the policeman's lips as he drank.

'We'd like you to help us,' he said, when he had finished.

She shivered inwardly, hoped that her tremor did not show. 'How could I do that?'

The younger one smiled. 'There's Scots boys being killed in Ireland. Plenty of our lads are over there.'

Catriona said nothing.

'Tell us what you know about Devlin,' the other one said. 'All that you know.'

She thought for a moment. 'I'll tell you all I know about Liam Devlin. He came over here twenty years ago, and he was a carter's lad. He earned a few pennies a week, which he sent home, because the family farm isn't a farm so much as a heap of stones.'

'We know that,' the inspector said, 'we know all about that.'

'Let me finish,' Catriona said. 'He did well, because he's clever. I don't know how he started, I've only known ... I only knew him for a year or so. But he kept his family and he bought his father's farm. I met him when I started a coffee stall outside the Britannia Theatre. He helped me then. When my sister left me with her baby, he gave me his kitchen so that I could start my business. He used to take me out to the country. When I was ... when I ...' She paused then, trying to find the words to tell them about McGinlay.

'Go on,' the inspector said.

'When I ... I started selling pies and bridies at the dockyards, one of the men, I thought he was a union man, he was bullying me. I didn't know what to do. Liam helped me then.'

'What did he do?'

'Nothing.' She brushed the hair from her eyes. 'He made me realize that I was being wrongfully treated, that was all. He gave me ...'

'What did he give you?'

'He gave me strength. He was a good man. He loved his country, he loved his family and he loved me. That's all I know. He told me once ...'

'What did he tell you?'

She had been going to tell them how he had said he had never held a gun. 'That when the war was over, we'd go back to Ireland, that's all. He believed in democracy, you see. He believed in democracy and in justice and in his people as well.' She stopped when she realized that she was shouting; that as she mourned Liam's death she had also taken on some of his rage.

The silence echoed then. The policemen looked at each other and shrugged.

She thought of Liam, feeling a rush of fury at his death. He had been trapped, she knew that now, stalked like a deer until he was run to ground in a place where he could not hide. She did not know if he had stolen explosives; it did not matter now whether he had or had not.

She lifted her head and faced them.

The policemen rose to leave.

'Remember,' the younger one said at the door. 'It's our boys over there. It's Scots boys who're being killed.'

She shook her head at the senselessness of it all.

'If only you'd cared as much about the men who were killed in France ...'

When they were gone she waited for a minute and then locked the kitchen and went to the market to see Donoghue. He was closing his stall; when he saw her he nodded and led her over to a quiet corner.

'The police've been round,' she said, her teeth chattering.

'I know, lass. I saw them.'

'Donoghue, I ...'

'Lass, if you want my advice, don't talk tae them, an' don't talk tae anybody else, either.'

'I didn't, Donoghue. They wanted to know about the explosives. They think Liam was stealing explosives.'

He cut her off then, with a look as cold as ice. 'God's sake, Catriona, ye'll have us both in gaol. Don't talk about it, not a bluidy word, d'ye hear? Jist forgit a' about it, whatever it is.'

Catriona shivered.

'It's no' our war, lass. Best no' tae tak' sides.'

The letter came the following morning.

'Dear Miss Nicolson,' it read. 'As our brother's heirs, we wish to sell the premises at Shipbank Lane and so we would be obliged if you could vacate them at your earliest convenience.'

She saw Dierdre's signature and wondered what Terry would say if she knew.

The letter meant nothing to her and so she tore it into fragments and tossed them into the fire, watching the brief puff of smoke as the paper flared and then turned to dust.

It was two days before Christmas; the new decade would bring better times.

Chapter Eight

*I*n the dead of winter, when frost made the pavements treacherous, night fell in mid-afternoon, turning the Briggait into a strange sort of hinterland lit by the weak glow of gas lamps. In the shadows ragged men leant against walls and spat their despair onto the pavement in strands of phlegm that made dark streaks against the stone. Catriona walked along quickly, purposefully, trying to overcome her creeping sense of hopelessness.

The lights were on in Shipbank Lane; through the window she could see Eithne showing a man in a bowler hat how the boiler worked. Deirdre was standing with her arms folded across her chest looking pleased with herself.

Catriona knocked on the door. Deirdre opened it and looked at her as if she resented her even breathing. 'What do you want?' she asked sharply.

'I came to collect the things I left in the kitchen.'

Deirdre stared at her for a minute. 'You'll have to wait. We're busy with the buyer.' The door slammed shut and Catriona stood in the lane, her teeth chattering with cold. Liam's face swam before her eyes: *'They're bitter old maids, Catriona, jealous bitches the pair of them. I'd not even give them the time of day, if they weren't my sisters'.*

Oh, God, Liam, she asked herself, why did you have to die?

Far along the lane she saw Donoghue standing warming his hands at the brazier outside the market. He looked in her direction and she shrank back into the shadows; he'd only ask her what was the matter and she did not want to tell him yet. He was kind, for all his gruffness; he had let her set up her stall beside his own in the market and he did not charge her any more rent than a couple of cups of tea. He would be angry at what Deirdre and Eithne were doing; he would know, as well as she did, that Liam would not have wanted that.

Something about her sadness made her want to be alone, to be able to feel the hurt in peace. There was no one who could fill the gap that Liam had left; nobody so gentle, who knew her so well. There had been poetry in Liam's soul that had been deeper than his anger; she had wanted to tell the policemen that but the words would not come and she knew too that even if she had found them they would not have listened.

The door opened, a thrusting sound that startled her into the realization that she had been crying. The buyer stood there telling Deirdre that he would pick up the keys in the morning, once they had handed the deeds to his solicitor who would give them a bank draft for the purchase price.

Catriona stood aside to let him pass.

'You'd best come in,' Deirdre said.

Catriona walked into the familiar room, strangely cold now that the fire was unlit and the ovens empty. In a pile on a chair she saw some old copies of *The Worker* and the cloth cap that Liam always wore when he went to work.

'Please,' she asked hesitantly, 'could I have that?'

Deirdre looked at Eithne, who shrugged. 'I suppose. It'll just get cleared out otherwise.'

Catriona picked up the cap, folded it and put it into her pocket. Working quickly, she stacked her trays and utensils into an empty flour sack. In the larder there was still a sack half full of flour and a couple of pounds of butter, some lentils and dried peas. She picked up the flour and butter but left everything else.

'That's all,' she said.

Eithne was already holding the door open. 'Goodbye, then.'

'Good riddance,' Deirdre spat.

Catriona turned round. 'I loved him, you know.'

Deirdre shrugged. 'You used him. Everyone did.'

'Maybe you,' Catriona said quietly, 'not me.'

Sleet fell outside, blurred against the night; as she walked home she felt the wind quicken and the sleet turn into snow.

The close seemed empty because the children were indoors having their tea; as she walked in Kate was talking to the landlady, her voice rising in anger. 'I tell you, you can't put the rents up again.'

'I kin dae what I bluidy like. Ye can pay easy, ye an' yer men. That's no' a house ye keep, it's a bloody pub.'

Catriona slipped past, too tired for an argument. She knew that the city was talking about pulling down the building; the health inspectors had already been and condemned it as unfit. Maloney had told her that MacKenzie was advising the corporation on the price they should pay for the land. She worried about that until she reasoned that if the corporation bought the building for redevelopment, they would have to rehouse the tenants.

Jess was sitting by the fire, singing a lullaby to Jamie, who had fallen asleep in her arms. Very gently she rose and put him in his cot, telling Catriona in a whisper to take off her wet clothes else she'd catch her death.

'The landlady's talking about putting the rent up,' Catriona said very quietly.

'So I've heard,' Jess replied, 'but Jack'll be up Rutherglen depot soon, an' we're out of here, please God.'

Catriona walked up to her room, grateful that Jamie still slept. Once she had settled him in his cot, she sat at the table and began to work out how many bridies she could make in her oven, baking in batches. If she kept going at the slip dock and gave up the other side of the river she could manage, she thought, until the spring, until she found a place she could afford.

Kate's voice rose from the stairwell and Jess's in reply; the close wouldn't be the same if Jess left. Jamie stirred; she picked him up, whispering words of comfort.

Jess's soft voice cut into her own from the door. 'Don't worry, me an' Kate were thinking. We'll bake bridies fir ye till ye git anither place.'

Catriona's face flushed. 'Thank you,' she murmured, 'thank you so much.'

'Dinna e'en mention it,' Jess said. 'We've tae cook a meal onyway, so it's no bother at all.'

Davy Calvert got his job on the railway; he was so proud of his LNER uniform that he wore it when he came to the coffee stall to say he couldn't take her down to the docks any more. She told him not to worry, because without Liam's kitchen she would no longer make soup and could manage easily by herself.

Each morning she took a gross or so of pies and bridies down to the slip dock on the tram. In the afternoon she bought the *Evening News* as soon as it came out, looking for a kitchen to rent, or a shop somewhere; she had written to every factor who had property in the city centre, but the rents were always too high. In the bank she had more than £100; she added a pound or two each week, but it was not enough and she did not know when it would be. Late at night, as Jamie slept, she lay awake and worried. Allan's chest was always bad in the winter and she sent Annie money for the doctor and plenty of warm vests.

Two months after Liam died she woke early one morning after a fractured sleep, and realized that her breasts were tender and that she had not bled. Touching her stomach, she felt a gentle mound; tears came to her eyes.

She went to Dr Jack's office on the Trongate. 'I'm pregnant,' she told him.

He knew that she was not married, but said nothing, just asked her how long.

'Ten weeks,' she replied. She knew to the day, to the hour, to the minute almost.

'It's early yet,' he said, 'but to make sure, I'd best examine you.'

'Examine me?'

He smiled gently. 'I need to check your womb, to make sure that everything is fine. But I'm sure it will be.'

She felt embarrassed, blushed and looked away. No man had ever touched her there, only Liam.

'I've examined hundreds of women, Catriona. We doctors do it every day, but if you'd rather see a woman, you could go to the child health clinic in the Gallowgate and see Dr Logan. I'll write you a note, and you can go to see her now.'

Catriona went to the clinic and waited, and then took her clothes off and lay terribly prone on a couch as the young lady doctor examined her internally and then felt her breasts.

'I'll write you a note,' Dr Logan said when she had finished and Catriona was dressing. 'Dr Jack will still be at his surgery, if you hurry.'

Dr Jack was leaving as she arrived, but when he saw her he took her back inside.

'Now, let me see,' he said, as he opened the note and read it. 'Why was it you thought you were pregnant?'

'I . . . I haven't bled, since . . .'

He got up and asked the receptionist to make a pot of tea, complaining about the way that the trams rattled his windows until the woman came in with a tray. He poured the tea himself, waiting for Catriona to drink hers before he spoke again.

'I'm sorry,' he said, slowly, 'usually, for someone in your position, I would say this is good news, but for you I guess it isn't.'

'What isn't?' she asked. Since she had realized that she was pregnant, she had been in a comfortable daze; Liam was dead, but a little of him had survived. The future had lost its portent, for some reason that she could not understand.

'You aren't pregnant.'

'*What?*'

'You aren't pregnant. If you were, Dr Logan would have felt it from the shape of your womb, but you aren't carrying a child. I must confess, I didn't think you were, because I've got an instinct for these things, but I had to get you examined in case there was a growth or something.'

Catriona wept bitterly then. Dr Jack patted her hand and waited until the tears finally slowed, then he handed her a hankerchief and another cup of tea.

'I don't know you very well, although I met your sister,'

he said. 'She told me a little about you. Why don't you tell me some more?'

The question surprised her. She thought for a moment. 'There's not much to tell, really.'

'I'm sure there is. You come from Skye, don't you? Why don't you tell me about that?'

Very slowly, she found herself telling him the story of her life and it sounded so sad as she repeated it all that she found herself crying again.

Outside, night fell and icy rain played a drumbeat on the windows, the noise outside dying as the shops closed and people went home.

'I must go,' she said as she heard the Tron clock strike seven. 'You must be busy.'

He smiled. 'I've always got time to listen.'

The silence that followed made her think.

'What are you going to do now?' he asked, after a time.

'Now?'

'After you leave here.'

She thought a little more, and told him that she would go home and tell Jamie his bedtime story, then rinse his clothes and her blouse, make herself ready for bed and sleep, she hoped. Tomorrow she would rise early and see to the baby, then start making bridies for the dinnertime trade. And worry about the future and the feeling of emptiness deep inside her in the space where Liam's baby should have been.

'You see a lot of life as a doctor,' he said, 'and a lot of death too. I remember thirty years ago, in the old Trongate, typhoid would strike and take all of a mother's children. It shouldn't've happened, of course, if they'd been healthy, well fed to begin with, they could survive an infection like that. But if they were healthy and clean they wouldn't've had the disease in the first place. Sometimes a mother or a father would ask me why. I never knew.' He shrugged helplessly and she saw the distant look of pain in his eyes.

'It must feel to you as if everyone you've ever loved has died. That's why you wanted a baby; you needed to have something left. It's the hardest thing in the world to do, to mourn the dead; don't ask me how because it's not something I've ever done. I've only watched others. My own family's rudely healthy, all of them. All I can tell you is to let yourself mourn, let yourself feel grief, anger, sadness, all of these things. If you mourn, then you will heal, but let the dead die; don't keep them alive with regrets or thoughts of what might have been. Will you try to do that, Catriona?'

Slowly, she said that she would.

He put the papers on his desk in a drawer, got up and extinguished the gas light before he opened the door for her. 'Come to see me again if you need to. I'm here all the time. And try not to look too far into the future, just take each day as it comes and let the future take care of itself.'

Two days later she was sitting at home, sewing a smock for Jamie, when she heard heavy footsteps on the stairs and a knock at the door.

A man stood there in an apron and boots. She thought he was deadly pale at first until she saw that a film of flour covered him from head to foot.

'Are ye the wee lass who does the bridies?' he asked.

She said that she was.

'I'm Jimmy Grieves, the baker fra' the lane, two doors down fra' Devlin's place,' he said.

She asked him in and gave him her chair as she put a kettle on for tea.

'I hope ye dinna think I'm taking liberties,' he said, 'but I heard thae two put ye out, and I was thinking, ma bread ovens, I put the dough on to prove at nicht an' I'm finished the baking by six in the morn, ye could use the ovens acos they're warm a' morning and naebdy uses them.'

'I'd pay you rent,' she said quickly, anxious to grab the chance before he changed his mind.

'The Devil ye will. I only do bread an' rolls, but I could do wi' someone to make bridies and pies. If ye could make them, I could sell them. Ye could get a barra boy tae tak them down the docks wi' you. I saw ye the morn, wi' thae big baskets on the tram.'

It had been a struggle to make the bridies in batches and then get them to the docks; by the time she arrived they were cold and though nobody complained she knew that the men missed their hot pies.

'What d'ye say, lass?'

'Yes,' she said quickly. 'I make the pastry in the afternoon and mix the filling; they only take half an hour to bake in the morning but they're better if they're hot.'

'And can ye do me a gross a day, till we see how they go? I'll charge thruppence, a penny fir me and tuppence fir ye. Is that fair?'

'It's more than fair.'

'See an' it's a bluidy sin, the rents they're charging. An' ye ken thae two put ye out fir a Jewish rag merchant? I've naithing agin' ony man, but I mind a time when we helped oursel'.'

At first Catriona was still in too much of a daze to realize that her trade had been saved, made better even. She saw that at the end of the second week when she counted her money and found she had made a little more than when she had Liam's kitchen.

Her life regained its routine. In the afternoon the grocer's and butcher's cart delivered to Jimmy Grieves's bakery and she made pastry and the fillings for baking the following morning when the bakehouse was rich with the smell of freshly baked bread. She went to the pitch outside St Enoch's station where the barrow lads plied their trade and hired one called Titch McKillop, a boy of about fourteen, of small wiry build with a thatch of red hair, who made his way about the streets of Glasgow using his barrow as a scythe to cut a path through the traffic. Titch came to the bakery at eleven and set off down Clyde Street whooping and yelling, cursing anyone who got in his way. He was famous amongst the barrow lads for having knocked down a policeman at Jamaica Street, and escaping across the bridge to the other side of the Clyde before the policeman could get on his feet again and give chase.

Just before twelve she met Titch at the slip dock; the

bridies and pies were still warm because she wrapped them in paper and then sawdust to keep the heat in.

Titch's quick wit made her smile, even laugh sometimes though it was not easy because the pain was still very raw. As he saw her crossing the street he would clamber on to one of the capstans and roar, 'World's greatest hot pies, only fourpence; hot bridies, sixpence', keeping up the yells until the barrow was empty. He took it as a personal insult if just one pie remained when the hooter went for the end of the dinner break.

As each day passed she felt that she had healed a little, that even if the hurt never left her, in time it would at least fade.

Catriona did not go to see Dr Jack again, but one day when she saw him on his rounds she stopped and thanked him; he told her that it was nothing and wished her good luck.

One Sunday at the beginning of March, when the wind was blowing a gale down Shipbank Lane, scattering rags and tearing bunting from the stalls, Donoghue caught her early as she was putting water on for the tea stall.

'See, Catriona,' he said, 'you look like a bloody ghost. Awa' you an' take the wee lad down the coast for the day.'

She looked at him as if he was mad, because nobody went down the coast until the spring.

'Awa an' see my cousin Aggie,' he said, putting his hand into his pocket and giving her some coins. 'There'll be naebdy in the market today. Wi' this wind, they don't need to buy stuff, they just need to wait for the wind to blow it off the stalls and catch it at the bottom of the lane. See?'

He took off, swearing, after a small boy who had run away with a pair of pyjama bottoms, gripping him by the neck just as he rounded the corner into Jail Square. Donoghue got the pyjama bottoms back, but the boy slipped out of his grasp and fled, calling him names.

He returned, winded. 'See what I mean? Come on, lass, away ye go. I've got a couple of things for Aggie that you can take. It would cost as much to post them.'

Catriona handed the money back to him. 'I can manage, Donoghue.'

'It's up to yersel', Catriona, but take a couple of bob anyway, to pay for yer tea.'

On the train she found a seat by the window in an empty compartment and sat down, holding Jamie on her knee.

The whistle blew as the train eased out of the station, the cranking of the wheels slow until they were across the river when the engine note changed and the houses by the track flew past in a blur. As the country unfolded, she saw the rich green of new grass, some early lambs in a field, crows picking at a freshly planted wheatfield. The harsh aura of the city in winter receded; she felt herself lighten as if a weight had been lifted.

She held Jamie up to the window and showed him grazing cows and the stripes made on raw earth by the plough. He was fifteen months old now, just beginning to talk. He called Catriona 'Trilly' and Jess 'Ess'. Catriona remembered Allan calling her mother and was glad for a while that Jamie did not, until she realized that he did not know what a mother was.

He laughed in the way that babies do when they see something new; she let him stand on her lap and make patterns in the condensation on the window.

With a sudden start, she realized that nearly a year had passed since Ailish had left, and she had heard nothing of her, nothing at all. Sometimes, at night, she felt a pang of worry that changed to anger as she remembered what her sister had done.

The train swayed around a corner; Jamie slipped and fell back into her lap and she caught him, laughing his look of astonishment.

Largs took her by surprise when the train pulled into the station. So early in the year, without any visitors or hawkers on the seafront, the town was forlorn in the grey light of morning, slapped by surging spray from the steely sea. She walked along the promenade, tasting the salt of the sea, feeling the wind buffeting her face. The parcel Donoghue had given her was not heavy, but it was cumbersome, so she crossed the road and waited for quite a few minutes before she found a passer-by who pointed out the street where Donoghue's cousin Aggie lived. Walking past the cafes and the ice-cream shops, boarded up for the winter, she felt like a trespasser on the stage of a play that had closed.

The street where Donoghue's cousin lived was full of little souvenir shops and dress shops at the beginning, then a grocer's, a butcher's and a hardware store crowded together to mark the place where the holiday trade ended and normality began. Further on, she walked past a row of houses and then paused to read the address on the parcel. Turning back, she found a little shop with windows so dusty that she couldn't see what it was, beyond a Closed sign that hung dispiritedly at an angle behind the door.

There was no bell. She knocked gently on the glass, harder when she realized that the sound was almost drowned by the wind.

After an age, she saw a glimmer of light and heard the rustle of keys, and then the door opened and a little old lady peered at her through pebble-thick glasses.

'Can you not see I'm closed,' she began, before she saw the parcel in Catriona's hand. 'Did that scallywag send you all that way on a day like this? Come in, lass. You must be Catriona. He wrote me about you.'

Catriona walked through the shop, past tables topped by upended chairs and a counter rimmed with dust, then up a set of steep stairs behind Aggie, who paused and rubbed her hips at the top. 'I'm too stiff with the rheumatisy to do this much longer,' she said, opening the door on a living room made stuffy by a huge, roaring fire. 'Well,' she continued, taking the parcel and cutting the paper open with a pair of scissors, 'let's see what the glaikit laddie's sent me this time.'

She fumbled with the contents and then held up a pair of thick ecru lace curtains. 'No' bad I suppose, but awfy hard to keep clean. But d'ye no' think yon would be better as a tablecloth, lass? I can't get round to this new thing of hanging lace up on my windows.'

Catriona shifted Jamie from one arm to the other; he was tired after the journey and beginning to fall asleep.

'Och, lass, what am I thinking of? Put the wee lad down on the sofa and take yourself a seat while I put the kettle on. You'll take a bite of lunch? Will the wain take a wee drop soup or would she like some custard? Is it a lad or a lass?'

'He's a boy,' Catriona said, as she settled Jamie on a cushion. 'He's tired; I think it must be the fresh air.'

'The air's great down here,' Aggie shouted from the kitchen. 'I don't know how you manage in the city, so I don't. I keep telling Donoghue to retire for the sake of his health, but he'll not hear of it. He says he'll be a rich man one day, but I said, aye, he'll be rich when the Kaiser's been canonized. Some chance!'

Catriona heard the sounds of a meal being prepared; pots simmering, plates rattling and a muffled curse when something dropped on the floor. 'Can I help you?' she asked, walking to the kitchen door.

'Ach, it's no' right, wi' you being the guest, but if you could pour the soup whilst I set the table. I've got rheumatisy every place, even my hands. I can manage to set the table, but I'm not so good with holding pots.'

Catriona poured the soup and carried the bowls through. Aggie talked on about everything as she ate and then some more as she fed Jamie the egg custard she had made. 'Will the wee lad take a bit rice pudding? An' jam? I've a bit put by that I had for my supper yesterday.'

Catriona smiled and watched the old woman's pleasure as Jamie made his way through a plate of rice pudding and jam, smacking his lips when he had finished. Afterwards, they drank a cup of tea as Aggie told stories about Donoghue in the old days, when she was young and he just a boy playing hookey from the village school.

'I'd best be getting back,' Catriona said when Aggie paused briefly to pour more tea.

'What, already? But you've no' even seen the place yet.' Aggie got up and went over to a chest of drawers, flicking through a pile of letters until she found the right one.

'Donoghue said that you've a tea stall, and he thought maybe you'd take this place off me. He wrote just last week and said he'd send you down as soon as he could.'

Catriona felt her interest rise, the feeling so rare these days that she did not recognize it at first. 'He didn't say anything to me.'

'Isn't that just the thing? I've been telling him for years I wanted rid of the place and he tells me he's found just the person but he's no' even told you. That's him, isn't it? Daft as a brush.'

From where she sat Catriona could see the branches of a tree. Rising and looking out, she saw a little yard, overgrown with grass, with a hen run at the end and a big oak tree whose branches moved gently in the breeze.

'A guid wee place it was, a real wee palace in its time, but I've let it go, these past few years, Catriona. I'm that stiff wi' rheumatisy, an' it's no' worth the bother, when your heart's no' in it. I've got my pension now, an' some savings, an' I bought a beautiful wee bungalow just up the road, but I don't want the place to go to just anyone, and Donoghue said, no' to worry, he'd find the right person.'

Catriona began to think. Closing her eyes, she saw the yard tidied up, a little garden beneath the tree where Jamie could play and hens in the hen run again, laying fresh eggs.

'It was a dairy when we started, my mother an' me, but I made it into a tearoom when she died thirty year ago. It's a great wee place in the summer, in the winter it just ticks over, but you could make a good living for yourself here, if you work hard.'

'How much?' Catriona asked her.

'What d'you mean, how much?'

'How much rent, Miss ... Aggie? I couldn't afford to buy it, but I could afford to rent it, maybe.'

'Och, I don't know, the solicitor chappie, he said I should get two hundred for it. I want to sell, really, to be rid of the place. I'm too old now to be bothered.'

'I couldn't manage to buy it, not just yet, but I could lease it for a year or two at fifty pounds a year, and if it did well, I'd buy it then.'

'Och, fifty is far too much. Mind you, I used to make four or five pounds a week in the summer, once I'd paid the girls.'

'I think fifty pounds would be fair,' Catriona said quickly, praying that Aggie would not change her mind.

'There's this room,' Aggie was saying, 'and the wee kitchen and then a bathroom and three bedrooms upstairs. Downstairs there's a big kitchen behind the shop and a storeroom that backs out into the yard. There's WCs for the customers an' that. You could have the tables and that; all the crockery, though you could do with some new, the kitchen stuff and what have you.'

'Would you take fifty pounds a year?' Catriona asked. 'I'll pay the rates and I'll sign a lease for two years.'

Aggie sat down. 'Ach, why not, lass? Donoghue says you'll make a go of the place, an' I don't want to let it go to a stranger. Mind you, you'll have your work cut out putting the place to rights. It's no' been open for eighteen months.'

Catriona went upstairs to see the bedrooms, and downstairs to the shop and kitchen. The range was in good order beneath the dirt, there was plenty of space and a big cool larder, the storeroom and a little office with space for a desk. In the tearoom, she counted a dozen tables, each for four people, with space for a few more if she moved the glass counter.

'I used to put the cakes in that,' Aggie said. 'They used to go up to the counter to choose what they wanted. But you'll find your own way of doing things, lass.'

Catriona was looking at the fading paint, the dust ingrained on the moulded ceiling, trying to work out how long it would take to get the place clean, how much it would cost to have it freshly painted.

'When will you ... when can I move in?'

'Och, lass, as soon's you like. My bungalow's ready and furnished. I'm just waiting for the curtains. A couple of weeks, say? Next week if you like. You want to be ready for the season starting, so you'd best come down as soon as you can.'

Walking back to the station, Catriona saw the clouds glow and then a column of light breached the sky and sunlight danced on the waves. The rain was over, the streets looked shiny and clean and as the train pulled out of the station she saw a rainbow hanging in the sky before the colours faded into the advent of night.

'Thank you,' she said to Donoghue when she got back home. He was standing at his stall in the gale, the market still stubbornly open despite the weather and the empty streets.

'Ach, lass.' He looked away from her. 'You needed a break, an' you've done Aggie a favour. You've needed a break for a long while, lass. But don't forget your pals in the market, eh? Come back and see us fra' time to time?'

'I will,' she said, 'and I'll always be grateful, Donoghue, always.'

'Ach, lass, awa' an' make us a cup of tea, else we'll both be greeting.'

After she had settled Jamie with Jess she went down to St Enoch's Square and found Titch McKillop sheltering under his upturned barrow.

'Canna go home,' he said miserably, 'there's a train in at half eight, an' there's aye punters on it.'

She saw his nimble fingers, the alertness in the eyes that darted from side to side, the legs that would never quite straighten because of the blight of childhood rickets.

'Titch,' she said, 'how'd you like to learn to make pies yourself?'

'What? I'm no' a sissy. I might be wee, but I'm no' daft. Leaving, are ye? I thocht ye might. You've been a guid gaffer, mind.' He guffawed carelessly, but there was an edge of bitterness in the easy way he grinned.

'I make ten pounds a week from the docks, more in a good week. If I go, you could take over.'

'That's wumman's work.'

'Jimmy Grieves bakes for a living.'

Titch got up and led her round the station, so that no one would hear what she said.

'You could sell it, ye ken. The hawkers sell their pitches on Argyle Street.'

He was just fourteen, she knew now, the same age she had been when she started. His mother was a washerwoman; he had five brothers and sisters still at school and a father dead somewhere in the mud of Flanders.

'I'd rather ...' she began. 'It was only ever a good idea, Titch.'

'Start the morn, like?' He looked around to check his barrow, snorted and rubbed his nose with his sleeve. 'Might as well try.'

'Five o'clock,' she said, 'at Grieves's in the lane.' She would have to talk to Jimmy Grieves about it, but she knew he would agree.

On Friday she stood at the slip dock with Titch, serving dinnertime pies and bridies for the last time. As she finished, one of the men came up, looking embarrassed. 'See, hen,' he mumbled, 'we ken ye're leaving, an' we didna want ye tae go wi' out a wee somethin' tae say we wish ye aw' the best.'

The men, her customers, stood in a semicircle around her as she unwrapped the big glass rolling pin and the huge wooden spoon.

'Oh,' she murmured, taken aback for a moment. 'I really...' She felt her voice crack; she paused and swallowed the sob that rose in her throat. 'I'm sorry to be leaving you all.'

A voice rose from the back of the crowd. 'Haud yer wheesht, lass. Ye've no' seen the last of us yet. An' nane o' yer fancy prices doon the watter. Ony mair than sixpence fir a pie, an' we'll start a picket.'

'Nicolson's on Castle Street,' she said, 'I'll give you a cup of tea as well.'

The whistle went and for the last time she watched them go back into the yards.

'Come on,' Titch said, 'there's the Aberdeen train in half an hour.'

'You go on,' she said.

'I'll see ye the morn.'

'You will not, Titch. You'll see me round the market maybe, but you're on your own tomorrow.'

'Aye,' he said. 'I forgot. But thanks, Miss, and thanks fra' my ma an' aw'. She says she'll help wi' the bridies if I canna manage.'

Catriona watched him run into the traffic, threading between the trams and cars, clipping a cart horse on the shin and nearly getting clipped himself by the carter.

Walking back to the Briggait, she passed the quay where she had arrived years before and stood for a time, gazing at the river, remembering most of all her aching feet and the shock of arriving at Mrs Gordon's. The crowds weaved around her, the racket familiar now, no longer frightening. A single tear rolled down her cheek and then she turned and walked on along the Clyde, watching the seagulls wheeling and diving, the flow of the river as remorseless as time.

As she turned into the close the landlady was waiting for her. 'Yer stuff,' she whined, 'ye'll be leaving yer bits an' pieces?'

'No,' Catriona said firmly, 'Donoghue's collecting them, if he hasn't been already.'

'I want the key back,' the woman said, 'mind and chap my door wi' it afore ye leave.'

The door banged and Kate's opened. 'I'll walk you to the station,' she said, as Catriona noticed that she had her good coat on and her hair squashed into quiescence beneath a tiny straw hat.

Jess was standing holding Jamie with his crib and a small bag at her feet. Catriona had already taken her case to the station.

'Goodbye, Jess,' she said, and then, quickly, 'I don't mean that. I mean I'll see you soon.'

'Aye, lass. I wish ye aw' the luck in the world.'

'God bless, Jess.'

'God bless you, Catriona, and the wee one.' She patted Jamie's head and then kissed him on the brow.

Kate picked up the crib. 'I'll take that.'

Donoghue had already been to collect her furniture and the place was as bare as it had been when she rented it.

'He says he'll give you ten shillings for it,' Kate said, 'unless you want him to send it down for you.'

Catriona shook her head. Donoghue had charged her only sixpence in the first place. She knocked on the landlady's door and put the key through the letter box.

'It's all changing, the aul' place. I doubt it'll last more than a year or two,' Kate remarked.

Catriona turned into the lane, knocked on Jimmy Grieves's window and waved her last farewell. He ran out of the shop and handed her £3 for the morning's pies. Titch McKillop was already there, covered from head to foot in pastry floor.

'The lad'll learn,' Jimmy said, 'at least, he'll not want for trying.'

For a moment, Catriona's certainty faltered. Kate saw her hesitation and gripped her arm. 'Come on, we'll miss the train.'

'Am I doing the right thing?' she wondered aloud.

'You'll not know until you try it.'

They reached the station just in time to collect Catriona's bag before the train for the coast was due to leave. 'Good luck,' Kate said again, 'I'll come down at the fair.'

Catriona stared out of the carriage window, watching the city as it faded, street by street, into the growing green of spring.

Aggie was waiting for her. 'Here's the keys, lass. And a receipt for fifty pounds. You'll get the lease from the solicitor on Monday. I don't know why you want to bother with all that.'

'I'd rather things were straight,' Catriona said uncertainly.

'Well,' Aggie said, 'I'll leave you to it. I've left bedding and the like, 'cos there's no room in my place, an' there's a pot of stew on the stove for you. I left tea and milk and bread as well.'

'That's awfully good of you,' Catriona said.

'Well,' Aggie said again, 'as I said, good luck, lass, and mind and come to see me. I'll pop by in a few days to see how you're getting on.'

The door rattled closed and Catriona noticed that the wood was warped. Outside, a man was going round with a pole, lighting the gas lamps. As he passed the window a strange blueish hue fell over the empty tearoom, giving it an air of desolation.

Catriona picked up Jamie's crib and began to carry him upstairs before she stopped and changed her mind. Going back to the tearoom, she settled him in the kitchen, where she could see him through the open door.

Taking off her coat and hat, she put on an apron and rolled up her sleeves. 'There's nothing that can't be put right with a bit of soap and water, Jamie,' she said.

Working in the sallow gaslight, she began to dust and sweep. It was after midnight when she finished and she sat down at one of the tables, looking out at the empty street. The light hit the window at an angle; she saw the veneer of grime, and scratches on the glass.

She made a cup of tea and a sandwich at the kitchen table; the room was warm since she had lit the range.

As the clock struck one she got up and walked around. The tables were rickety; when she put her hand down on them they tilted slightly. Two of the chairs had broken legs. The glass of the counter was chipped and stained. She eased it around until it stood against the wall and saw that she could get another two tables in that space.

She knelt down and wiped a patch of floor; the wood was solid at least, with wax and a lot of polishing it would recover.

She closed her eyes and saw the walls painted, with maybe oak-framed mirrors to give the sensation of space, the tables covered with snowy white linen with a little vase with fresh daisies on each. The outside would have to be painted, but that wasn't much, she would find someone to write 'Nicolson's' in smart navy blue letters, or even a carpenter to carve a sign like the one that hung outside Treron's. She picked up a pencil and paper and began to write a list of things to do, yawning occasionally as she worked.

The light of dawn crept into the cafe, though she was

unaware until the gaslight was extinguished and she realized the night had passed.

She wrapped Jamie warmly in his shawl and carried him out into the grey cold morning, down the street until she stood on the promenade, looking at the gulls wheeling over the blue-black sea. The sun had not risen yet; morning was the faintest glow behind the hills beyond the town.

In the chill she felt the need of a shawl, and clasped her thin jacket tightly to her. The fishing boats were tied up in the little harbour on the other side of the pier; the air smelt cleanly of salt.

For a moment she doubted herself, doubted the resolve that had made her leave the city to come here to this little town. Without the holiday makers and the sun, the streets of Largs were shadowy, as quiet and grim as the grave.

When the first rays of the rising sun fell warm on her back, she remembered the dream, knew now that the chance was hers. She looked back and saw the silver crescendo above the hills, heard the cries of the birds as the day began. As she slowly walked back towards Castle Street she saw the first of the fishing boats set off for the day, its wake cutting a dark triangle in the gilded sea.

Gently, the town came awake to the sun.

Chapter Nine

*I*t took a week to clean the cafe, the kitchen and the rooms above, but when Catriona was finished the place was spotless. The kitchen range had been black leaded and the rack of pots gleamed, the floor was polished to a shine; the fittings of the gaslights sparkled. The larder smelled of carbolic and bleach; the yard grass had been cut and the weeds cleared, the hen run made ready. Catriona went to a farm just outside the town and bought a dozen good layers which the farmer promised to bring round when he delivered her milk and butter. She opened an account with the grocer, to deliver, and she could buy fresh fish at the pier every evening when the boats came in.

At the hardware store she asked for a painter and eventually an old man came round carrying a ladder on his back. 'Five pounds,' he said, when she asked him how much it would cost to paint the cafe; ten pounds for the surrounds of the window, the sign and the front door.

'How much?' she gasped.

He scratched the wood and a few splinters fell away. 'The wood's rotten, y'see,' he said, 'it'll all have to be replaced. If you leave it, the window'll fall out.'

She hesitated.

'Take your time,' he said, 'suits me,' and he picked up his ladder and ambled off down the street.

Remembering MacKenzie, WS, she looked at the lease and saw that fixtures and fittings were the responsibility of the tenant, repair of the premises that of the landlord. Thinking of Aggie with her rheumatism, her little bungalow and her pension of ten shillings a month, Catriona knew that her face would crumple into confusion when told that repairs to the shop would cost ten pounds. Liam, she knew, could have fixed it in a moment with wood and a few easy swings of a hammer. She had watched him mend a broken shop door in the market in minutes and charge only a shilling for his trouble.

The thought of Liam brought a dull pain to the pit of her stomach; she sat down and cupped her face in her hands as she remembered. She had buried herself in work these last few months, but she still felt the hollow inside where his child should have been, the echo in her soul where his loss hurt so much.

Tears came to her eyes; she blinked to dissipate them, tried to stem the memory with thoughts of something else. Briskly, she got up and went through to the kitchen, where she put the kettle on for tea. After his walk early in the morning, Jamie was napping in his cot. She looked over at him, glad that he still slept most of the day, momentarily afraid at the realization that in a few months more he would begin to walk. By then, the tearoom would be open and she wondered how she would find the time to care for him along with everything else until she remembered that Maire would leave school in the summer and would come to join her then. The kettle puffed; she took it off the flame and made her tea, sat down and began to drink.

Along the counter, she had laid out her baking things, the big brown mixing bowl next to the wooden spoon and ladle, the salt cellar and sugar jar, the rolling board for pastry, all as they had been in Shipbank Lane. For a moment she looked for the space on the wall where the hook should have been for Liam to hang his cap and jacket. The emptiness trapped her then and tears came again, a wave of sadness that she could not staunch.

For a long time she sobbed into her folded arms, as the tea cooled and formed a skin.

Jamie woke up and his cries cut into hers. She went and picked him up and held him close, crying her heart out until she realized that he would not stop until she did.

'It's all right, little one,' she whispered, smoothing the soft hair on the top of his head. He looked at her in confusion, reached out and touched her chin. The gesture renewed her grief, the feeling of loss, the fear that with Liam gone no one would ever touch her with love again. She began to sob once more, then stopped herself. Outside, the sun had begun to shine, the light filtering in through the kitchen window. She put Jamie down on a rug by the fireside and began to measure out flour, sugar and currants, to bake some scones just to make sure that she hadn't lost her touch.

'To hell with fifteen pounds,' she said aloud.

The men who had worked for Liam were still in Glasgow. She knew the place they met, outside the Shipbank Inn. One of them would come down and fix the window and the door, probably do the painting as well for a fraction of what the local man would charge. But she did not want to go back to the old places, did not want to stoke the embers of her pain.

As she put the scones in the oven she heard the door rattle, went through and saw Aggie Donoghue standing uncertainly on the threshold.

'My,' she said as Catriona let her in, 'you've done a good job with the oul' place.'

'Just soap and water.'

'I mind,' Aggie said, 'when I started. My mother used to wash the tablecloths every night and polish the cutlery. The place was like a palace. You've found the cloths, have you? Good linen, they are. I left all the things I thought you could use.'

Catriona fumbled for words, because when she had found the cloths and washed them, even bleached them several times, she could not get rid of the stains and tide marks from the linen being folded and left so long in a grimy cupboard. That was another thing she had to buy, with new crockery to replace the cracked and chipped cups.

'Would you like a cup of tea?' she asked.

'I would that.' Aggie sat down and took off her hat. 'I just thought I'd drop in on my way to the post, see how you're getting on, like. The doctor gave me something for the rheumatisy and I'm not so stiff this morning.'

Catriona made the tea and put some of the freshly baked scones on a plate.

'You make a good scone,' Aggie said, once they had cooled enough to be eaten. 'Go down well, do scones, wi' the locals. That's the folks from here. The trippers, they like their cakes. But you need to have the locals as well, if you're staying open in the off season.'

Catriona was wondering how to broach the subject of the rotting window frame.

'I'll be just fine,' Aggie was saying, 'with your rent and my pension. Not too much, just enough to get by.'

The rent was fair, and ten pounds a lot of money. She could not ask her, not yet.

'When are you opening?' Aggie asked.

'The first week in April, I thought. Just after Easter. Everything'll be ready then.'

'You'll be taking the girls on?'

'I was hoping I could manage myself.'

'Ha!' Aggie exclaimed. 'You might for a week or two, but once it gets busy you'll need a girl to serve the tables, with yourself in the kitchen. Custom won't wait, you know. If you're not quick, they'll get up and go some place else. And you've the wee lad to watch out for.'

'I've a sister at home. She'll be coming down soon.'

Aggie shook her head. 'That's where you'll go wrong, lass. They don't like that, the locals don't. If you've a local girl working, the locals'll come in, but if it's all strangers, they'll not.'

'But the summer trade isn't local.'

'No, but the rest of the year it is. You need them, lass. I made a good living off the people of Largs. But it's a wee place, clannish like. They don't take to strangers.' She patted Catriona's hand. 'Take my advice, lass, hire a couple of local girls. Etta and Janet and Gracie, those were the ones I had. Janet's married, now, but the other two'll be round soon's they see you're open. I met Etta's mother and she said the girls couldn't wait to start again.'

Catriona thought of her carefully worked out budget, and wondered if she could afford to pay wages as well.

The old woman finished her tea, picked up the scone crumbs from the plate and slipped then into her mouth. 'Jist mind what I say, Catriona, an' tak' on a couple of the local girls when ye open. That'll see ye richt wi' the people o' Largs.'

Catriona stood at the door watching Aggie's slow progress down the street, her passage marked by the tapping of her walking stick on the cobblestones; then she went back to her books and added the wages to everything else.

Annie's letter came on the day she went to Glasgow to buy new tablecloths and china, also to find someone to fix the rotting window frame. Liam's men would be glad to help, they would welcome her like a long-lost friend; she was not looking forward to seeing them, though, too afraid of the pain the memory would bring.

She opened the letter on the train, when Jamie was sleeping, lulled by the rhythm of the wheels. Annie's letters always brought her pleasure; that would help her through the day:

> Sine's serious with this lad of hers. I think they'll be wed next year, when she turns sixteen. She doesn't know how lucky she is, with the lads dead in the war, or maybe she does. I'm so happy for her, he's a good man. Maire's about to finish school in the summer. When I asked her about coming to you, she blushed and said she wanted to see Sine wed and then she bit her lip, as if she'd said something she shouldn't have. She wants to come next year; Allan says he can't wait, but he can, of course. He's been better since the warmer weather, so you've to stop sending the money because we don't need it and I'm sure with all you're doing, you do. Iain's got his pension now and he's managing to do a bit of work. Your da helps a lot, honestly. He comes every morning and takes Iain down to the fields and helps him at the planting. Iain can't do much, but he planted the potatoes this year. He was so proud of himself and he's getting better all the time.

Triona, I want to wish you all the luck in the world with your tearoom. I know things will work out for you; you've worked hard enough, after all. When I read your letter I couldn't help thinking of Mor, and how proud she'd be of you, as we all are.

Allan and your sisters send their love; Allan says he'll write soon. He's waiting for the school prize day, because he thinks he'll win the prize and he wants to tell you himself. Miss Anderson told him the other day that he is just as clever as you are and he walked back from school as if he was six feet tall.

With love from Annie and everybody at home.

Except my father, Catriona thought bitterly. Since the twins had been killed he had not written, not even at Christmas. Every month, when she sent the money home, she wondered what he would do with it, what he would do if it stopped. But she couldn't do that, didn't dare because it might hurt Sine or Maire or Allan, maybe all of them.

Tom no longer cared for any of them any more.

She had chosen a Saturday to go to the market because all the stalls would be open and she might be lucky enough to find a dozen matching tablecloths, and sometimes an Irishwoman sold crockery on the pavement outside the market building. Liam's workers would be in the inn during the afternoon, she could send a message and ask one of them if he would fix the window.

On her way along Argyle Street she stopped at St Enoch's Square and left a message for Titch McKillop to meet her later at the market with his barrow to help her back to the station.

Donoghue was standing at his stall, his arms folded defiantly. On Saturday mornings he kept his prices high – for the chancers, he said, the passing trade that came to Paddy's to see if there was a bargain to be had. This early there were only children and a few old women raking through the tables of rags.

'I kenned ye'd miss us,' he said, winking. This time he

went to get the tea himself as she watched his stall. Quickly, he scanned the list of things she needed. 'I've a tea set still in the box' he said, 'but I canny mind whether it's a dozen or jist half.'

'I need forty-eight,' she said grimly, 'more if you can manage.'

'Can ye gie me a week? I've got teaspoons, I can get knives an' forks fra' a lad I ken at the Central Hotel. He wis saying they got new and thaurs boxes o' stuff they want tae get rid of. Mibbe get some cups fra them as well.'

'What happened to the woman who used to be here?'

'I dinna ken, Catriona. I think she's back home, but she only ever had the odd plate for sale, never any twa the same.'

She looked through a pile of women's clothes, found a couple of maids' dresses. 'How much?'

'You dinna have to ask. I sold the coffee stall for a fiver, ye ken, so yer credit's good.'

For the first time that day, she smiled. 'How good, Dono-ghue?'

'Och.' He made a great play of thinking, counting up on his fingers, spitting when he got the imaginary sum wrong and then starting again. 'About four dozen cups, saucers and plates good, an' a few knives an' forks. An' a' the maids' dresses ye can find in the pile. About a' I canny do is aprons. Ye ken I'm nae guid wi' anything white. I'm going up to the lock-up in a minute, I'll see if there's awt there.'

On the pavement nearby she found Ina and the other rag women and started to browse through their bundles. The call went along the line and after a while she had three aprons of different sizes and five damask tablecloths of differ-ent designs. Ina held one up to the light. 'Thing is, Catriona, if you put another cloth on top, it'll look as good as new.' She paid sixpence each and a shilling for the aprons, and counted herself lucky. Ina promised more in a week or two; she'd watch out for good things and post them to her.

'I bet you don't remember me,' a voice said in Gaelic, familiar yet quaint because it was years since she had spoken that language.

She wheeled round. 'Rory?'

He was smiling broadly, still the same after all these years. His shirt was open, his jacket slung carelessly over his shoulder. His hair still flopped over his forehead though there was a thin patch either side where it had begun to recede. She moved to throw herself into his arms, but stopped when she remembered they were in the thick of Paddy's Market. He smiled as if he knew what she had been about to do, and bent to give her a cautious peck on the cheek.

'I thought I'd lost you, little girl. I went to *bagradh* MacKenzie, got chased like a rent defaulter, but an old man called Maloney told me you'd be here. When I came, you'd gone too. I was just back to try to find out where, when I saw you, right as day.'

'Rory?' She felt tears prickle her eyes for the time that was past, for the warmth of the friendship she'd thought she had lost.

'You thought I was gone with the war.'

'I did not, Rory MacDonald. I knew you hadn't, but I didn't know where you were, either.'

His eyes fell onto Jamie. 'Who's this?'

'Jamie,' she said, and then, to explain, 'Ailish's son.'

'Ah.' He understood, without her having to tell him.

They linked arms and walked down the lane to the quiet end of the market. She looked at him, thinking how little he had changed, smiling when he said the same to her.

'What happened to you during the war?' Laughing, they realized they had asked the same question at once. Rory's face changed; he knew about the twins, knew how much she had been hurt. In the Atlantic, he said, he had been torpedoed once and lucky the rest of the time. His brother was running the family croft; he was going to start a haulage yard with a couple of trucks he bought cheap from a sergeant major he knew in the HLI. There wasn't any work in the island, but he had money saved from the war to start in the south.

In a rush she told him about her cafe, about the stained linen and the rotting window. He smiled and gripped her hand, took her round the corner to an old army van with canvas sides that fluttered in the wind. He had all the time in the world, he said, plenty of time to drive her and Jamie home to Largs; he wouldn't dream of letting her struggle on the train with all the things she had bought. He could easily fix the rotting window frame; she felt gratitude surge, and again suppressed the urge to hug him.

In the van she caught him looking at her.

'What is it?' she asked, in the easy way she could talk to an old friend.

He looked at the mirror, and then the road before him. 'You looked so sad, just before I met you. As if you'd lost somebody who was dear to you.'

Her eyes dipped. 'I was just tired, Rory. Starting a tea-room, it's a lot of work. And a lot of risk.'

'Still sending money home?'

Her silence told him that she was.

'I sent some the other week. A cow died calving. A late gale took the roof off and that bastard factor charged them a fiver for the wood.'

'You don't want to go home yourself?'

'Where's home, Catriona? I've been away from Skye for thirteen years. This yard I'm starting, if it works I'll not have to worry about cows dying or roofs coming off.'

I used to love you once, she realized, looking at his strong profile, before the memory of Liam drove the thought from her mind. She had grown up now, was no longer the little island girl with hair streaming down her back. Rory was special to all the island girls, but he had remembered her and sought her out; she was glad of that, to know that her friend was back again.

Rory repaired the window frame and the warped door, fixed the rickety tables and chairs, put new shelves in the kitchen. Once that was done, he took her round to the builder's yard and asked her what colour she wanted the walls. 'Blue,' she replied, thinking of the elegant dim of Miss Cranston's.

'That shop of yours's no' well lit,' the builder said, 'blue'd make it look awfy gloomy.'

Catriona thought again. 'White?'

'Aye,' the builder said, 'I've plenty of white.'

'I don't think he's got any colours,' Rory whispered as the man went into a shed and clanked for ages before he came back with some cans of white paint.

Catriona was wondering where she could find some cheap prints to hang on the wall, or vases for flowers to give the tearoom a touch of colour. Once she had paid for everything, even with Rory's help, she would have little money left and she wanted to keep some in the bank in case anything happened at home.

Rory nudged her and pointed; leaning against the wall of the shed were some dusty mirrors still wrapped in brown paper.

'Excuse me.' She cleared her throat as the builder wrote out a receipt for the paint. 'How much are the mirrors?'

The builder snorted. 'I dinna ken, lass, to tell the truth. Some flyboy ordered them and then skipped afore I delivered. They've been here since afore the war. If ye want them, I could let them go for a couple of pounds. But they're big, mind you, five feet by three, each of them.'

Rory carried them out to the van, muttering about a thieves' bargain.

When the painting was finished and the mirrors hung, the cafe seemed empty. Rory looked around. 'Maybe you were right about the blue walls.'

Catriona smiled to herself and told him to come back in two weeks, on the day before she opened.

Way along the shore road, after the promenade changed into a wide street lined on one side by the sea and on the other by villas, there was a house with a wonderful garden and two conservatories that even in the early spring were a riot of colour. Palm trees lined the driveway; she had studied them for a long time before she recognized them from the books of stories of the Holy Land that she had won as school

231

prizes. Catriona walked past several times before she saw a gardener at work, clipping the yew hedge.

'Hello,' she began diffidently. 'These flowers in the conservatory, where did you find them?'

The gardener stood up and rubbed the crick in his back. 'The whole world over, lass. That one there, that's roses for the rose garden round the back. You can't see it from here. The other is orchids and exotics from Panama, the Americas, where have you. Miss Cochrane, she's travelled the world to get her plants.'

Catriona's face fell. 'I couldn't find some to buy in Largs?'

'Ach, lass, come in and have a look at them. The Miss wouldn't mind if I gave you a cutting, I'm sure.'

He opened the gate and led her up the drive. 'I'm Robbie Thompson,' he said, 'I've worked with the Cochranes all my life and when the young Miss moved here, I came down with her. I was at Carnlachan, that's the big house up Stirling way.'

The orchid house was stifling; after a few minutes beads of perspiration formed on Catriona's brow. 'It's the heating,' Robbie said, pointing to two huge pipes that ran the length of the wooden floor. 'Orchids need heat, and a lot of moisture in the air. They're from the jungle, see.'

The jewel bright colours shimmered in the haze, the perfume overpowering in its intensity. Outside again, Catriona gulped the chill sea air. The rose house was cooler, the perfume gentle. 'Miss Cochrane breeds hybrids,' Robbie said, 'and she propagates the bushes here.' There were flowers in every shade of red, from the palest pink to deep crimson, big white cabbage roses and little yellow buds still tightly coiled.

'These are perpetuals,' Robbie said, passing a bank of flowers, 'they bloom from February to November. She just grows the cuttings here and plants the bushes outside in the spring.' He showed Catriona Austrian roses, Gloire de Dijon and Reine d'Angleterre, Mrs Bosanquet, Smith's Yellow, Persian Yellow, budding flowers that smelled faintly of tea.

Outside, behind the house, the rose garden was fragrant and fresh.

'Seen enough?' Robbie asked her. 'If you come back in a few weeks when they're in full bloom, that's a sight for sore eyes.'

'I wonder,' Catriona said uncertainly, finding determination because the idea had a momentum of its own, 'where could I get some? Not the flowers, but the bushes in the conservatory.'

'I don't know, lass. See, the rose isn't an indoor plant, not really. These you see, they're dwarf roses. Miss Cochrane's been hybridizing them herself.'

Catriona had a vision of her tearoom with roses in planters along the walls, cut roses in vases on the tables. Just a few buds in each, enough so that the perfume would flavour the air.

'I could give you some,' he said. 'There's plenty of them. In fact, I was about to clear some out, but the dwarfs, they don't do so well in the garden.'

'Oh, could you? Would Miss Cochrane mind?'

Robbie smiled. 'She wouldn't mind at all. She'd be glad of a use for them. It's been a hobby of hers, breeding dwarf roses to grow indoors, but most folks don't have the patience for it. I could give you cut flowers as well. She gives them to the church in spring, but there's aye plenty.'

'I'm opening a tearoom,' Catriona explained. 'The one that Aggie Donoghue used to have. I'd need plants to put in planters, and cut roses for the tables.'

'I could manage that, right enough. And the Miss, she wouldn't mind.'

'But I'd have to pay you. You'd have to ask Miss Cochrane.'

Robbie laughed. 'As I says, I've been with her all my working days, and I know she won't mind, but I'll tell her, if you insist. She'll be tickled, right chuffed. But it's a lot of work, mind. Growing roses indoors isn't easy; you've got to take care of them.'

'I'll manage,' she said, 'if you help me.'

'That I will, lass.'

Catriona walked home, humming to herself, wondering

where she could find planters to fix to the walls, and pots to hold the roses.

The tearooms along the promenade were getting ready for the summer season. One by one she had visited them and studied their menus. The tea they served was thick and dark, stewed so long that it tasted stale. The baking was mediocre, the scones and cakes often hard at the edges because they were baked early in the morning and then left under glass covers. For dinner they served fish – fried, steamed, poached or baked. Everywhere charged the same; 10d for baked whiting, 1/- for fried cod and chips.

Etta and Gracie had arrived on her doorstep a few days after Rory finished the painting. 'Aggie said you'd want us for waitresses, like,' Etta said shyly. Gracie stared glacially at the stark white walls, the old tables that looked shabby without a covering.

Catriona asked them in.

'We usually start in May,' Gracie said, 'but we can start early if you like.'

'May should be soon enough,' Catriona said.

'Our wages,' Gracie went on, 'ten shillings a week an' the tips, an' a bonus o' a week's wages at the end of the season. A half day off a week and we don't start on Sundays till midday.'

'Is that what Miss Donoghue paid you?'

Gracie looked away. Etta's mouth opened, closing again when Gracie nudged her. 'That's what they get at the Pavilion Cafe on the promenade,' Gracie said, with a note of aggression in her voice that made Catriona recoil. 'An' the uniforms. You supply the uniforms.'

Etta stood in silence, looking down at the floor.

'I was going to pay eight shillings a week,' Catriona said. 'My opening hours are ten to eight, noon on a Sunday, with two half days off a week.'

Gracie sniffed.

'Perhaps you'd be better at the Pavilion.'

'I've worked here the last few year, I've aye worked at Aggie's.'

'The Pavilion's opening hours are longer. I can't pay the wages you want.'

'We keep the tips, an' get our meals on duty.'

'I'm sorry,' Catriona said firmly, 'but I think you'd be better off at the Pavilion, Gracie.'

For a moment Gracie tried to stare her down and then turned on her heel and stalked out, slamming the door in her wake. Etta remained, perched uncertainly on one leg, rubbing her calf with her toe. Outside the window, Gracie gestured impatiently for Etta to join her.

'Why don't you sit down,' Catriona said, 'and we'll have a chat.'

Etta looked at Gracie hesitantly, and then sat.

'She's a bit tough, is our Gracie,' she said. Catriona was thinking of the stern waitresses at Miss Cranston's, like schoolmistresses only more forbidding.

'She's courting Jock the now,' Etta said. 'She'll be merrit soon, she'd no' last the season anyhow.'

Catriona gave Etta a job, and told her that perhaps she would take on somebody else during the season.

Slowly, the pieces were falling into place.

Donoghue had sent down two cases of crockery and cutlery with Rory. The crockery was the old style of the Central Hotel; the rims of the plates and saucers were decorated with CH in an ornate copperplate script; Catriona thought that if you didn't look too hard the CH looked like CN. From the ragwomen she had collected a dozen tablecloths and plenty of napkins, but of differing ages so that even after several washings and bleachings the linen was shaded from off-white to a dull ivory. Catriona experimented with the lighter cloths near the window, the darker ones further in, but the effect was not right, the tables looked shabby. She counted her money again, wondered if she could afford new linen and agonized over whether to spend some of the money she had put aside.

Robbie Thompson brought round a barrowful of dwarf rose bushes the week before she was due to open. In the

hardware store Catriona had found some wrought-iron planters, which she nailed to the wall herself, and then she bought
a couple of old barrels from the fish merchant, which she
rolled back to her tearoom and buffed until the wood shone
and the metal casings gleamed.

She explained to Robbie what she wanted; he thought for
a moment, his head cocked to one side. 'They're tempera-
mental, the dwarves,' he said, 'no' as tolerant as yer aspidistras. They might not take.'

'They'll take,' Catriona told him.

'It's worth a try,' Robbie said as he lifted the plants
tenderly and set them in the planters, leaving the biggest for
the twin barrels on either side of the kitchen door.

When they were finished, the flowers broke the stark
expanse of the walls, the greenery reflected gently in the
mirrors almost as if the whole room was a garden.

'Aye,' Robbie said, 'I'll gie ye this, lass, ye've got taste.'

She put her hand in her apron pocket for the pound note
she had saved for him, but he waved it away, saying that she
could give him a bowl of soup next week when he came to
make sure that the roses were thriving.

Catriona looked around, satisfied, until her eyes fell on the
tablecloths. The linen looked tired, despite all her efforts;
the unmatched, uneven colours spoiled the effect she had
tried so hard to achieve.

That evening she counted her money again and found she
had ten pounds left over after putting aside enough for the
first month's bills. Finding the number of the pub where
Donoghue drank in the Gallowgate, she took Jamie in her
arms and raced to the post office to use the public phone.

Donoghue came on the line, delighted to hear from her.
She took a deep breath, and asked him the favour she
wanted.

'Twa dozen *pink* tablecloths? Mother of God, woman,
whaur on earth dae I find *pink* tablecloths?'

'I don't know, Donoghue, but if anyone can, you will.'

'Aye, well, I'm no' so sure about that. No' sure at a', but
I'll see whit I can dae.'

A package arrived at the railway station with the last train on Saturday. A porter brought it round and she opened it, finding four dozen tablecloths in just the right shade of pale pink, and a gross of napkins to match.

Donoghue sent a note to tell her that she owed the foreman of the dyeworks a drink or two. She sent him two pounds and told him to buy himself one as well.

On Sunday she took Jamie down to the seafront to wait for Rory. It was a fine day, and she walked the length of the shore twice before Rory's lorry chugged into view, trailing a streak of charred smoke. He saw her and waved, then parked it gingerly by the side of the road.

'Bitch's still burning oil,' he said as he jumped down from the cab. 'Damned if I know why.'

She looked at him and smiled. There was a ring of grime around his hands where he had washed them, and another around his neck. Without asking she knew that he had spent the morning tinkering with the engine, probably the day before as well.

'It was working fine last time.'

'Ah, this's a new one. I got a contract, see, from the Chryston colliery. I've taken on two drivers and bought another truck.'

They walked to the tearoom as he told her about the yard he had leased just outside Cumbernauld.

'I'm opening tomorrow,' she said, as they reached the door.

Rory stopped and stared at the sign that read The Rose Tearoom. On either side of it was a flowering bush, and below was a glass frame holding a menu.

She had left the lamps lit and as she opened the door, Rory stood back.

'What is it? What's the matter?'

Each table was a pool of pink, with a vase holding a single blossom; the planters around the walls glanced off the mirrors and the smell of roses hung in the air. The effect was elegant and muted, rarefied and expensive.

Rory shook his head.

Catriona's lip puckered. 'What's wrong?'

He shook his head again. 'There's nothing wrong. Nothing wrong at all.'

She was looking at him intently. 'I was hoping that you'd be my first customer, Rory.'

He grinned broadly. 'I painted the walls, remember? I was hoping I'd get my tea for free.'

'I didn't mean I wanted you to pay.'

There was something very fragile about her in that moment, making him want to wrap his arms around her and chase all of her cares away. Briefly he remembered the island girl on the ferry so many years ago, the way she had defied her troubles then, the way she still did.

'I meant, if you sat down at a table, you could order your tea from the menu.'

'God's sake, Catriona, you wouldn't want to have your customers seeing you serve a tinker like me!'

She picked up a menu and thrust it at him. 'But Rory, look at my prices. I'm cheaper than anyone else in Largs. Just a penny, mind, but cheaper. And you're not a tinker, anyway.'

He looked down at the workman's overalls he always wore, clean but stained, still smelling faintly of engine oil. 'I'd've thought it was worth a few pence more to have tea in a place like this.'

'Yes, but ...' Jamie shifted in her arms, and she put him down, watching him carefully to make sure he didn't knock into a table as he began to crawl.

'Fact is, Catriona, I wouldn't want to sit down at one of your tables dressed like this.'

Jamie was closing on one of the barrels; she ran over and scooped him up.

'I mean, my dungarees're clean, but they might still be a bit dirty.'

She laughed, and held open the door to the kitchen. 'You washed them yourself, did you? Come on, we'll eat through here.'

Rory was used to shipboard food, dried herrings, pickled herrings, fresh stewed herrings on a good day and always biscuits that tasted of sawdust. On shore he ate at Maggie Drummond's, or some place like it, where the taste of the food was washed away with pints of bitter ale. Catriona served him steak and kidney pudding with fresh new potatoes, then cinnamon apple pastries, then a slab of the Dundee cake she had cooked the week before and soaked in rum. She wasn't sure what his taste was, so she served him a choice on one of the three-tiered cake stands she had bought for afternoon tea. Rory ate the lot, then sat back and sighed as she poured coffee.

'Reckon I'd pay for that,' he said.

'The steak and kidney pudding isn't on the menu,' she said, 'but everything else is.'

'Where did you learn to cook, Triona?'

She smiled. 'Here and there. You haven't told me if you like it, yet.'

'Like what?'

'My tearoom.'

He got up and stood at the doorway. 'You've worked a miracle, girl.' He went over to Jamie's cot and picked him up, tickling his chin. 'I thought it was just going to be a wee teashop, like Maggie's but not so uncouth. It's very special, Catriona. You should be proud of yourself.'

She blushed and picked up the menu when he sat down again. 'You see, you can have tea and cakes for sixpence, or coffee and cakes. A high tea won't cost more than a shilling.'

'But this is a toffs' place, Triona. Toffs can afford to pay more.'

She winced. 'It's not for toffs, Rory. It's for people like you and me.'

'But you could charge a penny more and they'd never even notice.'

Her face fell and he sensed he had disturbed a memory. 'D'you remember Lachlan Maclean?' she asked him.

'He thought for a moment. 'I don't think I do.'

'He joined the army. There were ten from The Braes that joined together and they were all killed at the Somme.'

'I remember that.'

'Well, Lachlan came to see me in Glasgow when he joined up. He took me into a tearoom and it cost one and sixpence for tea and cakes. I felt so guilty about it. I don't want my tearoom to make anyone feel like that.'

Rory grinned. 'I remember Lachlan now. He was the type that gets the rest of us called stupid teuchters.'

Her eyes flashed angrily. 'He wasn't stupid, Rory. Just kind, and too trusting for his own good.'

He held up his hand. 'I didn't mean it like that.'

'What did you mean?'

He scratched the back of his neck. 'I mean, oh, I don't know what I mean. I mean there's people who don't ever see further than the crofts and the summer fishing. Who don't ever see the world beyond. Like they're scared of it, or something.'

'What's wrong with that?'

'Nothing, Catriona. Nothing at all. But people who do, people like us, we're different, Catriona.'

'Different, perhaps. But no better than anyone else.'

He felt her mood change, darken like the sun in the face of a storm.

She got up and cleared the dishes, washed them quickly then put the plates on a rack to drain and dried the cutlery and put it back into its place. He watched her, wondering why she defended Lachlan so fiercely; he had been just a lad, the kind who never grows fully into manhood, who'd take whatever life gave him and be content with it, not daring to risk anything in the quest for something else. Catriona would not, could not have been happy with a man like that.

She was feeding Jamie now, a milky pudding that slipped from the edge of his mouth and trickled down his chin, where she caught it with a handkerchief. Rory watched her until she finished, and then she took Jamie up to his cot.

He had that lorry to work on back in the yard, and another he had not even started yet. With the yard and the lorries and the men he had taken on, he had only pounds left of the hundreds he'd saved during the war; it would be years yet before he had the kind of security he needed to take on a woman like that. Or any woman at all, because he was not the sort of man who would send his son to sea at the age of twelve, or daughter to work as a maid when the toil would rub the shine off her beauty before she had reached marrying age.

All he had was a promise and even that was based on a risk so great that it made even him tremble inwardly when he thought about it.

Catriona came running down the stairs, her eyes bright again.

'Well, Rory, do you think my tearoom will work?'

'Like I said, it's a miracle.'

'But will it work?'

'Will it work? Of course it'll work. By the summer you'll have a queue a mile long.'

She laughed and hugged herself. 'I doubt it. If I make enough to get by, save a little.' Her face became serious. 'I had to do it, Rory. I had to start out for myself.'

He looked through the window, surprised to see night falling, to realize that so much time had passed. 'You and me both, girl. The only chances we get are those we give to ourselves.'

At the door he bent down to kiss her fleetingly on the cheek.

'Come again soon, Rory.'

'I will, Catriona. God bless.'

The Rose Tearoom opened and a whole hour passed before the first customers came in and asked for cups of tea. Catriona carried the pot over and set it down on the table with the cups.

'Just a cup I wanted,' one of the women said.

'I serve tea in pots,' Catriona replied, 'it's the same price, but you can help yourself to another cup if you like.'

The women looked at each other and started to talk in hushed voices that made Catriona feel like an eavesdropper.

The first few days seemed very slow. The same women

came back the next day and the next again; it was Wednesday when she sold her first bowl of soup at lunchtime and then later a plate of sandwiches and cakes to a pair of early day trippers.

Aggie popped her head around the door, said she couldn't stop because she was on her way to the doctor's. 'It's quiet as the grave the first few weeks,' she said, 'it'll be a month afore yer trade picks up.'

Catriona waited nervously, counting the shillings and pennies at the end of each day, not the pounds she had hoped for. At the end of the first week, she had only coppers left after she paid her expenses, a fraction of what she had made with her stalls.

On the Tuesday of her second week she watched a huge car coast up and down Castle Street before it stopped at her tearoom and the chauffeur opened the door to let a spry old lady step out. Catriona watched in amazement as she looked at the window and then walked in.

'I'm Miss Cochrane,' she said, 'I've been dying to see what you've done with my roses.'

'Oh, please,' Catriona said, holding a chair for her. 'Do sit down.'

Miss Cochrane looked around. 'This is delightful, my dear, quite delightful.'

Catriona served her tea and fresh scones, brown bread and chicken sandwiches, some rich fruit cake she had baked to Mrs Beaton's recipe.

'Will you join me?' Miss Cochrane asked.

Catriona sat down and found herself talking about the chocolate cake she was trying to bake, the almond slice that drooped in the middle, the cherries that sank without trace in the sponge that was otherwise perfect.

Miss Cochrane waved her hand dismissively. 'You can obviously cook, girl. Cake-making is an art in itself, so my chef tells me. He does a wonderful sachertorte; you must come and see him some time to get the recipe. Just tell Wilkins or Thompson, they'll arrange it. Now tell me, do you do luncheons?'

'Of course,' Catriona said.

'Would it be too much trouble to let me have a luncheon here next Monday? It would mean closing for your other customers, but only between half past twelve and two. It's the meeting of the Ladies' Red Cross Committee and we have lunch afterwards. I usually have it at home, but it would make a nice change to come here.'

'What would you like?' Catriona asked.

'Oh, whatever.' Miss Cochrane waved her hand airily. 'Just something light, and plenty of scones and cakes. That was wonderful, dear,' she said as she rose, 'if you just see Wilkins, he'll pay the bill.'

'I couldn't' Catriona protested, thinking about the roses.

Miss Cochrane's eyebrow arched in a manner that did not allow for argument. 'Of course you must, my dear. My roses grow for fun, but this? This is a business.'

Something light, Catriona thought, pacing the kitchen after the tearoom closed. Not soup and bridies, or even the chicken parcels she made. Miss Cranston served roast chicken, whiting poached in a light sauce, salmon with an airy mayonnaise. She had a copy of Mrs Beaton and another book that she had put to one side because the recipes were so elaborate. Mrs Campbell had told her about the creamed leek and potato soup that was served chilled in the household where she once worked. She had described it as an affectation, a terrible waste of good, wholesome food. Catriona thought for a moment and suddenly the idea came to her, of a menu of chilled soup and then cold chicken in aspic or mousse of salmon. It was a bit early for salmon, but Rory would know where one could be found. A man like Rory could always find salmon. She dashed off a note to him and posted it, telling him to bring her two on Sunday, and then sent a note to Etta, asking her to start work at the weekend.

On Monday she waited nervously until the Daimler glided to a halt, followed by a procession of other cars. The chicken in aspic was perfect, the salmon mousse light as a cloud. The soup was chilling on an ice block from the fishmonger's; to go with coffee she had made little apple tarts and dainty cinnamon scones.

Miss Cochrane treated her ladies like a mother hen. She ushered them in and sat them at tables, clucked derisively when someone complained that the soup was cold.

'I could heat it up,' Catriona said quickly

'Nonsense,' Miss Cochrane said, 'it's meant to be like this. It was an excellent idea to serve vichyssoise.'

Catriona watched nervously as Etta changed the soup bowls to dinner plates and then carried through the platters of salmon and chicken with little bowls of buttered new potatoes and parsleyed beans. Miss Cochrane's guests were to have a choice, but some of them asked for a little of each.

After the main course, Catriona served coffee herself, trying to melt into the backdrop behind the chatter. Before, she had been too nervous to write out the bill for Wilkins; as two o'clock struck she scribbled out a note that said: 'Twenty Lunches at 1/0 ... £1.'

Etta was washing dishes, unconcerned. 'They enjoyed that, they did, Missus Nicolson.'

'Call me Catriona,' she said quickly. 'How can you tell?'

'Just look at them. It's the back of two, an' they're still not finished. My sister used to work at the Pavilion an' she says they don't want the food to be too good there, 'cos folks stay too long an' it's no' good for business.'

Catriona wanted to hug her. Picking up the coffee pot, she refilled the cups and served more pastries.

It was after three o'clock when the ladies left and the tearoom opened again for normal business.

Wilkins brought her a note a short time later, enclosing five pounds. 'I want to thank you for a most delicious lunch,' Miss Cochrane wrote. 'On the assumption you got your sums wrong, I am enclosing this because I certainly would not expect to pay less for a lunch like that. With grateful thanks, Louise Alicia Cochrane.'

'I've never seen food like that afore,' Etta said as she took her apron off. 'I didna ken ye could cook like that.'

Catriona put the money in the box and locked it. 'Nor did I,' she said softly, after the door had closed behind Etta.

*

After that the Rose Tearoom was busy, so busy that Catriona rarely had time to think beyond the immediacies of preparing the food and serving it, making sure that the waitresses smiled politely and the roses in the vases were fresh. Robbie Thompson came on Monday mornings to nurture the bushes; she collected an armful of blossoms twice a week and in return gave Robbie 7/6d and his lunch on his day off. Etta was rushed off her feet at first until Catriona found two other waitresses, young girls straight from school who smiled easily and worked willingly. Catriona made sure that she paid just over the going rate; she was fair but not generous to the girls.

Rory arrived one Sunday; she was so busy she did not see him for an hour, noticed him only when Etta tutted about the man who was spending ages over just one cup of tea.

She ushered him through to the kitchen, leaving him there at the table with soup and a chicken pasty until the rush ended when the tearoom closed at six o'clock. It was twenty past before she went back to find Rory with his sleeves rolled up washing dishes, Etta with a sheepish expression saying that he had insisted.

'Oh, Lord, Rory,' she said, sinking down into a chair, 'will you ever forgive me?'

'Only if I can have some steak pudding for my tea.'

'You can't, but would roast beef do instead?'

'I suppose.'

Etta checked that all the tables were clear, and then left with the other girls.

Rory sat down and began to eat as Catriona carried Jamie's cot in from the garden.

'I've been so busy,' she said.

'Don't I know it? I've been down here twice and I couldn't even get a table.'

'I'm sorry.'

'Don't be.' He patted her hand. 'I'm glad you're doing well.'

As he ate she told him about Miss Cochrane's lunch, that she had been busy all the time since then, although the season proper had not started yet.

'You're going to be rich,' he said.

'Just so long as I make enough to buy the tearooms at the end of the year.'

He grinned and told her that his yard was doing well, that he had bought another half dozen lorries from the Cameron Highlanders and taken on more men. Once he finished his meal, she cleared away the dishes and then took him upstairs to the living room, settling him on a sofa as she made tea.

'You're tired, Triona,' he said when he saw her yawning.

'I'm fine, Rory.'

'You are not, girl. I'd best away and let you get some sleep.'

She was so exhausted that she did not have the strength to argue.

'Come again soon,' she said at the doorway. 'I'll make a steak and kidney pudding for you.'

'Don't you worry, I will.'

The summer rush started and Catriona's days began to run together, punctuated only by a few hours of sleep. In July, during the Glasgow Fair, queues formed because of an article in the *Evening News* that described the most delightful seaside cafe, serving delicious teas in a room perfumed by roses. Catriona, dreadfully embarrassed, apologized profusely to her waiting customers and said discreetly that she would not be offended if they went instead to one of the cafes on the front.

'Whit?' a woman said. 'Ah can buy a tea any day, but ah canny drink it in a room fu' o' roses.'

When they eventually sat down and gave their order, they would look around and then tell each other that it was a braw place, a real palace, a right good find with the prices so reasonable too.

Catriona knew then that her instinct had been right, that all the hard work was worth it.

'You should put the prices up,' Etta said at the end of an exhausting day. 'It'd no' be quite as busy, an' you'd take the same money.'

246

That week, Catriona gave the waitresses a two-shilling bonus, something she promised them every week during the high season. She extended her opening hours from 10 a.m. to 10 p.m. and took on Etta's two young sisters to wash the dishes and keep the kitchen clean. Although she had not done her accounts yet, she was putting fifty or sixty pounds into the bank each week, after the bills had been paid.

She did not put up her prices.

She still remembered her dockworkers, the working men and their families whose few hours at the seaside during the Glasgow Fair made the only break in a long, hard year.

It was the end of September when trade slowed, but even then she was able to give one of the waitresses a job through the winter and keep another on to help her in the kitchen.

Robbie Thompson came and took away the roses, replacing the plants with azalias and cherries that bloomed right through the winter.

She handed him an envelope in which she had put a five-pound note.

'Ach, lass,' he said, 'ye dinna need tae do that. It's been a richt pleasure tae help ye.'

'Please,' she said, as she handed him a letter for Miss Cochrane, to thank her as well.

'Like I says, lass, it's thanks enough fir us both tae see yon smile on yer face.'

Once she finished her accounts, she found that she had made a profit of nearly eight hundred pounds. She asked Aggie Donoghue if she was still willing to sell the premises for £200 and when Aggie agreed, Catriona went to the solicitor, Mr Hendry, to arrange it. On the day she got the title deeds she kept them in her apron pocket, only putting them away in her desk when she realized they would get stained. She hired the local painter to freshen up the paintwork, then paid the electricity company to have electric lighting installed. Every day, after she had taken Jamie for his walk along the seafront, she would stand in the street for ages and gaze at her tearoom, almost unable to believe that it was truly hers.

Finally, she wrote home and told Maire and Allan that she had a home ready for them at last. Allan replied, in carefully joined up writing, to tell her that he and Maire would come in the spring, once Sine was safely wed.

Rory came down in October, amazed that in the afternoon the tearoom was quiet, but on that day an icy gale blew in from the sea, driving streaks of rain down the windlashed streets.

'How are you?' he asked, feeling his heart lift at her smile as he walked in the door.

'Did you get my letter?'

'I did that. I would've come sooner but I've been working on the trucks. It's the busy time, y'see, for coal, with the winter coming.'

Etta brought some coffee and a piece of the new chocolate cake that Catriona made from a recipe from Miss Cochrane's chef.

'I don't suppose you've got any steak pudding?'

'Aha,' she said, 'that's where you're wrong. I've had a steak pudding waiting for you the last few weeks, but you didn't come. There's one on now, we can have it later once the tearoom's closed.'

He watched her chat to the last of the customers, then followed her as she turned out the lights and went upstairs.

'I never thought I'd be glad to have a quiet day,' she said, 'but I am now.'

The table in the sitting room was already laid; he sat there as she brought him a huge plate of pudding, with potatoes, carrots and mushrooms.

Rory was wearing a carefully pressed tweed suit, a sporting suit the tailor had told him, not that he knew the difference. He had seen himself just once in the tailor's mirror and thought there was too much of the toff about him, but it was too late; he had already paid the money.

Outside there was a brand new Austin, registration number KA 45; a car he had bought because he didn't want to park his filthy coal truck outside Catriona's tearoom.

She still wore a maid's dark dress, though no longer with an apron. Rory felt the stiff collar of his shirt tight against his neck; he rubbed his finger around inside to loosen it, then gave up and undid the tie instead.

He wondered if she noticed the effort he had made.

She was washing Jamie's hands and face in a bowl on the kitchen table; he heard the splashing sounds as he ate. Once Jamie was changed and dried, she rocked him in her arms until he slept, then, putting her finger to her lips, carried him to his cot.

Rory carried his dishes through to the kitchen and began to rinse them himself.

'Rory,' she exclaimed, exasperated. 'Away and sit down and let me do that. You'll ruin your new suit.'

He laughed. 'I was wondering if you'd noticed, if you ever would.'

'I noticed soon's you came in the door.'

They sat down on opposite chairs, either side of the fire. She asked him how his yard was going and he told her about the new contracts he had, the new trucks he had bought, and the men he had taken on. 'I'm up to my neck in hock,' he said, almost defiantly.

Her face sharpened in concern.

'I had to do it, Catriona. If I hadn't taken the contracts, somebody else would've. There's all these trucks from the war, going begging with no use for them, and all the mines want proper transport, not horses and carts anymore. It's quicker, you see. And cheaper. I borrowed the money from the bank at five per cent. I'll pay them back in a year or two.' He explained that he had started a company, a limited company that limited his liability for debts.

Catriona had gone pale at the mention of the word.

'It's all about risk, see. Taking a chance.'

'But you could lose everything.'

'Then I'd just start again.'

'I don't know, Rory.'

'I'll make it, you'll see.'

'I know you will.'

She told him her own news, that Maire and Allan were coming down in the summer, once Sine had married Archie MacLellan. 'It's so strange,' she said, 'thinking of Sine getting married. But she's almost sixteen, after all. She's old enough.'

'Have you ever thought of getting married yourself, Triona?'

Her face flashed pain for a moment; he sensed the deep well of sadness in her that he had seen before, could have kicked himself for hurting her for no reason. As it was, owing a thousand pounds, even Lachlan Maclean would have been a better prospect than he was. Jealousy reared briefly; he still could not believe that Lachlan had meant anything to her at all.

She trembled just slightly, and hazarded a smile. 'There's trouble at home, Rory.'

He cut her off; told her he knew that. He was relieved that it was her family who pained her and not anyone else. Since she had told him about Lachlan, he had asked around, found out that Lachlan had been saying he was going to marry her. He did not believe it, but he knew that her kindness would not have made it easy for her to turn down Lachlan, that her loyalty would make her mourn his death almost as much as if she was grieving.

'I've had to do what I could. I haven't had time to think about things like that.'

'Nor me, Triona.'

Her eyes twinkled. 'I've heard stories about you, Rory MacDonald.'

He blanched. 'Catriona! I work the night through on my trucks. I hardly get an hour's sleep before the next day starts again. I don't even have the time to eat. Soup and a sandwich most days, that's all.'

'There's always a meal for you here.'

'I know that.' He paused, looking at his hands which he had meshed together. 'I was thinking, Triona, would you like to come home at Christmas?'

'Home?'

'Just for a couple of days. We'll drive up in the car. It takes less than a day.'

'I don't know.' She thought for a moment. 'It's Jamie, you see.'

'My mother'd take him.'

She thought for a moment longer. 'To hell with that, Rory. I'll take him myself, and stay with Annie. I'd love to come, Rory. I really would.'

She hugged him as he left; the perfume of her, the scent of baking and cooking, the faintest hint of flowers, stayed with him all the way back to the yard.

The telegram came on a grim day in November, the telegraph boy knocking the door so hard that he sounded just like the hailstones that had fallen during the night.

It was six o'clock in the morning, late for Catriona who usually rose before the crack of dawn, but the summer had tired her and she felt a delicious sense of wellbeing in the knowledge that she could sleep a little more.

'Telegram,' he yelled through the door.

'What?' Catriona got up, throwing a wrap over her nightgown as she ran down the stairs.

'Are you sure it's for me?'

'Nicolson, yes? C. Nicolson, Castle Street? It's for you, Missus, right enough.'

As she took the envelope she noticed that it was splattered with rain because she had kept the boy waiting for so long.

The dull dread gripped her stomach then, as she fumbled with the flimsy paper to open it.

She read the line once and then sat down to read it again:

'Allan very sick. Please come. Love Annie.'

'No,' she whispered, 'please God, no.'

The tears came and she crumpled up into a ball, rocking to and fro in the chair as the legs creaked and threatened to splinter, making loud cracking sounds that rang through her head. After a moment she collected herself, dried her tears and threw her coat over her nightgown, then went to the post office to use the phone.

The phone at Rory's yard rang for ever before a man answered, telling her gruffly that Mr MacDonald was away, would not be back until the evening.

The postmistress overheard her. 'Miss Nicolson,' she said, 'the boat leaves Greenock at ten and I could get one of the men to take you there.'

'The train would be quicker.'

'I wouldn't risk it, Miss Nicolson. That wind last night, there's trees down, blocking the line. It could take all day to clear them.'

When Etta came at eight o'clock she found Catriona dry-eyed, already packed for the journey home.

'Please,' she asked, 'can you stay here and look after Jamie?'

'I'll take him home to Ma,' she replied. 'Don't worry, Missus. He'll be fine wi' us.'

Chapter Ten

'*I* can hold it a few hours, lass,' the ferry captain said, ''till eight o'clock tonight, but no' much longer.'

The mist was low on the hills, a light rain falling. Catriona stepped down onto the quayside and looked around, seeing nobody familiar. Running into the town, she found the merchant Macleod outside his shop, his eyes narrowing as he saw her.

'You've a van,' she began.

'It's away at Sleat,' he said, 'won't be back till the evening.'

She turned away, walked into the square and saw a man she vaguely remembered.

'Please,' she said, 'I need to get to The Braes. D'you know anyone with a car?'

He started to smile in the lazy way that islanders used to deal with tourists, then recognized her as a native when she repeated the question in Gaelic.

'What's the matter, girl?'

'My brother's sick,' she said, 'very sick. I have to get home, maybe bring him back here.'

He whistled to one of the men at the harbour, and told him to fetch Cameron. 'He's just gone down the road, lass. We'll have him back in a minute.'

She reached for her purse, then recalled that he would be insulted if she offered anything.

'You work down there?' He nodded to the south.

'Yes. I didn't know, I only got the telegram yesterday.'

A van rolled over the cobbled square, reeking of fish and salt. The man helped her in and wished her luck. Cameron, driving, recognized her as her father's daughter. 'Don't worry, lass, we'll have you in Braes in no time.'

The land rolled past jerkily, like a newsreel. Reaching the crest of the hill, she saw her village, autumn bleak on this dull day against the slate-grey sky.

'Up top?' he asked, gesturing towards her father's croft.

'No,' she said, directing him to Annie MacDonald's.

'I'll wait here,' he said, turning the engine off. 'If you need me, just yell.'

Annie's door opened when she heard the van. Catriona saw her standing there, rubbing her hands together.

'He was asking for you,' she said, 'I've called the doctor, I asked the post to get him four days past, but he's not come yet.'

Catriona entered the cottage and saw that Iain and his sons were sitting on the far side, away from Allan's mattress beside the fire. The cottage smelled of boiling water and iodine from the seaweed poultice that was simmering on the heat.

Allan was as pale as the sheet he lay against; hardly awake, he tried to say something, coughed then tried again.

'Wheesht,' Annie whispered, 'Triona's here now.'

Catriona saw that he was struggling to smile. She went to him and felt the fire in his brow, saw the dark streaks underneath his eyes. The sound of his breath was like raking coal. She stood up, feeling gratitude surge for Annie. Fever was feared more than anything in the islands, more even than witchcraft. If there was fever in a house, people stayed away, for fear of catching it. It was considered an act of bravery to deliver food to a house where there was fever, even to leave it outside for the sick to fetch for themselves.

'Marsaili was afraid for her young ones,' Annie said. Catriona knew then that she had put Allan out of the house.

'Where's my father?'

'I've not seen him for days.'

Catriona was thinking of the hospitals in the south, of the doctors who had cured men from the war who had contracted typhoid and lung disease. The islanders had no faith in hospitals and little in the doctors; yet there was nothing here beyond age-old remedies and hope.

Allan's face was turned towards her; she felt his trust, his will. She knelt beside him again. 'Could you manage to get onto the boat?'

He nodded once, smiling weakly.

Annie went to the press. 'I'll get some clothes for him. You can take these blankets.' As Allan struggled to sit up, Catriona saw how thin he was, and realized that although he was twelve years old now she could carry him herself.

She went outside and told Cameron. There wasn't room for Allan in the front, but he had a tarpaulin in the back and he went to find some hay to make a bed.

When she told him about the fever, he nodded grimly, saying that he had survived it in the trenches; it wouldn't strike him now.

Before she reached the door of her father's cottage, Marsaili pulled it open and stood barring her way. Catriona pushed her aside and saw her father, hunched over the fire. He turned towards her, but his eyes were glazed with whisky.

Maire rushed to her and Catriona saw that she had been weeping. 'Fetch your clothes,' she said, 'I'm taking Allan home.'

Her father mumbled something, words that made no sense.

'Where's Sine?' she asked Maire.

Marsaili was standing on the doorstep. 'I want you out of here. Not that it's you, mind, but I don't want the little ones to get the fever.'

Sine ran up, out of breath. She had been washing clothes in the stream and her hands were raw with the cold.

'I'm taking Allan,' Catriona said. 'Do you want to come with us?'

Sine hesitated.

Her father stood then, swaying until he steadied himself. 'Get out, the lot of you. Get to hell, why don't you?'

The words whipped Catriona; her head jerked back as if she had been hit.

'You too, Sine,' he snarled, 'away to hell, the lot of you.'

Maire had a little bundle underneath her arm; she slipped out of the cottage and waited. Sine thought for a moment and then went to the press and took out her spare blouse and her nightgown.

'Don't look at me,' Tom Nicolson slurred, the words almost indistinguishable. 'Wasn't me that gave him the fever. Wasn't me that made him sickly. Can't have fever in the house, not with the young ones.'

Catriona was shaking. 'Father, Da,' she said softly, 'don't you remember anything?'

'Whassat?' he mumbled. 'Whaddyou mean?'

'Don't you remember Mother, don't you remember Mor?'

For a moment he swayed as if caught off balance. 'Don't you say that,' he muttered. 'Don't anybody say that.'

'Ma wouldn't have done that. Ma went to people with fever, you remember that.'

Tom sat down again, his head nodding to and fro like the cuckoo in a clock.

Catriona walked out, ignoring Marsaili. Maire and Sine were at the end of the path.

'Catriona,' Sine began, 'I'm going to wed Archie Mac-Lellan. I'll go and stay with his mother.'

Catriona looked at her; she needed time to talk but she had none. 'Are you sure, Sine?' The years had turned her into a pretty girl with hair the colour of the sun and open, laughing eyes. Sine was like Ailish, but she had no time for vanity, Catriona knew; her hands told the story of hard work. As Sine put her hand to her brow to brush away a strand of hair, Catriona saw the rough, red, callused skin of a woman twice her sister's age.

'Archie's a good man,' Sine said. 'He'll get a croft in time, if anybody does.'

'Will you stay with his mother till you're wed? I'll send you money.'

She shook her head. 'Catriona, you don't need to.'

Catriona hugged her and felt the years apart, the time that had made young women of the sisters she had left as children.

'I'll not be here for your wedding,' she said.

'You will too,' Sine said, 'because you're always here with us, in our hearts.'

Annie was waiting for them. 'He's all ready,' she said, 'Iain'll carry him out.'

'No,' Catriona said, 'I will.' She drew Annie aside. 'I'll send money. Will you make sure that Sine has a good wedding?'

Annie looked away and brushed her eye. 'Of course. I'll pray for you. For you all.'

Allan was as light as a feather. In the back of the van Cameron had laid down straw. She cradled her brother in her arms and drew a blanket over him. Maire climbed up and sat beside her. The van started; Catriona felt every jolt as she watched the land fade. Passing the familiar landmarks, she felt herself passing through time, wishing that she could peel back the years and the mistakes she had made.

Money doesn't matter, she thought, the slum in the Briggait didn't matter because if Allan had been there with her, he wouldn't have sickened like this.

Maire was looking at her, her brown eyes soft with tears.

'It was very quick,' she said, 'he got a cold a week ago and the next day he couldn't get up. Da took him to the doctor a while back and he said it was just an abscess.'

Catriona was praying silently, to Mor or God, whoever would listen, to give Allan strength to survive the journey.

When they reached Portree Cameron would not even let her pay him for his petrol.

'Good luck, lass,' he said, 'I'll wish you God speed.'

The captain gave her a cabin close to the boiler room, and told her that the weather looked good, that the sea shouldn't be too rough.

Catriona clasped her brother's hand. 'Allan,' she whispered, 'it won't be so much longer. The worst is over now.'

His eyelids flickered and he slept.

Rory was waiting at Greenock with his car. 'I got your message,' he said.

'Rory, please, just take us home, as quickly as you can.'

At the tearoom she asked Etta for the doctor's address, and told Maire to go in and help herself to some food.

The doctor's house wasn't far away, but his waiting room was already full. A nurse was measuring liquid into bottles as Catriona walked in.

'Please,' Catriona said, 'my little brother's outside in the car. He's very sick.'

The nurse looked at her for a moment.

'Please,' Catriona asked again.

The nurse put down the bottle, dried her hands and followed her out.

'What's the matter?'

'He's fevered, he's been coughing blood.'

The nurse opened the door and saw Allan. 'Oh, my God,' she said, 'you were right not to bring him in.'

Her manner changed as she picked Allan up and gently carried him into the doctor's house through a side door. 'I'll just get the doctor, if you wait a minute.'

The doctor came, brisk footsteps against the linoleum. The room felt so cold that Catriona had begun to shiver.

He looked at Allan briefly, then turned to her. 'How long's he been like this?'

'I . . .' She wrapped her arms around her chest and hugged herself defensively. 'I don't know. I got a telegram saying he was ill. We're from Skye. My sister says he got a cold last week.'

The doctor lifted Allan's shirt and began to listen to his chest, removing the stethoscope after a moment or two as if the action was a formality.

Catriona's anxiety overwhelmed her. 'Did I do the right thing?'

The doctor looked at her as if he did not understand.

'Bringing him here. I thought he'd be better here than at home.'

The nurse hovered, holding a bowl of disinfectant. The doctor was taking Allan's pulse.

'I wasn't sure,' Catriona said in a small voice. 'He seemed so terribly ill.'

'He's been ill for some time,' the doctor said, 'must've been to be in this state.'

Catriona looked at Allan, lying silently as the doctor examined him. Quickly, she asked the question in Gaelic; Allan nodded and said he'd not been feeling well for months but he didn't want to worry anyone.

The doctor said something to the nurse and then turned to her. 'It's very advanced, you know.'

'What is?'

'Tuberculosis. Your brother's illness.'

'What's tuberculosis?' she asked. The word meant nothing to her. 'I don't know,' she said, 'I didn't know. You see, I live here, down here. Two years ago, I sent money for the doctor, for medicines, but he got better. They told me he got better.'

The nurse gripped her arm and helped her to sit down.

'Did you bring him from Skye?' she asked, in a voice that sounded kind.

'Yes,' Catriona said dully, 'on the boat. They'd called the doctor, but ... I thought I'd bring him back with me. You can cure him, can't you? Can't you?'

'We'll send him to the sanatorium,' the doctor said, 'the Alexandra. Don't worry, it won't cost you a penny.'

'I don't mind,' Catriona said quickly. 'I can afford to pay.'

He smiled sadly. 'Miss Nicolson, I doubt it would make any difference. The disease is far advanced, in both lungs. I've never seen it as bad as this.'

'But he'd have a better chance.'

'Miss, perhaps ...' The nurse bent down and whispered something into his ear. 'There's a sanatorium down the coast,' he said, 'at Ardrossan. The matron there is the best tubercular nurse in the country. I'll go to see if they will take him.'

Catriona went to Allan, held his hand and mopped his brow. He was sleeping again, in that strange state he had been in during the journey. 'You're going to get better,' she whispered, 'you will.' His hand tightened slightly on hers; she knew that he would, if he had a chance.

259

The nurse came in with warm, sweet tea, forcing her to sit down and drink as she mopped Allan's brow. 'It isn't your fault,' she said, 'a disease is nobody's fault. You mustn't blame yourself.'

'I should have known.'

'How could you?'

The doctor came back and said that Allan could be admitted to Carnbrae that afternoon, that the matron was sending an ambulance to collect him.

'I'll go with him,' Catriona said.

The doctor seemed about to argue, but stopped when he saw the determination on her face.

Carnbrae Sanatorium was a sandstone villa set in grounds in which honeysuckle grew and a stream bubbled gently beneath ornamental wooden bridges carved in the Chinese fashion. Catriona dimly noticed patients in day beds on the veranda, others walking over the lawn. As two nurses helped Allan into a wheelchair, a woman in a matron's cap introduced herself as Miss Logan.

'Please,' Catriona said, 'can you save my brother?'

'I promise you,' the matron said, 'I'll do the best I can.'

Rory, who had followed the ambulance to Ardrossan, drove her home. The journey passed in silence; as Rory turned into Castle Street, Catriona realized that she had bitten her nails to the quick. She thanked him; he touched her cheek lightly.

'Don't worry,' he said, 'I'll come on Sunday.'

After he left, she remembered that this was the busiest time of his year.

Indoors she found Maire sitting beside the unlit fire. Etta had put Jamie to bed; when Catriona went to his room, he stirred briefly and then settled again. She thanked Etta and sent her home, telling her to take two days off.

'Maire,' she asked, 'why didn't you light the fire?'

Maire looked uncertain and Catriona remembered her own shock when she arrived at Mrs Gordon's. Briskly, she lit the fire and then the lights; she looked at Maire and saw her bare feet under the ragged skirt, the shawl tightly clutched to her chest.

'This is your home,' Catriona said softly, kneeling in front of her sister and taking her hands. 'In the morning we'll get some new clothes for you, shoes and a warm coat for the winter.'

Maire was sobbing silently. 'How is Allan?' she asked after a while.

'He's in hospital with tuberculosis, phthisis they call it.'

'Will he die?'

'I won't let him, Maire.'

Maire began to sob again; Catriona left her for a moment to light the fire in her room.

'You're rich,' Maire said when Catriona came back with warm milk and honey. 'Allan said that you would be but Sine told him not to talk nonsense.'

'I am not,' Catriona said, 'this place was a midden a few months ago.'

'Who's the baby? What happened to Ailish?'

Catriona thought for a while and then she told her.

'Ailish said ...' Maire began, her voice tailing off into a murmur.

'Ailish said what?'

Maire looked down at her hands clasped in her lap. 'After the twins died, it was terrible, Catriona. Da stated to drink, he drank so much that he was never sober, always drunk, and Marsaili was on at Ailish. Ailish used to stand up to her, used to fight her 'cept sometimes Da would tell them to shut up 'cos they hurt his head. Ailish said we'd go down to you but Annie said we couldn't because you'd not be earning much more than you sent home. So Ailish just went anyway. Then she wrote to us and said the city was terrible, almost as bad as home. She said she was going to America, but she didn't tell us she'd had a baby.'

The fire had begun to give off heat; Maire had taken off her shawl and was warming her hands before the flames.

'Maire,' Catriona started, fumbling for the words, 'Maire, Ailish took the money I'd saved to get us a place to live. That was how she got to America.'

Maire shook her head.

'She did.'

'I don't doubt it, Triona. I just don't know why.'

Catriona brushed her hair back with her hand. 'It was money for all of you. I saved for the twins first, 'cos I thought they could build a cottage on Angus's croft. After they died, I was saving to get a place to live. Then Ailish came, and I couldn't find anywhere, not with her being pregnant. We ended up in a slum.'

Maire touched her hand. 'It doesn't matter.'

'But it does, Maire. Don't you see? I should've had you down two years ago. If I'd done that, Allan wouldn't be as sick as he is.'

'You don't know that, Triona.'

'I do, Maire. Liam told me, Liam told me that I should give you the choice, but I didn't want to. I didn't want anybody to have to live there but me.'

'Who's Liam?'

Catriona shook her head; so much time had passed, there was so much that Maire did not know

'Oh. Liam, Liam Devlin. He was a man, Maire, an Irishman. A great, big, wonderful Irishman. He had a building in Shipbank Lane, and when Ailish went to America he let me use his kitchen for free to start my bridie stall.'

'Bridie stall? I thought you were a lawyer's clerk.'

'Oh, I was, but I gave that up when Ailish left. I started a coffee stall when we went to the Briggait; I made more money at that in a night than I did in a week in a law office. I met Liam then. When Ailish left, I did a round selling pies and bridies down by the docks.' She found herself smiling at the memory. 'That's how I made enough money to start this place. You see, after the war, there wasn't a flat to be rented for love or money to a single woman. So I had to make enough to get a place of my own.'

'And Liam, what happened to him?'

Catriona flinched. 'He died, Maire, in the war in Ireland. Almost a year ago to this day.'

'You loved him, didn't you?'

'Oh, Maire, yes I did.'

Maire came to her and held her whilst she cried. After a while, Maire went through to the little kitchen and made mugs of honey and milk. 'You know,' she said, 'I always thought it was you and Rory MacDonald.'

Catriona grinned. 'When I left home at first, I thought the sun rose and set on Rory MacDonald but then, well, he went away and I met Liam. Rory's just a friend, now.'

'Catriona, what you said about Ailish. And Allan and me. We wanted to see Sine wed, first. We both did. You see, she's been, she's been like you once were for us. So don't blame Ailish or yourself, not for that, not for anything. If you want to blame anyone, blame Da or Marsaili.'

'Oh, Maire,' she said, 'I'm so glad you're here.'

Rory came on Saturday night, as they were eating their evening meal.

Maire got up to get him some food.

'Catriona,' he began, as she looked at him with a face so sad that he squirmed inside, 'what can I do?'

She tried to smile; he could have cried for her. 'Allan's very ill, Rory. I can't see him this week, but the matron says I can go next Sunday. I can get the train.'

'The hell you will, girl. I'll pick you up and take you there.'

Maire put his food down then, sousled herrings with shredded cabbage and stovies.

'No,' he said, 'I haven't time.' He had a coal lorry waiting outside, work still to be done, though the thought of a hot meal made his mouth water.

Catriona walked downstairs with him, her own meal hardly touched.

'Go and get some sleep,' he said, 'you look like a ghost.'

She smiled grimly. 'No. I'm going to start on the kitchen. The doctor's sending the public health inspector. I've got to make sure everything's clean.' She stifled a sob.

He crushed her into his arms. 'Place's spotless; they'll see that.'

'Don't, Rory.' She pushed him away. 'Allan could've given me TB and I could give it to you.'

'Catriona, God's sake . . .' He tried to hug her again, but she put up a hand to stop him.

'The inspector's coming round on Monday morning.'

She rolled up the sleeves of her blouse, then put an apron over her skirt. 'You'd best go, Rory, and let me get on with it.'

'What d'you have to do?'

'I'm going to wash the ceiling and the walls, then scrub them down with carbolic to kill the germs. Then I'll do the oven, the pantry and the floor.'

'There's time enough to do all that tomorrow.'

She shook her head. 'There isn't, Rory. I'm opening tomorrow. Carbolic stinks. It'd sicken the customer. If I do it tonight, the smell has time to clear.' She put her head to one side, as if she was thinking. 'I wasn't expecting you till tomorrow either.'

He smiled. 'I had an hour spare. I thought I'd come early, see if I could help.'

'Thank you, but you can't.'

'I can so.' He took his jacket off, rolled up his sleeves. 'If you've a chair, pet, I'll start on the ceiling, while you do the walls. We'll be finished in no time.'

Suddenly she slumped into a chair, put her head into her hands and began to sob. 'Oh, Rory,' she murmured, 'I couldn't take it if Allan died.'

He could think of nothing to say, so he held her hand.

'I'd rather it was me in there than him.'

'Ssshhh, Triona, it doesn't help him if you start thinking like that.'

'But he could die, Rory.'

He took a deep breath and decided on a risk. 'I don't think he will, pet.'

'Why not?' Her eyes sparkled with tears.

'Because I know him, girl. He's a brave wee lad. He's got your strength. He'll fight it, believe me.'

'I don't know what to believe any more, Rory.'

'Believe in him if you have a choice.'

He filled a bucket from the tap, took a cake of soap and rubbed it in the water until suds rose. Then, standing on a chair, he began to lather the walls carefully, cleaning every inch.

'I'll help you,' Catriona said.

He grinned. 'Thank you, but you can't,' he mimicked, so perfectly that she had to laugh at herself.

She got up to begin on the oven. Maire came down to see what they were doing and offered to start on the floor but Catriona told her to go to bed, and see to Jamie if he woke up.

'Rory,' she said, as she scoured the metal, 'what about the lorry?'

'The lorry can wait, Triona.'

'You haven't eaten any dinner.'

He grinned again. 'You can make me breakfast instead.'

Once every surface and object in the kitchen had been scrubbed, she got the bottle of carbolic she'd bought from the chemist, opened it and gagged as the sour, sharp smell spread through the room. Rory tied a napkin around his face, soaked a rag in the carbolic and began to work, washing for a second time everything he had washed already. Catriona wetted the mop and wiped the floor.

When they finished she opened the kitchen door to a fragile dawn, the breeze rushing into the room and taking the edge off the disinfectant sting.

She turned to Rory. 'What would you like for breakfast?'

'Ach.' She had made coffee midway through the night, that had kept him going. 'I don't think I could manage anything yet, Triona. I'll have to give my nose a while to get over the phenol.' He rinsed his hands in fresh water and rolled down his sleeves.

They walked together down to the front, where he had left his lorry. Early mist lay over the firth; the little island called Great Cumbrae timidly peered through the veil, shy as a bride on her wedding day. In the distance the hills of Bute rose lazily to face the morning. The rising sun crested the brae then kissed the sea, sending ripples of light trembling across the water.

Catriona felt hope again. She turned to Rory. 'I'll never be able to thank you,' she said.

'You don't have to.' He grasped her hand for a moment before he turned to open the lorry door.

She shook her head. 'I wouldn't've made it if you hadn't helped.'

'Aha,' he said, smiling, 'that's a different story now,' before he came closer and whispered in her ear: 'Don't talk nonsense. You're stronger than that.'

With a cheery wave, he was off. She stood watching his lorry until it vanished and then walked home slowly, so grateful that she had him for a friend.

She rang his yard on Monday afternoon and told him in a small voice that the health inspector had said the tearoom was fine, also that neither she nor Maire had contracted the disease.

During that month Allan's lungs began to bleed, but he held on grimly, clung to his life with a will so strong that only his sister understood

Catriona visited the sanatorium every week; Rory took her and waited during the visiting hour. For a long time Allan was so weak that he could only hold her hand limply, he did not have the strength to talk. The nurses kept his room stiflingly warm and the only sound was the ragged croak from his chest.

All Catriona could do was to whisper words of encouragement and watch for the occasional flicker of his eyelids. When she got into the car to go home again, all she did was sob.

Rory would stop the car to try to comfort her.

'I remember,' she said once, 'there used to be seven of us. Ewan and Alec and Ailish, Sine and Maire and Allan.'

'I understand,' he said.

'How could you? Your brothers survived the war.'

'Yes,' he reasoned, 'but I've seen what it did to you.'

She swore then, fully, roundly, harshly. 'To hell with all that, Rory. I'm not going to let it do anything to me any more.'

During the first week in January Miss Logan told her that there was a little improvement. Catriona hardly listened to her at first, because she did not dare to believe he would recover.

Miss Logan said, 'I sense he has the moral strength he needs to beat his illness.'

Just then, Catriona could perceive no difference, except that his breathing was a little easier.

'It'll be years yet,' Miss Logan said, 'but I think he'll pull through.'

'Why do you say that?' Catriona asked at last.

'Because I've never seen a patient survive so many bleeds. He must want to live greatly, he would have died otherwise.'

At the end of the month Catriona received a bill for twenty guineas; the doctor's fees were £ 2/10/-.

Miss Logan told her that the nursing home had a benevolent fund, and if the fees became too much she must let her know.

Catriona bridled and said she could manage. Allan's life was too precious for her even to think of what it would cost.

When she got into the car that day to go home, for the first time in weeks she did not cry. When Rory hazarded a funny story, about one of his lorries breaking down in Chryston High Street and having to be dragged back to the yard by horses, she even laughed.

He watched her walk into the tearoom, smiling as if she hadn't a care in the world. Tiredly, he reversed the car and began the drive back to his yard, thinking of business again, of the bank loan and the broken-down truck, of the wages to be paid and bills to be met. Sometimes he wished he had not taken on quite so much, had more time to spend with the woman he loved. Yet he knew she was still hurting, still fragile despite the brave face she put on for the world. Only one person knew how he felt about Catriona; he had told his mother, at Christmas time, when he went home to spend the holiday with his family – the holiday he had hoped to spend with Catriona. His mother cautioned him to wait, to give Catriona time to heal the wounds of the war and of her own past. He had asked her how long; she had shrugged and told him that she did not know, but *he* would when the time was right.

The new year brought its own promise. Allan hadn't bled for a month and the ruddy bruises on his chest had begun to fade. His sputum was no longer crimson, but the more normal rusty phlegm characteristic of tuberculosis. On Skye, the factor had given Archie MacLellan a little cottage in the hills above Portree; Sine would marry him in May, when she turned sixteen. Maire's sadness faded; in Largs she began to smile again, to laugh even. Jamie was two years old and walking; and beginning to talk in a language somewhere between Gaelic and English. He had come to love his Aunt Maire almost as much as he loved Catriona.

On a Sunday in January Catriona took the train to see Allan, and returned in time to make Rory his dinner, for once. She had decided to close on Sundays for a month or two; the town was so quiet in the winter months.

Rory's face broadened into a smile when he saw the spread of steak and kidney pudding, stovies and mashed turnip, a chocolate cake covered with cream and cherries, and half a dozen different types of tart.

'Have to rush,' he said, as he sat down. 'Visiting stops at half past three.'

'I've been already,' Catriona told him. 'I took the train. I didn't want to spoil your meal.'

Rory began to eat and didn't stop until he had finished all of the pastries and Maire was gaping at him in astonishment.

'I wanted to thank you,' Catriona said. 'You don't have to come every Sunday any more. I can manage myself now that Allan's so much better.'

'I won't hear of it,' he said, 'I enjoy the drive.'

'But you must be busy, Rory.'

'No,' he lied. In fact he was doing deliveries on Sundays to the city foundries; he started before dawn and did not finish until after midnight because of the hours he took off to go to Largs.

'Well,' she said, as she helped Maire clear the table, 'you must come at noon from now on so that we can feed you first.'

'Rory fancies you like the devil,' Maire whispered in the kitchen as they were washing up.

'That's nonsense,' Catriona said, 'he's just got a kind heart.'

In the third week in January the tearoom suddenly became quieter than quiet. It began on a Monday when a wind as strong as a gale blew in from the sea, lashing the front with spray; there were no customers that day, beyond a man with binoculars who came in at midday for a bowl of warming soup. He spoke with a thick accent; Etta said she thought he was a spy until he told Catriona that he was a biologist who had come to watch the winter birds.

On Tuesday, nobody came at all, although the wind was down a bit and the sun broke the clouds for an hour or two in the early afternoon. On that day, as usual, Catriona had baked a batch of scones for the ladies who liked to buy half a dozen because they were so busy with the Church Guild that they had no time to bake their own. The scones cooled on the griddle; the icing of the chocolate cake hardened and the chicken savouries congealed. At closing time Catriona packed a box for Alice and another for Etta. In the larder, she kept cakes for two days, but she always made scones and savouries fresh.

'It's the time of year,' Maire said, 'isn't it? The weather, and there's no visitors.'

'There's always trade from the town,' Catriona said tersely, thinking of the fashion that Miss Cochrane had started.

The pattern continued through the week; by Friday, when she did her accounts, there was nothing to bank and only bills to pay. Catriona began to worry, but told herself it was just the season. The January winds were bitter cold; people walked through the streets bent against the wind, their cheeks buffeted raw and their lips tightened against chilblains. These southerners were soft, prey to the winter; they wouldn't want to stay out for longer than they had to, away from their own firesides. She told herself that, then remembered December when there had been solid, driving rain for a week and the tearoom was packed with shoppers taking a break from the weather.

Robbie Thompson came in to give her some potted chrysanths and a few tight rosebuds from the hothouse. For the first time ever, she had to take his money from the cash she had withdrawn to pay the bills and not from the takings.

'How's Miss Cochrane?' she asked, because the Daimler hadn't drawn to a halt outside since before Christmas and she missed her chats with the jolly old lady.

'She's away to Amazonia, mind? There was a wee note with your Christmas card.'

'Is that where the house is in Stirling?'

Robbie smiled gently. 'Amazonia's in South America, in Brazil. She's gone to collect orchids.'

Catriona felt gauche and regretted asking him.

'Is there aucht the matter, lass?' he asked.

'I don't know,' she replied. 'It's gone so quiet all of a sudden. I don't know why.'

Etta hesitated after she had been given her wages, shifting from foot to foot. She was in her coat, ready to leave, dithering for some reason as if she had something to say. Maire came in then with Jamie; she had taken him for a walk to watch the angry sea. His face was flushed and he was laughing.

'D'you know,' Maire said, as she took off her coat and shook it in front of the kitchen fire, sending droplets of water to singe on the flames, 'that woman Mrs Wallace? The nice one who used to come in every day for a cup of hot chocolate?'

'Yes,' Catriona said distractedly.

'Well, she was down buying fish and I saw her and went over to say hello, but as soon as she saw me she crossed the road and hurried away, as if I had the plague.'

Catriona's attention fixed on her sister. 'Are you sure?'

'Yes. She saw me and she sort of stopped, then when she saw me walking towards her she turned away.'

Alice had finished sweeping the floor of the tearoom. She came in and took her wages, thanked Catriona and said she would see her the next day.

Etta was still standing there, biting her lip.

'What is it, Etta?'

'Well, Missus, you'll not be wanting me any more, will you? Wi' the trade like it is, there's aucht to do and it's a waste of money paying my wages.'

'The trade'll pick up, Etta, next week or the next again. You'll see.' Catriona could feel her own certainty wavering, but she believed in herself; she had no choice.

'My da doesn't want me working here any more,' Etta blurted. 'He didn't want me to come in this week, but I said I had to. I told him it wasn't your fault, like. You're clean, Missus.'

Catriona's eyes narrowed. 'Clean, Etta? What do you mean?'

'Well, they're saying ... they're saying that your brother's got the consumption, and it's not safe here because there's disease.'

Catriona became deadly calm then; only Maire knew that was the mask of her anger. 'You know, Etta,' she said slowly. 'That happened three months ago and the only ones at risk were Maire and me because we were the only ones with him. We had our tests and we're clear; I burnt the clothes I'd worn and so did Maire. The doctor says there's no risk at all, the risk of TB comes from being coughed on by a stranger and bad sanitary conditions, and you know yourself how clean this place is. It's not typhoid or smallpox, Etta. Allan got TB long before he came to Largs; he's never even been in the tearoom because we took him straight to the doctor's and then to the sanatorium.'

'Folks is scared, but,' Etta said. 'Folks is scared of consumption and you've got to see that, and my da says I've not to work here 'cos he'd rather I was on the parish than in my grave.'

'Who's saying all this, Etta?'

'Folks, Missus, everyone.'

'*Who, Etta?*'

She looked away. 'It was Gracie that started it, Missus. Our Gracie, my cousin, mind?'

'I remember,' Catriona said tersely.

'She started saying he'd the fever and I telt her it wasn't the fever, it was the consumption.' Etta looked ashamed. 'I didna ken, Missus, truly, I didna ken. I never dreamt she'd do what she's done.'

Catriona got up and rubbed the crick in her neck. 'Do you want to stop working here, Etta? Do you want to leave your job?'

'No, Missus. That's what I told my da. I told him it was good working here, that I didna want to leave, but he says I must for the sake of my health.'

'Well, you go on home then, and don't worry about it. I'll come round to see your da later and I'll make sure he understands.'

'Don't, Missus, I wouldn't, if I was you. He's that feart, I doubt he'd let you in the house.'

'I'll speak to him outside then, Etta. Just you go home and leave it to me.'

She saw Etta's father that evening; he was still in his LMS uniform, back from his work at the station where he was a ticket collector. The family lived in one of the row of railway cottages; when his wife opened the door, Catriona caught a whiff of sweat and stale cabbage. She felt the insult of being left on the doorstep as Mrs Douglas went to fetch her husband.

'Mr Douglas,' she began, when he came out puffing at his pipe, blowing smoke at her face.

'There's aucht to say, lass,' he said gruffly, 'I'm sorry fir ye, but like I says, I won't let Etta be at any risk.'

'But there's no risk, Mr Douglas.'

'I'll not take a chance with consumption. Nobody would.' He sucked at his pipe, exhaled a cloud of smoke. 'That's aw' I've got tae say, Missus. My tea's ready the now, if ye please.'

'Wait!' Catriona thought hard. 'Mr Douglas, has anybody in your family ever been ill?'

'No' wi' the consumption, lass.'

'But you work at the station, don't you? The people there, the passengers, how d'you know you won't catch TB from one of them?'

His eyes narrowed. 'I don't, lass, but I ken that Etta could from your brother.'

Catriona shook her head. 'That's where you're wrong, Mr Douglas. Allan was never in the tearoom. I took him straight to hospital. Only my sister and I could've caught it, and we didn't because we've had our tests and we're clear.'

'Aye, but ye still could.'

'Mr Douglas, the public health inspectors would've closed me down, if there was any risk. Don't you see? I'd be closed down tomorrow if there was any chance that Etta or anyone else would get TB.'

He sucked on his pipe again, saying nothing.

'Ask the doctor, if you don't believe me. You've more chance of catching TB at the station than Etta has at my tearoom.'

Mr Douglas scratched his head. 'Mibbe I'll do that, lass. But richt now my tea's waiting, so I'll say cheerie-bye.'

She began to trudge home, feeling the icy sea wind bite at her face. At the end of the street she heard footsteps and turned to see Etta running towards her.

'Missus,' Etta gasped, breathless, 'ye've no' to worry, Missus. My ma said it was daft, so it was. My da didna ken the health inspector had been.'

'Etta, I wouldn't let you take the risk of catching TB. Or anyone else.'

'That't whit my ma says. She jist telt ma da tae stop being a silly bigot, an' he jist humphs, like. But he'll come roun',

Missus. I'll be back at work on Monday.' Etta frowned. 'Ye still want me, don't ye? Ye'll no' be giving me ma cards?'

'I still want you, Etta. Don't worry, I understand.'

As she walked the rest of the way home, through empty streets where the sounds of life spilled through tightly closed windows, she felt a rush of anger at the ignorance that bred so much fear.

Maire had her meal ready, a plate of herrings grilled in oatmeal and freshly baked soda bread that tasted stale and dry.

'I don't know what I'm going to do,' Catriona said, when she had eaten all she could.

Maire cleared the plates and brought through a pot of tea.

The upstairs sitting room was cosy with a rug by the fire and two soft armchairs, but it felt cold then as she began to sip her tea. Even in the dark winter nights Catriona rarely put the lights on, preferring the light of the fire, familiar from home, softer than the electric lights she'd had installed last year. In the low light Maire looked so young, her face as soft as a budding rose. Catriona caught the lines threaded across her brow; she didn't want her sister to have to worry, to age when she was young. In the mirror in the bathroom she had caught a glimpse of her own face, seen the dark shadows beneath her eyes and lines that ran either side of her mouth. I'm getting old, she thought in a flash; in March she would be twenty-two. She tried to relax her face, watching the lines fade and youth come again, and remembering Kate telling her not to become bitter.

She got up and snapped the lights on.

'If people think they'll catch TB ...'

'That's not true,' Maire said.

'It isn't, but if they think it is, they'll stay away.'

The furrows on Maire's brow deepened. 'Not for ever, Catriona.'

Catriona was thinking of the money in the bank, of how long it would last with Allan's hospital bills if she had nothing to put in.

'It's just gossip,' Maire said, 'it'll pass, like the wind. The customers'll come back, you'll see.'

'This girl, Gracie, the one who started it. I wouldn't give her a job, you see – because she's a bitch. And because she's a bitch, she's spreading the rumours. I should've given her the job, maybe.' She smiled wryly.

'Don't be daft, Catriona.'

'I don't want you worrying, Maire.'

'I won't, Catriona. You see, I believe in you.'

She looked away quickly, before Maire saw the doubt in her eyes.

When she went to Carnbrae that Sunday, Allan was being nursed on the veranda, wrapped up warmly against the wind from the sea. The sun had punctured the clouds; she felt a sudden rush of hope because of the tremulous colour she saw in his cheeks. Miss Logan believed in fresh air, and cajolled her patients out in all weathers to exercise their fragile lungs; nature, she said, was a better healer than anything the doctors had come up with yet. Catriona trusted her now, because she saw that Allan was getting better. Beneath the matron's brisk manner there was something very tender in the way that she cared for her patient. The sister told Catriona that Miss Logan herself had sat with him through the night during his bleeds, when his life had hung by a fragile thread. Allan told her that nurse Cicely sat with him and told him stories that never ended; he had to fight to hear the end of the story.

Catriona shuddered when she realized how close he had been.

She began to read him a letter from Sine; she was getting married in May. As always when Catriona began to speak of the island his face changed because he remembered the pain.

'I'm starting school,' he said, looking not at her but at the fat, tame pigeons that waddled over the lawn. Every two hours the patients were served warm milk or beef tea and trays of freshly baked sponges and scones. Sometimes, some of them dodged the nurses and fed the pigeons instead.

'That's good,' she said, brushing his hair from his brow. During the months in hospital, his hair had grown; the nurse had cut it by putting a bowl over his head and trimming the protruding edges, making him look like a monk.

'A tutor's coming,' he went on, 'I'll catch up soon, I promise you.'

'Allan, it doesn't matter. All that matters is getting well.'

He turned away again; she sensed that something was troubling him deeply.

'I can't walk, Triona.'

She rose and came around to the other side of the day bed so that she could see his face.

'Don't turn away again, Allan,' she said, 'listen to me. You will walk again.'

He looked deep into his eyes. 'Will I?'

'You will. In time. Your muscles are weak, but they'll grow strong again.'

Miss Logan had told her that the immobility would hit him hard once he began to recover, that because he was so young, he would not understand.

'Trust me,' she whispered.

'I always did, Triona. I knew you'd get me better.'

She had stayed too long, she realized when the nurses came out to bring the patients in for their evening meal. Rory always went for a walk along the shore, but he would have been waiting now for the best part of an hour.

'I have to go,' she said.

'Please, will you tell the nurse I don't like tapioca?'

She did as he asked, then stopped at Miss Logan's office.

'I haven't had this month's bill yet,' she said.

The matron frowned. 'It's already paid, Miss Nicolson. Just let me check.' She flicked through a ledger on her desk. 'Here it is: a year's fees, paid by Mr MacDonald at the beginning of the month. The young man who drives you down. He's a relative, is he not? He gave me to believe that he's Allan's uncle.'

'Yes,' Catriona said, backing out of the office. 'I forgot. How silly of me.'

In the car she studied Rory's hard profile, the sharp angle of his jaw. In the bright sunlight his hair was shot with colour, like Liam's, like her father's, but Rory was a different kind of man. He did not talk a lot, though he laughed easily; he preferred his coal trucks to the Austin, because a truck was more useful than a car.

'Why?' she asked. She did not have to say more for him to know what she was talking about.

He put his arm out of the window to signal as he stopped at a junction. Liam never stopped at a junction, he would slow down and then accelerate into the traffic, cursing impatiently. The difference between them struck her then, more than before, as she watched Rory's careful, precise movements.

'The money was in the bank. Better it went to some use.'

'I thought you'd borrowed from the bank.'

'I've done well. I've nearly paid them back.'

'I'll pay you back.'

'You will not, Catriona.'

'I will so.'

He slowed down to pass a horse and cart, careful not to surprise the animal. 'I've had a good year, Catriona, a very good year. You've had a lot of trouble.'

'I can manage.'

A look of exasperation flashed across his face. 'Catriona, I ...'

'Rory, I'll give you the money back. I'll write a cheque out when we get home.'

'Catriona, for God's sake. Why won't you let me help you?'

She thought for a moment, and realized that she did not know herself.

The road twisted, suddenly another cart hove into view and he swerved around it, tyres screeching because he was going too fast. She was sitting calmly beside him, and hardly noticed the sudden movement.

'God damn you, woman!'

She flinched.

'I didn't mean it like that. I meant, I nearly clipped the side of that cart, because I wasn't watching where I was going. I was watching you instead.'

'Rory, I've always managed myself. I . . .'

He pulled into the side of the road. 'Catriona, please, let me help you. Pay me back, if you like, but wait for the summer. Wait until the tearoom's busy again.'

'What do you know about that?' she asked sharply.

'Nothing,' he said, ''cept you said it was quiet just now.'

She was thinking of what the tearoom was worth, if the trade did not come back. If it was still quiet in March, she had decided to put it on the market, sell up and move elsewhere. If the worst came to the worst, she and Maire could always work as maids, and there would be enough in the bank to pay for Allan. She gritted her teeth because, despite everything, she loved Largs, loved her tearoom. 'If you don't mind,' she said, in a voice so small that it was almost a whisper.

'Course I don't.' He touched her hand, grinning broadly.

A few days later she met the district nurse as she was coming out of the dairy, where Catriona had cancelled her order for butter and milk. She had already given the hens back to the farmer, because she could not use the eggs.

'How's your brother?' the nurse asked, her grey eyes warm with concern.

Catriona smiled at the mention of Allan, because on Sunday he had been eating when she visited and his weight chart had finally steadied.

'He's . . .' she began, hesitating when she thought of his waif-like form. In the depths of her soul she believed that he would recover, but she hesitated to put all that hope into words. 'He hasn't had a bleed for two months,' she finished lamely. 'He's eating, a little; he's talking again.'

'I passed your tearoom the other day. It looked awfully quiet.'

Catriona flinched. 'People are staying away. They heard about his illness.'

'Oh.' The nurse turned up the collar of her coat. She put her hands on the handlebars of her bicycle, which she had propped against the kerbstone. 'You're staying open, though?'

'Yes. I have to.'

Catriona walked back, trying to smile at the people in the street, even when they turned away to avoid her.

At noon that day she heard the tearoom door opening. Going through from the kitchen, she found the nurse standing there, rubbing her hands. 'I thought,' she said, 'that I'd drop in here for a bowl of soup. It's five miles home otherwise, and half the babies in the town have come down with the croup.'

'You can sit by the fire if you like,' Catriona said. 'If you give me your coat I'll put it into the kitchen to dry.'

The nurse handed her the coat. 'If it's all the same to you, lass, I'll sit by the window. I like to sit and watch the world go by.'

Catriona went through to the kitchen, where Maire was heating the soup she had made for their own dinner.

'I used to come here in the summer,' the nurse called through, 'but I came one day and the queue stretched halfway down the street. I lost the habit after that. Daft, because you serve the best soup in Largs. But I'll come in every day now, and so will Nurse Cunningham.'

'Thank you,' Catriona said as she put down the bowl of chicken broth with a plate of soda bread, still warm from the oven.

The nurse clasped her hand briefly. 'Don't worry, lass. We'll see you through this.'

Catriona walked away quickly, so that the nurse would not see the tears streaming down her cheeks.

Her customers came back slowly, almost ashamed as they sat down and ordered tea and scones or coffee and cakes. Catriona served them herself, smiling all the time, for all the world as if nothing had happened.

No one ever asked how Allan was; no one mentioned her brother. Consumption was unmentionable; its stigma clung to the working classes, to the slums of Glasgow and the miners' cottages. In sanatoriums like Carnbrae, the rich recovered in genteel seclusion, the poor rarely recovered at all.

Catriona put the hard times behind her, trying not to think of how close she had come to losing it all.

The summer began, a few weekend visitors at first and then crowds who arrived by train or boat and thronged the streets, waking the town from its winter torpor.

Catriona started work at five in the morning and did not stop until late at night. Maire learned quickly; her native island charm delighted the customers, she had an easy, unhurried way about her that made them feel like her guests.

They were both used to hard work, had been almost all of their lives; Maire shared the task of caring for Jamie and made the long, busy days of the season almost fun.

Gracie Douglas's engagement was broken; her fiancé heard that she had gone to a dance with a tourist and then come home in the early hours of the morning, brushing bracken out of her skirt. Catriona felt a quiet satisfaction when she heard Etta tell Alice about it in the kitchen one day.

'You knew,' Maire said to her when they sat down for a cup of tea before the afternoon rush.

'Maybe,' Catriona said thoughtfully, 'maybe she'll think before she goes spreading tales again.' Robbie Thompson had told her the story; she had thought for a long time before she had passed it on to Jock Robertson, the fiancé, who was as innocent and defenceless as a hayfield ripening in the sun.

There was something evil about Gracie Douglas; Catriona had met her sort before, and long since tired of women like that.

'You have to be tough,' she said, 'else Gracie and her kind'd walk all over you.'

'Like Marsaili walked over Da?'

'That's in the past,' Catriona said briskly, rising and going over to the kitchen table where a large bowl of oatmeal was waiting to be made into biscuits.

The stranger arrived in June, a young man with olive skin and eyes as big as a spaniel's, who wandered up and down Castle Street aimlessly all day like driftwood caught on the tide.

'He's lost,' Maire said when she noticed him pass the window for the umpteenth time.

'Maybe he's a spy,' Etta said.

Catriona laughed because Etta's war wasn't over yet, she still remembered the stories of German saboteurs stalking the Clyde.

The man walked up the street, turning at the point where the shops ended and the houses began, and then walked down again. Reaching the tearoom again, he waited for an age and then shyly pushed open the door.

Etta dissolved into giggles and rushed into the kitchen. It was closing time and the streets had long emptied as the boats and trains went back to the city.

He had money in his hand; only coppers, Catriona saw, a few farthings and a penny or two. '*Prego*,' he stammered, '*caffè*?'

Catriona showed him to a table as he brushed his jacket apologetically. He was carrying a bag, or so it seemed, but when she looked closer she saw that it was a bundle of clothes, bound up with string. 'Go and get some soup,' she told Alice, 'and a couple of pasties.'

Alice just stared at him, so Maire went instead.

'No, no,' he said, when he saw the food. 'No money. Only *caffè*.'

'It's all right,' Catriona said, 'eat, if you are hungry.'

He nodded his head deferentially and then began to eat like a man who had not touched food for days. Maire brought more soup and bread, then leftover sandwiches and a pot of coffee.

The church clock chimed eight, and Etta and Alice left.

'I'll send my father,' Etta said, 'just tell him that if he makes any trouble.'

'He's got nowhere to go,' Maire whispered as he rose and began to thank them in a language they did not understand.

'Maire, we can't ...'

'There's the shed. It's cold at night, you know that.'

He's a stranger, Catriona thought, like a lowlander, forgetting for a moment her native mores, the custom of her people that permitted no one to go hungry or without shelter.

The man looked like a peasant, bred of simple rural folk. She sensed that he would not abuse her hospitality or her trust.

'Please,' she said, leading him through the kitchen into the garden and showing him the shed. Maire brought some blankets and a pillow. He tried so hard to thank them that he began to sob instead.

'People will talk,' Catriona said, back in the kitchen. 'He can't stay for long.'

'I doubt that anyone'll ever dare say anything about you ever again,' Maire said logically.

In the morning, in disjointed words and gestures, he explained that his name was Joe, that he was Italian and that he made ice cream.

Catriona began to think.

'Take him to the shops,' she told Maire. 'The fishmonger sells ice and he can get thick cream from the diary.' She had tried it herself several times but never achieved the texture of the Italian ice cream Liam had bought her in Glasgow.

Joe returned and, gesticulating wildly, closeted himself at the back of the pantry. Just after lunch he came out with a dish of vanilla, rich and light and smooth, and strawberry that tasted simply of heaven.

It was the best ice cream Catriona had ever tasted. Her interest quickened.

'Maire,' she said, 'how on earth do I explain to him that I want to give him a job?'

Chapter Eleven

*I*t took Allan four years to recover from tuberculosis. The illness changed him into an old man, grey-skinned and hollow-voiced; as he recovered he grew young again, though quieter and more serious than most boys of his age.

On the day that he left Carnbrae, Miss Logan and the nurses lined up with the medical superintendent and the resident doctor to wave him goodbye.

Catriona tried to thank the matron, but when she felt her voice crack she hugged her instead; the slight, dimple-cheeked woman was crying as well.

Allan stood waiting, ill at ease in unfamiliar outdoor clothes; the sanatorium had been his home for four years, the only place he had known besides the little cottage on Skye.

Catriona drove home slowly, watching his expression change as he saw a man on a bicycle, and a girl with cropped hair and the fringed dress of a flapper.

'I didn't know you could drive,' he said, watching the tense way she gripped the wheel. She had oversteered once and ended up in a hen run; she was still trying to regain her confidence.

'Why not?' she smiled. 'I watched Rory so often, there's not so much to it.'

The car was a second-hand Morris that roared like a lion when the gears were changed, rolled along the road like a thunderstorm on the level, coughed and protested at every little hill.

Allan knew the Rose Tearoom already because she had described every inch of it to him, told him stories about Miss Cochrane and Robbie Thompson and then taken him tubs of Joe's ice cream.

The Rose Tearoom was straining at the edges now, full every day between March and November and with a steady trade in the winter months. Since Joe's Ices had come into being, there wasn't enough room for it all and so Catriona had taken over an old newsagent's stall down the road where Joe sold his ices, and during the summer months there were always waitresses running in between the two places with customers' orders or more wafers for Joe.

They were all waiting, Maire and Rory and Jamie and Joe, with a huge ice-cream cake made especially to welcome Allan home.

Allan walked in and sat down. He was shaking slightly, too excited to eat the baked chicken she had made, or much more than a dish of ice cream. He was still thin, but growing rapidly. His sputum was clear of infection and had been for months; the doctors had promised her no recurrence.

'I never thought,' he said, when the hubbub had died down and the little party ended, 'I didn't think I'd see this day, you know.'

There were already traces of a man in the boy, in the way he blinked back his tears and tried to swallow away the tremor in his voice.

Catriona squeezed his hand. 'It's over now, Allan.' He was sixteen years old; she hated to think of how little of his childhood was left. In the sanatorium he had worked hard, done so well that Glasgow High had given him a scholarship for his final year; he was already talking about applying to the University.

Jamie was gazing at him wide-eyed, wondering at this new uncle who was still young enough to be a friend.

'Can you play marbles?' he asked.

Catriona reached for her purse and gave Allan some money. 'If you go down to the front, you'll find jugglers and coconut stalls and all sorts. The shove ha'penny is supposed to be a swindle.'

Allan grinned; she thanked God that he still had the capacity for fun. As he walked down the street with Jamie she couldn't help thinking how alike they looked, yet how different their lives had been.

Maire and Joe went back to work; Rory yawned and stretched. 'I should be away, too. I've two lorries off the road.'

She smiled; Rory always had a lorry off the road, but his yard was doing well – when his lorries were going he had them on the road almost twenty-four hours a day.

'D'you want another coffee before you go?'

'I wouldn't mind some more apple pie.'

She sat with him as he ate.

'You've changed, Triona,' he said. There was a lightness to her face that he hadn't seen for years, hadn't seen ever before when he thought of it.

She cupped her chin in her hands. 'I didn't know it would be so hard, Rory. Nor that it would take so long.' She frowned, trembling just a little; a tear formed in her eye and rolled very slowly down her cheek. She brushed it away impatiently. 'Daft, amn't I? I shouldn't be crying on a day like this.'

Rory never knew what to do when women cried, he would walk away if he could because the show of emotion confused him, but with Catriona he never had. Over the years he had hugged her, comforted her, cajoled her back to happiness or at least equilibrium and helped her to resurrect the courage that surged within her fragile body, that had held her through the bad times, when a lesser mortal would have given up. He had never hesitated to go to her before, to wrap his arms around her and give her what strength he had, but he hesitated now. When he had seen her walk in with Allan, he had known that the bad times were over at last, that he could tell her now what he felt, what he wanted; that the time had come to take her into his arms and never let her go.

She was smiling now, through her tears.

He had waited so long for the moment that when it came he was not ready for it; instead he fumbled in his pocket for a handkerchief. He always kept a clean one for Catriona; all the times that he had waited for her outside Carnbrae he had never failed her, always until this day when, expecting joy, he had forgotten and all he could find was the dirty rag that he used to wipe grease from the battery leads. For a moment he peered at it, searching for a clean bit, then he cursed roundly and put it back into his pocket.

She laughed, like running water, and wiped her face with the back of her hand instead.

'Oh, Rory, forgive me,' she said, 'it's too much happiness, all at once.'

He fumbled for the words but failed to find them. 'I'd best away, Triona. These bloody trucks.'

'I'll never find a way to thank you, Rory.'

'Ach, to hell with that.' He jangled the car keys in his pocket. 'Tell that scallywag I'll be down on Sunday, as usual.'

'Yes,' she said, rising to walk with him to the door. He had become close to Jamie, almost as close as the father the boy had never known.

'We'll go along to Fairlie. With Allan. If you've a moment, maybe you'll come too?'

'Yes, Rory,' she said, 'I'd like that.'

He got into his car and drove slowly along the front, looking for two young boys at play, feeling like a child himself.

The lawyer's letter came out of the blue a few days later, a brisk note that asked her to contact their Mr Sinclair, who had a matter he wished to discuss with her. She recognized the form from her MacKenzie MacLure days; the lawyer had a client who wished to buy her business, she would politely tell him that she was not interested. She began to write the letter and then decided it would be easier to call instead.

'I'm very sorry,' she said, as she was shown into Sinclair's office, 'but my tearoom isn't for sale.'

The lawyer took off his half-moon glasses and began to rub them methodically with an ink-stained hankerchief.

'I wasn't intending to make an offer for your tearoom, Mrs Nicolson,' he said as he brushed a speck of dust from the glasses and put them on again.

'Miss Nicolson,' she said quickly.

'Miss Nicolson?'

'My supposed son is actually my nephew. My older son is actually my youngest brother. If you understand.'

The expression upon his face made it clear that he did not. 'Quite. As I was saying, I wasn't about to make an offer for your tearoom, but rather I have been instructed to ask you if you would have an interest in someone else's.'

'I might, Mr Sinclair. It would very much depend upon whose, and how much they want for it.'

'Can I ask you to keep this discussion confidential?'

She nodded.

'My client is the Wilson family, of Wilson's Dining Rooms.'

Catriona thought of the great barn-like building towards the end of the promenade, a vast mausoleum that served badly cooked meals and thick tea the colour of tar. It had been successful once, years before at the turn of the century when the proprietors put on music-hall acts, but there was a careless air about it now, as if nobody could be bothered with it. The paint was peeling and the windows dirty; she had watched its custom fade even in the few years she had been in Largs.

'The premises have great potential, and a very good reputation to build on.'

'Had,' she said quickly.

'Beg pardon, Miss Nicolson?'

'Wilson's Dining Rooms had a good reputation. They no longer have it.'

'Maybe so, but the site is an excellent one.'

'Most of the trippers don't go so far along the promenade.'

'They used to in the old days, I assure you. And they would again.'

'How much is your client asking, Mr Sinclair?'

'I would consider a price of five thousand pounds reasonable for the premises and the goodwill. Mrs Wilson is ailing and the sons, I'm afraid, have no interest in the business.

They are of the opinion that it would be best to sell to someone who has the interest and capacity to manage such an enterprise.'

'Could I have some time to think about this, Mr Sinclair?'

'Of course, you can have a week or two, but I would want your answer by the end of the month because if you are not interested I intend to place the property on the open market.'

Catriona thanked him and walked out into the sunshine of a spring afternoon. The wind was fresh, clean smelling, the promenade empty but for a few strollers. She walked across to the Pavilion Tearooms; Wilson's was only a hundred yards away, but so tired and dull that it could have been a warehouse.

She closed her eyes and saw fresh paint, flags maybe, her name in big letters, a corner arcade where Joe could sell ice cream to passers-by and to customers in the restaurant.

Walking closer, she saw an 'open' sign, hanging at an angle, pushed at a door that opened only reluctantly and walked into the gloom.

A waitress came over and took her order for tea, uninterestedly at first and then looking at her sharply, as if to ask what she was doing there.

The dining rooms were built in the shape of a U around a rectangular courtyard facing the sea where once there had been a bandstand. The room itself was vast, maybe a hundred and fifty feet long and fifty wide, the tables set out in regimented rows almost like marching soldiers. At the back of the room a tea urn threw up clouds of steam; the place smelled of vinegar and dust.

Catriona saw the ceiling replastered and painted white to reflect the light that would come in the windows once the faded lace curtains were thrown out; a decent carpet, tablecloths and polished cutlery, perhaps potted palm trees between the tables to cast pleasant shade in the high summer. She could put a canopy over the courtyard and have some tables in the open air. This place cried out for love and attention; the dining room had space for a hundred tables, with room in the courtyard for two dozen more. The kitchens were big enough to cook for an army.

Five thousand pounds, she thought, tracing the figures in the dust of the table as the waitress put down a cracked cup of tea and a bill for sixpence. Catriona handed her the money, rubbing out the figures before the woman saw them.

In her bank she had more than two thousand pounds; she had thought of it as a fortune but now realized it was not enough. Her tearoom was worth perhaps another thousand, so a mortgage on it would raise a fair amount, but she was more than two thousand pounds short. Several more thousands short, if she counted the cost of renovations.

The image faded, surged again when she decided that she would try to make it real.

She left the waitress a farthing and walked out into the sunshine, humming a tune.

Sunday was a day of bright, early sunshine; the breeze was quick and fresh.

Rory's face fell when Catriona told him that the girl who washed dishes had come down with the flu and she would have to do them herself.

'It doesn't matter.' He shrugged as she handed him the picnic basket she had packed. Allan and Jamie were waiting, Jamie with his bucket and spade, Allan with a hookline and sinker.

'D'you have time for a walk along the front later?' she asked Rory.

'Of course,' he said, wondering why she wanted to do that.

When he got back from Fairlie with the boys the lunchtime rush was over, the dishes clean and neatly stacked. Catriona removed her apron and put on her jacket, then took his arm and marched him firmly towards the promenade. He caught a glimpse of the old determination in her, that mixture of optimism and brawn that he had been so taken with when she started her tearoom five years before. 'What's with the seafront all of a sudden?' he asked.

She smiled to herself. 'You'll see.'

They passed the stalls, the organ grinder with his monkey, the fly boys from Glasgow with their three-card trick, the gnarled old gypsy selling good-luck charms for sixpence each or three for a shilling. Catriona stepped nimbly around her, then stopped just before the awning of the puppet theatre. 'See that place,' she said, pointing over the road towards the dilapidated building he had hardly noticed in all the time he had been coming to Largs.

'Which place?' he asked her.

'Wilson's Dining Rooms.'

Rory squinted. 'That's your competition?'

'I want to buy it.'

He turned to look at her.

'It's for sale, Rory. It's been offered to me.'

'Let's go and have a look.'

She hesitated, then realized that the Wilsons already knew of her interest; after all, they had asked their solicitor to sell it to her.

Inside, once Rory's eyes had adjusted to the gloom, he peered at the ceiling, noted the damp patches and then the paint peeling off the walls. The merchant navy served a better afternoon tea.

'Take more than a lick of paint to put this place to rights.'

'But don't you see?'

'All I see is dust, Catriona.' He made a play of wiping his eyes.

Her eyes were sparkling. 'Rory, just imagine, once it's sorted. I'd get plants, great big potted flowering plants. And hang fans from the ceiling. In the summer I could serve tea outdoors, in the courtyard.'

'How much do they want for it?'

Her face fell. 'I can't afford it. I've put in an offer to lease.'

'You could borrow the money . . .'

She frowned and dropped her voice a couple of tones: 'You have a perfectly good tearoom already, Miss Nicolson. Taking on Wilson's would be stretching yourself too far.'

'I see.'

'They'd only lend me twenty per cent of the value, Rory. Any more and they would want a mortgage on the Rose Tearoom. I've decided I won't risk that.'

He felt anger rise, because the bank had lent him money when he had no more than two trucks and a contract, and had taken his business as security for the loan. Three years ago, he had owed several thousands; it was only in the last few months he had been free of debt.

'Catriona,' he began, 'I mean, don't you think . . .'

'Think what?'

He smiled, wondering if now was the time to ask her, if she would accept marriage to him in lieu of this dump.

'I know I could do it,' she said, 'I know I could make it work.'

'I'm sure you could,' he said, 'but . . .'

'No "buts", Rory. You sound just like the man at the bank.'

'I didn't mean to, Catriona. I just mean there's other things in life besides tearooms. There are other things you could do with your time.'

'This is what I want to do, Rory.'

'Are you sure about that?'

She nodded. 'Everything else's been for other people. This is something I want to do for myself.'

He seemed to think for a minute, then called the waitress to pay the bill. They walked into daylight again, blinking against the brightness after the gloom indoors.

'It's so wrong,' Catriona said.

'What is?'

'Everything about that place is wrong. With that high ceiling and the windows, it should be bright and airy. If they threw away the curtains, they'd catch the light of the sea. But the way it is, it feels like a mausoleum. People don't come down here for that. They come for something that's special, a bit different.' She turned back and glared at the shabby doors. 'You can't even tell if it's open or not.'

'I could lend you some money,' he began, abandoning the

promise he had made to himself to borrow no more once his loan was paid off.

'I don't want you to, Rory. I didn't bring you down here for that.'

'Why did you bring me down, then?'

'Because I wanted to know what you think. If you think it would work.'

'I'm sure it would,' he said slowly, 'but it'd cost a fortune in repairs.'

'That's just it.' She folded her arms over her chest. 'That's what the bank manager said. He went on about the depression, about the threat of strikes. He said the whole country could stop dead. There'd be no holiday makers, no day trippers either.'

Rory grinned. 'I doubt that.'

'Why?'

'He's right about the depression. He's right there'll be strikes. But there's more men in work than out of it, Catriona. They'll still have money to spend, they'll still come down here. The men who'll strike, they've always been poor. I doubt it would make much difference to your trade, either way.'

'Are you sure?'

'There's nothing sure in this world, girl. You know that.'

'I'm sure it would work,' she said, 'I have a feeling.'

'Well, do it, then.'

'I'm not borrowing your money, Rory.'

He nudged her playfully. 'Be like that, Catriona. See if I care.'

After he left, she thought it over again and again, until the figures spinning in her head made no sense, no sense at all. Only one thing was sure: if her offer of a lease was rejected, she could not afford the purchase price.

When she had told the bank manager that if she did not make an offer the premises would be put on the market, he had sighed tiredly. 'I imagine it'll still be on the market this time next year, Miss Nicolson. If it is, I will consider backing you then.'

The Rose Tearoom was thriving, after all, that alone made enough to care for all of her needs. She could not risk Allan's wellbeing, nor Jamie's, nor Maire's, come to that; she sighed and cursed the fates that had left so many futures in her hands.

Allan noticed how quiet she was when they were sitting in the garden, taking tea in the last of the sun. 'What's the matter?' he asked.

'Oh, nothing,' she said, 'nothing at all. Just a dream. A daydream, really. Nothing important. Nothing at all.'

She smiled. 'Come on, let's go for a walk.' They linked arms and wandered down to the seafront.

Far to the west, the sky had turned pink, gilding the sea and the islands beyond. Where they stood on the pebbled shore, all was quiet but for the call of birds. There was a serenity about it all that was almost like home.

Allan squinted at the ebbing waves. 'There's oyster beds out there,' he said, 'just before low tide.'

She laughed aloud. 'You can take a bucket tomorrow morning.' She could not get used to the lowland custom that held oysters as a great delicacy, an expensive indulgence of the middle classes.

She had not told him about Wilson's and she would not, not when her dream could put the future of them all at risk.

Annie's letter cleared the thought from her mind, all thought for a while, until the shock subsided.

Ailish had written to Annie from America to ask for Catriona's address.

The letter came in the middle of the month, lying innocently on the mat behind the tearoom door. Catriona opened it smiling, then her face changed.

Allan stopped eating his toast. 'What's the matter?'

She folded the letter and put it in her apron pocket. Allan had grown up beyond his years in the sanatorium; he had seen death and felt its close proximity, become wise to emotions that other boys of his age had not experienced. Sometimes he was a boy, running across the shore, playing in a rowing boat; she was trying to nurture his youth, trying to give him back his childhood.

'Is there trouble at home?'

'No trouble, Allan. Nothing to worry about.'

She left the table and started the day's baking. Allan finished his breakfast and helped Jamie to put his shoes on.

'Why don't you go over to Cumbrae?' she said. 'The boat leaves the pier at ten. I'll pack you some sandwiches.'

The tearoom had a rhythm of its own. The morning built up to a crescendo at noon which lasted until two, when there was a brief lull before afternoon tea. Catriona took a break then, to play with Jamie and talk to Allan, and do her business errands if there were any. The letter stayed in her pocket until then, the stiff folds rustling against her skirt as she walked.

When Marie was counting the takings from lunch and the girls were washing dishes, Catriona poured herself a glass of lemonade and went out into the garden, where she sat in the shade of the oak tree and read the letter again.

Annie had copied out Ailish's address in Brooklyn, New York.

Catriona stared at the words and tried to imagine Ailish living there. Over the years her anger had faded but the hurt still remained.

She stared at the letter for ages then folded it again and put it in her desk in the living room upstairs. Annie had not given Ailish Catriona's address, and would forward any letter Catriona wrote to her sister.

'I don't know what she wants,' Annie had written.

I do, Catriona thought. Ailish would want the solace of forgiveness, perhaps also the love of the son she had abandoned.

Now, when she thought of the months they had lived together in the Briggait, she thought of herself as being innocent then, believing as she did in the ties of family, in trust.

She hadn't wanted Jamie at first, hadn't loved him but thought of him as a burden, a problem that could not be solved. Love had come later, when she felt the purity of his affection and knew that she could not blame him for his mother. She felt guilt now, sometimes, guilt that perhaps by withholding her love for a few months she had harmed him in some way.

Over the years she had tried to find the words to explain to him the complex relationship between them, to tell him who he really was. The questions would come later, she knew, and lies would build up a fragile facade that could easily shatter and wound them both.

He called her Mother, of course, Ma when he was asking for something, Mama when he had been hurt and wanted to be hugged. At first, he had called her Trina, but when he came to Largs and people spoke to him about his mother he began to call her that, and she did not have the heart to tell him not to.

In the summer of last year she had taken him down to the promenade to hear the band and afterwards at home she had sat him down on her knee and said she wanted to tell him something. He was going to school in September and she knew that when he came to hear other children talking about their fathers, the questions would start.

'I love you very much,' she began, uncertainly, 'and I am your mother, but you were born to my sister, Jamie.'

He was sitting sideways on her lap, she watched his eyes drop and then slowly rise to look at her.

'My sister was your mother at first,' she went on quickly now, wanting to get it all out, all over with. 'It was the war then and your father was killed. Ailish ... Ailish was ill. She couldn't care for you, and so I did.'

Jamie's eyes were wide and puzzled.

'So, though I'm your mother, I'm also your aunt.'

'Why?' he asked.

'Why what, Jamie?'

'Why are you my aunt?'

'Because, Jamie, you were born to my sister and that makes me your aunt. But my sister, your mother, couldn't care for you as a mother, so I became your mother too. Do you understand?'

His little head shook slowly.

She tried to explain again, though she knew the words would make no sense to him, not until the time when he realized the difference.

'When you go to school,' she said, 'the other boys will talk about their fathers, and they'll ask you about your father. Your father is dead, Jamie, killed in the war like so many others. You had two uncles who died in the war too. But it doesn't make you any different, Jamie, you're just the same as the other boys. Just you don't have a father, that's all.'

'Rory,' he said in a small voice. 'Rory could be my father.'

She smiled. 'Rory's your friend, your best friend, Jamie. But when you go to school, you'll make other friends.'

He went to school and she worried and fretted until he came home one day and said in a matter of fact way that there were two other boys in his class whose fathers had been killed in the war, and several more in the class above.

'Where was my father killed?' he asked Catriona, the question no more significant than any other of the intrigues of childhood.

'Lys,' she replied quickly. 'Your father was killed at the Battle of Lys.'

Now, as she heard the hum in the tearoom build up with the afternoon custom, she put her doubts aside and went to get on with her work. Ailish's letter would not come for months, if ever. Only time would bring the answers to the questions she wanted to ask.

The lawyer's messenger stood in the tearoom, rubbing his nose with the sleeve of his shirt.

'Please, Miss Nicolson, Missus, ye've to come tae see Mister Hendry as soon as ye can.'

Catriona was on the point of writing to Sinclair, WS, to tell him that she did not want to buy Wilson's Dining Rooms. The vague deadline that he had given her of two weeks would expire that afternoon; she had watched the time go by, regretting the chance that faded with each hour that passed.

She said: 'I'm very busy just now. I'll come round tomorrow morning, first thing.'

'Mister Hendry says ye've to come now, Missus. The day. He tell me to tell ye to come the day.'

Catriona looked at the clock and took off her apron. She had twenty minutes before the lunchtime rush. Maire could cope, if she came back quickly.

Passing Joe's ice-cream stall, she watched him piling a cone high for a child, much more than the penny the mother gave him was worth. Joe had a habit of doing that, he would rather give away ice-cream than sell it. He spoke English well now, if haltingly. She had discovered that his real name was Guiseppe Valente; he was a cousin of the famed Napolis of Glasgow. There was a tangled relationship within the family, a feud founded on the technicalities of making ice cream; Joe was ranged against his uncle, Luigi Napoli. They had argued and Luigi had thrown Joe out, or Joe had left; she was not sure which, but Luigi had come to Largs one day to make amends. The two men had sobbed like babies and rocked in each other's arms – then started the feud again over a confection of dark chocolate and walnut.

Mayhem reigned briefly until Catriona broke up the fracas by wielding a rolling pin. Luigi straightened his tie and threatened to cast Joe for ever from the bosom of the family; Joe retorted that Luigi would never dare walk down the streets of Castellammare again.

Afterwards, Joe said that it was just a little family squabble, nothing at all to worry about.

She was still smiling to herself when she was shown into Mr Hendry's office. He was the second of the two lawyers in Largs, and had made out the original lease for the Rose Tearooms and later handled the purchase for her; because she trusted him she had asked him if he would make an offer to lease Wilson's but the offer had been turned down.

'Pursuant to the matter we discussed last week' he began in his judicious way, then smiled at her smiling at him. 'Forgive me, I meant, if you remember we were talking about Wilson's Dining Rooms? My son tells me that I talk like a textbook. I must get out of the habit. In any case, we've been approached by a party who would be agreeable to lending you the necessary funds.'

'I beg your pardon?' Catriona stammered.

'A lender, Miss Nicolson, who would be happy to lend you the money required.'

'Can I ask who?'

He coughed. 'I'm not at liberty to disclose that. All I can assure you is that it is someone with ample resources to make the loan. The party would be willing to lend you ten thousand pounds at five per cent, repayable over five years with interest charged only on the capital outstanding. The loan would be secured against the property purchased. The terms are simple; in fact, I would go so far as to say that the terms are generous.'

The shock hit her in a wave, she had the feeling of drifting on the tide.

Mr Hendry was reading out a draft agreement, legalistic terms that floated over her; though through years of familiarity with the law she understood the meaning, she did not understand why.

'Is it Rory,' she wondered aloud, 'Rory MacDonald?'

'As I said, I cannot tell you who it is, but I can say that it is not a Mr MacDonald.' Briskly he continued reading the terms.

'Please,' she said, when he paused for a moment, 'what would happen if . . .' The question tailed off. She was thinking of recession, of the threat of a general strike, of the bank manager's dire predictions for the summer trade. She would risk everything she had for Wilson's Dining Rooms, but not Allan's future, nor Maire's, nor Jamie's.

'I was coming to that,' he said, 'and this is where I feel that the terms of this proposal are extremely generous. It is a condition of the proposal that you continue to manage the Rose Tearoom and the property you own in Castle Street would not be at risk in the event of a default.'

Joy surged; she felt dizzy, faint, had to quell an urge to hug the lawyer and tell him that her dream had come true.

He had stopped talking and was looking at her, and she saw a gentle smile break his professional facade. 'Are you agreeable, Miss Nicolson? I can assure you that ...'

'Oh, yes,' she said, 'yes. I am agreeable, Mr Hendry. In fact, I am overwhelmed.'

'Now,' he went on, 'the purchase price. The sum asked is too high. At least a thousand pounds too high.'

'I won't need ten thousand pounds,' she said quickly. 'I'd hope to do it for much less.'

'It's a big building, Miss Nicolson. You mustn't underestimate the cost of repairs. Now, our friend Mr Sinclair has indicated that he is going to put the property on the open market if you do not come up with an offer today. I'm tempted to suggest that we let him do that, because I doubt there would be any interest at the price he's asking.'

'No,' she said quickly. Wilson's Dining Rooms was too precious to risk losing on a chance.

'Well then, will you contact Mr Sinclair and negotiate a price, or shall I?'

'I will,' she said, determined to do it herself.

By the time the church bells had chimed one o'clock, she had negotiated a purchase price of £3,250. When she told Mr Hendry he said he doubted he could have done better himself.

It would take a month to complete the sale, but he promised to try to arrange access as soon as possible.

The Rose Tearoom always wilted slightly just after lunch. In the heat of the day, the roses on the tables looked tired until they were refreshed with ice water, the tables themselves dishevelled with dishes and crumbs. As she walked in, Catriona saw Maire's sigh of relief.

'Come,' she said, taking her sister by the arm, 'let the girls finish that.'

Maire never felt it was right to leave any of the work to Etta and Alice and the two new girls Catriona had taken on.

'Come on,' Catriona said, 'they'll manage. I pay them, don't forget.'

She took a couple of dishes and dried them and then two helpings of Joe's sharp lemon sorbet from the brand-new refrigerator.

Even out in the yard, the air was still and hot. Maire sat down and slipped off her shoes.

'What is it, Catriona?'

'Let's wait for Allan.' He was washing dishes because he had taken pity on Alice, frazzled by the heat, who was sitting in a chair fanning herself with a copy of the *Largs Advertiser*.

Allan came and gulped down a pint of lemonade.

'I've bought Wilson's Dining Rooms.'

'You've done what?'

'Wilson's Dining Rooms, that dusty old place at the end of the promenade. I've bought the building. Next year it will be Nicolson's.'

'Nicolson's Dining Rooms?' Maire asked.

'No, just Nicolson's. We'll serve food like we do here, except we'll do dinners and high teas, or lunches and dinners. I'm going to make a proper palm court in the old courtyard, and Joe will have plenty of room for his ice cream.'

'What about here?'

'You're going to manage the tearooms here, Maire. Or perhaps Etta will. Either of you could do it. We'll just have two tearooms instead of one.'

'Wilson's is in an awful mess,' Allan said slowly.

'I know. That's what's so wonderful about it. When it opens next Easter, it's going to be best cafe Largs has ever seen.'

A month later Catriona put the closed sign permanently on the doors of Wilson's Dining Rooms and walked into the cavernous interior, where her footsteps echoed around the walls.

The tables stood in martial rows, covered with dust and the grime of years.

Even in summer the restaurant was cool, cold even. Opening a door, she walked into the kitchen and sat down before the vast iron coal range.

That will have to go, she thought, making a note. Joe's refrigerators ran on gas; gas cookers would be better. The kitchen had plenty of storage place, a good cool larder, but nothing else.

Joe wanted her to buy a coffee-maker imported from Italy; it was expensive but very fast. As yet she was undecided, but nothing would make her prepare tea in an urn and the thought of ordering a gross of teapots was daunting, not counting the cost of the coffee machine. She was trying to budget, having difficulty working out the figures.

Walking back into the restaurant, she let her imagination fly, saw the tables rearranged in zigzags with fresh white cloths and polished cutlery, the room filled with the light of the sea and potted plants, if she could find ones big enough. Robbie Thompson had promised her young palm trees for the courtyard – it would be her Palm Court – but he didn't know that the trees would grow indoors, maybe ficus would be better.

The mahogany columns dividing the room had been painted white, now faded to a dirty cream. She would strip that and the wood of the walls, install brass fittings and polished planters. The gaslights were scorched and rusting in places; she wanted new electric lights with frosted glass shades that would soften the glare.

Methodically she made a note to get a painter's estimate; one for the kitchen range, hot water and refrigeration; another for electric light and the fittings. At Mr Hendry's insistence a surveyor had checked the building and because of dampness in the roof and the need to repair the plumbing the cost had been reduced by another £250, but the repairs had already cost more than that.

The door rattled; she saw Allan and Jamie outside, blurred by the grimy glass.

'It's very dusty,' she said, opening the door. Miss Logan had told her to be careful that Allan didn't breathe dirty air.

He looked around, and shook his head as Jamie began to play aeroplanes amongst the tables.

'It's going to be wonderful,' she said.

He had something in his hand. Looking down, she saw a lobster threshing helplessly in a bucket of salt water.

'For tea,' he said.

She laughed.

Rory came down that weekend, once work on Wilson's had started and the whole place was swathed in dust sheets and sawdust. She had not seen him for weeks; he looked around as if he did not believe it, a funny expression upon his face – half grin, half scowl.

They were standing at the door from the kitchen into the restaurant; the ceiling was marked with chalk and festooned with electric wires.

'What's the matter?' Catriona asked. 'You see, once the electricity's in, all the paint'll be stripped off the wood. It's mahogany and oak underneath.' She went to one of the pillars and scraped with her fingernails, chipping off layers of stained paint.

'It isn't that.' He tried to smile.

'It'll look wonderful. It really will.'

'I know it will, Triona.'

He was thinking about the work it would take, about how long it would be, about how she was spinning around these days, so busy with the tearoom and her new restaurant that she hardly had time to draw breath.

'It was lucky I got the money,' she said quietly; she had come so close to losing it.

Rory knew about the money; he had known before she did. Once he knew what she wanted he had sent down a builder friend to look over the building, and with the builder's estimate in hand, he had borrowed the money himself. Then, when he found the lawyer who acted for her, he explained what he wanted him to do, only to find that someone else had already done it.

'Our Miss Nicolson is a very popular young lady,' the lawyer had said, 'I've just had another party on to me with exactly the same request.'

Rory's jealousy had flared briefly and he had badgered

the man until he was assured that the 'other party' was not another man. He had confessed to the lawyer that he intended to marry Miss Nicolson himself. The lawyer had wished him luck, but wondered if she would have the time. Rory wondered that himself. As his mother had said in a letter, it was time for him to get married now, to settle down himself. His business was as secure as he could make it, though times were hard in Chryston, in the coal mines; he did not know what the next year would bring, the next month come to that.

'Come on,' he said, 'dust's getting in my eyes.'

'I've got a steak pudding for you,' she said, smiling.

They drifted along the seafront, watching the organ grinder's monkey and the crowds knotted around the games of chance where a farthing gambled might yield a toffee bar or a packet of cigarettes.

'D'you ever get lonesome, Catriona?' he began.

She turned to him: 'What on earth do you mean by that?'

Taken aback, he asked if she had ever thought of getting wed.

Catriona stopped. The pain of Liam still hurt somewhere deep inside. Ireland was a free state now, but the Unionists had taken a bite out of the country and clung to the northernmost part of it; the civil war was over but she often wondered if Liam would have wanted to live in a country that was divided, if he could have given up his dreams of a people's republic.

Remembering their time together, she had sensed that she would never have married him, that she was afraid that his love for his country would lead to his death.

But she had lost love once and her psyche was too fragile to risk the loss of love again; she still missed Liam so, when she thought of him.

'Once,' she said, shivering slightly as the sun slid behind a cloud. 'Only once, a very long time ago.'

Rory grinned. 'Come on, Catriona. I know about that.'

'What do you know?' she asked, the pain of the memory clouding her eyes.

'I know about Lachlan Maclean,' he said. 'He was boasting that he would marry you. But you wouldn't've married him, Catriona. You couldn't've. Lachlan Maclean would've bored you to death.'

She shook her head, her mind shifting from grief to a vague recollection of sadness. 'Whoever said anything about Lachlan Maclean, Rory?'

'You did, Triona. Don't you remember? That day before you opened the tearoom . . .'

'It wasn't Lachie, Rory. It was never Lachie. I was going to marry a man called Liam Devlin. He was Irish. He was killed there, a few months before I met up with you again.'

He turned away. His stomach felt like he'd been kicked by a cow. He started to vomit, swallowed bile. The image of Largs on a sunny day stilled, sound faded to a whisper. A man began to laugh and then another. He thought they were laughing at him.

'Rory, Rory?' Catriona began to shake him, tugging at his arm. 'Rory? Are you all right?'

His mouth dry, he tried to speak. 'Yes,' he mumbled, avoiding her eyes.

'Are you really? You've gone awfully pale.'

He struggled to smile. 'I'm fine, Catriona.'

She took his arm. 'Come on, you'll be better once you've got some food inside you.'

'I've just remembered,' he said, 'I've a man going up north tomorrow and the clutch's slipping. I have to get back.'

'But I've made . . .'

With one last look at her, he waved then began to run, loping across the road with an easy stride. He did not stop until he reached his car.

Catriona walked home thoughtfully, wondering what had got into him.

'Where's Rory?' Maire asked.

'I don't know. He just took off like a bat out of hell.' She checked the pudding in the steamer, then turned to Jamie and asked him to invite Joe to eat with them in Rory's place.

Rory drove along the coast road aimlessly until he reached Greenock and the familiarity of the docks, where he found a seamen's club that could serve drink on Sundays. He drank solidly until midnight, then left. A passing policeman found him vomiting into a gutter. Recognizing his accent, he did not arrest him but hitched him up and threw Rory's limp arm around his own strong shoulder.

'What's the matter, laddie?' he asked softly, adding that he was from Islay himself.

'Woman,' Rory mumbled.

'Women,' the policeman repeated.

'No. *A* woman,' Rory slurred, 'one woman. Just one.'

'Ach, laddie,' the policeman said, with all the stoic logic of the islands, the logic born of the ocean and rocks, 'it could haff been worse. It could haff been two.'

For the first time since his childhood, Rory had to blink back the tears that came to his eyes.

Catriona's twenty-sixth birthday had passed that year, and she would not have known it but for the birthday cake Maire had baked and the present of a silver hairbrush that the youngsters had bought from the jeweller along the street. Birthdays were never marked in the islands by more than good wishes, but she had taken on the custom for Allan and Jamie and they had planned for her own in secret, which pleased her.

At the end of the summer Maire and Joe held a surprise party; they had planned one for her birthday, they confessed, but their plans had gone awry when she got tied up with her new restaurant.

Rory did not come to the party; he sent a note instead. Catriona felt a little hurt, because he still came down to see Jamie and Allan, but he always missed her, somehow. She was pleased with what she had achieved that year. The work on the dining rooms was going well; in the spring, when Nicolson's opened, it would be the biggest, brightest cafe in Largs.

Allan, bronzed with the sun and more healthy than she

could remember, was looking forward to his last year of school. Jamie no longer complained about his own school; if Allan enjoyed it, so would he.

The letter came at the end of September. So much time had passed that she had almost forgotten; she had hoped so much that Ailish would not write again. It came in a bulky packet from Skye with Annie's thready writing on the label but only another letter inside. 'Personal to Miss Catriona Nicolson', the envelope said; she put it aside to be read during the evening, when she would have a little time to think.

Her hands were shaking when she opened the envelope, so much that she tore off the top corner of the letter. Ailish wrote:

> Dear Catriona,
> I have wanted to write for years, but I was afraid to. I still am, but I know that, if I don't, I never will. I suppose I can't ask you to forgive me, but I can ask you to try to understand, because I was very young then and I have grown up now. What I did was wrong and I have no excuse, but if you let me have your address, then I will send you the money that I took.
> I suppose also that I do not have the right to ask after my son, but I have to because I've missed him so much over the years. I suppose you had him adopted, but I'd like to know that he is safe.
> I'm getting married soon. I told my fiancé about it all, and it was he who urged me not to be afraid of the past. I think that's all I have to say, except to send you my love and also my very deep regrets.
> With love from your sister Ailish.

Catriona put down the letter, thinking in passing that Ailish had learned how to spell.

'Can I read it?' Maire asked.

'Of course.' Catriona went to the window, where she could see night rolling in over the hills. She thought of the helpless look on Ailish's face when Jamie had cried, her own despair when she had opened her savings box and found her money gone. It wasn't the loss but the hurt that she remembered; what Ailish had taken wasn't money, but hopes and dreams and, most of all, trust.

'What should I do?' she asked Maire.

'Ailish is Ailish,' Maire said after a long time. 'Whatever she meant, I doubt she intended to hurt you.'

'She left me with a baby, for God's sake. I had a job to do and his father was dead. And no money. If I'd had that money . . .'

She stopped suddenly, listening to the sound of her anger reverberating around the room.

'You managed,' Maire said softly.

'For God's sake, Maire, I had no choice.'

'You had as much choice as any of us did.'

'Tell Allan that,' Catriona said bitterly. 'He's the one who suffered.'

'That was fate, Catriona. Not Ailish.'

Catriona sat down. 'What are you saying?'

Maire said nothing.

'Are you saying I should forgive her?'

Maire thought for a time. 'I'm saying that you can't hate her for ever.'

'I don't hate her, Ailish. I never did. It's just . . . it's just that I don't like to remember, that's all.'

Maire came to her. 'Catriona, if Ailish hadn't left you like that, would you ever have found this place in Largs?'

Catriona went to her desk and wrote a brief letter:

Dear Ailish,

I'm glad to know that you are well. Your son will turn seven this Christmas; he's a fine young boy and doing very well at school. I did not get him adopted, I brought him up myself. You put my name on his birth certificate as his mother, after all. Please do not bother to send me any money because I do not need it.

Yours sincerely, Catriona.

When Ailish's reply came, she burnt the letter without opening it.

Christmas came; the holiday passed quietly. Catriona, Maire and Joe had a festive meal together, then snoozed through the afternoon as Allan helped Jamie to play with his new Meccano set. She had invited Rory as well, but he was going home for a day or two. The presents had been Rory's idea; she had teased him about taking on the heathen lowland customs, but then she had bought presents too and realized what a good idea it was.

The work on Nicolson's was almost finished. All that was left to be done was to paint the exterior and put up the canopies and the big gold letters that bore her name.

Catriona walked into the vast room on Boxing Day morning and was pleased with the feel of burnished brass and wood. With the windows still whitewashed the restaurant was gloomy, but she knew that in the spring it would feel light and fresh.

In between the In and Out doors to the kitchen, she had installed a long counter for drinks and pastries, coffees and teas. The waitresses would have to go to the kitchen only for meals; all other orders would be served on the spot.

In an alcove at one side she had installed chilled cabinets for Joe's ice cream; Nicolson's would serve eighteen flavours, six more than anywhere else in the country. There was a counter for chocolates that she had ordered from Belgium and another for gateaux and cakes.

The coffee-maker looked like a small steam engine. It made espresso that she thought was bitter but the cappuccino tasted like a dream. She had ordered crockery and cutlery embossed with her name, feeling shy and proud when she unwrapped the first plate and read the writing: 'Nicolson's of Largs'.

The menus had arrived from the printer and also the special ones which read: 'The Palm Court at Nicolson's of Largs'.

One day in Glasgow she had visited two restaurants and a

cinema with a palm court; only *her* palm court had real palm trees, not just potted miniatures.

She went into the laundry and took a snowy linen tablecloth to lay just one table to see how the menus and plates would look.

Smiling to herself she switched on the coffee-maker and made just one coffee which she sat and drank all by herself.

Walking back to Castle Street, she could not wait for the winter to pass. In the tearoom she paused to talk to a lonely old lady for a minute before she walked through to the kitchen, where she stopped and stared in surprise.

Jamie was wheeling his way around in circles on a strange contraption that was halfway between a bogie and a bike.

'What's this?' she asked. 'Where did he get that?'

Maire looked at Allan. 'The post brought it from America,' she said. 'He said, he's sorry, it should have been here by Christmas, but it got held up at the docks.'

'You shouldn't have . . .' Catriona began.

'We didn't,' Allan said quickly. 'The post brought it round at half past ten and Jamie was in the kitchen himself.'

Jamie was whooping, ringing a bell that made a hollow sound like a whistle as he paddled round and round.

'This came too.'

Catriona quickly read the letter and put it down in anger.

'You're going to have to tell him,' Maire said quietly.

'Yes,' Catriona admitted, 'I suppose I must.'

Chapter Twelve

*O*n the day that Nicolson's opened, Catriona walked down to the shore and watched the shadows of clouds passing over the sea. It was April and the wind was fresh, the morning crisp still with the hint of winter. She took a deep breath and turned round, seeing the big glass windows topped by her name in letters two feet tall. The name was repeated twice along the length of the cafe on the promenade, split neatly in two by the canopy over the Palm Court. The wrought-iron tables there were bare, because it was too early in the year to take tea alfresco, but as she walked back she saw the slender Phoenix palms and the gracious Washington palms, the bougainvillea on the trellis and the little potted trees that later in the season would bear lemons and kumquats.

Already, she had entertained Largs to tea, the women of the Red Cross and the Ladies' Guild, the corporation and the kirk elders, the lawyers, accountants, even the bank manager who had expressed his fervent good wishes and the hope that his refusal to lend her money would not prejudice their business relationship in future. As she watched them eat and drink, she felt the thrill of elation that augured success and pinched herself hard to remember the loan that still had four years to run.

Largs approved of Nicolson's, even liked the new cafe that had arrogantly set itself at the end of the promenade. The local paper welcomed the innovation and had wished her luck in her latest endeavour; the paper carried a picture of the Provost vigorously shaking her hand. Looking at that, Catriona was both embarrassed and proud.

Inside, the cafe was cool and fresh, with an air of elegance that felt natural despite the months of work that had gone into it. The marching rows of tables had been broken up into groups arranged around indoor plants that she had chosen with Robbie Thompson. There were jacob's coats and Philippine medusas, cool red and green leaves under the ferns like jacarandas; in alcoves by the windows she had planted strelitzias and anthuriums, which would bloom into bird-of-paradise and flamingo flowers in the height of summer. Some of the plants had come from Miss Cochrane's conservatories, but she had bought more from the Botanical Gardens in Glasgow. The vast emptiness of Wilson's Dining Rooms had become an indoor garden, oasis from the sun and shelter from the rain, sanctuary from the weather, whatever it was.

Catriona looked around and was pleased with what she had achieved. Sharp morning sunlight cascaded in from the windows, burnishing the brass and mahogany, gilding the silver cutlery on the winter-white tablecloths. The waitresses were waiting nervously in their crisp new uniforms, lined up like servants until she told them to sit down and have a cup of tea. She had chosen ten girls out of more than a hundred she had interviewed; they each had ten tables to work but when the season started in earnest she planned to take on at least ten more.

She paid the best wages in Largs now, five shillings a week over the going rate because she did not dare risk her success on surliness. When she advertised in the paper the queue stretched almost to the Pavilion; bewildered at first she had talked to each applicant carefully, watching more the way she smiled than anything else. It hurt to turn down anyone, to watch the way a girl's face fell when she said she could not offer her work. The slump was biting now; she had hired two experienced chefs to supervise a dozen boys and girls in the kitchen, and been appalled to discover that most of them supported a family on the wages she paid for a junior.

Maire came and touched her shoulder gently, pointing to the clock. Catriona went to the doors and opened them, threw the switch that lit the cafe and Joe's Ice Cream Bar. From a hiding place behind a fortunella tree she watched the first customers come in and sit down, ponder the menu for an age before they decided on coffee and cake, ordering a second cup after they'd drunk the first. It was a quiet day, so early in the year; she didn't expect to be busy but at lunchtime she and Maire had to help the waitresses and the tempo kept up all afternoon. It was evening when she managed to go round to the Rose Tearoom where Etta and Josie were clearing up after a slow day that was normal for the time of year.

'It's the novelty,' she said, counting the takings which came to £96. She had estimated half of that for weekdays in the spring.

'It's success,' Maire said, more confident than she.

Catriona rubbed the muscles in the back of her neck that were taut with strain. She felt a movement beside her and turned to see Jamie in his pyjamas, ready for bed. There was a hesitant look on his face; she had been so busy that day, so busy for so many days that she hardly had time for him beyond seeing that he was clothed and fed.

'I got all my sums right,' he said. 'I know the twelve times table.'

She felt a rush of remorse. 'Come,' she said, taking his hand. 'I'll tell you a story.'

Once the story was over, as she listened to his prayers, she vowed that she would make time for him each evening to listen to all the things that had happened during the day.

Jamie was seven years old now, growing up so quickly and easily that she thought he had overcome the limbo of his parenthood without the torment she had feared.

She had explained, briefly, that the mechanical truck had come from his mother in America; he had nodded as if he wanted to know no more than that.

'He was asking Joe about America,' Maire said as they sat down to supper.

Catriona smiled, because once Joe learnt English he'd told them that he had taken the train to Largs en route to America. He had supposed he could catch a boat there and work his way to New York.

'Jamie wanted to know how far New York is from Arran, if he could see it if he climbed Goat Fell,' Maire went on. 'Joe told him to look at the moon, it's nearly as far as that.'

'He hasn't said anything to me.'

Maire smiled wryly. 'He gets dizzy just trying to keep up with you.'

'I know,' Catriona said. 'I'm going to make more time for him. Don't worry.'

She went to her desk to write to Allan, in Glasgow while he sat his final exams. She wanted him to know that Nicolson's first day had been a success.

The rattling at the tearoom door downstairs cut into her thoughts. 'I'll go,' she said quickly.

Rory was standing there, a sheepish smile on his face. 'I tried to come down earlier, but I couldn't get away. I thought you didn't close till eight.'

She hadn't seen him for months, nearly a year in fact.

'I got your letter,' he said.

'I thought you were trying to avoid me, Rory MacDonald. Every Sunday, I'd try to get back in time, but you'd always just gone.'

'Ach.' He looked away. 'You know how it is.'

She called up to Maire and asked her to watch Jamie while she went out.

Rory grinned. 'You mean you're opening again, just for me?'

They linked arms and walked towards the seafront. Nicolson's stood out in a blaze of light, its name visible from just about everywhere in Largs.

'Well, you did it,' Rory said.

She smiled. 'Wait until you see inside.'

She fiddled with a bunch of keys, opened the door and stood aside.

Rory walked in. He had been frightened for her, when he thought of the magnitude of what she had taken on. Once his feelings had steadied, he had rationalized that he had no right to blame her for having another man; he reasoned that he could not, but still felt anger and pain because she had. He smiled that quaint, lopsided grin of his. 'It's magic, Triona. But I always knew it would be.'

'Come on,' she said, leading him to a table shaded by a palm tree, 'you can have gateau and coffee, unless you're hungry.'

He thought of the double fish supper he'd eaten at lunch-time that had sunk, heavy and undigested, to the pit of his stomach.

The cake was light and moist, filled with cream and candied fruits with a faint hint of alcohol; he did not usually like cakes, but he liked this one.

She tilted her head to one side, balancing her chin in her hand as she watched him. 'I thought you were going to put a hex on me, Rory MacDonald. If you didn't turn up I was quite sure I'd have bad luck all year round.'

He laughed aloud. 'I've been busy, really.'

'Especially at three o'clock on Sunday afternoons. All I've seen of you this year is the tail end of a lorry going like the clappers.'

His face reddened. 'Jamie. You know what he's like.'

'You've been very good to him.'

He winced. 'He's a fine wee lad. And Allan's a fine big lad, come to that.'

She was looking at him in a way that made him think she could see straight inside his head.

At Christmas his mother, expecting a happy announce-ment, had cursed him for a fool. 'You daft bugger,' she'd raved, 'you silly eejit. You let Tom Nicolson wallop you and then you tell Catriona Nicolson not to write to you when you go off to war, and you expect her to wait for you despite that? Woman's not a fool, Rory. It's well seen she's not as silly as you are.'

'But you don't understand,' he had told her, 'Catriona's special. She's different. She's not like other girls.'

'Every woman is the same deep down, Rory MacDonald. You left her, remember. You hurt her first.'

'I did not, Ma. I never hurt her.'

'You did too, Rory MacDonald. Unless I'm going off in my dotage, my guess is the girl wanted you once just as much as you want her. Thing is, she grew up and you didn't.'

'She's different, Ma,' he said again. 'She's loyal. She loved him. I doubt she'd love anyone after that.'

'You men,' his mother spat, 'daft fools the lot of you. Whores or madonnas, that's all women are to you. D'you never realize that we can be both at once?'

Now he looked at the woman opposite him, at the way she smiled, at the way curls crept out of her plaited hair and tumbled anarchically about her face.

'You're my best friend in the whole world, Catriona,' he blurted, cursing himself for being such a child.

Her face broke into the widest smile: 'Thank God for that, Rory. You're my best friend too.'

There's hope, he thought, somewhere, somehow; struggling to change the subject he told her that the General Strike was official, the news had been in the evening paper.

'No,' she murmured.

'Yes. Every union man in the country is out from the third of next month.'

'Will it last?'

'I'm not sure, Triona. Sometimes I wish it would.'

She looked at him quizzically.

'If you worked down the mines,' he asked, 'would you take a cut in your wages?'

'I suppose not, Rory. But I doubt a strike will change anything.'

He sighed. 'You're right, girl. The pit-owners are out to break the power of the unions. And they will, because union or no, there's not a man who'll let his child go hungry if there's work to be had, however little he's paid.'

She trembled slightly. 'Will it come to that?'

'I hope not. But the country can survive a general strike right now, despite what they say. The country can survive and the government can survive. It's the working man who can't. It's him who'll pay the price in the end.'

'But Rory, your business, what'll you do if there's no coal to deliver?'

He grinned and patted her hand. 'There's always a use for trucks, Triona. I'll survive it.'

She looked at him and saw for the first time the deep lines etched across his forehead, the dark shadows underneath his eyes. 'Will you have to lay off your drivers?'

'God sakes, Catriona, what sort of man do you think I am? I'm keeping them on. I owe them that.'

'But if there's no work . . .'

'I can still pay them. The strike won't last for ever. Not the General Strike, anyway. They'll be out then. It's the strikes in the mines. That's what's stopping the coal.'

'But the mines've been on strike for months.'

'Some have. Some haven't. I'm managing, Catriona. I didn't come down here to talk about that.'

She lifted the dishes and rinsed them quickly, and then walked with him back along the shore.

Once he left she thought of how harried he had looked, how many times he had told her how busy he was; she cursed herself for selfishness, for not realizing the trouble he had.

'I wouldn't worry about it,' Maire said, when Catriona told her about the strikes and what it meant to him. 'Rory will manage. A man like that alway manages. Like Da did.'

'Maire,' Catriona said, 'Da didn't manage. That was why I left, remember?'

'Da always had money in his pocket,' Maire said.

'Usually it was mine,' Catriona said bitterly. She had worked hard for that money, so hard; she had worked harder for that than for anything else in her life.

The strike began, as Rory predicted. Catriona expected the worst, but nothing stopped in Largs apart from the railways. Day trippers still came, exultant that they had thwarted the strikers. One day, a bus full of people heading for Greenock arrived when their student driver had got lost and gave up when the vehicle ran out of fuel. It was all very funny, the way people got out on the seafront, cursing and swearing because they had never intended to come to Largs at all, whilst the student took off at a run, vanishing up a side street before any of his passengers caught up with him.

Catriona took pity on them and offered them tea whilst she tried to ring the bus company to find another driver. Half the day passed before another bus arrived, by chance, and took the passengers back to where they had started.

In the cities, things were grim. People were killed in accidents caused by amateur drivers, working men became beggars as the government said the hungry only had themselves to blame. Before the strike started, she had written to Jess to ask her and her children to stay in Largs for the duration; the reply came after the strike had ended with the news that they had managed through, although it had been a hard ten days. The government rejoiced and so did the newspapers.

At the end of the month, when she counted her takings, Catriona thanked God for the motor car. With the high season still to come, she would have enough to meet the loan payment that fell due in the autumn.

It was a few weeks before the school holidays started when Jamie asked her if she would answer a question. 'Of course,' she said, thoughtlessly, wondering what on earth he could want to ask.

'Anything at all?'

'Anything at all,' she told him.

'What's my mother like?'

'Why d'you ask that?' she replied, playing for time.

'I'd like to know,' he said, his face serious.

'Your mother's my sister Ailish. She's two years younger than I am. She's very pretty. You wouldn't know we were sisters, if you saw us together.'

'You're pretty, Ma.'

'Not like Ailish. Ailish looks like an actress.'

'Like Greta Garbo?'

'Maybe Mary Pickford.' Jamie paid acute attention to the cinema, though he had only seen a few Chaplin films and

The Thief of Bagdad. 'Ailish is as pretty as she is, but when you were born, she was very young and your father had died, and ...'

'She was ill, you said.'

'She couldn't take care of you herself,' Catriona said, trying to get over the lie. 'I was a little older and I was working, so I took care of you. The rest you know.'

'Can I see her?'

'When you're older, Jamie. America's a very long way away.'

'She wants to see me. She said in the letter.'

'She does, Jamie, but she knows you're too young.'

'You could take me. Willie Brown's da took him to America.'

'That was because they were going to live there.'

'We could go and come back. The boat takes a week.'

'Not now,' she said, 'I haven't time now. I've my work and you've to go to school.'

'I don't go to school in the holidays.'

'Jamie ...' She touched his arm, but he shrugged her away and hid his face in the pillow.

'Jamie?'

He said nothing, so she stayed with him, watching over him until his anger faded and he slid gently into sleep.

'Jamie wants to go to America,' she said to Maire when she went downstairs.

Maire looked up from the account book she was working on. 'He's been talking to Joe about it for ages.'

'He was upset when I said he couldn't go.'

Maire finished the column and closed the book. 'Why not?'

'Why not what?'

'Why can't Jamie go to America?'

'Maire, for pity's sake, I've just opened the biggest cafe in Largs, I owe ten thousand pounds, I don't know who to. I can't leave just yet.'

Maire rested her chin on her hands. 'When will you be able to?'

'Not for years yet.'

Maire was looking at her intently. 'You don't want to go at all, do you?'

'I don't, if you want to know the truth.'

They stared at each other for a long time. 'You think I should,' Catriona said finally.

'I understand why he wants to go and I understand why Ailish wants to see him.'

'You take him then.' Catriona got up and began to pace. 'The Fair's next month. There might be another strike. If Ailish wants to see him, why can't she come here?'

Maire began to file her nails, making little rounded points at the tip of each finger. 'She's afraid of what you'd do if she did.'

Catriona spun round. 'How d'you know that?'

Maire sighed. 'She's been writing to me. She asked me to talk to you, to try to explain . . .'

'To explain what? What right does she have to write to you?'

'Catriona, for God's sake, she's my sister too! For God's sake,' she said again, standing up to face Catriona. 'You've got to forgive her some time.'

Catriona sat down. 'I forgave her long ago, Maire. Jamie's just curious. Seeing her would only upset him.'

'Not seeing her would upset him more. It's been on his mind for ages, Triona.'

'She should never've sent him that bogie.'

'Maybe not, but it's done now. You can't take back the past and convince him it was a dream.'

Catriona thought of the look on Jamie's face when he turned away from her, of how hurt he had been. The image stayed with her until she slept, and recurred as soon as she woke up the following day.

Early in the morning Catriona took Jamie to school and then drove out of Largs, up the hill road that led over the moors to farmland and eventually the industrial sprawl that surrounded Glasgow. She had never been to Chryston before; she followed what she thought was the railway line until she ended in a siding, cursing. A line worker going home from the early shift directed her towards the village and she found Rory's yard just outside the mine, as he had described it. The colliery was still on strike, and she was jeered by pickets until she rolled down the window and explained that she was not going to the mine.

The yard was full of lorries, men standing idle. She got out diffidently, asked for Rory and was told to wait.

He came towards her smiling, and led her into a hut where he began to brew tea.

'What's happening?' she asked him.

He brushed his brow with his arm, leaving a greasy streak across his forehead. 'Nothing, the usual. The men've come out because management's sacked a union steward. There's no coal coming out of the mine. I'm just ringing round to find which mine is working, then I'll be able to send my men out on jobs.' He swore as the kettle boiled and scalded him with its steam. 'It's been like this for months.'

'I see.'

'Do you? If you drove a hundred yards down that road, you'd find children begging.'

'I didn't see that.'

He handed her a grimy mug, then took it back because he had forgotten to wash it.

'It doesn't matter, Rory. I didn't come here for tea.'

'Why did you come?'

She shook her head. 'To see how you were, that's all.'

His face tightened. 'I'm getting by, but only just. It'll break soon, the strike. It'll have to.'

She could see fatigue etched in the hollows below his eyes, the hard look that had not been there even a month ago.

'You don't want it to, do you?'

'No, if you want the truth. But I've worked too hard to let all this go to waste.' He had carefully washed and rinsed a mug; he poured some tea, checking that it was not too strong.

'I'm thinking of going to America,' she said as she waited for the tea to cool; she had wanted his help to solve the dilemma.

'Jamie would like that,' he said, smiling.

She scowled. 'Can you tell me, Rory, why Jamie told everyone in the world that he wanted to go to America before he told me?'

'He didn't want to ask you. So he asked us all what we thought.'

'And what do you think?'

'I told him the only way to find out was to ask you himself. Allan said you would.'

'*Allan said I would?*'

He smiled. 'Allan thinks you can work miracles. They both do. You know that.'

'Does Allan want to go to America too?'

'No. Allan wants to spend the summer brushing up his Greek. He's got some daft idea about getting through university in two years, not three.'

'Oh well,' she said, amazed at how little she had known about it all, 'I suppose I'd better go, Rory.'

'I suppose you had. I'd take him, Triona, but, God's my judge, if I left this place for a day, it'd fall apart.'

'Can I do anything?'

'A miracle, perhaps?'

She grinned. 'I would, if I could. You know that.'

'It would take more than that to put all this right.' He looked away, but not before she saw his rage.

'There's always leftovers at Nicolson's. If I get Joe to drive up in the evening ... These children who are begging, you could feed them at least.'

'That'd help,' he said, 'these bastards that own the mines, they'd have the children down the mines again, if they had the chance.'

She knew then that he was feeding the hungry children out of his own pocket, probably clothing them as well. Her own problems were slight in comparison.

On the way home she booked two passages on a steamer of the Stoddart line, second-class tourist, for New York.

*

Two weeks later Catriona stood on a pier in New York, holding Jamie with one hand, her suitcase in the other. Jamie was jumping up and down, his eyes running over the crowds. 'Where's my mother?'

'Shh, not yet,' Catriona hushed him. 'We'll go to see her once we've settled in.' She had asked the purser to find her a taxi – Rory had warned her about the sharks and tricksters who hung around the city's quays.

'When?' he insisted.

One of the crewmen came then, cutting off her answer as he picked up her suitcase and led her towards a cab.

The driver spoke with an accent so nasal that every word sounded like a sneeze. She had to repeat the phrase 'Gramercy Park' three times before he understood her and even then she wasn't sure he did, but he took off so fast that he must have known where he was going. New York passed in a flash, a market laden with fruits and vegetables then a glimpse of an enormous bridge before he turned into a maze of streets and then just as abruptly into an avenue lined with music halls and more people than she had ever seen in her life before. Jamie clasped her hand tightly and she watched his head tilt up to find the sky above the buildings, his eyes closing reflexively as the sun shone through a canyon between two office blocks.

'Ya evah bin heah?' the driver asked, twice, before she understood what he had said.

The traffic flowed like a river in spate, so fast that she had to avert her eyes for fear that they would collide.

'No,' she admitted, hoping that the purser had vetted him thoroughly and he was not one of Rory's scamps.

'Gramoicy Poik's noice,' he said, passing through a junction at breakneck speed, against a traffic signal she thought, but he only pressed the rubber bulb of the hooter fixed to the door of the cab.

'Ya immigrants?' he asked, as he skidded into a leafy square.

'No,' she said, thankful that he had stopped, 'just visitors.'

The hotel was small and tasteful, as Miss Cochrane had

described it; she said she always stayed there, because she could not abide the grand hotels of New York.

Catriona was appalled that the room she booked cost more than a hundred dollars a week, until she remembered she got more than four dollars for a pound.

'Can we see my mother now?' Jamie asked as she found the bathroom off the bedroom and the cot in the alcove made up for him.

It was evening; the ochre light of the sunset made long shadows of the trees in the park, gilding the windows of the houses on the other side. She opened the window and heard the distant city sounds, birdsong above the screech of the traffic.

'Tomorrow,' she said, 'you need a good sleep first.'

Once he was bathed and in his bed, she had to sit with him for ages.

'I'm so excited,' he said.

'I know,' she whispered, brushing the hair from his brow. 'It won't be long now. Hardly any time at all, once you're asleep.'

When he slept, Catriona took a slip of paper from her bag and crept out of the room. Using the phone in the manager's office, she called Ailish to say they would see her tomorrow, turning down her sister's offer to collect them from the hotel.

Back in her room she watched Jamie sleeping, praying silently that she had done the right thing.

'I owe you this,' she whispered, thinking of how close she had come to giving him up.

Half the world away from home, she remembered the girl who had fled the Briggait, and the girl she herself had been at the time, trembling for a moment before she realized also that in the years that had passed she, too, had grown up.

In the morning Jamie was too excited to eat his breakfast, too excited to do anything more than walk around the park with her, watching pigeons chase after crumbs.

The taxi came and she helped him in, sharing his awe as they crossed the bridge that soared above the East River.

When they reached Brooklyn his hand tightened around hers and she saw that his face had paled.

'How much longer?' he whispered. She asked the driver the same question. 'Acoupla minutes,' he told her.

On Bedford Avenue the cherry trees were in bloom; between the trees iron lamp posts held electrical lights, five globe-shaped bulbs to each column, blossoms shed from the trees danced and fluttered in the wake of the traffic.

She saw the building Ailish had described.

A man was waiting as the taxi scythed to a halt. Running forward he took a bill from his pocket and paid the driver before she had a chance to find her wallet.

'I'm Benny,' he said, as he pulled the door open, 'Benny Santino, your sister's husband-to-be. Hey, kid!' and he had picked up Jamie, swinging him into his barrel-like arms. 'I'm your ... I'm your, well, I guess I'm your pal for the moment. That okay?'

Jamie nodded, dumbstruck and shy.

He led them into the Imperial Apartments, pressing the elevator button as Jamie watched, intrigued.

'Ailish is over the moon,' Benny said to Catriona, 'she's been in a daze since she got your telegram. You don't know how much this means to her.'

The elevator came and Catriona stepped into it, biting her lip as the carriage began to ascend.

'This is nothing,' Benny said to Jamie, as the cables whirred. 'In Manhattan they're building a place that'll be a hundred storeys tall.'

The elevator clicked to a stop and beyond the wrought-iron gate Catriona saw Ailish standing before an open apartment door, wringing her hands nervously. Jamie clutched her hand and disappeared behind her skirt.

Benny strode out of the carriage and Catriona saw that he was only Ailish's height, though because of his build he seemed taller.

Ailish was looking at a little gold watch on her wrist. 'Benny, you should get to the office.'

'Na,' he said carelessly, 'on a day like this the office can wait.'

Catriona's eyes met Ailish's briefly; in that moment she realized that her sister had changed.

'Come on,' Benny said, leading them through the open door.

The apartment was light and airy, sunlight tumbled in through windows set high in the walls. The living room was painted ivory with a blonde carpet; two linen-covered sofas faced each other over a patterned rug and there was a stand full of potted plants below the window.

'The heat,' Ailish said apologetically. 'I should pull the blinds down, but it makes the place so gloomy.'

She looked so different now, with her hair in a bob that reached her shoulders and a soft wool dress in a colour that matched her eyes. Catriona had expected a flapper, heavily painted with a very short skirt, an extrapolation of the girl who had painted her lips wild scarlet to go dancing on Saturday night. She looked away quickly, before Ailish caught her surprise.

'Jamie,' Benny said to the trembling figure still behind Catriona, 'would you like a Coca-Cola, or a pop?'

'Lord,' Ailish said, 'I'm forgetting myself. Catriona, sit down please. Would you like coffee or tea?'

Catriona prised Jamie out from behind her and sat down on the edge of a sofa.

'Hello,' Ailish said to Jamie. He did not reply beyond sticking his thumb in his mouth. Very gently, Benny took Ailish by the arm and led her through to the kitchen. The gesture touched Catriona; he's a good man, she thought, he really loves her. Momentarily, she wondered why.

Benny came back, sat down and began to ease Jamie into conversation about school and ships and cars.

Ailish came in with a tray of coffee and biscuits and a tall glass of lemonade for Jamie. As she poured, her hands trembled; Catriona felt sorry for her despite her resolve.

'Here,' she said, as Ailish spilt the milk, 'let me.'

Ailish turned away, brushing her eye.

'Annie said,' she said, after a while, 'Annie said you've a tearoom in Largs.'

'Two tearooms now,' Catriona said, 'a tearoom and a big cafe on the seafront.'

'I always knew you would make it,' Ailish said.

Catriona ignored the remark.

'Annie said Sine's married,' Ailish went on.

'Five years ago. She's got children now, a boy and a girl. Maire lives with me in Largs. Allan's going to Glasgow University in October to study law.'

'Lord,' Ailish said, 'we have to talk.'

Benny looked up. He had been sitting on the floor with Jamie, tracing a diagram on the nap of the carpet. 'Jamie,' he said, 'why don't you and me go to find an ice cream? We'll go for a walk on the esplanade and you can see all of New York.'

Jamie nodded mutely; as yet he hadn't said a word or even cast a second glance at his mother.

'I'll come with you,' Catriona said, feeling his unease.

He forced a smile and shook his head.

After they left, Ailish touched her arm. 'Come,' she said, 'my bedroom is cooler.'

Her bedroom was as pale as the living room and there was an empty air to it, as if it was hardly used. Catriona realized then that Benny was not sleeping with her, that their courtship was as formal as the carefully laid out room.

'Benny's Italian,' Ailish said quickly. 'His parents stick to the old ways. It was two years before he took me to meet them. Catholics, you see. But I'm taking instruction at St James's.'

'Do you believe?' Catriona asked her.

'I believe in Benny. It took me a while to get over the other things.'

Catriona looked over the dressing table with the silver comb and brush, the glass bottle of perfume and a pot of cold cream.

'Do you love him?'

Ailish looked as if she'd been struck. 'Of course I do, but you don't care about that.'

'I care,' Catriona said softly, 'but I didn't think you cared that I did.'

Ailish sat down, legs folded, on a cushion on the floor. 'Oh, God, Catriona, where do I start?'

Catriona looked away. 'Ailish, it's in the past.'

'But it isn't, Catriona. It isn't now and it never will be. Jamie ... he's been with me every moment of every day. Even though I hardly know him now. He's still with me, deep inside.' Her face twisted into a sad little smile. 'He cried so much then. And I could never comfort him. I thought it was me.'

'I expected you to come back,' Catriona said slowly. 'At first I didn't think you'd really do it.'

'I nearly didn't,' Ailish said, 'but the ship left at ten that morning. I knew a girl on it, I just went along with her. I left the rest of your money with the man in the ticket office. He promised you'd get it. It was Benny who told me what a fool I was.'

Catriona said nothing.

'And then, when I got to New York, I was going to come back, but I thought you'd've already given him up for adoption, that he'd already be gone.'

'I nearly did but I couldn't.'

'Catriona ...'

'What, Ailish?'

'Will you ever forgive me?'

Her eyes were imploring. Catriona looked away. 'I already have. It's in the past, Ailish. I'm glad you've done well.'

Ailish shrugged. 'I didn't really. I stayed in the Christian Women's Hostel at first. For years until I met Benny. I worked in a shop in New York. He's an accountant, he's got his own office. After we met, I went to work with him and then I found the place here. Benny's like me, you see. There's trouble in his family, too.'

'Benny looks just fine to me.'

'Benny's brother is one of the biggest bootleggers in New York. You know what that means? He wanted Benny in with him, but Benny went to night school and did his accountant's exams.'

'There wasn't trouble in our family, Ailish.'

'Oh, no? What about Da?'

'You always had me.'

'But don't you see, Catriona? I thought you blamed me for Jamie. I thought you didn't care.'

Catriona looked at her sister, the stranger, remembered her coming to Glasgow, and knew now that she could not blame her for what had happened then.

'You know,' she said, slowly, 'there was a time when I did. I blamed you for taking my money. I blamed you because Allan was ill. But, you see, there were so many consequences. If you hadn't gone, I would never have found my tearoom in Largs. And other things. Not all of them were bad.'

Ailish was sobbing quietly.

'But Jamie,' Ailish said, 'Jamie suffered.'

'Jamie didn't suffer. He was too young to understand.'

Catriona went to her sister and put her arm around her. 'Ailish, you never knew this before. Nobody did. When Mor, when our mother died, I was there. I went to her and she asked me to promise that I would care for you all. And I did. I did the best I could. When you left, after you left, I thought that if I'd failed you, I'd also failed her. I was angry about that. But I didn't fail. You've shown me that.'

'Catriona, how could you even think that?'

Catriona smiled. 'You see, my life, my own life, it's only starting now. All of these years, I wasn't myself, you know. I was always trying to be someone else.'

She wanted to see New York so much, to taste the exuberance she felt in the streets, touch the promise that drew so many to these shores. But Jamie's shyness did not fade, his silence became more acute each moment he spent with Ailish. When they got back to the hotel he went to bed and she phoned the shipping company and booked passage on the next boat home.

Benny came with Ailish on Saturday morning and drove them around Manhattan, to the Woolworth Tower and Central Park, past the department stores on Fifth Avenue and the mansions crowding Park Avenue. After Jamie had eaten his first hot dog, they took the ferry to the Statue of Liberty and climbed the stairs to the top.

Looking down, Jamie went pale and was sick; Benny carried him all the way back to the boat.

'Oh, God,' Ailish said.

'It doesn't matter,' Catriona said, 'he'll be over it in a minute. I was getting dizzy myself.'

'I'm a Brooklyn boy, ya see,' Benny said, once the ferry had docked and the colour in Jamie's cheeks had returned, 'a Brooklyn boy, born and bred. The only time I was here I met Ailish at the lake in Central Park. Pure luck, it was. One of my brother's drivers got busted and I had to go to the courthouse to bail him out but when I got there they said it would be the end of the day before they had the papers ready, so I went up to the park. Family business. Ya know all about the family business.'

Catriona nodded, but the truth was that she didn't want to, because she liked Benny too much.

Ailish took Jamie to Loeser's and bought him canvas shoes and cotton print shirts, tracks and a train driven by clockwork. On the way to the Navy Yard to see the ships, Benny passed Wallabout Market. Catriona asked him to stop and got out to look at the farmers' carts loaded with pumpkins and watermelons, eggplants and peppers, string beans and lima beans, sweet potatoes, more vegetables than she had ever seen in her life before.

On Sunday they went to Coney Island, where the sun was so hot that a haze rose in ripples from the roads.

'Place isn't the same,' Benny said as they walked along Surf Avenue, past the seafood bars and the card sharks working the holiday crowds.

'You always say that,' Ailish said.

'If you'd seen Dreamland, you'd know' he said. 'The island's not the same since Dreamland burned down.'

He turned into Luna Park, an extravaganza of turrets, towers and pagodas, a huge plaster dragon that soared above the crowds. 'Dreamland was special,' he said as he bought their tickets. 'This, this is just tawdry.'

Jamie was too young to notice the flaking paint, the chipped plaster. When an elephant sashayed past, he cried out in delight.

Catriona was thinking about the sheer braggadocio of the placards that promised the world in tableau for just a quarter. Coney Island was loud, brash, brazen as a streetwalker, with all the strident honesty of a pavement hawker. The spectacle was enjoyable for what it was, a maelstrom of sound and colour with as much taste as the dirt-brown row houses that lined the railway track along Flatbush Avenue. There was a charisma about it all, a sort of style in the way the amusement parks and ice-cream parlours jostled together like market stalls; it would be too much for Largs, or anywhere else but where it was.

At last Jamie laughed, and grabbed Ailish's hand as he ran from stand to stand; for once Catriona did not count the candies or the lollipops or the spun-sugar cornets that came in all the colours of the rainbow.

Afterwards, sitting in a restaurant, she saw him smiling at Ailish and was touched by the look of relief on her sister's face.

'Place's gone to the dogs,' Benny was saying. 'When I was Jamie's age, my uncle Emilio used to take us to the Manhattan Beach. What a restaurant that was; the menu there, you could read it like a book. Thirty lobster dishes, fifty steaks, twenty-four different flavours of ice cream.'

The waitress came and looked vaguely sad as she listened to him reminiscing.

'A knickerbocker glory,' Benny said, 'boy's gotta have a knickerbocker glory.'

The knickerbocker glory came, ice cream, fruit, syrup and wafers piled into a glass that was a foot and a half tall.

'He'll be sick again,' Catriona said.

'That's half the fun of Coney Island,' Benny said, 'being sick afterwards.'

Ailish nudged him and he fell silent for a moment.

Catriona looked at the menu again and ordered a chocolate nut fudge sundae. When the waitress brought it she asked for a copy of the menu to take home with her.

'Ailish,' she said, leaning over to talk to her sister as Jamie worked doggedly though the whipped cream on top, 'd'you know where to buy glasses like these?'

'I can find out,' Ailish said, 'but I've only ever seen them at the island.'

'There's a place on Mulberry Street,' Benny said, 'sells them wholesale, but you could ask for half a dozen.'

'I'll take you tomorrow,' Ailish said, 'if Benny'll give me the day off work.' It surprised Catriona to think of her working in an accountant's office, but so many things about Ailish had changed.

'We're going home tomorrow,' Jamie piped up as he speared the cherry at the bottom of the glass.

Ailish looked hurt.

'It seemed best,' Catriona said.

'I've changed my mind,' Jamie said as he finished the cherry. 'Can we stay on now?'

Benny and Ailish came to collect them at Gramercy Park and drove them to the pier where the transatlantic ship was berthed.

Benny looked anxious until he saw a truck; he waved to the driver. 'Glasses,' he said, 'I got you a coupla gross of glories, sundaes and splits. Specially packed for export. Company's Italian, see?'

'I must pay you.'

'Na, you're family now, or you will be come September.'

Catriona did not want a long-drawn-out farewell; she did not want to make promises that she did not intend to keep.

'You could come to visit us in Largs,' she said.

'When Prohibition ends,' Benny said. ''Till then, I gotta watch out for the family business. Bail 'em out of jail when they get caught.'

They shook hands uneasily. Out of the corner of her eye Catriona saw Ailish bending down to speak to Jamie. 'I know,' she was saying, 'that you don't think I love you, but I do. I've loved you all of your life and I always will. I want you to know that, any time you need to. Ailish loves you, and so does Benny. Anything you need, anything you want, you only have to ask.'

Catriona loved Ailish then, and realized that the ties had never broken and never would. Jamie reached up to hug his mother and then he spun around and ran for their cabin.

'God bless,' Catriona said as she hugged her sister. 'I love you, Ailish. I really do.'

Ailish could hardly speak for tears. 'We'll meet again, Triona. Triona?'

'Yes, Ailish. Of course we will.'

As the ship slid away from the pier she waved until the figures there had shrunk to the size of flies.

In the cabin she teased Jamie until he was smiling again.

'I needed to see her, you see,' he said.

'Yes, Jamie,' she replied. 'I needed that too.'

He looked at her through tear-stained eyes. 'But I'm glad,' he said, 'I'm so glad that you're my mother.'

At that moment she could have hugged him to death.

Back in Largs, Catriona went into Nicolson's through the delivery door, having left Jamie at the Rose Tearoom, telling Etta all about his holiday in New York. After the voyage home she felt young again; seeing Ailish well had cleansed her mind of the residue of worry that had been with her all of these years.

The kitchen had an air of subdued panic as always; the chef was dressing salmon for the evening buffet with two boys beside him slicing cucumber and making flowers out of bundles of chives and tomato flesh.

She watched them unnoticed for a moment, sensing something different, something not quite right. Some of the kitchen lads were missing; the lunchtime dishes were still not washed, though it was past four o'clock.

Walking into the restaurant she saw Maire bent over the cashier's booth, her face breaking into a smile as she saw her sister. Catriona waved and mouthed the words 'in a minute' and strode on, noticing with annoyance that some of the tables had not been cleared.

Zena, the bright red-haired girl she had hired as a waitress and then promoted to supervisor, was clearing the tables herself.

'Where's the girls?' Catriona asked.

'Oh, Missus,' Zena said, looking up, 'thank goodness you're back. Hettie and Chrissie are on their break and Mary's gone round the shops with Jean.'

'What are they doing round the shops?'

Zena bit her lip. 'I'm not right sure, Missus. Mr Joe sent them.'

Catriona went back to her office, pausing on the way to ask two of the kitchen girls to help Zena with the tables.

Maire followed her a moment later. 'How was New York?' she asked, 'How's Ailish?' before she noticed the look on Catriona's face.

'What happened?' Catriona asked. She had already flicked through the daily accounts and seen that takings had fallen.

'A few problems. Nothing much,' Maire said.

'What sort of problems?'

Maire blushed and looked away. 'You'd best ask Joe.'

'I'd rather ask you.'

'I've left the cash desk.'

'Ask Zena to take over.'

'She's clearing the tables.' Maire's fluster increased.

'All right,' Catriona said, 'we'll talk later.'

'I'm glad you're back,' Maire said as she went out.

Catriona put an apron over her dress and went to help Zena. The air in the restaurant was still and hot; she turned on the ceiling fans and wedged the doors open so that fresh air could circulate. They worked in silence for twenty minutes until all the tables had been cleared and set again. By then, Catriona's brow was moist with sweat; Zena's face was flushed.

'I've been thinking,' Catriona said as they went to the staff room for some lemonade, 'these dresses are far too heavy for the summer.'

'Oh, aye, Missus,' Zena said, 'I'm fair biling, an' it slows ye down.'

'I'll go round to Lindsey's in a minute and see if they've got anything cooler. If not, I'll get some sent from Glasgow.'

'I'm fair wabbit,' Zena said as she sat down. 'An' it's only half past four.'

Catriona had sensed something of herself in Zena when she had given her the job. She was older than the other girls, married, with four children and looking for work because her husband had lost his railway job after an accident. Catriona had hesitated at first because she was only paying waitress's wages and Zena was worth more than that; she had taken her on because of her air of determination and then watched with satisfaction the crisp efficiency with which she went about her work.

Catriona waited until the high colour had faded from Zena's cheeks before she asked what had happened. Zena shifted uncomfortably and looked at the clock. 'It's nearly a quarter off five, Missus, I should be getting back.'

Because Nicolson's opened at ten in the morning and in the summer did not close until ten at night, the girls had two breaks of fifteen minutes in the morning and evening and half an hour after the lunchtime rush.

'You've fifteen minutes, yet,' she said quietly.

'Missus, it's no' my place.'

'If I ask you, it is.'

Zena rose resolutely. 'It's been chaos, Missus. I'm that glad ye're back. Ye'll get the place to rights in no time.' She was out of the door before Catriona could stop her.

Catriona went to the office, where she looked at the account books again. The daily takings were down an average of £50; since she had been away Nicolson's had lost a thousand pounds. There was still as much food being paid for; the problem was that it was not being sold.

She put her head in her hands, then checked the figures again.

Downstairs, Joe was nowhere to be found; the head chef would tell her only that it had been mayhem.

She stood in the middle of the kitchen, watching the way that nobody's eyes met hers. 'Stop that,' she said to the chefs and the kitchen girls. 'I said, stop it!' she shouted as the clacking and whirring sounds died. 'Now,' she went on, her eyes swinging around the room, 'which one of you is going to tell me what happened?'

Nobody said a word.

She asked again; just then Maire's head appeared through the swing doors.

'I'll be back,' Catriona promised as she walked along to the office with Maire.

Maire wanted her to promise not to sack anyone, least of all Joe.

'Just tell me what happened,' Catriona said tersely.

Maire did. 'Joe has a habit of giving away ice creams,' she began.

'I know that.'

Joe's generosity had gone awry, and from morning to night Nicolson's had been filled with hordes of screaming children, none of whom paid – and of course, the ones who *would* have paid did not because of that; there had been one bad egg in a tray from a farmer and a whole batch of ice cream had been ruined. Joe had chased the farmer, waving a rolling pin, threatening bodily harm; the farmer had complained to the police and Joe had been arrested, and was awaiting trial.

'My God.' Catriona put her head in her hands. 'Is he in gaol? Is that where he is?'

'No,' Maire said, 'I bailed him out. I thought you'd've wanted that.'

'I'd've left him to rot.'

'You don't mean that,' Maire said.

'Is that all?'

'Well, the farmer won't supply us any more, and nor will anyone else. That's where the girls are. They go around the shops buying what we need.'

'Which nobody eats, Maire. I don't suppose you've noticed, but nobody's had much time for our paying customers.'

Maire flushed. 'It's not that bad, Catriona. It's really only the Paisley Fair people, and they've gone back, now.'

'It's bad enough,' Catriona said, putting on her jacket and picking up her bag.

'Joe's been taking food to Rory,' Maire shouted after her. 'He's up there now.'

On her way to the farmer, she found Allan working in the public library.

'I've won the year medal,' he said, 'I'm dux of Glasgow High. Can you believe it?'

'I never doubted you would do it, Allan,' she said quietly.

'Are you angry with Maire?'

'I wish to hell I'd left you in charge.'

It was late in the evening when she got back to the Rose Tearoom. Both Jamie and Allan had already gone to bed. Maire was waiting in the living room.

'You promised,' Catriona began, 'you promised you'd take care of everything.'

'It just happened.'

'You let it happen, Maire.'

'I didn't, Catriona.'

'Who did then?' Her anger rang around the room as Maire flinched. 'Joe?'

'Not Joe,' Maire said, 'it wasn't Joe.'

'For God's sake, don't start defending him. His family's been in this business for generations. He knows how it works.'

Maire shook her head. 'It was the farmer who caused the trouble. Joe's just too kind-hearted, that's all.'

'Kind-hearted? He nearly bankrupts me and you call him kind-hearted?'

'He only gave away a few ice creams, Catriona.'

'He only cost me a thousand pounds, you mean. And attacked one of my suppliers, terrified the man so much that now the whole of the town's calling him mad.'

'He isn't mad, Catriona, don't say that.'

'What the hell is he, then? The second coming?'

Maire flinched. 'You know what his temper's like. He'll go to gaol for it, Mr Hendry said. It isn't fair.'

'It would serve him right if he did, Maire. But I've been to the farmer and he's calmed down about it. He accepts that Joe didn't mean to make threats. I've been to the police and the fiscal and the charges are dropped. The farmer'll supply us again, and so will the dairy and the butcher and the grocer and the fishmonger. But I'm sacking Joe, Maire. His ice cream isn't worth it if that's the trouble it causes.'

Maire's eyes narrowed. 'Don't do that, Catriona. I mean it. If you sack Joe, I'll walk out too.'

Catriona did not believe her and said so.

'I meant what I said!' Maire yelled as she strode out of the room, slamming the door.

'I don't care if you do!' Catriona roared after her.

The cool night air calmed her and dried the tears in her eyes. Over the moors she saw the moon high in the sky, grazing the watery peatland; as she drove past, the grass blurred and rustled, waved by the wake of her car.

Rory was still working, as she'd guessed he would be, though it was in the early hours of the morning when she reached his yard.

'The worst is over,' he said, wiping the grease from his hands with a rag. 'I've got foundry contracts now, delivering to factories. There's work for the men without the coal.'

'The strike's over, isn't it?'

'This time, it is. How was America?'

She told him about the trouble with Joe, about the chaos he had caused with his free ice cream; she almost laughed herself, once she saw how funny it was. It seemed petty to rue the thousand pounds she had lost, when Rory had lost so much more, keeping on his men when there was no work for them to do. She told him about Benny, the honest bootlegger, trying to keep his brother out of jail.

'I'm happy for Ailish,' he said when she had finished.

'So am I, Rory.'

'Ach.' He flicked through a pile of papers and handed her

one, his bank statement, which said that he had a balance of £1/11/9. 'I'm just about back to where I started, girl,' he said, a note of bitterness in his voice.

'Not quite,' she said, 'you've got the yard, all these trucks.'

'Things're so bad, I couldn't sell them even if I wanted too.'

'How much have you lost, Rory?'

'I've never counted, Catriona. I'm just lucky I'm still on the go.'

She yawned, suddenly tired.

'Joe kept the children fed,' he said quickly. 'Not everyone's as good at business as you. I mean, you haven't actually lost, have you? You just haven't made as much as you expected to.'

'I hate being in debt,' she said quietly.

'I know that, but sometimes there isn't a choice, Triona.'

'I can't help being angry with Joe, Rory.'

He hunkered down beside her, taking her soft, white hands in his own, rough, scarred ones. 'Let me tell you something I've learned, Catriona, something I've learned about life. All these chances you get, and you think each one is the only one, that isn't true, girl.'

'It isn't?'

'It's not. In the years I've had this yard, I've learned that. My back's been to the wall I don't know how many times, and every time something comes up. There's always another chance, if you keep your eyes open, if you keep on looking. There's always another chance with things like that. There's only one thing in life that you never get a second chance at, and that's people. Make a mistake with someone, and you'll never get the chance again. Do it wrong and you won't get back the past. D'you see that?'

She looked at him for a long time.

'Have you ever watched Maire and Joe together, Triona? Do you know what that pair means to each other?'

'I never thought about it, Rory.'

His face creased into a smile. 'Ach, girl, I'm havering. Being poor again's turned my head.'

She smiled back at him. 'Rory, I . . .'

He cut her off with a wave of his hand, turning away embarrassed. She wanted to talk some more, but he had fallen silent. In all the years she had known Rory she had never known him to be like that.

She found Maire and Joe early the next morning, talking in the back garden of the Rose Tearoom.

Joe stood up straight when he saw her, as if preparing himself to meet his doom.

'It doesn't matter,' she said, 'we'll say no more about it.'

Maire spun around and looked at her as if she had gone mad.

'Why didn't you tell me?' Catriona asked them.

'Tell you what?' Maire asked.

'About you two,' she said, 'you didn't tell me you had fallen in love.'

Chapter Thirteen

*R*ory came down at the end of high summer, on a day when the sun was so hot that heat rippled up from the pavement in sinuous waves, making the seascape sway like a mirage. On days like that Catriona opened the high windows to let the sea breeze in; with that and the fans and the shade of the plants, the interior usually stayed cool and fresh but on that day the wind faded to a whisper and then died completely. The waitresses served iced water in tall jugs and handed out little paper fans for the clientele to cool themselves.

The beach was thronged like Paddy's Market; the sea was full of children, some bathing fully dressed.

Rory sat in the Palm Court, waiting for her to take a rest. The restaurant was busy all afternoon, and she managed to join him only after high tea had been served, when the day trippers on the front were beginning to queue for the steamers back to the city.

'I'm sorry,' she said as she sat down.

'It doesn't matter. I enjoy the sun. How are you?'

She made a gesture with her hands. 'Joe and Maire are getting married at Christmas. They're going to live above the Rose Tearoom and Jamie and I will move in here. Jamie's back to school tomorrow. Allan starts university next month.'

'I know that,' he said, 'I've just seen the pair of them.'

'Can you imagine Allan a lawyer?'

'Whyever not? He's got the Nicolson brains.'

She smiled again. 'I bought him a flat in Hyndland.'

'Not the one you tried to rent all those years ago?'

'In the same road, Rory. It's only two rooms and a kitchen and bathroom.'

'But how are you?' he asked again.

'I've just told you, haven't I?'

'You've told me about everybody else. Not a word about yourself.'

She thought for a moment. 'I'm fine, Rory. I made up the loss. The loan instalment's paid and there's plenty in the bank. How are you?'

He looked away for a moment; in that instant she saw the dark shadows under his eyes and the strand of grey in his hair. The way he had aged shocked her all of a sudden, made her wonder at the years that had passed, at how much longer she might have of youth before she, too, faded into middle age.

Zena came in a rush and served him the concoction of peaches, sorbet and mint leaves drenched in brandy that was Joe's version of an adult sundae; Catriona had iced tea with a cucumber sandwich.

He cheered up then and began to tell her stories of the island that he had heard on his trip home, had her laughing at the saga of Hamish and the dyke and Lord MacDonald's cousin's shooting party. The time passed and slowly the chatter from the restaurant died; she felt her usual impulse to join in the work but suppressed it because she was enjoying herself. When the meal service stopped at eight o'clock she saw that Zena and Maire were managing just fine.

Rory talked on about nothing much; she had been listening for hours when she realized something was wrong, that there was a deep unease beneath his happy banter.

'Rory,' she said, when he paused for breath, 'what's the matter?'

The sun was sliding far to the west, cutting a track in the sea towards the Cumbraes and Arran beyond. It was not yet sunset, but the interlude of calm at the end of the day when the gulls wheeled in lazy circles over the water and the trail of the last home-going steamer was far away. The town was quiet then, content with itself and comfortable as a pair of old slippers. The sting of the heat was gone but the air was warm, bits of waste paper surfing the puffs of wind along the

341

front. Catriona watched a child's paper windmill cartwheel over again and again until it rested beneath a chair and a patrolling gull swooped down to see if it was edible.

The trippers were gone, so were the holiday makers, only the people who lived there all year round remained; in the cool of the evening they came out to watch the scenery, to remind themselves that it belonged to them and them alone.

Rory was smiling, not a true smile but the grin a man makes because anything else would betray something he would rather keep to himself.

'What is it?' she asked again.

He touched his lip with his tongue, looked from one side to the other and then at her: 'I'm going bust, Triona. Wednesday of this week, the yard goes bankrupt.'

'No,' she said reflexively.

'Oh, yes,' he said, 'I don't joke about things like that.'

Catriona said nothing for a moment, feeling cold despite the heat.

'I'd no idea,' she said then, helplessly. 'I thought you were managing.'

'I was,' he said. 'It wasn't that. It was Corbett's Ironworks. They went bankrupt last month. They owe me three thousand pounds, but I'll be lucky to get as many pennies. A bad debt, the accountant calls it. The slump. God's sake, Catriona, the company's been in business for nearly a hundred years.'

She was thinking of the money she had in her own bank account.

'The bank won't carry my loan any longer,' he said, 'I've enough cash to pay this week's wages, that's all. The bank'll come in Wednesday. They'll get their money back if they sell the trucks. There might be a little left over. I'll start again . . .'

'How much do you need, Rory?'

'The devil with that, Triona.'

'Rory, don't be a bloody fool.'

'I didn't come here to borrow your money.'

'D'you remember that time you paid Allan's hospital bills, and you wouldn't let me pay you back?'

342

'That was nothing, Triona. That was a favour for a friend. You paid me back in the end, remember?'

'How much do you need, Rory?'

'Three thousand pounds, Triona. But, God knows, I'm not taking it off you.'

'Rory, if you don't let me lend you the money, that's the end of us as friends.'

He sat back and thought for a while. 'I couldn't.'

'How many men will you put out of work if you don't?' She went to her office and got her chequebook; he still protested. 'You'd do it for me,' she said as she began to write.

'I would,' he agreed. 'I'll have the money back to you as soon as I can, Catriona. Within the year. My business's solid, or it soon will be.'

She shook her head. 'I don't care so much about the money, Rory. You're more important to me than that.'

Maire married Joe in the Catholic chapel in Largs on 2 January 1927.

The ceremony was a simple one, the ritual the confirmation of the love that seemed so natural, once Catriona had recognized it.

After the service she held a reception in the Rose Tearoom, which was adorned with fragrant orchids from Miss Cochrane's hothouse.

There were few guests, only Rory and some of the staff from Nicolson's, Joe's uncle and cousins from Glasgow, tearful and contrite now that the family quarrel was made up.

Joe loved Maire so much; the emotion shone from his eyes and tamed his mercurial temper, was obvious in every gesture he made, every word that he spoke.

As Catriona watched them she felt not envy but a sense of loss, regret that she had lost the love she had before it had a chance to mature. Joe was taking Maire home to visit Naples; that evening they would take the train to Glasgow to spend their wedding night in the Central Hotel and then the following day they would begin the long journey south.

In December Catriona had taken Maire to the city and bought her a going-away outfit, also some pretty things for her trousseau.

As the couple left for the station everyone gathered outside to wave them off. Allan had booked a taxi to take them and made sure that the hotel's porter would collect them from the train at the other end.

Maire hugged Catriona. 'I'll never know how to thank you,' she murmured.

'You don't have to say a word,' Catriona replied.

Joe brushed a tear from his eye and they were off, the car trailed by dozens of children chasing the pennies Joe threw from the window.

'That's it,' Allan said. The tearoom felt empty now, lonely in a way. Joe's uncle opened a new bottle of wine and started telling another story in his quaint mixture of Italian and Glaswegian. Everybody laughed. Catriona stood at the back of the room and watched as the revelries began again, happy but also sad. Her sisters were all married now, embarked on new lives; of them all, only she and Allan were left alone. Allan was in his first year of university and already he was changing, his speech becoming measured and considered, the hallmark of a lawyer. He would be successful, she knew: his character was as if he had been born to be a lawyer, he was cautious and precise, almost pedantic at times. The illness that had robbed him of his youth had made him thoughtful and infinitely patient, but there was also compassion in his soul, ingrained by hard experience, that would enable him to stand apart from the MacKenzies of this world.

She watched him pouring wine, first for the women and then for the men; he was chivalrous in attending to Zena, Etta and Josie, the employees who might have felt left out if he had been careless of them.

She was proud of him, proud of all the Nicolsons, even herself. If Mor had been there, or the twins, who had fallen so early off the helter-skelter of life, they would have been proud too, she thought, before she recalled the strange ways of fate: if her mother and the twins had not died, she would not be as she was now.

The only sorrow left was her father. Her estrangement from him left a void at the core of her soul; she wanted to make it up but the hurt was too great, the memory of the way he'd abandoned Allan and the rest of them too raw.

She still sent money, five pounds a month, but didn't know what he did with it because he never wrote and nor did she, the only contact between them was a banknote in an envelope every four weeks. She yearned for her island, for the familiarity of home and the majesty of the land, but she had another home now and a life far apart.

It was late and as the party waned she gave Allan the car keys to take the girls home and then put a pot of coffee on for Rory and Luigi, who faced the drive to Glasgow.

As she waited for the water to heat, Rory joined her in the kitchen.

'Catriona,' he said slowly.

She studied the gas flame below the coffee pot; she did not want him to see that she had been crying.

'Yes, Rory?'

'Business is picking up. I'll have the money for you in a couple of weeks.'

'Your business can't be that good,' she said, a shade too sharply. She did not want to talk about money at this of all times.

'I've more'n fifty trucks, Triona. I make good money, so long's nobody else goes bust. And that's the end of the strikes for a while.'

'Does that mean the workers won?' she asked, her voice ripe with derision.

'No,' he said patiently. 'It means the strike funds're exhausted, and so are the men. What's the matter, Catriona?'

'The strikes hurt you as much as they hurt anyone,' she spat. 'You nearly went bankrupt for the unions, Rory. Did they ever thank you for that?' She hated the bitter note in her voice; she did not mean to sound like that.

345

She was still staring at the coffee pot as it fizzled and coughed. 'Excuse me,' she said, lifting it and brushing past.

He was still sitting there when she got back. 'Come on,' he said, pulling out a chair for her. She sat reluctantly, avoiding his eyes and then, remembering she had left the coffee behind, rose to make another pot.

He watched her make it; she poured one mug for him and another for herself.

'The men stood by me,' he said.

She arched an eyebrow.

'They did. When I was going bust they held a meeting and voted to work without pay until I got back on my feet again. It wouldn't've made a difference, Triona. I'd've had no use for my drivers if the bank had taken my trucks.'

She swore.

He folded his arms on the table and looked at her.

'It isn't that,' she said, 'it isn't your men or the unions or your trucks.'

'What is it, then?'

'I'm lonely,' she said, 'and I hate it, being lonely. It's what I hate most of all.'

He unfolded his arms and, very gently, put his hand over hers. 'Catriona, will you marry me?'

She looked at him and shook her head. 'I didn't mean it like that, Rory. I'm not in the mood for one of your jokes.'

Inside, he was shaking.

There was a commotion in the tearoom. Luigi's laughter rang out on top of Etta's cries. Catriona got up to see what was happening.

'I'm serious,' Rory said, 'I've never been more serious in my life.' He waited for her answer for a long time before he realized that she had not even heard him, that she had gone through to the tearoom.

Allan came through for some more ice. Joe's cousin Matteo had another bottle of grappa; Luigi had vowed to drink it straight.

'Are you all right?' he said to Rory. 'You look as if you've had a bit too much.'

'Not yet,' Rory said, 'but I soon will have.'

A speywife came into the restaurant one winter's day, a bent old gypsy fortune teller with bundles of white heather in a sack over her shoulder; she plied her trade on the promenade with the others every year but Catriona had never seen her before.

Catriona served her herself because Zena was on her teabreak; the other girls shied away because they were scared of gypsy magic and of the curses that were said to flow from the speywife's lips if you didn't cross her palm with silver.

'Sit down,' the speywife said when Catriona went to clear the plates away. 'I've something to tell you.'

'I don't want my fortune read,' Catriona said quickly; she was superstitious of prophecy, as all islanders were.

'Sit down,' the speywife said again. 'I'm not asking you for money, lass, but there's something I want to tell you.'

Catriona heard one of the waitresses tittering, and turned around angrily before she sat down, which politeness to her customer demanded.

The speywife gripped her hand with fingers that were bent and gnarled with age.

'You think you're alone, lass,' she said in a voice that was hoarse, almost a whisper. 'You think you're alone, that you're not loved, but you are, lass. You're surrounded by love.'

'My family's with me,' Catriona said. 'They love me.'

'I don't mean that, girl. There's love you don't see. An older man, far away. Your father. He loves you, and it's breaking his heart. You can't go to him, because he's so proud. You'll have to wait for him to come to you, but he will.'

Catriona swallowed; she began to shiver.

'You haven't yet met the man who will love you, I don't think. There was one, but you turned him away.'

'Who?' Catriona asked sharply, surprised by the need she heard in her voice.

347

The gypsy's eyes turned rheumy. 'There was a man who loved you who died, lass. He died in war, but not the Great War. You know who I'm talking about, don't you?'

'No ... ' Catriona whispered.

'Don't lie to me,' the gypsy said sharply. 'Ignore me if you will, but don't lie to me.' She shook her head, and finished her tea. 'There's hard times coming, but joy will follow, as surely as night follows day. Never doubt yourself, girl. That's all I've got to say.'

The speywife got up and left, and Catriona watched her slow, crabbed walk along the promenade until she turned into the road to the station.

'What'd she say, Missus?' one of the waitresses asked.

'Nothing,' Catriona said quickly.

'How much'd it cost?'

'Nothing,' Catriona said, before she looked around and realized that she had not been paid for the tea and scones.

The storm came in March. At midday the sky looked angry; by two o'clock the children were sent away from school and told to hurry home before the rainclouds broke. It was dark as night then, the restaurant as deserted as the streets that were whipped by wind as wild as Catriona had ever seen in the lowlands.

She locked the doors against the gale and went upstairs, listening to the radio until the reception failed during the six o'clock news.

At midnight Jamie crept into her bed, frightened by the sound of the wind. 'It's nothing,' she whispered, 'it will all be over in the morning.'

During the night she heard a crash, or so she thought; but, not wanting to disturb Jamie, she did not get up.

When she woke again the storm had spent itself and the early sun was drying the rain-slicked streets. She got up slowly, careful of Jamie, then dressed and went down to the kitchen to make a cup of coffee.

She felt the breeze then, pushing against the swing doors from the restaurant. Walking through, she saw that the canopy of the Palm Court had been ripped off and blown away, shattering the windows and leaving a gaping hole in the centre of the room.

Stunned, she sat down, then stood up and futilely straightened the cloth on one of the tables that had not been knocked over.

There was glass everywhere, and jagged fragments of wood and metal from the struts that had been torn away.

A voice reminded her that she was insured, the premium paid last month as always. In the office she found the policy and read the clause that insured the building, its fixtures and fittings and contents against fire, theft, and all risks including storms.

It doesn't matter, she told herself; with work, everything could be put right. She made Jamie's breakfast, took it upstairs and sat with him until it was eaten and he was ready for school.

'The wind blew down the Palm Court,' she said, 'but it doesn't matter.'

'Can I stay at home and help you fix it?' There was a hopeful look on his face, because he did not like school; like Ailish, he resented the discipline of learning.

'No, you can't, Jamie. You can go to school and have your dinner there, because it'll be chaos here.'

'Will Rory come?' he asked when he saw the damage. 'Rory could fix it, no trouble at all.'

She looked at him; Rory came to see him on Sundays, but he had begun to miss her again. 'He could,' she said slowly, 'but I'm not going to ask him.'

'Why not?'

'Because there'll be trees down blocking the roads, Jamie. Because he's got other work to do apart from ours.'

Once he was gone she rang Hendry's first to ask the lawyer to help her file the claim, then the builder and the glazier, the joiners and decorators.

The lawyer came first, Andy Hendry, old Mr Hendry's son who had taken over his father's firm at Christmas when the old man retired. Catriona liked his easy manner, the efficient way he listed the damage and told her which estimates she would need before he could submit the claim.

'You're fully insured,' he said, 'my father made sure of that. Thank God.'

The damage would cost thousands to put right.

The staff were shocked, talking together in whispers. 'Will ye be layin' us off, Missus?' one asked her. 'No,' she replied, 'of course not.'

Once she had put up the 'closed' signs, the clear-up began. Two of the chefs put on strong leather gloves and began to prise the shards of glass away from the frames, making a big pile of fragments in the builder's cart. Others began to sweep, dust and clean; the task was daunting because most of the tables had been overturned and table-cloths, napkins and even cutlery had blown into unruly piles that had silted up against the walls. Only the back of the restaurant was relatively unscathed; in a week or so she could open again, Catriona thought, if she put up screens to hide the worst of it.

Robbie Thompson almost cried when he saw the plants, the mess of soil and greenery that had once been *Ananas variegatus* and *Fortunella japonica*, bougainvillea and slender palm trees. He got to work immediately, gently pulling away broken glass and wood, picking up the plants as tenderly as a mother would handle a hurt child. Once he had cleared the worst of the mess, he saved most of them with the exception of a once gracious phoenix palm whose trunk had been neatly sliced in half.

The builders had put up their ladders and scaffolding; as they began work on the structure Catriona went to her office to tally what had been lost.

The storm had been the worst to hit Largs for years; as word spread of the damage of Nicolson's, the staff's brothers and fathers came to help. There were now twenty or more people working with the waitresses and kitchen staff; she had promised each a pound a day and their meals until the place was put right.

In just a few hours the damage had been reduced from

devastation to neat piles of rubble; she would be able to reopen the restaurant in a day or two, the Palm Court maybe by the beginning of next month.

The glazier had already been, and she had asked him for moulded glass awnings with steel struts to replace the canvas that had ripped apart; it would be expensive, he said, but she told him it would be cheaper in the long run to make the entire building safe from storms.

It was lunchtime when she heard a crash and then a cry. One of the waitresses rushed through: 'Come quick, Missus, there's been an accident.'

She saw at once what had happened; one of the lads had stood on a table to pull down a bit of metal frame, had slipped somehow and fallen onto a pile of glass. His right leg was nigh severed at the thigh, blood pumping out in a gushing fountain surging in time with the beat of his heart. Zena was bent over him, vainly trying to stem the flow with her apron.

Catriona pushed her away; swallowing her horror at the sight of the bone through the wound she grabbed a tablecloth which she twisted around the boy's leg again and again, holding it tight until the flow of blood ceased.

'Get the doctor,' she hissed, through lips taut with strain; the boy was barely conscious, pale with shock.

'Oh, Missus,' Zena said, frozen to the spot.

'Get the doctor,' Catriona said again.

'He's on his way,' someone replied. She could feel the blood pulsing beneath the bandage; she drew it tighter and the boy gasped with pain. The glass had cut right through to the bone; half the leg was cut away but, lying face down, he couldn't see that.

He began to shiver; she sent one of the girls for blankets from her room.

'Where's the doctor?' she asked, then heard a car, driven fast, come screeching to a halt.

'Who is it?' the doctor asked.

Catriona did not know. 'Wee Rab Duncan,' somebody said. She flinched. He was a brother of one of the waitresses, the family a poor one because their father had been wounded at Ypres.

'Oh,' the doctor said, as he knelt beside the boy. 'Call an ambulance, will you? I'll go with him myself.'

Catriona leaned over to talk to Rab. 'You'll be all right now. The doctor is here and there's an ambulance coming.'

'Missus, Missus? I'm gey sorry abou' all the blood.'

She turned away quickly. 'Don't worry about that.'

In the evening she went to visit his parents at their cottage in the lee of the hills behind Largs.

'I'm Catriona Nicolson,' she said hesitantly as Mrs Duncan opened the door.

'I ken fine who ye are, lass,' Mrs Duncan said, 'ye'd best come in.'

She walked into a room hardly bigger than the one she had rented in the Briggait, furnished the same way around a coal-fired range. Emma, the waitress who worked for her, smiled shyly as she put the kettle on.

A man sat on a chair; as he struggled up to welcome her she noticed that he'd lost both legs and walked on wooden ones strapped to stumps.

'Please,' she said, 'don't bother.'

'I must thank ye, lass. Ye saved the lad's life.'

'Doctor's just been,' his mother said. 'He said you put a toornickey aroun' him an' if ye hadny, he'd'a bled tae death.'

'I did nothing,' Catriona said. 'He was trying to help me.'

Emma served tea.

His father told her that Rab had lost his leg. The nerves were cut and so were the muscles, and despite what they'd learned in the war the surgeons could not repair the damage.

'Jist bad luck, it wis,' his mother said, 'twa men in the family an' the pair o' them wi' only wan leg between them. His faither's no' worked the last ten year an' I suppose Rab'll no' get the chance either.'

'He will,' Catriona said. 'I'll give him a job.'

'I didna mean that, lass. I wasna asking ye; it's jist bad luck, ye ken.'

'Rab will work,' Catriona said. 'I'll give him a job in Nicolson's once he's left school. He can help in the office.'

'Lass,' his father said, 'we wasnae asking ye fir awthing.'

'I'm insured,' Catriona said, as she took her chequebook from her bag. Usually she didn't carry it with her but she had just been to the builder to pay him something on account. Quickly, she wrote out a cheque for £500.

'This won't pay for his leg,' she said, 'but it will make things easier.'

'Lass, we couldna,' Rab's father said.

'You must,' she said, as she rose to leave. 'It isn't for you, it's for him.'

She left quickly, before they could argue. The insurance would not cover the payment, she knew, because it covered her staff, not casual workers, but her conscience told her that she had to help.

Andy Hendry cursed her for a fool; he told her that, if they sued, she had already lost the case for herself.

'I don't give a damn,' she said. 'Amn't I insured for liability, something like that?'

The Palm Court opened again in April; Nicolson's was as good as new, even better with the courtyard rebuilt as a conservatory with moulded glass and steel struts that would withstand any storm.

The ice-cream sundaes in the American glasses brought people in, but the slump was biting now, there were millions out of work and Catriona knew she would be lucky if her business held up. The takings for the first weeks of April were similar to last year's; she contented herself with that.

At the end of the month a smartly dressed man asked to see her. His card said: 'Alex. MacFarlane, Director, MacFarlane's Pleasure Cruises'.

'I've been thinking, Miss Nicolson,' he said as she served him coffee in her office, 'your cafe here is as much of an attraction as my cruise ships; if we join forces, we would be unbeatable.'

'What do you mean by that?' she asked as she studied the

gold links on his shirt cuffs and the high shine of his shoes. He seemed prosperous, if a little ostentatious for her taste.

'Well,' he said, waving his hand towards the coast, 'there's Largs, and then there's Rothesay, Dunoon, Ardrossan, all these places. Plenty to choose from for the day doon the watter, as they say in my home town.' He paused to smile then, but not before she had caught the hard, guttural note of the slums beneath the Kelvinside finesse he affected.

'That's good, isn't it?' she began, before he cut in.

'With all that competition, prices are keen, but I think a day trip to Largs with high tea at Nicolson's would be unbeatable, don't you?'

'My trade is good,' she said, 'as you can see.'

'Ah, but I can make it better, Miss Nicolson. I can give you fifty customers for high tea, every day, seven days a week between June and September.'

'And what would you want in return?'

'What does a high tea cost, Miss Nicolson?'

'That depends on what they eat, Mr MacFarlane.'

He began to outline a proposal for him to sell tickets in Glasgow for a cruise to Largs and high tea at Nicolson's; he would pay her two shillings for each ticket sold and in return she would supply the high tea.

Catriona began to think not about the main cafe but of the function room at the side that was empty now; MacFarlane's customers could create a use for that during the day. As the boat docked at 2.30 and left at 4.30, the waitresses would not be too busy because the normal high tea customers did not come until after that.

'What do you say?' he asked jovially, holding his hand out for her to shake.

'I'll think about it,' she said. 'They couldn't have the run of the menu, but I could give them a very good meal for that.'

'Miss Nicolson, my trade is working people. All they want is to have tea here.'

'And how would you pay?' she asked.

'Monthly, when you submit the ticket stubs.'

'I'd want trade references.'

'Of course.' He pulled out two letters, one from the harbourmaster at Glasgow and another from a shipyard.

'I'd rather you paid weekly.'

'I do all my accounts on a monthly basis.'

'I'd want a banker's reference.'

He wrote down the name and address of his bank. 'Are we agreed then?'

'I'll have my lawyer draw up a contract.'

'No,' he said, 'I'll see to that.'

The papers came a week later and she signed them, her mind already on other things. A few days later she agreed two other contracts, one for dinners for passengers on the evening boat, another for lunches with a tour company that sold day trips on the trains to Largs.

The summer began; Joe's sundaes, frappés, splits and knicker-bocker glories started a new fashion in Largs. The American glasses were twice as big as Scottish ones; everyone wanted to try one version and then another, the local children saved up for theirs and she gave tokens for banana splits and chocolate sundaes to the school for prizes for the sports day.

One Sunday afternoon she was walking through the restaurant when a voice rose behind her: 'See yon wumman? She owes me a tanner since seven year ago!'

She spun round and saw a sharply suited young man with bright red hair and his arm slung around the shoulder of a bleached blonde whose lipstick was melting in the heat.

'Aye,' the man said, 'thaur she is, the scunner, an' I bet she doesna e'en mind me either. Catriona Nicolson, I'd ken ye onywhere, an' I'll thank ye for my tanner back.'

'Titch?' she said, 'Titch McKillop?' He had grown into a man since she had last seen him, but his hair was the same, and so was his smile.

'Aye,' he said, 'the very same. See ye, Catriona?' He adjusted his posture and began to mimic her voice: '"Now, Titch, I'm going to Paddy's and I'll need your barrow to get me back to the station. Three o'clock, mind, and don't be late. I have to catch the train back."'

Helpless with laughter, Catriona collapsed into a chair beside him.

Titch held out his open palm. 'My tanner, thanks. It bluidy rained that afternoon, an' I bluidy waited, but you never did turn up, ye scunner, ye! I should mak' it twa tanners, fir the soaking I got.'

She reached into her pocket for her money, but he told her to put it away.

'I met a friend,' she said, 'from home. I hadn't seen him since the start of the war. I forgot about you till I got back here. I'm sorry.'

'Ach, dinna mind,' he said, 'Donoghue said ye'd met a pal, but I waited jist acos ye telt me tae.' His face softened, and he smiled at her. 'It wis a guid thing ye did fir us, Catriona. McKillop's the biggest pieman in Glesca now.'

'I'm glad,' she said; she could see he was a success.

'I'm in the Gorbals, Partick, Govan. Five branches an' growing fast. That's me.'

The blonde got up; they talked until she returned and put a proprietorial hand on Titch's shoulder. 'This is Mary,' he said, 'the best wee Mary in Carter's Close.'

'I'm the only Mary in Carter's Close!' she snapped, nudging him with her elbow as Titch winked at Catriona.

He looked over to the function room set aside for the people who came on MacFarlane's steamers.

'You doin' business wi' Alex?' he asked.

'High teas,' she replied.

'He's a flyboy, that. I'd watch him.'

'Don't worry,' she said, 'I do.'

After Titch left she realized that the banker's reference had not arrived yet; she made a note to herself to send a reminder. But MacFarlane had paid his bills so far; during the month of July he planned to send her at least a hundred customers every day, two hundred during the Fair.

It was mid August when she realized that MacFarlane's bill, for nearly £600, had not been paid. She was about to ring his office when he arrived in the restaurant, profusely apologetic.

'I had trouble with one of the boats,' he said, 'the engine needs reconditioned and it's had to go into dock. Knocked me right out, last month.'

'You've been paid for the tickets already,' she said.

'Aye, but I didn't expect this to happen. Will you give me until the end of the month?'

She thought for a moment. 'I'm not happy about it, Mr MacFarlane.'

'Miss Nicolson, I'm booked solid right through this month. Soon's I have the money, you'll get it.'

'I'd rather you paid something on account.'

'I've a dry-dock bill of three thousand pounds to meet. Like I said, you'll get the money at the end of the month.'

That evening she checked her accounts. Although business had been steady through the summer, better than she had a right to expect, once she had paid for the new glass canopy she had spent £2,000 that was not covered by the insurance. The loan payment was due in September, but by then Rory would have repaid the money she had loaned him; the payment would easily be covered.

At the end of August MacFarlane's bill had grown to nearly £700; when she tried to phone his office the operator told her that the phone had been disconnected.

The other companies she dealt with had not paid their August bills, either. She tried their numbers and found the phones there also cut off. At the station the LMS manager told her that Bridie's Tours was owned by Alex MacFarlane. Fearfully, she called the office of the shipping company and discovered that Moonlight Voyages had belonged to him as well.

She rang Andy Hendry and left the details with his secretary. Within half an hour he phoned back: 'You've been robbed,' he said.

Shakily she searched through her pockets until she found the number of McKillop's Bakery.

'Titch,' she said, 'remember what you said about MacFarlane?'

'Ha!' he laughed. 'Yon's jist gone. Scarpered, like. Done a runner.'

'What do you mean?'

'MacFarlane's done a moonlicht flit, Catriona. Boy's gone, wi' about hauf o' Glesca chasing efter him.'

'Oh, God.' Reflexively, she put down the phone.

'Catriona, Catriona?' Titch McKillop said.

'She picked it up again.

'What's the matter?' Titch asked her.

'He owes me nearly fifteen hundred pounds!' she wailed.

'I telt ye tae watch him, and ye said ye did.'

'I did,' she said, 'but I didn't know he was the other two as well. How could I?'

'Ye shoulda been more careful,' he said, 'an' I'm surprised it's me wha's tellin' ye that.'

Cursing herself, she rang Rory's yard and then, not getting through to him, got into her car and drove there.

Rory was not there, but his cousin Niall was in the office.

'Catriona,' he said, 'I haven't see you for years.'

She cut him off. 'Where's Rory?'

'Ach, he's away, Catriona. He'll be back in a while.'

'When?'

'A while.' He shrugged.

'Today, tomorrow, next week, next month?'

Niall switched to English. 'Rory iss away for a week or two. I don't know anything more than that, Catriona, except you haff lost your manners since you went to the lowlands because you haffen't effen asked me how I am.'

'*Galach*, Niall, don't give me that nonsense. I want to know where Rory is and I want to know now.'

Niall shrugged and turned away. 'I shall make you some tea, Catriona. Maybe it's to wet your tongue you need. Maybe that iss why you haff lost your temper.'

'Niall, I haven't lost my temper yet, but I soon will if you don't tell me what's happening. I'm not a lowlander, you know. I'm not that daft.'

He seemed to think for a minute, then he took the kettle off the fire and got a bottle of whisky from Rory's filing cabinet. Catriona's eyes narrowed. 'I don't need that.'

'I do,' he said, taking a gulp before he switched back to

358

Gaelic. 'Rory said not to tell you, you see. He said: "Don't let Catriona know, for God's sake." He's off to America with Charlie Mackenzie and some of the others.'

'Charlie Mackenzie?'

'Charlie who has the Dunvegan ferry. They heard that whisky was fetching a very good price in America this year, so they decided to take some over. Some of Sorley's, and some of the others'. Half of Skye's got money on it.' He paused then, considering. 'Maybe a few of us. Rory, he said he could do with the money. And we could do with it too.'

Catriona was gazing at him. 'You mean they've taken the ferry to America?'

Niall shrugged. 'They have.'

'For God's sake, Niall, what are they thinking of? They'd've been better on skates than in that tin can.'

'They got there safely, Catriona. Rory sent me a cable last week, from Canada. They've been to America, and they're coming home.'

'When?'

Niall shrugged. 'I don't know that, Catriona.'

'You let me know the minute they get back.'

'I don't know if Rory would want that.'

'I do, Niall. If you don't tell me, I'll make your life hell.'

'And how would you do that?' he asked her.

'Just pray to God you never find out.'

Late that night, very late, after she had checked the figures again and again, she knew that she could pay the instalment due on the loan, but not the balance she had hoped to pay off.

Joe came up to see her before he left Nicolson's, to tell her that the cafe had had a good day and that all was well. He lingered at the door for a moment, once she had thanked him.

'What is it?' she asked.

He came and sat opposite her. 'Luigi will give me the money to give you if you need it.' His English had improved since he had married Maire.

She pushed her hair back. 'I'm not going to borrow any more.'

'I did not say "borrow", Catriona. I said "give".'

'I don't need it, Joe. I can pay the loan.'

'You are family. You're my sister. You give so much to me, to other people. Why won't you let us give something back?'

She thought for a moment. 'You see, Joe,' she said, 'Nicolson's is mine. I want to keep it like that. I don't want anyone to help, or give me anything. I made it what it is, and I want to keep it myself. Do you understand?'

'I do, of course.'

'Maybe I'm selfish.'

'You are not selfish. It is not selfish to keep something like this for yourself. It is only sense.'

'I've been thinking, Joe. If you and Maire like, I'd help you to buy a place for yourself . . .'

He laughed. 'I don't want that. I want Maire alone, a few bambinos, then maybe I think about a business for my sons. When Luigi and Matteo die, they have only daughters. In time, maybe their business will come to me. I don't care. I have enough as I am.' He smiled. 'Maybe you change your mind, Catriona. Maybe you think I'm not good for your sister after all.'

'You're fine,' she said, 'I'm glad she has you.'

As he walked to the door she asked him if he knew about Rory.

'What about Rory?' he asked, surprised.

'This trip to America.'

'I gave Rory a few pounds, yes, but no more than I'd put on a horse.'

She swore in Gaelic, called him the bastard progeny of a mangy dog, the detritus of a landlord's anus.

'Don't say that,' he said quickly. 'You see, I live with Maire. I know what it means.'

She was too worried to be really angry, to fight any more than she had already done.

Before she went to bed she wrote out a cheque for the loan

payment and left it downstairs for the kitchen lad to take round to Mr Hendry next day. Passing the room where Jamie slept, she looked at him for a long time, wondering how she would explain Rory's death to him, if it came to that.

She was still distracted a few days later when she saw Miss Cochrane's Daimler coming to a halt outside. Forcing a smile, she went to welcome her.

It was early in the day and the restaurant was quiet. She served Miss Cochrane herself, as she always did, taking her a slice of the *tarte tatin* she had baked that morning, and a little dish of Joe's latest flavour of ice cream. Miss Cochrane loved the ice cream, a mocha-coffee walnut that Maire liked but Joe thought would be a little too tart for Largs; she seemed to struggle over the tarte, so much that Catriona moved to take the plate away.

'Don't do that,' Miss Cochrane said quickly, 'it tastes so nice. It's just that I always feel so full these days. I'll finish it, if you give me time.'

Catriona loved to sit and chat with Miss Cochrane, she never could spend as much time with her as she wanted to. The old lady was spry and alert, with an interesting slant in her opinions, and she was not scared to be different or unconventional if she felt like it. She had an individuality that Catriona envied, because her business did not allow her to be like that.

That day, though her eyes still sparkled, there was a pale cast to her skin under the weather-beaten veneer of a lifetime's Amazonian expeditions.

'How are you?' Catriona asked her.

'*Comme ci, comme ça*, this way and that. I woke up this morning with some energy so I decided to use it to come here. At my age, you can't complain.'

'I'm glad you did.'

'How are you, my dear?'

Catriona grimaced and then told her, in a few terse words, of Rory's antics in America. Their relationship was like that;

although months, sometimes years passed between their visits, when they talked, they talked about everything.

'How wonderful,' Miss Cochrane said when she finished. 'I think that's absolutely splendid. It's like something Jerome K. Jerome would've thought up. Three men go bootlegging to America in the Dunvegan ferry. It's magic, magic!'

Catriona winced. She had phoned the coastguard that morning, as she had phoned him every morning, only to be told the same thing; as far as he knew, there was clear weather over the Atlantic, all the way to Nova Scotia.

'I'm so worried,' she said.

'But you mustn't worry so, my dear. That's the only thing you do that is wrong. This Rory, is he strong?'

'I suppose,' Catriona said, 'you've seen him, haven't you? In fact, you met him. He's the one who moved his lorry one day outside the tearooms when you couldn't park in the Daimler.'

'Ah. He *is* strong, my dear. You mustn't worry about him. He'll make it. Strong men always do. It's what the male of the species does throughout nature; they seek danger, my dear. They have the need to prove themselves.'

'Rory doesn't.'

'They all do, my dear. Take my word for it. If it wasn't for men there'd be no war, but then there'd be no love either – at least, not that sort of love.'

Catriona smiled. 'When I was a child, Rory was my sweetheart.'

Miss Cochrane's expression became distant, even vaguely sad. 'That's one thing I've never had, my dear. Mind you, I've had everything else, just about. I've learned a lot from nature. We should be like the flowers, my dear, the lilies and the orchids, just lie around looking beautiful and wait for the wind or insects to pollinate us to keep the species on the go. I'd rather be pollinated by the wind, myself. Bees sting. You must let me know when this Rory gets back. I'd love to meet him properly.'

'He'll have to explain himself to me first.'

'Don't be too hard on him.'

'It's hard not to be. If you care for someone.'

Miss Cochrane's eyes misted.

'You see, he needed the money. For his business. He's in haulage. The strikes hit him hard.'

'That's the irony of it,' Miss Cochrane said, 'money's the only thing you care about only if you haven't got it. If you have, it means nothing, nothing at all.'

Catriona smiled. 'I've never thought about it like that.'

'It's true, though, if you think about it.'

'I suppose it is.'

'But, dear, I mustn't become maudlin. I came to beg a cutting of your strelitzia, if you have one to spare.'

'Of course. I'll send one with Robbie.'

Nicolson's was filling up for morning coffee; their time together had come to an end. Miss Cochrane looked around. 'It's a miracle, you know, Catriona. What you've done with this place. It really is.'

Catriona blushed deeply, shrugged off the compliment with an easy shake of her head and then rose to get on with the work of the day. Miss Cochrane sat on for an hour or more, beside a Meyers lemon tree that was just beginning to fruit, as if soaking in the gentle atmosphere of the Palm Court, which was shaded from the wind but not from the sun. As she went about her chores, Catriona turned occasionally and saw the old lady watching her, with a look on her face that could have been pride.

When she cleared the table after Miss Cochrane had gone, the tarte was still uneaten; a little note beside it said it was not the tarte, but her digestion.

Later that day, Catriona sent a strelitzia up with Robbie; also a tub of the mocha ice cream for Miss Cochrane's refrigerator because Joe had decided not to put it on the menu after all.

Niall phoned her two weeks later: 'For God's sakes, Catriona, don't say I told you, but they got back this morning. Rory's here now.'

She thanked him and put the phone down, left Zena in

charge of Nicolson's and went out to her car. Robbie was pruning the plants in the Palm Court, and called out as she raced past that Miss Cochrane had asked her to drop by at the villa, if she had time.

'Right now, I have to go to Chryston,' she replied, 'but I'll drop in on the way back.'

It was the second time he had asked her, but she hadn't had a minute. She had sent more ice cream and a blooming bird of paradise plant instead.

'You do that, lass,' he said, 'she'd come to see you, but she's not so well these days.'

Catriona felt fear in the pit of her stomach, but it was swept away by her anger at Rory. It had been simmering for weeks, and now she felt it quicken and begin to boil.

By the time she arrived in Chryston she knew what Rory meant when he said that his business was sound. She had passed at least a dozen of his trucks and as she reached the yard she had to stop to let two more drive out.

Rory was in the office with some of his pals; she heard their jubilant voices, and saw Rory in the lighted interior. She did not go in at first, but watched for a while as they drank and laughed, seeing that he was strong again, his face bronzed with the sun. Whatever had happened on that voyage across the Atlantic, he had got his vigour back, his sense of fun.

Rain began to fall. Still she watched from the shadows of one of his sheds. After a while the door opened and a couple of men spilled out, heading for the station and then, she thought, the boat back home.

'Bloody fools,' she called after them, so quietly that they did not hear.

The strains of a song rose from the office, an old song, a stupid one; she remembered it from many years ago, her father singing it when the shinty team won the Camanachd. The chorus, mockingly, spoke of bravery and guts; the islanders had whistled the tune as they went off to the war.

At last, when she had a grip of herself, she walked to the office and went in. Rory was sitting behind his desk; Niall took one look at her and fled.

'Catriona,' Rory said, pleased to see her.

'You fool,' she said, 'you stupid fool. You bloody idiot.'

He was taken aback. 'I didn't know ...' he began.

'Rory, for God's sake. Half of my staff took bets on you just like they bet on horses.'

'They *invested*, Catriona. They did not bet.' He grinned. 'It paid off. It paid bloody well.'

'How well would it have paid if you'd sunk to the bottom of the Atlantic?' she yelled.

He laughed then, carelessly. He had his pride, the island pride, like her father's and that of the men who had answered the call to arms.

'God's sake, Catriona, I know the Atlantic better than you know your way home. I'd never've done it if there'd been any risk.'

'Oh, no? And what about the bootleggers you sold it to? Don't you know they'd shoot you as soon as look at you? You're such a fool, Rory. You're a fool because you didn't see the risk.'

'Catriona –' he grinned broadly – 'I'm not that daft. The Eyeties we sold it to, they're expecting us to go with another load next month. They're not going to shoot us. The golden goose, you know.'

'And are you going?'

He bridled. 'I might.'

She turned to leave.

'Catriona,' he said, 'the money. The money I owe you.'

'I don't want it,' she said, 'if that's what it cost, I don't want it. You can keep it.'

He grabbed her arm. 'What the hell's got into you?'

'Just leave me alone, Rory. Let me go.' The worry had drained her; she no longer cared about anything, she felt like seaweed, stranded and drained by the tide.

'Wait,' he said, opening a drawer and finding a slip of paper. 'Here's a bank draft for the money. It was here all the time. Niall would've given you it if I didn't get back. The payment's not due till the end of the month, is it?'

She did not take it.

'I don't understand,' he said.

'Oh, don't you? Well, let me explain, Rory. I haven't had an easy year, but you haven't seen me so you don't know that. I wanted to pay the loan off, but when it came to it I was lucky to make the instalment due. I didn't count on the money I lent you, I never did, but when I discovered what you'd done, I've never been so angry in my life. Or so afraid.'

'There was no risk, Catriona.'

'There was, Rory. The risk was great. It always is, when you make money like that.'

'There wasn't a risk,' he said again.

'Oh, no? If there was no risk, why didn't you tell me what you were going to do, then?'

He pushed the bank draft into her hands; for a moment she looked at it then she ripped it up.

'Catriona, that's a bank draft, that was three thousand pounds!'

'If you take the pieces to the bank, they'll give you the money.'

He sat down, ignoring the bits of paper. 'Why are you so angry?'

'Remember what you said about chances, Rory? You'd've had another chance to get the money, but I'm not going to give you another chance with me.'

His face hardened all of a sudden. 'You have no right either, Catriona. You have no right to run my life, to tell me what to do.'

'I won't any longer, Rory. Don't worry about that.' She spun on her heel and strode out of the door. He ran after her, catching her just as she reached her car.

'Catriona, you don't understand,' he said, 'I've enough money now for anything, to buy you the whole of Largs if that's what you want.'

'I *don't* want,' she said, 'I never did. If you'd known me, you would've known that.'

He watched her drive away, knowing then that the risk of the ocean was nothing like the risk of love. The adventure had been cleansing, though, the chance he had taken had washed away the worst of the hurt: of the years of waiting and hoping and then of asking a question and realizing that she had not even heard.

A few miles along the road Catriona stopped the car. The rain was over and the sun shone on a field of ripened wheat; at the far edge she could see a cottar with his scythe just beginning to harvest the fruits of the soil.

She watched him for a while, thinking of Rory and the things she had said, things she did not really mean but that had spilled out with her anger anyway.

The war had been over for nearly ten years, but the wounds had not healed; the loss had been so great, as if her generation had been torn apart.

She looked at the cottar again; he was young, maybe too young to know. He would have a father at home, or maybe a brother who could tell him, perhaps. As he moved closer she saw that he was just a boy, Jamie's age or even younger, taking a day off school to help with the harvest.

He could have been Liam's son.

Rory had never been touched by death; he was one of the lucky ones. She should have known, known that the luck which had held him through the war would have seen him through a little more.

In time, maybe, she would laugh at it like Miss Cochrane had, but not yet; the trouble with Rory was that he did not know the meaning of death, nor how much even the thought of it frightened her.

She drove home tiredly. Passing the Cochrane villa, she remembered her promise, turned into the driveway and parked beside the Austin already there. She didn't know whose it was, and wondered vaguely if the other visitor would make it inconvenient for her.

Miss Simpson, the housekeeper, opened the door, her eyes rimmed with tears. 'Ach, lass,' she said as she held the door wide, 'you're a mite late, but come awa' anyway.'

'Late?'

'Aye, lass. The Missus, she passed away just an hour ago. That's the doctor's car ben, but he couldna do aucht for her. It was peaceful, he said.'

Catriona leaned against the cold mahogany of the hall, smelling the wood and the beeswax, tasting the air that hinted of death, before her own tears came and she tasted them instead.

Chapter Fourteen

Old Mr Hendry looked at her in that way of his: a smile gently set on his lips and his eyes peering over the half moon glasses he wore to enable him to make sense of the world around him. He was retired, but he had written to ask her to see him; she had agreed, of course, although she did not know why.

'You've done very well, Miss Nicolson,' he said, 'in fact, you've done better than any of us dared hope. You've built up a business that's better than anything we've ever seen in Largs, despite the depression.'

Catriona relaxed, settled back into the deeply upholstered leather chair and let out a sigh of relief. She had been worried that it was something about the loan, that the lender had decided to call it in, perhaps. But if it had been something bad, he would have told her so first.

'It hasn't been an easy year,' she said.

'It has not,' Mr Hendry agreed, 'but you survived it. You've earned the respect of the town and way beyond.'

She smiled; he watched the way her face lightened around her dancing eyes.

'There's something I have to tell you,' he said.

'And here I was, thinking you'd asked me here just to flatter me.'

Aloysius Gregory Hendry was sixty-five years old, forty of them married, but even so she made him blush.

The lawyer got up and walked to a window overlooking the pier. For a moment he studied the seabirds wheeling overhead, the sky quilted with clouds. Then he turned back to her.

'The loan has been cancelled,' he said, adding quickly as he saw her shock, 'I don't mean foreclosure. It's been turned into a gift.'

'*What?*'

He returned to his desk, avoiding her eyes. 'Your payments went into a trust account that we – the firm – supervised. We've just been instructed to close the account and hand the balance over to you. There's a shade over eleven thousand pounds in it, with your payments and the bank interest and the balance of loan that you never used.'

Catriona, stunned for a moment, could not speak.

'But who,' she asked, finally, 'who on earth did that?'

'Miss Nicolson, I'm not at liberty to tell you, and please don't press me, because I never will be.' He was still avoiding her eyes; she could get no clue from his expression.

'It wasn't Rory MacDonald,' she said, making a statement. He had paid the money he owed her into her bank account; she did not know if he had retrieved the banker's draft she had torn up.

'I've already told you that,' Mr Hendry said. 'Beyond that, I'm not saying another word.'

Her thoughts tumbled, running in torrents until with blinding clarity she realized who it must have been.

Miss Cochrane's funeral had been a quiet one, with only her staff in Largs and Mr Hendry, a few dignitaries and the president and secretary of Ayrshire Red Cross. Just as the service began another Daimler glided to a halt outside and a man who Robbie said was Miss Cochrane's cousin, her father's heir, got out to pay his last respects.

The old lady was buried in the cemetery just outside the town, at a point on a hill where the view took in the sweep of the coast and the islands beyond. Robbie Thompson had planted a palm tree next to the grave, and a eucalyptus bush to give off its scent.

Only he and Catriona and the undertakers went to the burial; the other mourners left after paying their respects to the tall, dignified man who was her only living relative.

As Catriona left with Robbie she thought it was so sad to die that way, to leave this world without love. Robbie read her mind, though, because as they turned away he had looked at her and said that Miss Cochrane had been loved by him, if no one else.

'I loved her too,' Catriona said, regretting again that she had not had time to see her before she died.

Mr Hendry was talking: 'Your business is worth a good deal of money, Miss Nicolson. You must be very pleased with what you have achieved. You are a rich woman, now.'

'No,' Catriona said reflexively.

'But you most certainly are. Most certainly, yes. Nicolson's as a business is worth fifty thousand pounds if it's worth a penny, and you own it outright.'

'I didn't mean that,' Catriona said quickly, 'I meant, it was Miss Cochrane, wasn't it?'

The look on his face told her that it was.

'And at the end,' Catriona said, 'I didn't have time to see her. I didn't know she was dying, you see. That's why I said "no", Mr Hendry. There's a part of me that will always be poor.'

She walked out into the afternoon, into the fresh September wind that had the kick of winter. The sky was three shades of grey, darkest on top, with the heavy bulge that would soon turn to rain. Waves crashed against the pebbled shore, a carbonated sea that fizzled and cracked and sighed like a soda bottle with the top taken off. The rain began, making polka dots on the pavement, sending the organ grinder with the monkey scurrying for cover. The last of the day trippers shrugged and headed indoors to stem the loss of the weather with an early high tea.

Catriona walked on past Nicolson's to the villa where through the palm trees she could see Robbie Thompson at work in the conservatory.

She pushed opened the gate and walked up the drive. The house was closed now, all the servants gone except for Robbie; the curtains were drawn over the windows but through a gap she glimpsed dust sheets over the heavy oak furniture Miss Cochrane had loved.

'Robbie,' she said, as she watched him pruning an orchid carefully, cutting away the tall leaves that would drain the blossom of nourishment, 'I'm almost scared to ask you, but would you consider coming to work for me?'

He said nothing for a moment until he finished the task. 'I'll miss the orchids, lass. Most difficult plant in the world to grow, but when it does, by God, it's worth it.' He swept his arm around the conservatory: 'It's all going, every leaf of it. The Botanic in Glasgow's taking some, and Edinburgh University's having the rest. But I want to get them right, see? I'd not let the Missus's plants go without being properly pruned and cut.'

She asked him again if he'd like to come to work for her.

'I heard you first time, lass. I'm not being rude, just thinking about it. This place, it's going to the orphans, like. To the Quarriers Homes in Bridge of Weir, for holidays for the bairns. They're building a coupla dormitories out the back, and this here'll be a swimming pool. They've asked me to stay on, to be a caretaker. I'd keep the room in the gatehouse and be paid the same wage.'

He started on another plant, caressing the blooms tenderly before he began to snip away at the leaves. 'I've been here all my working life, just about. Since 1899, when she bought the place. She was in the prime of life then, the Missus, an' I was just a sixteen-year-old lad, wi' a couple of years wi' the gardener at Carnlachan. Her faither'd just died and left her the money and the business wi' yon who came to the funeral.'

Catriona wondered about the twists of fate, about why neither of them had ever wed.

'Like leaving home, it is. The only home I've ever known. I don't think I'd like it but, not wi'out the Missus and the plants.'

He snipped at a stem and handed her a single, perfect orchid, a flower that blushed crimson at its core and then lightened to shades of pink and violet at the edge of the petals, the labellum almost as dark as night against the brilliant orange of the pollen.

The flower reminded her of sunset over the sea.

'*Orchidaceae cymbidium cochrana*,' he said, 'she found that one way up the Amazon River. They named it after her. Proud as punch, she was, when she got the drawings from Kew with her name on it.'

'I'd give you a room,' she said, 'and you could try growing orchids in the Palm Court. I'd want you to do the plants, the roses for the tearooms. That's all. I'd pay you three pounds a week and your meals.'

'That'd be more than enough, lass. The Missus, she did me well with the will. She left us all that we'd not have to work any more, if we didn't want to. That's what I was thinking here, I'm not sure I want to be a caretaker, but I do like working with the plants.'

Catriona left Robbie and walked on to the edge of the town, to the point where the pavement disappeared into scrub and grass and, a bit below, a small rocky beach. The rain was holding now, the wind fresh against a pregnant sky. She sat on the grass and took off her shoes and stockings, then walked out onto the sands.

She felt the sadness then, the aching void of loss made worse by thoughts of what might have been had she not been so set on an objective that meant nothing to anyone but herself.

She knew then that Nicolson's had been hers from the moment she had walked in and put the closed sign up for ever over the tired and flaking notice that read 'Wilson's Dining Rooms.'

The feeling bubbled up inside her, simmering on the brink for a moment before it overwhelmed her and tumbled out in ruptured tears that mingled with the failing rain along with all the regrets and thoughts of what might have been.

The emotion was not dangerous, though, not as harsh as grief. Sadness brought its own remission, the sense of healing that came after the tears. As she sat in the rain crying, watching the blur of the surging tide, she could feel the dimensions of her loss, the pain that receded almost as soon as she let herself feel the depth of it.

That was the difference between sadness and grief; if sadness could be felt grief numbed feelings, threatened death not of the body but of the soul, like the walking dead she had seen in Glasgow after the war, the men with splintered bodies whose minds had gone as well, the women with eyes as empty as the winter sky who walked the streets like marionettes.

She had not let herself feel grief at first, because she sensed that the pain was too great, that it could take her mind away if she allowed it to. By the time she dared again, when she reached inside herself it was as if a part of her was gone.

As the waves pounded the shore, pulverizing into froth as they hit the sand, her grief faded into sadness; the dead lost their resonant echo and left Catriona free at last.

She walked home in that state, seeing the town almost anew, the gaudy tents and banners that frayed in the wind, the stateliness of Nicolson's, the genteel glass building at the start of the promenade that held the reflection of the sky.

This is my home, she thought for a moment, before she remembered her island, most of all the change of the seasons when you could watch the metamorphosis of the land, the vista untouched by roads or buildings or any of the other flotsam of man.

She heard her mother's voice, and for a moment stopped and listened to the silence, before she murmured that the dream had come true.

Slowly, she became used to the idea of her wealth. The money piled up in the bank now; more each month once she paid her bills and the staff's wages.

It was a pleasant feeling.

Marie's first baby was due in the New Year; she thought of using the function room to start an Italian trattoria but when Joe tried the recipes in the restaurant they learned that Largs would not yet tolerate pasta. Titch McKillop gave her the idea of starting a fish and chip shop in the old booth where Joe used to sell his ice cream; though it opened in October the takings were good right from the start.

Miss Cochrane was right about money, Catriona thought. Once you had it, it no longer meant so much.

For years she had spent nothing on herself. Her clothes were as functional as they had always been, plain, dark dresses that aged well and looked efficient; they cost 59/6 from the draper's in Castle Street. She still drove the old Morris, more confidently now; with Jamie she lived in the rooms above Nicolson's, though she would have to move out when Robbie Thompson left the villa because she had promised him a place to live as well as a job.

For weeks she looked around Largs at dour grey villas and pert little bungalows, but found nothing that was quite right for her needs. She was about to buy a house from a retired headmistress when Andy Hendry told her about a place in the next village that he thought she might like.

Fairlie was just a few miles along the coast from Largs, a little fishing village set against a hill; she had never seen it except in passing during the years when she had visited Allan in the sanatorium in Ardrossan. Rory used to take Jamie and Allan there to walk on the beach and fish for crabs from the little jetty.

'I'm not sure,' she said to Andy, 'it's a bit away.'

'Ten minutes in the car,' he said, 'come on and I'll show you.'

He drove her quickly along the main street, pointing out the post office and the shop, the little road that led to the jetty and the one that wound up the hill towards the school.

'Is there a beach?' she asked, more through politeness than interest.

'The beach here is rocky,' he said, 'but there's a long stretch of sands a bit away.'

The road turned; he slowed down and swung into a gap in the roadside wall, then along a drive shaded by oak trees, to a greystone villa set against a gentle lawn.

'It's too big,' she said.

'It isn't really,' he said, getting out of the car and walking up the steps to the front door. Cumbrae House was double fronted with a big oak door that groaned as he pushed it open, leading into a small tiled lobby with an inner door whose stained-glass insets had a Rennie Macintosh design.

Opening that, he stood aside to let her see the hall, with its parquet floor and wide, sweeping staircase against a tall window that let the morning sunlight tumble in.

There were two big rooms on the ground floor facing north, a dining room and a reception room with high ceilings and plenty of light, then towards the back of the house a family room and a breakfast room with a big, old-fashioned kitchen, and a suite of rooms for the housekeeper beyond that.

'See?' he said, opening the french doors of the family room and walking onto a terrace overlooking the garden; through the trees Catriona could see the sea and the rise of the Cumbraes. Walking to the garden wall, she stood on tiptoe and saw that a small incline led to the sea, where the incoming tide pounded against the rocks.

'How far does the tide come in?' she asked.

'This far, and no further.' He indicated a place with his hand, pointing to a tideline midway up the rocks. 'You're a few feet above high-water level.'

'Even in winter?'

'Even in winter.'

Upstairs he showed her the bedrooms, one with a changing room and bathroom, another for a child with a little room for a nanny.

'How much?' she asked when they returned to the car.

'Fifteen hundred,' he said.

She took a deep breath; there was something about the house that called out to her, that told her it would be a happy home.

'Do you want it?' Andy asked her.

'Yes,' she said, 'so long as Jamie agrees.'

She spoke to him that evening. 'It's a bit away,' she said, 'but I'd drive you in to school every morning and then back again, or Uncle Joe would. There's even a school in Fairlie you could go to if you want.'

'The Fairlie boys are daft. We beat them at football.'

'Well then, you can stay on at the school here. I'd drive you in any time you want. You could even get a bicycle and ride yourself. It's not so far.'

'Can I get the bus?' he asked.

'There's no need, Jamie. I can drive you.'

'But can I get the bus in the mornings, when I go to school?'

'If you want to, yes.'

'Smashing,' he said, 'I'd like to go, so long's I can go to school on the bus.'

When Andy Hendry brought the deed of purchase for her to sign, he asked her to go to the Christmas Ball with him.

'I don't know,' she said, thinking.

'Whyever not?'

He had asked her out a couple of times, but always diffidently, as if it didn't matter if she agreed or not. The thing was, she thought as she looked at him, that she was nearing thirty now, and he was much younger than that. He had only been admitted to the solicitor's roll the previous year, when he had finished his MA.

She decided to be frank. 'I'm older than I look, Andy. I'll be twenty-nine next year.'

He laughed. 'And you think I'm not? I was thirty in January, Catriona. I'm older than you. I was in the army during the war and I stayed in France for a couple of years after that. I only went to university when I was demobbed. Not that it matters, but does that change your mind?'

She blushed. 'Yes,' she said, 'but I would have said that anyway.'

She moved into the house in October, with Jamie, and hired Ellie Simpson, Miss Cochrane's former housekeeper, to take care of it while she was at work.

She furnished the reception room in shades of the softest grey, two comfortable sofas with light beech side tables, a plain, pale carpet and wispy silk curtains. The colour came from cushions covered with a rambling rose print and a mirror at the back of the room that caught and reflected the sky. In the spring she would fill vases with armfuls of flowers; over the cold months she grew winter cherry plants in planters beside the windows, twin aspidistras on either side of the fire. The dining room was similar and her bedroom was ivory, with curtains and upholstery in a wild print of muted blues and sage greens that made her think of Skye.

Jamie had his room painted blue; she made a study for Allan in the room beside hers but knew he would never live there, would only visit from time to time. She made the family room comfortable, with cushioned leather chairs and a big dresser to hold books and games.

In December, when she asked Marie and Joe for Christmas, Jamie asked if she would invite Rory too.

She turned away to hide the look on her face. Rory still came down to see Jamie on Sundays, but he had been avoiding her as she avoided him.

'You've rowed, haven't you?' Jamie said.

'We have.'

'Did he hurt you, Ma?'

She managed to smile. 'He didn't hurt me. We had an argument, that's all.'

'Did you hurt him?'

She hesitated. 'I didn't mean to.'

Jamie's face relaxed. 'Well, that's all right. If he didn't hurt you and you didn't hurt him, you can make it up, then.'

'Sometimes it isn't as easy as that,' she blundered.

'Yes, it is. I make up arguments all the time. If you don't make up arguments, you end up without friends.'

She went to her desk to begin composing a letter. Hours later, when the words would not come, she got into her car and drove to his yard instead. During the drive she thought of their row, and of the years of friendship that had preceded it. Jamie is right, she thought.

There had been times when she wished that her friendship with Rory would turn into something more.

In a way, she still did. There was an emptiness to her life, to the parts not filled by work or family. She thought of the fortune teller, remembering her conundrum. Andy Hendry was a candidate, but when he had taken her to the ball, the evening had been pleasant, but nothing else.

A lorry, one of Rory's, swept past her and in its wake her little car swayed. She gripped the steering wheel and swore at herself.

It was after six by the time she arrived. Because the gates of the yard were closed, she parked outside and walked towards the office. The lights were on and she could see Rory inside, sitting at his desk. His face was rimmed with grease, but he was smiling; she watched him for just a moment and felt the old emotions return. She had been senseless, perhaps, blamed him for something that he could not have known about. But she cared for him still; he was the only person beyond her family she had ever cared for deeply, in a way that almost amounted to love.

Rory could have been her brother. He was closer to her than a friend could ever be.

Smiling to herself, she remembered the years when she had loved him, when her young girl's mind had thought of almost nothing else.

Then there was the war, and then there was Liam; the only constant had been Rory, he was the rock to which she had anchored in those tumultuous times.

Just as she reached the door, he said something; she paused for a moment and wondered who he was talking to. She heard a woman's voice, tinkling laughter, then shrank back as she saw a girl going over to him, handing him something then giggling as he grabbed her and pulled her down on his knee. The desk scraped, papers thudded to the floor.

Averting her eyes, Catriona crept away and then, when she reached the road, ran to her car. The engine caught first time, still warm after the journey; she thanked God for that and then she stifled a sob.

Through the ragged hedge around the yard, she saw the office door opening and then Rory and the girl flashed briefly against the light before he switched it off. They linked hands and walked away; she watched them all the way along the road, silhouetted against street lights, until they turned into a house.

I have no right to be angry, she told herself, nor jealous, nor any of these things. For a moment longer she wondered, then she engaged the gears and began to drive home.

The following morning she wrote a bland note to Rory in which she did not mention their argument, but told him only that she had bought Cumbrae House, and hoped he would be able to join them for Christmas there. She added at the end that she would quite understand if he could not, but that Jamie and Allan would like him to be there.

His reply came two days later; he thanked her for the invitation but he was going to Skye, as he sometimes did.

'You're mad,' Jamie said when she told him. 'You should've married him when you had the chance.'

'I never did,' she said mechanically.

'Oh, yes,' he said assuredly. 'I asked Rory once. He said he *had* asked you, but you didn't even hear him. I asked him why he didn't ask you again, and he said he thought that it wasn't to be.' Jamie shrugged, as if to say who was he to understand such people?

'Jamie,' she said, 'Jamie?'

He had already gone to pack his kit for football practice at school later that day.

She told herself that it didn't matter, that she would make Christmas fun for them any way.

On Christmas Eve Maire's labour pains started; she gave birth to a baby daughter in the Cottage Hospital just ten hours later. Joe was alternately panicked and ecstatic; too elated to eat the elaborate meal that Catriona had prepared.

In the evening they were allowed to see her. 'I'm sorry,' she said woozily to Catriona, 'I'm so sorry that I've ruined your day.'

'It doesn't matter,' Catriona told her. The Nicolsons had developed a habit of having babies on Christmas Day.

The baby was christened Morag Catriona, after her aunt.

When the holiday was over she drove Allan back to university in the Morris.

They were struggling through the traffic on Byres Road when he asked: 'Why've you never married, Triona?'

Her hands tightened on the wheel. 'I never got the chance.'

'You mean no one ever asked you?'

'No,' she confessed. 'Someone did, but he died. It was a long time ago. There were forty thousand men killed from Glasgow alone, you know. Twenty thousand were bachelors. That means there's twenty thousand spinsters like me. Why d'you ask?'

He looked away, but not before she saw him blush.

'Allan, you're not courting, are you? Are you?'

A tram cranked to a halt before them, and she had to stop to let the passengers get off.

'Not really,' he said, after a long time. 'I've met someone, but she's like me.'

'What do you mean, "like me"?'

'I mean I'll have to work for a few years after I graduate before I'm ready to wed. Her too, because her father's a gamekeeper in Helensburgh and she's on a scholarship.'

'What's she like? Can I meet her?'

'Triona, it's not like that. Not yet. Her name's Louise, and she's going to be a doctor.'

'I'd like to meet her.'

'Maybe you will.'

'Allan, it isn't true,' she said quickly. 'You don't have to work. I have enough money for all of us.'

He turned and touched her cheek, the gesture strange for him because he so rarely touched anyone. She hoped that friendship with this girl, whoever she was, would change all that.

In his rooms he lit the gas range and made tea, and then fidgeted as he unpacked, saying that he wanted to get to the library because there was a book he needed for his lectures on metaphysics.

The look on his face told her that he had arranged to meet his girl somewhere and was longing to see her; Catriona left, feeling vaguely sad.

She left the car in Hyndland and took a tram into town, looking for a use for the hours she had planned to spend with Allan.

The winter sales were on, the reduction notices taking her back in time to the young girl who had pressed her face against the window glass and then drawn back, ashamed of the mark she had made with her breath.

Passing MacDonald's, she thought of Tia Macleod, whom she hadn't seen for nine years. She could have lunch with her, perhaps; they could talk over their memories. She wanted to know if the years had been as good to Tia as they had to her.

She asked the uniformed porter if Miss Macleod, of Ladies' Gowns, was in.

'Trade?' he asked sharply.

'I beg your pardon?'

'Are you trade, Miss? If you are, I must ask you to use the trade entrance.'

'No,' she said, 'I'm not trade, just an old friend.'

'In that case, I think that Miss Macleod left our firm some time ago. I believe she now works for a store in New York.'

Catriona stood for a moment, wondering what to do next. Suddenly she was annoyed at the doorman's manner, at the way he had treated her with tolerance, but not respect.

'Is there anything else, Miss?'

'Yes,' she said, 'this is a store, isn't it? I might be a customer. You never know.'

He opened the door with a flourish so elaborate that it was almost a grudge.

The store was lit softly by crystal chandeliers, hung from a ceiling four storeys above. Thick carpet soaked up all sound except that of money changing hands. Catriona wandered for a while, then found the baby department where she bought an Irish linen and lace dress for a price that made her gasp, a Wedgwood china baby's cup, and a little silver rattle that made a wonderful sound.

'Cash or charge?' the assistant asked her.

'Oh, cheque, I suppose,' said Catriona, delving in her bag.

'What name would you like engraved on the rattle?'

'I haven't time for that,' she said, 'I'll get it engraved in Largs.'

'We can have it done for you in a few moments,' the assistant said. 'The time it would take you to have a cup of tea.'

Catriona had nothing else to do. 'Morag Catriona,' she said quickly, 'Christmas Day, 1927.'

The assistant noted the inscription then handed it all to a waiting messenger boy.

'Can I have your address, Madam?' she asked as Catriona handed her the cheque.

'Catriona Nicolson,' she replied, 'of Nicolson's of Largs.'

The assistant's eyes widened as she turned away. Catriona smiled to herself, then stopped when she saw her reflection in a mirror suspended over a stand selling ladies' gloves.

She was young, lithe and slim, sensibly clad in her navy winter coat, with her hair pinned up under a winter hat. In these clothes she could have been anyone, most likely a nanny or even a maid. She was shocked; whatever she was, she was not that.

In the fashion department upstairs she found the sale rails, clothes squashed together, almost discarded because the spring fashions were in already, arranged in dainty groups above discreet little signs – new dresses started at fifteen guineas, tailored suits at several more.

She browsed through the racks for ages before she decided on a dark wool dress and perhaps a simple winter woollen suit, sharply reduced, she guessed, because most anyone who could afford to spend thirty-five guineas on an outfit would not fit into it.

One of the assistants joined her. 'Can I help you, Madam?'

'Not quite yet,' Catriona replied.

'That's quite a bargain,' the assistant said, stepping back but still hovering behind her.

'Tell me,' Catriona said, 'did you know someone called Tia Macleod?'

'Miss Macleod left years ago, Madam. She emigrated to New York.'

Catriona turned away from the clothes. 'I don't suppose,' she said, 'if you know if she was happy.'

The assistant's face changed. 'Are you a friend?'

'I was. Many years ago.'

'Well ... ' She moved closer. 'Miss Macleod ran off with Mr Campbell, that's Sir James's son, of Campbell, Stewart and MacDonald. That's a big firm on Ingram Street. Mr James, he was engaged to Mr Stewart's daughter. When he went off with Miss Macleod, it caused quite a stir.'

'But she was happy,' Catriona said.

'Oh, yes, Madam. I'm sure of that. They're married, now.'

'I'm glad about that.'

Catriona looked around and noticed on one of the displays the simplest suit she had ever seen, cut so that the cloth was not draped but fell in clean lines from the short, box-like jacket to a skirt with one deep pleat at the front. The silhouette was lean and slim; she sensed that it would look good on her.

'That suit,' the assistant said, 'the one you were looking at. It really is a bargain, Madam. You'd get years of wear out of it.'

Catriona pointed to the other and asked if she could try it instead.

'It's very expensive. It's new from France, you see.'

Catriona counted up, realizing that it cost the same as the two things she had been thinking about from the sale rail.

'Would you still like to try it?'

'Yes,' she said, 'I would.'

The assistant had to measure her because Catriona didn't even know her size. The suit fitted like a glove; it changed her into someone she hardly recognized, at first.

'Your shoes aren't right,' the assistant said, 'and you'd be better with light stockings.'

Catriona was looking at herself, thinking that the person she saw was the one she wanted to be, the person she already was, inside.

'Shall I run up to shoes and get you some?'

'Please,' she said.

When the assistant returned, Catriona had picked out two more suits, one walking suit in Prince of Wales tweed and a tailored gabardine in a shade of bronze that matched exactly the auburn highlights in her hair. Another assistant came to help, and then the manageress when the messenger came with the gift-wrapped rattle and whispered that her customer was *the* Miss Nicolson, of Nicolson's of Largs.

Why not? Catriona thought as she chose half a dozen suits and matching blouses, shoes and bags, a couple of afternoon dresses; a wonderfully light cashmere coat, swirling like the clouds as she moved, in a shade of green so gentle that wearing it made her feel she was being hugged.

'I'm not sure . . .' she began, as the manageress hovered expectantly.

'About what, Madam?' The woman's face suddenly looked racked by anxiety.

Catriona smiled. 'I keep on thinking that I really should buy some more things that I could wear at work. That suit, the light one, does it come in any other colours?'

'Well, no,' the manageress said, 'but I could have it made up. It would take two or three weeks, though. It is French.'

'I'd like that,' Catriona said. 'One in black, and perhaps one in that dark bronze, the same colour as the other one.'

The manageress turned to one of the assistants and told her to fetch the alteration hand from her lunch.

'Don't do that,' Catriona said quickly, 'I'm not in a hurry.'

She chose only one thing from the sale, a fur that was not really reduced but which the manageress offered her at half price. It was Russian sable, rare since the revolution; Catriona bought it for its power and also its glory. If the cashmere made her feel comforted, the sable made her feel as if she was loved.

After her measurements had been taken and noted, Catriona went through to the restaurant, where she ordered lightly poached sole for a very late lunch.

She was laughing quietly at herself when the waiter brought the meal.

'Is anything wrong, Ma'am?' he asked.

'No, no,' she said, 'everything's right.'

It was late afternoon when she left the store, accompanied by the manageress to the door, and she caught the look on the doorman's face when he saw the packages that dangled from each hand. She had taken only half of what she had bought, the rest would be delivered by MacDonald's van.

'Taxi, Ma'am?' he asked her.

'Yes,' she said, then changed her mind and decided to walk.

The Royal Exchange was peaceful that evening, as always, the buildings lit gently by gaslight, not as harsh as the electricity in the main thoroughfares.

For a long time she stood looking at the sign that said MacKenzie MacLure before she saw the office lights going off, and walked quickly away.

In a thoughtful mood she walked into the Central Hotel and asked for a room for the night.

The receptionist was sceptical until she gave her name as Catriona Nicolson, with the address of Nicolson's of Largs.

'Certainly, Miss Nicolson,' the man said, as he gave her a form to sign and called to a porter to carry her bags.

Once in her room she phoned Maire, who was giving Jamie his tea, and asked if he might spend the night with her, because she had decided to stay in the city.

Then, in the anonymity of the hotel room, she ran a bath and sank into waters perfumed by bath oil, and soaked for a long time before she stepped out and towelled herself dry. Very slowly she put on the stockings she had bought in MacDonald's, then the peach silk underthings that came wrapped in tissue in a box that was a gift in itself. In the mirror she saw her body, still lithe as a girl's; she ran her hands over her contours, smiling at herself.

She wanted to be loved then, to feel again the need that Liam had kindled so briefly before he had been killed. When she recognized the thought for what it was, she blushed deeply and dressed herself in a pearl-grey dress, cut simply with a short, pleated skirt.

She dined alone in the room, as the manager had suggested; it wasn't done for lone women to venture into the dining room.

In the morning she paid her bill and then had her hair cut at Daly's of Sauchiehall Street, where the stylist snipped her locks into a soft bob that just cleared her shoulders.

Hailing a taxi, she wrapped the sable around her and gathered up her bags, then directed the cab to Allan's flat where she got into her own car and drove off quickly, not wanting to answer any questions he might ask.

In Largs her life resumed its normal rhythm in the quiet months that preceded the summer rush. With Joe and the head chef she worked out new menus, and signed contracts with local merchants for the supply of foodstuffs over the coming year; at the end of January both Nicolson's and the Rose Tearoom closed for a week, whilst decorators freshened the paintwork, the carpets were cleaned, and the woodwork waxed and polished to a high sheen.

Jamie noticed the change in her first of all. 'You look different,' he said, on the day after she had come back from Glasgow.

'How?' She put her head to one side and rested her chin on her hand as she watched him demolish his tea.

'Nicer,' he said, between mouthfuls, 'like the lady in that film we saw.'

'I've been thinking,' she said, as he finished his fish and began on the apple dumpling. 'Would you like to go to school in Glasgow like Allan did?'

'What? Go all that way to school? I'd rather stay here.'

He finished the dumpling and gulped down a glass of milk. 'There's a football game on Saturday. I'm playing forward. Will you come to watch me? Will you wear your fur coat?'

'Yes, I'll come to watch you,' she replied, 'but, no, I won't wear my fur coat.'

'Aw, Ma . . .'

'It's not the thing for a school football game,' she told him firmly.

On Saturday she dressed warmly, then stood with all the other parents, cheering for Largs as the school battled with Saltcoats. Jamie scored one goal, then missed another; she was surprised that the boys watching cheered him anyway. Jamie's form master was there, a thin, studious man called Herbert McNeill, who was saved from pedantry because he knew how to smile.

After the match, as the team changed and showered, he joined her at tea.

'You must be very proud of Jamie,' he said.

'Yes.' She was surprised he had said that, because Jamie did not struggle or strive, he stayed resolutely in the middle of the class.

The teacher nodded to himself.

'You know,' she said, 'there's something about Jamie. Something very special.' She smiled. 'You musn't listen to me. Everyone thinks that of their children.'

'No, no,' he said quickly, 'you're right. I was thinking the same as we watched the game.'

Catriona blushed and began to thank him for his politeness.

'Miss Nicolson, I wasn't being polite. The special thing about Jamie is that he's the most contented boy in the school. He's not academically gifted, or particularly talented, but he has a way with people that makes him friends.'

He looked around and then went on: 'In terms of child psychology, he is secure and well adjusted. That is a very roundabout way of saying that he's happy.'

As he walked away, Catriona looked around dumbstruck, until she saw Jamie standing with some of his friends. She began to walk over, then hesitated and waved instead. He waved back, then began talking again. He was nine years old; not yet started on the way to becoming a man.

She began to walk home, smiling to herself. A car drew to a halt beside her, then the door opened and Rory called out. She spun around, smiling, until she noticed the woman beside him.

'I didn't know you liked football,' he said.

She pushed her hands into her pockets. 'I don't. I came because Jamie asked me to.'

'Oh,' Rory said.

'Your friend . . .' Catriona began.

'Just a friend,' he said, a shade too quickly. He looked towards the football field. 'Jamie asked me to come, too.'

'He scored a goal then missed another one,' she said.

'Oh.'

'It's cold, Rory. I'd best get away.'

'I'm sorry about Christmas,' he said.

She shook her head. 'See you, Rory.'

'See you, Catriona.' He began to walk around the car to open the passenger door, then called out to her. She looked back. 'You've had your hair cut,' he said, 'I like it like that.'

Annie's daughters Janet, Peggy and Elsbeth came down in April; Janet and Peggy had been toddlers when Catriona left, Elsbeth was born in 1914; there was no work at all for them on the island, and Catriona gladly gave them jobs at Nicolson's – Janet as a waitress and the others in the chocolate shop. Shortly after, when Janet told Catriona that Annie had given birth to a healthy baby boy, Catriona felt sad that she had never had a child herself.

The whole Macdonald family were exultant that Niall, Annie's eighteen-year-old son, had won a scholarship to St Andrews University to study divinity. Catriona remembered the baby who, a year younger than Allan, had piddled in her lap.

She smiled as she showed the girls how to do their new jobs, was proud of how quickly they learned and how good they were at caring for the people they served.

In May a reporter came down from the *Glasgow Herald*; she was embarrassed when she read she was famous, and

Nicolson's was described in the same elaborate phrases as the Willow Tearooms had once been.

In June the *Evening News* published a cartoon of a Glaswegian couple having tea down the water; the cafe was Nicolson's, and the boy with them was looking wistfully at the bird of paradise flowers; 'Hey, maw,' he asked, 'can ye eat the flo'ers an' aw?'

Two weeks later, Allan won the gold medal for metaphysics and also for jurisprudence.

After the ceremony Catriona caught a glimpse of Louise and managed to smile at her before Allan, embarrassed, whisked her away. The Dean of Faculty shook her hand and promised great things for his future.

The rush of the summer took the edge off the gnawing unease she had experienced all year, the feeling that she was adrift whilst everyone around her got on with their lives. Andy Hendry had courted her studiously; she had become almost embarrassed at the number of times she had to turn him down. Instead, she spent time with Titch McKillop and his passing parade of girlfriends; he wanted her to take shares in his new bakery, the biggest in Glasgow. She laughed and turned him down, telling him that he could have her recipes free for the sake of friendship. Titch asked for her name then, but she would not let him use that.

When the summer ended she felt mellow, vaguely regretful. That season, Nicolson's had done better than ever, but it was not the money she enjoyed so much as the work.

One day in mid September Catriona was standing in the alcove behind the serving counter in Nicolson's, idly watching afternoon tea being served.

She saw a waitress serving a couple at a table by the window then Janet hurrying over because the woman had made a complaint. She had seen the couple once or twice before, noticed them because of the woman's spoiled arrogance. They came with the yachts that each year raced in the Clyde.

Janet rushed up to the serving counter, banging a tray

down. '*Tigh na Galach!*' she spat. 'Chocolate cake, chocolate cake. That is chocolate cake.' She pointed to the cake on the plate, abandoned with just one forkful eaten.

'Yes,' Catriona said. 'That is chocolate cake.'

Janet picked up a server and hovered over the sachertorte and the gateaux; there were three chocolate gateaux, Black Forest with whipped cream, kirsch and cherries, mocha with coffee cream, and praline with chopped nuts and flaked, dark chocolate.

'Which one, d'you think?'

'Which one does she want?'

'She said, the chocolate cake with cream.'

'Take a slice of each,' Catriona advised, ' and ask her.'

Janet took three plates and strode off towards the table, returning a moment later with the cakes still on her tray.

'*Galach*, Lord have mercy; she's complaining about the coffee now.'

'I'll go,' Catriona said quickly, smiling. 'Don't worry, Janet. She's always like that.'

She was wearing a trim navy suit that day, with a blouse of silk just a shade darker; that morning she had applied to the Licensing Court for a public licence for a cocktail bar. The application had been granted without question; she wondered later why she had bothered but Andy Hendry, who had filed the application, told her it would be better if she was there.

Afterwards, they had lunch at the Rose Tearoom; she had left hurriedly when Andy became morose over his salmon soufflé after she told him that she was sorry, she simply did not have time to go to the dance at the Turnberry Hotel.

'Can I help you, Madam?' she asked, a shade too abruptly.

The woman sucked the long cigarette holder fixed to her lip and then waved her hand airily. 'I doubt it. Nobody else here has.'

'I'm very sorry,' the man said, 'really, it doesn't matter.'

'It does, John,' the woman snapped. 'I asked for a mocha and they bring me this?' She indicated the tiny coffee cup, negligently letting ash from her cigarette fall into it.

Catriona smiled thinly, reminding herself that they were customers.

'Amelia,' the man said; Catriona caught the look of apology in his eyes.

'Don't contradict me,' she snapped. 'I had mocha in Italy. It comes in a big cup with milk and it's got chocolate flakes on top.'

Catriona went to the counter and returned with a new cup.

'Ah,' the woman said, 'now we're getting somewhere. The silly girl couldn't have listened to what I said. That's mocha. Amn't I right?'

She was looking at Catriona now, eyes bright with triumph.

Catriona smiled diplomatically. 'If you ask for café au lait next time, Madam, you'll get this right away.'

'This is mocha,' she insisted.

'With milk,' Catriona said gently.

'What pretty flowers you have,' the woman said, turning to the strelitzia on her left.

'I'm so sorry,' the man said in a low voice. 'Please, don't blame your waitresses. And please, put the cakes on my bill.'

Catriona sensed he was about to say something else when out of the corner of her eye she saw a familiar figure outside, at the foot of the steps that led up to the Palm Court.

An old man was standing there, his head moving from side to side as he read the sign that said 'Nicolson's of Largs'. He bent to take off his cap, rubbing the hair on the back of his head as he did so.

He wore a tweed jacket and a clean shirt but no tie, and the collar of the shirt was tucked under the collar of his jacket on one side so that you could see the white skin of his chest underneath.

He was tall, but beginning to shrink with age, and the skin underneath his chin hung in loose folds, like a chicken's wing. His hair, once auburn, was white now, as white as the crests of the waves of the incoming sea.

Though he had dressed carefully, you could tell that he wasn't a lowlander, a city dweller, or a wealthy man.

The man next to her said something else, but Catriona didn't hear him as she rushed through the Palm Court, opening the door so quickly that a breeze frilled the nearby tables, making the difficult woman exclaim aloud.

'Da,' she said, throwing her arms around him, 'Da. Is it really you, Da?'

He hugged her tight for a moment before he stood back, looking into her eyes as he held her in his arms.

'Yes, Catriona. It's me, it really is.'

Chapter Fifteen

Driving to Fairlie, Catriona looked at the man sitting beside her.

Tom Nicolson was old now; she had recognized his aura rather than anything else, because the years had changed him, aged him and made him frail almost, though there was still a hard edge to his jaw that she could see as she edged through the traffic and then accelerated along the coast road out of the town.

His face was pale under the tan of summer, almost white on the brow where his cap shaded him from the sun. He was thinner than he had been, there was a gaunt quality to his face; when he sat down his shoulders slumped and she could hear him breathing.

Neither of them said anything during the journey. When she reached home she led him into the family room, where a fire burned brightly in the grate, lit by Ellie Simpson for Jamie when he came home from school.

'Are you hungry, Da?' she asked as she carried the tea tray through with a plate of biscuits and some scones.

'No,' he said, as he watched her pour and serve the tea, and then, as she offered him a biscuit, 'maybe a little, pet. I've not had a bite since I left home yesterday.'

She went through to the kitchen and heated some soup, cut bread and put some of the stew for Jamie's dinner on a plate.

'Let me,' Ellie said quickly. 'You go through and I'll bring it in to you.'

'No,' Catriona said, 'it's my father, you see.'

She put the food on the little folding table that Jamie and she used for cards and jigsaws in the winter months.

'This is too much for me,' Tom said, 'you don't eat so much when you get to my age.'

She watched him as he ate, the bent, gnarled fingers of his hand wrapped around the spoon, the way he wiped the bowl with bread after he'd finished as they always did on the island because food was too precious to waste even a drop.

He drank some water then and finished the stew although he had said he could not. She was pleased that a little colour had come back to his face.

Afterwards, he reached into his pocket and put his pipe to his lips.

'There's some tobacco somewhere,' she said, rising to fetch some of Robbie's, that he had forgotten when he had been down to lay the flowerbeds.

'Sit yourself down, pet. Take the weight off you feet. I'm not smoking awt but the air these days; anything else makes me cough.'

She wondered what more to offer him; he drank whisky but there was none in the house, no hard liquor and not even beer because the bottles she'd bought in the hope that Rory would come had been drunk by Robbie with his lunch. There was only a case of the rough red Neapolitan wine that Joe had sent from Italy, and a few bottles of the white that she occasionally drank herself.

'Would you like some wine, Da?' she blurted.

'Now, there's a thing, pet. That's a thing I've never tasted all my life, not ever in all my born days, but I'll take a glass with you, pet.'

They spoke Gaelic together, slipping easily into the language of her childhood; she loved its cadences, the gentle guttural rhythms that held the echoes of the wind and the sea.

When she returned to the room he was standing at the french windows, watching the breeze through the trees.

'Good earth,' he said, 'good soil,' as his eyes passed over the lawn and flowerbeds. The rhododendron bushes were just that, now, no longer the riot of colour they had been in the early summer; there were only a few roses left, shedding their petals amongst the leaves that had just begun to fall from the trees. Robbie had pruned back the plants and pulled out the weeds the week before, leaving the beds dark brown and moist against the grass.

There were two bottles of wine, red and white; she did not know which one he would prefer but she liked the white so she opened that first, serving it in a tumbler because her father was not the sort of man she could ever imagine drinking happily from a stemmed glass.

'This is Lacrima Christi,' she said, 'it means the Tears of Christ.'

He drank a little, then made a face. 'Ach, well, the papists, they'd bottle anything.'

She opened the red and gave him some of that.

'Maire and Joe,' she said, 'they'll come down with Morag. That's your granddaughter.'

'I came to see you, pet.'

'Then they'll come tomorrow.'

His expression told her that he did not care.

The door banged; Jamie ran in.

'Who's this?' Tom asked.

'This is Jamie,' she said, 'your grandson. Ailish's son.'

They had dinner together; only Jamie ate and afterwards he got up to go out again.

'That's your grandfather,' she said, as he was in the lobby putting on his wellington boots.

'Yes,' Jamie replied, 'but I told Gordon we'd go whelking. His father needs bait, you see.'

'Ach,' her father said, 'it's something, isn't it, pet, when you've grandchildren that age you haven't even seen?'

'Allan's at university,' she said. 'He'll be down at the weekend.'

'I've to get back tomorrow, pet. The hay's in, but I've to harvest the grain, yet.'

Outside, evening was coming; the sun had already slipped behind the Cumbraes and the sky had deepened a tone to usher in the night. The room rested in the shade; there was still light enough from the windows and the fire, she would wait a little longer before she turned on the lamps.

In the shadows, Tom looked old and tired. His face was marked with lines of toil and thought that hadn't been there before and something else; it cut Catriona to the quick to realize that he also looked sad.

She'd tried to hate him, sometimes, when Allan was ill, before that when she had left home herself. She had tried to wipe him from her memory as she remembered the pain she had borne because of him in the past.

She had disliked him, railed at him, derided him but never quite managed hate. In the years the feeling had faded to apathy, or so she thought, but even that was not true because every time the end of the month came around, she added a little spoken word of love to the envelope that she sent home.

Tom was a big, gruff man, garrulous sometimes but taciturn when it came to himself. His silence now spoke louder than any words.

She saw then that he was hurting and she went to him and he folded her into his arms and held her as he had done when she was a child.

'The dream came true, Da, you know, my dream?'

'It did that, pet,' he said thickly. 'But then, I never doubted it or you for a minute.'

'Oh, Da,' she murmured, 'why did it have to be like that?'

'Only God knows, my pet.'

His voice was ragged, his throat dry, so she rose to pour him more wine and then closed the curtains, lit the lamps and added a few more logs to the fire.

He stood and hitched up his trousers. 'I'd best take a trip outside, pet.'

She looked at him, laughing, and then led him through to the cloakroom below the stairs. 'I've got a WC, Da, hot running water and baths, all modern conveniences. D'you know how to use it?'

He shot her a glance that would have frozen anyone else. '*Galach*, Catriona, what d'you think I am, a Pict? They had these heathen things in that *galach* court in Edinburgh when they tried me and the lads for chucking a few stones at the factor, or was it tearing up a writ? I can't remember which. That was when they started to say that every time Tom Nicolson went off the island he ended up in gaol. You must remember that.'

He came back into the room and prodded the fire to heighten the flames.

'What I did was wrong,' he said, very slowly.

'It's in the past, Da.'

'I didn't want you to go, pet, I wanted to keep you with me. I didn't even want you to grow up, but I couldn't stop you. I saw it in a flash one day; I watched you down at the beach when you'd just turned fourteen and I heard Mor's voice telling me that it was time for you to go soon and I said, aloud, don't be daft, her place's with me. But you're my daughter, pet, not my wife; I had to let you go. I let you go the only way I knew how. I wanted you to know all that ...' His voice tailed off and he looked away for a while before he turned back to her.

Their eyes locked for a moment; she understood him then, for the first time in her life.

'You know,' he said, 'men are supposed to be strong, they say. Stronger and tougher than women, but it's not true, pet. The truth is that we are weaker. God knows that, if no one else. That's why he made women the childbearers. If all that had been left to us men, the Garden of Eden would have been the graveyard of the human race.' He grinned. 'The old ones knew that too, pet. Way back, they'd send the women to fight the battles. If Georgie Boy had done the same, that bluidy cousin of his would've gone packing, he'd've run all the way back to Berlin.'

'I love you, Da,' she said simply.

'I love you too, Catriona.'

As she lay in bed, she remembered the rhythms of life on the island, knew how hard it must have been for him to take the time to visit her and wondered why he had come just then. During the night she heard him coughing, came awake with the unfamiliar sound, but when she turned over she saw that although the sky was lightening dawn had not yet come and so she turned over and went back to sleep again.

In the morning her father walked out onto the terrace and stood testing the quality of the day. Once he had absorbed the taste of the wind, he walked over the lawn to the small kitchen garden where he knelt and parted the grass, his touch as gentle as if he had been stroking a woman's hair. With his fingers he dug into the earth and took some of the grains in his hand, rubbing the dark, moist soil and studying it for a time before he replaced it in the hollow he had dug and teased the grass back into place.

He stood up slowly, his limbs creaking.

'This is good ground, lass. You'll get a harvest from anything you plant.'

She thought of the harvests on Skye, the soil sometimes so thin that a man was lucky if at the end of summer he got back the seed he had planted. The earth was exhausted from the plantings, the same small ground being burdened with seed again and again without being allowed to lie fallow for a while as nature demanded. She remembered her father's rage when one of the papers said that the crofters did not understand the land, that its lack of productivity was the fault of those who worked it.

Jamie went off to school; from the house she heard the sound of Ellie Simpson turning on the Hoover.

Tom took her arm as they walked towards the gate that led to the shore.

'Are you busy today, pet; d'you have things to do?'

'No, Da. There's people to take care of it. There's Zena, she's the manageress, and Janet, Annie's Janet. There's even Joe. That's Maire's husband.'

'Maire. I suppose she's mad at me too.'

Catriona shook her head. 'You're wrong, Da. Maire's not one to bear a grudge. I'm the one that used to do that, but not any longer.'

'You've reason enough, lass.'

'There's never reason, Da. It's never worth it.'

They walked in silence for a while, along the thin, rocky beach until the sand melted into rocks and scrub.

'How well d'you know this place?' he asked her then.

'Not so well. I spend most of my time in Largs.'

He led her along the road beyond the village and then turned onto a farmside path that followed the sea past an old quern stone set into the ground.

'It's been years since that was used,' he said, as they gazed at it. 'Time was when it was good luck for the year that came with the first grain ground.' He knelt and touched the stone for luck, rubbed the dust with his finger but found only sand.

'Your mother held with Michaelmas and all that, but the kirkers said it was a popism. She used to say the prayers, though, when I brought her the first of the grain.'

Beyond the quern stone they crossed an old wooden bridge over a stream, passed some rocks set into the sand and then rounded a corner into some dunes.

Catriona saw the beach then, the long stretch of gilded sand that stretched towards the sea, far down from the tideline marked with flotsam and weed. She stopped and took her shoes and stockings off, and felt the cool of the sand under her feet. Tom wore no shoes; she wasn't surprised, since he rarely wore anything on his feet – only when the occasion demanded it, when he would otherwise be dismissed as a pauper.

'You've been here before.'

'Never,' she said, as her eyes travelled over the expanse of sand. There were seabirds wheeling above the shore, gulls and curlews, oystercatchers far away where she saw the rise of oysterbeds. Traversing the dunes, they discovered a duck's nest, long abandoned, with broken shells undisturbed.

She recognized the beach from the black rock that rose way down from the shore, that Rory had described to her, that had been Jamie's favourite place when he was a little boy, when Rory took him out every Sunday, when she was too busy with the tearoom.

'You've changed, Catriona,' her father said. 'Time was

when you'd've found this place in an instant, been down every day to gather mussels.'

'I've grown older, that's all. I've grown up.'

'You've forgotten, haven't you? You've forgotten the way we lived back then.'

'I never have and I never will. Those were the happiest days of my life, Da.'

'But after ... afterwards, you weren't so happy then.'

'There was always joy, Da. Always a little joy each day. I needed so little then. If I found a stray lobster trapped in a rock pool, that was enough.'

He smiled wistfully. 'Is there no joy in your life now, then?'

Catriona thought for a while before she answered. 'There's pleasure, Da, satisfaction, things like that. When you came yesterday, I felt joy then.'

He squeezed her arm. 'I'm glad about that.'

When they reached the end of the beach they stood for a moment gazing at the view before turning back. Tom looked at the sea and then up at the hill behind them.

'You know, lass, I bet on a good day you'd get a view up there.'

'Cocks Law,' she said, 'Rory goes there.'

'Rory?'

'Rory MacDonald. Rory from the ferry. He's in haulage now.'

'I know Rory.' He laughed. 'I boxed his ear once. He used to have the eye for you, he did.'

Catriona stopped dead. 'Da, you didn't.'

'I did too. I thought for a minute the wee blighter was going to box me back.'

'When was that?'

'Oh, let me see, years ago. Right after the war started, about the spring of 1915. Scunner went off to war then, if I remember. Of all the men that went to war, he's the one I hoped wouldn't come back.'

She remembered the funny look on Rory's face, the way he'd rubbed his jaw when she asked him to write to her, the way he had turned her down.

'Oh, Da,' she said.

Tom did not notice. 'You know, pet, there was another thing. The twins, they went like you did. One minute they were there and next they were gone. I nearly went after them. In fact, I did. I went to Inverness to join up, to keep them safe. I thought, the hell with it. I packed the young 'uns off to Annie and left Marsaili with the croft. I thought, you want fed, you grow food yourself. Bitch is, and I've never told anyone this, not even Annie, I got to Inverness, all that way, and some silly lowland bugger said I'd to have a medical exam. Over forty, it was the rules, he said. So I took this bloody medical exam and the bugger said, "You've failed, man." He said I'd a squint, I'm cross-eyed, I couldn't see to shoot straight. I told him, "You tell the stags that." He said it was the rules. I said I'd get a gun and shoot him to prove it. He called the guards and I was marched out. So ended your father's military career. One night in the glass-house in Fort George. They wouldn't let me out till I signed a bit of paper promising not to shoot the MO.

'The bloody bastards. If I'd been there, the twins wouldn't've died.'

He stopped talking and looked at her.

'I wanted you to know that.'

The last of her anger faded and drifted away on the wind. The landscape melted into her tears.

When he left she gave him the flask of Mor's whisky that she had kept safe for him all these years.

At Largs they stopped at Nicolson's and he said 'hello' and 'goodbye' to Maire and Joe and little Morag almost in the same breath.

'I wanted you to know the truth,' he said as she drove him to the pier at Greenock.

She looked away.

'My little oyster girl,' he said, as he hugged her on the quay. 'You'll come back, one day, won't you? You'll come back home?'

She touched her breast. 'There is a part of me that never left.'

'Ach,' he said, 'the blood is strong. Enough like you, girl, and we could get the land back. We could.'

Back in Largs she went round to Maire, in the little bungalow Joe had bought on the edge of town.

'I'm sorry,' she said.

Maire shrugged. 'Don't be. Da was always like that.'

The autumn of that year had a gentle quality; Catriona took pleasure from the bronzing of the leaves, the sense of peace that settled over the town when another busy summer had come to an end.

Her business was comfortable, secure now as a source of pride and wealth; the years of struggle and worry were over and retreating in her memory as quickly as a rainstorm passes once the sun comes out again.

The future stretched before her, unshaded by doubt.

Once Nicolson's and the tearoom rested in the hiatus of the autumn months, Catriona drove up to Glasgow to see her brother.

'I know you hate him,' she said, speaking of their father, 'but he's a changed man.' In a way, she hoped to heal the breach between them, the wound that had opened when Allan was born.

'I don't hate him,' Allan said, 'I don't even blame him for what happened.' He was wearing a dark suit; in a way he seemed like a boy dressed up as a man.

'It wasn't him,' he said, 'I mean, it wasn't him that put me out. He took me to the doctor time and again. He paid for all the medicines himself. When I got ill, really ill, he went for the doctor. He left me with Annie while he went and then Marsaili wouldn't let me back into the house. He nearly killed her. He would've done if it wasn't Marsaili had had his children.'

'Why didn't you tell me?'

He looked sad for a moment. 'I was scared of what you would do if you knew.'

Catriona blew her nose. Tom had told her that Marsaili's daughter worked in the hotel; her son had already gone to sea. He said they were fine young people, both of them, but she knew that he hardly cared – and nor did she.

She drove quickly out of Glasgow, in a rush to get home in time to make Jamie's tea before she remembered, as she passed Nicolson's, that he had a rehearsal of the school Christmas pantomime. Because it finished late, he was staying with Maire and Joe; that was just an excuse, she knew, to see Morag, whom he adored.

The day felt suddenly terribly vacant; the evening stretched before her, a yawning void.

She went into Nicolson's, watched the last of the afternoon teas being served as the girls discreetly cleared the tables, and felt that sense of relief that came over the restaurant as the last of the day's customers left. The noise grew then with the waitresses chattering and clattering as they put crockery and cutlery away in the serving hatches and threw table-cloths and napkins into laundry baskets to be washed and pressed.

Catriona smiled at them as they left, one by one, after Janet had checked each girl's area and made sure everything was done; Zena was having a few days off so Janet was in charge in her place.

'That's it,' she said to Janet as the last waitress filed out the door. There were still a few minutes to go before closing time, but Catriona always let the girls get away if they finished early because so often in the summer they had to stay late.

Janet shook her head. 'Not quite. There's someone in the Palm Court. I forgot about him till I sent Lily to clear up.'

They walked to the glass enclosure beyond the main restaurant. It had been Robbie's idea to install heating and keep the Palm Court open through the winter; it cost no more than having the plants in a greenhouse, and customers loved the winter garden he nurtured there. At night spot-lights shone on the greenery until midnight; Catriona often stood in the shadows behind them and watched life go by on the promenade.

At a table by the window a man sat staring at the sea, his fingers touching a cup of coffee that had long since gone cold.

'Damn!' Janet looked at her watch; it was just moments to six and she had a choir practice that night. It was a rule that customers were never hurried, never made to feel unwelcome no matter how long they dawdled. 'He's been there all afternoon,' she said tiredly. 'All he's had's a cup of coffee.'

'You go,' Catriona told her, 'I'll see to him.'

Janet hesitated.

'Don't worry,' Catriona said, 'Robbie's upstairs and Joe's with Douglas in the kitchen.'

Janet thanked her; Catriona listened to the click of her heels as she walked quickly away. Outside the restaurant, night was falling on a cloudy day; waves were pounding the sea wall, throwing froth against the darkening sky.

The man seemed far away, lost in thought. She saw smoke curling upwards from his cigarette, the stubs of many others in the ashtray beside him.

'Would you like another coffee?' she asked as she picked up the one he had forgotten and changed the ashtray with a deftness born of years of practice.

'I ... oh.' He looked at his watch, reminding himself of the passing of time. 'I'm very sorry,' he said, 'I mustn't keep you.'

He flexed his arms and sighed as he began to get up.

'It's no trouble,' she said, 'really,' as she noticed the hollows beneath his eyes, the emptiness inside them.

'No,' he said, his voice suddenly gaining strength. Then, looking at the windows, he saw the first streaks of rain lash down from the sky. 'Oh, Lord,' he said, 'you don't know where I could find a hotel?'

'I know of a very good place where you can have bed and breakfast,' she said, thinking of Zena, who took in guests during the summer months. 'I'll phone and make the arrangements while I get you another coffee.'

'It's silly, really,' he said, when she brought fresh coffee, 'but my car's open and there's something wrong with the hood.'

She purred sympathetically, not understanding what he meant.

'The rain,' he explained, 'I couldn't see, and I've to get back to Edinburgh.'

'You could take the train and leave your car at the garage.'

'That would complicate things more,' he said, 'I'd have to come to collect it.'

'They'd deliver it, if you asked them.'

'I'd rather wait out the rain.'

'Maybe you could have them look at the hood?' she ventured.

He smiled. 'You're very practical,' he said, looking at the cup of coffee on the table before him. 'Why don't you join me?'

Catriona got another coffee; she had nothing else to do that night. Returning to the table, she looked at the man again, noticing something familiar about him.

'You're Miss Nicolson, aren't you?' he asked. 'I'm Jack Ryan. We've met before, but maybe I shouldn't remind you.'

'I don't remember.'

'It was a few months ago. My wife complained about the chocolate cake, and then the coffee.'

'Oh,' Catriona said, remembering now.

'It wasn't you,' he said quickly, 'or the chocolate cake. Or the coffee.'

His face darkened then, for some reason, and Catriona had a premonition that she did not want to know any more. A sudden impulse urged her to rise and walk away, so strong that she actually moved in her seat before she suppressed it and took a sip of her coffee instead. She looked at him and saw a strong, clear face shaded by the kind of emotions that could be discussed only with loved ones or a stranger. This happened sometimes, in the limbo of a holiday town, a visitor would divulge things so private that inwardly she blushed as she listened and tried to understand. Over time, she had realized that she was not being asked for advice or solace, but rather being used as a confessor almost like a priest, the instant itself a moment of absolute honesty in the charade of human relationships, a brief consequence of time and place that would never be repeated.

'It's very peaceful here,' he said.

'Yes,' she agreed, watching a wave rise like a lion above the railings at the edge of the promenade and then crash on the asphalt with the orgiastic energy of a bursting balloon. Before the sea, the glass walls of the Palm Court held their reflection. Jack Ryan had very dark hair, almost black, over finely chiselled features; his face was smooth but there were more creases than there should have been for a man of his age, as if in his life he had laughed a lot and had also felt pain. His eyes were slate blue, almost as deep as the ocean. She watched him for a while, smiled as another breaker briefly swept his image away, and wondered for a moment what a man like him was doing married to a woman like his wife.

'I've been coming here for years,' he said. 'Amelia's – that's my wife – Amelia's brother sails from Gourock each year. We come to watch the races.'

Catriona smiled. 'I've seen you several times over the years.'

'I used to wonder who it was who created all this.' He looked around at the plants, the wickerwork chairs, the criss-crossed shadows of the palms on the windows.

She blushed. 'What brings you here now?'

His face resumed its expression of detached sadness. 'Amelia's in a mental home,' he said.

'Oh, my God. I'm so sorry.'

He smiled wistfully. 'Don't be. It's what she wanted.' He began to play with the thin gold band around his finger. 'I drove down here because it's so peaceful,' he said, 'such a nice place to be. It's away from everyone I know.' He was slipping the ring off and on his finger; he did that several times before he finally took it off and put it in his pocket.

'I'm so sorry,' she said again.

'Don't be.' He shook his head. 'The mental home, it's one

of these private places, very discreet and genteel. There's nothing of the asylum about it. It's where the idle rich go to rest their livers, or poor senile Aunt Harriet is left until she dies and leaves her money to her grasping relatives. Amelia wants to end our marriage. That is the way she's decided to do it.'

There was something terribly bitter in those words, as if all love and even affection had gone, and only contempt was left.

Catriona shivered.

He asked her if she had ever been married herself.

'I nearly married when I was young,' she said, 'I've only just realized I'm glad I didn't.'

'Why's that?'

'Because I didn't know who I was then; I didn't know what I could be. If I'd married, I'd never've known myself.'

He smiled. 'You don't know how lucky you are.'

'But he died, you see. I feel guilt about that.'

She saw that a skin had formed on his coffee, and got up to fetch him another. When she gave it to him, he took a sip before he spoke again.

'You should never feel guilt for being what you are,' he said.

'Sometimes it's not so easy to do that.'

She wondered how the roles had twisted, how she was suddenly confessing her secrets to him.

He sensed her disquiet. 'Amelia and I married the summer I graduated. She was eighteen then, I was twenty-three. After the honeymoon, she says, she didn't see me for a whole year.' He smiled. 'I'm a surgeon, you see. I was a houseman then, living at the hospital. After a couple of years I realized that I had married a stranger. We muddled through, fought a lot. I never fought for long because I could always go to work. A few years ago I became a consultant. That's when we realized that it didn't work and it never would.'

Catriona smiled sympathetically. 'Maybe, if she isn't well . . .'

'Oh, no,' he said, 'don't think that. It's what she wants; I thought I should play the loving husband for a while longer. But I went down to the hospital yesterday and her doctor tells me that I'm the cause of all her troubles and the sooner we're divorced, the better.' He laughed. 'That's what I mean about guilt. I should feel terrible guilt, but I don't. I just feel a tremendous sense of relief.'

He looked around at the rainswept windows, glacial mirrors of the night that trapped the tableau of their conversation endlessly, prism-like.

'You must think I'm terrible.'

'No.' Catriona had an eye-view of his wife, her spoilt, demanding, childish voice rising in protest not for a reason but for the attention it would gain. 'I think I understand.'

'I was driving around all day, aimlessly, thinking how dreadful I was, wondering if I would see horns growing the next time I looked in the mirror. You've brought me back to earth.'

They began to talk then, endlessly, not about his marriage but of life and being, his work and hers, the things that interested them both. Time passed not as normal but speeded up, like a Marx Brothers film, as if a leprechaun had tampered with the chimes of the clock. At one stage, when Catriona learned that he had not eaten since he had left the hospital in Edinburgh, she went to the fridge and gave him cold roast beef and mustard, some leftover bramble tart, apologizing because it was all that was left.

He ate ravenously, like a starved man, mopping up the shreds of beef with a doorstep-sized hunk of bread, sighing deeply when he had eaten the entire tart. 'You must be a fantastic cook,' he said.

'I manage,' she smiled.

They talked on, late into the night, ignoring the clock until the phone rang, rupturing the tranquillity of the darkened restaurant.

Catriona listened to a couple of rings, rising only when she realized that Joe and Douglas had left and that Robbie had long since gone to bed.

'Catriona?' Zena's voice asked. 'That guest you rang

about, is he still coming? It's just that it's after midnight and I was wondering if he'd changed his mind.'

'Gracious, yes,' Catriona replied. 'It's just that we've been chatting and I forgot the time.'

'I'll hang on, then.'

'No, Zena. If you leave the door open, I'll let him in.'

'What was that?' John Ryan asked when she returned to him.

'Your room,' she said.

'Oh, goodness, yes.' He looked at his watch, a thin gold disc around his wrist. 'I'd best get on.'

'Don't rush,' she said, as she cleared the debris of his meal. 'It's a friend of mine, someone who works here, in fact. She's left the door open and I'll take you there. Is there anything else you'd like?'

'I don't suppose I could have another coffee?'

'Of course. It'll just take a minute to heat up the machine.'

She watched the coffee froth on his lips, the faint line the bubbles left and how he licked them away with the tip of his tongue as a child might.

'It's been a very pleasant evening,' he said, taking his overcoat from the stand.

'I'll drive you to Zena's,' she said as she locked the doors behind her.

He stood and studied the air for a moment; the night had been refreshed by the rain, the sky scattered with a thousand stars.

'I'd rather walk, if you don't mind.'

'My car's here,' Catriona said, businesslike but instantly regretting it.

In the car park his was the only car beside hers, a long, low Bentley roadster spotted by the rain and shorn of its top. 'You see,' he said, as he opened the door and rainwater trickled out.

'You should have said.' She went to the shed where Robbie kept his gardening tools and found a tarpaulin to put over the top.

'I did,' he reminded her.

In the car she caught a glimpse of his face lit by the street lights, and felt suddenly shy to be sitting so close to him. The journey was very short, she thought.

At Zena's, she led him into the living room, then showed him the bathroom and the guest bedroom at the front of the house. Zena appeared, very tired, with a housecoat over her nightgown.

'This is Doctor Ryan,' Catriona whispered.

'Mister Ryan,' he corrected her.

'I thought you were a doctor?'

'I'm a surgeon. You spend six years to be called a doctor and then another six to get back to "Mr" again.'

At the threshold of the room, she felt his closeness keenly. 'Is there anything else you need?'

'A toothbrush?'

'Zena always leaves one on the dresser. She told me that.'

'Thank you,' he said, as he took the room key.

'Goodnight, Mr Ryan.'

'Goodnight, Miss Nicolson, but please call me Jack.'

She nodded briefly, and then she fled.

The colours of the new day were extra bright, she thought, as she opened the curtains and looked at the rain-washed grass and the wild autumn sea beyond.

Strangely aware of the man she had left at Zena's, Catriona found things to do that morning that kept her away from there and also Nicolson's car park. She visited the bank and the accountant's, then the butcher's to talk about orders for the Christmas functions, and the town corporation to ask how many were expected for the New Year dance. That done, and because it was only half past ten, she went to Andy Hendry's office to ask why she had not received his bill for attending the licensing court.

'I thought you were avoiding me,' he said, as he cleared some papers from his desk and asked his secretary for the file.

'Not at all,' she said too quickly, 'it's just that I've been busy, these last few weeks.'

The bill found, he asked diffidently if he could dare to invite her to the Chamber of Commerce's Christmas Ball and she replied carelessly that of course he could and she would be very pleased to go with him, quite forgetting the resolution that she had made to lead him no further along the byway of a relationship that he wanted but she did not.

That would mean a ballgown, she thought as she left, wondering whether to go up to Glasgow then or to leave it for another day. Thinking of Jamie, and that it was already nearly midday, she put the thought aside and went to the Rose Tearoom to have lunch and a talk to Etta about what had to be done in the quiet months before the season came round again.

It was after four when she reached Nicolson's, scanning the car park anxiously until she was certain that the Bentley was gone.

'Where 'ave you been?' Joe asked, the moment she walked in the door. 'Mister Ryan, he waited ages for you. I phoned everywhere and got as far as Hendry's. Andy said you may 'ave gone to Glasgow, so Mister Ryan said he had to go too. He asked me to give you this.'

The note thanked her for such a pleasant evening, and apologized that he could not wait to thank her in person. Catriona folded it carefully and put it in her pocket.

'Thanks, Joe.'

'Who is he, Catriona?'

'Nobody,' she said quickly, 'a man who got stuck in the rain, that's all.'

Joe was pacing up and down in the business suit that Maire made him wear when he wasn't crouched over a recipe or a tub of ice cream. He was thinking of the Christmas dances, deciding where to put the ornaments in the function room as Sheilagh Cameron, Catriona's new secretary, made notes. Catriona watched him for a while, thinking how marriage had changed him, bled the heat from his mercurial temper and soothed the rough edges of the pride that had been callused in places ever since he left his native land.

*

Marsaili's letter came in December, a few days before the Christmas dances began.

The writing on the envelope was unfamiliar, and thinking it came perhaps from a friend of a friend asking for a job she left it with all her other mail for Sheilagh to open and deal with.

The letter was on her desk in her personal folder when she had her morning coffee.

'Dear Catriona,' it said:

> Your father is a proud man as he has always been and he would not be pleased for me to write to you so please do not tell him that I have done so.
>
> I am writing to tell you that he has not been well this past month. He has seen the doctor so there will be his bill to pay. Things are not easy here as they never have been so I hope you will oblige me by sending some money to help.
>
> *Marsaili Nicolson*

Maire had joined her for coffee; she read the letter twice and then handed it back. 'What do you want to do?'

Catriona thought for a long time. 'I'd like to go home, find out what's really the matter.' Tom's last letter had been brief, almost stilted.

'Well, go then,' Maire said, simply.

'I can't leave Jamie.'

'Jamie is just fine with us, Triona. Joe and I'll watch things for you. I mean, we really will this time. And there's Zena and Sheilagh and Janet.'

'I suppose,' Catriona began. She felt strange then; an odd feeling had been lingering all day, since the moment she had woken. 'You will be careful, won't you?'

'God's sake, Catriona, we've grown up since those days. We both have.'

On the train north, in the anonymity of the first-class compartment that Sheilagh had booked, Catriona tried to wipe the fear from her mind.

The land flashed past in a whisper, the soft roll of the lowland farms, the rising crags of the hills beyond that gave a hint of the mountains to come. She sat back and closed her eyes, held the image of vibrant, vivid shadow that faded to blankness even as she tried, in vain, to keep it for ever. Opening them again, she saw the steward with morning coffee, biscuits and cakes on a tray.

He poured her coffee and then left her alone.

Catriona felt her father's death as the train rounded a bend that moved deep into the hills; she felt the shift in her consciousness then, in an instant, as the whistle keened and its distant echo bounced back from the heights.

She battled with the realization for a moment before she accepted it as fact.

A single tear formed in her eye, rolled all the way down her cheek and then spotted the lapel of her jacket as a rain drop might.

Why is it, she wondered, that I feel death, but never see it? Then she remembered the ebbing helplessness of her mother's death, the way that as she had watched she had wished for the power to turn back time.

The thought had been at the back of her mind ever since Tom had come to Largs. She had sensed it then but suppressed it because she had too much life still to live for Tom to die.

She still had things to say to him.

The steward came and took away the still full coffee cup, nodding briefly when she told him that she did not want another, and again after she said she did not feel like lunch.

She reached the island at night, remembering only when she looked at her watch that night came earlier there in the winter, that the distinctions of the seasons were sharper further north.

The land was a shadow of itself as the car wended the long road home from Kyleakin to The Braes. The driver was an estate worker, driving her home in return for ten shillings. She was glad he was not an islander, that he would not ask questions or even talk. She watched the moon rise starkly over the Cuillins, and caught their mighty reflection in Loch Sligahan. As the car turned off the road onto the track she felt the call of the land, heard its distant whisper welcoming her home.

Her village was as she had never seen it before, the little houses sharp-angled against the night, people grouped at Annie's door and beyond at her father's, the echoing silence that spoke so loudly of his death.

She got out and thanked the driver, hugged Annie briefly and Sine and Archie before she stood alone and spoke to the mourners.

She knew them all, though the years had changed them, had made rugged masks of their faces, had aged a generation in the blink of an eye. One by one she shook hands, hugged some, said a few words to others.

'He was a great man,' someone said; she could not remember who for a minute until the knowledge collided with the next in line.

Hamish-of-the-dykes had survived; God knows, he must be a hundred, she thought as he murmured his condolence along with a jest about stones.

Then Angus, her father's brother, stood there; she hadn't seen him for fourteen years, and had not thought of him either.

'It's been a long time,' she said.

'Ach, lass, it's always the brave who leave the nest. He was so proud of you, but you know that.'

She smiled weakly. Out of the corner of her eye she saw that there was no longer anyone outside Marsaili's house; everyone had come to her.

Annie ushered her in at last; she sat, too tired for a moment to say anything. Sine hugged her, then left to feed her children.

'It's shock, pet,' Annie said as she heated honey and milk.

'Away with that,' Iain said, easy now in his blindness, familiar with every object in the house. 'Would you not like a dram, pet?'

'I think I would,' she said, as she cupped the hot drink in her hands and felt its kindness ease the ache in her soul. In the light of the fire she saw that Annie had aged – there were fine lines drawn on her face, as a cartographer would mark the incline of a hill on a map.

'What're you thinking, pet?' Annie asked her.

'The time that's passed,' she said, 'so much time.'

'He was in no pain,' Iain said. 'The doctor told us that.'

They told her how Tom had been found sitting on the rocks overlooking the beach; a heart attack had killed him instantly, though his death had been expected because the doctor said that a cancer had begun to eat away at his lungs.

Annie went behind the curtain and came back with a little bundle of tiredness.

'This's Fionn,' she said, 'my youngest.'

'I'm not all blind,' Iain said.

Her father was buried the next morning, as a stormy chiaroscuro sky wiped out the colours and turned the land into shades of grey.

The minister said the same prayers as he was laid to rest in the graveyard next to Mor; the mourners were silent but as the earth dribbled into the grave a sigh rose that sounded like prayer and eulogy all at once. Her father had often railed against the Lord, but he had cherished his world.

A lone voice rose in song; Catriona recognized the words of the psalm that had been the anthem and epitaph of the Land League so many years ago. Her voice joined the others; the whole land, the whole landscape was filled with the music that Tom loved.

Is leis an Tighearna an talamh agus an lan,
an domhan agus iadsan a tha combuidh ann.

The earth is the Lord's, and the fullness thereof ... The words traced the majesty of the hills, swooped down towards the sea, floated for a long time before the wind caught and carried them away.

The sun broke the clouds then and shone briefly on the waves like a spotlight from the heavens before the sullen rainclouds banked again and extinguished forever the light of Tom's life.

A man came up to her, a stranger dressed in city clothes. He introduced himself as the lawyer from Portree; she bridled because on the islands lawyers invoked only the landlords' law, never the people's.

He told her that he acted for her father; she gasped and then swallowed her surprise.

He handed her some folded papers and a bankbook. 'Your father's will. He was most anxious that I gave it to you.'

She asked him about his bill. He said that it was already paid.

'The will,' he said, 'is quite simple. He wanted to leave everything to you, but I had to tell him that might not survive a challenge. Instead, he left the croft to Allan Nicolson, his eldest son. He had already put his money in your name.'

She flicked through the book and had read only a couple of entries before she realized that he had banked almost all the money she had sent him over the years.

Annie was standing beside her. 'He had his way, Tom did,' she said.

Catriona blinked back tears, of anger or sadness, she did not know which.

'Marsaili . . .' she said to the lawyer.

'Your father said you were to evict her, if you can. They were trying to divorce each other for adultery. She was holding out, he told me, because she wanted the money he had in the bank. He solved that by giving it to you. Her children are already provided for.' He paused. 'There was another woman, you know, and a child Tom acknowledged as his own. They've also been provided for.'

Catriona had heard enough. She thanked him and walked away.

In the afternoon she walked slowly up the path towards her father's house.

'Thank goodness you're here,' Marsaili said, rising from her chair as Catriona walked in.

Catriona looked around, seeing that nothing had changed except for a line of cheap glass ornaments on the dresser. 'You didn't even come to the funeral.'

'I've bills to pay,' Marsaili said, 'the doctor and the funeral and that. Tom's not brought a penny home for months.'

Catriona walked into the bedroom and saw the bed where her mother had died, that her father had left so many years ago.

'What do you want, Marsaili?'

'Well, nothing really, if you pay what Tom owes, that's all. I'll put the place up for sale, that'll tide me over.'

'You won't,' Catriona said. 'This is my father's flesh and blood. He bled for the land, but you don't know that.'

Her voice was a whip and Marsaili reared back.

'I am his wife.'

'You were trying to divorce him. The lawyer told me that.'

'I've a son to him. And a daughter.'

Catriona laughed at her.

'What do you want?' Marsaili asked.

'Just get your things and go, Marsaili.'

'And just where do you expect me to go to? I went through hell on earth with that man, he made me a laughing stock the length and breadth of the island when he stood up in church and baptized his bastard son.'

'The only bastard children he had were yours.'

'How dare you say that?' Marsaili shrieked.

'I'll say it again, if you like. Louder, if you want me to.' Catriona went to the door and opened it.

Marsaili stared at her for a moment and then brushed past her into the bedroom, where she took a bag from the chest.

'I've debts, God knows,' she whined, 'not even you can put me out without a penny.'

Catriona held the door wide for her and waited as she took the glass ornaments and then the pots and pans, tying them to her bag like a tinker.

'You've a friend in Portree. I know that,' Catriona said. 'Willie's already on the track, waiting to take you there.'

With Marsaili gone Catriona left the door open and let the wind in, to blow away the woman's musky traces.

Sine and Archie would move in and care for the house as it needed to be cared for, because the landlord had never made good on his wartime promise and crofts were more precious now than gold.

The phone rang the day after she got back to Largs.

'Catriona?' Rory said.

She gasped.

'I heard about it after the funeral. When I rang the island they said you'd already left.'

'I had to get back,' she said weakly.

'I'm sorry,' he said, 'not for Tom, never for Tom. But I'm sorry for you.'

'I'm not so bad, Rory. I'm managing. He came down, you know. He told me that he hit you. I was angry about that.'

Rory laughed. 'I nearly hit him back. I would've done if I'd been a year or two older. I suppose that's life, though. If you think about hitting someone, you never end up doing it.'

'How's your girlfriend?' she asked.

Rory said nothing for a while.

'Perhaps I shouldn't've asked,' she said.

'No, no. That was Ally you saw me with. She works in the office. That's all.'

'Oh, well,' she said.

'Do you need me?' Rory asked.

'Like I said, I'm managing, Rory. I don't feel too bad.'

'Oh, well,' he said, 'I'll say goodbye then.'

'Maybe I'll see you over Christmas?'

'Perhaps.'

She held the receiver for a long time, listening to the echo, before, very gently, she put it back on its hook.

'I'm sorry,' she said.

Chapter Sixteen

*J*ust after Easter, when Nicolson's was poised for the new season, Catriona had the feeling that someone was watching her. It was early in the evening, and she was about to close the restaurant for the day. Rab Duncan, the boy who had lost his leg in the accident, had left school and was working on the cashier's desk; he had mastered the till quickly and now she was instructing him how to complete the daily records that showed how much had been sold of the various foods, cakes and ice cream, how many cups of tea and coffee. There were special buttons on the till for each and at the end of the day, another button, when pressed, gave the total sales of each. The invention was American; Ailish had sent it as a present when Benny told her how well it worked.

'You see,' she explained, pressing the buttons for tea and coffee and noting the amount in the form she'd had printed, 'twelve pounds' worth of tea and fifteen of coffee. That's about average for the time of year. Hardly any ice cream.' She pressed a button and the display at the top read £5/17/6.

'Twelve pounds is a lot of cups of tea,' Rab said.

'Not so many. In the summer, we do thousands. That button often comes up seventy pounds or more.'

She tallied the other totals, for meals, snacks and pastries.

'Why d'you bother?' Rab asked.

She looked at him.

'I wasn't being funny, Missus. I just wondered why. Money comes to the same if you count it all at once.'

'It isn't so much the money we're taking,' she explained patiently. 'It's that it gives us a stock check, of sorts. We have a standing order with the grocer's but sometimes things go awry, like when we started doing cappuccinos everyone was drinking coffee and we didn't notice it until Joe told me that we'd just about run out. We serve so much every day that in the whole of Largs there wasn't enough to last us for more than a few hours and we were running around all over the place hunting coffee beans. And the fresh food like ice cream, we order so much cream and eggs every day; sometimes people don't buy so much and this tells us that, so we can cut the order. Understand?'

'I think so, but why don't you know anyway? I mean, Joe can tell how much ice cream's being sold by looking at it, and I watch the chefs filling the mocha machine.'

She smiled. 'This time of year isn't normal, Rab. This is very, very quiet. In the summer, some days we serve five thousand cups of tea, two thousand lunches and high teas, thousands of ice creams. When that happens, you'll be so busy working the till you won't have time to look around, never mind work out how much of what's being sold.'

He nodded carefully, as if he had thought about it, and she began to explain quickly about the waitress slips before she had that feeling again, and turned to look around, but nobody was there beyond a pair of women finishing their tea and a man standing at the chocolate counter.

'Why d'you do that?' Rab asked immediately, and then, when she sighed slightly, 'don't worry, Missus. My da always says I ask too many questions.'

'It doesn't matter, Rab. The reason is to make sure that all the waitresses are doing much the same work as the others. You just make a note of how many covers each has served so Zena knows if she needs to re-allocate the tables. Understand?'

'Yes. What do I do next?'

'Well, usually you wait until we're closed before you total the till, but since we've done it now, you just put the money in bags and take it up to Sheilagh and she puts it in the safe. Can you manage that?'

'Easy,' he said, wincing a little as he got off the stool and put his weight onto his wooden leg. Catriona watched him for a moment, holding his crutches in case he stumbled, but he managed manfully.

'Hello,' a voice said behind her.

She spun around, saw Jack Ryan and knew then why the man at the chocolate counter had seemed familiar.

'I was wondering when you'd notice me.'

Catriona blushed slightly. He had phoned her twice; each time Sheilagh had fielded the call and she was relieved that he had not called a third time. At Christmas he had sent a card with a little note and she had sent him one of the printed cards from Nicolson's of Largs in a polite if distant response.

'I was wondering,' he said, 'if I could take you to dinner?'

'I couldn't possibly, it's so short notice,' she said, not noticing Maire, who was standing watching her.

'I realize that,' he said, 'I did phone, but your secretary kept on telling me you were busy, so I thought the only way to see you was to come in person.'

'I'm sorry,' she said, 'I have been busy.'

'I've felt so guilty ever since I met you. You see, I never paid the bill.'

She laughed. 'I forgot about that.'

'Well, how about dinner tomorrow? I could stay in that boarding house. I'm sure they've got space for me.'

Catriona didn't know what to say.

Maire called sharply from behind the counter: 'Go,' she said tersely, in Gaelic, 'I can tell you want to.'

'No!' Catriona spat, in the same language. 'Leave me alone.'

'I'll do no such thing,' Maire said.

'What about Jamie?'

'What about him? He loves staying with us.'

Catriona felt herself being pulled inside, a force so strong that she put her hand out to steady herself.

Jack Ryan was standing there, a gentle smile on his face.

'Please,' he asked again.

'Yes,' she said finally, fearing that if she did not Maire would agree for her, and draw this man more into her life than she wanted him to come.

'I must change,' she said.

'You don't need to, Miss Nicolson. You're perfect as you are.'

She blushed deeply, looking down at the little beige suit she had bought in MacDonald's that she rarely wore to work but had worn that day because it seemed to leap towards her when she opened her wardrobe.

Jack Ryan settled her in the Bentley, closing her door before he walked around the car and got in.

'Is there anywhere special you'd like to go, Miss Nicolson?' he asked as he edged slowly out of the car park and then accelerated along the seafront.

'Please,' she said, 'call me Catriona. And no, there's nowhere in particular I'd like to go.'

'Only if you call me Jack,' he said. 'I thought, since you run the best restaurant on the coast, you might like to go to Glasgow for a change. There's a new restaurant I've heard about, and it's not so far to go.'

'I run a cafe more than a restaurant.'

'It's both,' he said decisively. 'Who was that boy you were talking to?'

'That's Rab,' she said, relieved that she had something to talk about. 'He hurt his leg in an accident when the Palm Court was blown down in a storm, and I gave him a job when he left school. But I'd've given him a job anyway. He's very bright.'

'So you gave him a job because of the accident?'

'Not really. I suppose so. A lot of glass was shattered in the storm. He climbed up to clear a bit of wood that was hanging and fell down and just about cut his leg off on the broken glass.' She paused and winced at the memory. 'It was the least I could do for him.'

'Don't say that,' he said quickly, 'men lose their legs every day at work, and the men who employ them rarely give a damn. I saw them all the time when I was at the infirmary; railwayman, factory workers, men from the docks.'

She watched the expressions on his face change, anger on top of the rapt attention he paid to the road.

'Ever been to Erskine, have you?'

'No, but I've heard about it.'

'You'd see them there, amputees. Thousands of them from the war. Most young and able-bodied otherwise, but they can't get a job because nobody'll give them a chance. Least of all, the country they fought for.' He laughed bitterly. 'Perhaps I shouldn't say that.'

'I agree with you,' she said softly.

'It makes me angry.'

He paused to change gears as the car started up the long, winding brae behind the town.

'I worked there, for a while,' he said, 'when I was a junior. I was very lucky to get the chance.'

'Lucky?'

'I learned how to do bone grafts. That's a way of healing injured limbs. The man who started Erskine, he taught me the technique.'

'Sir William Macewen,' she said.

'How did you know that?'

'He dug up all the willow trees in the university grounds to get the wood he needed. The University Court were going to sue him to get their trees back. I worked for the lawyer who drew up the writ.'

'I never knew that.'

'Oh, yes, but we had this wonderful messenger, you see. MacKenzie, that was the lawyer, he sent the messenger off with a threatening letter and the messenger came back and said that he couldn't find Macewen. By that time the University Court had had second thoughts.'

Jack Ryan laughed.

'Willie used to send us out at the dead of night, cutting down willow trees from people's gardens.'

'No!'

'He did, truly. Like grave robbers, we were. Around Erskine, there's a lot of estates. Macewen would see some likely samples and send us out at night to cut them down. We never did get caught.' His face changed. 'It was worth it, you know. If you could see a man's face when he started to walk again, even with all the pain of a wooden leg.'

He stopped talking then, and Catriona listened to the wind rushing past the car.

'I mustn't bore you,' he said.

'You weren't,' she told him.

'Orthopaedics,' he said, smiling, 'one of the loves of my life. Or so I'm told. That's the branch of surgery that fixes joints, limbs, bones. You can make a cripple walk again, make sure that a child doesn't limp for the rest of his life. I worked in an orthopeadic hospital in Boston for a year.'

'When was that?'

'I came back a few months before the first time I spoke to you. Amelia stayed in Edinburgh. It was after that we agreed to get the divorce.'

'If you can,' Catriona said, remembering the tortured law that kept couples trapped in loveless marriages, and how MacKenzie refused to take on any divorce actions at all.

'It won't be so bad in my case, or so the solicitor tells me, because I'm not going for a divorce, but an annulment. On the grounds of Amelia's health. Her doctor says she wasn't in fit state to undertake marriage vows, not to me or anyone else. The papers have been drawn up. It will all be over in a year, or maybe a little longer.'

The car glided through the night, as she waited for the air to clear.

'I got the hood fixed,' he said, when they reached the edge of the city sprawl. 'As you can see. The car's as old as Methuselah, the repairs far outweigh the original bits, but I'll never get another one because it was a present from someone very dear to me. My mother,' he added quickly. 'But perhaps I'll get another one and keep this in a garage for weekends.'

He must be very rich, she thought.

'It's a nice car,' she said weakly.

In Argyle Street he turned into Queen Street, then slowed as he passed Royal Exchange Square. 'The restaurant's there,' he said, pointing towards the far end of the square, 'but I'd better park here because it doesn't look like there's a space outside.'

Catriona stepped out into the cool of the evening, hearing the distant chatter of starlings far away, remembering the first time she had ever seen the square.

It was no different now, still haughty, poised, the Corinthian columns of the library a symbol of mercantile arrogance.

Jack Ryan took her arm, very gently, giving rise to a shiver that climbed her backbone before she drew a deep breath and concentrated on the sound of her heels on the cobblestones.

The restaurant was discreet outside, as reticent as a lawyer's office, the only mark of its presence a little brass plate on the wall before a doorman threw the door open and she walked into a softly lit room in which little Tiffany lamps threw pools of light onto tables dressed with silver and crystal.

A waiter led them through to a table beside the wall, seating her carefully and unfurling her napkin as Jack seated himself opposite.

'Would you like a drink?' he asked. 'Some champagne, perhaps?'

She flushed. 'Whatever. I don't drink an awful lot.'

The champagne came and fizzled comfortingly.

'Have you ever been here before?' Jack asked.

'No,' she said, and then, thinking that was not explanation enough, 'I hardly come up to Glasgow these days.'

'It's an oyster restaurant,' he said, 'very popular. Though they do fish and meat as well, if you don't like shellfish.'

'Oysters?' She smiled, then started to laugh.

'What's so funny?'

She told him.

They talked so easily that time sped past and the food was only a distraction from the attention they paid to each other.

The evening went on, the hum from the other diners faded to a whisper and then silence; it was only when the waiter came and offered yet another cup of coffee that they realized they were alone and the restaurant was about to close.

'I'm awfully sorry,' Jack said as he paid the bill.

'It's quite all right,' the maitre d' said generously, 'it is our pleasure that you enjoyed your meal.'

Outside the restaurant there was a group of children, ragged and scarred with the mark of the slums. 'I'm so sorry,' the restaurateur said, 'I'll chase them away if you'll give me a moment.'

'Don't bother,' Jack said. Outside, he reached into his pocket for change but then the oldest boy's face twisted into a snarl. 'Awa tae hell, Mister! We're no' beggin', jes' waitin' tae walk wur sister hame fra' work.'

Catriona laughed, proud of the city and of Jack.

'Oh, God,' he said, 'I probably got his sister the sack.'

She turned back and saw that the maitre d' had already locked the door. 'I doubt it. I don't think he heard.'

'Have you ever given anyone the sack, Catriona?'

'I sacked my brother-in-law and my sister once. Apart from that, never, but, you see, I take people on at first for the summer and then if it works out I give them a job.'

'What about your brother-in-law and sister?'

'They got married. It turned out they were in love.'

'Did you give them their jobs back?'

'They never actually left, Jack. I stormed off. It was years ago, the first year that I opened Nicolson's.'

'I remember that,' he said.

'You do not.'

'I do too. I told you, I've been going to Largs all the years I've been married. I first had tea with you nearly ten years ago, in the Rose Tearoom.'

She flushed crimson. 'Oh, no.'

'Oh, yes. Amelia and I were arguing even then. We would argue for so long and she would stand on the pier to hail her brother and I would go off to have tea at Miss Nicolson's. It was always a pleasure. After a year or two, I began to look forward to it. I wanted to see how much you had grown.'

'My God,' she murmured, 'I was so young. I was so serious then. I used to wear the same dresses, year in, year out. I was in MacDonald's a year ago when I caught a glimpse of myself in the mirror. I was appalled.'

'You were always very beautiful,' he said, very softly, so softly that at first she did not believe he had said it.

'It still seems early, doesn't it?' he said when they reached the car. 'Shall we find somewhere to go dancing?'

Catriona hesitated.

'Would you rather just talk?'

'I'm not in the mood for music,' she said, thinking that she wanted only to listen to him.

He helped her into the car, offering her his coat because it was cold after the warmth of the restaurant.

'There's a back road to the coast,' she said, 'if you go through Dalry. The view from the hill is meant to be wonderful.'

'Where's Dalry?'

'I don't know. I've never seen the view either but I've heard it's worth the going.'

He smiled and unfolded a map, staring at it for a few moments before he found the town and the road that led to it.

'Do you know where you're going?' she asked as they left the city heading in a slightly different direction.

'I think so.'

'I'm no good at reading maps. I never go anywhere until I've been there a few times on the train. I used to follow the railway lines but a couple of times I ended up in sidings.' She shrugged and then smiled at herself.

He glanced at her briefly. 'Don't say that. Don't ever say you're no good at anything. I bet you could read a map easily, but you've never really needed to and nobody's showed you how.'

'Perhaps you're right.' She felt comfortable then, at ease with herself.

Beyond Dalry he turned onto a side road that crested the hills and then wound lazily over a moor. The landscape seemed to last for ever, the plateau perfectly flat and featureless as if suspended on the edge of the earth.

'Maybe we've taken the wrong road,' she said.

'I don't think so.'

They drove on into the night, chasing the moon.

A flock of sheep was strewn across the track, frozen by the headlights into ragged statues with dazzling eyes. Jack slowed the car, touched the horn until they started and ran. One raced helter-skelter down the road in front of them, searching frantically for safety until he stopped and let it find its way.

After a few miles the plateau suddenly dipped down and she saw the view that Rory and then her father had told her about.

The sea was a mirror-echo of the land, holding the islands suspended as the sky held the stars.

The moon touched the Cumbraes and then grazed the hills of Arran beyond, as if devoured by the mountains before it could yaw west beyond the thrall of the land.

The car engine kicked and died, the stillness broken only by the ticking of the dashboard clock.

Jack opened the door and got out; as Catriona joined him she saw his face in the light of the moon.

'You were right,' he said.

They stood in silence for a while before they spoke at the same time and then stopped, gazing at each other.

He kissed her then, so softly that it felt like a dream at first, becoming real as she tasted the moisture of his lips, felt the incursion of his tongue as he drew her towards him and folded her into his arms.

It could have lasted for ever, would have done if he had not suddenly stopped and let his grip on her relax a little.

She opened her eyes then, saw him occupy all of the world, felt dizzy for a minute as if the earth had stopped spinning around its own axis and was spinning instead around his.

'I'm sorry,' he said, 'I didn't mean to . . .'

'Don't be,' she said, coughing to clear the frog from her throat. 'Don't ever be sorry for being yourself.'

Her sensibility reared then, all of a sudden, and told her with resonant clarity that she had fallen in love.

In the car again she felt shaky, too weak to talk. She looked at Jack, hearing another voice telling her this man was married, he was not hers to have.

Jack sighed, and then drove very slowly towards the coast. Going through Fairlie, he asked where she wanted him to take her.

'Nicolson's,' she said quickly. 'I have a flat above.'

'Oh.'

He came to a stop in the car park just by the side door.

'I . . . I have to see you again,' he began.

'I can't,' she said, opening the door.

'Please?' He gripped her hand.

She struggled just a little and he let her go immediately.

'I have no right to ask,' he said, 'but can I see you when . . . once the marriage's over?'

'Of course,' she said, stepping out of the car.

'Catriona!' he called after her, shattering the calm of the night.

She turned.

'I don't want to lose you,' he said in a softer voice.

She smiled and shook her head, then opened Nicolson's door and closed it behind her before she dared to take a breath.

The memory stayed raw in her mind; Jack Ryan defeated her efforts to try to forget him. In the end she rationed herself to thinking of him for only so long in a day; once that quota was used she determinedly set about thinking of something else.

At first she had expected him to telephone her, or write. When a week passed without either, she began to hope that he might have decided to give her the space she wanted. It was a flash, after all, a sensation only a moment long at the culmination of a pleasant evening; the emotion she felt was not love but perhaps a mixture of affection and empathy that had shifted the anchors of her equilibrium temporarily. As the days went past she began to hope, even believe that was true.

The package came on Monday morning, the address in writing that she did not recognize but knew instantly was his. The letters were small and precisely formed, sloping slightly to the right like the fence stakes of a field plundered by goats. The script was perfect, as legible as newsprint. For a moment she felt impelled to drop it into the wastepaper basket or, better still, back in the post with the information that the addressee had left and her whereabouts were unknown. She picked up a pen and started to write before she realized the deception would never pass the scrutiny of the post office at Largs, that the package would come back like a boomerang.

For a long time she stared at it, before Sheilagh Cameron's footsteps on the stairs reminded her of the passage of time.

Taking the silver letter opener that had been presented to her by the Chamber of Commerce last Christmas, she ripped open the package and a little velvet pouch tumbled out, followed by a book with a letter wrapped around it.

Dearest Catriona,

I would have sent you flowers, but you have so many already and besides anything that I would send would be already dead. I was walking along the street the other evening, thinking of you, as I usually do, and I saw this in the window of a shop. It reminded me of your eyes and the colour of your hair when light shines through it. The book is nothing, I was given it a long time ago and I didn't understand it then. But I do now.

With love from Jack.

She read the letter many times, especially the last line.

She opened the book first. The frontispiece read: *The Collected Works of Christopher Marlowe*; a paper label told her that it was given to Jack Michael Ryan as a prize for an essay when he had been in the sixth form of Fettes College.

She flicked through the pages and found a verse with

words so tender that tears came to her eyes and she could not read any more.

In the pouch was a little brooch, a Deco scroll of silver inset by amber stones with golden strands that glowed softly in the light.

It was a lovely thing, the type of jewellery she might have bought herself if the aching loneliness of her status had not prevented her from doing that.

Carefully she pinned it to the lapel of her jacket and then, changing her mind, at the base of her throat at the neck of her blouse. Then she called Sheilagh in and began the day's work.

Only Maire noticed it; Catriona silenced her with a glance when her mouth opened to ask about it.

The season was ripening to summer again; she was glad because the summer brought visitors, and plenty of work.

She felt light-headed, though, so light-headed that she agreed to let Titch McKillop use her recipe for walnut honey biscuits, and say on the label 'as served at Nicolson's of Largs'.

Jack Ryan came again on a Sunday in July.

Catriona was on the lawn beyond the veranda, reading a book. Allan had already gone back to Glasgow, and Jamie had gone to Largs to play with his friends.

The afternoon was hot, the sky a featureless expanse broken only by the sun; Catriona was unused to the ease of the weekend because for so many years she had worked all the way through it, but now she loved Sundays for the hours she spent at home with her boys, cooking meals for them, washing Jamie's socks and ironing Allan's shirts for the following week. Ellie Simpson sometimes did that, but so did Catriona because, to her, it was a labour of love.

In the drive a car rumbled to a stop against the gravel; turning the page she wondered vaguely who it was, thinking it was too early for Joe and Maire, who sometimes came for tea.

A shadow fell across her and she looked up into Jack's face.

Startled, she rose too quickly and nearly upended her wicker lounger.

'Please,' he said, 'don't get up.'

'How did you know where I lived?'

'Someone at Nicolson's told me. The man at the ice-cream counter. Joe?'

She frowned slightly.

'Catriona, I had to see you.'

She rose, hospitable through habit rather than choice. 'I'll bring you a chair. Would you like a cup of tea?'

'No, please.' He put up a hand to stop her. 'I'll be fine on the grass. But I'd love some lemonade.'

She poured some from the jug into a glass.

'I see you got my note.' His eyes were fixed on the brooch pinned to her chest. She opened her mouth to speak, but he told her to hush. 'I know,' he said, 'or rather, I don't know, but I can guess. And I've no right to ask anything of you, at least not yet.' He paused and drained the lemonade. 'The papers are in court. It should be over by the end of the year, they say. It's a complicated process.'

'I know that.' She had been to the library and looked up the law.

'I wanted you to know what was happening. The papers are in the car, if you want to see them.'

'I believe you, Jack.'

He sighed. 'So I thought, I thought, we could at least have tea now and then. To keep in touch, no more than that. Could we do that?'

'I think so,' she said.

'Thank God. I've driven down every Sunday for weeks. I didn't go in because I didn't want to press you, but then, I thought, the end's in sight. I thought, you had a right to know, if you feel anything like I feel for you.'

Catriona inclined her head slightly. 'I thought I saw your car a couple of times, but when I looked again it was gone. I wondered if I was dreaming.'

'You weren't. Unless you know anyone with a Bentley like mine.'

They smiled at each other.

Suddenly he reached for her and drew her into his arms. She looked at the sky and saw it begin to spin before his face crowded out the sun. Her eyes closed. She tasted his breath, the salt on his tongue; she felt the tweed of his jacket rough against her arm. Her skin began to tremble and sing; her body came alive and responded, she felt her own breath quicken in time with his. She wore only a light silk dress that day, gossamer almost, hardly anything beneath that. She cried out when she felt him glance against her breast, she felt his touch so keenly.

For a moment he paused.

'I love you,' he said, 'I wanted to tell you. I love you. So much.'

'I . . . ' She opened her eyes, blinked, pushed him away.

He looked hurt. 'I got carried away,' he said.

The buttons on her dress had opened; she turned away to do them up, thinking of the spectacle they had made, of Jamie.

'I'm sorry,' Jack said. 'Please look at me.'

Her blood was high; she felt the flush on her cheeks.

'Catriona, I truly didn't mean to do that.'

For a moment she said nothing, then she poured two more glasses of lemonade. 'You see,' she said thickly, 'I have a son, Jamie. He was my sister's, but I brought him up. He'll be back soon.'

He reached out to touch her but she drew away.

'I'll leave,' he said.

'Yes, please. Please do that.'

Watching him go, she wanted to call him back. If not for Jamie, she would have done that; she would not have stopped herself, in fact. She had lost control then, now she was afraid of herself. She ran into the house, up to the cool of her room, where she closed the curtains and cried.

Later, much later, she picked up the phone and called Rory. The phone rang for an age before he answered, but she hung on because she knew that he would.

'Are you busy?' she asked in a tiny voice.

435

'Just the trucks,' he said, 'as usual.'

'I thought with the money you made in America you wouldn't have to worry about broken-down trucks.'

'Aha,' he said, 'but I still do. I still work on them myself, when I have the time. A penance, of sorts, if you like. The prodigal son returns to his yard. The particular truck I'm working on, it's so old, it could be my father.'

'That's impossible,' she said.

'Maybe, but it acts like it.' He cleared his throat. 'Why did you call, Catriona?' His voice was lukewarm, not cold.

'D'you remember the last time you called me?'

'Yes.'

'D'you remember you asked me if I needed you?'

There was a pause. 'Yes,' he said.

'I need you now, Rory.'

'I'll be there in the time it takes me to drive down.'

She waited in the family room, pacing up and down, starting every time she heard a car. When a car door banged shortly afterwards, she ran to the front door and opened it, not thinking that hardly twenty minutes had passed.

Maire stood there, beside Joe's new SS, a car she had bought him when he won the Gold Medal in Paris for his raspberry peach sorbet.

Catriona wilted. 'Jack Ryan came,' she said.

'I know. Joe told me. That's why I drove down.'

'Where's Morag?'

'With her father. He's singing her songs in Italian, probably teaching her every rude word in the world.'

Then went to the kitchen for tea; it was Ellie Simpson's day off.

'Rory's coming,' Catriona said.

'You're in love with Jack.'

'He's married, Maire.'

Maire swore softly to herself. 'Why is Rory coming?'

'Because I asked him to.'

'Don't do it, Catriona.'

'Don't do what?'

They faced each other over the kitchen table until the

kettle squealed. 'I'm not going to see Jack again,' Catriona said as the water bubbled onto the leaves in the pot. 'It's time I made up my row with Rory.'

'You don't love Rory, Triona.'

'I did once. I still do in a way.'

'I think Jack Ryan loves you,' Maire said slowly.

'But he's married, Maire. He says the marriage'll be dissolved, but it won't be for months yet. Or years.'

'It's only a little time,' Maire said, 'you could give him that.'

Catriona shook her head. 'You don't understand, Maire. If I did, and if something went wrong, if it didn't happen, I couldn't bear the pain. It's dangerous, what I feel for him. I can't take the chance.'

Maire opened the kitchen door and let the sunlight tumble in, with the smell of the herbs that Robbie Thompson had planted in the little patch of kitchen garden. There were gulls poised on the wall; she found some stale bread, crumpled it, and threw it to them, watching as they dived and squabbled briefly before each one caught a bit.

She turned back to Catriona. 'You don't sound like my sister when you say things like that.'

Rory came, the sound of his tyres on the gravel like the hissing of snakes. He banged the car door, then bounded up the steps.

She was waiting for him. 'Come in,' she said.

In the living room he looked around. 'It's a nice place you have here, Catriona.'

She went to the kitchen and came back with a bottle of beer. The rays of the setting sun caught his hair and burnished it golden; for a time they sat in silence. Rory got up and looked out of the window, then he turned to her. 'You said you needed me, pet.'

'Oh, Rory, I do. I always did. But now, I no longer think I have the right to ask.'

He said nothing.

She was thinking that she would have loved him, that she

would have married him years ago, if only he had asked. She still would now, if not for what Maire had said, if she did not know that to do so would be a lie.

She did love him, but not like that.

'You could tell me what it is,' he said, 'let me decide that for myself.'

She looked away and began to speak in a very small voice. 'I wish we could go back to the old times, Rory. Way back, in Glasgow, before the war.'

'Why's that?'

She was thinking of the time when she met him, of how he had eased her into the frightening, cold world of the city, how he had carried her across the cobblestones to Maggie Drummond's. She remembered the blur of voices, the terrible noise, her own confusion that made it worse. She remembered the taste of the currants in the scone.

Then she remembered how hurt she had been when she saw his arm slung around Mary McLellan. Mary was married now, with children, so were the others, the women, that is. Most of the island men of her generation were dead.

Her childish love for Rory had surged and faltered; too many things had come in the way. There had been many years when she had been so tied up with other things that she had no time to think of her own future, but she had always thought that he would be a part of it.

Until now, when her whole life had been upended, turned upside-down by a man who had made the same mistake as her father, who had taken the wrong woman to be his wife.

Because she loved him, she had no right to Rory any more.

Rory came over, saw the tears in her eyes. 'I remember too.'

'But you don't, not the same way.'

'I think so, Triona. I loved you then. I still do, in a way. But I realized a while ago that it wouldn't work, not the way I thought it would.'

'Why's that?'

'Because, Catriona, you don't love me. Not like that.'

'But I do, Rory. I do love you.'

He put a finger to her lips. 'In a way, perhaps you do, but not the way I wanted you to.'

I wish to God I could, she thought.

Rory stood up. The beer bottle was empty; she went for another one but when she came back he said he had to drive home, he'd rather have a coffee instead.

In the kitchen, waiting for the water, she told him that Allan was graduating next week, and asked him to come to the ceremony.

'I can't,' he said. 'I got my dates mixed up. I've got a meeting with the council that day. Permission to build a new workshop in the yard.' He grinned. 'But I saw Allan last week. I congratulated him then.'

The coffee drunk, she walked to his car with him.

'Can we be friends, Rory?'

'Yes, pet. We'll always be friends.'

He got into his car and drove off, as the setting sun caught the metal and made it look on fire.

Jamie came in to the kitchen, shaking his head.

'Where've you been?' Catriona asked him.

'Around.'

'Did you see Rory?'

'Only when he was leaving. He said he'd to work on his trucks today. Are you going to marry him?'

She shook her head.

He pursed his lips. 'Oh, well.' She caught the disappointment on his face, and knew then that in his child's way he had been trying to get her to do that for years.

Rory drove through Largs, past Nicolson's with its summer flags and buntings, the restaurant still busy with holiday makers though the day trippers had long gone home. Catriona's face came to him, the mixture of apprehension, hope and determination that had touched him when he first befriended her, her emotions so raw that he felt them himself. Like twin tugs, they had met the tides and the storms, he'd thrown her a line every so often, she had thrown him a line once or twice. More than that, if he was truthful, because she had been his motivation then, the reason he had started his yard and nursed it through the years, not given up when it would have been easier to do that. Left to himself, he would have stayed with the ocean, with the mighty liners and the empty seas; he was happy there, he would have been content.

He stopped the car on a patch of scrub and watched the fragile waves stroke the shore. A dinghy way out was making for land, its sail frilled by the wind. The sailors were amateurs and the sea was being kind to them; the ocean would not let them get away with the diffident way they handled the craft. The ocean would rear up and sweep them away. For a moment he wanted to shout out to them and tell them to use the wind, to trim the sail and hold fast; they would be back in no time if they did that, but he knew that the tide and time would bring them back anyway and his advice might be dismissed as that of a crank.

He smiled to himself and rubbed his chin where the stubble was growing; although he had shaved that morning his skin felt like sandpaper there.

Suddenly he wished that he could reach into the past and grab back the years so that he could have his chance again. She had been his then, so very nearly, she'd have been his for the asking if he'd persisted, coaxed her into accepting him as a lover as well as a friend. He'd been so fraught then, so afraid of rejection that he had coasted along like the dinghy sailors on the forgiving, gentle waves of the bay when she had been the ocean all along. He should have known that. She was his no longer; she loved someone else.

Already a scab had formed over the raw edges of his wound and he knew that if he left it there, if he did not scratch or pick at it, it would flake away and leave a scar that might twinge but would not hurt in the same way it had hurt before. The Atlantic had done that; the knowledge that he still had the instinct to master the ocean, although he had forsaken his love for it many years ago.

As the sun set and the sky turned to indigo and then

violet, he pondered his fate for a time before he looked to the sea again and saw that the dinghy was safely ashore.

'So be it,' he said to himself, as he started the car and began his journey home.

At the graduation ceremony Allan, embarrassed, had his photograph taken with Catriona and Jamie, his cap and gown and the prizes he had won. He had been taken on as an apprentice by Bryce McArthur, the firm that had taken MacKenzie MacLure's place at the top in Glasgow.

Catriona had thought of booking a table at the oyster restaurant Jack had taken her to, but at the last moment changed her mind and made a reservation in the restaurant of the Central Hotel.

Just as they left the university she missed Allan and when she went looking, found him in conversation with a girl. She was slim, very young, with brown hair bundled into a bun and little round glasses set on the tip of her nose. Catriona thought she was plain until she saw her fine bone structure and the soft grey of her eyes.

Allan seemed mortified when she went up to them. 'This is Louise,' he murmured, staring at the ground.

Catriona looked at her and then at him. 'I'm very pleased to meet you,' she said, 'would you like to join us for a meal?'

Louise looked at Allan, who nodded. 'I'd like that,' she said, 'if it's no trouble.'

In the restaurant Louise sat beside her, with Allan and Jamie on the other side.

'We're the wrong way round,' Catriona said to her.

'What?'

'You're supposed to sit a man between two women. That's how they do it at functions in Largs.'

'Oh.' Louise looked ashamed. 'I haven't been to a restaurant before, or only once. Allan took me to one on my birthday.'

'I didn't mean it like that. I wanted to talk to you.'

Louise blushed. 'Really, I ... '

'You're going to be a doctor, Allan tells me.'

44I

'I hope so. It isn't easy sometimes. They keep on saying it's not a job for a woman.'

Allan was staring at her. 'We're going to get married,' he said suddenly. 'Once Louise qualifies.'

'But I'm going to work,' Louise said. 'When our children are at school. I'll volunteer at the child health clinics in the evenings until then.'

'I'll look after the children in the evenings,' Allan said.

Catriona looked from one to the other, realizing they had been planning it for years.

Driving back to Largs, Allan sat beside her. 'Why didn't you tell me?' she asked.

He shrugged. 'I was nervous. I was afraid you wouldn't like her.'

'You could ask her down for a week or two. Have a holiday, almost.'

'I'd like that. I'd like that very much.'

At the height of the Glasgow Fair, when Nicolson's was packed with customers, and more were waiting in the chocolate shop, the phone rang.

Catriona picked it up distractedly, wondering where Sheilagh was until she looked out of the window overlooking the restaurant and saw her helping the waitresses. She had been helping them herself, a moment before, until she remembered that she had to call the coffee merchant to remind him of the extra order she wanted delivered that day.

The line rumbled and hummed, she heard an operator's voice asking her to wait and then another one, softer this time, telling her that the connection was through. She felt a rush of fear when she realized the call was coming from Skye.

Annie's voice broke through the miles. 'I'm so sorry, Catriona,' she said, 'Janet said you're awfully busy these days.'

'It doesn't matter, Annie. What is it?'

'It's Fionn, Catriona. He can't walk. There's something wrong with him. The doctor wants to send him to Inverness for an operation.'

'Is he sick?'

'Not sick. It's his feet. They say he has to go to hospital. I don't know what to do, Catriona.'

The tremor in her friend's voice frightened Catriona; this was Annie, she thought, mother of fifteen, the best mother she had known, apart from her own.

'You see, I don't want to leave Iain.'

Catriona decided quickly. 'Can you wait a day or so?'

'The doctor wants me to take him there on Monday.'

'I'm coming, Annie,' she said, 'I'll drive up today. I'll be there late tonight, or tomorrow morning.'

Jamie came with her to read the map, with Allan's camera, which he had borrowed for the trip. He had never been home, never been to Skye. She had promised to take him often but the time was never right.

During the journey she told him about Annie, how she had been a mother to her and Allan all those years ago.

In the late evening, they reached the Kyle of Lochalsh and caught the last ferry over to Skye. He had been sleeping, but she woke him up for his first glimpse of the Cuillins. Though it was night the sky was pale primrose against the shadowed land, the water a silver mirror that echoed the sleeping hills.

Jamie yawned and looked around. 'Where are we?'

'On the road to Portree. We'll be at The Braes soon.'

He watched the sheep as they stumbled before the car, the winding track that jarred and jolted. As they reached The Braes, an old man doffed his cap at Catriona and she waved to him.

'Who's that?' Jamie asked.

'I can't remember his name,' she said.

The whole village were waiting when she arrived, but knowing of Annie's trouble they did not keep her. Only Sine came in with her; the others left, having seen what they had waited for – Tom Nicolson's daughter driving a car.

Sine hugged Jamie, told him she was his other aunt, and cuffed him playfully when he told her that she looked just like Ailish.

Annie was cradling the boy in her lap, crooning a song. When she heard them come in she put a finger to her lips to indicate that he was on his way to sleep.

'What happened?' Catriona whispered to Sine.

'He's not walking, and he should be. Annie told the nurse, the nurse told the doctor.'

Annie got up slowly and carried Fionn to his cot, behind the curtain.

'I'll just put the kettle on.'

Sine went to the baby, taking Catriona with her. Lifting the blanket, she showed her that Fionn's feet were fixed, as if he was standing on tiptoe, and twisted slightly around the ankles.

'He can't put his feet down on the floor when he tries to walk' she whispered, 'he screams if you try to make him.'

Catriona was looking at Annie, bustling around the fire, wondering why she hadn't noticed when she had had so many children before. As the water heated, Annie stood up and listened for a minute: 'That's him,' she said, 'he's off now.'

Iain was sitting in his chair, carving a pipe from a bit of briar.

Annie picked up the kettle. Catriona, who had watched her so many times before, wondered why she was taking so long about it. Her movements were slow, clumsy almost; when she lifted the kettle to pour water into the pot, some spilled and fizzled onto the grate.

Annie looked up, smiling.

Catriona saw it then, the milky veil over Annie's eyes, the way they seemed unfocused. She knew now why Annie hadn't noticed Fionn's feet before, that she couldn't see him properly because she was near blind herself.

'Shall I take Jamie with us?' Sine asked.

Catriona looked at Jamie, still sleepy after the journey, and nodded.

'You'll be fine with us,' Sine said to him, 'my Peter is just four years younger than you. You can bed down with him, and in the morning your uncle Archie'll take you out lobster fishing.'

Jamie's face brightened and they left.

'Why didn't you tell me, Annie?' Catriona asked softly.

'I only knew since this morning, when I went to town to see the doctor.'

'I didn't mean that,' Catriona said. 'I meant you.'

Annie looked around to Iain, took Catriona's hand and led her outside. 'He doesn't know, Catriona, and I can't tell him.'

'Why not?'

'I've been his eyes too, all these years. If he knew, it'd be like he was blinded again.'

Catriona looked at Annie's hands and saw that they were burned and scalded from cooking, cut because she could not see what she was doing.

'It's not so bad,' Annie said. 'I can still see a bit. I can see light and shade, the difference between night and day. I can manage.'

'What can I do, Annie?'

'Fionn,' she said. 'I can't take him to the hospital, and I can't let him go alone.'

Jack's voice came to Catriona: *'You can make a cripple walk again, make sure a child doesn't limp for the rest of his life.'*

'The doctor was saying that the doctor in Inverness isn't sure he can cure it, that maybe they'll have to send him to the children's hospital in the lowlands.'

'I'll take him, Annie,' Catriona said. 'I'll take him to a good doctor.'

'I'd never forgive myself, pet, not if my stupid eyes stopped him being able to walk.'

'Annie, I have a friend, a doctor at a children's hospital. I'll ask him. He'll help. I'm sure he will.'

Chapter Seventeen

Archie's brother Hamish drove her back to Largs in her car; Jamie had fallen in love with the island and wanted to stay with Sine for the holidays, and she had to care for little Fionn, who slept in her arms.

When she looked up at him she felt the burden of Annie's trust, the weight of her expectations. He woke up from time to time, and his face crumpled into confusion; she sang him Gaelic lullabies and held him close.

He was beginning to talk; before they left Annie had tried to explain to him but he was far too young to understand.

Hamish was a big man, a few years younger than his brother, who worked on the shoots in September and did what he could for the rest of the year. He had lobster pots and a boat; he said he managed fine but you could tell from the hard look on his face that he only just managed to survive.

When they reached Fairlie she thanked him, and tried to push some money into his hands for the boat home. He refused tersely, saying that people were vexed about Annie, vexed about what had happened to little Fionn. The whole village knew she could not see properly, the only people who did not were her husband and the district nurse who was supposed to help look after him.

Allan drove him to Greenock for the boat.

In the morning she went to the doctor's surgery in Largs, to a young doctor called MacDowell who looked at Fionn's feet and hmmed.

'What's the matter?' she asked him.

'It's a club foot. Club feet in fact, the same condition in both but it's not so bad in the left one. It should have been treated at birth.'

Catriona thought of the way babies were born in her village; friends helped, not professionals. Annie had brought many babies into the world apart from her own. After that, for months, babies were wrapped in shawls; the only person who would have seen Fionn's feet was his mother, and if she could not, then no one would.

'They were talking about an operation,' she said carefully.

'It's usually treated with a splint,' Dr MacDowell said, 'that pulls the foot into the right position. It's worn for six months or so and as the child grows, the tendons are stretched. Surgery is risky for a child of this age. I'd rather try the splint first. I'll order them from Glasgow, have them sent down on the train. If you come back this evening, I'll fit them then.'

She walked out into the sunshine, with the child in her arms. He was quiet and as she held him she felt his body tremble.

At Maire's she put him down on the rug with Morag Catriona and let them play together for a while. As Morag toddled, Fionn balanced on his knees and tried to copy her. When he tumbled over, Morag picked him up.

Maire watched him for few minutes when Catriona went to check on Nicolson's; Annie had begged her not to tell Janet, Elsbeth or Peggy, she did not want anyone worrying but for herself.

Walking back to Maire's, Catriona passed the fortune tellers and gypsies on the front. For a while she looked for the one who had prophesied her future, but the old woman wasn't there. The others did not know where she was, but promised a reading and all the luck in the world for sixpence.

Dr MacDowell fitted the splints, strange contraptions of metal and leather straps that made Fionn scream out. As the braces were put on, Fionn stayed silent, but once they were tightened he howled.

'They always do that,' the doctor roared over the wails. 'It takes a week or two for them to get used to it.'

447

Catriona drove round to Maire's. 'This isn't right,' she said, 'no child cries like that if he isn't in agony.'

Fionn's wails cut into Catriona's soul. For a moment she hesitated and then she took the splints off, wincing when she saw the vivid red weals they had made in only a few minutes.

Fionn's cries stopped; he smiled when she hugged him and ate his dinner contentedly.

In the morning she called the children's hospital in Edinburgh and asked for Jack. A secretary answered and said that he was in theatre. Catriona left no message, but said she would call back.

She called again at lunchtime and again in the afternoon. When the secretary told her she expected Mr Ryan to be in his office at five, she tried then, only to be told that he had gone to another hospital to see a child who was too sick to be moved.

'If you leave your name,' the secretary said, 'I'll give him a message.'

Catriona told her it was a personal call. The secretary said she did not know whether he would be back in the hospital that day.

The operator told her there were ten J. Ryans in the city; she tried each one in sequence and spoke to several strangers before she found two that didn't answer and decided that one of those number's must be Jack's. She found Jamie's old cot and put it in her own bedroom so that she could comfort Fionn if he wakened in the night.

Allan had gone to Glasgow to see Louise. Ellie Simpson made her a supper of scrambled eggs and fish that she did not eat. During the evening she listened to the news on the radio as she tried the Edinburgh numbers again and again. At midnight she went to bed.

In the early hours she heard a car on gravel, then a banging at the door, which she ran to answer.

Jack stood there, red-eyed and tired in the light of the moon. 'I didn't want to wake you,' he said, 'but my secretary said someone's been phoning. I thought it might be you.'

'It was,' she said, 'come in.'

In the kitchen she made coffee and asked if he had eaten. He waved aside her concern and asked what was the matter.

She told him briefly, apologizing for disturbing him. When she fetched Fionn, Jack examined his feet so gently that he didn't even wake up.

'You were right about the splints,' he said. 'It's far too late for them to do any good.'

'What, then?'

'He needs an operation, maybe two. In the right leg, his Achilles tendon'll have to be split and lengthened and the tendon in his foot stretched, maybe lengthened as well. In the left, it's not quite so bad. It might be enough for the tendons to be stretched under anaesthesia, or split and left to heal. The right needs a graft.'

'The doctor said an operation would be risky on a child of his age.'

He thought for a moment. 'It's true that there is a risk, but it's the only way to make him walk.'

'What's the risk?'

'Wound infection. A bad reaction to the anaesthetic.'

'What are his chances?'

'With the right surgeon, very good indeed. The anaesthesia will go very slowly, to make sure he's safe. The final risk is that the graft won't knit.'

'What's the chance of that?'

'Catriona, the man who taught me, he's got years of experience of doing grafts. I think he could do it. In fact, I'm sure he could. I'll phone him tomorrow, and you can see him the next day.'

'What's his name?'

'Callum Ferguson.'

She shivered. Briefly, he put his hand over hers, then drew it away.

'I'm sorry,' she said, 'I didn't want to trouble you.'

'It's no trouble, Catriona.'

'Are you hungry?'

He looked at his watch. 'I have to get back to Edinburgh.'

'You could stay here, I have a spare room. And I'd wake you in time.'

His face was pale, there were dark hollows underneath his eyes and deep lines radiated from them. For a moment he looked wistful, then his expression became resolute. 'Better not,' he said, 'the roads are empty now. It'll only take an hour and a half, or so.'

It was two o'clock in the morning. She wanted to tell him she was sorry she had pushed him away, told him to leave last time.

At the door he kissed her forehead fleetingly. 'You look so tired,' she whispered.

He smiled. 'It comes with the job. I can survive it.'

She felt guilty, and wondered if she had asked him to do too much. She wanted to tell him that she loved him, but it wasn't the time.

In the morning she called Allan at Bryce McArthur, to ask if Louise knew of a surgeon who could cure Fionn's feet in Glasgow, or if it was better to take him to the man in Edinburgh. He was sure Louise wouldn't know, because she was only a student, but agreed to ask her anyway.

In the evening he called back. Louise had asked the doctor in the children's clinic where she was volunteering over the summer. That doctor said Callum Ferguson in Edinburgh was the acknowledged expert. Another man from Edinburgh had been mentioned.

'Who's that?' Catriona asked.

'Jack Ryan. He's younger than Ferguson, but he's said to be almost as good.'

She felt her heart leap and dive all at once. When Jack phoned later to tell her that Callum Ferguson could see her either the next afternoon or the following morning, she said she would be there.

'Would you like me to meet your train?' he asked.

'No, no,' she said. 'I'll get a cab.'

*

Edinburgh Castle haunted the skyline, the old fortress as dominant of the landscape as it was of the past. She had never been to the capital before, her only connections that her father had once been gaoled there, and then, years later, Jack.

Fleetingly she looked up from the station and saw the dark castle walls reach towards the sky. Fionn was too young to recognize history.

The surgeon's consulting rooms were in his home in an elegant terrace in the Georgian New Town.

Callum Ferguson seemed a kind man, tall and bespectacled, with grey hair that frayed untidily over his collar. His manner was slightly harried; as she was shown in he rubbed the back of his neck then swept the papers upon his desk into a pile that left room for an empty note pad.

The nurse wore a uniform so stiff that it crackled like a tram. Catriona thought of Carnbrae, where the matron would not let the nurses starch their uniforms because the sound might disturb her patients.

The surgeon put Fionn on a couch and began to examine him. 'Yes, yes,' he said, after a few moments, '*talipes equinus valgus*. It's a rare condition, Miss Nicolson. Sometimes it does not become obvious until the child tries to walk.'

She took the splints, those dreadful contraptions, out of her bag and laid them on his desk.

'It's way too late for a Dennis Browne,' he said.

'Why did the doctor in Largs try to fit them, then?'

He rubbed the back of his neck again. 'It's the textbook treatment, but it only works within months of birth.'

'Can you fix it?'

He looked through his diary, then went through to the other room, where she heard him asking the nurse this and that. 'I can do it first thing on Friday morning, Miss Nicolson. There's a very good private children's nursing home, or at the children's hospital.'

'What's the difference?'

'In the nursing home, you can visit every day. In the hospital, only once a week.'

Friday was two days away.

'But I'd want him admitted today,' he said.

'Why?'

'Tests. To make sure he's healthy otherwise. I'm sure he's fine, but I want to be certain. The anaesthetist has to see him. I need to make sure he's not allergic to the antiseptic.'

He was so matter of fact about it, as if these things happened every day. She told him about Annie and her blindness, how she was the best mother in the world apart from that.

Once she had left Fionn in the nursing home she walked to the station and went home to pack her own bags. The surgeon had told her that Fionn would be in hospital for three, maybe six months. She could see him every day and they had a Gaelic-speaking nurse. She wrote to Annie, saying she had found a doctor who was seeing Fionn on Friday, and promised to phone Annie at four o'clock on Friday, at the post office in Portree. By then the operation would be over, and Annie no more worried than she had to be.

Fionn's operation began at eight o'clock in the morning. When she phoned at midday, from the hotel where she was staying, they told her he was still in surgery, not expected out for another hour or two.

Callum Ferguson called her at half past two to say the operation had been successful; she swallowed her tears of relief and then asked to see Fionn.

'Well, I suppose so,' the surgeon said, 'you're not really meant to on the day of the operation, but I'll leave word with the nurses. If you come quickly, I'll still be here.'

Fionn was a tiny ball of exhaustion, with a huge plaster on his right leg, a bandage on the left. 'That's the graft on his right leg,' the surgeon said. 'I stretched the tendon in the other leg. With exercise, I think that'll be enough to correct it.' He seemed pleased with himself.

Fionn was covered from chest to toe in purple paint. 'The antiseptic,' Ferguson said, 'to make sure he doesn't get infected.'

Fionn opened an eye, looked at her, then closed it again.

'With any luck he'll sleep for most of the next few days,' the doctor said.

'Is he in pain?'

'I don't think so. I've given him as much painkiller as you can safely give a child of that age. Once it wears off, the nurses can give him more. There's a doctor on duty through the night and I'll pop in to see him tomorrow.'

The connection to Skye took a long time. First the line was engaged, then it did not answer for ages; finally the postmistress picked it up, panting: 'Is that you, Catriona? Annie's here waiting. I just made her a cup of tea.'

Annie's voice wavered, then strengthened.

'Are you all right?' Catriona asked.

'Yes. Sine came with me. We had to get some hooks for the men.'

'Annie, Fionn had his operation today. It's over. They say it was a success.'

Annie began to cry. 'Oh, Catriona ... how can I thank you? When can Fionn come home?'

Catriona took a breath. 'Three to six months, Annie.'

'That long?'

'It takes that long for the tendon to heal. Remember, they've to teach him to walk, as well. But you can come down to see him. Sine would bring you, or Archie would. Even Jamie, when he comes home after the holidays.'

Annie was still crying. 'Catriona, I've never been to the lowlands, you know.'

'Annie, don't worry. I'll care for him. If you can wait.'

'Of course I can.'

Afterwards, she felt light-headed, light-hearted, although the sky above the castle was almost as dark as the stone itself.

Jack was waiting outside her hotel, his jacket slung over his shoulder and his collar undone, leaning against the flank of the Bentley.

'Would you like to come for a drive?' he asked.

The roof of the Bentley was down, the wind so strong that it blotted out all sound. In the background the roar was a basso profundo; the top notes teetered around her ears, whipping her hair into fronds.

She looked at him, he sensed her scrutiny and laughed as his hands tightened on the wheel and the car leapt forward, coursing the road like a hare in flight.

At North Berwick her skin tingled and she felt alive, as if she had just walked miles through a storm. He took her hand and led her down to the sands.

'I'm sorry,' she said.

'What on earth for?'

'For Fionn. I didn't mean to trouble you.'

'It was no trouble, Catriona. I'm glad you did. You see, that's my job. Like running Nicolson's is yours.'

She told him about Annie, about how she was blinded now and how much of a friend she had been over the years.

'What are you going to do?' he asked.

'I'll get a room somewhere, stay here until he's better. I can drive home every week. You see, I don't think Annie will come down. She's never been to the lowlands.'

'Her eyes,' he said. 'There's an operation to remove the cataracts. It would mean she could see, but she'd have to wear pebble glasses. Trouble is, it's risky. One slip, and she's blinded for life.'

'I don't think Annie would do it. Not yet, not until Fionn's better.'

They walked to the end of the sands, far away from the crowds, dwindling now in the face of the evening.

'I don't want you to think, Jack . . .' Catriona began, her voice tailing off when she realized the foolishness of what she was about to say.

'Think what?'

She took a breath. 'If I'm here, it's as if, it seems as if we're being thrown together.'

'I don't mind. I've already said that's what I want.'

'It feels like fate, Jack.'

'Well, if it's fate, why fight it?'

Catriona found a flat to rent, just two rooms, a kitchen and bathroom in a house in Morningside. It was a bleak little set of rooms, furnished in oppressive Victoriana, last rented by a university lecturer who had left only some books on geography and isoplethic lines around the enamel bath. The landlady was almost as inhospitable as Mrs Gordon, blaming her tenants for the indignity of having to let out parts of her home.

Catriona did not care, because the place was cheap and clean and quiet; she only wanted a place to sleep and to prepare the simple meals she ate when she was alone.

Jack came to see her often, usually at the end of his working day when she had visited Fionn at the nursing home. She made him tea, a snack sometimes, and apologized for the genteel squalor of her surroundings.

'It doesn't matter to me,' he said.

The landlady bumped into him one day and afterwards told Catriona that it was a rule of the house that male visitors left at a decent hour, though she would prefer that her friend did not visit at all.

More often they went for long walks through Edinburgh, in the Georgian elegance of the New Town, through the winding alleys around the castle and beside the Royal Mile.

'We could be seen together,' she said one evening when he took her hand.

'I don't give a tinker's,' he said, as they walked down the Mound.

'But your wife,' Catriona protested.

'Our marriage has been over for years.'

They walked down Princes Street together, in the shadow of the castle, cocooned by the gloaming of the Edinburgh night.

She felt so close to him then, so proud of him. She had learned things about him, that he was funny and clever and wise and kind, that though he could have gone into the family business he had chosen surgery instead, not because of the money, because he had plenty of that, or the power, but because he loved people, children most of all.

When she asked why he had no children of his own, he said that his wife did not want them, that she was too much of a child herself.

His family were bewildered by him, and in the cloistered world of Edinburgh medicine, where jobs often passed from father to son, he had been an outsider for a long time before he worked his way in. Amelia's father had been chief surgeon at one of the hospitals, he was still an Emeritus Professor, though he rarely operated. Jack said he was a sycophant, good with hospital trustees and the like but only mediocre with patients.

Amelia's father was not the reason for his marriage, he said, rather he had met Amelia just months after his mother died, and thought the fascination he felt for her amounted to love.

She thought of her own father when he said that.

When they reached the house on Morningside Drive, she did not leave him at the door, but asked him in.

'I feel like when I was a student,' he whispered. 'One night we climbed into the nurses' home.'

'What for?'

He winced. 'Matron's underthings. It was rumoured she left them to dry on a radiator. For a trophy, you see.'

She had a bottle of wine, but not a corkscrew. He edged it open with a penknife.

They sat on the floor by the fire. The firelight was forgiving; it made the room homely, despite the scuffed, careless furnishings. He did not touch her; for some reason she felt that he was scared to.

'I've been thinking,' he said, then paused for a moment. 'You see, Catriona, I don't want to have an affair with you.'

She trembled slightly.

'I don't think you want to have an affair with me,' he added.

'Why do you say that?'

'That time in Fairlie, you pushed me away. And when

we're out, you're always looking around, like we're children being naughty and you're afraid we might be seen.'

'It isn't that,' she said. 'In Fairlie, it was Jamie. It was too soon. I was scared of what I felt. Here, it's you.'

'How me?'

'Because a scandal could hurt you, if it got out.'

He shook his head. 'It happens. Everyone knows my marriage is over.'

'Why don't you want to have an affair with me, Jack?'

'Because I want much more than that, Catriona. I want to marry you. I want you to be my wife.'

The flames flickered, sending fleeting shadows over his face. His eyes glittered and held hers, without blinking. 'I mean, I could go down on bended knee and beg you. I could come at dawn and serenade you. I could shower you with diamonds and swathe you in furs. I though I'd ask you first.'

'Oh, yes.'

'I don't know if I could keep you in the style you're accustomed to, but I could keep a roof over your head and the wolves from our door.'

'Oh, no.'

Fear flashed over his face. 'A surgeon's salary isn't a fortune, but you can manage on it. You see, Amelia wants every penny I've got. I'd give her it to get rid of her. Maybe I shouldn't've asked you. Maybe it'll end up you keeping me.'

'Oh, no.'

'I didn't mean it. I wouldn't ask you to do that.'

'Jack.' She held her hand up to stop him. 'I didn't mean I didn't want to marry you. I meant I didn't care about my style, or your money. I'd marry you, whatever happened. I mean that. I said "Yes" long before I ever said "no". You didn't hear me, you silly fool.'

He gathered her into his arms, swept the hair from her forehead. 'Do you mean it?'

'Of course I do.'

'You see,' he said, slowly, 'I saw the lawyers the other

day. They say that Amelia has asked for an income of ten thousand pounds a year. I had offered her twenty-five thousand and the house.'

'That's a fortune, Jack. She can't ask for any more than that.'

'She can ask for whatever she wants, my beloved.'

'But you can't afford it. It's not reasonable.'

He looked sad. 'My grandfather left me a share of the family business. It's worth well over a hundred thousand pounds.'

'The stock market's crashed.'

He shook his head. 'Ryan's hasn't. It's a private company, the shares aren't traded. It owns buildings in Charlotte Square, land in Balerno, whole streets in Leith. You know those signs saying "Lothian Construction"? There's one in Princes Street, now, just along from Jenner's? That's my grandfather's company, the family business. Amelia knows that. She knows how much it's worth.'

For a long time he said nothing more, then kissed her – gently at first, hesitantly until she shifted slightly and let her body begin to melt into his.

The landlady hammered at the door then. When Catriona answered, the woman pointed at the clock in the hall, saying it was past the time she should be entertaining her friend.

Catriona opened her mouth to say that she paid rent enough to do as she chose, but the landlady swept away, indignant.

Jack touched her arm gently. 'It's not worth it,' he said. 'In a few more months it'll all be over.'

In September, when the school year began, Jamie came back from Skye, tanned and healthy. He had come down with Rory in a lorry, but when she asked how Rory was, he gave a noncommittal answer, as if Rory was no longer any of her business.

Six weeks after his operation, Fionn was still in plaster, still frightened. She sensed that he needed her, and told Jamie that.

In her absence Nicolson's had done well, and so had the tearoom. She now paid Zena a manageress's salary, and Joe and Maire shared the profits with her. She was no longer worried to leave them alone; she drove to Largs two or three times a week to check on things.

'Would you like to come to live in Edinburgh until Christmas?' she asked Jamie. 'You could go to school there.'

He looked at her as if she was mad. 'I'd rather stay with Aunt Maire and Joe.'

'Are you angry with me, Jamie?'

He mumbled something about a football game and his friends, shrugging off her comment that his shirt looked as if it could do with a wash.

'He's growing up,' Joe told her later.

'He's only ten,' she said.

'But he's beginning to become a man. Like the bird that leaves the nest. His mother reminds him of the child he was and he wants to leave all that behind.'

She drove back to Edinburgh, feeling mellow until a sense of joy swept over her when, driving in from the west, she saw the cragged outline of the castle against the sky.

On Saturday, after she had visited Fionn, Jack picked her up outside the nursing home and told her, mysteriously, that there was somewhere he wanted to take her.

'Where's that?' she asked, thinking that they had already been everywhere in and around Edinburgh.

'You'll see,' he said, and he would say no more.

Past the soft fields before Peebles, the landscape segued into rolling hills and low valleys that deepened to the velveted folds of the Pentlands. The road ran along the path of a stream for a while, then dove into a forest past Broughton, coming out again to bright sunshine on bracken-tousled slopes.

Jack turned onto a tiny track on the left of the road: 'Where are we going?' she asked again but, again, he only smiled.

The track climbed steeply then dived again, reaching first

a river and then a loch, the landscape so familiar that Catriona found herself thinking of Skye.

'What is it?' he asked, seeing her expression.

'It's like home, a little.'

'Funny, isn't it? You think there's nowhere on earth like Ardnamurchan, or the Mull of Kintyre, or Sgurr Alasdair on a spring evening, but if you look hard enough, you can always find something.'

'There's nowhere quite like home,' she said, smiling.

'You're right,' he said, 'but this is as close as you get within an hour of Edinburgh.'

He had stopped beside a river, swollen with the autumn rains; there was a forest nearby, not a real forest but a wood, the sort where you could just see the light through the trees. Beyond, hills rose towards the sky, grazed with clouds but blue in patches.

'Come,' he said, leading her down a path.

The woodland path was strewn with fallen leaves; wild mushrooms grew beneath the trees and the air was heady with the scent of pine.

'How did you find this place?' she asked.

'I used to come here with my mother when I was a boy; we'd go mushrooming and then I'd try to catch a trout as she made a fire and we cooked lunch in the open air. But I haven't been for years, not since . . .'

His voice tailed off and she knew that he was thinking of his mother's death. He had loved her so much that although she had died years ago, there were still echoes of her in his life, in the car that he cherished and an old, fading picture in his wallet, a steel schoolboy's watch that he kept in the breast pocket of his jacket because, he said, it kept better time than the other one. That was something they shared; when she spoke about her own mother he understood that she still missed Mor, and always would.

'Fifteen years, it must be,' he said, taking her hand. 'I came a couple of weeks ago and it was still the same.'

The track widened into a clearing; she saw the sky again, a little cottage resting amongst the trees.

'What's it called?' she asked. 'This place, I mean.'

'Talla,' he said. 'This is Talla.'

He looked deep into her eyes and then, without saying anything, lifted her up and carried her to the cottage, opening the door with one hand as she laughed.

The door opened into a small room, the proportions familiar to her from the island; there was a big, wide fireplace, two windows on opposite walls, another door that led to a bedroom and one at the back to a kitchen built on as a lean-to.

It had been recently painted, furnished like a room-set from a Wylie and Lochhead advertisement in the soft, muted colours she had chosen for her own house in Fairlie. The fire was set, but not lit; Jack took matches from his pocket and knelt down to see to it.

'Whose is it?' she asked, looking at the bland, unadorned walls, the oak dresser empty of everything except a pair of candlesticks.

Jack blew gently on the flame, waiting until he was sure it had taken before he put a brass guard over the fire, spreading a sheet of newspaper over that.

'It's ours,' he said, 'yours and mine.'

'What do you mean?'

'The title deeds are in both our names,' he said, going to the dresser, taking out some papers and showing her their names along the top. 'This is your copy.'

She smiled slowly, a little bemused.

'Come,' he said, leading her to one of the soft upholstered sofas placed opposite each other beside the fire. 'If you sit down, I'll explain all of it.'

She sat and he sat opposite her, so that he could watch the progress of the fire.

'I used to come to this cottage with my mother. It was abandoned then, and we used to peer inside and wonder who had lived here. I've thought of Talla a lot these months, because it was somewhere I wanted to bring you to; I never felt that about anyone before. In any case, I came down one day when I managed to pinch an hour or two. It was all just as I remembered it. So I went home and started to ask questions. I went to Scrimgeour Johnson, and they discovered who owned the land and so I managed to buy the cottage, for a pittance really, in both our names. Then I had to get it furnished, of course. I wanted you to do that, but I didn't want to spoil the surprise. So I phoned Jenner's and told them the colours you like, what I thought we'd need, and they did it for me. You can change it if you like, you can add bits and pieces to make it a home and not just a house. I want it to be that.'

He paused, and she looked around with a sense of wonder.

The fire was blazing now, the newspaper beginning to scorch, so he whipped it away, crumpled it into a ball and threw it into the flames; then he came and knelt at her feet.

'Catriona,' he said, taking her hands, 'did you ever read that book of poems I sent you?'

'How can you ask that?' She smiled. 'I read it almost every night.'

'You know the one, then: "Come live with me and be my Love, And we will all the pleasures prove"?'

She did not answer; she could not.

'That's what I want,' he said softly, 'if you will.'

'I will,' she said, 'you must know that.'

'It's not all I want, you know that too, but it's enough for the moment, until . . .'

'It's more than that,' she murmured, brushing the hair on top of his head. 'It's everything I've always wanted.'

'It's a promise, if you like.'

She inclined her head in assent, holding his eyes with her own.

He kissed her then, deeply, for longer than before; she pulled away gently and told him what she had wanted to say for months now: 'I'm not a virgin, Jack. I had a lover once, long ago.'

He smiled tenderly. 'I thought that, beloved. No woman who loves like you could stay a virgin for ever.'

Very gently, as they kissed again, he eased off her jacket and undid the buttons at the back of her dress. As she leant back dreamily he slipped off her shoes and traced her silk stockings until he found the suspenders at the top. Deftly, he unlatched them and slid the stockings off and then, taking her hand, drew her down until she knelt beside him on the hearth rug. She smiled, a little shy, still embarrassed by the newness of their intimacy, and reached to undo the buttons of his shirt.

'No,' he whispered, brushing her hand, aside, 'please. Let me.'

He lifted her dress off, sighed when he felt the fluid silk of her underslip. The material melted in his hands, slid off as fluently as water from the feathers of a bird; he unhooked her brassiere, French lace more for appearance' sake than anything else, then gently lifted her hips and soothed her panties off.

She closed her eyes and wrapped her arms around him, feeling his shirt soft against her skin, the scratchy gabardine of his trousers. She slid beneath him as easily as sand slides beneath the waves, her body thrilling to him when she felt his skin as he shrugged off his clothes. His touch was light as the summer breeze as he slowly traced the line of her body; he kissed her mouth, then the tip of her nose, then her eyelids. She trembled, felt hot and cold; his finger rounded the areola of her breast, burning her there. All of a sudden she wanted to touch him too, drew him to her as she felt clumsy and inept, like a virgin should be but much worse.

'I ...'

He kissed behind her ear, the base of her throat, the place where his hand had been then lower, the soft fall of her stomach.

She murmured, then his finger was there, so soft, so warm, parting her as she wanted to be, then a little more. For a moment she felt brazen, until her inhibition faltered and then died. She cried to him and he came to her, she screamed as the pleasure heightened, peaked then began again as if from the beginning. She clung to him, cried like a baby, felt his sweat fall on her and burn in between the rhythm of his body.

It was never ending, charged by electricity like a thunderstorm, without end but only pauses, like the trough between lightning and thunder. In the moments when he subsided she teased him, tormented him gently, felt like a lion tamer as she watched him come alive again.

She was herself no longer, not the prim Miss Nicolson but another woman, wild and free. When she first touched him hesitantly, felt the softness harden in her hand, then bent to taste him as he had tasted her, she looked at him. 'Is this me?' she asked. 'Is it really me?'

'It is,' he said. 'Oh yes, my love, it is.'

When she came back to herself she was resting in his arms in front of a fire that had become a mellow glow. Night seeped in from the cottage windows; hours had passed, she was not quite sure how many. In Jack's arms she was content, as she had never been before, as if she had found what she had been searching for all of her life, or been found herself.

He looked at her face and saw that her eyes were open. 'Are you hungry, precious, cold perhaps?'

'No,' she said quickly, 'Just happy, that's all.'

'There's a bedroom, just through the door, but it will be cold there, I haven't lit the fire.'

'It's perfect here.'

He smiled and shifted slightly. 'Don't move,' she said quickly.

He smiled again. 'My arm's dead, Trina, you've been sleeping on it for ages. It must be ten at night or later, because before that we made love for hours.'

She blushed a little when she thought of it.

'I don't want to move,' she murmured again, 'I don't want to move ever.'

'I'm starving, ravenous. I didn't eat this morning, not a thing. If I don't eat soon, I'll die.'

She got up slowly and draped his shirt around her. 'Is there any food?'

'There was,' he said, 'I had some sent down, but I think the men from Jenner's might've eaten it.' He grinned sheepishly. 'I didn't realize the cottage door was so small. They'd to take all the furniture apart and the door frame off before they could get it in. They'd to get a carpenter down to take the bed apart and put it together again. They were here all of yesterday doing it. They phoned me at the hospital about it, to say they weren't sure they could and would I take responsibility if it got damaged? I told them to do the best they could and to help themselves to the food in the larder.'

Lighting a candle from the fire, she went through into the kitchen and saw a proud new Aga and a larder, empty of everything except a little butter, coffee, tea and a tin of milk. There was wine, though, and liqueurs. She picked up a bottle of claret and a couple of glasses.

'Will this help?' she asked.

'Only for a moment. I feel like a car that's run out of petrol.'

He opened the bottle, drank a little after he had poured her glass, then shook his head vigorously. 'I can't drink any more of that, not on an empty stomach. I'd reel over if I did.'

She went back into the kitchen and put some coffee on.

'I should've told you,' he said, joining her, 'it's primitive here. There's no electricity, gas, no pumped water either, but there's a spring outside.'

The water had come from a jug on the kitchen table; she had expected that. 'It doesn't matter.'

'But don't worry. The stove runs on coal or wood, the roof's sound and there's even an enamel bath if you want to have one.'

'John, the cottage where I was born, it didn't even have an oven.'

He came over and hugged her, nuzzling her neck like a young colt.

'You can't eat me,' she laughed.

'Why not?' he asked, then: 'I've an idea, Trina. There's mushrooms in the woods; I could catch a trout if I'm lucky. Why don't we do that?'

*

465

The wood was lit by moonlight that made skeletal shadows of the trees, cast vascular patterns on the path below. Dressed in an old pair of Jack's trousers held round her narrow waist by a belt, Catriona looked around, listening to the sounds that animals made in the night. An owl whirred past, a squirrel chattered, in the undergrowth an otter swished past, entering the river with hardly a splash. A young deer bolted in fright, her presence only a flash of white and a flurry of leaves. A rabbit, nibbling away at a berry held between its forepaws, glared at the trespassers for a moment before it vanished.

'Here's chanterelles,' Jack said, brushing at the mossy ground, revealing yellow-gold shapes peeking out of the earth like scattered doubloons. 'I don't like them so much,' he said, bending down to pick a handful.

'How'd you know they're not poisonous?' Catriona asked.

He winked. 'Maybe they are. Maybe they're magic mushrooms that'll turn you into a faerie queen or a witch.'

He put the chanterelles in his pocket and led her deeper into the wood. 'I'm looking for *cèpes*,' he said.

'What's that?'

'Big, fat mushrooms. They're a great delicacy in France. My mother took us there on holiday once because she wanted us to see the Corniche and on the way home we stopped in Provence and ate *cèpe* omelette with fresh bread and butter and sharp white wine. I'd never tasted anything like it in my life. It was she who found them here.'

He walked on for a bit, his eyes sweeping the ground. After a time, he suddenly swooped down and cleared some leaves from the ground. 'See?'

The mushroom was bulbous, toffee brown on top with a thick pale stalk veined with white lines. 'A *cèpe*,' he said triumphantly.

'How did you see it?' she asked, laughing at the expression on his face.

'The colour and the texture of the cap. It's like the leaves, but not quite the same. It takes time.'

They wandered on, finding half a dozen more *cèpes*, then

they crossed into a field, scattering sheep, before climbing a dyke at the river's edge. Jack put a finger to his lips and rolled up his shirt sleeves. 'You mustn't frighten them,' he whispered, as he knelt on the riverbank, cautious that his shadow did not fall across the water.

'You're not going to guddle a trout?'

'I am too, why ever not?' he said, as he let his arm drop into the water. 'My native Irish blood sometimes comes out. It was my grandfather who taught me.'

'I thought only my father could do that,' she said, sitting on his jacket beside him.

'Shhh,' he hissed again, 'don't let them know I'm here.'

Hours later, he still had not caught a trout, but they had talked the night away easily.

'You know,' she said, 'I could be pregnant.'

'Would that be such a bad thing?'

She leant back, balancing on her elbows. 'Perhaps not, but it would make things difficult.'

'How d'you mean?'

'Your divorce. It might affect that.'

He winced when she mentioned that. 'I've told you, Catriona, it's not a divorce, it's a dissolution. That means we don't have to go through that torrid stuff about adultery. It makes no difference if you become pregnant. It wouldn't matter if you had triplets, for God's sake.'

'It would matter to them if their father was married to someone else.'

He turned away from the river. 'It would matter to me, too, beloved. But it'd make no difference to us. Not at the end, anyway. If it means anything to you, you could go to Dr Wallace's surgery in Chambers Street.'

'I'd be awfully embarrassed.'

'Don't be daft, Catriona. She's a woman, she's not a moralist. She even takes on working girls, so I've heard.'

There was an eddy on the surface of the river then, he turned to it and let his arm drift until a look of concentration spread over his face, making it as taut as a mask. His eyes narrowed, he held his breath for a moment and then with a cry he lifted a big fat trout from the river, stilling its death throes with a single blow from a rock.

'See,' he said, 'you didn't believe me.'

'But I do,' she assured him. 'Absolutely and implicitly, all of the time.'

He smiled and looked at his watch. 'It's after four, Trina. If we go up to Meggethead, we'll be able to see the dawn.'

Hand in hand they climbed a sloping track until they stood at the top of a low rise that faced Broad Law in the north and looked out towards St Mary's Loch and Ettrick Forest in the east. It was a primeval place, pagan almost, land as far as the eye could see in all directions that bore no trace of man.

Catriona shivered; Jack put his jacket around her shoulders as she looked around.

'Who owns all this?' she asked him.

'I don't know, Trina. It was the fiefdom of the earls of Ettrick and Lauderdale once; I bought the cottage from a farmer who didn't even know he owned it but Johnson found the earl's name on the title deeds, way back. He's the feudal superior, we've to pay him a tithe of a shilling a year or a newborn lamb in lieu of that.' He smiled at the quaintness of the custom. 'I left Johnson a fiver on account and told him to get on with it, so the feu's paid for the next hundred years, my dearest, by which time our grandchildren or maybe their children will've inherited.'

'Will that happen, d'you think?' She had vowed to talk no more about such things, but what he said demanded it.

'I don't think, I know,' he told her. 'In all of my life, I've never been so sure of anything as I am of you.'

The dawn came slowly, an almost imperceptible lightening of the sky at first, a translucence that edged in from the east and made the mist-draped hills glow very faintly, like a street lamp in fog, then a filament of the sun crested the hill and light spread across the earth, making the endless hills strips of gauze on gauze against the misted backdrop of the sky.

468

It was beautiful, so fragile that it took Catriona's breath away. She had seen the sun rise before, but never as tenderly as this.

She watched the landscape develop like a photograph, soft greys at first until contrast came with shadow and shape.

She remembered Liam Devlin then, a brief flash of sorrow as she thought of him on his hill outside Glasgow, a sight she had thought wonderful then that became trivial beside all of this.

Liam hovered for a moment, then his shadow left her life finally; in the years to come she would never think of him again, spontaneously, unless some remembered association brought him to her mind.

'What are you thinking of, precious?'

'Nothing,' she said quickly, 'a man I once loved, or thought I did, that's all.'

'He died, didn't he?'

'How do you know that?'

'Because I doubt you'd ever leave anyone, and I can't imagine a man leaving you.'

'He did die, Jack, but it wasn't love I felt for him, so much as gratitude.'

'Oh,' he said, smiling sadly. 'It was nothing so pure for me.'

'What was it then?'

'Lust, pure and simple.'

They walked back to the cottage together, no longer talking. Catriona cooked the trout and mushrooms, made little wheaten dumplings with some flour she found; he told her it was the best meal he had ever eaten, better even than the omelette in France. Afterwards, once the fire in the bedroom had been lit for a while, they went to bed and slept the sleep that only lovers know; when they thought they were dreaming, they realized that it was wakefulness, dreamlike only because they were together.

In November Fionn's plaster came off, and he took his first faltering steps in the arms of a nurse. At first he cried with the pain because his muscles were so wasted, but then, as the nurse gently exercised them while he lay on the bed, he grinned because he realized that the pain was only fleeting, that if he tried, he could manage to walk.

He took only a few steps at first, and then a few more every day, but Catriona noticed the improvement each time she visited. By the end of a fortnight he could manage to walk the length of the room, if a nurse walked beside him to help.

Callum Ferguson watched him carefully, sharing Fionn's exultation at the progress he made.

'He's so much better,' Catriona said.

The surgeon waited until Fionn had completed another length of the room. 'It'll take a while for the muscles to come back,' he said, 'but they will, in time. I've been thinking, Catriona, I could discharge him in a couple of weeks.'

She looked at him, catching the thoughtful look that came over his face as he considered it. 'You see, though he loves you, I sense he's missing his mother. Fourteen weeks is a long time for a boy who's not even two. But the treatment isn't over. He still needs exercises, and I think the tendon in his left leg could be stretched a little more. It's nearly there, but not quite. He still has difficulty standing flat on his left foot. So I was wondering if I could discharge him for a month over Christmas, then bring him back for another three months in the new year.'

'That would be wonderful,' Catriona said.

'But the problem is his mother. If she can't see properly, she won't be able to take care of him.'

Catriona thought for a moment, then told him that she would give Peggy or Elsbeth the time off, to go to Skye and help Annie to care for him.

'I'm coming down,' Annie said when Catriona told her, 'I'll come down to the lowlands to take him home.' Now that Fionn was better, she could tell the girls and let them at least meet their little brother. They had all left home before he was born.

*

On a Saturday at the end of the month Catriona met Annie and Elsbeth at Waverley Station. Annie was exultant, Elsbeth anxious to go to the nursing home quickly and learn the exercises. She wanted to take the train back that night, if she could.

'She's courting,' Annie whispered.

Fionn leapt into Annie's arms, crying with happiness. 'Ach, little one,' she crooned in Gaelic, 'what's all this? You know I didn't leave you.'

They left him at the nursing home for his final night and took Elsbeth to the station; on Sunday, Catriona would drive Annie to Largs and then Joe was taking them home in his SS.

In Catriona's rooms in Morningside, Annie cried for a while, then dried her eyes. She was dressed in the curious mixture of clothes that islanders always wore to go to the lowlands: a black straw hat from someone's mourning and a beautiful ivory silk Victorian blouse, culled from some Big House where it had been abandoned by a lady, underneath a jacket Catriona had sent Sine and a new tweed skirt that Annie's daughter Kirsty had made for her. To Catriona she looked wonderful, it was only when she saw the curious looks of strangers that she realized Annie looked like a woman from Edwardian times, or even before.

'There's someone I'd like you to meet,' she said diffidently.

'Who?'

'A man. Jack Ryan. I'm going to marry him.'

Annie's mouth curved into the broadest grin.

'He's married,' Catriona said quickly.

'Ach,' Annie said, 'things never come easy for you, pet, do they?'

'But aren't you angry, Annie?'

'Angry, Catriona? Why ever should I be angry with you? I trust you, pet, like I trust no one except Iain. You know the reasons, and if they're right for you, they're right for me.'

'He was very young, Annie.'

'Wasn't that the trouble with your father? The man was nearly fifty, and he still hadn't grown up.'

'Jack's grown up now,' she said, 'You'll see.'

Jack took them to dinner at a little restaurant off the Royal Mile. 'I thought,' he said to Annie, 'if you came all this way you'd like a nice dinner. If you can't see the castle, at least you can say you've had dinner in the shadow of its walls.'

Annie looked around, dimly perceiving the flocked walls and the silver. 'Catriona makes a good meal, you know.'

He smiled. 'I do.'

The waiter brought the menus and he ordered for them all. 'I'm not one for this nonsense,' Annie said, when the waiter brought *paupiettes de sole* so slippery that you had to chase them around the plate.

'I thought it was better than oysters,' Jack said. 'The first time I took Catriona to dinner, I took her to an oyster restaurant. They're considered a great delicacy down here.'

Annie laughed aloud.

'That was before I knew about my little oyster girl here.' He reached for Catriona's hand and squeezed it under the table.

Annie looked from one to the other. 'You're right for her,' she said to Jack. 'You're so right for each other. For God's sake, don't ever let any lowland nonsense draw you apart.'

'I won't,' Jack said gruffly.

The waiter brought a daube of beef, which Annie liked, and a claret, which she said went straight to her head.

She began to talk about her children, all fifteen of them, with twenty-four years between the eldest, Flora, and the youngest, who was Fionn.

Jack listened, fascinated.

She told them how they all grew up and how she got them over their childish aches and pains. She told him about iodine poultices for chests, carrageen for stomachs, and the seaweed bandage that mended even the deepest cut, even Niall's foot when he stood on the blade of a spade.

'Did you stitch it?' Jack asked.

'Lord, no, nobody holds with that. Causes an abscess. The weed cures it, that and time. And God. But you know. You're a doctor.'

'I'm beginning to wonder,' he said, 'if I'll ever know as much as you.'

'I'm only a mother.'

He asked if she ever wished she'd had fewer children. She told him that each one was a gift from God. He shook his head.

As they got up to leave he whispered to Catriona that Annie was the most wonderful woman he had ever met in his life, apart from her.

He took Annie's arm to help her down the step from the doorway, a look of anger passing over his face when a man coming in rudely brushed past. The man, who was older than Jack, said, 'Hello.' Jack merely nodded.

'Who was that?' Catriona asked when they were in the car, Annie in the front seat and her in the little one behind.

'Harry Kyle,' Jack said, 'the great Sir Henry, Professor Emeritus of Surgery. He happens to be Amelia's father as well.'

'I'm going to start a restaurant,' Catriona told Jack a few days later. Fionn had gone home with Annie but she was still in Edinburgh – playing truant, she said, from her life in Largs. She was going home for Christmas, for Jamie's school holidays, but coming back with Fionn in the new year.

'You don't need to,' he said offhandedly.

'But I'd like to. That place we went with Annie. I'm sure I could do just as well.'

'The dissolution'll be through by the end of January. We could be married a few weeks after that.'

She heard a warning bell ring in her head. 'There's Fionn,' she said, 'he's another three months, six perhaps. And then there's afterwards. I don't want to be a kept woman, you see.'

'I was hoping you'd have a baby or two. Three or four. Something like that.'

She smiled. 'I will, Jack. But apart from the hour or two I spend with Fionn, my day's empty. I need to do something with my time.'

'Yes, but, when we're married ... ' His voice tailed off and he looked up from the paper he was reading.

'Don't you see, Jack,' she said, 'if I have a restaurant here, then I have to be here too.'

'Now I understand,' he said, smiling, as he gathered her into his arms.

A few days later she found a building on South Charlotte Street, going cheap because of the slump. She signed the lease and briefed workmen, not spending too much, but just enough to create the ambience she wanted. She wanted to serve the kind of food she had eaten at the Rogano in Glasgow, but with lighter sauces and the kind of elaborate desserts they had perfected at Nicolson's. In Thin's she had found a copy of an Escoffier cookbook with ideas that inspired her own; plenty of good seafish came into the port at Leith and she could get oysters, lobsters, shellfish and game sent down from Skye. If she did, that would mean work for a few of the island men. She remembered Rory's lorries that took coal to the island and often came back empty.

For a long time she hesitated before she called to ask him about it.

'It's only a little,' she said, 'but it would help.'

'It would,' he said, 'I could do it for nothing. They go up and down the road anyway.'

'I'll pay,' she said quickly. 'They'd have to come to Edinburgh.'

'I was thinking of what it would mean back home,' he said, 'isn't that bastard in the Royal Hotel or whatever it's called these days, isn't he still paying sixpence for a gross of oysters, something stupid like that?'

'I don't know,' she said, 'but I'll pay fairly. I always do.'

Just as she was about to put the phone down, he said he had heard she had met someone.

She said that she had.

'Are you happy?'

'Yes, yes, I am.'

'Then I'm glad,' he said sincerely, 'very glad.'

'You must come through for a meal some day,' she said.

'I will, pet. Let me know when it's opening.'

Her restaurant arranged, she spent a final weekend at Talla with Jack and then went home.

On the second day of 1930 Catriona drove down to Talla early in the afternoon. She wanted to have a meal on and the fires lit before Jack arrived. He had been on call at the hospital over the holiday, and had said he might be an hour or two behind her because he had to see his lawyers once he had finished there. 'It's nothing serious,' he said, 'just Johnson fretting again.'

They had not seen each other for two weeks, a period that felt like a lifetime, though she had been with her family and tried to have fun. She had watched Jamie playing football, played games with Morag, and entertained a shy Louise to a dinner with Allan on New Year's Day.

Apart from Annie, only Maire knew the secret of her love affair. Maire was glad when Catriona told her she no longer had any doubts, that Jack's marriage would be over in a week or two. It was only her superstition that prevented her from making plans.

As Catriona turned onto the track to the cottage, she felt as if she was coming home. She was humming a tune when she braked sharply, with the sudden realization that something was wrong.

Jack's car was outside, although the cottage looked empty. For a moment she wondered if he was out hunting mushrooms before she remembered it was far too early in the year for that. Walking to the cottage, she saw that the door was slightly ajar.

Puzzled, she pushed it open before she saw Jack sitting in the cold of the living room, his head cupped in his hands.

He didn't notice her at first, only realized she was there when he heard the door closing.

'What is it?' she asked, 'whatever's wrong?'

His eyes were dark, sunken pools of anger, no longer steely blue but dark grey instead; they were red-rimmed, drawn, as if he had been crying.

He looked at her for a while as if he did not see her; it was only when she knelt at his feet and took his hand in hers that he reacted.

'Catriona,' he said thickly, 'I didn't expect you so early.'

'I wanted to surprise you.'

His face was flushed with pain.

'What's the matter? she asked, her own fear rising, 'what's happened?'

He stood up, rubbing the ache in his back. Because he stood so long at the operating table, he sometimes had a stiff back and when it ached, she rubbed it with Sloane's Liniment or Bay Rum.

'Sit down,' she said, 'I'll make you tea or something.'

'No,' he said, 'I need a drink.'

There was whisky, brandy, drambuie in decanters on the dresser; she went and held up the whisky questioningly and when he nodded, poured a measure.

'Now can you tell me?' she asked again, when he had taken a gulp of it. She had seen him sad before, but never like this: something terrible had happened, she knew, perhaps a child he had treated had died unexpectedly – it couldn't be anything else, he wasn't close enough to anyone but her to be hurt like that.

'Did something happen at the hospital?'

He shook his head vigorously. 'You know me, Trina, it isn't that.'

'What is it then?'

'It's Amelia,' he said, 'it's the dissolution. She's changed her mind. She won't go ahead with it. It's all off. Johnson's just told me.'

Catriona tried to keep the tremor out of her voice. 'She's threatened that before, hasn't she?'

Jack nodded. 'Once or twice.' He hadn't told her, but she had guessed.

'It might be she wants something,' Catriona said slowly.

'No,' he said, 'Johnson offered her about every penny I own. He's tried everything.'

'Oh,' she said. Then, after a while: 'It doesn't matter, Jack. You can get a divorce instead.'

'I've already asked her,' he said bitterly. 'The solicitors have. She won't agree to that either. You see, she's changed her mind about our marriage. She's decided she doesn't want to end it after all. She says she's still in love with me.'

He laughed bitterly, so bitterly that the sound was almost a cry.

Chapter Eighteen

*C*atriona went through to the kitchen, lit the stove, opened cupboards and began preparing a meal.

After a moment Jack came to the kitchen door. 'Come and sit down,' he said, 'we have to talk.'

'You need something to eat,' she said mechanically, 'you haven't eaten all day.'

'There'll be time later,' he said, grasping her arm and leading her back to the living room. The fire was unlit; the room felt cold. She knelt to put a match to the kindling, but he eased her aside, saying he would attend to it. She sat down, trembling. Once the fire was lit he went to the dresser and poured a brandy for her.

'I don't want that,' she said.

'It'll help,' he told her, 'trust me.'

'I did,' she said, bitterly, hating the sound her voice made.

He turned away, arched his back, said nothing for a long time. 'I suppose I deserved that,' he said, once he had poured himself another drink and sat down again. She saw that he put the glass on the side table by the sofa and made no move to drink from it.

The brandy warmed her, loosening the knot in her throat.

Jack reached into his briefcase and handed her two papers. She saw the headings, his wife's name and that of a hospital in the south, and pushed them aside before she could read any more. 'I don't want to see them, Jack.'

'Read them, please. For me.'

'I don't want to.'

'I think you should.'

'No, Jack.'

'Why not?'

'Because I don't want to know any more about Amelia than I already do!'

He sat down and rubbed his eyes. She apologized for shouting. 'You see,' he said, 'the first one said she was hysterical, immature, incapable of making an adult decision, even knowing her own mind. The other says she is perfectly capable, perfectly adult, that there's nothing wrong with her except melancholia because, he says, she's married to me.'

'Has she changed, Jack?'

'Only her doctors. The second one disagrees with the first. But I can't get the dissolution without her consent. I wish to God I could have her certified.'

'You said Amelia wasn't insane.'

'She isn't. She's spoilt, selfish, devious, mean. She's spent most of the last decade saying the worst mistake in her life was to have married me. Now, for some reason, she's changed her mind. Suddenly I'm to blame, and she's utterly blameless.'

'That doesn't change anything. Your marriage is still over.'

He handed her one more letter. 'Not as far as she's concerned, it isn't.'

Catriona read the letter slowly, word by word, then read it again. The letter was from Amelia's lawyer, asking Jack to give the marriage another chance.

Meanwhile, Jack read aloud the doctor's reports, sentences from one that contradicted the other. According to the first, she was hysterical, the second said she suffered from melancholia. One said that the marriage should be dissolved because Amelia did not understand the nature of the vows she had taken and had been the subject of 'undue influence' by her father. The other said she was completely sane, if in a state of despair, and blamed all of her problems on Jack. Her drinking was described as 'an escape mechanism from her troubled life'. Jack read on, then balled up the papers in disgust and tossed them into the hearth.

'Do you see what I mean, Catriona? Catriona?'

She was staring at the fire, at a flame wending its way

towards the chimney, a flame that appeared to die and then came to life again. For a long time she studied the flames, and then she put her head in her hands.

'Please, Catriona, don't cry.'

'I'm not crying,' she said, 'just thinking, that's all. Our dream's over now, Jack, isn't it? Isn't it?'

He gathered her into his arms. 'Our dream will never be over, dearest, not until my dying day.'

'It couldn't be her father, could it? Could he have persuaded her not to go through with it?'

'Ha, Harry Kyle's not in a state to persuade anybody to do anything these days. The old charlatan's in too much trouble himself.'

'Why's that?'

'He was operating on a woman the other day, the Lord Provost's wife, as it happened. He was supposed to be removing her womb because she has fibroids. When he was tying off arteries, he made a mistake and tied off the right renal artery as well. Only God knows how. It's the kind of mistake a houseman wouldn't make, never mind a supposed professor. But he made it and she died in the night. The right kidney was bloodless and the other one failed as well. He killed her, Catriona. It went down as surgical shock but it was Kyle's fault, there's no doubt.'

'Does he know?' she asked quietly. 'I mean, her husband?'

Jack's eyebrows lifted. 'Of course not. I hear they slept in separate houses, only met up at functions. But Kyle's finished, as it were. He'll have to retire. For God's sake, Catriona, don't mention it, though. If it got out, there'd be hell to pay.'

Catriona worked hard at preparing her restaurant in South Charlotte Street; she called it *Slainte*, the Gaelic word for health that is also used as a toast. Although she had started it for fun, almost, she needed it now to use up the empty hours, to soak up the nervous energy that held her in its thrall from the moment she woke to the time, often twenty or more hours later, when she fell into a fragmented, disturbed sleep. Fionn was back in the nursing home, but in April, May at the latest, he would be discharged with his legs healed; she could not leave Edinburgh until then, with its taunts and its hurts, its echoes of love that bounced off the grey stone streets swept by icy winds from the firth. She reminded herself she had taken a year's lease so she had to use it, or waste the money. But once Fionn was out of hospital she could leave it to a manager and go home herself. If she had to wait for Jack, she would rather do it in Largs.

She told him that one weekend, driving back from Talla; he stopped the car and reached for her, his face so raw that she wished she could swallow her words.

'I need you,' he said, holding her so tight she could not see his face. 'I need you so much.'

A lorry passed, its wake brushing the hood of the Bentley. After a moment he let her go.

'Do you want to leave me?' he asked.

She turned away. Her mind felt sometimes as if it had melted, she could no longer think of herself only, she had to think of him as well. 'It wouldn't be for long,' she began, then lifted her eyes and allowed them to meet his. Their souls met, merged in a moment; she touched his chest, felt his brawn under the cotton of his shirt, saw a knot of fine hairs creep out where a button had undone. She did it up and withdrew her hand.

'I don't want to leave you. It isn't that.'

'What is it, then?'

Her silence gave him the answer.

For a time, they sat thinking.

'I have no right to ask you to stay,' he said, 'but that's what I want.'

'Why?'

He rubbed his eyes, sighed. 'Because I'm afraid I might lose you.'

'Jack, you would never lose me. You will never lose me.'

Her hand reached out, met his, and found his gentle fingers, the touch so sure and deft.

'I'll stay,' she said.

He drove back single-handed, only letting hers go when he had to change gears.

She began the decoration of *Slainte*, nonchalant at first, with no clear idea of what she wanted, only to avoid rococo, gilt and flock. She had the walls stripped and painted a shade of pale grey, and laid a carpet in a darker shade. The lighting was harsh, so she had wall lamps fitted. Miss Cranston had retired years before, and she heard that Coopers were taking over the remnants of her business and selling the contents of her store. Driving to Glasgow, she discovered four dozen Macintosh chairs, broken, which she had repaired and polished. For the larger tables at the back of the room she bought simple oak carvers. She covered the tables with white linen clothes, set with ivory-handled cutlery and a Wemyss Ware service. For the empty walls she bought some paintings by an artist called Peploe, with colours so real that the images almost jumped out of the frames. She put a jug in the centre of each table, filled with flowers that picked up the tones of the pottery. There was a majestic old fireplace, in which she burned pine. The effect was of the countryside, a country house, perhaps.

Jack loved it.

Catriona knew then that she had not been thinking of her customers, but of the home she would like to make for him.

Slainte opened in February, serving seafood from the island, oysters and lobsters, baked mussels, also salmon and game; spring lamb and beef she bought in Edinburgh. She kept the main courses simple, the food very fresh and garnished with sauces that did not mask the taste; for desserts she served the rich fantasies that Nicolson's had become famous for. The restaurant's success surprised her at first; she had not expected it to become popular so fast. It didn't matter about the prices she charged, or that customers had sometimes to wait in the cocktail bar for a table; she had tapped the spirit of the age, which was beginning to recognize the difference between fashion and style.

The Scotsman, the haughty Edinburgh daily, ran a review which read, in part: 'Here is a restaurant that presents our native produce, superbly cooked so skilfully that the heavy sauces and embellishments of France would be a profligate excess. *Slainte* is a culinary masterpiece. Those who dismissed Miss Nicolson as proprietrix of a seaside cafe, the worthy if rather pedestrian successor to the renowned Miss Cranston, dismissed a lady who is one of the most accomplished and innovative restaurateurs of the day.'

After the review appeared *Slainte* was booked solid for a month ahead; the flood of reservations that followed inspired her to clear the basement and so double the number of tables, and to make up for the implied insult of asking her clients to dine downstairs, she installed a trio of musicians to play the ragtime music she had first heard on the sidewalks of Coney Island.

'I wish,' Jack said one day, 'that you weren't quite as busy as you are.' It was late in the evening; he always joined her for supper after the restaurant closed, but sometimes had to wait for hours.

'Don't you realize I have to be?' she replied. 'If I sat at home and thought all day, I'd go mad instead.'

'You'd never go mad,' he said.

Catriona turned away from him. 'Maybe I am mad. Maybe you're mad too. Maybe we were both mad to think that you'd get your annulment and live happily ever after.'

'Don't say that. For God's sake, don't ever say that.'

'It's true, isn't it?'

He followed her, eased her around until her eyes met his. 'I love you, Catriona. I love you more than I thought possible. I cannot, could not live without you. You love me too, don't you? Don't you?'

She told him that she did.

'Well, it makes no difference then. No matter what Amelia does, we'll be divorced eventually, and then I'll marry you. It changes nothing.'

'But it does,' she argued. 'She could make it last for ever. The scandal could ruin your career.'

'The only thing that could hurt my career, beloved, is if I lost you.'

Since Amelia had left the hospital he had moved out of the elegant Georgian house in the New Town which he had shared with her and into a tiny flat off the Lothian Road, not far from Catriona's lodgings in Morningside. He begged her to live with him openly, to forego the week-long separations between the precious hours they shared at Talla, but Catriona's sensibilities, and also her sense, would not allow her to do that. If Jack, devoted to his work to such an extent that he was oblivious to the mores of society, did not understand how divorce could crucify even the most brilliant career, she did.

Amelia came to *Slainte* one lunchtime; it was an early spring day with the sun bouncing off the pavements, the kind of day when sensible people stayed out of doors.

She sat at a side table with two women friends; the restaurant was busy with a brace of Court of Session judges, a duke, and the chairman of the board of the Bank of Scotland, so Catriona did not notice the trio until the other diners began to leave after two o'clock.

The women's voices were affected, high, their laughter forced and tinselly. Catriona had felt an atmosphere since lunch had started; she realized why much later, when she felt eyes drilling through her and saw Amelia's chiselled features, as cold and sharp as ice. Their eyes met for a moment; Catriona turned away first because she was talking to a businessman who wanted her recipe for lemon trout for his cook. Distractedly she took a pen and scribbled the recipe, telling him to ask his cook to phone her if it wasn't clear. The businessman thanked her and paid his bill, leaving a generous tip. Meantime, Amelia had hailed a waiter and ordered another bottle of chilled Chablis. Catriona caught the waiter *en route* and hissed that it was already past closing time, but he checked his watch and said there was a minute or two still to go. She went through to the kitchen and wilted in the steamy heat, listening to the noxious racket of Amelia's chatter long after all other customers had left.

It was her habit to talk to her guests after their meal, to make sure they had enjoyed it and offer another coffee, a liqueur or perhaps a *petit four*. Usually, it was to her that the bill was paid, though sometimes the maitre d' or a waiter took the money if she was otherwise engaged. She was determined not to talk to Amelia, not to allow her the condescension of giving money to her.

The maitre d' came through to the kitchen, looking askance at her when he saw that she was doggedly slicing fruit for a *confit* to go with the wild duck on the dinner menu.

'There's a table still on lunch,' he said.

'I know,' she replied, 'see to them, will you? I haven't time.'

Raising his eyebrows, he went through to the restaurant, coming back a while later and muttering about the lack of a tip.

That evening, when Jack came for supper after *Slainte* had closed, she stayed away from him even after all the staff had gone and they were left alone.

'What's the matter?' he asked as she began to roll napkins into rings and stack them ready for the following day.

'I've been thinking,' she said, 'perhaps you shouldn't come here.'

'Why ever not? I like to make sure you're home safely. You know that.'

'My own car's outside.'

He smiled. 'That's even more reason to take you in mine.' Her old Morris had become a joke between them, his scepticism of its mechanics matched only by her refusal to buy a new one because of her stubborn loyalty to the car that had served her for all these years. The engine coughed, the gears groaned and the brakes creaked, the whole machine threatened terminal collapse, particularly on cold days when the starter handle had to be turned for five minutes or longer before the old engine finally fizzled and sparked into life of a sort.

'Catriona,' he asked again, when he saw her tightly pursed lips, the absence of the smile he had expected, 'what on earth's happened?'

'Amelia was here today.'

He said nothing for a long time, then just, 'Oh.'

'Is that all?' she said, putting the napkins away and joining him at the table. 'Jack, she knows about us.'

'What makes you think that?'

'The way she looked at me.'

He rubbed his eyes, lifted the cup and drained the last of his coffee. 'Catriona, it's no big secret. She had to find out some time.'

'Jack . . .'

'Catriona, I was married to her for nearly fifteen years. Sham though it was, she knows me well enough to realize it's over. She must have left me fifty times over the years, again and again, and I was always there when she came back. Going to hospital was just another way of leaving me. But now I've left her, I've hurt her pride and she'll look around to find out why. It doesn't take a genius.'

'What d'you mean by that?'

He sighed deeply; tiredness was ingrained on his face. Jack started at the hospital at six thirty in the morning and stayed until the last of his patients had recovered from surgery; he often remained there late into the evening to talk to the nurses and the house doctor and worried patients. *Slainte* did not close until eleven and sometimes later; she often told him not to wait, that she would take a cab, but he insisted and she allowed him that because these moments at the end of the day were so precious. He told her he could cope with little sleep, that doctors learned to do without it at the same time as they learned their skills, but sometimes at Talla he was so tired that he would fall into bed and sleep the clock round.

She saw his tiredness and felt sympathy because of it, but stemmed the impulse to tell him that they would talk another time. The subject was too important to be put off.

'You remember,' he said, 'that day I first met you.'

'When your car hood wouldn't close and you couldn't drive home through the rain?'

He smiled and touched her hand. 'No, precious. Before that. When I was with Amelia and she made such a fuss that you came over to see what the matter was?'

'I remember.'

'Well, I've a habit of watching women. Or I *had* a habit of watching women until I met you. It's something most men do. It used to drive Amelia mad. I watched you that day, after you left us. It was when your father came and he was just an old man in not very good clothes and you ran to him and treated him like a king. I watched you, not just because you were a woman but because of the woman you were. Amelia noticed that.

'We started rowing that evening; we had never stopped, but there had been a truce of sorts, I can't remember why. Amelia said she knew I wanted you; she could be very perceptive that way. In any case, we went on rowing all week, even after we got back here. She went into hospital a couple of days later, claiming hysterics. I went to see her once, but her doctor said it would be better if I didn't. She was away for nearly two years, and when she comes back you're here. It doesn't take a genius to work it out.'

'Come on,' Catriona said, taking the jacket he had slung around the chair and placing it over his shoulders. 'We must get home, and you need some sleep.'

'It won't always be like this,' he said as he parked outside her lodging house, letting the engine idle as he kissed her gently on the brow. 'Soon, when I come home at night I'll come to you, and we'll never again have to part at the end of the day, I won't have to watch you walking away like a stranger.'

'I know,' she murmured, kissing him gently, touching the shadows under his eyes with the hope that she could ease his fatigue. 'I love you, Jack Ryan. I love you very, very much.'

'As I love you,' he said.

A couple of days later, when she walked to *Slainte* in the morning, there was a shiny new Armstrong-Siddeley waiting for her, with a note that read: 'If you insist on driving yourself, my love, at least in this you'll be safe.'

When Fionn was discharged from the nursing home, Catriona went to Fairlie for a couple of days; Janet and Elsbeth were taking him from there to Skye.

Her life was so full with Jack and *Slainte* that her other concerns had faded; she no longer worried about Allan at all and only a little about Jamie and her businesses in Largs. Allan and Louise sometimes came to see her for dinner on Friday evenings; Jamie had been once or twice on the train by himself. She had offered to drive him but he insisted that he was old enough. She felt a pang of regret when she realized that Joe was right: Jamie was growing up.

In Largs she asked Maire and Joe to come to a meeting, with Zena as well, at Nicolson's.

'I've been thinking,' she said, as she looked from one to the other, 'we've had a good year.'

Joe sighed.

'That was a good bonus you gave us,' Zena said. Catriona knew she was unsure why she was there.

'I've hardly been here myself,' she went on, 'but you know that. At first, I was scared the place would collapse, but it hasn't.'

She took papers from her briefcase, and went on quickly, 'I've turned Nicolson's of Largs into a limited company. These are shares, ten percent for each of you. I'll keep fifty, and Jamie and Allan have ten each.'

Zena didn't understand at first. 'But, Missus, Catriona, you always paid a good wage.'

'Yes, but your work's been more than good, Zena, especially since I've been away.'

Maire was gazing at her. 'Why, Catriona?'

'You know I've always thought of Nicolson's as mine. I realized over the last few months that it's yours as well. You've worked for it as much as I did. I thought it was the right thing to do.'

It was something Jack had said, something about the

morality of having money in the bank. He'd had money all of his life and had never thought of it until the depression, until hollow-jawed men formed long lines outside Employment Offices and children and women begged in the streets. Then he felt he had no right to it, he had not earned it, after all. If, all of a sudden, it wasn't there, he said he would not miss it. She told him that was wrong. He disagreed. 'If you have wealth,' he said, 'You have a duty to use it.'

Once upon a time she had thought that when she married Jack, she would sell Nicolson's, but then decided she could not do that, either. It had been a part of her life so long, she could not bear to lose it. If she did it this way she was making a gesture of faith in her future with Jack and also in the people who had helped her, the people who meant almost as much to her as he did.

'What about Etta?' Maire asked. She was thoughtful, fair-minded as always.

'Etta tells me she's getting married this year.' Catriona smiled. 'So I'm giving her a bonus, and her job back if she ever wants it. I'm keeping the Rose Tearoom, and Janet is going to look after it.'

Zena was stunned, almost crying. 'Oh, Catriona,' she said, 'when you were away all this time, I was that feart you would sell it.'

'Never,' Catriona said, 'I would never do that.'

'On the way back to Edinburgh she drove too fast, slowing down only when she narrowly missed a milk cart, feeling the familiar thrill when she saw the castle rising towards the sky and felt again Jack's closeness.

Allan came on Friday for dinner, without Louise, who had just qualified as a doctor and was in the thick of her house jobs. Catriona had asked him to come then because she wanted to give him his shares; she realized that something else was on his mind only after they had finished the meal and were drinking coffee in the living room that now made her feel as if she was staying in a museum.

'I must get somewhere decent to live,' she said as she

poured the coffee; normally he would have picked up a remark like that instantly, but now he just nodded.

'What is it?' she asked, once he had fended a couple of things she said with noncommittal grunts.

He thought for a moment. 'I'm leaving Bryce McArthur,' he said. 'I'm going to become an advocate instead.'

'Why's that?'

'It's the sharp end of the law,' he said, 'court work. Being a solicitor's like being a fairground spieler. You get the punters and take their money, somebody else does the work. And Bryce McArthur's commercial law. Contracts and tax, company formation, a little litigation. That's not what the law's for, Triona. The law's for people.'

She thought for a moment, hearing an echo of her father.

'I'm going out on my own. I'm going to do civil law, personal injury claims, maybe some work with the unions. I'll never make a fortune, Catriona, but I'll be doing what I believe in.'

'What does Louise say?'

'She's right behind me. I couldn't do it without her. She'll be paying the bills when I'm a pupil.' He laughed then and said he really didn't mean it, he had enough saved to see him through. 'What do you think?'

'I'm proud of you, but I always was.'

'That's not the only thing,' he said, serious again.

'What is it?'

'The Freemasons, Catriona. Ever heard of them?'

'Not really.' The phrase was vaguely familiar, no more than that.

'It's like a secret society, like a boys' club but for men. A lot of lawyers are in it, with politicians, landlords and the like. In the law, everybody's in it, just about. The law lords, most of the sheriffs, all the KCs. They shake hands a certain way and there's a ring Masons wear, most of them, a signet ring with a set of dividers over the scales of justice. Just about every judge I've met wears one of those.'

Catriona thought of MacKenzie suddenly, remembered the way he had stared at his ring when he told her she would never become a lawyer even if she passed her exams, and knew then what the power was she had sensed all along, the hidden consensus that governed the law.

'I see,' she said.

'They've asked me to join.'

'Do you want to join them, Allan?'

He put down his cup and began to pace the claustrophobic little room. 'Like I said, it's a secret society. There's all sorts of rules you have to obey, and the biggest one's its secrecy. You must never reveal what goes on in a meeting, no matter what it is. All sorts of things happen. KC s talk to judges, to opposing counsel. More cases are decided in the Lodge than in the Court of Session.'

'When I worked at MacKenzie's, a lot of cases were decided over the lunch bar at Lang's.'

'Catriona, for God's sake!' he exclaimed, exasperated. 'The law is meant to be impartial; Freemasonry is corrupt.'

'There's corruption in everything, Allan. Didn't you realize that?'

'No.' He sat down, looking very young suddenly. 'I knew the courts were old-fashioned, atavistic even. There's a lot of self-interest, cap-tipping to the gentry, things like that. Men aren't equal before the law because the law costs money. But I thought the general principle was there and we all agreed to it. I didn't realize that a man could get away with killing his wife because he and the judge on the case are in the same lodge. Oh, God.' He put his head in his hands. 'For God's sake, Catriona, forget I told you that.'

She remembered the case from the papers, the acquittal more startling than the trial itself. 'I think people guessed there was something wrong anyway.'

'But I was at the meeting, Catriona. I went through interest. It was the first time I'd been. I had a few drinks, that's all. I saw two men talking. I didn't realize they were the judge and the defendant until I read the trial report.'

She went to the window and closed it, though the house was set far back from the road. 'Are you going to join them, Allan, or have you joined already?'

491

'I haven't joined, Catriona. I won't.'

'Don't, then. Don't join them.'

'But I'm an officer of the court, Catriona. Under the court rules I should report the judge.'

She thought for a long time. 'Don't do that, either.'

'What *do* I do, Triona?'

'All you can do is forget about it. If you did anything, they'd deny it, they and all the others who were there. Forget it and don't fret about it.'

'A man got away with murder. That's the power they have.'

She shivered. 'Allan, I'm sorry. That's the only advice I can give you. If you want to report it, I'll back you all the way, but it'd make no difference. I'm sure it wouldn't.'

He smiled bitterly. 'I'm going to the bar, Catriona. I'll be the best bloody advocate this country's ever seen, but if I don't make the bench, it won't be because of my ability. It'll be because I won't join their stupid club.'

When he left he thanked her, saying that he couldn't have told anyone else, even Louise.

She was left with the feeling that she had not helped.

She was checking the wine bills a few days later when the maitre d' told her that one of the lunch guests had asked to see her.

'Do you know why?' she asked, a quarter of the way through a ten-page invoice that totalled nearly £400. She had already gone around each table and made sure everyone was happy.

'He didn't say, Ma'am, but I could ask him, if you like.'

Catriona noted a sub total and put the bill aside to be checked later. 'You'd better not,' she said, 'I'll go and see what he wants.'

The maitre d' pointed to an older man with steel-grey hair and the vivid features of a dedicated gourmand; he was marginally familiar to Catriona, but no more than that.

'How can I help you?' she asked, wondering where all his guests had gone because there had been five others at the table with him. 'I hope the meal was to your liking.'

'The meal was excellent as always,' he said, 'but I rather hoped that I could have a moment to discuss a personal matter with you. Is there anywhere a little more private?'

'Whatever you want to say can be said here,' she replied firmly, wondering if he was going to make a proposition of the sort she'd had with depressing frequency since she had opened *Slainte*.

'Why don't you sit down?' he said, indicating an empty chair but not rising to help her.

Catriona remained standing until he stood perfunctorily, bobbing his head.

'You can help yourself to some wine. I think there's a glass left in the bottle.'

She ignored him and folded her hands on the table, poised to listen to whatever he had to say.

'I'm Henry Harrison Kyle,' he said, as if she should recognize the name instantly. A moment passed before she did.

'Yes,' he said, 'you do know who I am. That said, we can do without further formalities. My daughter tells me you are having an affair with her husband, and I must say that your rather sordid little tryst is the gossip of all the city hospitals, even my own.'

'I'm not having an affair with anyone,' she said tersely, remembering what Jack had said at Talla, that their relationship was more than that.

'So be it.' He waved his hand dismissively. 'Whatever you call it, you do not deny a degree of acquaintance with him.'

She said nothing.

'Amelia is most distressed about it. He's had affairs before, but never so blatantly. I take it he's decamped and left her stranded. Amelia tells me he wants a divorce and I agree that it would be the best thing in the circumstances, but there's divorce and there's utter social humiliation. What Amelia is being put through is the latter and I will most certainly not stand by meekly whilst my daughter is made a female cuckold. Do I make myself clear, *Miss* Nicolson?'

There was a horrible emphasis to the Miss.

'I'm afraid you don't, Mr Harrison Kyle,' she said evenly, trying to play for time.

'Come, come, Miss Nicolson. Though you appear a mere maid, you must be in your thirties, and you must know what I mean.'

'I'm sorry, but I don't,' she said, as calmly as she could.

'Very well, I'll spell it out to you. If this marriage is to terminate, then it is to terminate in the manner that will cause least pain to my daughter. She is of a nervous disposition and she cannot take the humiliation that Jack Ryan is subjecting her to at the moment. There are ways of doing these things and I can guarantee you that Ryan will not get the divorce you want by flaunting this sordid little affair so much that Amelia is forced to cite his adultery and you as co-respondent.'

'Mr Harrison Kyle,' Catriona interrupted, 'as I've said, you're making far too many assumptions.'

'You're the one who's making assumptions,' he spat, decorum lapsing as he reached to pour himself another armagnac from the bottle the waiter had left on the table. 'Amelia refuses utterly to even consider divorcing Jack on the grounds of adultery. She is the one who would have to raise the action and she refuses to do so. *Ergo*, no divorce, no matter how long your little dalliance lasts. The pair of you could have senile dementia and Amelia would still be Jack's wife and you would still have the legal status of a streetwalker. Do I make myself clear?'

Catriona caught a glimpse of the ring on his finger, saw the dividers superimposed upon the scales. The fuse of her temper lit then, began to fizzle and flare as she took a breath and urged herself to stay calm. 'As I've said, Mr Harrison Kyle, you are not making yourself entirely clear.'

He finished the brandy in one swallow, winced and put the crystal glass down on the table so hard that it cracked. 'Well, *Miss* Nicolson, let me spell it out. Young Jack Ryan is a fine surgeon who's done well for himself so far, but he won't go much further without the good grace of his elders, and he's liable to lose that if he continues as he does.'

'How dare you,' she said, very quietly. 'How dare you come into my restaurant and make threats?'

'Oh, I dare, I can assure you of that. You take my word, Miss Nicolson. This dalliance goes on a moment longer, and Ryan'll be out of a job.'

He made a move to leave, but she stopped him, then poured him another armagnac.

'Aha,' he said, 'I see you've decided to be sensible. I could do that, you know. I could put Ryan out of his job.'

'I thought you were retired,' she said sweetly.

'Semi-retired. I am on the hospital management board, also the board of the College and the General Medical Council.'

She drew breath for a moment, thinking that she'd had enough threats from him, that she wasn't scared of his titles, or silly clubs, come to that. Freemasonry was not so strong in medicine; she had asked Jack and he told her that.

He became amicable all of a sudden and patted her hand, too sure of himself to see her repugnance. 'Don't worry, my dear. I'm quite happy to make up any financial loss you might have. You're a businesswoman, after all. You know that, really, you have no choice.'

'You have no choice either,' she said, so quietly that he had to lean across the table to hear her.

'What did you say?' he asked, far too loud.

'I said, you've no choice either, *Mister* Harrison Kyle. Your daughter is a drunk, and everybody knows it. She's had affairs, and everybody knows that too. She's cuckolded him twenty times or more. She's deranged ...'

'I beg your pardon, Miss Nicolson!'

Catriona held her hand up. 'She was in the hospital, what's it called? The one in Dumfries? According to them, she's got just about every neurosis in the book. And as for you and your string of offices, I wonder just how long they'd all last if anyone found out about the Lord Provost's wife? I don't mean anyone, because of course your colleagues already know, don't they? That's why you've got all these positions and titles, so you won't have time to operate any more, because Sweeney Todd was a better surgeon than you are. Your mistakes are too embarrassing to admit in public, so you get kicked upstairs with a nice little sinecure like an old horse gets put out to grass. But it won't last, Mr Kyle, not for a moment, not if I told the Lord Provost how his wife died and he started asking the questions someone should've asked long ago. Do I make myself clear, *Mister* Harrison Kyle?'

If he had been flushed before, he was crimson now, his temple flayed by a blood vessel throbbing much faster that his sclerotic arteries were comfortable with.

'You wouldn't do it,' he reasoned, 'you couldn't. There wasn't an autopsy.'

'He could always have the body exhumed.'

'It would have decomposed.'

'Pathologists can do wonders these days. I wouldn't take the risk.'

He went pale then, and tugged at the tablecloth. 'You're nothing, a little girl, that's all. A cook. Nobody would listen.'

'Just try me,' she said, 'just make one more threat against Jack, say one word against him – because I'll find out. You know that. Just a whisper, Mr Harrison Kyle, and I'll go to the Lord Provost *and* the board of management and the papers, and tell them as well.'

Somehow, he regained his composure and reached for his wallet. 'I haven't paid the bill.'

Catriona shook her head. 'Please don't bother. I would rather you did not come again.'

His expression was childlike in its hurt. 'My God. You're not blackballing me, are you?'

'Nothing like that. It's just I prefer to have customers that I can treat as friends.'

She held the door open and watched him walk down towards Princes Street. As he reached the main thoroughfare he seemed to think for a moment, and then revive somehow, because when he walked on there was a noticeable spring in his step.

Catriona, worried, wondered whether she had gone too far, but realized she would never know. Medicine was too good at keeping secrets; if Harrison Kyle was as devious as he seemed, he could do something to hurt Jack in such a way that she would never find out.

And she couldn't tell Jack either, because she had broken a confidence of sorts.

As spring became summer and the sun shone relentlessly on the city streets she began to yearn for the autumn, to feel the breeze again. There was no wind in the city, the days passed lethargically as if time itself was slowing down. Five months had elapsed, and Jack was still no nearer his divorce.

In the middle of June she drove down to Talla on a weekday afternoon and walked through the woods in search of wild mushrooms. The country air was fresh and cool by the river; there had been a squall of rain earlier, so slight that she had not felt it in the city but it made the trees damp and as she walked the heavy branches touched her face and she felt the moisture on the leaves. In the open spaces she could breathe again and feel at peace with herself.

The *cèpes* needed rain, she knew that, more than there had been; there were only a few little ones, as plump and lush as baby piglets. She picked some, but left most to grow and drop their spores on the ground. She had found a book on the French countryside that told how to dry wild mushrooms, or preserve them in wine vinegar; she wanted to gather enough to use through the winter to flavour stocks and sauces. She had known almost nothing about haute cuisine when she started *Slainte*, but she was an expert now, she had become fascinated by the art of food, by the work of Escoffier and the continental masters. Sometimes, on Saturday nights, she would try out new ideas for Jack, the light, airy sauces that she favoured and then a hopelessly rich, elaborate pudding so full of sugar it would give him all the energy he needed for the coming week. As time went by, and the lawyers achieved nothing more than a growing pile of paper, she began to long for the time when it would all be at an end and they could marry and get on with their lives. She wanted to be able to make his dinner every day, to be there for him in the evening when he came home from the hospital, the desire so mundane that it made her smile at herself. In her life Catriona had defied convention and it was strange now to want nothing more than the most normal desire any woman can have. Jack was impatient with society, he would have abandoned the facade of separation and lived openly with her; she would not do that because she feared the wrath of the establishment that she had so often seen in the past.

A woman like Amelia could sin repeatedly and be forgiven; a woman like Catriona could not sin at all.

She reached the cottage all of a sudden, as the clearing in the trees let in the sunlight again; Jack's car was parked there, beside hers, the engine still warm and giving off heat waves that rippled the air.

With a whoop of joy she fell into his arms.

'How?' she asked, a moment later, once he had noticed the *cèpes* and begged her to make an omelette for his tea.

'I had to go to a meeting about the new hospital,' he said, 'it was so tedious that I sneaked out to phone Sandra and she phoned me twenty minutes later so I could make an excuse about a patient and get away.' He grinned. 'But, not to worry, Fergus is there to take care of it all.' Sandra was his theatre sister, the only person who knew of their affair. They had met once, by accident, whilst Jack and Catriona were out walking. Sandra had clasped her hand warmly, telling her if she ever needed to reach Jack to leave a message at the hospital with her.

'There isn't really a patient?'

'Course not. I looked out of the window at lunchtime and I thought it was such a gorgeous day that we'd be able to get away and play hookey for the afternoon, but when I phoned *Slainte* they said you'd already gone.'

'How did you know I was here?'

He patted his heart. 'I always know where you are, my dearest.'

She smiled; he loved to watch the way her face changed when he began to make love to her, the slow suffusion of pleasure, relaxation that spread across her features, the way her eyelids closed like a butterfly's wings.

She shivered slightly as her silk blouse fell off, as light as a cloud as it fluttered towards the floor. Sighing deeply, she began to unclothe him as gently as he was unclothing her. They melded easily on the fireside rug, in a pool of light that tumbled in through the window, their attraction so strong that it had a force of its own. It was not just that he made love to her, or she to him, but something more than that; the power that drew them together grew stronger with each day.

All through the afternoon they made love, as the sun moved across the floor and hit the far wall of the cottage, lighting the bumps and clefts in the plaster over the ancient brickwork.

'I love you so,' he said as he leant over her, untangling the knots in her hair.

'I must get it cut,' she said, thinking of practicalities, of getting dressed and going out into the spotlight of the day.

'Must you?'

'Perhaps not,' she said, 'perhaps I'll let it grow like when I was young.'

'You are young still,' he told her, 'you are still my oyster girl.'

As they embraced, finally, in the space between their cars, Catriona started because of a flutter in the undergrowth, then blinked when a flare of harsh light momentarily struck her eyes.

'What is it?' he asked, all concerned because her face was screwed up tight, like a child's.

'I don't know,' she said, 'nothing, just the sun, I suppose.'

Three weeks later Jack's lawyers wrote to tell him that Amelia had refused to end the marriage on the terms he had suggested, of his cruelty towards her and neglect because of his career, which he was willing to admit was tantamount to desertion.

He told Catriona at the end of a day when she had

worked from dawn to after dusk because the chef and his assistants had gone down with summer flu.

She swore at him, then apologized.

He poured her a glass of wine. 'Swear again,' he said, 'I did too. I don't know what to do next.'

'Sue her for adultery?'

He winced. 'I had a word with Harry the other day. The old boy begged me not to. I suppose it'd be the last resort, but I'd have to send private detectives after her, to catch her in the act. All she would have to do is stay at home and keep the curtains closed. And she could counter-sue me. God knows what'd happen then. I don't want you mixed up with it, dearest.'

Catriona was thinking of Harry Kyle, relieved that she had called his bluff.

'Piles has changed his tune,' Jack said.

'Piles?'

'It's Harry's nickname at the hospital. I've never seen him so humble before. Mind you, he said he'd dyspepsia. He drinks far too much these days.'

They sat in silence for a minute, subdued.

'It's just a negotiating tactic,' Jack said after a while. 'I stopped paying her charge accounts, you see. I was paying an allowance into her bank instead, and Amelia doesn't like that. Amelia hates even thinking about money, never mind counting it, though God knows, she hardly needed to, I was giving her so much. So this letter came and at the end of it there was a little bit about how inconvenient it was for her to have to shop at Jenner's and pay cash or, God forbid, write out a cheque instead. I told them to tell her I'll let her charge things again but only if she'll reconsider the grounds for the divorce petition. Once she hears about that, she's bound to change her mind.'

They left *Slainte* then and drove to Catriona's lodging house in silence. She pecked his cheek perfunctorily, because the news about Amelia made her feel temporarily anaesthetized, emotionally close to death.

*

She phoned Sandra the next afternoon while Jack was at the clinic, and told her she was going to Largs. Sandra replied that the clinic was running late anyway, and if Jack had any sense he would go to bed and have an early night.

Sandra was like that, very matter of fact.

'Are you all right?' she asked.

'I'm fine,' Catriona said, 'a touch of summer flu, perhaps. I don't want to stay at work and infect the customers.'

Driving out of the city, she felt a sense of relief, ignoring the little voice that told her she was running away.

In Largs, Maire made lemon tea, sharp and healing. Jamie whooped with excitement when he saw her and immediately asked if he could spend the summer in Skye.

Catriona's heart lightened; for a time she had been torn between Jamie and Jack, she felt guilty about the time she had been away from him.

Jamie was going out in a rowboat with a friend; she told him not to go out too far.

Maire shook her head. 'We hardly see him either, Catriona. He comes in for his meals, and then he's away again. Joe says it's normal. They go off for long talks. His voice is breaking. Did you hear that?'

She winced at the thought of adolescence; that always reminded her of the twins.

'You look worried,' Maire said.

She sighed and unburdened herself, watching the minute hand complete a half circuit of the clock before she had finished.

'He still loves you,' Maire said.

'Yes, but Amelia can make his divorce take for ever.'

'You love him.'

'Of course I do. What has love got to do with it?'

Maire grinned. 'It's all that matters, Triona.'

'There could be a terrible scandal. It could ruin Jack's career.'

'What does he say about it?'

'He says it couldn't ruin his career, that I matter more anyway. He puts all his brains into his work, his mind's like spaghetti when it comes to mundane things that he feels don't matter.'

'He's right, in a way,' Maire said. 'Scandals pass.'

'Have you seen Allan?' Catriona asked.

Maire smiled. 'Only once. With Louise. The pair came down and sat in Nicolson's all day agonizing about their wedding.'

'I thought they were going to get married quite soon.'

'Well, no. Louise got a good job in the hospital, and she says she'll lose it if she suddenly becomes Mrs Nicolson.'

'No!'

'Yes. Apparently if there's anything worse than a woman doctor, it's a married woman doctor.'

'I got the impression they had everything worked out.'

'Allan's pretty coy about it, but I think they're living together.'

'My God. Maybe Jack's right. Maybe *we* should do that.'

By the time she got back to Edinburgh, she really did have flu. She did not go to *Slainte* for three days, and refused to answer the door to Jack, telling him through it that she was infectious, and if he got it too he would give it to his patients.

Jack argued and cajoled, but she prevailed. The truth was that she did not want to see him because she wanted only to stay in bed. She felt lousy and, worse, she looked it.

He sent a bunch of roses every day, with silly notes and a box of twopenny terribles to amuse her. On the fourth day he left a note in the morning threatening to break down the door if she did not let him in that night.

That evening they went to Talla, and Jack made her hot toddies and fed her aspirin for the headache.

'How long?' she asked him. She had never been ill in her life.

'It's a virus going around. It lasts four or five days, and you feel pretty rough for a few days after that. But you'll live.'

He made her feel cosseted, precious. He teased away her angst about her looks, and heated water so that she could have a bath and wash her hair.

She staggered into *Slainte* on Monday, when the fever had gone, though she still felt weak. The trouble with *Slainte* was that the staff were strangers to her, though they worked well enough she did not trust them as she trusted her people in Largs. The maitre d' traditionally helped himself to port after lunch and brandy after dinner, sometimes the whole bottle if she wasn't looking, on the ground that it was nearly finished anyway. She spent lunch time in her office off the kitchen, going over the accounts, learning that she had lost a case of wine and probably a couple of pounds into each waiter's pocket. The petty larceny left her with a feeling of distaste; though it was considered almost a perk of the job she had always prided herself that her staff did not steal because it was as much in their interests as hers that the business thrived. The waiters she employed now were different though, their interest was not in her success but about how they could get the capital they needed to start a restaurant themselves. She felt very cynical when she thought about it.

The maitre d' came as she heard the sound of the tables being cleared. 'There's someone asking for you, Madam.'

She hated that word, ignored it whenever she could. 'It's not the same man, is it?'

'No, Madam. It's a woman this time.'

She walked through to the restaurant, dragging her hand through her hair to pull it into a semblance of order. Because she felt so tired and had only come in to see to things in the office, she had not worn a smart working suit, but rather a comfortable sweater and a pleated tweed skirt with walking brogues.

Amelia stood there, smiling prettily, her hair perfect; she was dressed in a suit that Catriona had seen in Jenner's window for seventy-five guineas. It was a Paris original, silk lined, trimmed with sheared Persian lamb.

'Miss Nicolson,' she began, 'Catriona, isn't it?'

Catriona agreed that she was.

'I won't take up any more of your valuable time' Amelia said carefully, 'but, you see, I wanted to tell you before anyone else did.'

'Tell me what?' Catriona asked tiredly.

'I'm pregnant,' Amelia said. 'Jack and I, my husband and I have decided to make a new start. I wanted you to know, before it all came round as a rumour.'

Catriona felt her legs melt, the room started to spin; she caught herself in a mirror and saw that the shock did not yet show in her face.

'I beg your pardon?' she said.

'I'm pregnant,' Amelia simpered, patting her stomach gently. Catriona looked down and saw the faint rise of the first trimester.

'Well,' she said, 'wonders will never cease. And it's Jack's, you say? Why don't you be honest for once, Amelia? I'd just as soon believe it's the second immaculate conception.'

Amelia's mouth opened; she gasped like a landed fish. 'I ... I ... I ...'

Catriona gripped her firmly by the arm. 'Just get out,' she said, 'and don't you ever dare to come back here to say anything like that.'

Jack found her late that night, when her certainty had given way to doubt.

'What is it?' he asked when he saw her ashen look.

She said nothing, just poured herself a brandy to go along with his. The restaurant was empty; long after closing time, it felt as forlorn as a theatrical masquerade caught suddenly in the unyielding light of day.

'What is it?' he asked again, once she had downed the brandy and was looking gloomily into the middle distance.

'Can I ask you a question,' she said, 'and will you tell me the truth, will you promise to, whatever it is?'

'Of course I will,' he said, smiling at the childish riddle, becoming serious when he realized how earnest she was. 'Go on,' he said, 'I promise you.'

'Have you seen Amelia? – I don't mean that, but have you gone to see her at all recently, in private, for any reason at all?'

He looked appalled. 'Of course not. Why ever do you ask me that?'

'She's pregnant.'

'She can't be.'

'She is. I've seen enough pregnant women to know that.'

'You can't think, you don't think . . .'

'I didn't think, Jack, that's why I'm telling you.'

'You must have done,' he said, putting his head in his hands. 'You wouldn't have asked otherwise.'

They rowed then, for the first time ever. Catriona threw bitter words at him that she would regret for the rest of her life. Meaningless words, she didn't even believe them as she said them, but she felt the need to strike out because she had been so badly hurt herself.

It meant nothing to him, he told her later, when they were cocooned in her office with the electric fire the only light.

He would forgive her, of course, not that he had ever blamed her, he would not blame her, obviously.

'Oh, God,' she said, falling into his arms. 'When will it end, Jack? When will it end?'

'Soon,' he said, 'very soon.'

'And if not?'

'I'll make it end,' he murmured. 'We'll go away, you and me. We'll go away to America. You can get a divorce there without all this trouble. And I can find a job there and you can run a restaurant; we'll make a new life for ourselves and leave all this behind.'

'I need you,' she murmured. 'I need you so much.'

'I need you too,' he said, as he dried her tears and began to untangle her clothes.

Afterwards, she lay dreamily in his arms, feeling the damp on her body dry in the thin warmth of the fire, remembering that she hadn't used the diaphragm from the doctor on Chambers Street, thinking that it wouldn't matter, because it was only the first time. Or, perhaps, the second. The first had been at Talla the week before.

Chapter Nineteen

*I*n the autumn Talla faded to bronze on gold, the dying leaves against the parched grass of the hills, the bracken drying to the colour of tobacco. In the distance heather flowers washed the mountains indigo; after sunset the colours melted into nothingness.

Talla had always been a haven of peace, the place where their love was not hidden or tainted, but as brilliant and free as the water in the streams that tumbled from the hills. By a consensus they had never voiced, Amelia was not mentioned there, nor the difficulties about Jack's marriage, after that one time when he had spoken of his despair. As the days passed, though, as their love affair entered its second year, Catriona became imbued with a sense of finity about it all, that somehow events, which were out of her control, were racing towards a climax which she and Jack were powerless to change.

The strands of control which she had held, however loosely, seemed to be slipping from her grasp and flying away like thistledown in the wind. In Edinburgh, during the week, she and Jack would sit in *Slainte* until the early hours, talking sometimes but more often silent, taking the comfort they could from each other. At Talla they were often silent too, communicating by touch not words; when Jack's frustration threatened to overwhelm him he became mute, rather than contaminate this precious place with talk of the tainted ritual of divorce. Catriona understood that, and was grateful to him for it; she tried to live for each day, not to think of the future.

There was a strength in her way beyond the boundaries ascribed to her gender; Jack was surprised by that at first and then in awe of it before he came to love that part of her as much as he loved the others, because only with a woman as strong as Catriona could he have a true partnership rather than a relationship of dependency.

'You know,' she said, one day in *Slainte*, 'I'm happy just as we are.'

'What d'you mean by that?'

'Well, we have each other, we have almost as much of each other as we'd have if we were married, but Amelia's using the fact that she can prevent it to hurt you. If you stopped pressing her she might stop resisting, Jack. She might realize that she wants the divorce as much as you do.'

He thought for a moment. 'Perhaps.'

'So if you tell the lawyers to stop pressing her, and just ignore her for a while, she'd change her mind. She's bound to.'

'Maybe,' he said, 'but she's like a child, you know. There's nothing she wants more than something she knows she can't have.'

'Children grow up, Jack.'

He shook his head. 'Amelia won't.' He lifted her hand and began to trace circles on it with his finger. 'You say we have each other now, that we have almost as much of each other as we'll have when we're married, but that's not true. When I wake up in the morning, you aren't there and I miss you. You aren't there when I get home from work and it isn't home without you, I could never have a home unless you were with me. I feel lonely in the mornings when I get up and shave, like there's a part of me missing. It's with me all the time until I get to work, and it's there again when I leave it. And here we are, like two strangers in an empty restaurant, meeting in secret when I want to shout out to the whole world that I love you, that I want you to be my wife. Do you understand, dearest?'

She blinked. 'I do.'

'I don't want to wait any longer for that. And Amelia can't ... she won't ...'

His voice faded. Amelia was pregnant, had become so by the simple mechanism of ensnaring one of Jack's ward clerks, a lad just out of medical school who could not believe his luck when Amelia chanced upon him at a hospital ball and seduced him hurriedly in a linen cupboard. Because of Catriona, Jack had left the ball as soon as obligation allowed; Amelia had gone later, in her usual décolletage and state of exuberant drunkenness. It was the talk of the hospital, but Jack had been the last to know. It could have given him grounds to sue her for adultery, but the lawyer said he would need witnesses to what had transpired in the linen cupboard, or at least to Amelia and the lad emerging in a state of dishevelment. There seemed to be none, although everyone knew what had happened. The scandal would have been dreadful; the young doctor hadn't known Amelia was Jack's wife and he fainted clean away when he was told. He was the innocent party in it all, if such a term could be applied. He fainted again when Jack cornered him and told him not to worry; it took Sandra five minutes to revive him. Jack still wanted a divorce that would not involve any third parties; he no longer cared what Amelia said about him.

Catriona thought it would be bound to end soon, because Amelia would give birth early in the new year; he told her not to bank on it because Amelia drank so much that she was likely to miscarry before she reached term. The callousness of that appalled Catriona, until Sandra told her that Amelia had been in the private wing of the Simpson Memorial several times, when she had miscarried Jack's children. It had been the talk of the hospital, until her father had put around the word that Amelia suffered from endometrial hyperplasia and so needed frequent D & Cs and threatened a suit for defamation upon anyone who suggested otherwise. Knowing that, Catriona could only guess at the depths of Jack's pain.

Amelia still insisted that Jack was the father; there was little chance of proving otherwise.

Catriona went around the restaurant putting out the lights, checking that the fridge door was shut and all the gas burners extinguished.

'Come,' she said, putting his coat around his shoulders.

He flexed his back tiredly and yawned. 'Maybe,' he said, 'maybe this time she'll be careful, actually go through with it. I hope to God she does for the sake of the child.'

'Don't think about it,' Catriona said.

'I try not to, but it's all so bloody sad.'

Catriona put her finger to his lips to silence him.

His mood changed to cynicism when he got into the car. 'Bloody hell,' he said, starting the engine. 'Home again, to an empty room, a cold bed – and another letter from Amelia's lawyers, I 'spect. And the thing is, precious, they've the cheek to make all these demands and at the end of it there's always another demand, for me to pay their bloody bill as well! I mean, for Christ's sake, what sort of people are they?'

She began to laugh then, hysterically, as he blundered on. 'What is it?' he said angrily, when he had stopped at the junction of Princes Street and Lothian Road. 'It isn't funny, not a bit of it. It's not even remotely funny. It's pathetic, for God's sake.'

'But it is,' she said helplessly, 'it's really terribly funny. It's just dawned on me. All you have to do to stop all this is stop paying Amelia's lawyer's bills. And then they'll stop writing all these letters.'

Jack's face straightened suddenly; the anger faded and then he began to laugh so hard that he had to pull the car to the side of the road.

They laughed for so long that a passing policeman stopped and asked them what was the matter, and made Jack get out of the car and touch his nose with his eyes closed until Jack managed to persuade him that he was not drunk.

At the end of October Jack took a week's holiday; they decided to spend the time at Talla.

Catriona was quite happy to leave *Slainte* to the manager; she had become sceptical about Edinburgh society and no longer cared for her customers as she had for the people she entertained in Largs. The country was in the depth of a recession, the worst slump in history; there were millions unemployed, thousands of hunger marchers on the streets in search of the chance to work, but the national establishment continued oblivious to all that, more concerned about the quality and vintage of the wine they were served than the squalor and despair in the city's slums and everywhere else.

Jack cared; with a few of his colleagues he sent students to distribute food in the poor areas of the city and Leith, and he kept many of his little patients in hospital for longer than necessary because he knew how bad the conditions were outside. He railed in anger because diseases that they had started to combat were appearing again; rickets, scurvy, polio and TB all flourished in malnourished children, there were outbreaks of typhoid and typhus, and dozens died because of measles, mumps and whooping cough, the sort of illness that a healthy child threw off in a blink. Health officers toured the slums, reporting families with only a single turnip in the cupboard, others who had not eaten for days; the problem was so great that the government dithered and left too much to charity or chance.

Catriona sent all *Slainte's* leftovers to the Salvation Army and more besides, but, when one day there was a protest march in the capital and collectors stood outside the restaurant to ask for donations, an MP called a passing constable and asked him to remove the obstruction. Later, Catriona gave the restaurant's lunch takings to the hunger marchers and apologized on her customers' behalf.

She was looking forward to her holiday at Talla, could hardly wait as she handed over the restaurant to the maitre d' and then went to her lawyers to sign the lease for another year. It was a Tuesday; already a precious day was gone but Jack had to stay on at the hospital to care for a very sick boy and she used the time to deal with all the little things that she had been putting off.

He phoned her from the inn at Broughton to tell her he was on his way; she left *Slainte* shortly afterwards, feeling a delicious sense of freedom as she drove out of the city, then a thrill an hour later as she turned onto the track that led to their cottage and saw Jack's Bentley through the trees.

He was waiting for her at the door, wearing an open-necked shirt and the old corduroy trousers he favoured; she loved him like that, so much, when he was relaxed and carefree as a child.

'Is the wee boy all right?' she asked first of all, as he opened her car door.

Jack winced. 'I'm not sure. I had to take out his kidney in the end. Please God, he'll survive.'

He was very humble about his work, he always credited success to God rather than himself.

The child had rickets, TB in his kidney and myriad secondary infections as well, brought on by poverty and made worse by the worry that suffused his tiny mind because his da was out of work and his mother in the hospital having lost a child. Jack had not wanted to operate, she knew, because the shock of surgery was perhaps more than the boy could take.

He kissed her softly, then lifted her case out of the car. The front door was open already; she walked in then stopped abruptly, astonished by the mound of Jenner's boxes piled high on the floor.

'What on earth?' she asked.

Jack grinned sheepishly and rubbed his neck. 'Ach, what the hell. I was about to take them all up to the post and send them back, but you can have them, if you like.'

'Have what?'

He waved his arms magnanimously. 'This.'

She sat down and took the glass of wine he poured for her.

He picked up a bag at random, tipping out a tidal wave of silken underwear in all the colours of the rainbow. She picked up a ribboned brassiere. 'Jack, you know I don't like black. Or red or white for that matter.'

He looked sheepish. 'I realized that later. I didn't choose them myself. I just asked the assistant to pack a selection.'

There were garters, suspenders, panties, nightgowns and negligees in organza and satin and silk. She flicked through the pile, picking out only the few in the peach and ivory shades she liked and packing the rest, carefully, in the tissue it came in, gazing distastefully at the pile of tarty scarlet and black. 'You don't expect me to doll myself up like a French maid in a farce, for God's sake.'

'Certainly not,' he said, making a face as she packed the last of the funereal lace. 'I hate the stuff, if you want to know.'

'Why did you buy it then? Have you gone mad?'

'Only slightly.' He drained the wine and poured himself a whisky.

'Why, Jack?'

He did not reply, so she asked him again.

'Oh, well,' he said, 'I suppose I had better tell you. I got Jenner's bill, or rather, Amelia's bill from Jenner's. They sent it to my office and I got it just after I'd finished up on Colin. He was still drowsy, and I had to wait until he'd come round properly. So I checked on him and realized that I'd better wait another day but I'd nothing else to do meantime so I went down to Jenner's and asked them how on earth any woman could run up a bill of more than fifteen thousand pounds in less than three months.'

'*Fifteen thousand pounds?*'

'Fifteen thousand pounds.' He went to the bedroom and came back with a sheaf of papers bearing the store's letter-head. 'It turns out that my wife, not content with her efforts to destroy my reputation, has decided to bankrupt me as well. She's furnished the house from basement to attic yet again, and apart from that she toured all the fashion departments and picked out one of everything in every single colour it came in. That's about a hundred suits, half as many coats, countless dresses, God knows how many ball-gowns. She spent a hundred and fifty pounds on shoes alone.'

Catriona's face had turned pale. 'You don't have to pay,' she said, 'by law she can only buy what's necessary in terms of food and so on. She can't do that.'

Jack stared at her balefully. 'That's what I thought too. It turns out that Jenner's phoned my secretary last month, as soon as they saw what she was doing. The silly little brat seems to have said it was just fine. She said something to me, but I was on my way to theatre, I wasn't paying any attention to her. I told her not to worry me about it.'

'You don't have to pay. That's ridiculous.'

'Alas, my dearest, I do, or so my lawyers tell me. There's certain things I can do, of course, but that's in the long term. Right now, all I can do is to pay.'

'Can you do that?'

'Unfortunately, yes. I haven't touched my dividends from the company for God knows how long. Apparently, I've enough in the bank and I can write out a cheque just like that.' He made another face; he lived on just his surgeon's salary, because he did not want to use the money from the family company.

Catriona had not been able to understand Jack's attitude to money at first, she hardly did now because his experience was so far from her own. Once she asked him why, if he didn't want to have anything to do with the company, he didn't sell the shares or give them to his brothers; he told her she did not understand, that because it was the family company he had to keep his shares even if he didn't want them. He was a Liberal, leaning towards the ILP; he held his shares in Ryan's Lothian Construction Company almost like the thief in biblical times bore his own cross.

'So, you see' he went on, 'I paid Jenner's all that and I put a limit on Amelia's account to make sure she doesn't do it again and when I was walking back down the stairs, I passed the ladies' department, and I saw something I thought you would like, so I stopped to buy it. I wrote the cheque out, and then I thought how rarely I'd bought you anything, how little I've given you since we've been together . . .'

'That's nonsense, Jack. There's here, the car, the brooch you sent me, all the books . . .'

'But that's nothing, my love. It comes only to a few pounds . . .'

'Nearly a thousand for the car.'

He waved his hand dismissively. 'It wasn't much, Catriona, and the car was for me as much as you, because I

513

wanted to be sure you'd be safe, that you wouldn't break down somewhere. I've given you nothing much, nothing like what I want to give you.'

'Jack, don't ever say that. You've given me the most precious thing I have.'

He interrupted her again; he was so engrossed in his explanation he did not see that her temper was faltering, beginning to flare. 'I don't know, beloved, it's maybe the Irish peasant tinker in me, the illiterate tinker who wants to clothe his woman from the inside out, to take care of her every need, but so often when I've been rushing here and there, I've seen something in a shop or in the street that I wanted you to have and I haven't had the time to get it, and there I was, in the best shop in the country, furious at what Amelia had done, and I thought, well, if she had one of everything, then so would you, and, apart from that, I bought you one other thing, the one thing that I really liked and apparently it was the only thing she didn't want ...'

Catriona was not listening to him any longer. She got up and strode through to the tiny bedroom, and saw the bed piled high with boxes and bags. She began to rip them open at random, giving rise to a torrent of shoes and clothes and bags. As she opened box after box, she became so angry that she began to weep. She picked up a fragile stiletto, hurled it so hard at the wall that the plaster chipped and the heel broke and the crimson leather left a ruddy stain on the paint.

'Catriona ...' Jack stood in the doorway, watching her. She picked up the shoe again, hammered it against the wall until the sole tore off and the straps came apart. She picked a pair of boots then and hurled them on the floor, then when nothing happened against the window, again when it didn't break until she heard the satisfying tinkle of fractured glass.

'Catriona,' he said again, but she didn't hear him, she was so busy tearing an alligator bag apart. It was a vile thing, brazenly shiny, as corrupt and devious as the animal whose skin had made it, the putrid stench of skin and tanning acids rising once she had ripped out the silken lining and was pummelling the gold-plated silver catch against the floor to smash the whole thing into smithereens. But it had been well made, for some unknown reason, crafted lovingly by someone who cared about the work, and she could not destroy it, no matter how hard she tried, so instead she gathered up the pieces and cast the whole devilish artefact upon the fire, poking the flames until it smouldered and burned.

Jack stood aside to let her pass, watched her struggle to destroy it and waited until she sat back on her heels when the flames rose.

'Are you finished?' he asked as she wiped her face, leaving a grey streak that stretched from cheek to cheek.

'No,' she said determinedly, as she got up and headed for the bedroom again. He stood aside again as she stalked into the room, scanning the scattered items for what she was going to destroy next. She paused then for a moment, started then stopped, and fell down exhausted on the bed.

He stood watching her for a long time, going to her only when her tears of anger stopped and the tears of sadness began.

'Oh, Jack,' she whimpered, 'oh, God, oh, Jack. What on earth's she doing to us? What on earth's she doing, that we do this to ourselves?'

He let her cry until she had sobbed her tears dry, then went slowly around the room, piling everything back into bags and boxes.

'We'll build a bonfire,' he said. 'We'll build it now and burn it all and watch the flames.'

'No,' she said, 'don't do that.'

'What, then?'

She tried to smile, looking so wan that it made his heart ache. 'We'll pack it all up and send it back to Jenner's and if they won't take it we'll give it to the Salvation Army or a church jumble sale.'

He struggled to smile as well. 'I told you, I went slightly mad. I went mad in the way that only I could; you could never go mad like that, you couldn't be as careless.'

'No.' She was smiling sadly, shaking her head. 'You didn't go mad, not really.'

He laughed aloud. 'Maybe that pair of quacks down the road should have looked at me and not Amelia.'

He looked so fragile that she nearly began to cry again. 'Don't say that, Jack. Don't ever say that again.'

The sky had faded into evening; an owl sounded plaintively through the open window. 'Come on,' she said, 'I've some oysters and a rib of beef to make a daube Provençale.'

'You don't have to do it yet.'

'I do, if we want to eat this side of midnight. As it is, it'll be almost then before it's cooked.'

He helped her up, quelling his instinct to make love to her, because he was afraid she might push him away.

As she began to slice shallots and braise garlic he fetched glass, hammer and nails from the shed and started to reglaze the window, not that he had done anything like that ever before but he thought he could on the ground that if he could manage a passing good graft to repair a badly broken femur he could surely put window glass back into the frame. Three panes lay in fragments on the floor before he managed it and by then the meal was in the oven, spreading comfort throughout the cottage.

Catriona washed and changed her clothes, filed the torn nail that had caught on the clasp of the alligator bag and tied her hair securely at the nape of her neck.

'I love you so' he said, when they sat in front of the fire, amidst the debris of his spree, drinking a bottle of crisp young Beaujolais.

She picked up an armful of clothes and began to fold them carefully. He put down his glass and helped her; after a while they restored a semblance of order to the room.

'I don't think I dare send them back to Jenner's,' he said, 'I'd rather the Sally had them, if you don't mind.'

She shook her head. 'I don't really care, Jack, so long as I never see them again.' She turned to the last few bags, frowning when a pale oyster wool crepe outfit tumbled out. 'I'd've liked that suit.'

'Well, keep it then.'

'No. Never. I wouldn't wear anything Amelia has.'

Jack shrugged. 'I can understand that, I suppose.'

She got up and served the meal by candlelight.

'You said you got something specially for me,' she said, when they were having coffee beside the fire.

'Oh, yes.' He got up. 'I forgot about that.' From the wardrobe he brought a wispy light coat in a colour that looked like water in the firelight. Unfolding it, he showed her that it was a simple trench coat, lined with shirred mink.

'Oh, Jack,' she said, trying it on. 'I love that.'

He smiled. 'I'm glad.'

When they went to bed he cradled her in his arms.

As she lay there, she asked him the question that had been nagging at her all night. 'What you said about Amelia trying to destroy your reputation, does that matter?'

He smiled. 'Trust you to think of that. No, it doesn't. Not really. There's nothing I've done that anyone can say anything about so it's all no more than a lot of nasty gossip. Amelia knows nothing because she never bothered to find out, and since Piles was eased out he can only snipe from the sidelines. So don't worry about it, precious, please.'

Just before she closed her eyes to fall asleep she noticed a pile of Jenner's bags stacked against the wall, thought how pathetic they looked, and realized that no matter how they cleared everything up, the little cottage had been besmirched by the detritus of Jack's divorce.

She thought of the future then, and shivered; Jack hugged her tightly, then began to kiss her, to love her; she seemed strange, then, but when he opened his eyes and looked at her, he realized that she had fallen asleep.

That hurt him, for a while, until he remembered that she'd had bad flu, that she worked terribly hard. When he studied her skin, it seemed paler than usual. Assuming she was anaemic, he, too, went to sleep.

The magic of Talla was gone; they knew that the next day when they began to argue about nothing much as Jack loaded the Jenner's bags in his car to take up to the post office where he would call the Salvation Army to collect them.

It was something he said about his Irish roots, the stringy, sinewy flesh of his arms made strong by his heritage of potatoes and hope. There was nothing to it, but it upset Catriona, made her feel for a moment that he was disparaging her past.

'My people are peasants too,' she spat, 'illiterate fools by your standards.'

'I didn't mean it like that,' he said, trying to fold her into his arms, but she pushed him away.

'If you didn't mean it, you shouldn't've said it. But I'm proud of what I am, Jack. Illiterate peasant or not. My language is a flowering tree and yours is only barren seed that falls on stony ground.' She cursed him then in Gaelic, and he shrank away from the vituperation of the sound she made.

'Illiterate peasants or no, I don't know anyone who ever got into the kind of mess you got into with Amelia.'

He looked away. 'God's sake, Catriona. I told you. There's nothing in this world as blind as lust.'

'As blind as the man who lusts,' she corrected him, remembering then her father, as blind, blinder than Jack had ever been.

'I'm sorry' she said, later.

'It doesn't matter,' he said, starting the car. They dropped the packages at the post and then drove to Peebles, where they wandered around the town and then ate a tasteless meal at the Hydro.

'We should go away,' he said, 'drive north and find a hotel somewhere. As if we're really married. Nobody would know.'

'I would,' she said bitterly.

On Friday morning Catriona said she had to go to *Slainte*, not because she needed to, but because she wanted to get away. The cottage felt claustrophic, suddenly. She drove aimlessly for a while, stopped by a field, got out and walked. The wind was keen; it whipped her hair and began to spit rain. Jack's face swam before her; she still loved him but the pain felt as if it was cutting into her soul.

There had been a time when they had laughed together over the lawyers' antics and Amelia's demands. Way back, in the spring, after she had refused to agree to the dissolution. It was a waiting game, the lawyers said; Jack shrugged and paid them, praying that they would win. Then Amelia's pregnancy and protestations that Jack was the father; he had only a slim chance of proving that he was not. It was his word against hers, the lawyer said, there were no conclusive tests and Jack, being a doctor, knew that anyway. Amelia would triumph through deception and the law was powerless to stop her.

The law could not force Jack to live with her, he could live with Catriona openly or they could go somewhere else, perhaps to America, but that would be running away — and Catriona had never run away from anything in her life.

These thoughts churned through Catriona's mind. Hours later, she got into her car and drove back, unable to decide anything.

Jack was pacing the cottage. The room was tidy, his clothes folded on the bed as if he was ready to leave.

'This isn't working,' he said.

'I know.' She went into the kitchen to make coffee.

He watched her from the door. 'I looked forward to this for so long, Catriona.'

'I did too, Jack.'

'I can't stand the way we're narking at each other.'

'I don't like it either.'

She put the coffee mugs on the tray, and added a slice of cake for him.

'I think we should go back to Edinburgh.'

'That's all right,' she said. 'But I'll stay, if you don't mind, because I hate that place where I live.'

He stood up. 'I'll get along, then.'

She watched him pack his things and check the kitchen window was securely shut. 'Don't worry,' she said, 'I'll see to all that.'

He waited at the door, hesitant all of a sudden.

'Jack,' she blurted, 'don't you love me any more?'

'Oh, Triona, for the love of God, how can you ever ask me that?' He put down his bag and came to her, folding her into his arms, and for the first time in days she welcomed his touch.

'I adore you, Catriona. I worship you, respect you, love you to distraction.'

She cried when they made love; there were tears in his eyes afterwards. 'What's happening to us?' he asked.

She thought for a moment, as the flames of the fire wove a mesh around them. 'Only God knows,' she murmured. 'I love you as much as I ever did. More, even. I love you more each day. D'you know that?'

'Only because that's the way I love you. You know, that's the first time we've made love all week. You kept on falling asleep on me. I thought, I was afraid you'd gone off me.'

She smiled. 'No, never. I'm just very tired.'

'I didn't want to wake you up again.'

'I wouldn't've minded.'

'That was why I was going to leave. I couldn't bear to lose you, Catriona.'

He was tracing a line over her abdomen, across the hollow of her pelvis and the slight rise of her stomach.

'It's not a dream any more,' she said, 'it's real. And you have to work very hard to make a dream become real. I know about that.'

His expression had changed, she didn't notice at first until his touch changed too; she looked then and saw his face suffused by wonder. Very gently, he palpated her breasts. 'What was that you said about putting on some weight?'

'It was nothing, Jack. I always do when autumn comes, because I'm not so busy. I couldn't get my coffee skirt zipped up the other day, but I've skipped puddings since then so I'll be able to get into it when I get back.'

'The devil you will, my love. You won't be wearing that suit again for eight or nine months at least.' He parted her legs, began to probe in a way that made her sit up, astonished. 'Jack!'

'Just a minute.'

'How dare you! What on earth?'

He finished, put his finger to her lips. 'You're pregnant, my darling. At least ten weeks, twelve weeks pregnant. You mean you didn't know?'

'Of course not ...' Her voice tailed off. 'I didn't think ...'

'Well, you are, I promise you.'

'But Jack ...'

He folded her into his arms. 'No buts, Catriona. No "buts", no "ifs"; you're pregnant, and that's the end of it.'

'Oh, Lord, Jack,' she murmured, falling into his arms. 'What do we do?'

'What do you mean, what do we do? We do what everybody does. You go along to see old Farquhar to make sure you're all right, and then we'll go out and buy young Ryan some baby clothes and a crib, what have you, a house as well, and then we sit back and wait for the happy event.'

'But Jack ...'

'Oh, bugger that!' he exclaimed. 'Don't you dare even mention Amelia. The woman drinks so much that all of her vital organs are headed for the anatomy museum as proof positive of the dreaded consequences of the demon drink. I'm still her next of kin, so if the worst comes to the worst I'll bundle her back off to that place in Dumfries. Even Piles says she's getting out of hand and there's the child to think of, if she hasn't lost it already – and Farquhar's told her that her life's in danger if she doesn't stop. The police caught her the other day in her car, she was trying to drive up the Mound and she was so drunk she ended up on Platform Ten at Waverley Station instead. She's a menace to herself and everyone else. And she's quite happy there, you know. It's not a real hospital at all, it's a cross between a public park and a twenty-four-hour vaudeville act.'

'Jack.' She put her finger to his lips. 'I wasn't thinking about her, I was thinking about us.'

He ignored her and carried on. 'It's what might be best to do, precious. Apart from anything else, I've been talking to my friend Horace at the Royal Edinburgh and he says she's bonkers and she'll never get better unless she gets some decent treatment.'

'I thought she was just supposed to be sad.'

'The melancholia was just an act. Any case, that madman she sees, he's changed his mind since then, says she's manic now. Horace says she mightn't be as bad as that, she might just be a classic neurotic, all that Freudian stuff, God knows what. I don't know, but Horace does. No one can be as unhappy and discontented as Amelia is unless there's something wrong with them. Any sane person would manage to change it. It doesn't matter anyway, it's not my problem any more. I don't even want to think about it.' He shook his head and changed the subject rapidly: 'You must make an appointment to see Farquhar soon's we go back. In fact, I'll ring him tomorrow from the village, and I'll come with you.'

'He'll get confused,' she said, 'Amelia's already seeing him.'

'Fingers never gets confused when he's dealing with pregnant woman. It's other people that bewilder him.'

'Fingers?'

'He's called that because of the way he teaches students to palpate the gravid uterus. He holds up his finger and wiggles it and says that it tells you more than any textbook ever can. It causes all sorts of ribaldry amongst the students. But he's very good at his job.'

'But won't we confuse him, you and me and Amelia?'

'Lord, no. He'll be absolutely fascinated with you. He won't give a damn about anything else. He's so old he's probably forgotten about all that, anyway. I think if the Holy Mother turned up on his doorstep he wouldn't be the least bit fazed so long's she wasn't showing any sign of pre-eclampsia.'

They were woken, very early, by someone hammering at the door. Jack answered the knock, bleary eyed, in his pyjamas and robe, nearly falling as he was thrown aside.

A man pushed past him and a camera light flashed. Catriona sat up in bed as another man pushed a set of papers into her hand. Jack, stunned, saw the horror on her face and then grabbed the man by the scruff of the neck and threw him out of the cottage. There was a policeman there, the constable from the village.

'I wouldna do that, Sur, Mister Ryan, Sur. Yon's a sheriff officer, an' he's entitilt tae serve his papers.'

Catriona swore in Gaelic, and got up with a sheet wrapped around her as the other man backed out of the cottage. Jack followed him, swinging his fist threateningly.

'Don't, Jack!' She grabbed his fist and clung to it as he tried to shrug her off.

'I don't bloody care!' he roared, 'I don't bloody care! I'm going to kill him. D'you realize she's pregnant, you thugs?'

The policeman ushered them away quickly, a car engine surged and they were gone.

Catriona eased Jack into a chair and took the papers from his hand.

Amelia Ryan, pursuer, Jack Ryan, defender, Catriona Nicolson, co-respondent; divorce sought on the grounds of adultery of defender with co-respondent, citing witnesses, a private detective, documentary evidence in the form of photographs, her Amstrong-Siddeley next to Jack's Bentley, against the sunset and then in the morning, the two of them embracing the day she had seen a flash in the bushes.

Catriona felt faint, her guts convulsed and she ran to the kitchen and vomited into the basin, still retching long after her stomach had voided.

Tenderly, Jack comforted her and eased hot sweet tea between her lips when he had taken her back into the living room and sat her beside the dying embers of the fire.

'Precious, beloved,' he whispered, 'don't even look at it. I'll make Amelia stop it. I don't care what it takes.'

Once they were back in the city, at work again, Catriona realized that she had left some papers behind, the lease of *Slainte* and the restaurant accounts, Rory's contract for the supply of shellfish. The lawyers needed the lease; she asked them to send a messenger to fetch it, then realized how silly the request must have sounded and went herself.

On the way back, the postman in Talla village stopped her, asking her to sign for a letter addressed to Jack. She did so thoughtlessly, assuming it was something about the cottage, a bill perhaps.

Ripping it open carelessly, she felt sick when she saw the heading, and had to drive the car a few yards down the road until she was out of the postman's eyeshot before she could stop to read it properly.

The letter was from the General Medical Council. Jack had been summonsed to answer a charge of infamous conduct; exactly what conduct was not specified. She read it again, noticing only the name of Henry Harrison Kyle, FRCS, KBE, amongst those on the panel who would hear the charge against Jack.

Back at *Slainte* she went into the office, closed the door firmly and then phoned Allan at the advocate's chambers where he was doing his pupillage.

'Can you ask Louise what the General Medical Council is?' she blurted, when he came onto the line.

'I can tell you that,' he said happily. 'It maintains the medical register. That's a list of all the doctors licensed to practise.'

'Does it do anything else?'

'Why d'you want to know?'

Allan knew nothing of Jack, or her affair with him. She thought rapidly. 'It was something I overheard in the restaurant. Something about a disciplinary panel.'

'They can also strike doctors off.'

'What's that?'

'If they're negligent, or drunks, or they cause a scandal, perhaps. The Medical Council strikes them off the register, and they can't practise any more. Like the Law Society can stop a lawyer, or the Faculty of Advocates could stop me.'

The line echoed. 'Oh,' she said.

'What's wrong, Catriona?'

'Nothing,' she blustered. 'It's just a story I overheard, like I said. Gossip, that's all.'

'I've never known you to gossip.'

'Well, I do now,' she said firmly, putting down the phone.

She left the restaurant, then began to wander aimlessly through Charlotte Square, then along Queen Street. It was in the afternoon, Jack was at work and would be there for hours.

She passed Callum Ferguson's house, then turned at the end of the street and went back again.

His car drew to a halt and he got out, harried as usual. 'Mr Ferguson,' she called from the other side of the road.

'Catriona, how are you? How's little Fionn?'

'He's fine,' she said, 'but could I ask you a question?'

'Of course you can.'

'Can you tell me about the General Medical Council?'

'Why on earth d'you want to know about them?'

She hesitated. 'It doesn't matter. I'm sorry I troubled you.'

'Well, I can tell you what I think of them.'

'What's that?'

'They are a bunch of old fogeys. A clique of old men with nothing better to do with their time than make prognostications that nobody listens to. They're supposed to uphold medical standards, but they don't. I don't think most of them would know a medical standard if it reared up and hit them in the face. They sit there in Harley Street, penalizing good doctors and letting charlatans off the hook. They have as much relevance to modern medical practice as the dodo. That's my opinion, mind you. For God's sake don't quote me, else they'd strike me off.'

She thanked him and walked away.

Back in her office she read the summons again, and saw that it was just a notice to tell Jack that he would be called to answer the charge in the summer term, nearly a year away. Pretending to be a secretary, she called the GMC and was told that was normal, to give the offending doctor time to prepare his defence to the charge.

She folded the paper carefully, then locked it at the back of the safe. There was enough time, she prayed, to do something about it without troubling Jack.

*

Jack took her to see Farquhar Henderson the next day. He was as nervous as she was, pacing the waiting room as she endured the internal examination, let Farquhar palpate her abdomen and insides and then listen to her innards with a trumpet.

'It's early yet,' he said, 'too early to hear the heart beat, but you've a healthy baby in there, my dear.'

He was a kind old man with hands as gentle as the wind and a manner so calming that she quite forgot her unease.

'When was your last period?' he asked when she was seated in front of his desk and the nurse had gone to get Jack.

She had to think before she could tell him.

'Hmmm. That's only nine weeks. I'd have thought it was longer than that.'

'Is there anything wrong?' she asked anxiously.

'No, my dear. I'd have thought it was thirteen weeks, but it doesn't matter at this stage. It just means a very healthy baby is growing inside you.'

Jack helped her into his car afterwards, handling her as carefully if she was a freshly laid egg. He hesitated before he drove away, flexing his right hand before he grasped the wheel.

'I've nothing else to do today,' he said, 'd'you fancy a walk up Arthur's Seat?'

Once they reached the hill he did not get out at once.

'I've a confession to make,' he told her.

'Oh, what's that?'

He rubbed his hand again, and she saw that a livid bruise stretched across his knuckles.

'Before I tell you, will you promise me one thing? Will you promise me that, whatever I do in future, you'll never, ever give me legal advice again?'

'Why's that, Jack?'

'Because, my dearest, what you said about not paying Amelia's solicitors, I thought that was the most sensible thing I'd heard in ages, so that's what I did. When they sent their bill, I got the girl to send it back with a compliments slip, no remittance. They puffed a bit, but I thought they'd run out of steam when they realized they'd run out of money. Not a bit of it. I was in theatre this morning, and there was a commotion outside and this wee probationer nurse comes and tells Sandra there're some people to talk to me. So Sandra tells them to wait and I get on with my list. I thought it was something about a patient, something like that. After I'd finished, still in my gown, there they are in the changing room. Two men and a pair of coppers. One handed me a paper, like that time in Talla. I didn't read it, I just saw Amelia's name written all over the top. I was so angry, I was still keyed up from theatre, thinking about the last patient, and there they were with all their nonsense about Amelia. So I decked him.'

'You did *what*?'

'I decked him, beloved, hit him hard on the nose, so hard he fell to the ground. Next thing there's a copper clinging to each of my arms and I'm being marched off to court. Right past the wards. Of course, our little scallywags, the ones that can walk, they started following me like I'm the Pied Piper. It was chaos. Matron was furious. The sheriff officer, the one I decked, he was taken to the Royal by ambulance to fix his broken nose. So I'm frogmarched to court and there I discover that Buchanan Atcheson, respected Writers and legal representatives of my wife, have filed some bloody order that I have to pay them or else I go bankrupt and they end up with all my assets. I don't know what. By this time, I'm puffing like everybody else and eventually young Michael Scrimgeour turns up and tells me I better pay up, so I write out the cheque and then I have to listen to a long homily from the police sergeant who's apparently already had a word with his colleague at Talla who tells me that if I assault any more court officers I'll end up in the dock myself. That's it.'

Catriona was horrified, so horrified that she laughed hysterically; Jack smiled too, he seemed to think it was funny.

'So I go back to the hospital to change my clothes and

there's Matron incandescent because the *Evening News* has already been on to her about the Surgeon Arrested at Children's Hospital, Accused of Assault, and all the children are clapping and cheering, "You gie him yin, Mister Jack! Gie him a belter!"'

Jack laughed then. Catriona looked away and tried to giggle. 'I suppose it *is* funny,' she said carefully.

'I suppose so,' he said, 'perhaps. But my reputation won't be ruined, you'll be glad to know. I whipped the editor's daughter's appendix out last year, and because of that he's prepared to take a lenient view of it. Plus Sandra assured him that the court officer – whoever he was – well, she and the nurses were going to say he hit me first.'

Next afternoon there was a knock at her door. She usually spent all day at *Slainte*, but she had come home for a nap. She answered it groggily, wondering who it was.

Allan stood there, briefcase in hand.

'D'you have a case here?' she asked him.

He shook his head. 'I came to see you. I know there's something wrong.'

She let him in and went to make tea in the kitchen alcove off the living room. 'Really, Allan, you should have phoned me.'

'Where were you two weeks ago?' he demanded, and then, without giving her a chance to reply: 'That man at *Slainte* said you were on holiday. I thought you'd be at home. Louise and I drove down, but you weren't in Fairlie, and you weren't in Largs, either.'

'I went down on Monday ...' she began.

'We even came here, but of course you weren't here. That's not you, Catriona.'

'What did you want to see me about?'

'I hadn't seen you for a while. Louise and I, we're getting married next summer. She's decided to go into general practice and there's a woman in Glasgow who'll take her on. You haven't told me where you were, yet.'

She looked out of the window at the relentless sky.

'I am your brother,' Allan said.

'My younger brother,' she corrected him. 'You don't have the right to come here and ask me to account for my time.'

'Would you rather I left?' he asked, very softly.

She turned back to him and went to sit on the chair opposite his. The words came, haltingly at first, then faster, like a car engine warms up. She told him about Jack, and how their love affair had begun, how things had changed when Amelia had changed her mind but by then it was too late; they were too deeply in love to part. She told him everything, except that she was going to have a baby.

Allan listened intently, saying when she had finished, 'I'd like to meet him.'

'First promise me that you won't tell him about the GMC.'

Eventually, Allan said that he would not.

She got up and asked the landlady if she could use her phone. 'It's my brother,' she said, reading the look on the woman's face. 'He's a lawyer. Ask him if you disbelieve me.'

Grudgingly, she gave her consent, and listened as Catriona spoke to Sandra at the hospital.

'He won't be long,' she told Allan. 'Apparently, he's just finishing his rounds.'

'You look terrible,' he said. 'I've never seen you look so tired.'

They waited until Jack arrived. She wanted to go to the shops for food to cook Allan a meal, but he said he was not hungry.

Jack arrived, the smile wiped from his face when he saw Allan's grim expression. Catriona saw him looking over her brother with his doctor's eye for any sign of the tuberculosis that had nearly killed him in his youth.

The two men shook hands, but the gesture was perfunctory.

She made coffee and tried to chat; Allan waited until she was seated again, and then he shook his head.

'You bloody fool,' he said to Jack.

Jack was taken aback. He hesitated for a moment and then asked Allan what he meant by that.

Allan shook his head again. 'You don't even read the bible.'

'Nor do you,' Catriona spat.

He smiled cynically. 'That wasn't what I meant. I wasn't going to give you a little homily on the sin of adultery either. Adultery's got nothing to do with it. It sounds like the pair of them were committing adultery for all of their married life.'

'Now just a minute,' Jack began, but Allan cut him of with a wave of his hand.

'It's jealousy, don't you see? Jealousy and pride, two of the deadly sins. It's so simple, and neither of you realized it.'

Catriona said nothing, nor did Jack.

'I mean, she wanted out of the marriage anyway. She wanted pastures new. The process she chose was the simplest way of doing that. Not strictly legal, but that's irrelevant. It was within months, within weeks, in fact, of the hearing. You had only to wait for a few more days, and you went and started an affair.'

'She didn't know,' Jack said, 'she had no way of knowing.'

'You're wrong,' Allan said, 'I'll bet you anything she found out. I don't know how, but I know she did.'

Jack fell silent. Catriona reached for his hand. 'Allan, you mustn't moralize.'

'I'm not moralizing, for God's sake, Catriona. I'm just dealing with the facts.' He had begun to shout; he stopped to get a grip on himself. 'I don't handle divorces, but I know the basics. This sort of thing, the trick your wife tried with the dissolution, it happens. Sometimes it works. The other thing that happens quite a lot is that one party, often the woman, suffers an attack of pride or jealousy; she becomes colder then, realizes that she can drag the whole thing out for ever.'

'I'm not so sure it matters now,' Jack said, 'she says she's divorcing me for adultery anyway, citing Catriona as co-respondent.'

Allan's eyebrows lifted. 'She can withdraw her petition. I imagine that she will.'

Jack looked away; Catriona caught the gesture. 'What is it?' she asked him.

'Johnson phoned me today. Apparently she's already done that.'

Allan did not smile.

'What can I do?' Jack asked him.

'What she's doing to you. You can petition for divorce on the grounds of adultery, cruelty, desertion. With witnesses. The other thing would be to have her declared insane.'

Jack had thought about it, threatened it once, but in the cold light of day he could not bring himself to do that.

Catriona went through to make more coffee, because she could think of nothing else.

Allan joined her. 'I want you to come home for a couple of weeks,' he said, 'come to Fairlie and let it all die down.'

'Maybe,' she said.

'I'll find out about the GMC,' he whispered.

Jack asked Allan if he would like to go out for a meal; Allan looked at him as if he was mad. After he left, Jack told her he was a good lawyer; Catriona was still coming to terms with the realization that her little brother had grown up.

Catriona left for Fairlie the next day. She had convinced Jack that it was the right thing to do, for a while at least. Her morning sickness had started so she left *Slainte* with the manager, but because of the baby she had already decided to sell it.

Jack smiled and told her that going away for a day or two would be good for her.

Out of the city, her fatigue lifted; as the powerful car clipped the miles she rolled down the window and let the slipstream tangle her hair and buffet life into her tired skin.

As she drove down the hill to Largs she saw the sweep of the coast, the view she had always loved; she felt her soul lift, as if she was home again. The feeling was strange, because she had never felt that about Largs before, only for her island.

Walking into Nicolson's, she saw Robbie working on one of his plants, an *Ananas variegatus* that had borne fruit at last. The plant was four years old or more, she could not remember but it was one of the originals that had survived the storm; when Robbie saw her he smiled broadly and held up a lush, ripe pineapple, which he had sliced off for her.

In the Palm Court the lemon trees gave off their pungent, heady scent.

The waitresses saw her and gathered around like hens; she had tea and a dish of the new tea-rose sorbet that Joe was going to try as a dessert at the Red Cross Dinner.

'You look tired,' Joe said tenderly. 'You must come back to us. The city is no good for you.'

She looked around carefully, saw that the carpet was worn in places and made a note to order a replacement and also, perhaps, some new china. The service she had ordered when Nicolson's had opened was still in use; she thought something more colourful would look nice in the summer.

She watched Zena weave amongst the tables, as poised as an ice skater, smiling deftly at the afternoon customers.

'Old place could do with having you back,' Robbie said.

She smiled, but did not answer. As she looked around she felt a pang of such acuity that tears came to her eyes.

Zena walked back to her table, as crisply efficient as she herself had once been. 'Maire's round at the tearoom with Mr McKillop, Catriona. They say: d'you want to go to them or will they come round here?'

'I'll go there,' she said quickly; she had forgotten all about Titch and his biscuits.

In the Rose Tearoom she looked around at the freshly painted walls, the sheen of the woodwork, the dainty arrangement of autumn blooms on the tables. Janet and her sisters had done well, she thought.

She stopped dead when she saw Rory sitting with Maire and Titch.

He smiled broadly, not noticing her discomfiture. 'I came down with a lorry, Triona, and decided to come in for tea. It's been a long time.'

'Yes,' she said. He had never been to *Slainte*, though she had sent him a card when it opened.

'I must get away,' he said.

'No. Please don't. Please finish your tea.'

'I already have,' he said, pointing to the empty plate as he rose to go.

She watched him walk away, as tall and proud as ever.

Titch was dissecting a piece of cherry cake with surgical precision. 'See, mibbe we'll hae tae chop the cherries smaller. I'm tryin' tae make yer cherry cake, Catriona, but the cherries aye sink.'

She laughed. 'I haven't seen my biscuits yet.'

He frowned as if he had forgotten something, then delved into his pocket and handed her some papers. 'Ye've tae sign at the crosses,' he said.

'What does it mean?'

'I dinna bluidy ken. Ask yer brother. I get tae use yer name and yer biscuits, ye get ten per cent o' the profit.'

Maire grinned. 'He ran into Allan when he came down to ask about the cherry cake.'

'I see.'

'Do you want anything, Catriona?'

'No, Maire, I'm a bit tired. I'll go home, then come back later.'

'Catriona, tell me,' Titch repeated. 'I've tried yer recipe fir cherry cake, and the bloody things sink. Why's that?'

His bakery was one of the biggest in Glasgow now, doing well despite the recession.

'Ye ken, Catriona. I see that look on yer face,' Titch said, ruffling her hair.

'I do,' she said. 'You mustn't let the mixture lie. You fold the cherries in just before you put the cake in the oven, and they won't sink all the way.'

'Aw, hell,' he said. 'I wis that busy counting the cherries, makin' sure I'd get my money back when I got aroun' tae selling it.'

She got up to leave, telling Maire she would see her later.

Titch followed, and drew her into a doorway along the

street. 'I hope ye dinna mind me sayin' this, but ye're in the club, Catriona, are ye no'?'

'How d'you know?'

'I've haud that mony tellin' me that, I can tell a pregnant wumman wi' ma eyes closed.'

Titch wasn't married yet, but he was considered the best catch in the Gallowgate, and just about everywhere else.

'I am, Titch,' she told him, 'but it isn't what you think.'

'Ach, lass, dinna mind me. But see, Catriona, if things dinna work oot fur ye, see an' I'd mak' an honest wumman o' ye ony day, an' I wouldna e'en touch ye, mind!'

She laughed and thanked him.

In the evening she ate dinner with Joe and Maire, Jamie and Morag, then drove alone to Fairlie, because Jamie had a football practice.

Ellie Simpson knew she was coming; the fire was burning brightly, and there was a supper tray with sandwiches and Dundee cake.

Because she wasn't hungry, she tore up the sandwiches and threw them out on the lawn, where the birds would find them. The cake went back in the tin.

Ellie was in her room, reading a book. Catriona apologized for disturbing her, then said she hoped that the housekeeper didn't mind, because she had been away for so long.

'It's nothing to me, Miss Nicolson, nothing at all. The old Miss, she used to go to South America for years on end, sometimes. At least you're in Edinburgh; we can reach you on the phone, if need be.'

Catriona walked back to the sitting room wondering if Ellie called her the young Miss to differentiate her from her other spinster employer.

A while later Allan arrived.

She got up. 'I was expecting you to phone.'

He sat down, telling her not to bother making tea.

He still wasn't certain what infamous conduct meant, whether or not Jack might be guilty of it.

'He's done nothing wrong,' she said angrily, 'nothing at all.'

534

Very gently, he calmed her down, then asked her to tell him again what had happened at Talla and then later at the children's hospital, when Amelia's lawyers had sent the sheriff officers with a court order to force him to pay their fees.

She did so.

'That might be it,' he said.

'I doubt it. The summons said nothing. I thought it was Jack's adultery.'

'If somebody with a lot of clout laid the charge that might start it,' he said, 'but adultery isn't enough, unless you were his patient. You see, infamous conduct is one of two things. One is breach of his professional code of conduct, gross negligence or something of the sort.'

'He's never done anything like that.'

'I know. His professional reputation is impeccable. The other reason is if he's ever committed a criminal offence.'

'Don't be ridiculous.'

'That's it, Catriona.'

'What is?'

'He has committed a criminal offence. He assaulted a sheriff officer whilst on court duty. To impede a sheriff officer is an offence in itself, but Jack went further. He didn't just hit him. He hit him in front of witnesses. The summons came a few days later. That could be it, Catriona.'

'But he wasn't charged or anything.'

'He doesn't necessarily have to be. To have behaved like that is enough.'

'But how would Amelia know?'

'They were sent by her lawyers, weren't they? And if that wasn't enough, Jack went and hit them twice.'

She put her head in her hands. He went to her and prised them apart so that he could look at her face.

'Don't worry,' he said, 'with a good lawyer he might get a warning. There's a chance, a good one, that he won't get struck off.'

'Even that'll break his heart.'

Allan smiled wryly: 'Don't you see the irony of it, Catriona?'

'What irony?'

'It's the selfsame thing that da was tried for, fifty years ago. He was convicted and he spent three months in gaol. That's the other thing about Jack. Apart from being a good surgeon, he's also got the reputation of being a bit of a maverick.'

Harry Kyle was a charlatan, a fraud almost, but he was conservative, a pillar of the establishment in fact.

Jack phoned her two days later. 'I miss you,' he said.

'I miss you.'

'I need you.'

'I need you too, Jack. I'm coming back.'

Much as she loved Largs, the separation had made her realize that she loved him more.

Chapter Twenty

Jack traced the rise on her stomach. It was December and they were at Talla, lying on cushions bunched up by the fire. Catriona was over three months pregnant now, still living in the gloomy flat in Morningside until the sale of *Slainte* was finalized; Jack wanted to find her somewhere else but she told him it wasn't worth it, because her baby was coming soon.

When she told him that she would go back to Fairlie, then have her baby at the cottage hospital in Largs, he winced.

She was torn over the future; she felt like iron filings trapped between magnetic poles, like the display she had seen in a shop window. She told him that.

'You worry too much,' Jack said.

'I'm not worried at all, just thinking.'

'I've been thinking too. I was thinking, if it means as much to you as it does, then we must live in Fairlie.'

She looked at him. 'How can we do that?'

'Simple, dearest. We'll get a place here, maybe a flat, and I'll stay in town during the week and come down on Friday night. If I get up early on Monday, it's only an hour or two to drive here.'

'Three hours,' she said, 'and I thought you wanted me to be with you when you got up in the morning, when you came home at night.'

He shrugged. 'I've done without you for so long, I could live with that.'

They both knew now that whatever happened, his divorce would not be heard until the autumn term, after she had given birth.

'I'm not an Edinburgh person, you see,' she said.

He grinned. 'I've had enough of Edinburgh people to last me a lifetime.'

'How can you say that? You're one of them.'

'Not really. I'm an Edinburgh doctor, that's different.' He continued to explore her stomach, rearranging her clothes when he was sure that all was well. 'I was thinking, anyway, we might be better living out of Edinburgh for a bit, in any case. Once you're on the road, Fairlie isn't so much further, but the thing is, I need to be close to the hospital during the week.'

'I know that.'

'Later, we'll buy a house here. There's plenty of good schools in Edinburgh.'

'There's a good school in Fairlie, for heaven's sake.'

'I mean, a *good* school, Catriona.'

Sometimes Jack could be insular about the city, assuming that just because it was the capital it was better for that reason alone. Catriona's thoughts drifted back to her own childhood, to the magic of the island, the education she'd had in Miss Anderson's classroom, as thorough and rigorous as it would have been anywhere else.

'I'd like to give our children what I had,' she said dreamily.

Jack did not understand what she meant.

'It was magical, you see. The island, when I was young. So peaceful and gentle. So safe.'

'I'd do anything in the world for you, Catriona, but I don't see how I could do that. I'd have to work as a general practitioner and I wouldn't know where to start; I don't know how to work a croft, either. You'd end up keeping me.'

She ruffled his hair playfully and went to check the meal that was cooking in the oven.

After they'd eaten, Jack fell silent.

His face had changed; it was set, angular in the firelight.

'What is it, Jack?'

'Nothing, precious, nothing at all.' He handed her the milk and honey that he made for her at bedtime.

She asked him again, cajoled him until he held up his hand in a gesture of truce.

'All right, dearest, but I don't want you to worry about it. There's a surgeon's job coming up at the new Crippled Children's Hospital, and I applied for it. I wasn't sure I'd get it, but I thought I'd get an interview. I've got the experience, after all, as good as anyone's. But I didn't even get that. I had the letter yesterday – you can read it if you like.'

He reached into his trouser pocket and handed her a crumpled piece of paper.

Catriona read the letter quickly and gave it back to him. 'What did you expect?'

'Not this.' He jabbed the letter with his finger: '"Dear Mr Ryan, blah, blah, blah. Thank you for sending us your application et cetera, we thank you for your interest in the position but in this instance we regret to tell you that the appointments board have decided not to consider your application further."'

'What's wrong with that?'

'Catriona! It's a form rejection letter, the kind they send to people who are completely unsuitable. I'm a consultant surgeon, well qualified for the job. Most of the appointments board know me already. It's a snub, a calculated insult.'

She thought for a minute. 'Are you sure, Jack? You're not overreacting?'

'Catriona ... ' His eyes met hers for a moment, then he went to the dresser and began to search through the drawer where he kept all the house deeds. Finding a letter, he handed it to her.

'Dear Jack,' it read, 'we were delighted to receive your application and to know of your interest in the hospital. It was a pleasure to meet you ...'

Catriona scanned it quickly: it was a letter of rejection that was as pleasant as anything of that nature could be; it fulsomely praised Jack's skills as a surgeon, explained that he had not been appointed to the post of medical director at the children's hospital in Glasgow because the job entailed a great deal of administrative work and so Jack, by his own admission a dreadful administrator, would be wasted in that post. It ended by expressing the hope that, if the hospital succeeded in its long-term plan to appoint a manager to oversee all such work, and free doctors to attend to their patients, then Jack would be considered 'with our earnest interest' for the job of chief surgeon.

'Oh, Jack,' she murmured, knowing the opportunity lost, 'couldn't you have done the administration for once? Couldn't you have managed it, just for me?'

His face fell when she said that, and she wished instantly that she could take back her words. The trouble with Jack was, he was too honest for that.

'My secretary would've rumbled me,' he said ruefully. 'Once they found out, they could've had me up for fraud.'

'It doesn't matter,' she said, as they got up to go to bed. 'Don't worry. Something else will come up.'

She still had not told him about the GMC.

Christmas was coming; Catriona had agreed with the buyer of *Slainte* that she would continue to run the restaurant until the end of January, when he would take over, keeping on all of her staff.

In the end, the lease and the business had been sold for £20,000 – an enormous sum, she thought, since she had started it a year ago on a fraction of that. The weekly takings averaged £2,000, of which a third was profit if the staff were watched carefully; the restaurant was always busy, usually filled to capacity.

'You earn more in a year than I do,' Jack said when he watched her completing her tax return.

'Yes,' she said, 'but you do more good.'

'I don't know about that,' he pondered. 'You keep dozens of people in work. You give a small fortune to charity.'

'I feel guilty,' she said. 'I make so much and there's so many thousands who don't know where their next meal is coming from.'

When she walked down Princes Street she saw the unemployed who had become beggars, the hope of a generation squandered on the forlorn promise of victory in the Great War.

The city made her angry, with its flippant disregard for reality, the way that its business continued oblivious to the plight of the people.

The shops were adorned for the season, with gaudy fripperies to encourage consumption more than faith. Presbyterian Scotland had traditionally been sceptical of Christmas, of anything that smacked of Popish revelry, but that reticence had been abandoned in the face of blatant opportunism. Everywhere, there were exhortations to buy, to enjoy, to give to one another but not to the poor.

Catriona had dressed *Slainte* with pine cones and paper roses, a triptych of baubled trees in the window, and the comfort of a glowing log fire inside. There were holly branches on the walls, bright red napkins on the tables with little cards that wished her clientele seasonal greetings; there had been a crown of mistletoe dangling from the ceiling until a drunken banker had tried to kiss her beneath it, berating her for prudery when she squirmed free of his grasp.

One week before Christmas there was a party at the children's hospital with clowns, magicians and minstrels, students dressed as fairies and doctors as Santa Claus. Catriona made little Christmas cakes and chocolate logs, and dainty little many-coloured fruit jellies for the children who could not eat solid food. Sandra collected it all early in the morning, having commandeered an ambulance; she extracted Catriona's promise that she would come later to join in the fun. She had never been to the hospital, and Jack had told her that if she did not come he would bodily drag her there himself.

During lunch she toured the restaurant as usual, already dressed for the party in a bright red dress, fielding compliments with her usual aplomb. Having sold *Slainte*, she was bored with it now, impatient of the demands that it made on her time.

As she watched the last puddings leaving the kitchen, the maitre d' came to tell her that Mrs Ryan was a guest at a table that must have been booked by one of her friends.

'What shall I do about it, Madam?'

'Funny,' she said, 'I didn't notice her just now.'

'She was in the ah-hem, Madam. I didn't notice her either, until the waiter pointed her out. Shall I ask her to leave?'

'No,' Catriona said quickly, 'let her have her meal, but make a note of who booked the table and don't give them one if they call again.'

She waited until lunch was over before she got ready to leave. In the alcove just behind the serving doors, the maitre d' was watching the last of the diners.

'Is she still here?' Catriona asked.

'I'm afraid so, Madam. They've just started another bottle of champagne. Apart from that, everybody's gone.'

Catriona looked and saw Amelia, face flushed, talking animatedly with a couple of women. She had been drinking.

'Damn,' she said, turning to leave by the kitchen door that led to a lane behind the street. There she saw Rory's van, driven by a man she knew from Portree, just beginning its delivery of shellfish and plump island geese. Because of the journey, the shellfish were packed in ice to keep them fresh; slimy water oozed from the cases, turning the floor into a treacherous expanse that could be traversed only by the kitchen lads who wore rubber-soled boots. She looked at her own red patent sandals with heels as slender as a bird's leg.

'Drat,' she said, turning again and, head down, striding through the restaurant.

'Miss Nicolson!' Amelia said sharply, getting up despite one of her friends putting a hand on her arm to restrain her. 'Miss Nicolson, I'd like to have a word with you.'

Catriona deflected her with a harassed gesture and walked on.

Amelia shrugged off her friend and grabbed Catriona's sleeve. 'Don't you dare ignore me when I talk to you.'

Catriona could smell drink on her breath, the cloying sweet sour of champagne indigestion.

'I'm sorry, but I don't have time.'

Amelia's friend came to her side. 'Come on darling, sit down and have another drink.'

'Stay out of this!' Amelia spat.

Catriona twisted out of her grip and ran for the door. Amelia spun on her heel and ran after her, grabbing her hair. 'You bitch,' she said, 'you'll listen to me. I'll make you.'

'Leave me alone,' Catriona said, wincing at the pain of having her hair pulled, lifting her hand to untangle Amelia's. Amelia drew up her other hand and hit Catriona sharply on the face.

'I said, listen to me.'

Catriona saw the madness in her eyes then, the penetrating stare of sight and blindness all at once, the pupils dilated like an animal's. 'Amelia,' she said softly, 'I'm busy now, but if you want to talk to me you can come round later and we'll have a chat. Come tomorrow if you like.'

'Amelia,' the other woman said, 'don't be so bloody boring. Leave her alone.'

'I'm never boring,' Amelia said, looking deep into Catriona's eyes, fixing her with a gaze horrific in its intensity. 'Never boring,' she said again, just a little slurred, but then Catriona remembered Jack saying that Amelia could hold her drink, drink all night like a man and you'd never notice the effect until she exploded like a firework.

Catriona, sensing danger, put her hand out to touch Amelia's, as she would try to calm a child.

Amelia's eyes narrowed and for a moment Catriona thought she had succeeded – until in a flash Amelia had grabbed a glass from the table and pushed it into her face, then again when it did not smash.

Catriona fell to the floor, trying to deflect the blows with her arms, tasting the warm rush of blood on her face. She was aware only of that, and the animal smell of Amelia's body on top of hers, not the rushing feet of the waiters, the arms trying to pull Amelia away, the hobnailed boots of the policeman who succeeded in restraining her and putting handcuffs around her wrists.

Amelia was bundled out of the restaurant screaming, her friends in tow insisting that she, Mrs Jack Ryan, the daughter of Sir Henry Harrison Kyle, could not be lawfully treated like that.

'You don't know who she is,' one of them reasoned, in a voice as brittle as the broken glass, 'her father's a knight, a professor of surgery.'

'Don't bloody care,' the policeman wheezed. 'If her pa's a bloody surgeon she should know not to cut people up like that.'

They left in a tangle; Catriona heard the horn of the police car outside, and then the maitre d' picked up a piece of paper and set off after them: '*Mesdames, s'il vous plait, l'addition.* You haven't paid the bill!'

Catriona began to laugh hysterically. The kitchen maid came with a napkin and iced water, and wiped the blood off her face. 'It's no' that bad, Missus, there's just a wee cut. It'll no' e'en be noticed, after it's healed.'

Catriona rose shakily, looked at herself in a mirror and saw bruising, the dark red line of the cut just below her ear.

'Come on, Missus Nicolson,' the chef said, 'my car's aroun' the back, I'll tak' ye up the Royal an' git ye sortit. The polis'll be wantin' tae talk tae ye, efter that.'

She was still shaking, drinking the tea the kitchen maid had given her.

The maitre d' came back, fussing about the bill. 'It'll have to come from his wages,' he said, speaking of the waiter who had served the women. This was a rule he had insisted on, not Catriona – that the bill of the occasional customer who skipped must be paid by the waiter who had served them.

'No,' she said.

'It bluidy will so,' he went on, lapsing then into the harsh vowels of Leith, 'four bottles o' champers, an' no' jist the Moët, bloody Dom Perignon that wis, sixteen quid fir booze alone, he's no getting awa' wi' that, Miss Nicolson, wee limmer can pay it back at ten shillin' a week, he kin weel afford it wi' the Christmas tips he's gettin'.'

'It doesn't matter about the bill,' she said quietly.

'It effing matters tae me. This is a restaurant, no' the bloody Seamen's Benevolent Society.'

She got up and walked slowly through to the ladies' room and saw that apart from the swelling her face didn't look too bad, that the blood had soaked into the satin of her dress, looking more like a pattern than what it was.

'I have to go,' she said, picking up the bag she had dropped in the mêlée and draping a scarf around her throat.

'But Missus Nicolson, yer face, the polis,' the chef said.

'It'll have to wait. I've an appointment, and I'm already late.'

She walked into the main hall of the children's hospital, through the decorations and the gaggle of children watching the clowns. The nurses were there, and some of the doctors, but she could not see Jack. She had never been there before, but she knew it well from listening to him. Walking along a corridor, she passed the surgical wards, heading for the theatre where she hoped to find Sandra. A sister stopped her, officiously asking who she was just as Sandra appeared, wearing an angel's crown in the place of her cap.

Catriona waved and then drew her aside.

'I was wondering where you'd got to,' Sandra said, 'so was Jack, but he's up in the ward with wee Colin. He's just taken a turn for the worse, on this day of all. He was sick after lunch and he started crying when sister said he couldn't go to the party. Come on,' she said, taking Catriona's arm. 'I'll take you up to see him.'

Catriona kept her head on one side, so that Sandra would not see the other.

'It's pandemonium,' Sandra said, to a backdrop of cheers and whistles, 'always is this time of year, but they love it, the wee souls.'

Her voice dropped as they reached the top of the stairs. 'The bairns up here are pretty sick, it's not fair really, 'cos they can't join in the fun.'

She stopped at a door with a window set into it, high up.

'There's Jack,' she said, standing aside.

545

Catriona stood on tiptoe to see properly. Jack was seated on the side of a bed, holding the hand of the boy in it. The boy was propped up on pillows, his face shades of ivory and grey. Jack was talking intently, smiling every now and then, watching the child's reaction. Catriona could see he was trying to respond, but when he tried to say something, a cough came out instead. Jack stopped talking and lifted him upright, holding a jar to his lips as he spat out some phlegm, then settled him back on the pillows when the coughing fit had eased. Taking a cloth from the bowl at the bedside, he wiped the boy's forehead and then his lips. A nurse went up to him with a dish of jelly; Jack looked at the boy, and then shook his head.

Sandra shook her head too. 'He's not going to make it, Catriona. Such a pity, the wee mite.'

'What do you mean?' Catriona asked her foolishly.

Sandra looked at her for a moment. 'He's dying. I doubt he'll make it through the night. His lungs, you see. There's TB in his lungs, as well as his kidneys. He's got pneumonia now, despite all we did.'

She took her arm and tried to lead her away, but Catriona was watching the way that Jack cared for the child. She felt then the helplessness, the anger of being faced with death. 'There must be something,' she said.

Sandra shook her head. 'If there is, we don't know about it. Jack tried everything, you know. If he did any more it'd be for himself, not the lad.'

Catriona turned then, forgetting herself; Sandra immediately touched her face to steady it so that she could have a closer look.

'It doesn't matter,' Catriona said, 'it's only a scratch.'

'It's a laceration,' Sandra said, 'it'll need cleaned and stitched, 'less you want a scar that'll stretch the whole left side of your neck. What happened?'

Catriona looked away.

'Come on,' Sandra said, taking her arm. 'We'll go and see Paddy Matheson. Paddy's a whizz at stitching cuts like that.'

*

Jack would not come to see her in *Slainte* that night, Catriona knew, because the child he had tried to save was dying. She left the restaurant early, after she had spoken to the police, so exhausted that she called for a taxi to take her home.

She could not sleep though, and watched the night pass in the claustrophic living room, from the stillness of the small hours until a chlorite dawn bleached the sky. She felt curiously alert, despite not having slept; the events of the day before replayed endlessly in her head as she watched the milkman delivering his bottles and then the postman on his rounds.

The police had been waiting in her office at *Slainte* when she returned from the hospital with her skin stinging from antiseptic and feeling tight. Paddy Matheson had put ten tiny stitches in the cut, close together so that it would heal neatly. 'It's superficial,' he said, once he had examined it, 'she only cut the flesh, nothing else. But you're lucky, because a fraction to one side and it'd've cut the nerve, to the other she'd've slashed the jugular. You could have been dead.'

She had told him what happened; she'd had to, in the end. Sandra said it was important. Once she told him about the champagne glass, she was X-rayed this way and that to make sure that no glass remained within the wound. She kept on telling them that it was just a little cut.

After that, the police had taken a long statement even after she had told them that no great harm had been done and that she did not want to press charges. The older policeman, a detective, told her that after she had been arrested Amelia had kicked a constable and kneed a sergeant in the groin, so she would be charged with that; they needed Catriona's statement so that they could prove her arrest was just.

Catriona felt sordid after the process ended, in need of a long, deep bath in hot, scented, water. There was only the chipped enamel of the tub in Morningside with its concentric rings of ingrained dirt; she bathed there when she got back, but did not feel clean afterwards.

At dawn, facing the emptiness of the day ahead, her

feeling of being adrift crystallized into a more definite thought. Jack was the sole purpose of her being here; without him her life had no more permanence than a gypsy's.

She had felt the same thing, long ago; the limbo that comes from living in rented rooms filled by furniture that belongs to someone else. It had not mattered before, she had been young then, without ties beyond the promises she had made to herself. Her life had not yet gained the quality of finity that comes with the passage of years.

It mattered now because of her pregnancy, because of the instinct that told her to begin the building of the nest. Like a refugee, she had begun to hoard things; the kitchen cupboards were crammed with tins of soup, and more flour, syrup and currants than she could use in several years.

Realizing that, she remembered her mother, the way that when her pregnancy progressed to its sixth month or so, she began to nest like a magpie, hoarding meal and grain, harassing her father if the potato pit was not full, garnering eiderdown from the beach and calico and thread to make a bed and clothing for the coming life.

Tears came to her eyes when she recognized the pathos of Mor's determination, how simple her joy had been. In the poverty of their lives, riches were a few eider feathers or a knot of new wool. Her father had anticipated all that, huffing and cursing as was his wont but catering for all Mor's whims and requests with a patient smile. She missed home then, missed the love that had once surrounded her. Jack was a gifted surgeon and a wealthy man; he loved her but he did not cherish her enough. Sometimes, it was as if he did not know that joy never came from money, but only from love.

Once she had bathed again and eaten breakfast, she continued her vigil at the window, staring at a world blurred by the smear of condensation.

Halfway through the morning, a car door slammed outside. She saw Jack walking up the path, his collar folded against his face. She went to the door and opened it.

Jack's face was raw with pain. Although he rarely visited

her there, she welcomed him and went to make hot chocolate once she had settled him by the fire.

'Colin's dead,' he said as she handed him the mug.

'I know,' she said.

'How?'

'The children's party. I was there. Sandra told me he was terribly ill.'

'Oh.' He slumped back into the chair. 'I'd forgotten that.'

She knelt at his feet and touched his free hand. 'You did all you could, Jack.'

He shook his head. 'I don't know. I could've cut the tuberculosis out of his lung, but I didn't think he could stand it. I was hoping he'd pull through. He might've done, if he hadn't got pneumonia.'

'Jack . . .'

He always took the death of his patients so hard, almost as if he was mourning a child of his own. It had only happened twice in the time she had known him; she had expected him to be inured against death, because he saw it so often. The last time it'd happened, she had said that, but he told her she was wrong: if a patient, a child, died, it meant that he had failed. What he felt was not grief but an inner anger that, in its way, hurt almost as much.

Over the weeks they had talked about Colin until she knew his tormented body almost as well as Jack did. For a while, it had looked as if he might survive.

'Herbert McIntyre agreed with you,' she tried, 'right from the start. In fact, he wouldn't even've tried, would he? He didn't think Colin would survive the operation, and he did.'

'Ach,' he spat, 'McIntyre'd leave a burst appendix, just about. He's such an optimist. "Leave it to nature, my boy. she aye knows better than anyone of us."' Jack cleared his throat and glared at the fire.

'If you hadn't tried, he would've died sooner.'

His eyes met hers. 'So I gave him a couple more months of lying in bed in hospital? He died just the same. Don't forget that.'

She sat on the chair opposite his, waiting until he had thawed. After a while, he cleared his throat again. 'He died just after six, just after dawn. It's strange, that, y'know. They usually die at the dead of night, Catriona. If they make it to the morning, they usually make it through the day ahead.'

Jack stared out of the window at the banked grey sky. 'I told him yesterday, just lie back and go to sleep, Colin. Just lie back and dream, and d'you know what he said, Trina? He said, "I donny want tae, Mister Jack, acos if I slept, I'm no' sure I'd wake again, an' I donny want to die."' Jack paused, swallowing a sob. 'He fought so hard, Catriona. And just think about the life he had. He's had nothing, nothing at all, and even so the poor wee tyke didn't want to part with it.' He blundered on, so angry that his face hardened into a mask.

There was nothing she could say in consolation, she knew that. When Jack was sad or angry, he went almost manic, would not listen to anything until he had calmed down and worked things out for himself.

'I shouldn't be so angry, Trina,' he said after a while. 'I should be used to it by now.'

'If you weren't angry,' she told him, 'you wouldn't be human.'

'Thank God I've got you,' he said, 'nobody else ever understood.'

She made more hot chocolate, then an omelette for his lunch. Though it was Saturday, and they should have gone to Talla, Jack did not seem to want to make a move. After they had eaten, Catriona sat down, saying she felt like a wrung-out dishrag.

It was then that he noticed the scar just behind her jaw, that she had tried to hide with her hair.

'What's that?' he asked. 'What happened to you?'

She told him as quickly as she could.

'So that was it,' he said. 'I had her lawyers on to me yesterday, Piles after that. Messages only, I couldn't return the calls. So she's banged up then? Serve her bloody well right, too. But it's a nuisance that it happened. God only knows what it will do to the divorce.'

Catriona's eyes narrowed. 'Jack, she was completely mad. She could've killed me.'

'But she didn't, did she? It's only a cut, Catriona. It'll heal, and the scar will fade.'

'The doctor who stitched it said she missed the jugular by half an inch.'

'Yes, well, if you get stabbed in the neck, there's always a risk of that. It's as well she missed, isn't it? But I wish you hadn't said anything to the police.'

'They said I had to make a statement. They needed it because she assaulted them and they were going to charge her for that. I had nothing to do with it.'

'Catriona, you've worked in the law. You know better than that.'

'I do not, Jack. She stabbed me, remember? In my own restaurant. I could've bled to death. It's lucky I didn't. What else was I supposed to do?'

'You should have called me, told me about it. You've got Scrimgeour's number. You could've called them.'

She took a deep breath. 'Jack, if you remember, you were with Colin. I wasn't going to disturb you. And Scrimgeour was the last person on my mind.'

'Well, Catriona.' He brushed his hair back, as if the matter was at an end. 'I just wished you'd waited. You should've thought about the divorce. It could've been useful. But I don't suppose it matters now.'

'Get out,' she said coldly.

'What?' Stark amazement spread over his face.

'I said get out, Jack. You've made me very angry and rather than have a row, I'd like to be on my own.'

'Why?' he asked, bemused. 'Why are you angry?'

'For God's sake. I'm pregnant, Jack, due to give birth in the summer. I'm not sure when, but I do know that it will be before we marry ... '

'That's not my fault,' he said quickly. 'I mean, if it's my fault, it's also yours. It's nobody's fault, for God's sake. It's the most natural thing in the world, and I'm overjoyed about it. Aren't you?'

She took a deep breath. 'I am glad,' she said, 'but I'd rather I was married, that we could live together like normal people, like a man and wife, that Farquhar's secretary didn't look at me in a strange way when I give my name, that when I go to buy myself a maternity dress, I don't have to pretend it's for my sister.'

'But all that doesn't matter,' he said, 'none of that matters. All that matters is you and the baby. Whatever happens now, however bad it is, I'll make it up to you as soon as I can. I've promised you that. You do believe me, don't you?'

'I believe you want to,' she said tersely, 'but yesterday, as I was on the way to the party at your hospital, not because I wanted to go – I didn't, but you insisted that I did – if it wasn't for that this'd never have happened because I'd've waited in the back until Amelia went, until midnight if I had to because she was sodden drunk ...'

'She wasn't drinking, was she? She told Farquhar she wasn't.'

'Whatever she said to Farquhar, Jack, she was stone drunk, I promise you. In any case, if it hadn't been for your stupid party that you weren't even at, I would've been perfectly all right, but as it was I had to leave the restaurant and on the way I was accosted by a madwoman ...'

'She isn't mad, she's hysterical.'

'I assure you, Jack, she's mad. I was accosted by a madwoman and near stabbed to death.' He started to interrupt again then but she put up a hand to stop him. 'I should've gone to hospital there and then but I didn't because I would've been late and I thought you might've missed me and come looking for me. Now, I quite understand why you didn't and why you couldn't and I don't blame you at all for that. What I am annoyed about is that, lucky or not, I was stabbed in the neck and I lost quite a bit of blood, not enough to make me faint but enough to make me shaky, but after that I just brushed myself off and soldiered on because I didn't want to worry you or upset you, that once I'd been treated I went back to my restaurant to find half of the Edinburgh police waiting for me, that though I didn't want to and I told them that, I told them what happened because it seems to me they had a right to know, and after all of that, you have the temerity to sit here and tell me I should have said nothing because otherwise you could have used it in your stupid divorce?' Her voice had been rising to a crescendo all this time; she realized too late that she was screaming, as she told him for a second time to get out; then the landlady started hammering at the door.

They stopped, staring at each other.

'Just leave,' she said, as calmly as she could.

'But Catriona . . . '

'No buts, Jack. Just leave.'

She did not bother to see him out, she just hugged herself by the fireside until her trembling had eased.

The landlady knocked again, calling through the door when Catriona did not answer. 'That was quite enough, Miss Nicolson. I can't have my house disturbed by raucous arguments. I'll have you out if it happens again.'

'*Tigh na Galach*,' Catriona spat.

'What was that?'

'Go to hell.'

They had planned to spend Christmas at Talla, or at least, the holiday after Christmas Day, which Catriona would spend in Largs. Jack had already lopped the top off a pine tree and set it in a bucket of soil in the living room, ready for her to dress with ribbon and baubles. She had already packed his present, as he had hers, she thought, because she had seen him sneaking furtively into the shed when he thought she was not looking.

Catriona drove to Largs that afternoon, without leaving a message anywhere. By the time she arrived Jack had phoned Nicolson's three times, finally leaving a message that he was on his way.

She got back into her car and drove to Glasgow, where she took a hotel room for the night and then spent the next day buying extravagant presents for all of her family.

She met Allan and Louise; Allan wasn't coming to Largs because Louise was working, so he was making Christmas dinner for her at their flat instead. Allan asked her about the GMC, but she told him that the hearing wasn't for six months yet; they hadn't even set the date. She changed the subject to the latest development in the divorce case, ad-libbing frantically.

When she phoned Nicolson's, Joe told her that Jack had gone.

When she arrived there was a letter waiting for her, just delivered from Edinburgh.

My dearest Catriona,

I love you. I'm so sorry about what I did, I didn't mean to, the last person in the world I would be careless of is you. It was the unmentionable – my divorce, that is. I thought if she had done that to you, she'd gone too far, that at last she might have done something that the lawyers can actually do something about. It was reflexive; as soon as the words were out, I regretted them. I've become obsessive about the divorce, but I've had to be. That and a sleepless night spent watching a wee boy die, I wasn't myself, I was more of a puppet. That's not an excuse; it's an explanation. Whatever happens, I won't do that again.

In any case, when I got back I discovered she's been put in the asylum. She's been certified, not at my request, but her father's. I feel sick about it, if you can understand; madness isn't something I would inflict on anyone, even her. It's all very sad. I haven't called the lawyers yet. I suppose, in time, they'll find a way of working all of it out. Please don't leave me. Please come back. Only you matter to me, nothing else does.

With all my love, Jack.

On Christmas Day, having dinner at Maire's, she tried to tell Jamie that she was in love with someone. He blushed, looked away, did everything to avoid her explanations.

His voice was breaking wildly, and would transcend an octave in a word.

Joe shook his head when she asked him to help. 'It's impossible, Catriona. He's just beginning to know lust, it'll take another ten years before he even thinks about love.'

Just before he went to bed, Jamie came to her. 'This man,' he began diffidently, 'will I like him?'

'I think you will. I do.'

'Oh, well, I'm glad, then,' he said. 'It's time you married somebody.'

'Happy New Year,' Jack said on the second day of 1931.

'I'm sorry,' she replied. A snowstorm had trapped her in Largs, though she had wanted to come back sooner; the roads were so treacherous that she would not let him collect her, either.

'You didn't get your Christmas present,' he said ruefully.

'Ah, but I'm old enough to wait. And you didn't get yours either.' She felt herself smiling, because she loved him again. 'Yours was only a fisherman's sweater. I knitted it myself. You said you wanted that.'

'I do, my love.'

'I'm not good at knitting. It's full of knots.'

'I'll love the knots.'

He took a little box from his pocket. 'This isn't your Christmas gift, Trina. It's something I should have given you a long time ago.'

It was a wonderful old engagement ring, of a pearl surrounded by pavé diamonds.

'It's beautiful,' she murmured.

'It was my mother's,' he told her. 'I'd to fight off both my brothers to get it for you.'

'I wouldn't want you to fight anyone for me.'

He looked guilty. 'I'd fight lions for you, my beloved. In fact, I went through that storm for you.'

'What?'

'I did. I decided that wild horses couldn't keep me away any longer, so I got into the car and started driving. I skidded and landed in a ditch. The car was towed to the nearest garage. By cart horses. I won't get it back till next week.'

'I told you not to. The radio said the road was blocked.' She hugged him, knowing now that he knew about joy.

'I'm sorry. Next Christmas, we'll be together.'

'Next Christmas, we'll have a child,' she said quietly, breaking her vow to remain within the present.

'So I can't drive you home,' he said, after he had given her his Christmas gift as well, a bracelet set with sapphires the colour of a summer sky.

'It doesn't matter. You can drive my car, if you like.'

Because he had not eaten all day, she grilled a fillet of sole, served it with lemon and chive butter and a salad, with a big chunk of french bread.

'I feel better now,' he said, once he had eaten.

'What's wrong?' she asked, noticing the deepening lines upon his face, the bruised hollows beneath his eyes.

He sighed and rested his chin on his hands. 'How do you feel about emigrating?' he asked her.

The question took her aback. 'I don't know,' she said slowly. 'I thought you didn't want to leave here.'

'I might have to,' he said sombrely.

'Tell me why?'

He sighed again. 'There was a case conference last week. There's one every month. We talk about the patients, about the ones we've helped and the ones we haven't. Colin came up. I said, because the kidney was so badly damaged, I had no option but to remove it. Everybody agreed with me. Then Piles piped up and said the boy's only chance was medical treatment – that the operation killed him, if you like.'

'That's not true, Jack.'

'That's what I think. There is no medical treatment for TB, really, it's good nursing care only, you know that. The kidney was tuberculosed, and there was a secondary infection, an abscess that was draining into his bladder. He'd've died within twenty-four hours if I hadn't cut it out. But Piles raved on. He called me negligent, for God's sake.'

'That's rubbish, Jack.'

'Yes, but he is a professor, God knows what else, and his word does carry some weight.'

'Jack, he's a charlatan. Everybody knows that.'

'The trustees don't. The management committee don't. I can't have him going around making accusations like that.'

'You could sue him for slander.'

'Catriona, please. No legal advice.'

She looked hurt and he softened.

'I didn't mean it like that.'

'I'm not giving you legal advice, Jack, and for that matter I wasn't the last time, but he's talking nonsense, and he's got to be stopped. You did nothing wrong.'

Jack rubbed his neck tiredly. 'I know that, Trina, but the fact is that Piles is Piles and it looks awful, a Professor Emeritus of Surgery saying the surgeons in the children's hospital don't know what they're doing.'

'But, Jack, McIntyre saw Colin too. He was in theatre when you were operating. It was his case as much as yours.'

'I was the surgeon in charge, Trina.'

'Yes, but if Piles is saying you were wrong, he's saying that McIntyre's wrong, and he's a professor too.'

'Trina, who was wrong hardly matters. Colin didn't die because of anything to do with his kidneys. He died of pneumonia caused by TB aggravated by malnourishment. That's the pathologist's report, clear as day. They can't question that. They're trying to say that the surgery weakened him, but that's nonsense, too. The pneumonia set in a couple of days before he died, months after the surgery. He was a very sick child and we did our best to save him, but he was just too sick and too frail to fight any longer. That's it. But Piles raving on about it could cause all sorts of trouble.'

'But can't McIntyre do something about?'

Jack winced. 'You know McIntyre, he just wants a quiet life. But he's trying. I've just left him at the New Club. Piles is there and they're going to work it all out over a few ports. Herbert's bloody mad about it, because today's his day for the Operatic Society and instead he's at the New Club dining Piles.' His face twisted into a grimace as he mimicked the professor. '"What bloody nonsense is this, lad? If you're fighting with your wife can't you sort it out in private, like the rest of us? Do you have to bring in the entire department of surgery? Do you have any idea what this nonsense will cost, if the trustees get word of it?" I mean, Christ's sake, Trina, the trustees aren't doctors. They don't know the facts. If Piles is going around making trouble, they'll listen, if nobody else does.'

She let him talk on, only half listening as she wondered if there was anything she could actually do.

'You don't really want to emigrate,' she said after he had finished.

'God, no,' he said. 'I couldn't stand America, it's so noisy over there. But there's this mess, and the divorce. I might have to if it gets any worse.'

Farquhar had given her some news that day, but she did not tell Jack. He told her that he thought she might be having twins, but it would be week or so yet before he was sure.

Catriona drifted on, through the days, taking long walks in the parks, spending her evenings easing Jack's angst. At the end of January she received a letter with unfamiliar handwriting on the envelope, and when she opened it only a newspaper cutting tumbled out. She had to read it several times before she realized its significance; it was a notice from *The Scotsman*, at the time of her funeral, which reported that the Lord Provost's wife had been cremated.

On her last day in *Slainte* she went into her office and phoned the GMC for a second time, this time pretending to be Sir Harrison Kyle's secretary. She asked the clerk who answered to confirm the dates of the disciplinary panel meetings in the summer. He did so; quaking then, Catriona asked him to confirm the details of the infamous conduct charge against Jack Ryan, FRCS. The clerk went away, she heard footsteps, drawers being opened and then the flicker of papers. He picked up the phone and offered to phone her back; she insisted on waiting. After an age, the clerk picked up the phone again and told her that the file was empty, that Sir Henry had merely stated that the charge would be brought. He had apparently forgotten to provide details. The clerk asked her to remind him to do so, and told her that Sir Henry would not be on the particular panel that heard the charge, since he himself had brought the matter to the Council's attention. She could strike out the date from his diary.

'Yes,' Catriona said, 'I certainly will do that.'

At the beginning of February Farquhar told her he was certain, he could definitely hear two separate heart beats inside her womb.

She was very quiet when she was given the news.

'Is anything wrong?' he asked.

She shook her head.

'I know it isn't easy for you,' he said.

She winced. 'Amelia's father . . .'

'Don't worry about him,' he said, 'everybody knows about Amelia. And Harry Kyle. Everybody's on your side, Catriona. You and Jack, you deserve all the happiness in the world. All this will pass, like a bad smell in the wind.'

'But Harry Kyle's making trouble for Jack.'

'Harry Kyle can't make trouble for a man like Jack.'

She flinched.

'My dear, in Edinburgh, we've always prided ourselves on rearing the best medical men in the world. Sometimes we throw out a bad 'un. Usually they drift off, find a small town where the population's so decrepit that the worst of their efforts will not make any difference. Harry Kyle was competent once, but he was never gifted. During the war the best men went to help the soldiers. Harry stayed behind. Like scum in water, he floated to the top. But nobody has any illusions about him. He's well known for being what he is.'

She told him about the GMC, and Harry's charge of infamous conduct.

Farquhar's face darkened. 'I doubt it'd stick, Catriona, not if the truth came out.'

'The truth doesn't always come out,' she said slowly.

'Tell Jack,' he said. 'That's the first thing to do. Tell Jack, and then we'll all help him fight it.'

'I can't do that.'

'Whyever not, my dear?'

'Because it would break his heart.'

It took a long time to reach Sir Henry Harrison Kyle, shivering in the icy cold of the entrance hall of the house in Morningside, with the landlady listening to every word. The phone was only for incoming calls, not outgoing; Catriona had to negotiate each time she wanted to use it and even then the landlady listened in to make sure it was only a short, local call.

The maid answered again and so Catriona put the phone down without giving her name.

'I don't know what all this nonsense is,' the landlady said.

'Like I said,' Catriona explained, 'it's a personal call. I can't just leave a message.'

The landlady looked her up and down, then peered at her inquisitively from the edge of her pince-nez. 'You're not in trouble, are you, chasing some poor fellow to pay the price?'

Catriona sighed deeply, too tired to be angry. In the sixth month of her pregnancy, she felt bloated, ugly; worst of all, she had a fatigue the depths of which she had never known before. Rising in the morning was such a struggle, she felt like a dying fish floating to the surface; on seeing daylight, cotton grey, her torpor felt like stagnant water. 'It's natural,' Farquhar had told her, 'the most normal thing in the world. You must rest for your babies. You must remember that you are an elderly primagravida, after all.'

'What's that?' she asked, curiosity for once overcoming her lethargy.

'You are thirty-one, my dear. That's old for your first, and twins are twice the weight to carry.'

'I'll be thirty-two soon,' she had told him pedantically.

'You are, aren't you?' the landlady whined. 'In that state, and you're using my phone to make demands of the father.'

'All right,' Catriona said, exhausted, 'think that if you want to.'

560

'I won't have it,' the landlady said, arms folded. 'This is a decent house.'

'Don't worry,' Catriona snapped, 'I'll be out of it momentarily.'

She got through to Sir Henry on her fifth attempt. She explained briskly who she was and when she heard the sharp intake of breath, asked to see him.

The Kyles lived in a Grecian folly on the edge of the New Town; when she rang the bell Sir Henry answered the door himself, ushering her into a study just off the hall.

'You must be quiet,' he said, 'and quick. Amelia is sick, and it wouldn't do for her to know you are here.'

His daughter's presence hung in the air, making it tense as if a storm was coming. The scar on Catriona's neck twinged.

'I know,' she said. 'I'll be as quick as I can. The thing is this: this charge against Jack, you're behind it, aren't you?'

Sir Henry meshed his fingers and cracked the joints. 'I am Professor Emeritus of Surgery, young lady. It is my duty to uphold professional standards.'

'But Jack's the best, you know that. The charge is concocted.'

'Concocted?' Sir Henry raised a sceptical eyebrow. 'I'm not so sure of that. Like all of us, he is obliged to behave in a way that befits his status. Assaulting court officers is hardly a way of doing that.'

Catriona rubbed the scar on her neck, fading now, but still visible. 'Jack wasn't the only one guilty of assault,' she said.

'My daughter is a different matter. Sadly, she has lost her mind, temporarily, as a result of her husband's sustained mental cruelty. There is professional testimony to that effect.'

Catriona gazed at him, wondering what to say.

'You see, Miss Nicolson, your threats didn't have any effect.'

You're seeing me, she thought, that means I still have something.

'You should have left when I advised you to. If you had, none of this would have happened.'

That's it, she thought, taking a breath.

'Mr Kyle,' she began.

'*Sir* Henry!' he barked.

'Sir Henry. Jack is an excellent surgeon, you know that. The question of his behaviour is something else. If the charge is to be laid, then he has a right to answer it. When he does, I will make sure that the truth comes out.'

'What truth?' he barked.

'Your professional testimony. There is also professional testimony to the effect that you, not Jack, are the cause of your daughter's problems. There is testimony to the fact that you personally threatened Jack. And me, for that matter. There is still the question of the Lord Provost's wife.'

He laughed aloud then. 'The silly bitch had herself cremated.'

'That does not matter. The allegation remains. The purpose of a court hearing, or a Council hearing, is to establish the truth. I am quite happy to give my side of it.'

'You're a cook. They wouldn't listen to you.'

'They might not listen, but they would have to hear me. I wouldn't like it all to be played out in the papers. Would you, *Sir* Henry?'

He sat down suddenly, then smiled, the gesture so alien that it seemed like a grimace.

She felt a rush of hatred, so strong that she had to clasp her hands together to stop herself from reaching out to strike him.

'Miss Nicolson,' he said, placatory all of a sudden, 'I do not question what you say about Ryan. It is my daughter who concerns me.'

She gazed at him.

'Ryan's just a young Turk. He thinks surgery is the cure for everything. Ha!' he laughed. 'That's nonsense if there ever was nonsense. Surgery cannot correct the basic flaws in the human physique. It cannot make up for bad breeding, the poor physical specimens that throng our hospitals nowadays.'

Catching his theme, he became animated. 'The healing knife, what nonsense that is. I believed in it too, of a time, until I realized that no surgeon can make up for the degeneration of age, for the natal state of some of our species.'

He paused and tapped a book on his desk; Catriona could see only that it came from Germany because the title was printed in a thick, gothic script. 'Eugenics,' he said, 'the art of conservation of the race through breeding. I'd never have become a surgeon if I'd understood that when I began.'

A jolt ran through her, a vagrant memory of the horror of war.

'All these supposedly great advances in surgery, and the result was a bunch of men with warped and absent limbs, useless to society in any meaningful sense of the word. It would have been better for us all to let them die. And most were sorry specimens in the first place, which is where eugenics comes in. A licence to procreate would do more for health than medicine ever did. But I'm digressing, aren't I? I sense you didn't come for a learned debate.'

Catriona felt bile rise, and struggled to swallow the bad taste in her mouth.

'But since you raised the matter yourself you should know that the woman who died presented with the most minor of feminine ailments,' he went on sonorously. 'She had a little pain and the passage of some blood. Iron would have sufficed but she wanted surgery. Women should accept the frailties of their gender. It is arrogance to demand respite from nature.'

The man's mad, she thought, a raving lunatic. Every bit as crazy as his daughter. For the first time ever, she felt a splinter of sympathy for Amelia Kyle.

'I'm so sorry,' she said, 'it must be awful to realize that your life's work has been in vain.'

He stopped dead and scowled at her, not certain what she meant. She wondered then if she had been right about him, if Harry Kyle had the intelligence to play Jack just like a sporting angler reels in a fish.

'If I were to leave,' Catriona began, holding her hands over her stomach to guard the life growing there, 'could these allegations be dealt with discreetly, without any fuss?'

'It might be possible,' he conceded.

'I would have to be sure,' she said. 'And you would have to stop hounding him about Colin.'

He thought for a moment. 'That case, ah, it was bad blood, you know, no more than that. Eugenics would not have permitted procreation of a strain as weak as that. As for the Council, the Council has quite enough on its hands already, without considering the antics of Ryan. It's quite possible that his problems will vanish, my dear. I would not trouble myself further, if I were you.'

'I would have to be sure,' she said again.

'Ah, I see that you're healthy, strong, the kind of blood that is needed these days. Too many woman are weak. They moan about such little things. You can be sure, Miss Nicolson. You have my word that neither matter will progress further if you keep your part of our bargain.'

She handed him the paper she had already prepared and waited until he had signed it. The language was not perfect, but she knew enough of the law for it to be effective.

That done, she stumbled out into the shy sunlight of early spring, the air so cold that it made her gasp. She gripped the railing at the side of the house for a while, until her nausea eased and then, very slowly, she walked away.

In the post office she put a call through to a Glasgow number. When it answered, she took a deep breath. 'Titch,' she said, 'this is Catriona. Will you help me?'

Jack felt her absence when he had finished in theatre. He had notes to write, letters to answer, but he left all that and walked into the glacial sunlight of the late afternoon, feeling the cold nip at his nostrils.

It was the end of the week and he had wanted to go to Talla, but as he got into his car he sensed that she would not be there. Driving past the house in Morningside, he saw curtains half open on an empty window.

Talla was as Catriona had left it. The Armstrong-Siddeley was parked there, with the keys on the mantelpiece indoors.

He stumbled in, poured a drink and sat down before he opened the letter on top of the bundle of papers. Glancing at them, he saw a deed of gift by which Catriona Nicolson transferred her share in the property known as Burn Cottage, Talla, Peeblesshire to him, Jack Ryan.

The letter was short; reading it hurt his eyes.

My love,

What can I say, except I've known for a while that it would come to this, and so instead of fighting it any longer I am leaving in the hope that by so doing I will achieve a truce that will, in the end, lead to peace. I love you still, I always will. Don't come after me, please. Let me be for a time, let fate take its course, because I believe that this parting will not be for ever.

My love, please pray for me, and for the time to come when we will be together again.

With all my love,

Catriona.

For a time he sat motionless, the glass drained in his hand. He cried then, sobbed like a baby, threw the glass against the wall and watched it fracture into shards. He left it there, just like that, left everything but the key of the bank deposit box in which she said she had left his mother's engagement ring.

He went to the hospital, took out the rotas and began to reschedule duties so that he could have some time away. Finding Sandra scrubbing the theatre walls, he told her that he was leaving for a week or two, that he would return when he could.

'Don't be bloody mad,' she said, 'that wee girl's coming in for you to excise that dermoid cyst.'

'Herbert can do it,' he said, 'he's the professor, after all.'

'He's seen her, Jack, and he says you've to do it.'

'It won't matter, Sandra. Knowing my luck of late, it'll turn malignant.'

'It might. It might not. If you try, you give her a chance. The best she's got. I tell you this, Jack, if you leave now, then I'll walk out with you. Only thing is, when you decide to come back, I won't.'

'What do you mean?'

'I could get a better job, one that pays more money. I'd've packed this in years ago if I hadn't been working with you. And if I'm not, then it's not worth the bother.'

'Don't be daft, Sandra. There's other surgeons here, plenty of them.'

'None as good as you, Jack. None that's so much fun to work with.'

He left the hospital then, taking the little girl's notes and X-rays with him.

On Sunday, in the evening, he was studying an anatomy chart, planning his route to the cyst, how he could cut it out without damaging muscles, blood vessels or nerves.

The phone rang and he picked it up, giving his name mechanically.

'Jack, it's Farquhar,' the voice said, 'you couldn't come down to the Simpson, could you?'

His heart leapt, palpitated and then settled. 'It's not Catriona, is it, for mercy's sake?'

'God, no, nothing like that. Woman's strong as an ox. She'll have these twins of hers, no trouble . . .'

'Twins, did you say?'

'Didn't she tell you? But that isn't why I'm calling, Jack. It's Amelia, not Catriona.'

Jack sighed. 'Go on. You may as well tell me.'

'I'd rather you come down, if you've got a moment.'

'I haven't a split second, Farquhar. I've a wee four year old tomorrow, with a cyst the size of a crab apple on the base of her skull. It's a dermoid, so I've got to get it out. You know the sort of thing.'

'I can imagine. Oh, well, hell, Jack. Amelia's dead. I might as well tell you now.'

'Dead?' His heart flipped again, but not with fear. 'What happened?'

'She gave birth last night, a bonny wee girl. She wasn't well, you know; after that fracas she had with Catriona her

566

father had her up in the asylum. They kept her there for a while, only let her out because Harry got round-the-clock nurses. I had her in for a couple of weeks. It was mayhem, even in her own room. They had her on chloral hydrate up the road, but I stopped that. I had to, for the little one. Like I said, she gave birth last night, and we gave her a good strong dose to knock her out. The nurses went in every half hour. She was asleep an hour ago, next time they went in she was out of the window. She fell through the conservatory. Thank God, there were no patients there. But it wasn't a pretty sight, you can imagine. She must have lost half her blood in ten seconds flat.'

'Yes,' Jack said dully. 'Farquhar, what can I do?'

'Do? It's a bit late for that, Jack. Having known Amelia, I think it always was. You should talk to Horace about it. He knows better than I do. Dementia praecox, he said it was, schizophrenia as they call it these days.'

'I'm sorry, Farquhar.'

'I'm sorry too, Jack. She seemed quiet enough. If she'd been in the asylum, they might have managed. But this is a maternity hospital, we don't have facilities for lunatics.'

The word echoed along the telephone wire, as absolute and final as the news of her death.

'Don't worry, Farquhar. I don't blame you. And I doubt Piles will either. You did all you could. You can't be blamed.'

'There's the baby, Jack. A bonny wee lass. Technically she's yours.'

'Biologically, she isn't.'

The obstetrician sighed. 'I could put the wee mite up for adoption. Harry was going to take it in, get a nursemaid and all that, but I doubt he'll want her, now.'

'Do that, Farquhar. I'll sign the papers. You'll find a good home, won't you?' Jack's voice cracked then, he was holding the phone so tight that his knuckles were white.

For a long time he sat there, as the day ended and street lights went on. The anatomy book lay open on his lap, the X-rays as well, but he could no longer concentrate on them.

He closed the book and put the film back in the file, telling himself that he already knew the case as well as he ever would, though he couldn't be sure what the cyst had done until he got inside. He looked at the clock and saw that it was only half past eight, he had an hour and a half to spare before he went to bed at ten to get the eight hours of solid sleep he needed before a major operation.

Catriona, he thought; I have to tell Catriona. Pain struck him then, a spasm of regret, not grief. For a moment he mourned the lovable, puzzled, puzzling child who had been Amelia before she was trapped by a disease so terrible that medicine had only just put a name to it and could as yet offer no cure.

He picked up the phone then remembered that there were no phones at The Braes; he looked up Allan Nicolson's number in his address book.

Allan answered his phone on the second ring.

'This is Jack Ryan. I hope I'm not disturbing you.'

'Not at all,' Allan said levelly.

'I have to find Catriona. She's in Skye, isn't she?'

There was a moment's pause on the line.

'In fact, she's here,' Allan said. 'But she's fast asleep and I don't want to wake her.'

'No, don't do that,' Jack said quickly. 'But if you tell her, when she wakes. Tell her I phoned. Even better, I'll send her a telegram and she'll get it in the morning.'

'I'll make sure she does,' Allan lied.

'Please,' Jack said, 'tell her I love her. Tell her that as soon you can.'

'I will do,' Allan said. 'When I see her.'

'I'm operating tomorrow morning, but I'll be free in the afternoon.'

'She has to go to Largs tomorrow. Her business. She can't cancel it because she's to sign some papers. But she'll be in touch with you after that, I'm sure. By the end of the day or maybe the next one.'

'The operation I'm doing tomorrow, it's a tricky one. It'll be a day or two before I can leave the patient.'

'Don't worry, I'll give her the message,' Allan said, adding 'and the telegram' as he replaced the handset.

Jack dictated the telegram to the operator, then asked her to connect him to Horace's home, then the hospital when there was no reply. He found Horace there, at his desk, hard at work on a Sunday evening.

'I know,' Horace said, 'Farquhar called just after he spoke to you.'

'The diagnosis,' Jack asked him. 'Farquhar told me. Were you certain?'

Horace sighed. 'As certain as we can ever be. It's not surgery, Jack. You can't open up the mind and take a look inside.'

'But were you sure?'

'We had her here for more than a year, Jack. As an outpatient and then in the hospital, when she got worse. Nobody wants to make a diagnosis like that. We tried analysis, hypnosis, every conceivable technique. Nothing worked. She began to deteriorate markedly. We might have managed, if it hadn't been for the pregnancy. But because of that, we couldn't give her the drugs.'

'Why, Horace?'

'Nobody knows, Jack. The Freudians put it down to childhood trauma, repression of the id by the ego, so on. I think it's a disease of the brain, myself. A malfunction like Addison's disease. It resists every known treatment. With time, the symptoms get worse. Amelia wasn't so bad, when we saw her at first. A few affectations, mild paranoia, that sort of thing. After a while, she began to hear voices, see things that weren't there. One moment she was God, the next the concubine of the Devil. We tried, God knows. It's hell's own prognosis. The only thing is sedation. If they're sedated enough, sometimes the symptoms recede. But it always comes back, like cancer. We were never hopeful about Amelia, anyway. The tragedy was that she had her lucid moments, she knew then that she was ill. That was why she became suicidal. She wanted to die, because she couldn't handle the pain of the illness, and because she was afraid of it her illness got worse. It was a vicious circle, Jack. She broke it the only way she could.'

'I should've known, Horace. I should've helped her more than I did.'

'Jack, nobody could've helped her. Nobody knew.'

'But I should have seen it. Catriona did.'

'Jack, you're a surgeon, no psychiatrist.'

'She had psychiatrists, for God's sake. They were treating her for hysteria, melancholia, even mania – everything but what she had.'

'That can all be part of it,' Horace said wisely. 'But if it's schizophrenia the symptoms get worse.'

'It was that bloody hospital she was in. They should have seen it there.'

Horace coughed discreetly. 'It was a private hospital, Jack, wasn't it? Sometimes at these places they give patients the treatment they want rather than the treatment they need. You know that.'

'I'll sue them, Horace. I'll have them struck off. Quacks? They don't even know the meaning of the word. I'll make them look so stupid they'll wish they'd never been born ...'

'Jack, JACK?'

He paused midstream.

'Sleep on it first, eh, before you do anything?'

Jack thanked him and put the phone down.

Going to the cabinet, he poured a drink for himself, returning the liquid to the bottle when he remembered the operation he had to perform.

The clock chimed nine times. He had just enough time to go again over the technique he would use the following day. Going to his books, the only things he'd bothered to take from the house he had shared with Amelia, he pulled out his old anatomy notes, found Jimmy Jamieson's drawing of the base of the skull in the child, and began to study it carefully, to make certain all the structures were fixed in his mind.

Epilogue

*T*itch drove her home in the end, no more than that. He came to Morningside and collected her and the few possessions that she did not want to leave behind, then drove behind her to Talla, where she left her Armstrong-Siddeley, the deeds to the cottage, the key to the safety deposit box that held the ring, and her note.

She felt the call of the land then, the magic of Talla in the spring, the voice that asked her not to leave and, when she did, echoed and beseeched her to return. Though the land there was empty, had been for centuries, she knew that her people had once lived there, had made the lonely hills a home.

Seeing Skye for the first time, Titch reminisced about his grandmother, and became maudlin when he saw the majesty of the land at sunset. She laughed at him, but she was glad that he understood the power it had.

Annie welcomed her, so did Sine and Archie and their gaggle of children, one for each year of their married lives.

They understood without her telling them; when she told Annie that she was having twins, Annie only remarked that it ran in the family.

She was home again, where nothing would trouble her. If the gossips talked, then Annie or Sine would silence them; both, when the need arose, had tongues as sharp as hunting knives.

There was a dance that night in the next village; they wanted her to go but she said that with her pregnancy she was in no fit state to jig.

'Ha,' Annie said, 'you can keep me company then.'

Annie was as blind as a bat now, but she had been to the doctor and he had arranged for her to go to the eye hospital in the south.

'I would've done that,' Catriona said, but Annie told her that she had done enough already.

They all went to the dance together, walking through the sunset, hearing the music long before they reached the village hall.

Iain spun her around one frightening time, then let her be with Annie when he went to talk with the men.

Catriona watched the configuration of dancers like the fragments of a carousel, constantly changing as the music spun on. After a time the pattern settled. 'You must tell me,' Annie said, 'who's going off with who.'

She watched Titch with Fiona, Annie's pretty eighteen-year-old daughter, who had worked as a maid in Broadford Hospital and was now thinking of going to do nursing at a hospital in the lowlands. Catriona shot Titch a warning look and he replied with one that told her not to fret.

She told Annie, who nodded knowingly.

She saw Hamish, Archie's Hamish, tenously holding the girl from the post, his grip tightening once the music ended. She smiled at him and he smiled back; he was doing well with his lobsters now. She bought most of them.

She told Annie, who nodded knowingly.

She saw Eileen MacInnes's daughter squeal when Willie the carter put his hand on her bottom.

She turned to tell Annie, who knew already; all she wanted to know was who had pinched Jessie.

Then, at the back of the hall, she saw Rory, with a tall girl whose dark red hair, when she danced, flared like a winter sunset. As the reel closed on her, the girl flashed past and Catriona caught a hint of green eyes and a face flushed with happiness. She said nothing.

'Is that Rory?' Annie asked.

'Yes, Annie.'

'I was going to tell you, he's seeing a bit of the teacher. A nice girl she is. She's from the lowlands, but her parents are from Lewis.'

Miss Anderson had retired a few years ago.

'Catriona?'

'I'm glad,' she said, 'so happy for them.'

'Are you really?'

'Truly.' She paused, and a wistful expression came over her face that Annie did not see, but perceived all the same. 'You see,' she explained, 'I never danced with Jack.'

Annie gripped her hand firmly. 'Don't worry, pet. The time will come when you will. That's why I'm getting my eyes done. I need to see so I can watch your wedding.'

They walked out together into a night that was chill but not cold, and astonishingly beautiful. Back by Annie's fireside, they talked some more, until Iain came in with the men and told Annie that Fiona had been safely wrested from the clutches of Titch McKillop, who was bedding down at Sine's for the night. Fiona came in and went to bed, saying something about a promise to get up to watch the dawn with him.

'Ach, havers,' Annie said, 'does the sun not rise in the city the same way that it rises here?'

Catriona took a deep breath and then sat back in her chair by the fire, fell asleep and did not wake until dawn had come, when she found that Annie had wedged her legs on a high stool so they would rest too, and wrapped the rest of her in thick woollen rugs.

She walked out into the fragile morning, where she could be alone with the land and the things that she loved. On the path above the beach she heard the cry of a newborn seal, the crackle of an eider duck. She thought of Allan, rising to go to his work, still smarting from the row they had had. Titch had taken her to him first, had insisted upon it. Her brother had not helped, though, he had hindered her. He had come out with a lecture on the law and patience and she had bridled at his pedantry, gone for him like a wildcat when he said that he blamed Jack.

Allan did not even know why she was angry with him. Louise would explain, she thought — she hoped.

She had left then, dragging Titch with her. Because she was sleepy they'd stopped at a hotel in Fort William, then driven home slowly through the glens.

She had reached the rocks above the beach now; she stopped, winded, to take a breath.

The tide was way, way out; she walked for half a mile or more before she felt soft waves lapping at her feet, the water cool but not icy. She had passed the oyster beds long ago; this far out there were only sandworms and stranded jellyfish.

There was one at her feet now, a great fat bloated mass trailing fronds like fairground streamers, the poison sacs lurid against the pale *of the sand. With the tip of her toe she touched the body and watched it contract, knowing that the beast would come to life again when the tide recaptured it. Walking back, memories flared, memories of childhood and her mother, vagrant trails of pain that she no longer wanted to recall.*

She remembered that day, the day after her mother died, when she felt Mor come back to life and talk to her, the day four years later when she had seen her father and had been sure that he had seen her but he had slipped away, as if embarrassed. Catriona shivered, and hugged herself against the breeze.

She wanted her mother now; she needed her. She stopped and listened, but no sound came to her over the soft hum of the sea. After a long time, she spoke aloud: 'Mama, are you there? I need to hear you, Mama. I need help. I'm going to have babies, Mama, two of them, and I'm not married and I don't know what . . .'

The silence was so absolute, so profound that she could hear her heart beat. She waited for a long time before she turned to walk away.

The geese came then, a whole flock of them flew overhead; it was late in the year for them, too late, and so she stared in wonder for a moment before she understood.

Mor came to her then and told her that everything would be all right, to care about nothing because she was loved. In an instant Catriona found herself babbling, telling her mother about the things that had happened over the years, about how Allan was a lawyer and Sine and Ailish and Maire were all married, that Tom had died but not before he had made up his rift with her. About everything that had happened to her. Even Jack.

The geese drifted away then, shrank and become point sized before they vanished entirely into the sky. 'I know all that,' Mor said, her voice fading as her laughter echoed against the hills.

The wind turned fresh then, so Catriona headed for home.

Halfway to the rocks she saw a young girl, and felt a sense of déjà vu so sharp that she exclaimed out loud.

'Are the oysters good?' She could think of nothing else to say.

'Not bad, for the time of year.' She stood up straight, arched her back. 'Better this week than they were last, but not as good as this time last year.'

'*You come here often?*'

The girl smiled. '*Every day. Mussels and whelks as well. It's not meat, but it's food, just the same.*'

'*I used to gather oysters too.*'

The girl's bucket was full now; she picked it up and they walked together towards the rocks.

'*What's your name?*' Catriona asked.

The girl smiled again. '*I'm Katy McNicol. You're not from around here, are you? Everybody knows that.*'

'*I've been away,*' Catriona said, '*but I was born here.*'

'*I know that from your accent.*' Up the sands a way, Katy stopped and picked up the other bucket. '*I was born and raised in The Braes too. My da was Peter McNicol; he was shot in the head in the war and he couldn't move properly after that, though he must've been able to when he sired me, right enough. He died a while back, and we lost his pension. My ma spins wool, knits some of it, takes in washing for tourists and the like, but I come here most days. It helps out. Mind you, I could kill folks when they call me tinker just because I gather fodder from the beach.*'

'*I wouldn't bother with people like that,*' Catriona said.

'*Don't worry,*' Katy said, at the top of the beach, '*I don't. D'you know what, Missus?*'

'*Tell me,*' Catriona said.

'*There was a girl once, before my time. Her folks were poor, like we all are, and she used to gather shellfish every day, rain or shine, summer and winter. In any case, it was her ma who died, and her da, a right one he was, he married again, a girl just a few years older than his daughter. And the daughter she went away then, went down to the city and nobody heard anything of her for years except they knew she still sent money home to her da. D'you know what, Missus? D'you know what happened to her? She worked right hard down there and she started a tearoom in a place called Largs, a great big restaurant after that. She's got a restaurant in Edinburgh as well. You can sell oysters to her, to Rory. They pay a fair price. She worked right hard, but she did it, she did all of that and all she started off as was a little oyster girl. She's in America now, so they say. She's a millionairess, they say. I don't know all about her, Missus, but if you were here a while ago you might know her, though she must be a few years older than you.*'

575

'I've heard that story somewhere,' Catriona said, 'but I'm not sure that every bit of it's true.'

'Oh, but it is, Missus. It's as true as the day itself. You can go down to Largs and see for yourself, a great big sign all along the promenade, Nicolson's of Largs. That's right enough, because my ma says it is, and there's plenty who've seen it for themselves. Janet Macdonald works there, with Elsbeth and Peggy. Allan Nicolson, the lawyer, he's her brother. And Big Rory MacDonald, he's her best friend. I asked Rory if it was true one day and he said it was, every word. So you see, Missus, I don't mind at all, I don't mind gathering oysters, I just keep on thinking of that girl and what she did, because if I can do half as well, it'll be worth it. Every bit of it.' She grinned. 'I even sell oysters to Rory for her sometimes, if I've got a few to spare. Not today, though. I need these for the wee ones.'

Catriona watched her go, the hard cut of her jaw slicing the wind, her shoulders as taut as the sails of a yacht. Good luck to you, Katy, she thought; if that was not enough, she could always offer a little help.

Way up on the rocks, at the place where you could sit and watch the tide, she found Rory, who had been watching her.

'Hello,' he said softly.

'Hello, Rory. I didn't see you.'

He grinned. 'The last year or two, I've felt as if you've forgotten me.'

'I could never do that,' she said quickly.

He would not let her sit on the cold rock until he had folded his jacket into a cushion for her.

'I'm pregnant,' she said.

'Chrissakes, Catriona. I'm not blind.'

She looked at him and sensed anger, regret, something like that.

'Titch is here,' she said.

'Ha. Don't I know that? I'm just back from digging that Alfa of his out of the peat on the other side of the hill. Daft bugger decided to go bloody sightseeing in his car, of all things.'

'I haven't seen him since yesterday.'

'You'd never've seen him again if old Hamish hadn't been up early as usual, and off to see about that bloody dyke of his. He heard the cries, and there's McKillop and some woman gallumphing around in the peats like a pair of cart horses and that wee Alfa sinking fast.'

576

'Oh, Lord. Did you get the car out of it, or only Titch?'

'Both in the end, though we shouldn't've bothered. First the girl, and it was Annie's daughter Fiona and she should've had more sense. Then McKillop, who looked as close to his pater familias the rat as I have ever seen him, and then the Alfa. It was bogging, though. I think he's wrecked the suspension. It must be the air's gone to his head. He was prancing around, talking about the dawn, and there's me and Willie and Tam and two horses trying to edge out the car, and Hamish directing operations from the rear like he always does. Hamish goes up to Titch and offers him a wee dram out of his flask, and Titch starts reciting poetry. Mental, the pair of them.'

She watched his profile in the sharpness of the early sun, the earth beyond reflected in his eyes.

'So we're still friends, then?'

'Sure we are. Don't be stupid.'

'Rory, what is it?'

He looked down at her belly, and then at her. 'What happened?'

She sighed. 'I loved him, Rory. I still do.'

'You should've married him, girl.'

'I couldn't.'

'If you had a row, you should make it up.'

'It's not always as easy as that.'

'You said "loved", past tense, Triona. Love isn't something that dies. Love never dies.'

'That's true,' she said slowly.

He smiled almost sadly, as the rising sun silvered the ridges of his face. In the distance, for a moment, the Cuillins, poised on the edge of darkness, blanked completely before the day flared and caught them in the face. The mountains rose then like marble lions, though more perfect than anything that could have been formed by man.

For a moment they watched the day as it developed.

'I saw you last night,' she said. 'I'm glad.'

His smile became real then. 'I was wrong about chances,' he said. 'I got another one after all.' He thought for a moment. 'Funny how things turn out, eh?'

'Don't waste it,' she said, 'your chance, I mean.'

'Don't you waste yours either, girl.'

'Maybe I won't get another one,' she said sombrely.

'Oh, no,' he said, 'that was where I was wrong. You might not get a second chance with everyone, but you do with someone you love. If they love you back, that is.'

'He does,' she said slowly. 'He loves me and I love him.'

'Well then,' he said. 'I'd best away, get on with work, things like that. I only came up for the dance.'

She moved to give him his jacket back.

'No, pet,' he said, 'you sit here, if you want to. The day's just starting. Watch it for a moment yet. You can always give it back later.'

She felt so small then, so lonely once he had gone, and sad too, at the love they might have shared if she had known. He loved her more than she loved him. She hated that fact for its betrayal; if she could have chosen to, she would have loved him back.

The infant sun crested the mountains; she felt its tender warmth heat her face as its first slanted rays danced like will-o'-the-wisps upon the distant sea.

'Love's never wasted,' Mor said, 'not even the tiniest bit of it.'

'But I wasted Rory's love,' Catriona whispered, 'Jack's too.'

'You wasted nothing,' Mor said, before silence came again.

Catriona thought of the rows she'd had with Jack, over little things, nothing that mattered now that she thought about it.

It wasn't true that he did not cherish her, it wasn't true that he did not know the value of joy. She thought of the day when she had been struggling along Princes Street with a pair of shopping bags and he had screeched to a halt beside her, though he had been on his way to the Royal to see a child too sick to be moved. 'Go on,' she'd said, 'don't be daft. I can manage.' 'You will not,' he told her, 'I'll take your bags at least.' And the flat in Morningside, he knew how much she hated it, when she had found another in the New Town with a garden he had wanted to rent it for her, though the rent was exorbitant, much more than she was prepared to pay. He told her then that money didn't matter. Only she did.

He'd loved her so, he still did; he would have cherished her too, if she had let him – the brief spasm of aloneness that had hurt her was in her mind, not his.

I must tell him, she thought, *write a letter or, better still, go to Portree and telephone.*

A thought struck her with the force of a blow; that letter she had written, it had been so final, she'd said things she didn't mean, made it sound as if love was at an end.

That wasn't what she had wanted to say, she had only wanted to say that she couldn't bear to be in Edinburgh, not with all the trouble with Amelia, the threat to his career; she had parried that the only way she knew how.

I must tell him, she thought, *I must tell him that it isn't for ever, that the time will come when we'll be together.* She could not bear to face the future without him as a part of it.

She rose slowly, clumsy as a whale, headed for the village and then, seeing the light on the sands went there instead, to compose her mind, to think exactly what it was she would say to him.

It was a Wednesday, already five days had passed, too many, but there had been that nonsense with Allan and then Titch's meandering drive on the journey north.

For the first time in more than a year she had no idea what Jack was doing, the operations he had to do that day, the follow-ups on patients of the day before.

She was halfway back to the water's edge when she heard a cry behind her, turned and saw a telegraph boy racing towards her, then another, and another behind him.

Twelve telegraph boys in all, every lad who ever worked at the post in Portree, though most were part time because there wasn't enough business to give any one of them a decent job.

She waited, amazed, until the first one reached her.

'You're Catriona Nicolson,' he said, 'Catriona Nicolson of Largs who comes from The Braes.'

'I am,' she told him.

'Thank God for that,' he said, 'it's an awful trouble we've had this morning. Twenty grams we've had in all, all addressed to a Miss Catriona Nicolson of Largs, who comes from The Braes, but the sender, they didn't know where The Braes is, so they sent one to every single village from Portree to Breakish to make sure it reached whoever it was. We've been up since midnight, Miss. They all came in different times, we've been running here and there until *we managed to work out they were all for the same person.'*

She looked at the rumpled paper he held in his hand.

'Can I read it?' she asked.

'Of course you can,' he said, handing it to her.

The other lads, grouped behind him, watched her as she opened the flimsy envelope. She turned to read it in private then realized that they would know what it contained anyway, that if they didn't they'd find out soon enough from Maggie MacDonald, the telegraphist in Portree.

CATRIONA NICOLSON, BALMEANACH, BRAES, SKYE: CATRIONA NICOLSON OF NICOLSON'S OF LARGS. MY LOVE, IT IS ALL OVER, I CANNOT TELL YOU WHY SO PLEASE DO NOT ASK. MARRY ME, WILL YOU? WILL YOU MARRY ME NOW?

'Oh, yes,' she murmured, 'yes, I will.'

'Thank God for that,' the telegraph lad said. 'If you want to send him a telegram, Missus, I hope you've got the right address.' The lads looked at each other, grinning, and then headed back towards the track to Portree.

'Wait,' Catriona said, 'if you come with me I'll get you some breakfast. You must be hungry if you've come all this way.'

They looked at each other. 'Right enough, Missus, we could do with a bite.'

'You know Annie Macdonald's,' she said, 'go on there. I'll follow you.'

As she waddled up the beach, she saw a man in the distance, running towards her with his coat flapping around his knees; she began to move towards him, as fast as she could, her gait as clumsy as a milking cow's.

He waved frantically, his voice rising over the wind. 'Don't run, Trina. Wait for me to come to you.'

She waited until he reached her and swung her around in his arms.

'How d'you know where I was?'

'Rory told me. I remembered him and rang his office. They rang him here. He rang me back last night. I've been driving here since then.'

The doubts left her then, all of them.

A long time later, he let her go.

'Amelia?'

'She died, Catriona.'

'Oh.'

He took her hands in his. 'I got that job in Glasgow, precious. Starting in October ...'

'Is that what you want, Jack? You don't mind leaving Edinburgh?'

He smiled. 'I thought, I love Nicolson's almost as much as you do. I thought a change would be good for both of us.'

'Do you want to leave Edinburgh?'

He put his arms around her. 'It's funny in a way. I'm not sure yet. It's up to you. I was thinking, I could even set up a practice here. If it means so much to you.'

'No, Jack. We can come for holidays. When we retire, perhaps.'

'It's so wonderful,' he said, squeezing her tight. 'Even old Piles sent me a letter apologizing, promising no more nonsense.'

She smiled to herself; she would tell him all some time, but not yet.

'He's gone to Switzerland,' he said, 'he went last week in fact. He won't be back for months, he says.' Amelia's solicitors had told him that her father would not return to handle the funeral arrangements. They had offered to do so and he had agreed thankfully, had even sent a cheque for their bill.

'Come,' she said, 'let's walk for a while.'

'There's something I want to do,' he said.

'What's that?'

'I wanted to gather oysters, my love. I want to gather oysters with you.'

She laughed and then they walked over the sands. 'This beach is special,' she said, 'you see, it's a magical place, a place where, if you dream, you dream comes true ...'